ALTAR OF R

A NOVEL OF SUSPENSE

VOLUME TWO OF THE WORLD WAR TWO TRILOGY

TO THE READER

This is the story of the Italian Campaign and Nazi Occupation of Rome in 1943-1944. It is told through the eyes of General Robert T. Frederick of the U.S.-Canadian First Special Service Force, the precursor to the modern Special Forces, Pope Pius XII, Waffen-SS Colonel Eugen Dollmann, Rome Gestapo Chief Herbert Kappler, and others whose deeds and words have been recorded by history. However, the history you will find in these pages may be different from the one you've heard before, as it is based largely upon recently released documents and the last decade of research by a new generation of historians. More than fifty historical figures populate the pages of *Altar of Resistance*, and the story unfolds through the unique viewpoints of the four major factions that grappled for control of the Eternal City: the Allies, trying to capture Rome as the first Axis prize of war but encountering stiff opposition; the German Occupiers, trying to throw the Allies back into the sea while holding Rome hostage and using it as a staging ground and supply line to the front; the Vatican, represented by Pius XII, codenamed the "Chief," deeply involved in the secret plot to remove Hitler from power while struggling to maintain Vatican impartiality, save Rome from destruction, and protect its Jewish and Christian population from extermination; and finally, the Roman Partisans, fighting to drive out the Germans and liberate their sacred city.

With regard to the major events of the Italian Campaign and the living, breathing historical figures representing the above four factions, I have tried to travel back in time like H.G. Wells and recreate them with meticulous fidelity. Where possible, I have taken the actual quotes of the participants or large portions of their words from transcripts, interviews, and government documents. For the reader, the result is an immersion in the spoken words, sights, sounds, smells, pageantry, and brutality of the war in Italy.

Altar of Resistance is the tragic yet uplifting tale of how the American and British Armies fought and bled their way towards the Eternal City while Rome's top secret agent—Pope Pius XII, leader of the Vatican's Church of Spies—orchestrated events behind the scenes in an attempt to thwart German oppression, overthrow the Führer, and usher in a viable post-Hitler government. I hope you enjoy reading this historical work as much as I enjoyed writing it. But more importantly, I hope you learn something new and interesting about WWII and the men and women who fought in it.

Praise for Samuel Marquis

#1 *Denver Post* Bestselling Author
Foreword Reviews' Book of the Year Winner (HM)
Beverly Hills Books Awards Winner & Award-Winning Finalist
Next Generation Indie Book Awards Winner
& Award-Winning Finalist
USA Best Book Award-Winning Finalist

"*The Coalition* has a lot of good action and suspense, an unusual female assassin, and the potential to be another *The Day After Tomorrow* [the runaway bestseller by Allan Folsom]."
—James Patterson, #1 *New York Times* Bestselling Author

"*Altar of Resistance* is a gripping and densely packed thriller dramatizing the Allied Italian campaign...reminiscent of Herman Wouk's *The Winds of War*."
—Kirkus Reviews

"Marquis is a student of history, always creative, [and] never boring....A good comparison might be Tom Clancy."
—Military.com

"In his novels *Blind Thrust* and *Cluster of Lies*, Samuel Marquis vividly combines the excitement of the best modern techno-thrillers, an education in geology, and a clarifying reminder that the choices each of us make have a profound impact on our precious planet."
—Ambassador Marc Grossman, Former U.S. Under Secretary of State

"*Blind Thrust* kept me up until 1 a.m. two nights in a row. I could not put it down. An intriguing mystery that intertwined geology, fracking, and places in Colorado that I know well. Great fun."
—Governor Roy R. Romer, 39th Governor of Colorado

"*The Coalition* starts with a bang, revs up its engines, and never stops until the explosive ending….Perfect for fans of James Patterson, David Baldacci, and Vince Flynn."—Foreword Reviews

"Old-time spy buffs will appreciate the tradecraft and attention to detail, while adventure enthusiasts will enjoy the unique perspective and setting for a WWII story….[A] combination of *The Great Escape*, *Public Enemies*, a genuine old-time Western, and a John Le Carré novel."
—BlueInk Review (for *Bodyguard of Deception*, Book 1 of WWII Trilogy)

"*The Coalition* by Samuel Marquis is a riveting novel by an uncommonly gifted writer. This is the stuff from which blockbuster movies are made! Very highly recommended."
—Midwest Book Review - The Mystery/Suspense Shelf

"Readers looking for an unapologetic historical action book should tear through this volume."
—Kirkus Reviews (for *Bodyguard of Deception*)

"*Cluster of Lies* has a twisty plot that grabs hold from the beginning and never let's go. A true page turner! I'm already looking forward to the next Joe Higheagle adventure."
—Robert Bailey, Author of *The Professor* and *Between Black and White*

"With *Blind Thrust*, *Cluster of Lies*, and his other works, Samuel Marquis has written true breakout novels that compare favorably with—and even exceed—recent thrillers on the *New York Times* Bestseller List."—Pat LoBrutto, Former Editor for Stephen King and Eric Van Lustbader (Bourne Series)

"Samuel Marquis picks up his World War II trilogy with *Altar of Resistance*, a well-researched and explosive ride through war-torn Rome with Nazis, booming battles, and intense cat-and-mouse chases....Grounded in historical fact but spiced up with thrilling imagination with the fate of the world in balance."
—Foreword Reviews

"The science of earthquakes is truly fascinating, and Marquis has captured this science and packaged it into a really fine thriller 'against the clock' style for almost anyone to pick up and enjoy, and readers will no doubt want more from Higheagle and his intrepid grandfather once they have devoured this installment."
—SP Review (for *Blind Thrust*)

"Reminiscent of *The Day of the Jackal*...with a high level of authentic detail. Skyler is a convincing sniper, and also a nicely conflicted one."
—Donald Maass, Author of Writing 21st Century Fiction (for *The Coalition*)

"In *Cluster of Lies*, Samuel Marquis touches all the bases. He starts with a murder and the action doesn't let up until the very last page in this compelling environmental thriller that is often uncomfortably realistic."
—Charles Salzberg, Author of *The Henry Swann Detective Series*

"*The Devil's Brigade (*formerly *The Slush Pile Brigade)*, by Samuel Marquis, is a hilarious and exciting read filled with one crazy turn after another....The author slams on the accelerator early in the story and doesn't let up, forcing the reader to flip the pages frantically. And once it's over, it's still hard to catch one's breath."
—SP Review - 4.5-Star Review

By Samuel Marquis

NICK LASSITER-SKYLER INTERNATIONAL ESPIONAGE SERIES

THE DEVIL'S BRIGADE
THE COALITION
THE FOURTH PULARCHEK

WORLD WAR TWO TRILOGY

BODYGUARD OF DECEPTION
ALTAR OF RESISTANCE
SPIES OF THE MIDNIGHT SUN (JANUARY 2018)

JOE HIGHEAGLE ENVIRONMENTAL SLEUTH SERIES

BLIND THRUST
CLUSTER OF LIES

ALTAR OF RESISTANCE

A NOVEL OF SUSPENSE

VOLUME TWO OF THE WORLD WAR TWO TRILOGY

SAMUEL MARQUIS

MOUNT SOPRIS PUBLISHING

ALTAR OF RESISTANCE
VOLUME TWO OF THE WORLD WAR TWO TRILOGY

MOUNT SOPRIS PUBLISHING
Trade paper: ISBN 978-1-943593-03-3
Kindle: ISBN 978-1-943593-07-1
EPub: ISBN 978-1-943593-11-8

Second Mount Sopris Publishing Premium Printing: February 2017
Cover Design: Christian Fuenfhausen (http://cefdesign.com)
Formatting: Rik Hall (www.WildSeasFormatting.com)
Printed in the United States of America

To Order Samuel Marquis Books and Contact Samuel:

Visit Samuel Marquis's website, join his mailing list, learn about his forthcoming novels and book events, and order his books at www.samuelmarquisbooks.com. Please send fan mail to samuelmarquisbooks@gmail.com. Thank you for your support!

ATTENTION: ORGANIZATIONS AND CORPORATIONS
Mount Sopris Publishing books may be purchased for educational, business, or sales promotional use. For information, please email the Special Markets Department at samuelmarquisbooks@gmail.com.

Dedication

For the "Fighting General," Robert Tyrone Frederick, and the other officers and enlisted men of the U.S. and Canadian First Special Service Force.

And for the much-misunderstood and maligned Pope Pius XII (Eugenio Pacelli, codenamed the "Chief"), who was deeply involved in three plots to remove Adolf Hitler from power (including Claus von Stauffenberg's famous July 20, 1944, Operation Valkyrie Plot), and who helped ensure that eighty-five percent of Italy's Jewish population was spared from Nazi extermination, the highest survival percentage of any country in Europe during the Holocaust, with the exception of Denmark.

Altar of Resistance

Why hadn't the pope done more to resist Hitler? Critics posited cowardice, insensitivity, political calculation, anti-Semitism, and apathy; some just said Pius was a Nazi, and left it at that. Catholic apologists countered that the pope was silenced and paralyzed by a desire to save lives, since "a strong condemnation would have increased the persecution." Both sides in the debate generally agreed, however, that Pius did little or nothing to oppose the Nazis. Both sides were wrong. The entire Nazi era was marked by dramatic, if secret, Church resistance, in which the pope played a pivotal role. The signature element in this resistance was Pius XII's participation in the conspiracies to kill Adolf Hitler.

—Mark Riebling, intelligence expert and author of *Church of Spies: The Pope's Secret War Against Hitler*

The Eternal City was far more important to the Allies than merely as the capital city of their former enemy. Militarily, Rome was of considerable strategic importance for its road and rail net and nearby airfields. The immense political and cultural significance of the Italian capital also made its capture of psychological value to the Allies.

—Carlo D'Este, *Fatal Decision: Anzio and the Battle for Rome*

Why did it take you so long? the Italians asked, and the answer could only be: *Because so many of us died to set you free.*

—The Allied liberators in Rick Atkinson's *The Day of Battle: The War in Sicily and Italy, 1943–1944*, in response to the recurring question from the newly freed Roman populace: *We are so happy to see you at last. Why did it take you so long?*

Our men were going to get to Rome all right. There was no question about that. But the way was cruel. No one who had not seen that mud, those dark skies, those forbidding ridges and ghostlike clouds that unveiled and then quickly hid the enemy, had the right to be impatient with the progress along the road to Rome.

—Ernie Pyle, U.S. War Correspondent

The problem of reprisals was raised and resolved once and for all at the beginning of the Partisan war in Italy as it had been in France and in the other countries occupied by the Nazis. To accept the blackmail of reprisals meant renouncing the struggle from the outset. One had to react to Nazi reprisals on a one-by-one basis without submitting to the enemy's threat.... We represented a component of a fighting army. We were in fact participants at the highest level of command of that army.... We had but one duty: to keep on fighting.

—Giorgio Amendola, Roman Resistance Leader

Cast of Characters

FICTIONAL CHARACTERS

Standartenführer Wilhelm Friedrich Ernst Hollmann: Waffen-SS colonel and diplomatic liaison officer for Rome's upper echelons, German father of John Bridger and Teresa.
Marchesa Bianca Manuela Di Domenico (formerly Bianca Hollmann): Royal Italian mother of John Bridger and Teresa.
Captain-Major John Bridger (formerly Gunther Hollmann): American officer and spy in First Special Service Force, son of Wilhelm and Bianca, immigrated to America from Italy in 1936.
Teresa Sabrina Di Domenico (formerly Teresa Hollmann): Roman royal turned Partisan known as the *Inglesina* (The English Girl), daughter of Wilhelm and Bianca, biological daughter of Colonel Di Domenico.
Colonel Giovanni Vassalli Di Domenico: Italian chief of the Clandestine Military Front of the Resistance, Teresa's biological father and John Bridger's stepfather.
Beppo (Giuseppe Valenti): Roman Partisan with Teresa in National Liberation Committee (CLN) and also her lover.
Major-Colonel Walther Hollmann: Field Officer in Wehrmacht Hermann Göring Division on Italian Southern Front, younger brother of Wilhelm.
Lieutenant Peter Savoyan: American Fifth Army intelligence officer, head of Office of Strategic Services (OSS) Rome.

MAJOR REAL HISTORICAL FIGURES

The Vatican

Pope Pius XII: Roman-born Eugenio Pacelli, world's highest ranking leader involved in plots to assassinate Adolf Hitler, codenamed the "Chief."
Cardinal Luigi Maglione: Secretary of State, reliably pro-American.
Monsignor Giovanni Battista Montini: Undersecretary for Ordinary Affairs, future Pope Paul VI.
Monsignor Domenico Tardini: Undersecretary for Extraordinary Affairs.
Monsignor Hugh O'Flaherty: Irish priest in Congregation of the Holy Office, key figure in Vatican Escape Line for Allied POWs and refugees, codenamed "Golf."
Father Robert Leiber: German Jesuit priest, Pius's private secretary and closest advisor, one of German Colonel Claus von Stauffenberg's two spy cutouts with Pius in Rome, codenamed "Gregor."
Father Pankratius Pfeiffer (Padre Pancrazio): Bavarian Abbot-General of the Order of Salvatorians, liaison with German authorities.

Count Giuseppe Dalla Torre: Director/chief editor of L'Osservatore Romano
Bernardino Nogara: Vatican financial manager and secret representative to the Roman Resistance *Comitato di Liberazione Nazionale* (National Liberation Committee, CLN).
Rector Roberto Ronca: Rector of the Roman Seminary and secret Vatican representative to CLN.
Monsignor Arborio Mella St. Elias: Master of the Chamber (*Maestro di Camera).*

Rome's Jewish Leaders

Ugo Foà: President of Rome's Jewish community.
Dante Almansi: Deputy to Ugo Foà.
Israel Zolli: Chief Rabbi of Rome.

The First Special Service Force (FSSF)

Colonel-Brigadier General Robert Tyrone Frederick: American Commander of First U.S.-Canadian Special Service Force, known as the "Fighting General."
Lieutenant Colonel T.C. MacWilliam: Canadian, mild-mannered history professor in peacetime.
Lieutenant-Captain Gus Heilman: American, self-appointed mayor of "Gusville" at Anzio, former football star at the University of Virginia and tavern owner.
Sergeant Tommy Prince: Canadian scout, Ojibwa Native of the Saulteaux tribe from the Brokenhead Reservation, Scanterbury, Manitoba.
Sergeant Guy Van Ausdale: Apache-American, hard rock miner from Arizona in peacetime.
Lieutenant Finn Roll: Norwegian, intelligence officer and interrogator.

The German SS and Regular Army (Wehrmacht) Occupiers

Lieutenant Colonel Herbert Kappler: Chief of the Gestapo in Rome and Nazi rival of Hollmann.
Polizeiführer General Karl Wolff: Head of the SS in Italy, Colonel Wilhelm Hollmann's boss.
Captain Erich Priebke: Kappler's closest aide and second-in-command, a social climber and vicious torturer, a man of divided loyalty and provider of useful intelligence information to Hollmann.
Field Marshal Albert Kesselring: Supreme Wehrmacht Commander on Southern Italian Front, known as "Smiling Albert," respected by Allies as a formidable opponent.
Lieutenant General Kurt Mälzer: Commandant of Rome, corpulent self-styled "King of Rome."
Captain Theodor Dannecker: SS "Jewish expert" on a mission from Berlin for Rome's roundup (*Judenaktion*).
Major Hellmuth Dobbrick: Police battalion commander of SS *Polizeiregiment Bozen*.

The Foreign Diplomats, Spies, Activists, and Plotters against Hitler

Sir D'Arcy Osborne: British Minister to the Holy See, key figure in Pope-backed plots against Hitler and Vatican Escape Line, codenamed "Mount."
Harold H. Tittmann: United States Chargé d'Affaires to the Holy See.
Major Sam Derry: Escaped British POW, Military Head of Vatican Escape Line.
Baron Ernst von Weizsäcker: German Ambassador to the Holy See, a cautious anti-Hitlerite.
Albrecht von Kessel: Weizsäcker's closest aide, a vocal anti-Nazi in private circles.
Consul Eitel Friedrich Möllhausen: Thirty-year-old acting head of the German Embassy in Rome, a non-member of the Nazi Party with penchant for aiding Jews.
Josef Müller: Attorney and leader of the German Catholic Resistance to Hitler with close ties to Pius and the Vatican, imprisoned by Nazis, codenamed "Herr X."
Lieutenant Colonel Claus von Stauffenberg: Catholic German Army leader of failed July 20, 1944, Pius-backed plot to assassinate Adolf Hitler and remove the Nazi Party from power.
Paul Franken: German Abwehr agent, one of Stauffenberg's two spy cutouts with Pius in Rome.

The Roman Resistance, Italian Fascist Police, and "Black" Nobility

Giorgio Amendola: Communist leader of the Military Council of the National Liberation Committee, commander of CLN GAP's throughout Central Italy.
Riccardo Bauer: Action Party leader of Military Council of CLN.
Sandro Pertini: Socialist leader of Military Council of CLN.
Cervo (Maurizio Giglio): Roman police lieutenant and Allied double agent secretly running the OSS's Radio Vittoria with Peter Savoyan.
Princess Enza Pignatelli Aragona Cortes: Member of Rome's black nobility, friend of Teresa.
Pietro Koch: Head of the Rome Special Police Unit (the Koch Gang), ex-Italian army officer of German origin and self-proclaimed "doctor" and adventurer.
Pietro Caruso: Rome's brutal Chief of Police (*Questore*).
Alfredo Troia: Renegade Tuscan monk, posed as a priest Don Ildefonso during the December 21, 1943 Koch Gang raid upon the Seminario Lombardo.
Laura Nucci: Fascist Italian film star, SS-Captain Erich Priebke's mistress.

The Allied Commanders

Lieutenant General Mark Wayne Clark: Commander, United States Fifth Army.
Major General Geoffrey T. Keyes: Commander, II Corps, Fifth Army.
Major General Lucian K. Truscott: Commander, VI Corps, Fifth Army.
Brigadier General William "Wild Bill" Donovan: Chief of Office of Strategic Services (OSS), forerunner of the CIA.

PROLOGUE

INNSBRUCK, AUSTRIA
SEPTEMBER 8, 1932

ON THE DAY THEIR FAMILY WAS RIPPED APART, Gunther Hollmann and his younger sister Teresa were let out of school a half hour early. A broken water line had flooded the dirt-covered playground where the children congregated after school, and the superintendent, not wanting the students mucking around in the mud and tracking it all over the streets and sidewalks, sent them home early.

With their schoolbooks in their rucksacks, Gunther and Teresa—ages fourteen and ten—hopped on their bicycles and set out down the path that led to the mighty Inn River. A tree-lined promenade ran along its length all the way from the east to the west side of the Tyrolean capital bounded on the north and south by the Alps. The city's name—Innsbruck—was derived from the first medieval bridge built across the fast-running alpine watercourse, tinged an olive green in the spring and summer.

When Gunther and Teresa reached the river, they turned right and headed upstream on the wide promenade that ran along the north bank. It was a resplendent day: the sky was an untrammeled blue, and the rows of houses and commercial buildings across the river twinkled in the late summer sunshine. The tall, narrow medieval houses, painted in lively pastel colors and supported by sloping buttresses, always made Gunther feel as though he had traveled back in time to the era of chivalrous knights and damsels in distress. Beyond the rows of houses was the *Alstadt*—Old Town—with the impressive Hofburg castle and the twin bell towers of the Baroque Cathedral of St. Jakob stretching towards the heavens.

Along the streets and sidewalks, Innsbruck bustled with activity: men and women going from one place or another for business, as well as those out for a simple stroll, many sporting ruddy cheeks and classic Tyrolean vestments. After biking along the promenade for several minutes, they turned right onto Burgstadl. From there, they peddled up the hill and struck left onto Schneeburggasse until they came to their spacious Tyrolean villa looking out over the river valley and historic town of Innsbruck. The classic Bavarian stucco and timber architecture, cobblestone walkways, and decorative figurines, woodwork, and emblems of the Holy See revealed the wealth, prestige, and proud Roman Catholic tradition of the Hollmann family. Adding to the aura of opulence were the priceless Tintoretto, Jacob von Ruisdael, Holbein, and Rosetti oils hanging inside the villa. Their father was the town's chief of police and a prominent political figure and landholder; their mother a wealthy marchesa of the royal Bellomo family of Rome.

As they put their bicycles away in the garage, Gunther was surprised to see their father's sleek black Mercedes parked inside. Normally, he didn't arrive home until six o'clock, and often later. Gunther felt a spring in his step as he and Teresa headed for the house, climbed up the cobbled stairs, and crossed the wooden deck. Perhaps his father would kick a soccer ball around or work on a model airplane with him before dinner, as he sometimes did.

But his enthusiasm was dampened by the sound of his mother's and father's voices coming from inside the villa. Though they were not shouting at one another, they were definitely quarreling. This in itself was surprising since his parents only rarely fought, with his Italian-born-and-raised mother usually doing most of the yelling. Their unusually hostile voices on this occasion, however, made him instantly curious as to what they were fighting about. With the windows wide open, he and Teresa could hear them clearly. He put his finger to his lips, instructing his little sister to keep quiet, and the two of them crept forward to eavesdrop.

ψψψ

"You are a whore," his father said emphatically to his mother. "I don't know what else to call you after what you've done."

The ugly word sent a shockwave through Gunther's body. He turned to cover his sister's ears, but she pushed him away.

"No, I want to hear," she whispered adamantly, her mouth set in a stubborn line.

"Fine, but you had better be quiet," the boy warned her quietly. "And don't blame me if you hear something you wished you hadn't."

"I don't care. I want to hear what they say," she repeated, and they inched closer to the open window, peering over the sill.

He saw his father fling a manila envelope on the antique side table next to the stylish chaise lounge where his mother was sitting. She wrinkled her nose at the sight of the envelope. But then, to Gunther's surprise, she opened it up, withdrew a set of photographs, and quietly examined them. It took her several minutes to look through them all, and at least three times she gasped in startlement. When she was finished, she put the photographs back into the envelope and set it down on the side table next to a pair of porcelain snuff boxes and an encrusted vase containing an exotic bouquet of peacock feathers and palm leaves. From her face, Gunther could tell she was embarrassed and angry.

"So, you had a private detective follow me?" she said to his father. "I guess I should have expected as much from the chief of police."

"If your children saw those pictures, they would renounce you as their mother. And don't try and tell me that this hasn't been going on with Di Domenico for years because I know it has."

"Then don't you try and deny that you have not one, but two mistresses, neither of whom is over the age of twenty-three."

His mother had caught his father by surprise, Gunther saw at once. But his father quickly recovered his composure.

"Don't try and turn this around, Bianca," he snapped back. "This isn't about me—this is about *your* infidelity."

"Like hell it is. If anyone has been whoring about, it is you, not me."

"You have no proof. You are just trying to deflect the situation."

"What, you think you are the only person in all of Austria who can hire a private detective? You have been living a lie just as much as me. Do you deny that you have two mistresses?"

"I don't have to take this. You're trying to turn this back onto me."

"Oh, so I'm supposed to roll over and accept your infidelities, but I am a whore?"

"It is different for a man. You know that."

Gunther looked again at his little sister; it pained him that his parents could act so treacherously towards one another and he didn't want her to hear any more. Once again he tried to cover her ears, but for the second time she pushed his hands away.

"So we have both sinned against God," he heard his father say. "The question is what should we do about it?"

"Oh no, you're not getting off that easy," replied his mother testily. "We are just getting started."

"What on earth are you talking about?"

"I know about your wife. Or, I should say, your first wife."

This time Wilhelm Friedrich Ernst Hollmann—paragon of virtue as the chief of the Innsbruck Police, leader in the Christian Social Party and Roman Catholic community, and head of the German-Austrian Alpine Club—was at a complete loss for words. To Gunther, he looked as if he had been punched in the gut. The revelation that his father had a previous wife was startling, but what was even more shocking was that his mother could exert such control over his powerful father as to render him speechless. He had a sudden sick feeling that his family was falling into some terrible abyss from which it would never resurface.

Finally, his father spoke. "How did you find out?"

"Your beloved Monika Stauffer of Vienna contacted me. You abandoned her and she wants money. Actually, what she wants is *more* money because you have already been paying her off all these years to keep her quiet."

His father looked completely deflated. For several seconds, he said nothing, just held his head in his hands. "My God, what have we done?"

"I'll tell you what we've done. For fifteen years of marriage, we have both been living a double life—and now the game is up."

Her admission of equal responsibility for the failure of their marriage did little to mollify his father. He slumped further into the sofa, a defeated man that Gunther hardly recognized. He still couldn't believe that his father had been married to someone else all these years while also wedded to his mother. In fact, the entire conversation was so strange and unexpected that it was as if his parents were imposters. Who were these people? Was it possible that he was dreaming and this was all some sort of nightmare?

"So you know the truth," his father said somberly. "I always knew this terrible day would come."

"I want an Annulment, Wilhelm. I have already spoken to my uncle about it."

His father jumped up from the sofa. "What? You told Antonio about this!"

"Of course, I spoke with him. He *is*, after all, the Bishop of Siena."

"Why did you have to get your uncle involved?"

"Because I want a *quiet* Annulment without a lot of fuss. Antonio can be counted on to handle this matter discreetly to preserve the Bellomo family name. Good heavens, don't you realize that you cannot be married to two women at once? If anyone finds out, you will be excommunicated."

"You certainly have it all figured out, don't you?"

"Your beloved Monika told me everything."

"Did she now?"

"I know you only married her out of desperation. You were a young, naïve lieutenant back then, on leave during the Great War after winning your Iron Cross. You married her without your parents' knowledge or blessing because you thought you were going to die in those brutal trenches. I can sympathize with your predicament, Wilhelm, but I'm afraid it doesn't change anything. You have lied to me all these years and this allows me to quietly be rid of you. Do you know what this would do to my family's reputation in Rome if the truth ever came out? My father is absolutely furious and wants to strangle you."

"I should have known you'd tell your damned father. You've always been daddy's girl and I'm sure he's the one that put you up to this."

Gunther looked down again at his little sister. Now she appeared genuinely frightened. Despite her young age, she understood the destructive magnitude of what was taking place. Their family that had seemed so happy all these years was coming unraveled before their very eyes. For the first time, he realized how cleverly his parents had hidden their true feelings towards one another from him and Teresa. It was as if all these years they had been acting out roles that contradicted their true nature and they had deliberately duped their own children.

And today was the day of reckoning.

"It pains me to say this, Wilhelm, but I realize now that I have never really loved you. My heart was always meant for the captain."

"The captain? That Fascist son of a bitch Di Domenico is no military officer!"

"You're one to criticize. When were you going to tell me that you had joined the Nazi Party? I heard it from Count Stroheim. You know perfectly well that it is illegal to join the Party here in Austria."

"I don't care about the damned Nazis. I only joined because it will mean advancement. Mark my words, Hitler will be chancellor soon and those who have joined the Party will see their stars rise."

"You always were self-centered. The only reason you married me was so you could waltz around in the best social circles."

"You know perfectly well that I am quite wealthy on my own, thank you. And I didn't marry you for your money, Marchesa, I can guarantee that. I married you because I happened to have fallen deeply in love with you. And to be quite honest, a part of me loves you still. I almost don't believe it myself, but there it is."

"With two mistresses, you certainly have a strange way of showing it. But it doesn't matter. I am leaving you and taking the children with me to Rome."

"Don't tell me you are going to actually live with that filthy Lothario?"

"Giovanni and I will probably marry. But that is no concern of yours. All you need to know is that we are leaving this week and my uncle is annulling our marriage. The children don't need to know anything more than you have a previous marriage and, by God's sacred law, we cannot remain husband and wife."

He stepped towards her, his face pleading. "You can't do this. You can't take the children away from me. They mean the world to me!"

"You should have thought of that before you became a bigamist and serial womanizer. At least I did it for love, but you, Wilhelm...." She left the harsh words unfinished.

"But none of them have meant anything to me."

"It's too late to beg. And I must say it's most unbecoming for the chief of police."

"If you do this, you'll regret it."

"Oh really? And why is that?"

"Because I will tell Teresa who her true father is."

Gunther watched with a mixture of fascination and horror as the full brunt of his father's words struck his mother. Like his father a moment earlier, she had been completely blindsided.

"I think it's only fair, Bianca, that our daughter knows you have been lying to her for the past eleven years as well."

Feeling a mixture of shock and revulsion, he looked down again at his sister, whose eyes were now filled with tears. Suddenly, he wished they had never come home from school early. They should have gone to the park to play or headed to a friend's house. Then they wouldn't have heard any of this terrible talk.

"You wouldn't dare do such a thing!" protested the marchesa.

"I believe she has a right to know that her father is a pompous Italian ass that her mother has been secretly carrying on an affair with for over a decade. Did you really think that you were going to get away with it?"

He saw the blood drain from his mother's face. Now her normally imperious voice was nothing more than a strained whisper.

"How did you find out?"

"Blood type. Yours and mine are both Type A, but Teresa's is B. Actually, it's B-negative, which is less than two percent of the Austrian and Italian populations."

"So?"

"So B-negative also happens to be the blood type of your beloved Captain Di Domenico. I was able to obtain his military records."

"You bastard."

"As the Americans like to say, I believe that's the pot calling the kettle black. Don't act so surprised, my dear Bianca. As you have so often said, I am the chief of the Innsbruck Police and getting people's records is my business."

Gunther shook his head in dismay, not wanting to believe what he was hearing. It was an outrage, a repudiation of his and Teresa's entire lives. Their family was a sham. It was bad enough that his parents had cheated on one another, but it was far worse that the lies on both sides had been building up for years. Had his parents ever truly loved one another? Or had it been a marriage built on convenience, laziness, or to gain some sort of social advantage since they both came from wealth and title?

He felt as though a stake had been driven through his heart.

"I am getting an Annulment, Wilhelm. That is the only honorable way out for us both."

"Fine, but the children will stay here with me in Innsbruck."

"How dare you! They'll never accept that. They want to be with me!"

"Not when they find out how you've been lying to them all these years."

"You wouldn't dare!"

"That's where you're wrong, my dear. And remember, the Church doesn't take too kindly to giving out Annulments and awarding the children to a cheating wife. Perhaps we will both be excommunicated."

"You are a cold-hearted bastard, Wilhelm. You would keep my own children from me?"

"You're forgetting that they're my children too."

"Teresa isn't."

"She's more mine than that bastard Di Domenico. I raised her. Blood doesn't mean a damned thing once you've spent a decade raising a daughter. Who taught her how to perform arithmetic, ride a bike, swat a tennis ball, climb a mountain, and ski down a glacier? I don't recall seeing you or your Italian Lothario out there with Teresa. Besides, Di Domenico will never love her as I do."

"You are wrong. Giovanni is a good man. He will love them both."

"On the contrary, he is nothing but a sperm-donor and home-wrecker. You want your Italian lover and Annulment, then you will have to give up something—and that is the children. You cannot have all three."

"Damn you to hell, Wilhelm! You are doing this to spite me!"

They were both up and on their feet, glowering at one another. Gunther realized that a part of him hated them for keeping dreadful secrets from him and Teresa all these years. But he was also desperate to hear how it would all end. He leaned closer to the window, tilting his ear towards the opening, his eyes fixed on his parents. Behind him, he felt his little sister edging closer too. Instead of being sad or scared, she, too, was mesmerized. What was taking place was the most shocking thing either of them had ever experienced and they were transfixed.

It was then that the room turned eerily quiet. He had a terrible feeling something bad was about to happen.

His mother reached into her purse and pulled out a pistol.

He stared at her in shock, unable to believe his eyes. Where did his mother get a gun? And why was she suddenly acting so crazy? It couldn't possibly be just because his father wanted to retain custody of him and Teresa here in Innsbruck.

He gulped hard, feeling all sense of hope, and sanity, vanish. Out of the corner of his eye, he saw Teresa pull away from the window and curl up on the deck with her hands over her ears. This was too much for her. It was too much for him, too, he suddenly realized, and he cursed himself again for snooping on his parents in the first place.

What happened next was like someone else's nightmare unfolding before his eyes as his mother pointed the gun at his father. It seemed impossible that she knew how to even fire such a weapon, but, to his surprise, the pistol looked supple and compliant in her hands and her expression was one of firm resolve.

His father shook his head in disbelief. "Where the hell did you get that?"

"You know damn well where I got it. Tucked beneath your bedside table drawer. What, you didn't think I knew where the police chief keeps his spare?"

"My God, you've been planning this for some time, haven't you?"

His mother said nothing, but her look said it all.

"You would shoot down your own husband?"

"I will not let you steal my children from me, and me and my father will not allow you to dishonor the Bellomo family name. So you leave me no choice but to rid myself of you."

"No, something isn't right. You're overreacting."

"Why can't you understand that I will not let you take my children from me or disgrace my family's name?"

"No, that's not what's driving you to this extreme. What is really going on, Bianca?"

"Stop talking. I just need to end this."

"You'll never get away with it. You can't claim shooting me was an accident. No one will ever believe—"

"Shut up!" his mother cut his father off. There were tears in her eyes. She held the gun with two hands and widened her stance in preparation to deliver the fatal shot. "It is you who have driven me to this, you bastard!"

"But this is too much. Why...why are you doing this, Bianca?"

"Shut up, I said!"

Gunther saw that his mother's hands gripping the pistol were trembling.

"How can I shut up? Despite my many mistakes, you're my wife and I still love you. I may have been a failure as a husband, but know this: I have always loved you."

"I'm pointing a gun at you and you still love me? It is you who has gone mad. If I don't shoot you now, our children's lives will be ruined!"

"Ruined? What do you mean ruined? What is this really about?"

"I said shut your mouth!"

"They will lock you away in prison for the rest of your life, Bianca. Think of what you are doing. I am the fucking chief of police!"

"I said keep quiet!"

"If you go through with this, you and your children will be cursed for the rest of your lives. Mark my words, if you pull that trigger you will curse us all to damnation here on earth and in the afterlife. And that includes your precious Captain Di Domenico and the entire Bellomo family. No one—and I mean no one—will be spared!"

This drew of look of mortification from his mother and she took an involuntary step back. Despite how determined she appeared to be, clearly his father had caught her by surprise with his threat of a family curse, a hex that would not merely have an adverse impact upon the immediate Hollmann family, but would also bring sickness, sorrow, and suffering to the Di Domenico and Bellomo lines as well. He saw his mother's face pale, for curses were not something to be taken lightly, particularly when made by someone that had suffered a true injustice. This was no last-minute, desperate muttering by his father to save his own skin nor was it a lot of hocus-pocus; Roman Catholic Church doctrine made it abundantly clear that curses were real and especially effective when someone had been genuinely wronged. Only fools didn't believe in them or take them seriously, and they did so at their own peril.

But then his mother's face again hardened with resolve and he knew she was going to go through with shooting his father. He couldn't believe that his parents' life together had come down to this horrible moment, and that he and Teresa and their extended families would be cursed for the rest of their lives.

He couldn't bear to watch. He turned away from the window and slid to the wooden deck. Next to him, Teresa was still curled up into a ball, quietly rocking.

Don't do it, Mother! Don't kill our Father!

He heard a gunshot.

The blast of the weapon sent a shudder through his whole body. Teresa moaned and sobbed and rocked back and forth on the wooden deck.

Another gunshot rang out, and this time he heard his father groan and the sound of his body collapsing to the floor.

Oh my God, what have you done, Mother! What have you done!

He wanted to leap to his feet, charge into the house, and force her to stop. But he was still frozen with fear.

And then he heard two more gunshots, delivered one right after another. The sound of the gun was different this time, a deeper-pitch.

A second gun? But how?

Still in a state of shock, he was unable to believe what he had just heard and equally unable to make any kind of movement. But after a moment, he summoned enough courage to rise to his feet and peer through the window.

His father lay face down on the floor. A crimson pool of blood grew like an inkblot around his gunshot face and he clutched a smoking pistol in his right hand. Above him with two neat red blots on her freshly starched white blouse, a look of disbelief on her face, and her own gun in her left hand stood his mother.

My God, they've shot one another!

And then his mother, too, collapsed to the hardwood floor, the gun dropping from her hand and skidding across the floor.

He jerked open the screen door and ran inside, his heart racing madly.

"What have you done? What have you done?"

He knelt down to lend aid to his father and mother, who now lay next to one another. Behind him he heard a scream.

He turned to see, outside on the wooden deck, Teresa peering in through the open window and wailing at the top of her lungs.

It was then he knew for certain.

We are truly cursed. We are cursed to damnation here on earth and in the afterlife.

PART 1

THE ROUNDUP

CHAPTER 1

VATICAN CITY, ROME
OCTOBER 14, 1943

POPE PIUS XII—ROMAN-BORN EUGENIO PACELLI—stared worriedly out the window of his papal library at St. Peter's Square, the Tiber River, and the Eternal City beyond. He was dressed in his habitual holy vestments as the Vicar of Christ and Father of Rome: a snow-white cassock, sash, and snug-fitting skull cap; flat red slippers; a golden cross glittering with diamonds and sapphires at his chest; and the Fisherman's Ring he wore on the third finger of his right hand. But despite his saintly appearance, he felt like a prisoner.

A prisoner of a world at war.

Beneath his window, in the open space between the embrace of the Bernini colonnades, a bold line of white paint demarcated the perimeter of Vatican City and, in effect, the physical boundaries of his prison. On the Rome side of the curved white line stood German Wehrmacht soldiers in *feldgrau*, black boots, and steel helmets, with *Maschinenpistole* 40 light submachine guns, or Schmeissers as the Allies called them, on their shoulders. On the other side stood the Papal Swiss Guards, wearing ruffled tunics, plumed hats, and white gloves, armed with only antique swords and medieval pikes. To the north, further beyond the white line in the direction of the Monastery of the Order of Salvatorians, a senior German SS officer stepped from an idling Opel Admiral Cabriolet and barked out orders to a soldier standing in front of a convoy of military trucks. The SS officer's jet-black uniform and jackboots gleamed in the October sunlight, and his skull-and-crossbones insignia leered hideously from his lapel.

Pope Pius XII frowned. It was strange to think that the Holy See now bordered Hitler's Third Reich, but that was the predicament he now found himself. Though a longstanding Germanophile from his twelve years as apostolic nuncio to the Fatherland early in his career, he did not like these new interlopers, these new occupiers of Rome, these violent Nazis that had besieged his beloved city. But he reserved his greatest animosity for their Führer.

In fact, for four years now, the *defensor civitatis*—the defender of Rome as he was now called by its citizenry—had been deeply involved in an ongoing, highly secretive plot to topple Adolf Hitler and his Nazi regime. Since September 1939, Pius XII had acted as a secret intermediary between German generals plotting to overthrow Hitler and the British government. Very few affiliated with the Holy See were even aware that he had committed himself to the tyrannicide of the Führer. In fact, no one in the Secretariat of State—not even his closest advisors, Secretary of State Maglione, Undersecretary for Ordinary Affairs Montini, or Undersecretary for Extraordinary Affairs Tardini—had been let in on the secret. And that was how Eugenio Pacelli—once a boy wandering the streets of Rome and now the city's Supreme Pontiff—wanted to keep it.

His code name was the "Chief."

His war to topple Hitler was a secret war, his Catholic church a Church of Spies, and Vatican City, with its warren of diplomats, was *"un covo di spie"*—a cave of spies, as Benito Mussolini disparagingly referred to the Holy See. Since Italy's surrender and armistice with the Allies on September 8, the Germans had occupied Rome, the royal family and most of the government had fled the capital, and the Pope was the only remaining leader in the city that had been declared "open" a month earlier. Vatican City was surrounded on all sides by German troops and the Italian *Nazifascisti* that did their bidding. Meanwhile, the Allied Army was still far to the south facing Kesselring's Wehrmacht war machine at the Volturno Line, a prepared defensive position and death trap spanning the width of Italy north of Naples.

The Holy Father shook his head, turned away from the window, and returned to his desk. As he sat down and folded his hands, he was silhouetted by sunbeams, lending him an aura of light and spirituality in a world filled with darkness. Upon his desk rested objects both sacrosanct and mundane: a golden crucifix, an Olivetti Studio 42 typewriter, a wax candle, a silver plaque, and a gold-plated rotary telephone with finger-holes in royal blue. The plaque bore a special inscription declaring the desk a gift from the German bishops for Pacelli's twelve years of service as nuncio in Berlin. Across from him in a cane-backed chair sat Father Robert Leiber, a whisper of a man wearing an ebony soutane. The German Jesuit priest, who served as Pius's private secretary and closest advisor and taught at the Gregorian University, had been faithfully loyal to him for more than a decade. As the Pope's most trusted confidante, the *éminence gris* acted as the intermediary between Pius XII and the German Resistance, both dedicated to the removal of Hitler from power.

His codename was "Gregor."

"We have word from our contacts," said Leiber to begin the clandestine meeting, pulling out several sheets of paper devoid of official Vatican water-markings and handing them to the Pope. "Our friends have put together another plan to bring about the change we seek."

The Chief nodded as he took the papers from his private secretary. The only sound in the room was the quiet ticking of the Rococo clock in the corner as Pius pulled a pair of gold-rimmed reading glasses from his cassock and began to peruse the secret documents. He knew perfectly well that the *change* Leiber was referring to was the liquidation of Adolf Hitler. Thus far, Pius had participated in two plots to eliminate the Führer, and both times he had held midnight meetings in his papal apartments with British diplomat Sir D'Arcy Osborne to try and bring off a coup in Berlin. But the first plot fizzled when German generals lost their nerve, and the second failed when the fuse on a bomb on Hitler's plane froze; regrettably, the aircraft had been forced to unexpectedly climb to a frigid high altitude to evade

Allied flak. This would be the third coup attempt, and the Pope could only hope that this time the German conspirators could pull it off successfully.

"The attempt is to take place this week or next," said Leiber as Pius continued to read. "As you can see, our contacts are hoping the situation on the Russian front has stabilized before they move forward."

"I take it if there is no stabilization then they will abandon the plot?"

"Correct, Your Eminence."

"Timing is everything, it would seem."

"Yes, it appears so."

The room was silent for an extended time as he flipped to the second page of the secret document and continued to read. "This von Stauffenberg interests me," he said eventually, as if talking to himself, before flipping to the third page, reading for a moment, and then looking up. "What else do you know about him?"

"Only what is in the file there, Your Eminence. He is a lieutenant colonel in the Wehrmacht, a member of the German Catholic nobility, and the driving force behind the plot to assassinate Hitler and take control of Germany. He was badly wounded in battle in Tunisia last spring. He lost a hand, his left eye, and a pair of fingers on his other hand. But he has recovered from his wounds sufficiently to assume personal command of the operation. He is close to Generals von Tresckow and Oster, as well as Canaris, and is devoted to the cause, I am told. The operation is called Valkyrie."

"Operation Valkyrie. After the Norse myth?"

"Yes, Your Eminence."

"So there shall be a new ruler in Valhalla, and Stauffenberg gets to choose who shall be slain and who shall live?"

"It does seem rather appropriate, doesn't it?"

Nodding in affirmation, Pius continued to read. After a moment, he flipped to the fourth page of the document and read it before looking up a second time.

"Valkyrie, Valkyrie. It says here that after Hitler is eliminated, the plan is for General Olbricht's Home Army to block the main Reich communications center, and that if this can be done only a full-fledged SS counterassault can stop them."

"Quite right, Your Eminence. And to prevent that, the regional Wehrmacht military commanders must disarm the SS and arrest the local Nazi party leaders with lightning speed. To ensure secrecy, only a select few among the plotters inside Germany will be privy to every intimate detail of the plan. Officers not approved as need-to-know operatives at X-hour are to call in to headquarters in Berlin, where Stauffenberg will provide up-to-date briefings on the ongoing status of the operation. By this point, Stauffenberg will have liberated our friend Müller from prison. As we have discussed, Müller will then be flown here to Rome as swiftly as possible to work with you to publicly announce and secure a worldwide armistice following Hitler's death and the successful coup."

"It is an ambitious plan. Unfortunately, success has thus far eluded us."

Leiber nodded. Pius leaned back in his chair, steepled his fingers together, and assumed a thoughtful pose. Since the first plot to eliminate Hitler, the Vatican's primary contact in the German Resistance had been Josef Müller, a Catholic lawyer with ties to the Holy See. The Pope had decreed that, in the event of an overthrow, Müller would serve as the Vatican's special emissary to the post-Hitler government, with the title and status of ambassador-designate. Upon demonstrating to the world that Germany had new political leadership, Müller would work with the Pope and Holy See to mediate with the Allies. But with Müller's capture in April and subsequent imprisonment by the SS, the new clandestine cutouts here in Rome were Albrecht von Kessel, the First Secretary at the Reich Mission to the Holy See, and German Abwehr intelligence agent Paul Franken.

Posing as a history professor for the German-language school on the Via Nomentana, Franken interacted with the Holy See on a routine basis and had established discreet contacts with British and U.S. diplomats. To provide cover for his espionage activities, Franken received a stipend from Rome's German Research Association to edit papal nunciature reports. But in reality, the Catholic Franken took over Müller's Vatican contacts along with Kessel, who served directly under the Embassy Secretary to the Ambassador to the Holy See, Ernst von Weizsäcker. A strident anti-Nazi in the private salons of his more liberal and trustworthy German diplomatic colleagues, Kessel—or "Teddy" as he was called by those close to him—loathed Hitler and, along with Franken, kept the Pope and the Vatican well-briefed on plans to remove the Nazi leader from power.

Pius knew he was taking great risk in continuing to support the liquidation of Hitler. In directly involving himself in the conspiracy, he was once again putting not only himself and his aides, but the entire Roman Catholic Church, in danger. Never before in the history of the papacy had a Supreme Pontiff engaged in such a perilous conspiracy to take down a tyrant by force. The stakes were huge and unprecedented. If the Germans found out, the Holy See's official position as a strictly neutral and impartial party would be destroyed, confirming Nazi suspicions of the Vatican as a den of spies. But he felt he had to take the risk because, with the allies bogged down far to the south near Naples, it seemed the only chance to bring the war to a swift end.

He cleared his throat. "God promised Abraham that He would spare Sodom from destruction if ten righteous men could be found in the city," he declared. "Stauffenberg and the generals are hoping, for their sake, that God will not destroy Germany for Hitler's sins. I pray for their success. The Führer is many things, but he is above all else a stain upon humanity and all that is good and moral in this world. In the name of the Heavenly Father, he must cease to be at the helm of Germany."

"Yes, Your Eminence."

"I give my official blessing to the new plan, Father. Inform Colonel Stauffenberg and the others that, once again, they can count on me."

"Thank you, Your Eminence. Will you also be conveying your support of the operation to our English friends?" Leiber was referring specifically to Sir D'Arcy Osborne. The British Minister to the Holy See had been fully briefed on the two previous plots and, with the Pope's blessing as well as administrative and financial support, was helping run a secret Vatican Escape Line for Allied POWs along with the Irish Monsignor Hugh O'Flaherty.

"Not yet. I would like to see the plot more definitively hashed out. The

British have always been skeptical, so we will need to be on solid footing."

Leiber nodded and they fell into silence. Pius read over the last paragraph of notes again and then looked up. As he did so, he caught his reflection in the glass window behind his secretary. His skin was pale as parchment, dark circles ringed his eyes, and his skeletal face was taut as a drum beneath his wire-rim glasses. He had grown more and more emaciated as the war had dragged on, with the effect that he now presented a cadaverous picture of the Vicar of Christ shouldering the sufferings of those that had fallen under the wrath of Hitler's Third Reich.

He thought about the plot. He had carefully studied the Catholic teachings on tyrannicide, and he knew that he was operating within the parameters of Church doctrine. The three most important prerequisites were: the removal of a tyrant must improve conditions; the tyrant must be the primary instigator of unjust policies; and all peaceful means of removing him must have been explored and exhausted before raising a hand against him. All three prerequisites had been met. All the same, Pius still felt guilty. Like the Allies, he longed for Hitler's removal and the end of the war, but he knew he had stepped well beyond the line that separated papal diplomacy from papal "plotting." After all, he was a key instrument in the ongoing spy operation to liquidate Hitler and was secretly flouting time-honored Vatican neutrality, at grave risk to himself and others.

For four years and three separate assassination plots now, he had been the lone constant amongst the German conspirators and the Western Allies—as their top secret foreign agent. He had officially sanctioned the removal of the Nazi leader and had negotiated on the plotters' behalf with the British government for a post-coup peace treaty. By lending his much sought-after moral authority to the cause, he was the driving force behind the attempts to overthrow the Nazi regime, and his leadership was critical for a successful coup in the eyes of both the conspirators and the British. He and he alone provided the moral justification for the assassination of Hitler under the accepted Catholic Church doctrine of tyrannicide. In the end, he wanted the same thing as the German Resistance and the Allies: the removal of Hitler and his replacement by "any government without Hitler," as he had told the Resistance leaders since the very beginning.

He read through the document one more time. As he was finishing up, he heard the low hum of airplane engines. He looked across his desk at Father Leiber, fearing the worst: that Allied bombers were coming to drop a new deadly payload onto the Eternal City. He rose from his seat and went with his private secretary to the window, opened it, and stepped out onto his papal balcony. In the sky to the south, he saw an airborne battle, a dogfight, taking place between a German fighter-bomber and an American fighter. He breathed a sigh of relief that there were no Allied heavy bombers, but he was still not pleased at this encroachment upon the city of his birth. He pursed his lips together and squinted into the sunlight, deeply pained by the sight of these monstrous dragonflies of death flying so close to Rome and the Holy See, noisily spitting out machine-gun bullets.

He hated this war, hated it with all of his ethereal being. In his eyes, war was not the way of Christ, and was ultimately nothing but a cancer of the human spirit. He watched as the two planes raced across a backdrop of rolling, olive-colored hills, then rose again towards the heavens, their tail exhaust plumes streaking, spiraling, and crisscrossing the pastel blue sky, the color of a Fra Angelico fresco.

After a moment, he looked away from the distant airplanes and glanced down at the German soldiers with their MP 40 Schmeissers patrolling the white line demarcating the limits of his Vatican prison, and beyond them the terrifying SS officer in the jet-black uniform. Despite Eugenio Pacelli's strictly observed public impartiality to the Axis and Allied powers and his hatred of war, he knew which side he was on. And more importantly, he knew without a doubt which side God Almighty was on.

He looked again in the distance at the dogfight.

The two planes arced acrobatically across the sky, darting in and out of puffy white clouds. And then, quite suddenly, the German Focke-Wulf 190 with the black Nazi cross on a white background burst into flames, nosedived towards the trees, and disappeared out of sight. There was a tremendous explosion and a cloud of black smoke appeared along the horizon above the tree line.

Then there was nothing but silence.

"The American has won," observed Leiber.

"No," said Pius firmly. "No one wins in times like these."

Father Leiber dipped his head. "I see your point, Your Eminence."

He turned away from the distant smoke and looked down at the Germans in their *feldgrau* and their jackboots marching along the white line delineating the boundary of his prison. "Nonetheless, Father," he said, "we want our American and British friends to hurry to Rome. There is much at stake." He pictured the face of the tyrannical murderer with the narrow bristly mustache who was destroying his beloved Europe and mercilessly killing its inhabitants. "And there is not a moment to lose."

He then turned away from the window, looked directly at the secretary, and spoke in German, one of the six languages with which he was fluent.

"*Wir gedenken des Führers, uns zu entledigen*," he said in a low voice.

The Jesuit priest and spy codenamed Gregor nodded.

Pius nodded in return and silently repeated the words to himself in English: *We are thinking of the Führer, that we may be rid of him.*

"Go now, Father, and relay my message to our German friends. You have my backing and my blessing. I wish there was another way, but there is not. Go now in peace."

"Yes, Holy Father," said Leiber. "But before I go, I must remind you to do one last thing."

"And what is that?"

"To destroy the evidence and burn the pages."

"Yes, of course."

And with that, Pope Pius XII—the Chief, the Vicar of Christ, and the Father of Rome—stepped to his desk, took the Operation Valkyrie briefing notes, and set fire to them with a lit candle. He then carefully disposed of the last vestiges of the charred remains, without burning his fingers, in the small metal trash bin at the side of his desk.

"There," he said when finished. "Now you can tell Kessel and Franken that you saw the Holy Father burn the pages with his own hand."

CHAPTER 2

TYRRHENIAN COAST WEST-CENTRAL ITALY OCTOBER 15, 1943

THE B-24 LIBERATOR knifed through the rainless night sky eighty miles southwest of Vatican City and the Eternal City of Rome. A pregnant moon and smattering of stars cast a thin, silvery iridescence on the snout of the American heavy bomber, making it appear like a stalking barracuda. Powered by four Pratt & Whitney R-1830 radial engines, the B-24 could hit the needle at three hundred miles per hour, brandished wings wide enough to bridge the Tiber, and was, on account of its lengthy range, the ideal plane to drop clandestine operatives behind enemy lines. Tonight—with Naples having been liberated by Allied forces only two weeks earlier and the U.S. Fifth and British Eighth Armies slugging their way up the boot of Italy—the bomber carried two passengers in addition to its normal flight crew.

Two very important passengers.

One was an American spy. The other a commando with the First Special Service Force, a joint American-Canadian brigade specifically trained for cold weather insertion, mountain combat, and covert operations behind enemy lines. Poised to be airdropped more than one hundred miles north of the Italian front, the two operatives had been handpicked to be the eyes and ears on the ground for Brigadier General Mark Clark's U.S. Fifth Army and General William "Wild Bill" Donovan's newly created U.S. intelligence outfit, the Office of Strategic Services. The commando officer—Captain John Bridger—and his OSS-spy companion donned assault-black jump suits and were equipped with two different types of firearms. They also wore a pair of the newly invented "infrared light devices"—night-vision goggles, some called them—and jump packs as dark as their uniforms and charcoal faces.

Bridger felt his ears pop as the B-24 dipped its cruising altitude from nine thousand feet to just above two thousand to avoid German radar. Soon thereafter, the bomber banked sharply to the left and began a zigzagging flight pattern to avoid searchlights and antiaircraft batteries along the Tyrrhenian Coast. To ensure that Nazi air defenses and shore batteries could not detect a pattern, Allied pilots seldom flew the same route in Italy, or in other countries in Axis-occupied Europe. The mechanical roar of the B-24's engines dampened the sounds of the pilot, navigator, bombardier, and jumpmaster talking to one another through Bridger's radio headset. He glanced to his left at his comrade-in-arms, Lieutenant Peter

Savoyan, as they prepared themselves mentally to take a literal leap of faith out into the darkened sky. Their objective was to land, safe and sound, within their drop zone on the Italian mainland in the dead of night—a fifty-fifty proposition at best.

Bridger inhaled a deep breath of air to settle his nerves. During his First Special Service Force training, he had completed only three practice jumps at Fort William Henry Harrison in Helena, Montana. And during one of them he had sprained his ankle—and that had been during a daytime jump. But it was too late to worry about his lack of parachute training now.

Through his headset, he heard the navigator alerting him and Savoyan that they were approaching the drop zone, located in empty farmland one mile northeast of *Villaggio dei Pescatori*, a small fishing village along the coast. The pilot brought the B-24 below a thousand feet to search for the lights Bridger's ground-based reception committee would illuminate to signal the location of the drop zone: two bonfires blazing like a pair of panther's eyes. Bridger noticed that the voices coming over the intercom carried a note of urgency now that they were in hostile territory and nearing the target area. Noisy bombers circling overhead tended to attract attention and draw antiaircraft fire, and the SS was always on the lookout for Resistance officers being dropped behind enemy lines. The bastards were even known to set bonfires on the ground to lure Allied spies into a trap and capture them.

At seven hundred feet, the pilot leveled off the plane. He began to circle and lowered his wing flaps to slow the B-24 to 130 miles per hour, just barely above the speed at which the contraption could stall and plummet to earth. And then the red light in the cabin flashed, signaling Bridger and Savoyan that they should get ready to jump.

The jumpmaster shouted out the order, "Action stations!" and lifted the plywood cover off the trap door called a Joe hole. Feeling a flare of excitement, Bridger took another deep breath to steady his nerves. The roar of the Pratt and Whitney engines was ear-piercing as a pocket of air turbulence jostled the plane.

With their static lines hooked, Bridger and Savoyan took their leg bags and stepped forward to sit around the lip of the Joe hole. They moved unsteadily as they neared the opening, fighting against the tremendous but unseen force of the airstream. Once seated, the air rushed past their dangling legs, flapping their jump suits furiously and tearing their breath away.

Bridger stared down at the Italian coastline and, beyond, the Eternal City of Rome. As a boy, he had spent considerable time in the Holy City founded by Romulus and Remus along the banks of the Tiber, and he had lived there full-time from the age of fourteen to eighteen after fleeing Innsbruck. Back then he had been known as Gunther Hollmann, but he had a new identity now, an identity he had forged following his teenage exodus to America. Gunther Hollmann of Austria and Rome was now an American named John Bridger, a name he had not chosen at random. Peering down at Italian soil with the wind flapping his jump suit, he found it ironic that he was returning to the European continent not as one of its citizens, but as a U.S. military officer. He was here in Italy to liberate the legendary city that he had loved and admired growing up as a boy.

Looking down through the Joe hole, Bridger could now see the fires on the ground demarking their drop zone. Everywhere else was darkness, the unforgiving nighttime oblivion that he remembered only too well from the last of his three training jumps back at Fort Harrison. Bridger felt a powerful churning in his stomach, his heart pounding, as he made his final preparations to leap off into the blackness.

And then the red light extinguished, and a green light flashed.

The jumpmaster shouted, "Go! Go! Go!" and smacked each man on the shoulder. Bridger jumped through the hole, the static line attached to his parachute opening it automatically, with Savoyan right behind him.

He was hit instantly by the slipstream. Even wearing his helmet and night-vision goggles, the blast of air hit his face like a freight train and the parachute harness jerked savagely upon his shoulders. Hearing the rustle of silk, he peered up to see his chute obediently fluttering open into the darkened night. He and Savoyan continued to float downwards, the physical forms of the two paratroopers congealing occasionally from the darkness as the light of the full moon and stars caught them in silhouette during their rapid descent.

At four hundred feet, they pulled down hard on their front risers, drew their feet together, raised their knees, brought their elbows in tight to their bodies, and braced themselves for the landing both men knew would come all too quickly in a seven-hundred-foot nighttime jump. With the receding B-24's starboard lights flickering like fireflies above them, Bridger prayed to himself that the bonfires on the ground below were not a trap set by the enemy as they drifted down through the still night. To his right, he saw the little Italian hamlet of *Villaggio dei Pescatori* winking back at them to the west of the two separate ground fires.

As they closed in on *terra firma*, Bridger felt his heart racing in anticipation of the landing. With his night-vision goggles, the terrestrial world came to him in various shades of fluorescent green, giving the land below an otherworldly glow. As they continued to drift downward, the twenty-six year old Special Forces captain studied the luminous green outlines of the houses and roads of the village proper and the outlying farmhouses, getting a feel for the terrain while keeping a wary eye for signs of a German patrol.

If they were spotted from the ground at this point, they would be sitting ducks. It was imperative that they touch down unseen by anyone except their reception committee: the Italian Resistance contacts from the *Fronte Militare Clandestino della Resistenza*. The partisans were supposed to meet them along the edge of the open field with the pair of bonfires, one and a half miles northeast of the fishing village.

That was the plan.

But war was the most unpredictable of human endeavors. So when Bridger saw that they were going to miss their drop zone and he heard shouting voices and barking dogs, he knew that their top secret operation on Italian soil was no longer a secret at all.

CHAPTER 3

NORTHEAST OF VILLAGIO DEI PESCATORI
OCTOBER 15, 1943

WHEN THEY REACHED the edge of the clearing and stashed their chutes, Bridger could tell the enemy was rapidly closing in on them. The sounds of the barking dogs, sharp Teutonic voices, and clomping boots on the needly carpet of pine forest were growing louder. It was only because of the strong westerly sea breeze that he and his OSS companion had missed their original drop zone. But what a stroke of luck. Because the German patrol was on foot, it had to cover the much-longer distance to their actual landing site, which was located in the open field several hundred yards northwest of the original drop zone.

But the Germans were still hot on their tail and there was no time to lose. And they were platoon-strength at least, converging towards him and Lieutenant Savoyan from the woods to their left. Their thumping boots and guttural voices slashed through the quiet night like a *blitzkrieg*.

They were moving fast with the dogs.

"We have to move!" he snapped to Savoyan. "Let's go—now!"

"But where's our man?"

"Luigi probably double-crossed us. Or the SS snatched him and forced him to talk. Either way we're blown. Truth is we got lucky. If we hadn't missed our drop zone, we would have been captured by now. Come on, this way, let's go!"

Leaving their parachutes concealed beneath a thin layer of brush, they dashed northward in the opposite direction from the encroaching enemy. They were well inland from the fishing village, traversing the thick pine forest planted at the direction of Pope Clement IX in the 1660s as a way to protect the coastland and soak up the brackish muck near the mouth of the Tiber. A decade earlier, Mussolini—the self-proclaimed Il Duce—had ordered the surrounding coastal swampland drained; and by the beginning of the war, houses and verdant pine sprouted up all along the Tyrrhenian Coast. For Bridger, the good news was that by missing their drop zone, they were deeper into the thick forest and closer to the Eternal City, which lay only fifteen miles to the east of the coast. With a little luck, they would be able to elude the German patrol and push on to Rome by the light of the full moon.

They ran through the forest, keeping to the shadows. Behind them, the German patrol showed no sign of slowing down; Bridger could see flashlights flitting to and fro in their wake. A moment later, there was a flurry of activity as half a dozen flashlights converged on a single point. He heard excited voices, dogs barking frantically, orders shouted out.

"Damn, they found the chutes. Now the dogs will have our scent. We have to move faster!"

They picked up their pace to a run.

Only after a half mile, when they could no longer hear the dogs, did they reduce their pace, and then they held at a steady jog for another mile before slowing to a brisk walk. Soon Bridger heard the soft nicker of horses and the burble of flowing water. Peering through the trees, he saw a farmhouse along a small creek.

Taking a wide berth around the farm, they kept moving northward, quickening their pace again to a light jog. It was a warm evening and the full moon was crisp and bright. They soon came upon a small village. The *terra cotta* rooftops of perhaps a dozen houses and pinnacled spires of the town church glowed silvery in the moonlight. The streets were empty and shrouded in velvety darkness. It was surprisingly still and quiet. The only sounds besides the rush of the creek were the occasional snort of a horse or mule, or the distant yap of a stray dog.

And then suddenly, a German convoy appeared.

The lead vehicle was a black Mercedes-Benz 770 W150—a massive, eight-cylinder, 7,655 cc-engine luxury car favored by upper echelon members of the German High Command, the *Oberkommando der Wehrmacht,* as well as high-ranking Nazi Party officials, including Hitler himself. The sleek vehicle came to a sudden stop and out stepped a commanding, middle-aged man with a prominent scar on his cheek and wearing the jet-black uniform of an SS colonel. He immediately began barking out orders to the troops disgorging from the fleet of heavy trucks lined up behind him. There was something about the man, something in the way he—

No, it can't be! It can't be him! It's not possible!

But if it wasn't possible then why did the man look exactly like his father—Wilhelm Friedrich Ernst Hollmann of Innsbruck—once you adjusted for the passage of eleven years? He gulped hard, unable to believe his eyes, and strained for a better look. But the Nazi colonel with the puckered red scar on his face stepped quickly into the shadows next to the church and Bridger could no longer make out his features.

That can't be him, he told himself.

Savoyan was looking at him. "What's going on, Captain? You look as though you've seen a ghost."

It can't be my father. There's no fucking way!

He remembered back to that terrifying day in Innsbruck eleven years ago.

We are truly cursed. We are cursed to damnation here on earth and in the afterlife.

"We've got to get closer," he blurted, feeling a wave of sudden desperation.

Savoyan was still staring at him. "But Captain, we can't go closer. We've got to get the hell out of here. They're searching the whole area."

"No, I need to see that officer up close."

"The Nazi colonel? Why in the hell do you want to do that? That Gestapo son of a bitch will kill us on sight."

"I just need to see his face."

"You're talking crazy, Captain. The place is crawling with Krauts."

"I just need to see his face again, damnit!"

"Who the hell do you think he is? Someone you know?"

He took a deep, invisible breath. "I'm not sure but...but I think it's my...my father."

"Your father?"

He still couldn't believe he was saying it either. It just wasn't possible!

"But I thought you said your father was dead."

"He is, more or less."

"What do you mean *more or less*? You told me your father was killed in Innsbruck when you were a kid, long before the war. You said that your mother shot him in the goddamned head and he died right in front of you and your sister Teresa. That *is* what you told me, John."

"I know what I said."

"But now you're telling me that he didn't actually die? So he's alive?"

"All I know is to me he's dead. In fact, so is my whole family. My father died that day in Innsbruck, and my mother and sister seven years ago when I left Rome for America. You know the goddamned story, Peter."

"Yeah, I know the story. But you shouldn't talk that way about your mother and sister. You know that they care about—"

"Look, I don't need a lecture right now. I just need to see his face, all right? I need to know for sure."

The sound of voices and barking dogs drifted up again from behind, slowly picking up in resonance. The Germans were coming up fast, a couple hundred yards now at most.

"We can't stay here, John, and you goddamn know it. We have to go—now!"

Bridger hesitated. He wanted desperately to take a closer look at the SS officer, but knew that Savoyan was right and they should get the hell out of here. In all likelihood, he was letting his imagination get the better of him. Had setting foot once again on European soil, so close to Innsbruck and Rome where he had grown up, subconsciously made him want to see his father? Or was he just losing it?

"Goddamnit, Captain, we've got to go now! The Krauts are coming and the dogs have our scent!"

Maybe I am just seeing ghosts. "Okay, okay," he said, and they dashed across the road and into the dense forest on the other side.

CHAPTER 4

NORTHEAST OF VILLAGGIO DEI PESCATORI

OCTOBER 15, 1943

CLINGING TO THE THICK-TRUNKED PINES, they pushed first north then east along a game trail. Luckily, the dogs seemed to have lost their scent at the road and the bulk of the German troops headed southeast to cut off their escape, giving them a clear path to Rome, at least for the time being. They ran hard, quickly putting distance between themselves and their pursuers. Within fifteen minutes, Bridger could no longer hear any sounds coming from the Germans and called a brief halt to allow them to catch their breath.

A minute of quiet recuperation passed before he had the feeling that something wasn't right. Though he could no longer hear any sounds, not even the distant barking of the German shepherds, he still felt a vague presence. He had the uncanny feeling they were being watched.

He methodically scanned the area for signs of the enemy, but he saw nothing.

Then again, it was so dark in the woods how could he be certain? The only illumination was from the moon. It cast a silvery glow along the tops of the neat rows of pine trees and the lone farmhouse visible in the distance, before pinching out into soot-black night. He pricked his ear alertly to listen. He heard the hoot of an owl, but nothing else.

He told himself that he was worrying over nothing.

But the feeling didn't go away.

"Let's keep moving," he said quietly.

Lieutenant Savoyan sensed his discomfort. "Is everything all right?"

"Yeah, just being cautious. We need to keep moving."

They continued on at the standard brisk First Special Service Force walking pace of five miles per hour. At first he felt secure, but after they had gone a quarter mile the uneasiness returned. Taking evasive maneuvers, they darted around a series of rocky outcrops and stands of trees, hid out several times and waited, but there was still no sign of anyone following them. All the same, he couldn't shake the feeling that they were being shadowed and in possible danger. It wasn't just a presence; it felt like they were being stalked.

He thought of the man with the scar. Was it his father? Was he following them? Had Wilhelm Hollmann, former police chief of Innsbruck and now a Nazi colonel, returned to his life like some sort of ghost after an eleven year absence?

The thought sent a chill up his spine as he heard, or thought he heard, a noise to their left.

He raised his hand, bringing them to a halt. Again, he searched the shadows and strained his ears to listen.

Nothing except a faint rustling of branches from the wind.

He pulled out his snub-nosed Beretta pistol; Savoyan followed suit.

They started off again, pistols in hand. But they hadn't gone five paces when Bridger heard the sound again. This time he could swear he had heard the snap of a twig along with the soft scrape of a boot on the ground. Without stopping, he peered over his shoulder, expecting for someone to appear, but there was no one.

He brought them to another halt, again straining his ears to listen.

"Who do you think it is?" the lieutenant whispered.

"I don't know. But I think we're about to find out."

He continued to scan the shadows. Still nothing. The woods and farmland to the south stretched vast and empty behind them, with only faint pools of light sneaking through the piney canopy and cover of low clouds scudding in from the east. Should they sneak away quietly, or fire off a warning round and make a run for it? He knew it was best not to panic, but the urge to flee was overwhelming. He thought again of the man with the scar; he definitely was one scary-looking son of a bitch. But was it his father?

They resumed moving forward, faster now. Instinct told Bridger they were still being followed.

They accelerated their pace.

But to his horror, he heard a noise again. This time it was unmistakable: the sound of footsteps, coming up from behind them.

He brought Savoyan to another halt and turned abruptly. As before the sound stopped.

He probed the shadows. "Who's there?" he queried in flawless German. Then he tried it in equally fluent Italian. *"Chi c'è?"*

There was no reply.

He continued searching the darkness, but saw nothing. He still felt a tickling sensation on the back of his neck, as if someone was reaching out to touch him.

We should keep moving and get the hell out of—

He heard the footsteps behind them again. This time they were coming up fast.

They both stopped and turned, clutching their Berettas in two-handed grips.

But they were too late.

Out of the corner of his eye, Bridger saw a terrible, swift slash of shadow. The pistol was knocked from his hand and he was restrained by two pairs of strong arms. In a flash of moonlight, he saw Savoyan taken with equal alacrity and quickly disarmed by two more darkly-dressed men, one of them a hulking mass of brute strength with a clean-shaven head.

Bridger struggled to free himself, but his opponents' grip was like a vise, and he and the lieutenant were quickly rendered helpless. After a moment, he realized that further resistance was futile and allowed his body to relax. If they were here to kill him, they would have already done so.

"Very wise choice to surrender without a fight, Captain Bridger," said a voice behind him, spoken in smooth Italian. "We have been expecting you—and Lieutenant Savoyan as well."

Bridger felt the powerful arms release him. He turned to see the apparent leader emerge from the shadows, a bearded man in a dark-blue uniform illuminated by the moonlight. "The spotted cuckoo is flying to Sicily," he said to the man, reciting his code sign phrase.

"No, it is spring and he flies north," came the countersign reply. "Unfortunately, our code has been compromised, Captain Bridger. It is totally worthless. We have both been double-crossed, it would seem."

"Why should I trust you?"

Now the man switched to heavily-accented English. "Because my men and I here are with the National Liberation Committee," he replied, referring to the Roman Resistance group consisting of militant liberals, Communists, and Socialists. "Or, as we call it here in occupied Italy, the *Comitato di Liberazione Nazionale*."

"Just because you speak garbled English doesn't mean you're with the CLN or that we can trust you," said Bridger pointedly in Italian.

"True enough, but I would swear on the tomb of St. Peter himself that your contact Luigi is the one that sold you down the river. In fact, he was, until recently, a member of the *Servizio Informazione Militare*. The secret service of Mussolini's Fascist regime. Unfortunately, Luigi Fontane and others like him are nothing but unreliable soldiers of fortune. They would sell their own mother to ensure their own survival. Especially now that Italy has surrendered to the Allies, Mussolini is a German puppet living in exile in northern Italy, and the Nazis have occupied Rome."

"So you say. But you still haven't given me proof."

"I guess you'll just have to trust me then."

Bridger realized that he and Savoyan had little choice but to do just that. All the same, his gut told him the man was telling the truth. "So how did Luigi double-cross us? You're saying he's a Nazi collaborator?"

"He alerted Colonel Kappler, the head of the Gestapo in Rome, that you were coming. That's why half the SS in Italy is out searching for you. You're lucky your *Americano* airmen couldn't hit a drop zone if it was lit up by a hundred bonfires. That is what saved your ass."

"I'll be sure to thank the pilot with a fine bottle of Monfortino when I see him next time."

The four Italians chuckled. "I am liking you already, *Capitano* Bridger. Now get out of those commando outfits and put on some proper Italian clothes." He signaled one of his men, who tossed them a stuffed backpack. "You don't want to look like American spies when you hit the streets of Rome, do you?"

"Most certainly not."

He and Savoyan quickly took off their black, one-piece paratrooper uniforms and exchanged them for neatly pressed Italian sharkskin suits, cleverly planted with loose strands of Italian tobacco in the pockets, and brown leather shoes hand-tooled in Siena.

"Yes, that is much better," said the partisan leader when they were finished.

"Why if I didn't know better, I'd say you were a couple of respectable Fascist monarch sons. I think you'll blend right in."

"I'm glad you approve. Now since you're having so much fun at our expense, what should we call you?"

"You can call me Cervo. But my name is Lieutenant Maurizio Giglio of the Rome Police."

"A double agent—now that *is* convenient."

"Not when you get caught by Kappler's Gestapo, it isn't. That's when convenience is a word that does not exist. But we should not worry about such things. This is a time of celebration. Welcome to Italy, Captain Bridger and Lieutenant Savoyan. The Roman Resistance is at your service."

Bridger couldn't help a little smile. "Now that's what I like to hear, Captain. Let's go to Rome. It's been seven years since I last saw the Colosseum. Tell me it's still standing."

"Yes, of course it is. But only because your pilots are as inaccurate at dropping bombs as they are at hitting drop zones."

The Italians chuckled again, and the brawny leader pointed up at the full moon. "There is one last thing I should tell you before we go. You do know *why* you have reached us safely even though you were double-crossed, don't you?"

He followed Cervo's gaze up to the radiant, bulging moon. "Divine intervention?" he ventured, thinking it must be a trick question or the guy was pulling his leg.

"We Italians call it the *Roman Moon*." His voice was sweet and melodic like a strumming harp.

"You're talking about the full moon?"

"I'm talking about the protective power of the gods. It happens only during the new or full moon in times of war, and the moon's protection is offered only to the righteous. That is the Roman Moon."

"A bit superstitious, wouldn't you say?" said Savoyan with a wry grin.

"No, even Catholic true believers swear by it. You see, in ancient Rome Mars and Juno—the Roman gods of war—were always striving to deliver a secure peace and, in their efforts to do this, they imparted a special power to the righteous. Today that is us, the partisans, and you, our liberators the Allies, my friends. The Roman Moon protects us like *lorica segmentata*—that is, the body armor of the centurion in the days of old."

Bridger was intrigued. "And this special protection only happens during the new or full moon, you say?"

"Yes, my American friends. Tonight, we are protected by the gods just like the Legions of old. Tonight we are invincible."

"Invincible?"

Cervo smiled up into the brilliant moonlight. "I would never joke about something like that in this terrible time of war, *Capitano*. Now let's make for Rome, shall we?"

CHAPTER 5

GESTAPO HEADQUARTERS
VIA TASSO 145, ROME
OCTOBER 16, 1943

AT 0449 HOURS ON THE DAY OF THE JEWISH ROUNDUP, Waffen-SS Colonel Wilhelm Friedrich Ernst Hollmann stepped into the office of Lieutenant Colonel Herbert Kappler, chief of the Gestapo in Rome. Hollmann wore a black leather uniform with a peaked cap bearing a *Heer*-style eagle together with an SS-*Totenkopf*, and in the death's-head holster at his hip, he carried a 1939 Walther PPK 7.65-mm SS officer's pistol. In 1942, Himmler had ordered most all of the black SS uniforms recalled, stripped of insignia, and replaced by grey-green *feldgrau* uniforms; but Hollmann liked wearing black, so he had a Roman tailor make him a special black-leather outfit that borrowed equal parts from the Waffen-SS Panzer Troop double-breasted uniform and the Gestapo police unit uniform that were still allowed in the field. Fortunately, Himmler liked the arrangement and never forbade him from wearing it.

The outfit made Hollmann look absolutely terrifying. But in reality, the *standartenführer* was the furthest thing from a rabid Nazi. Ever the gracious socialite, fluent in German, Italian, English, and French, he was a bon viveur with a weakness for fine Italian wine and beautiful women. In fact, he had used the SS purely as a means to a pleasant existence without ever believing at all in National Socialism. Officially, the Bavarian was the liaison officer between the highest echelons of the SS and the fascist hierarchy, the Roman aristocracy, and the Vatican. Unofficially, Hollmann didn't have a clue what his official duties were—or what side he was truly on. Although he was certain that he was not fighting for the same cause as the Gestapo police chief seated at the desk in front of him.

Lieutenant Colonel Herbert Kappler's Gestapo headquarters had been only recently converted from the German Embassy's Cultural Center, and it included more than a dozen offices, a twenty-cell prison, a sound-proofed interrogation center, and a life-sized portrait of the Führer in the lobby. In only a month's time, since the German occupiers had seized Rome, the name Via Tasso had struck fear into the hearts of the Roman populace as a place of unmitigated police brutality and torture. The citizens of the Eternal City—particularly anti-Fascists, partisans, Jews, Communists, surrendered Italian Army soldiers and intelligence agents, and those harboring escaped Allied soldiers—were already aware that very bad things were happening behind the closed doors and sound-proofed torture rooms of the new Gestapo headquarters.

When Kappler saw his unexpected visitor, he sat upright in his chair with a look of irritation. "What brings you here at this early hour, *Standartenführer*?" His lean, hawk-like face bore a three-inch dueling scar on his cheek that turned red and looked like a hissing snake when he became agitated. "You wouldn't be looking over my shoulder again on behalf of General Wolff, would you?" he then added perfunctorily, referring to Hollmann's immediate boss, General Karl Wolff, the head of all German SS troops and police in Italy.

"Of course I'm looking over your shoulder—that's what I do." With an air of aristocratic entitlement, Hollmann took a seat in the finely upholstered chair situated in front of Kappler's massive mahogany desk. "I've been briefed on the roundup operation. But of course, Captain Dannecker hasn't told me everything. I thought you might fill me in—Herbert."

Kappler frowned. Hollmann suppressed a smile; he knew how much Kappler hated being addressed by his given name. The colonel delighted in knowing this and did so just to irritate him during his unannounced visits to Via Tasso.

"Why don't you start off by telling me when the roundup will commence?"

"At dawn." Kappler looked at his watch. "A half hour from now."

"Dannecker is handling it personally?"

The Gestapo chief nodded. Dannecker was Captain Theodor Dannecker, the so-called "Jewish expert" who had been brought in specifically to handle the special *Judenaktion* assignment, along with nearly fifty officers and soldiers that had previously served with him in the *Einsatzgruppen*, Himmler's mobile SS death squads. Under Dannecker's direction, the Jews of Rome—an estimated 8,000 souls—were to be rousted from their beds at gunpoint and shipped off in box cars on a one-way trip to the east. Though Hollmann had known for more than a year that when Jews were shipped in that direction they never returned, two weeks ago was the first time he had seen an official SS document on the systematic "Final Solution" taking place in Poland. He was glad that he was far removed from the ongoing horrors transpiring in the occupied countries. He thought the physical destruction of European Jewry was not only morally reprehensible, but a damned waste of time and resources, when there was a hard-fought war to be won. But he wasn't the one in charge of making such decisions.

Kappler continued, "Dannecker has made a master list of every Jew in Rome with their name, date of birth, address, phone number, place of work, and any other available information obtained from the synagogue records. Dannecker and his men are going to cordon off the twenty-four zones within the ghetto and the Trastevere district and round up all of the Jews in each zone."

"How are they going to round them up?"

"At each zone, a squad of troops will be posted and arresting officers will be dispatched to knock on the doors of every Jew on the list. Each one will be given a card instructing him or her about the transfer process, and they will be given twenty minutes to pack their things. Once packed, they will be loaded onto the trucks posted at strategic locations, cross streets, and squares within the zones. The destination of these vehicles will be the Collegio Militare," he added, referring to the military school fronting the Tiber less than a quarter mile from the Vatican that would serve as the holding pen for the *Judenaktion*. “They will be held at the college until Dannecker has cleared them for deportation by rail.”

“Where will they be sent?”

He held up the official order. “It says here that the Jews are to be used as hostages and will be sent to the work camp at Mauthausen.”

“And you actually believe that? You know perfectly well they will be sent to Auschwitz.”

“That is not my concern. Like you, Herr Hollmann, I never wanted to have anything to do with this. I have partisans, military deserters, and Vatican spies to contend with and do not need to concern myself with a bunch of harmless Jews.”

“Unfortunately, fate has ensured our mutual involvement in this regrettable deportation matter. My job is to keep an eye on Dannecker and his hooligans. I need to know if they lay a hand on a single protesting Roman Christian citizen during the roundup. Especially anyone from the black set.” He was referring to the Roman Catholic aristocracy that supported the Italian monarchy and the papal authority vested in the Pope. Since the time of Garibaldi, this elite group had been metaphorically represented by ‘black-colored’ priestly garb and was often referred to as the ‘black set’ or the ‘black nobility.’ “Our task as occupiers is already difficult enough—and I want to know if the only thing to come out of this for us is more enemies to deal with. As you noted, the partisan forces are already building up. All this nonsense may result in is turning us all into targets.”

“Finally, that is something we can agree on,” said Kappler.

Hollmann nodded and silently appraised his Gestapo counterpart. Despite their black SS uniforms and physical similarity, the two men could not have been more different. It was largely for this reason that they loathed one another. Born in 1896 in Regensburg perched at the edge of the Bavarian Forest, Hollmann was the son of a wealthy German lawyer and claimed a titled Italian and Austrian ancestry on his mother’s side. Like many German aristocratic dynasties, the family lost much of their fortune following the Great War, but a portion of its wealth, the old titles, and blue-blood identity were retained and young Wilhelm was accepted into the posh intellectual and social life of Munich and Vienna. He enrolled at the University of Munich, where he graduated impressively with a doctorate in the new field of criminal science while simultaneously becoming an expert in art history as well as Renaissance Romance literature. Following his diverse university studies, he married a titled Roman marchesa and became a wealthy landowner and police chief of Innsbruck. But that life was behind him now. Now he was a middle-aged bachelor with a new, reconstructed face and a weakness for Roman high society, a man known for his diplomatic light touch, calmness under fire, erudition, cynical wit, Machiavellian cunning, and, not surprisingly, his vanity. The former police chief of Innsbruck and titled Austrian landowner was now quite comfortable in his role as a drawing-room soldier with access to the wealthy of Rome and the uppermost strata of the Holy See.

In contrast, his rival Kappler seated before him was the son of a working-class Stuttgart chauffeur, but of Swedish origin, and had long been steeped in a militant police culture. In his spare time, the gray-eyed Gestapo chief collected

Etruscan vases and loved roses, dogs, photography, and his buxom mistress Helen Brouwer—and argued incessantly with his wife, Leonore, whom he was actively trying to divorce. Unable to father a child, the thing he cherished most in the world was their adopted son, Wolfgang, an "experimental" child of the *Lebensborn*—Himmler's baby-farm scheme to genetically engineer perfect Germans by mating male and female specimens believed to possess the purest Aryan blood. Blond haired with blue eyes and burgeoning muscles, the child could have been the type specimen for the depraved Nazi program. Unlike Hollmann, Kappler was zealously dedicated to the Fatherland. He truly believed in the Third Reich, and was ready to carry out orders unquestioningly. He disliked Hollmann precisely because of the Bavarian's "drawing-room soldier" personae, and he was envious not only of Hollmann's superior education but because he was the favorite of General Wolff.

They also differed greatly in their views concerning the "Jewish Question." Hollmann felt no animosity whatsoever towards the Jews of Europe, and he was only here to serve as the eyes and ears of his boss Wolff, not to take part in the roundup. While Kappler would lay his life down for the Fatherland and despised the Jews, Hollmann had become Himmler's personal representative in Rome only so he could live in comfort in his beloved Eternal City and be as far away as possible from the front lines and the atrocities he knew were taking place in Occupied Poland and Russia.

But there was another reason Wilhelm Hollmann had secured a posting in Rome. And it was deeply personal.

Kappler broke the silence. "You know I tried to stop this roundup, but Berlin wouldn't listen. Damn fools."

Hollmann gave a smirk. "You know you did nothing of the kind, Herbert. You extorted fifty kilograms of gold from Rome's Jewish community with the promise that none of their people would be rounded up and deported. Now, despite the fact that Chief Rabbi Zolli, Jewish Community President Foà, and his deputy Almansi have paid your fiendish ransom, the Jews are still going to be sent off to their deaths."

"You bastard," snorted Kappler, rising up from his seat. "You can't talk to me like that."

"I'll talk to you anyway I please. Remember, I am your superior officer and am here on behalf of General Wolff, who expects a full briefing. However, in the spirit of cooperation, I will let you in on a little secret. My sources tell me that the Pope offered Foà and the other Jewish leaders whatever amount of gold might be needed towards the fifty kilograms you demanded. But they ended up not requiring the Vatican's assistance. They were apparently able to raise the full amount on their own."

"The Pope did that? That's a violation of Vatican neutrality!"

"Indeed, it is. But I demand you say nothing and keep this information to yourself."

"Could prove diplomatically useful one day, is that it?"

"Yes, and I wouldn't pat yourself on the back pretending your gold ransom was a philanthropic attempt to prevent the forthcoming roundup and inevitable deportations that will follow. All you did was make the Jews here in Rome feel safe when they are, in fact, anything but safe. They are about to be roused out of their beds, rounded up like cattle, herded off at gunpoint to a collection point, and then shipped in boxcars to the east where we both know they will be gassed or worked to death. They certainly will never return home to Rome."

"I tried to stop it, I tell you."

"Come now, Herbert. Don't delude yourself. You have many commendable qualities, but altruism and the ability to question authority are not among them."

"I've had enough of your insolence. I want you out of my office." As Hollmann had expected, the scar on Kappler's cheek reddened like a hissing snake.

He decided to try and calm the Gestapo chief down. "Oh, quit your posturing. I'm just being honest with you because I know you are of valuable service here in Rome and to the Reich. I know you tried to do what you thought was right. But in the end, I'm afraid you didn't succeed. And now we have Dannecker and his Jew hunters swarming our fair city. I know that you love Rome nearly as much as I do, and for that I admire you. So for the time being, we just have to hope that the roundup won't incite an angry mob or stir up the Pope."

As expected, the complimentary tone achieved a mollifying effect and Kappler's face seemed to relax. "Oh, we won't have to worry about the Vatican," replied the Gestapo chief. "It's the Roman people and the partisans that I'm worried about."

"You don't think the Pope will vigorously protest?"

"I doubt it. From what I understand he is a Germanophile from his time as papal nuncio before the war."

"I would say he is more concerned with maintaining coveted Vatican neutrality. But that doesn't mean he won't issue a strong denunciation. After all, this roundup will be taking place beneath his very windows."

"Ten to one he doesn't speak out. Did he utter a word of public protest when we first took the city and Field Marshal Kesselring proclaimed Rome a war zone? Or when Kesselring declared martial law and placed the citizenry under his command? Why these days Rome is no more an Open City with no air bombing or military traffic than Paris—and yet Italy's beloved Pope hasn't uttered a word of public protest."

"I believe you misjudge the man. I can personally vouch for the fact that he *has* spoken privately with our diplomatic authorities, and there's no doubt they're concerned. In fact, Möllhausen and Weizsäcker are worried that he will make a public declaration against the roundup on Vatican Radio." He was referring to the head of the German Embassy in Rome and the German Ambassador to the Holy See, respectively, who had direct access to the Pope and were dedicated to protecting German and Vatican relations.

"Well, I believe they are worrying over nothing. The Pope won't publicly protest the roundup. Though he apparently has no love for our Führer, he would not dare to provoke his wrath and risk the destruction of his beloved city."

"You surprise me, Herbert. I didn't know politics was in your blood. You may be right, the Pope may not issue any sort of public condemnation. As we know, he is a cautious man and quiet diplomacy appears to be his weapon of choice. But I would not confuse public silence on his part with inaction. It is my understanding that when Italy quit the war and switched sides, the Vatican began hiding not only former Italian soldiers and Jews, but American and British soldiers that have escaped from the POW camps. In fact, my sources tell me that the Vatican is hiding two British officers and Israel Zolli the Chief Rabbi of Rome himself. Clearly, the Pope doesn't just condone these activities—he has issued commands to his priests and nuns to actively take these people in and feed, clothe, fund, and hide them. Again, so much for Vatican neutrality."

"That's what my informants tell me, too. Regarding the POWs, it is the work of that damned Irishman Father O'Flaherty, and other priests like him."

"No, hiding away Allied POWs is ultimately the work of Pius. Priests like O'Flaherty do their clandestine work only with the Pope's official blessing."

"If that is true, then that is precisely why your boss General Wolff should seize the Vatican. It would make our job here in Italy easier and would rid us of this den of spies once and for all."

"Herbert, Herbert. You have much to learn about diplomacy. You possess too much of the lion and not enough of the fox, I'm afraid."

"And you have much to learn about the intelligence business."

"Oh, I think it's safe to say I know a thing or two," said Hollmann with a competitive wink, and they fell into a brief silence. He looked at the raindrops dribbling down the window pane. After a moment, a book caught his eye in the bookcase next to the window. It was a leatherbound copy of *All Quiet on the Western Front*, an authentic bestselling German novel about World War One now banned in the Fatherland because it captured all too accurately the brutality of war and severe hardships faced by the front-line soldier. *Good for you, Herbert; you have a little subversion in you after all.*

Kappler broke through his thoughts: "Mark my words, I will catch O'Flaherty and his ilk in the act one of these days. Then I regret to say, I will have to hand him over to Captain Priebke and have him escorted to the basement."

Hollmann knew what that meant. The *obersturmbannführer's* closest aide and second-in-command, Erich Priebke, had, in only a month's time, already established a fearsome reputation as the Torquemada of Via Tasso. On two occasions thus far during the German Occupation, Hollmann had ventured down to the windowless basement of Gestapo headquarters and witnessed firsthand the ruthless interrogations ordered by Kappler. But he could never take the sight of torture for very long. Proficient at getting captives to talk by both physical and chemical means, Priebke and the rest of Kappler's Gestapo interrogators subjected partisan and anti-Fascist prisoners to unspeakably inhumane treatment, pounding them with spiked mallets, burning their feet and stomachs with lighted gas, and yanking their teeth out with dentists' tools. The special soundproofed room in the basement muffled the sounds of the victims' screaming to startling effect. Hollmann dreaded going down there, though at the same time he understood how important harsh but effective interrogation techniques were to Kappler's efforts to keep Rome safe for German troops and to instill fear into the partisans.

"Is there anything else I should report to General Wolff?" he then asked

Kappler, not wanting to be here at Via Tasso any longer than necessary.

"Just one thing. I received a tip two days ago from an informant."

"Who?"

"A detestable but generally reliable Fascist and former military staff member. For a sizable fee, he warned me of two American spies reportedly being air-dropped west of Rome near the coast. My men and I investigated later that night, but unfortunately we just missed them. We found their parachutes and discarded jump suits, and our dogs were hot on their scent. But a group of partisans came to their aid and they ended up getting away. We believe they were headed for Rome."

"I see," said Hollmann. Regrettably, he would have to deliver yet more bad news to his direct superior, *Polizeiführer* Karl Wolff.

He rose from his seat, signaling that the meeting was over. "I must be on my way to make my report to the general. Please be sure to keep me informed throughout the day of the roundup, and let me know if there are any new developments with the two spies. The general insists upon keeping a close eye on the state of Rome and mood of its citizenry."

Kappler rose from his seat and clicked his heels. "I bid you adieu then, *Standartenführer*. Give my regards to General Wolff." He gave the official Hitler salute, but did not exclaim, *Heil Hitler*!

Returning the salute half-heartedly, Hollmann left the building. He was driven by his Italian chauffer, Mario, through the empty streets in his Mercedes staff car to his office at Villa Napoleon, which served as the German headquarters for the delegation to the Vatican. When he reached his office on the second floor, he went to the window and stared out into the rainy darkness, not yet suffused with predawn light.

These were troubling times indeed with roundups and prowling partisans in the Eternal City, the Allies creeping towards Cassino, and a war in Europe that was killing millions. How would it all end? Would there be a Thousand-Year Reich, or would the Fatherland suffer ignominious defeat? He listened to the thin crackle of distant thunder, thinking of how the war would unfold if he was in command of all German forces instead of that maniac in Berlin, before his thoughts turned to Kappler's patrol the night before last along the Tyrrhenian Coast. It had been a fruitless excursion, but he was still curious about the spies. Who were these men and what did they hope to achieve by dropping behind enemy lines? Were they attempting to set up radio communication with the partisans to report on enemy strength and movements? Did they have a connection to the Vatican? In short, what was this dangerous game they were playing?

And what about this ill-advised Jewish roundup? How could the German High Command make such an error in judgment by antagonizing the Vatican and a whole city of people, Jew and Gentile alike? But he knew that, like a runaway train, the roundup—and its expected deleterious aftermath—could not be stopped. Himmler and Kaltenbrunner, the bastards, would not allow it.

Under the very windows of their protective Pope, the Jews of Rome were in mortal danger—and most of them didn't even know it.

CHAPTER 6

PIAZZA NAVONA AND JEWISH GHETTO, ROME OCTOBER 16, 1943

FAST ASLEEP in her bedroom at Palazzo Bellomo, her parents' luxurious villa overlooking Piazza Navona, Teresa Sabrina Di Domenico—known in her previous life in Austria as Teresa Hollmann before taking her biological father's last name when her mother remarried—was awoken by the family house servant Carla and told that there was an urgent phone call waiting for her. The person on the other end of the line, she was informed, was her close friend Princess Enza Pignatelli Aragona Cortes. Pulling on her silk robe, Teresa followed Carla into the anteroom of her father's office and picked up the white telephone on the credenza. Her father was Colonel Giovanni Vassalli Di Domenico—chief of the Clandestine Military Front of the Resistance—and like the monarchist Badoglio regime that he supported, he had gone into hiding shortly after Italy's surrender on September 8 to avoid persecution from the German occupiers. She had not seen him in a month.

"Enza, what is it? What is going on?" she asked her friend without preamble.

"Teresa, you must listen to me. I just received an urgent call from someone who resides near the ghetto. She told me that the Germans are arresting all the Jews in the area and taking them away in trucks."

"But I thought the gold ransom paid to Colonel Kappler made them safe?"

"Apparently not. My friend at the German embassy just told me that Kappler is not the one in charge of the roundup. It is being handled by an SS Captain named Dannecker, though Kappler approved it."

Teresa felt a cold chill run down her spine. "What do you want me to do?"

"I am going to speak in person with the Pope. Only he has the authority to put a stop to this atrocity."

"The Pope?"

"Yes, and I need you to drive me and speak to him with me. You, too, are close to the Holy Father, and to get there quickly we are going to need your fast little Fiat that has not been seized by the Nazis."

Teresa thought through the logic. With events already set in motion, could they possibly get in touch with Pius in time for him to intercede on behalf of these poor people? Would the Pope even receive her and Enza unannounced? It was true that she and the princess, as devout Catholics and members of the black nobility involved with many charitable endeavors in the city, were on excellent terms with the highest ecclesiastical circles of Rome. In fact, she and the princess both knew

Pope Pius XII quite well, having been his students before his accession and gaining a private audience with him on several occasions since the war began regarding charitable activities and the plight of the Roman people. And it was also true that she had one of the few cars in Rome that had yet to be requisitioned by the Germans. But would His Eminence see them when they had no appointment and he was consumed with the affairs of the Church and war?

"Teresa, we must go together now. You and I must help the Pontiff save the Jews!"

"Yes, yes, Enza, I will pick you up in ten minutes."

"Good, I'll be waiting."

ψψψ

At 7:43 a.m. Teresa picked up the princess at her residence just off Piazza Borgondini on the Tiber's west bank. They quickly headed to the Jewish ghetto to see for themselves what was going on with the roundup. Before meeting with Pope Pius, they needed to verify with their own eyes the accuracy of the description provided by the princess's original caller.

As they drove along the boundaries of the Jewish ghetto, they could see that the SS had indeed encircled the entire ghetto, cordoning off every entrance and exit. At every street corner, uniformed Nazis stood armed with submachine guns next to waiting trucks. As they neared the gates of the Portico of Octavia, they saw that the SS guards were halting all foot and automobile traffic at the police line at the gate and other access points. To make sure they could take a close look at the roundup, Teresa kept the car idling across the street some distance away from the guards. She and the princess saw at once that the original report was accurate and they were witnessing a well-planned and massive operation on the part of the German occupiers.

The Jews of the city were indeed being rounded up from their homes against their will, made to stand in the rain like convicts, and crammed into canvas-covered trucks. Officers shuffled through the streets barking out orders with pistols and submachine guns in hand. The Germans had compiled lists and were entering the houses where Jews lived and forcing them out into the streets at gunpoint. Teresa saw that some of the people were still in their pajamas, being marched down the street in the pouring rain and thrown into the black-canvassed trucks. She didn't just see able-bodied men and women, but grandmothers begging for mercy, hobbling old men with canes, and frightened children clinging to their mothers' skirts. With the windows of the car rolled down, she could hear the SS barking out commands over the sound of their snarling German shepherds and the anguished cries, pleas for mercy, and words of prayer of the victims. Close enough to clearly see and hear what was going on, Teresa and her friend Princess Pignatelli just sat there incredulous in the car.

"My God," said the princess. "It's even worse than I imagined."

Suddenly, a pair of beefy SS guards motioned aggressively and started to approach their car from across the street.

"Quick, we have to get out of here!" cried Teresa, and she jerked the wheel to the right, gunned the little Fiat, and headed northwest on the Via del Portico d'Ottavia before the guards could stop her. Two hundred yards up the road, they blew out a sigh of relief. Thankfully, the Germans cared more about rounding up the Jews of Rome and maintaining the integrity of their checkpoints than they did one little Fiat with two nosy Italian women inside. Teresa and the princess drove in silence towards the Vatican, tears in their eyes and prayers in their hearts. Surely, the Pope would be able to intervene and save these people whose only crime was that they were born Hebrew.

Crossing the Tiber, the princess at last broke the melancholy silence: "Where do you think the Germans will send them once they are rounded up?"

"I don't know. But it can't be just for the labor service we have been hearing about. They were arresting women, children, the old, and disabled."

"I have heard about the death camps. Do you think they truly exist?"

"I don't know. But what is happening to our fellow Romans is too terrible for words."

As they approached the mist-shrouded Vatican—a neutral nation-state with extraterritorial status as recognized by international law—the magnificent dome of St. Peter's and Bernini's colonnade looked inconsequential and mournful in the gray morning light. The Swiss Guards, the Vatican's loyal protectors, were as usual patrolling the grounds with their ornamental pikes. Downshifting the nimble little Fiat, Teresa raced to the north entrance and parked. As soon as they scrambled from the vehicle, they were surprised to see Monsignor O'Flaherty walking towards the entrance. The Irish Roman Catholic priest and senior official of the Roman Curia had worked previously with them on behalf of the underprivileged of Rome.

"Father, do you know what's happening?" asked Teresa. "The Germans have barricaded the ghetto and are rounding up all the Jews."

"I'm afraid they're not just invading the ghetto." He pointed to the people being arrested and lined up in the piazza in front of an apartment building a mere two hundred yards from the north wall of the Vatican. Men, women, and children were being herded towards a pair of heavy trucks by armed German guards. "They're rounding people up right under the Pope's very own windows."

"This shouldn't be happening, Father," said the princess. "That's why we have come. We need to talk to His Eminence and ask him to put a stop to this."

"Follow me, I'll escort you inside," said the bulbous-nosed, tousle-haired Irishman, and they started for the entrance. But before they had taken three steps, a pair of canvas-topped trucks appeared. The vehicles slowed as they passed the historic Basilica, and Teresa and her companions paused a moment to watch. The German drivers, unfamiliar with Rome's streets, must have been either using the prominent landmark of Saint Peter's to navigate or were taking a brief sightseeing detour from their route to their final destination, which Teresa suspected was the nearby *Collegio Militare*. The military school fronting the Tiber was less than a quarter of a mile from the Vatican. Inside the trucks, Teresa could hear people screaming and banging, making one final plea for someone to intercede and come to their rescue. And then the vehicles resumed their course and disappeared from sight, and all hope evaporated.

"This is terrible, just terrible," said O'Flaherty.

"That's why the Holy Father must stop it before it is too late," said the princess.

"He will do all he can. I can guarantee that, my children."

Teresa looked at the priest, nodded hopefully, and wiped away the tears in her eyes. The forty-six year old monsignor was an important figure in the Roman Catholic Resistance. Working with Sir D'Arcy Osborne, the British Minister to the Holy See, he had hidden hundreds of escaped Allied soldiers, Jews, anti-Fascists, and other enemies of the Third Reich in various Vatican properties surrounding the Holy See. One of these individuals was Teresa's biological father, Colonel Di Domenico. Teresa's father had lived with her and her mother, the marchesa, up until early September. That's when Italy had surrendered to the Allies, the Germans marched in and seized Rome, and all those who had supported the monarchy or voiced opposition to the Nazis like her father became a threat to the occupiers and were hunted down like fugitives.

Father O'Flaherty led them briskly through the entrance, down three hushed corridors, and eventually managed to coax them past some startled lower-ranking officials to the coveted *Maestro di Camera*, Monsignor Arborio Mella St. Elias. Taking over for O'Flaherty, the Master of the Chamber then led them to Pius's private chapel, where they found the Pope kneeling in silent prayer. His expression evidenced surprise.

"Holy Father, we are sorry to interrupt, but it is urgent that we speak with you," said the princess.

He regarded her and Teresa for a moment before crossing himself and rising from his kneeling position. "Come, my children," he said. "Let us go to my study where we can talk in private."

CHAPTER 7

VATICAN

OCTOBER 16, 1943

"YOUR HOLINESS," Pignatelli said once they had taken their seats in the chairs facing the Pope's spacious desk. "Please, you must act immediately. The Germans are arresting the Jews and hauling them away in trucks. Only you can stop them."

Seeing the Supreme Pontiff's surprised reaction, Teresa could tell that this was the first he had heard of the SS roundup taking place this very moment on the streets of Rome. He shook his head in despair.

"Did you see this for yourself?" he asked.

"We both did, Your Eminence," said Teresa.

"A friend called me earlier this morning," explained the princess. "She said the Germans were raiding the ghetto, arresting all the Jews, and loading them onto military trucks. Not just able-bodied men, but entire families including women, children, and the elderly. I immediately called Teresa and we drove to the Portico of Octavia. The Nazis had cordoned off all of the streets, but we could clearly see what they were doing. It wasn't just happening in the ghetto. They are arresting people right outside the Vatican's walls as we speak. The trucks are driving right past your Swiss guards patrolling the grounds."

"It is a desperate situation, Your Holiness," quickly added Teresa. "We saw people, many still in their pajamas, being marched out into the rain and thrown into the trucks. There were frightened children clinging to their mothers and old women begging for mercy. We saw dozens of young men trying to flee across the river. You must help them, Your Holiness. They need your help badly."

"This isn't happening in France or Poland—it is happening right here in Rome," said the princess. "Right under your very windows, Your Holiness. This cannot be allowed to happen."

Again, he shook his head with dismay. "I don't understand this. The Germans promised not to touch the Jews in the city once they were paid their gold ransom. They gave their word."

"We *all* thought that the gold payment would provide the poor Jews with the security they needed, Your Holiness," said the princess. "But it appears that Colonel Kappler has gone back on his word."

"Today is the Shabbat during Sukkot," said Teresa. "The Germans deliberately chose this date to cast scorn upon the Jews."

"Yes, it would appear so. Luckily, two weeks ago I personally ordered Vatican clergy to open the sanctuaries of the Vatican City to all non-Aryans in need of refuge. Thankfully, Rabbi Zolli and many others took me up on my offer."

"Unfortunately most did not, Your Eminence," said the princess. "We must have seen dozens of families being rounded up and shoved into the waiting trucks. I do believe the Germans are trying to get their hands on every Jew in Rome."

"This situation saddens me beyond words. I only opened the sanctuaries as a precautionary measure. I firmly believed that the Germans would keep their promise and leave the Jews alone. And President Foà, Deputy Almansi, and many of the other leaders of the Jewish community believed the same."

"The ransom gave us all a false sense of security," said Teresa.

"It most certainly did. All the same, I can't help but feel responsible."

"No, no, this is not your fault, Your Eminence," said the princess. "This is the evil work of the Nazis, and no one else is to blame. You have opened your doors to Jews and Christians alike in this terrible war and all of Rome knows it."

"Thank you, my child. Your words mean a great deal to me. Now who is leading this roundup? Kappler?"

"No, it is an SS captain named Dannecker, the so-called 'Jewish expert.' He was brought in from Occupied France, I am told."

"How did you come by this information?"

"From my diplomat friend who works at the German Embassy."

"Does this friend have a name?"

"Karl Wollenweber. He even offered to bring me here, but I told him that I wanted Teresa to drive me instead so that we could both speak with you."

"Do you know where they are taking the prisoners?"

"We think it is the *Collegio Militare,"* said Teresa. "The trucks are right outside the walls of the Vatican and heading in that direction."

"This *razzia* is an affront to God, Your Eminence," said the princess. "The Germans must be stopped."

"And they will be. But unfortunately, this Dannecker and Kappler are men of great power in the city at this moment. In fact, right now with their weapons of violence and the backing of their Führer, they are more powerful than me, I'm afraid. So we must tread carefully. These are dangerous times, and this is going to have to be handled firmly but quietly through formal diplomatic channels."

Her friend Enza shook her head sadly. "I feel terrible, Your Eminence. We should have known the Germans would pull a trick such as this."

"Yes, but as I alluded to before, even the Jewish community never expected them to actually go through with such brazen treachery. Not here in Rome. The gold ransom was paid and the Germans gave assurances. That's all any of us had to go by. But I will take care of this. I promise I will do all I can."

"Thank you, Your Grace," said the princess.

"Yes, thank you, Your Holiness," echoed Teresa.

He picked up the phone at his desk, dialed a number, and spoke into the mouthpiece to the Secretary of State of the Holy See, Cardinal Maglione, instructing him to immediately summon German Ambassador Weizsäcker. After a few head nods and more words, he hung up and looked back at his visitors.

"As I said, I will do all I can. Now go in peace."

And with that, he showed them out with what Teresa could tell was a very heavy heart.

CHAPTER 8

PIAZZA LOVATELLI

OCTOBER 16, 1943

JOHN BRIDGER couldn't believe his eyes as he peered down into the piazza below. In only the last two minutes, an army of submachine-gun-wielding SS troops had swooped in on heavy trucks, barricaded off the street, and were conducting an aggressive door-to-door search and arresting people.

He turned towards Savoyan, who had just stepped from the *gabinetto*. The OSS lieutenant raised an eyebrow.

"Something wrong?"

"There's Germans everywhere! Quick, take a look!"

He pulled the curtain back another inch as Savoyan stepped quickly to the window. "Jesus! Who the hell are they after?"

"I don't know, but we can't wait to find out. They'll be breaking down our door any second now."

"I'll bet they're rounding up men for labor service. Let's take a peek out back."

Dashing quickly to the apartment's rear bedroom, Bridger pulled back the curtain. He didn't see any movement on the street behind them and there was no sign of the Germans, but that didn't mean an SS squad wasn't assembling out of view or waiting in nearby trucks. He wiped the fog from the window to get a better look, but the visibility was still poor with the heavy rain and water droplets on the glass. Part of his view of the street was obstructed. But from what he could tell, the escape route behind the house was a better option than the piazza. Then he saw a pair of young men dashing down the street and he knew it was probably their *only* escape option.

"We have to go now! Grab your things!"

Having spent last night planning for this eventuality, the two spies quickly gathered up only their essentials, which were already packed: their guns, spare magazines, stilettos, spare clothing, toilet kits, and raincoats. They then grabbed their false papers. Their short-wave radio was safe with their fellow OSS operative Cervo. Though they were both terrified of being caught and tortured by the Gestapo, there was no evidence of panic in their movements. They worked with calm mechanical efficiency, like the well-trained soldier-spies they were.

When they had everything, Bridger checked his watch. Less than three minutes had passed since the Germans had arrived and already he and Savoyan were prepared to leave. But then they heard shouting voices coming from downstairs along with the sound of breaking glass and objects being overturned.

The bastards had already busted into their building and were rounding up people.

"Quick, we have to get the hell out of here!" he said to Savoyan.

Now the pounding of feet echoed on the stairs and down the hallway: the Germans were on their floor now, banging on doors. He went to the rear window, drew back the curtain, and peered down at the street.

A truck screeched to a halt and a squad of square-jawed SS troops leapt out and started chasing three young men who were trying to escape.

A cold hand closed over his heart. They were trapped on both sides now. But at least the SS squad was running away from the piazza.

They had no choice but to make a dash for it.

Bridger quietly opened the window. Then they climbed down the fire stairs to the street level and ducked into a narrow side street just as another German patrol raced in from the west. They waited for the Germans to fan out down the street and enter a pair of buildings before starting off again, heading north on Via dei Funari towards Largo di Torre Argentina.

They walked at a brisk but reasonable pace for several blocks, trying to remain inconspicuous though that wasn't easy as they were the only non-Germans on the street and the enemy seemed to be everywhere. For Bridger, it was surreal to see the Rome he had loved transformed into such a dangerous place.

They turned right onto Via Paganica, made their way cautiously to Piazza dei Calcarari, and from there to the edge of the Largo di Torre Argentina. Standing before them were the ruins of the four ancient Republican temples and the Curia of the Theater of Pompey where Julius Caesar had been assassinated at the hands of Cassius and Brutus. Along the way, they were forced to duck into a doorway to avoid being spotted by a Roman Fascist foot patrol as a German truck filled with screaming captives rumbled past. Catching a quick glimpse of the prisoners, Bridger saw from their appearance and clothing that they were Jews. It was then he realized that the Germans were not after ex-Italian army soldiers, Communists, or anti-Fascists for work details, but rather Jewish civilians—men, woman, and children, including the elderly.

Suddenly, a black Mercedes-Benz bearing two miniature Nazi flags turned a corner and came roaring down the street at them. Taken off guard, they didn't even have a chance to hide themselves in a doorway and simply froze. The car continued to race towards them. A small pack of wild Roman cats scattered at the roar of the engine. The scrawny animals took cover behind the six remnant columns of the circular temple built by Roman Consul Quintus Lutatius Catulus in 101 B.C.

"Shit!" groaned Savoyan.

"Just act natural. Our papers are in order."

"Yeah, but we're carrying guns and packs filled with clothes."

"That may be, but we're still two loyal Fascists in sharkskin suits who speak fluent Italian. Let me do the talking."

The Mercedes screeched to a halt in front of them. There were two men in the car: the driver, an Italian in civilian dress, and a German officer in the backseat. The officer, wearing a black uniform with the insignia of an SS colonel, stepped from the rear of the vehicle, pulled out his pistol, and commanded them to halt or be shot. Bridger had a strong feeling of déjà vu. At first, he thought the man was the commanding Nazi officer he had seen two nights ago along the coast, the man he had thought was his father. But then he saw that the officer before him couldn't possibly be his father because his face looked nothing like his father's face. And yet, somehow the profile of his body and way he moved was exactly like the father he remembered. But how was that possible? And then the SS colonel's face flashed with recognition and he spoke out, in of all languages, English.

"Gunther?"

Bridger felt his whole body go still, like a sail that has suddenly lost all wind. The voice! It told him everything he needed to know; it belonged unmistakably to his father. And yet, he still couldn't believe his ears and was unable to speak.

"Gunther, my son…what…what are you doing here?"

Still, he was unable to respond. It couldn't be his father. *My father is dead!* a voice screamed inside him. *Or is it that I want him to be dead?*

Now Savoyan was staring at him. "This man is your father?" he whispered accusingly in Italian. "You've got to be kidding me."

"I…he…I don't know what to say," replied Bridger, also in Italian. He looked at the man; the face looked nothing like his father's face. It was too sharp and angular, and it was plastic-looking. Almost like it was fake. A wax-figure face.

"Gunther, you must answer my question. What are you doing here in Rome?"

With sudden clarity, he understood that it really was his father. The face may not have been his father's face, but everything else was the same. After the terrible shooting in Innsbruck, his father must have had his face surgically reconstructed. And now, in order to get out of this desperate predicament they now found themselves, Bridger knew he had no other choice but to lie and use his blood relationship to his father to his advantage.

"Why I live here," he said, as if affronted. "Rome is my city—as you perfectly well know."

His father shook his head, and the gesture, though not a sharp rebuke, reminded Bridger of when he was young and he had done something to displease his father.

"Don't lie to me, Gunther. I am your father and you can't fool me. I also happen to be a colonel in the SS here in Rome, and I can tell you that you are in serious danger out here in the open on these streets. Today especially."

For several seconds, Bridger didn't respond. It was strangely surreal to have his father back in his life, addressing him like when he was a boy growing up in Innsbruck. For some reason, the stern, patriarchal tone filled him with anger. He stepped towards him aggressively, just as a pair of heads poked timidly out of the shuttered windows of the houses lining the narrow street to see what was going on.

"To play it safe, maybe I should just kill you then."

To his surprise, his father held his ground, looking as tall, stolid, and imperturbable as he had looked back in Austria when Bridger was a little boy named Gunther. "That certainly wouldn't be a surprise. Shooting me seems to run in the family."

"Yes, but I am a much better shot than Mother. Trust me."

"I'm sure you have been well-trained by the Americans. If there's one thing they know how to do over there, it is shoot a gun. Most of them are gangsters."

"I am no American, and even if I was, you obviously don't know a damned thing about America."

"I know that you have lived there since you were eighteen. And I know a great many other things about you. In fact, I—"

"Shut up! You had another wife and lied to us all. If I were Mother, I would have shot you myself. And then, you had the nerve to shoot her."

"I shot your mother in self-defense. She tried to kill me and she ended up living, didn't she?"

"It doesn't matter who shot who first. You're the one who started it all with your other wife and your goddamned mistresses. You ruined Teresa's and my childhoods, you bastard. You ruined us for life!"

His father said nothing. His face darkened with shame. Bridger glanced at the Italian driver in the car. He was listening to the conversation intently, hanging on every word, and Bridger knew he would get no trouble from him.

"Don't you have anything to say, you bastard?"

"Only this. Did you ever ask yourself how your mother, the marchesa, was able to shoot me down in cold blood and then get away with it? How she was able to steal my children away from me and force me to disappear from their lives even though all I did was defend myself? Well, did you?"

It was Bridger's turn to be shocked.

"I'll tell you how. She had the best legal defense team in all of Europe and her father's vast fortune and political influence behind her. Not only did I have to have reconstructive facial surgery, but I was forced to agree to never see you children again." He looked at him accusingly. "And here all these years, you thought I was the one who was in the wrong. But I tell you, it is the other way around."

"I don't believe you. I don't believe any of this."

"You can believe what you want, but I am telling the truth."

"I still don't believe you. Now drop your weapon and put your hands over your head."

"I'm not in the habit of giving up my gun. Not even to my own flesh and blood."

"Shut up. You're not my fucking father. Now put the gun down."

"Very well. To avoid another disgraceful family shooting, I suppose I will comply."

Slowly and deliberately, his father set his Walther PPK SS pistol gently on the pavement. Keeping his Beretta trained on him, Bridger stepped forward, picked up the gun, and stuffed it in his pocket.

"This will make a great war souvenir."

"You shouldn't be doing this." He shook his head. "My very own son."

"Don't call me *your son.* I may have been once, but not anymore. I would never be the son of a fucking Nazi."

"Let's get the hell out of here," said Peter Savoyan, looking around worriedly. A handful of Romans were now staring at them from the open windows down the street. "We don't have time for this."

"Your spy friend is right, my son. There are police and soldiers on the prowl everywhere. You will never get away."

"You heard him. We have to go, damnit!"

Bridger shot his partner a look. "I just need one more question answered." He looked back at his father. "What about this roundup that's taking place? Is it a labor roundup, or is the SS trying to break the Resistance?"

"They are rounding up the Jews. And I have nothing to do with it. In fact, I tried to stop it."

"Then what are you doing here?"

"I was heading to the ghetto to assess the situation and report my findings to my superiors on how the roundup is conducted."

"Why?"

"Because it's my job to know the mood of the city and its citizenry. Counterintelligence and liaison work is my business—and I'm damn good at it. That's how I know that it was you and your friend here that were airdropped along the coast two nights ago. The head of the Gestapo here in Rome, Colonel Kappler, found your discarded parachutes and your jump suits. You are lucky the partisans got you out of there in time. Otherwise, you would be in Kappler's basement at Via Tasso being interrogated by his infamous second-in-command Priebke. You should know that the young captain takes his work quite seriously and has already gained quite a reputation as the Torquemada of Rome."

"We have to go now, goddamnit! There's a truck coming!" pleaded Savoyan.

Bridger glanced over his shoulder. A heavy, black-canvas-topped truck turned left and drove in the opposite direction, surprisingly leaving them alone. It was early morning with many people still asleep, and luckily they had escaped into a section of Rome without many Jews or others wanted by the authorities. All the same, it was still dangerous. He turned back and glowered at his father.

"I told you I am a Roman."

"No, you're not. You stole away to America in 1936 at the age of eighteen to live with your uncle in Chicago. After two years of working as a cook, oil field roustabout, and miner in the American West, you changed your name to John Bridger, became a U.S. citizen, and enrolled at Notre Dame. I am told that the name Bridger comes from the famous frontier scout and Indian fighter Jim Bridger. I must say I heartily approve. And now, at the ripe old age of twenty-six, you are an officer in some branch of the U.S. Army, I don't know which. But I promise you I will find out shortly."

"But how did you…?"

"I told you I am in the intelligence business. What, you didn't think I would keep track of my one and only son all these years? I told you I am good at what I do. So you must stop lying to me."

"That's not going to happen. I don't trust you."

"It makes sense the Americans would send you here to Rome. You are fluent in German and Italian. And who is your friend here? Is he your radio operator?"

"I'm not telling you a damned thing." He turned to Savoyan. "Let's go. I've heard enough from this Nazi asshole who claims to be my father.

"I don't *claim* to be your father, Gunther. I *am* your father. And I always will be. Remember, blood is thicker than water. It is the very thing that binds us. That is why if you are taken prisoner by the Gestapo, you must tell them you are an informant working for me, SS-Colonel Wilhelm Hollmann. You changed your name to put your past behind you. But the past seems to have caught up with us both and we find ourselves united together again, as father and son."

"Fuck you. I don't need your help."

"Ah, but someday you might. I *am* your father, Gunther, and despite what you may think of me, I love you. And I will *always* love you."

Bridger felt all the anger and resentment of his aborted childhood suddenly rise up in him like a tempest.

"Damn you to hell! You and mother ruined my life!"

He drove the butt of his pistol into his father's temple, catching him partly in the right eye and knocking him hard to the street. To Bridger's startlement, his father's head struck the cobblestone road hard and his body instantly went limp.

Bridger stood above him, chest heaving, his mind filled with rage. He knew his father wasn't dead, just unconscious since he was still breathing, but a part of him wished the bastard *was* dead.

"You're not my father, you Nazi piece of shit! You're not my fucking father!" he screamed down at the motionless body.

And then he and Savoyan turned and dashed away, making for Piazza Navona on foot. But as he ran, the past came back to him in a terrible torrent. He couldn't get the nightmarish words out of his mind as he pictured the wax-figure of a man he had just left behind in the gutter, this Frankenstein monster with a reconstructed face that somehow *was* his father. Nor could he forget the horrifying images of that gruesome day eleven years ago in Innsbruck that had created that monster.

We are truly cursed, said the voice in his head, as he knelt next to his fallen father and mother and Teresa screamed from the window. *We are cursed to damnation here on earth and in the afterlife.*

CHAPTER 9

LARGO DI TORRE ARGENTINA AND PIAZZA NAVONA OCTOBER 16, 1943

HE FELT someone gently shaking him and thought he heard Captain Priebke's voice. It came to him like a dream, but he knew he wasn't dreaming. The voice and the shaking were too real and could mean only one thing.

He was actually alive.

He tried to open his eyes, but could manage to open only his left. The other was swollen shut. Peering through his good eye, the world came to him in a blur, like the first streaks of predawn. He felt gentle raindrops on his face. The faint light, bleeding down between the buildings, cast a gloomy gray tint on everything around him, lending the empty street an airy, ghostly quality.

Where am I? And where did my driver go?

Feeling dreamy and lightheaded, he slowly realized that his body was propped up against a wall. Nearby, he heard two muffled voices—his Italian chauffer Mario was telling Priebke something. He turned towards the voices and felt a sharp pain shoot through his head.

He let out a fierce groan.

My head—I was struck in the head. And then he remembered who had done it: his own damned son!

"*Herr Standartenführer*, are you all right? It's me, Captain Priebke."

The pair of figures, up until now nothing but a blur, came into slight focus out of his good eye. Hollmann forced himself to concentrate, but the world around him was still fuzzy. He blinked several times and squinted.

Standing now before him with his chauffer was Kappler's second-in-command, a true specimen of Aryan perfection: tall, blond, blue-eyed, a veritable *Lebensborn* who was known to carry a loaded, self-cocking Mauser *Hahn Selbstspanner* in his leather SS holster and another in his right boot as a backup piece. Despite being a devout Roman Catholic, as well as married with two young boys, the thirty-year-old Erich Priebke was quickly gaining a reputation throughout the city for bedding wealthy Fascist women and, with equal enthusiasm, brutally torturing enemies of the Reich. With his steely gaze, erect posture, immaculate grooming, and spotless SS uniform, he somehow managed to simultaneously carry himself with an aura of Nordic chivalry and Neanderthal thuggery. Personally, Hollmann loathed the young man, but he had to admit he had his uses. Priebke was an inveterate social climber, desperate to improve not only his rank in the SS, but his standing within Rome's aristocratic Fascist set within which Hollmann was well-connected. Although the captain worked for Herbert Kappler, the head of the Gestapo, he also served as an informant and occasional muscle for Hollmann, knowing that the colonel was number two to Karl Wolff, the head of all the SS in Italy.

"You are lucky that my men and I happened to be patrolling the area. We will catch these bastards, Colonel," said the strikingly handsome and cultivated SS captain, who had spent his formative years as a waiter at the Savoy Hotel in London and on the Italian Riviera and was renowned for his ability at waltzing. For the first time, Hollmann noticed the pair of SS troops in gray uniforms standing patiently a dozen feet from him, awaiting Priebke's orders. "Can you tell me who did this to you?"

Hollmann tried to force his mind to work, but he was still groggy. He looked at Mario; thankfully, his loyal Italian chauffeur had told the Gestapo police captain nothing except that they had been ambushed.

"Colonel, who did this to you? Partisans? Jews? We ourselves just caught a pair of escaped Italian POWs."

Hollmann touched his temple gently and looked at Priebke and Mario dumbly, still trying to clear the cobwebs. He thought back to his son Gunther moving quickly towards him, his teeth gritted with anger and hand raised to strike a blow with the butt of his Beretta.

My God, he moved fast!

"Sir, who was it? Who did this to you?"

He thought: *Do I dare turn in my own son?*

"Did you get a look at them?"

He tried to speak. "No…I mean, yes…they were partisans."

"How many were there?"

"Three."

"Three? You're quite certain it was three."

"Yes, three Italian partisans."

"*Italian* partisans? But, Colonel, what other kind is there?"

"I don't know, goddamnit—my head still hurts. Now help me up."

Priebke and Mario leaned down and hauled him to his feet. But as Hollmann stood up, he was struck with a sudden realization.

Damnit, I know where Gunther is headed!

"Captain, I appreciate your coming to my aid from your patrol, but I am fine now and have an urgent matter to attend to. Come, Mario."

The chauffeur opened the rear door for him. He stepped inside the Mercedes. "Piazza Navona," he said to Mario, who closed the door and hopped into the driver's seat. Hollmann then rolled down his window to deliver a parting word.

"Thank you, Captain," he said to Priebke, his senses fully recovered and mind now grinding aggressively forward.

"*Jawohl, Herr Colonel.*" Priebke clicked his boots and raised his right arm in the official Führer salute. "*Heil Hitler!*"

Hollmann suppressed a roll of his eyes. "Go now, Mario," he instructed his chauffeur. "Let's get out of here."

"Yes, Colonel."

The Mercedes raced off, moving like a racehorse through the light drizzle. They quickly left behind the four Republican temples, surrendering the remains of the Theater of Pompey in the Largo di Torre Argentina to the army of wild felines that had taken over the historic site.

When they reached the Corso Vittorio Emanuele, they drove west until they reached Corso del Rinascimento, where Mario downshifted and skidded on the slick pavement before turning north again. The Mercedes' eight-cylinder, 7,655-cc engine roared as it zoomed towards Piazza Navona. All of Hollmann's thoughts were on his son Gunther, who for the last seven years had lived a secret life in America. It was only fitting that his son now went by the name John Bridger, taken in honor of the legendary frontier scout Jim Bridger. Hollmann remembered reading Karl May to him back in Innsbruck. The American Western adventure stories of the nineteenth-century German writer had obviously left a lasting impression on the boy.

Like him, his son had created a new persona for himself since the family tragedy. After the shooting, subsequent legal wrangling, and its eventual resolution, Gunther had lived four years with his mother, his sister Teresa, his stepfather Di Domenico, and the extended royal Bellomo family in Rome, before running away at the age of eighteen to live with one of his Italian uncles in America. Hollmann had secretly kept close tabs on him over the years through his handful of contacts in Rome and the German-American Bund in the United States. But since December 1941, when Hitler declared war on the U.S., he no longer had access to sensitive materials from his American contacts and had to rely on intercepting letter correspondence between his former wife and his two children. For the past eleven years, he had kept his ex-wife and daughter Teresa under sporadic surveillance, including checking their mail. Since his recovery from his gunshot wounds, he had moved from Innsbruck to Vienna, then from Vienna to Rome. The last information regarding his son that he had been able to track down was that he had graduated from Notre Dame and joined the U.S. officer's school in Georgia in 1942. But where had he gone from there? What unit had he been assigned to? It had to have been an elite unit given the fact that he had been airdropped far behind enemy lines into Occupied Italy.

He couldn't help but feel fatherly pride that his son had turned into such a clever, well-trained, and strapping young man even though he was fighting on the side of the enemy. But what would he do if he actually caught his son? Would he be forced to interrogate and torture him for information? Could he bring himself to hand over his own flesh and blood to Kappler and his Gestapo? It made him deeply uneasy to think about how far he might be compelled to go, especially if pressed into action by his bosses Himmler, Kaltenbrunner, and Wolff in the name of the Third Reich.

With these thoughts heavy on his mind, he had Mario park his Mercedes half on the street, half on the sidewalk in front of a large palatial estate overlooking Piazza Navona. With his duel swastika flags on his automobile, no Roman would dare tamper with the vehicle or question its presence here. He thought about quickly bandaging the cut on his face, but he didn't have anything handy and would have to make due in his current state.

Should I even go through with this? He rolled down his car window and peered up at the Italianate façade of the colossal, twenty-room, art-filled palace that had belonged to the Bellomo family for more than two centuries. *It has been eleven years, and you are technically under court order not to go anywhere near them. How could this possibly be a good idea?*

He took in Palazzo Bellomo. The palace was a thing of beauty with its arched stone lintels, balustrade balconies, floral and geometric motifs, ornamented white marble and terra-cotta, and judiciously distributed Corinthian porch columns. The home belonged to his ex-wife, the Marchesa Bianca Manuela Di Domenico, and her second husband and Teresa's biological father, Colonel Giovanni Di Domenico. As the chief of the Clandestine Military Front of the Resistance and an Italian monarchist officer in support of the new Badoglio regime, he was at the top of the Gestapo's list of enemies of the Reich, but he had gone into hiding and had yet to be captured. Like the marchesa's powerful father, Armando Bellomo, Di Domenico was part of Rome's black aristocracy that supported the Italian monarchy and the Vatican. For the past three weeks, Hollmann had kept the palace under periodic surveillance in the off-chance that the fugitive colonel would return for a visit. But given the manpower shortages due to the roundup, he had been forced to call off his surveillance team for the past several days.

You should just drive away right now. No good can come from this.

But his curiosity—and the sense that other secret motives had been at work on the day his wife had shot him—got the better of him. Before he could talk himself out of it and against his better judgement, he stepped from the Mercedes, strode up the cascading marble staircase to the front door, and rang the bell. An elderly butler in a conservative Italian tailcoat and white gloves appeared. He instantly pushed his way past the stunned servant, barking at him to summon the lady of the house and her daughter immediately for a word with a full colonel in the SS.

As the bald-headed servant dashed off timidly, Hollmann wiped away the mist clinging to his black leather uniform and stepped into a gracefully furnished Romanesque sitting room off the main dining room. The twelve-foot high room was gilded in gold leaf along the floors and ceilings. A pair of original Raphael oils and a Tintoretto hung resplendently from the walls, and a huge Tuscan rug with floral arrangements spread underfoot. With his SS quirt in hand, he began poking around impatiently at the snuff boxes, religious figurines, and family photographs on the marble mantels and rich mahogany side tables. He could already tell by the butler's surprised expression that his son Gunther had not come here after all, but Hollmann's visit could serve another purpose.

It could serve as a warning.

But should I be doing this? What if things turn violent like Innsbruck? Will Teresa even recognize me?

Since moving to Rome following the invasion of France in 1940, he had seen his ex-wife the marchesa and Teresa several times, but only from a cautious distance. He knew that they lived here at the historic Palazzo Bellomo, and he had long been looking for a pretext to drop in on them. Technically, the divorce agreement he had been blackmailed into signing by the marchesa and her powerful father had left him with a sizable income, but without the legal right to even visit his children and a restraining order for him never to come within fifty feet of his ex-wife. In addition, he had suffered the indignity of having to give up his job as the Innsbruck Police Chief and moving to Vienna, where he had assumed the role of that city's assistant chief of police. But now, with the German Occupation of Rome and the SS and German Army in charge of the country, the blackmail agreement no longer had any governing authority and he could do as he damn well pleased.

Now his son Gunther's presence in Rome gave him a compelling justification to visit his ex-wife and daughter. As did the fact that the marchesa's husband was an enemy of the Reich and much sought after by both the Gestapo and Fascist police. This gave him the pretext he needed. But it was the discovery of his son in Rome that provided a more urgent reason for his visit. He knew that, if he wanted to, he could drag his ex-wife into Via Tasso and have her interrogated by Priebke, but he had not yet resorted to such a drastic measure. The vengeful anger he had once felt towards her for shooting him and taking away his children—in short ruining his life—had dissipated long ago. He no longer pictured himself strangling her with his bare hands. During their marriage, she had always been a tempestuous woman; and he ultimately found that he was unable to hold her responsible for her inherently volatile nature, or for the strong-arm tactics of her powerful father, who had used his vast wealth to buy him off and make him disappear from his daughter's and grandchildren's lives.

In truth, Hollmann was actually allowing his ex-wife and daughter some perks that many other prominent Italian families, even those from the so-called "black set," did not have. While most automobiles had been confiscated by the German occupiers, and homes could be invaded and searched at the whim of the Gestapo and Fascist police, he had allowed his ex-wife to keep not merely one but two cars, and he had affixed a special SS-protected designation on their house forbidding unauthorized searches and seizures similar to those placed on protected Vatican properties. On the one hand, he was keeping a vigilant eye on them; on the other, he was ensuring them some comforts not available to other wealthy Romans of noble lineage.

His ex-wife and daughter appeared with the butler. The marchesa wore the same haughty expression that he had once known so well. At first, she didn't recognize him with his reconstructed face. Her expression then slowly changed from one of aristocratic contempt to shock and eventually to fear, all in a matter of seconds. But his daughter didn't recognize him at all. And yet, she seemed to realize that something significant and unusual was happening as she studied her mother's mixed reaction to his presence here at Palazzo Bellomo.

My God, this is actually happening, he thought. And then he realized that he had been waiting for this very moment for eleven long years.

CHAPTER 10

PALAZZO BELLOMO, PIAZZA NAVONA OCTOBER 16, 1943

HE LOOKED AT HIS EX-WIFE and saw the hate in her eyes. An image of her clutching a smoking gun replayed in his mind like the horrible, recurring nightmare it was. He took a deep breath to steel his nerves, and reminded himself to remain calm. She looked at him as if he was a common criminal, instead of the man who had once been her husband, served as a father to her children, and was now the second-ranking member of the SS in all of Italy who lorded over her occupied city. His daughter, on the other hand, bore a curious yet apprehensive expression. Clearly, she understood that this was not a routine SS visit, not the standard search or interrogation, but rather something else entirely.

"How dare you come into my house and snap at my servants!" roared the marchesa in her native tongue, her cheeks flushed red with the imperiousness he remembered so well from their marriage.

He ignored her and looked at his daughter. "Hello, Teresa. It's me, your father Wilhelm," he said, also speaking in Italian.

She stared at him in disbelief.

He touched his cheek. "My face…I…I've changed…after the accident, I had to have surgery," he spluttered feebly, feeling his emotions muddling his brain.

Incomprehension still clung to her face.

"How…how have you been?" he asked her.

The words were almost impossible for him to get out. But his ex-wife wouldn't even allow Teresa to answer.

"My God, it is you!" she gasped. "Damn you, Wilhelm. You are not allowed to have any contact with us. That was the agreement. Now get out of my house!"

"Calm down, Bianca. In case you haven't noticed, there is a war going on and the situation has changed. We—the German Army—control Rome now."

"I told you to get out of my house!"

"Stop being so melodramatic. I am not here to argue with you or harm anyone. I am here on official business—and to issue a friendly warning."

She rolled her eyes. "Friendly warning? You don't know the meaning of the word *friendly*."

"It's all right, Mother. Calm down," said Teresa. It pleased Hollmann to see his daughter behave with such aplomb under such awkward circumstances. She was more like him than his ex-wife, he could see from her calm demeanor. She looked him in the eye, and he could now see the recognition. "You're bleeding," she said to him, not tenderly, but with feeling. "Were you attacked?"

"Yes, and I will get to that in a minute. But first I need you both to listen. There are choices you must make in the coming days and, if you make the wrong ones, there is nothing that I can do to protect you."

"What are you talking about?" bristled his ex-wife.

"I am talking about your husband, the colonel—Teresa's biological father. We all know he has left here and gone into hiding. You two need to make sure that you do not help him in any way and that he does not attempt to come back here. Up until today, this villa has been under regular surveillance, and it will be again once the Jewish roundup that is at this very moment ongoing is complete and every able-bodied soldier is no longer needed. And it will remain under surveillance until Colonel Di Domenico and his officers are apprehended, so you should ensure that he stays away. Otherwise, I cannot help you and you will be treated very harshly, the both of you."

"Why are you telling us this? Is this some sort of trick?"

"That is just like you, Bianca, to think the worst of people. No, it is not a trick. I am giving you one chance and one chance only so take what I say to heart."

"But you are with the SS? Why would you help us?"

"Who says I am doing it for you? Perhaps I am doing it only for Teresa."

"I still don't trust you."

"That's fine, but for Teresa's sake, you had better listen to me. Because once you make your choice there can be no going back. First, this war between our two sides is a Faustian pact and it is important that you understand that. And second, I want you to know that I have seen our son Gunther."

His ex-wife's hand flew to her mouth. "Gunther? But he's in America."

"Not anymore. And he no longer calls himself Gunther, as you both are no doubt aware. He is an American soldier who goes by the name John Bridger."

Her lips trembled. "You…you saw him here in Rome?"

"Yes, and you need to send him on his way, too, if he shows up here." He pointed to his torn skin and swollen eye. "He is the one who did this to me."

"Good for him," hissed the marchesa triumphantly.

"Where did you see him?" asked his daughter.

"Near Torre Argentina. He was smuggled behind enemy lines and was almost captured by the new head of the Gestapo in our fair city, Colonel Kappler."

"*Our* fair city?" snorted the marchesa. "You're a German, you bastard. Rome is not your city, nor will it ever be."

"You know that I have Italian blood, too, and have always loved Rome, just as you do. And right now, we despicable Germans own this city. It might as well be named Hamburg."

"Stop arguing," interrupted Teresa. "I can't believe this is happening." She looked accusingly at her mother. "How long have you known *he* was here in Rome?"

The marchesa crossed her arms, saying nothing.

"How long have you known that…that Father was here?" his daughter persisted.

"This man is not your *father*. He is a colonel in the SS and nothing more."

"Stop lying to me. How long have you known he was here in Rome?"

His ex-wife looked guiltily towards the floor. For several tense seconds, she did not speak. "For over two years now," she said finally.

"My God, Mother, and you didn't tell me?"

"Why should I? He was forbidden by the agreement to see us. Don't you remember, he tried to shoot me? I didn't want him near me or my children."

Hollmann felt all the old anger returning. "It was self-defense, Bianca, and you damn well know it."

"Is that so? Do you want me to get the agreement you signed? It says in big, bold letters that you tried to shoot me and that *I* was the one who fought back in self-defense."

"Your father and his army of lawyers made me sign that false piece of paper eleven years ago—and I have regretted it every day since."

"They didn't make you sign anything. You did it for greed. Ten million lira is a lot of money for a police chief. I would venture that that's why you're here: you've probably spent it all, and have come back for more."

"Please stop it, Mother," cried Teresa. "I know you're lying. Gunther told me everything that happened. It was you who shot father first, and you have been lying about it ever since. That's why Gunther left us for America, and you know it. He was tormented by what you had done. And so am I."

"I'm not going to listen to any more of your insolence." She turned and glared at her ex-husband. "I want you out of my house this minute. All you are doing is causing us misery by stirring up the past."

"Very well, if you don't want to talk about the past, then you had better at least focus on the present. I cannot say this with more urgency: I am powerless to help you if you are found aiding or sheltering spies or enemies of the Reich."

"I don't need your damned protection."

"As I said, I am not doing this for you." He looked at his daughter. "I am doing it for Teresa."

"Why should we trust you? You and your SS brutes are the ones who told the Jews they would be safe if they paid a fifty-kilogram gold ransom. And then you backed out on the deal and are this very minute having them rounded up."

"I have nothing to do with that. I am a liaison officer, a diplomatic go-between, not a policeman. Colonel Kappler and Captain Dannecker are the ones behind this treachery with President Foà and his Jews. I am but a mediator."

"Damn you, you are a Nazi, and it is time for you to leave!"

"All right, I will go now. But remember, my reason for coming here was to warn you. Or at least to warn Teresa. She deserves a hell of a lot better mother than a woman who would shoot her father, force him to give up his children, and steal away to Rome to live with her lover."

"The only mistake I made was not killing you!"

Yes, but why did you shoot me? What actually drove you to take such a drastic measure?

"Stop it, the both of you!" cried Teresa.

"You should listen to your daughter, Bianca. She has more sense than you and she's only half your age."

Teresa snapped right back at him. "I told you *both* to stop it!"

He nodded his head obediently. He was angry at himself for letting his emotions get the better of him like his fiery ex-wife. In his view, the marchesa had only managed to escape a prison cell years ago because of her father's money and far-reaching political connections.

"Yes, you are right," he said to his daughter. "But one last piece of advice—stay away from that Father O'Flaherty, too. We know he runs an Allied POW escape network, and it is only a matter of time before we shut him and his operation down. He is not someone you want to associate with in times like these."

As his warning echoed, they fell into a strained silence. He looked into his daughter's eyes. He realized that deep down, he still wanted her love and approval, even though they had had no contact with one another for eleven years and they were now, technically, wartime enemies. With fond remembrance, he thought back to all the wonderful times he had held his little girl in his arms and swung her joyfully about. He remembered her tiny baby hands that had lovingly clasped him, her adoring worshipful eyes that had made him feel a deep sense of paternal purpose and happiness. He remembered teaching her to ski and ride a bike. He remembered going to her singing recitals. God, how he had loved to hear her sing? He had been so proud of her: his smart, talented, beautiful baby girl who had showed so much promise and whose entire life had stretched before her like a magnificent sunset. He realized in that moment that he was torn by a need to protect his daughter at all costs—and his desire to do his job to the best of his abilities and be a loyal German officer. He even felt a sense of familial loyalty to his wife, whom he pitied more than anything else, though he knew there was no reason he should have been sympathetic to her after what she had done to him.

The simple truth was he felt conflicted inside. Despite the suffering he had endured, he was desperate to protect his family and he wanted to somehow be a part of their lives again, even as merely a respectful adversary. He certainly didn't want Kappler and his Gestapo goons to mistakenly seize his ex-wife or daughter as enemies of the Reich and lock them away in the basement of Via Tasso or in Regina Coeli Prison. Nor did he want his son—despite the injury the young man had inflicted upon him—to be tortured or killed at the hands of Priebke or some other ruthless police interrogator.

"Please just do as I ask," he said, feeling a trickle of emotion playing through his system, adding to his sense of confusion. "Stay away from your husband, Gunther, and Father O'Flaherty. I cannot protect you if you associate with our enemies. That goes for you too, Teresa."

"I already told you, we don't want or need your damned protection," hissed the marchesa. "Now get out of our home and never come back."

"Yes, I will leave."

He looked at Teresa. She was torn just like him, he could tell, which somehow made him feel better. Then he looked back at his haughty ex-wife. *Avere la puzza sotto il naso*, he thought. *You still have your nose in the air; such a stubbornly exquisite specimen of the black nobility.*

"You may not want my protection right now, Marchesa, but I can promise you that one day you will. Good day to you both—and may God be with you."

CHAPTER 11

VATICAN CITY

OCTOBER 16, 1943

AT 11:53 A.M. THAT SAME DAY, Pius Pope Pius XII received Cardinal Maglione in his papal study for a debriefing on how the secretary of state's meeting had gone with Baron Ernst von Weizsäcker, the German Ambassador to the Holy See. He felt shaken from today's harrowing events and his heart was filled with dread as Maglione took his seat. Few in the Curia were delusional enough to think that, with Hitler and Himmler in power, the Jews would ever be safe in Rome, despite the payment of the gold ransom. But the roundup had nonetheless caught the Holy See and everyone else in the city flat-footed. Pius was still grappling to find a way to effectively counter the Germans and have the arrested Jews returned to their homes. It was the swiftness of the SS operation, the sudden stark reality that the dreaded arrests that had been whispered about for the past three weeks were actually happening, that caught everyone by surprise. It had precipitated an extremely frenetic and busy day for the Pope and his inner circle as they attempted to counter the Nazi menace.

"What did the German ambassador have to say, Luigi?" he asked his secretary of state to begin the meeting. "Please tell me."

"The ambassador already knew about the arrests," replied Maglione. "I asked him to intervene in favor of these poor people. I spoke to him in the name of humanity and Christian charity. I asked him to end this roundup and let the Jews return to their homes."

"And what was Weizsäcker's response?"

"His answer caught me somewhat by surprise. He replied to me, in all sincerity, saying with some emotion: 'I am always waiting for you to ask me: Why do you remain in this position of yours when you have to stand by and say nothing when your country does such unspeakable things as this?'"

"What did you say to him?"

"I told him that I would never presume to ask him such a question."

"Do you remember your exact words?"

"I said to him, 'Excellency, you who have a good and tender heart, try to save these many innocent people. It is painful for the Holy Father, painful beyond words, that right here in Rome, under the eyes of the Common Father, so many people are made to suffer only because of their Jewish descent.'"

"What was his response?"

"The ambassador, after reflection, asked me, 'What would the Holy See do if these things were to continue?' I informed him, quite directly, that the Holy See would not want to be faced with the need to express its disapproval."

Pius quietly nodded; he understood plainly the coded language his secretary of state had used with the German ambassador. Since the war had begun, the Pope had been in the midst of a conundrum when it came to wartime atrocities. The Vatican had been well-informed about the mass murder of Jews in Eastern Europe since mid-1942. Pius had spoken out against the atrocities during last year's Christmas address and on other occasions, but he had toned down his protests to maintain the appearance of honoring the Holy See's tradition of impartiality during times of war, even though he was actively engaged in the plots to remove Hitler from power and was devoted to the Allied cause. Cautious by nature and training, he held steadfast to the conservative policies of his predecessors, particularly those of Benedict XV who had presided during the difficult time of the Great War. These time-honored policies dictated that the Vatican remain publicly neutral so as to avoid alienating belligerent leaders and the Catholic population spread across the European theater of war. Pointing the finger at the Reich, he believed, would alienate the sizable Catholic minority in Germany, a country dear to his heart from having served as nuncio there in his younger years. Publicly condemning the atrocities perpetrated by one side or another would likely risk greater persecution to Catholics, Jews, and other innocent victims of the war. Singling out Germany, he felt, would provoke Hitler's wrath and thus more slaughter, which was precisely what had happened in 1942 during an ill-advised protest by Holland's bishops that led to the Nazis deporting 40,000 Dutch Jews.

He knew that, publicly, Hitler had to perform the same delicate tightrope act. There were millions of Catholics in Germany and Austria who would turn against the Reich if he directly offended or threatened the head of the Church. It was for this reason the Pope believed Hitler had recently put aside his plan to have General Wolff seize the Vatican, kidnap him, and put him under house arrest in Lichtenstein. The German diplomats in Rome had quietly informed Pius about the Führer's harebrained scheme two weeks earlier through discreet back channels. But he considered it unlikely that the Germans would take action against him or the Holy See when such a plot had the potential to backfire disastrously and arouse Catholic resistance throughout Europe. Then again, Hitler's erratic behavior made him capable of anything, and Pius was convinced that Europe would not be safe until the tyrant was removed from power.

"Please continue, Luigi. What did you say next?"

"I made it clear to the ambassador that you, as the Holy Father of Rome, must not be placed in a position of having to protest. But if the Holy See were forced to do so, it would trust in divine providence with regard to the consequences."

"And how did the ambassador take this warning?"

"He said that for more than four years now he had followed and admired the attitude of the Holy See. He said it had succeeded in steering the ship amid all shapes and sizes of rocks without running aground and, even though it had greater faith in the Allies, it has maintained a perfect equilibrium. But now, just as the ship was about to reach port, he said he had to ask himself if it was worth it for the Holy See to put it all at risk. He said he was thinking of the consequences that such a step by the Holy See would provoke at the very highest levels.”

Hitler, thought Pius miserably. *Until he is dead, these despicable acts will go on and on. No words can stop this mass murderer. But perhaps Stauffenberg can?*

Maglione went on, “I didn’t particularly like the ambassador’s tone of mild reproach when he accused us of having greater faith in the Allies than the Axis, though you and I both know it is true. So I told him that the Holy See, as the ambassador himself had just pointed out, has always been very prudent since the war began in our policy of impartiality. I reminded him that we pride ourselves in the fact that we had been very careful not to give the common German people the impression of having done the slightest thing against them in this terrible war.”

“What did he say to that?”

“He again reminded me that a formal papal protest would draw criticism and perhaps drastic action from the highest levels of the German government.”

The Pope leaned back in his chair at his desk, removed his wire-rim glasses, and rubbed his tired eyes. “Your implied threat of papal protest was the bucket of cold water Berlin needs to come to its senses. And the German ambassador’s counterthreat of provoking dire consequences from the “highest levels”—even without mentioning the Führer by name—was a gag order on me speaking out. It appears, Luigi, that this meeting of yours is the opening salvo in what will likely prove to be a huge showdown. And all because Hitler and his Nazis are incapable of leaving the poor Jews alone.”

“Or Catholics, Your Eminence. He is secretly killing the Catholics in Poland and elsewhere in large numbers as well, as you know.”

Yes, and he must be stopped. But how? Can Stauffenberg actually pull it off? When will he and the others make their move? And more importantly, are we destined to fail yet again? Surely, God Almighty wouldn’t allow such a thing, not a third time?

“Did the ambassador say how many people were arrested?”

“Well over a thousand souls, Your Eminence.”

“Were they taken to the Collegio Militare, as we thought?”

“Yes, that is where they are being held.”

“We will send someone to see to their welfare and report back to us. No doubt the Germans are not treating them well.”

“Yes, Your Eminence. I will see to it.”

Pius shook his head in dismay. The Germans were rounding up people right under his very windows. The military college abutted the wall that formed the outer perimeter of Vatican City. Was this a direct threat from the Nazis that they didn’t care whether or not he interceded? Were they sending a message that they would do as they pleased in Rome and were not at all intimidated by his power and influence upon world opinion? Did he have the moral authority to stop these madmen, or would it be solely up to the German Resistance and Allied armies?

“How did the meeting end?” he then asked, feeling an oppressive burden in a world that seemed to have gone mad with war and hate.

“He said he would try to find a diplomatic solution to the problem. I then thanked him for agreeing to do something for the Jews.”

“That was it? Was there anything else?”

"The ambassador made one final appeal. He requested that we keep word of the meeting private. He asked me if you, Your Eminence, would allow him *not* to report the conversation through official channels. I reassured him that I would say nothing of our conversation in official correspondence until we had worked out an acceptable solution."

"How did the meeting end?"

"I reminded him one last time that I was asking him to intervene for the sake of humanity. I left it to his judgment whether or not to mention our conversation, which had been conducted on good terms. As you will recall, we had in recent weeks been working together not only to prevent the expected persecution of the Jews, but to request reinforcements of German police forces in Rome to maintain order. And also to reach an agreement on the text of a statement to be issued by the Holy See at Berlin's request acknowledging the Germans' respect for the sovereignty of Vatican City."

"Do you believe that the ambassador will actually be able to orchestrate the release of the prisoners and their return to their homes?"

"I am unsure, Your Eminence. I believe he will do what he can. But I do not know if it is in his power to pull this off. We must trust in divine providence."

"Unfortunately, divine providence has its limits. We have to assume that we will not be successful in halting the German deportations. That's why we will, as the Americans like to say, have a backup plan."

"A backup plan?"

"I am hereby reissuing my order from two weeks ago for the Vatican to be opened to Rome's Jews, and for the convents and monasteries here in the city to provide hiding places as well as false identification papers and subsistence money to those being persecuted. The doors of all of our extraterritorial properties protected under the Lateran Treaty must be open to one and all. That is what we must do, and we will do it with increased zeal beginning today."

"Will this be an official written order, Your Eminence?"

"No, there can be nothing in writing in case that deranged madman changes his mind and actually makes good on his threat to seize the Vatican and all of our files. Or if, despite General Wolff's objections, the Führer tries to have me forcibly removed and sent to Lichtenstein. This work on behalf of our Savior must be done in secret. Otherwise, the Germans might discover for a fact that our neutrality is a sham and we favor the Allies."

"I understand."

"We will quietly perform our rescue work behind the scenes, but mark my words, we will be effective. And as always, the final decision of precisely what action to take at any given time and place will have to be decided by our priests and nuns at the local level. They will have the clearest picture of the inherent risks and possible retaliation by the Germans."

"Yes, Your Eminence. Unfortunately, I fear the situation is going to become even more precarious for us here in the Holy See under the Nazi Occupation."

"These are trying times for us all. But especially for the Hebrews."

"They have done nothing wrong. It should not be this way."

"No, it shouldn't." In the somber silence that followed, he wondered how it had come to this dismal fate for the Jews of Europe. It seemed unbelievable that they were being subjected to complete genocide in the east. In the last year, he had begun to hear about horrible sufferings and mass killings at a place in Upper Silesia Oswiecim in Poland. The Germans called the hell on earth Auschwitz. There was said to be a sign in German at the gate that read *Arbeit Macht Frei*—Work Sets You Free—which Pius found revolting given that the camp was not a place of work at all but rather a site of systematic industrialized mass killing on a scale never seen before in the annals of civilization. And now, in the fall of 1943, Catholic priests from all over Europe were telling him about such moral abominations every month. He desperately wanted to do something to halt the massacre of innocents. But without an army at his command, he knew there was only one thing he could do to perhaps put an end to it all, and that was remove Hitler from power. Only by cutting off the head of the snake could the unconscionable carnage be halted.

He looked at Maglione. He saw the pain and empathy on his face for the Jewish families rousted from their homes in the early morning hours. The plump secretary of state seated before him was his most trusted advisor, and the Pope always gave his counsel serious consideration even though they didn't always see eye to eye. Maglione was known for his dislike of Hitler and Nazism, as well as Mussolini and Fascism, and for his preference for the Allies and their democratic ideals. But the experienced cardinal also knew the value of diplomacy and the critical importance of maintaining at least the guise of Vatican neutrality.

Maglione had done a good job, the Pope realized, walking the diplomatic tightrope with the white-haired patriarch Baron von Weizsäcker. True, the protest had been delivered in the Vatican's standard coded, non-confrontational language, but the anti-Nazi German ambassador no doubt understood Maglione's meaning. If further mass raids on Rome's Jews continued, the Pope would have no choice but to go public with a forceful denouncement of Hitler and Nazi Germany. It was as simple as that. While admittedly nuanced, the threat had been made by Maglione to the ambassador, and it had been completely understood. There was no possibility of misinterpretation by the Germans.

And yet, Pius couldn't help but feel a sense of having not merely fallen short in the negotiations, but as if he had come up against an immovable force. Sadly, it felt to him as if the battle was already lost. He suspected that, for political reasons, it was too late for the rounded-up Jews and they would not be able to be saved. That pained him deeply. But the rescue of today's prisoners could not be the overarching goal. Thwarting Hitler and his *Endlösung*—Final Solution—for the Jews of Rome and Italy could not be viewed within the context of a single battle that needed to be won at all costs, but rather as a long, epic struggle in which overall success was measured by one thing and one thing only: the percentage of Jews and Catholics who did not meet their death at the hands of the SS out of the total population. If speaking out against Hitler and the Nazis resulted in greater persecution and mass murder, then speaking out was nothing but stupidity and rashness. At this point, the primary goal had to be long-term, and that was to get the Germans, especially Himmler himself, to back down from a public confrontation with the Curia and put an end to future roundups.

Though he had the moral, and to some extent, the political authority to defy Hitler, he knew that the Vatican's public façade of neutrality was precarious. Maintaining the Vatican's sovereignty, while surrounded by Kappler's Gestapo and *Feldmaresciallo* Kesselring's Wehrmacht army, was a dangerous enterprise, especially when he was so deeply involved in the German Resistance plot to remove Hitler from power. In his heart, he wanted to stop the Nazis in their tracks and demand that they return every arrested Jew to his or her home; but jurisprudence and diplomacy demanded a more nuanced, forward-thinking course of action.

All the same, he felt no reassurance in caution. In fact, a part of him despised it, and he couldn't help but feel like a coward. But Hitler and the Nazis were men of the wickedest design. Even with himself and the sympathetic German embassy working together to combat the persecution of the Jews, he knew that neither of them had control over the excesses of the Third Reich. Pius recalled his first impressions of Adolf Hitler during his diplomatic tenure in Germany. He had read *Mein Kampf* cover to cover and met the future dictator, and he saw them both for what they were: detestable and utterly dangerous. When Hitler began to flex his muscles in Munich in 1923, Nuncio Pacelli provided detailed reports on the up-and-coming Austrian and his growing Nazi movement to Rome. After the failed Munich Putsch in November of that year, the young future Pope wrote to the Vatican, "Hitler is bad news for Germany, he is bad news for the Catholic Church, and he is bad news for the Jews."

Now Pius knew, first hand, how prophetic his words had been.

CHAPTER 12

PALAZZO BELLOMO, PIAZZA NAVONA
OCTOBER 16, 1943

AFTER MAKING THE SIGN OF THE CROSS, Teresa dipped a piece of freshly baked bread into a small plate of olive oil and slowly ate it. In her mind, she went over what had just happened with her father. Her mother sat at the dining table next to her, staring out the window into the rainy piazza with a pensive expression on her face. Carla the house servant was busy in the *cucina* putting together a simple lunch of *insalate* and *gnocchi al telefono*. The encounter with her father had shaken the entire household, although her mother seemed more incensed at the intrusion of her ex-husband and the war into her cosseted world of nobility than intimidated by the SS colonel's authority.

Despite the surreal awkwardness of seeing her father again after so many years, Teresa couldn't help but be intrigued by the man. He was as she remembered him: physically imposing and commanding, yet somehow modest and soft-spoken. She was impressed with his ability to keep his wits about him and hold his emotions in check when he was being browbeaten by her mother. Such presence of mind in the face of incivility lent him strength of character in her eyes. But more importantly, she could tell that he still had strong feelings for her and still considered her his daughter.

She found him mesmerizing and wanted to see him again to talk to him about his life these past eleven years. Deep down, she had always felt that he had received the raw end of the deal following the shooting. He had lost his job and his children, while her mother had gotten off scot-free and not seen any jail time even though she had been the first to pull a gun and open fire.

Gunther had told her the whole sordid story when she was thirteen, before he had run away to America. Confused and angry, he didn't want to have anything more to do with the Bellomo family, and had set off to make a fresh start. After breaking into the marchesa's desk one night, he had discovered the legal agreement and supporting documents describing the entire cover-up. Like Teresa, he was traumatized by the shooting and subsequent legal battle, and was disgusted with the way their mother and powerful grandfather had manipulated the situation to their benefit. It seemed to Teresa and her brother that their father had given up everything and their mother almost nothing, except a large sum of hush money. But even that had been paid by the marchesa's wealthy father, Armando Bellomo.

After the incident, Gunther claimed their family was cursed. He said that their father had warned her mother that if she went through with it and pulled the trigger, their family would be cursed here on earth and in the afterlife. Having covered her ears during the episode, Teresa didn't actually hear her father invoke the curse. But having grown up as a strict Roman Catholic fully embracing the concept of "curses" in matters of moral theology, the threat of a hex had always frightened Teresa as a child and was very real to her, as it was to most practicing Catholics and others of strong religious faith. Consequently, upon her brother's youthful admission, she had fully expected any day that her life would be filled with sickness and misery, her enemies would prosper, and she would grow old in sadness and regret. But with the passing years and still no sign she was living a cursed existence, but rather the pleasant life of a daughter of a noble Roman family, she began to feel less and less that the family was truly cursed, even as her country became enveloped in war. All the same, in the back of her mind, she still greatly feared the family curse. She knew it was one of the reasons that Gunther had left her and her mother behind and forged a new life in the New World. He had genuinely believed in the Hollmann curse, and she couldn't help but feel that somehow it still hung over the family.

Suddenly, she heard a scream coming from the kitchen.

Her mother looked at her with shock. "Oh my God, he's back!"

Teresa was out of her chair in a flash and running for the kitchen, the marchesa close on her heels. She pushed open the door and—

"Don't be alarmed. It's just me and Peter!" a voice cried in Italian.

Teresa was stunned to see Carla clutching a kitchen knife, and beyond the house servant, her brother Gunther and Peter Savoyan, an American she had known in Rome during her youth. They were moving towards Carla with their hands up, trying to calm her down. She waved the knife at the two interlopers, warning them to back off, as the family butler, Vincenzo, came rushing in from a side door. After her father's visit, Teresa wasn't surprised to see Gunther here; her father had suspected he might try and make contact with her and her mother. All the same, seeing him in the flesh after all these years was still a shock.

"It's all right, Carla," she said. "They are friends."

"Gunther, is that really you?" exclaimed her mother, coming up from behind. "My God, it is!" and she rushed towards her son to take him in an embrace. "I thought you'd never come back!"

To Teresa's surprise, her brother held up his hands to keep the marchesa at bay. "Hold on, Mother. This is not a family reunion."

"What are you…how did you get in here?"

He tipped his head towards the servants. "Shouldn't we speak in private?"

"Yes, of course," said the marchesa. "Vincenzo, Carla, please excuse us. And not a word is to be uttered about this. Otherwise, the Germans will hang us all."

"Yes, Marchesa." They stepped from the kitchen.

Once they were gone, her brother looked at her mother. "You must listen to me. My name is no longer Gunther—it is John Bridger. I am an American soldier with the Fifth Army, and we need your help. You remember Peter, don't you, Mother? We were driven from our flat in Piazza Lovatelli and we need to get in contact with your husband, Colonel Di Domenico. That's the reason we're here."

Savoyan stepped forward and bowed his head gracefully. "Marchesa, my apologies for the unexpected intrusion. We made sure not to be seen and will be on our way quickly, I promise you."

"Peter's a lieutenant with the OSS, Mother."

"OSS?"

"The Office of Strategic Services, America's intelligence service. I'm working with Peter and the Italian partisans to set up an intelligence network here in Rome."

"We were supposed to meet with Colonel Di Domenico tonight, but I think that's out of the question with this city-wide roundup taking place," said Savoyan.

Bridger turned towards his sister. "You remember Peter too, don't you Teresa? I believe you two used to be sweet on one another."

She felt herself blush and smiled in embarrassment at Peter, whom she remembered kissing on her sixteenth birthday at the bottom of the Spanish Steps. The moment came back to her as if it had happened yesterday.

"Hello, Teresa," said the handsome Peter, who, like her brother, had filled out and matured into the body of a man since she had last seen him. She recalled that before the war Peter's parents had been American citizens living in Rome and that Peter's father had served as some sort of diplomat. But what she remembered most of all was their sweet summer adolescent romance five years ago and how sad she was when he had trundled off to Harvard in the fall.

"Hello, Peter," she said bashfully.

The marchesa looked at them with disapproval before turning her fierce gaze upon her son. "You obviously didn't come here, John Bridger, to make small talk. What is it that you want exactly? Your presence here puts us *all* in jeopardy."

"Yes, and we apologize for that. But the city is crawling with Germans, and we didn't know where else to go. You needn't worry though. As Peter said, no one saw us enter the villa. We snuck in through the servants' entrance."

"We don't care why you came, Brother. We are just glad to know you are safe," said Teresa, and she meant it. "But we have to be careful. The enemy is everywhere now that Italy has surrendered to the Allies. In fact, before you arrived, Father was here looking for you. He is a colonel in the SS, and he said he came upon you quite by accident on the street an hour ago. You should have seen his face. You gave him quite a whipping."

"Yes, when we were fleeing our flat, we ran into him. And then we came here, but unfortunately so did he. We saw his Mercedes parked out front and hid out across the piazza. We figured he'd come here, and waited until he left."

"With the Germans occupying Rome, there is no safe place in the city anymore," said her mother. "That's why my husband, too, has gone into hiding."

"Peter and I are going to have to find a new hideout ourselves. Piazza Lovatelli isn't safe right now and may not be for some time."

Teresa took a moment to study her brother and Peter. In their sharkskin suits, they could pass easily for native Italians from the Fascist set. All the same, it was obvious to her that their gleaming suits were nothing more than clever disguises. "What is your military rank and unit, Brother?"

"I'm a captain in the First Special Service Force."

"What is that?"

"An elite brigade of American and Canadian troops trained to fight in cold weather, mountains, and behind enemy lines" answered Savoyan. "Believe me, once the Germans get a taste of them in combat, they're going to wish they were back in Berlin eating schnitzel with Lili Marlene."

"Oh, so you two—one a commando, the other a spy—are actually knights in shining armor who have come to rescue Rome from our Nazi overlords?"

Bridger chuckled. "No, stuff like that only happens in the movies."

"You shouldn't joke like that," said her mother. "You don't know how precarious the situation is here in Rome. And I don't just mean with this terrible roundup of the Jews. We have a six o'clock curfew. Our identity papers are checked at every other street corner. Young men are constantly being pulled from the streets for Nazi military labor. And anybody who so much as whispers the word 'Resistance' is hunted down like a dog by Kappler's Gestapo."

"I have heard about this Kappler fellow. They say he should be avoided at all costs. But Peter and I just need a place to stay for a day or two, until we know whether or not our apartment was specifically targeted during the raid."

"Well, it is certainly not safe here," said the marchesa. "Our home is under surveillance, and our phones are being tapped. But I do have access to a small apartment near the Vatican. It is a protected extraterritorial property with a warning placard out front provided by the Germans to keep in good standing with the Pope. You can stay there, at least for a short while."

She summoned Vincenzo by tinkling a silver bell and had the butler fetch her spare set of keys.

"What can you tell us about the Resistance here in Rome," her brother then asked her mother. "Does the colonel have the partisan factions working together as reported?"

"The *Communista* in the Patriotic Action Group are difficult to control, but the different groups seem to be trying to work together. In my view, the Communists are more trouble than they are worth. They are the ones that create the divisions in the partisans. Mark my words, Communism will kill the Eternal City long before the brutal Germans."

"Sometimes, you have to strike a deal with the devil himself if you want to vanquish a ruthless enemy. Just look at Stalin and the Russians. In any case, we'll know soon enough who the true partisans in this city are, and those who are merely out for themselves."

They talked for a minute longer about the growing Resistance network in Rome before Vincenzo returned with the set of keys. Taking the keys from him, Teresa fished through them until she found the one for the apartment her mother wanted, a silver key with the symbol of the pontificate.

"The apartment's address is Viale Giulio Cesare 183. I'll show you a safe way out," said Teresa to her brother and Savoyan once Vincenzo had left again.

"All right, Little Sister, lead the way." He looked at the marchesa, whose lower lip was trembling with emotion. "Thank you, Mother, for helping us. You might not see me again for some time, so I bid you goodbye and good luck."

Her mother stepped toward him and took him in an embrace. Teresa saw tears well up in her eyes as she hugged her son ferociously.

"Please be careful," she said to him. "I don't want to lose you, Gunther. I love you. I know you are still angry at me for everything that happened, but I want you to know that you mean the world to me and I will always love you. If we don't see each other again, never forget that. Please."

He said nothing in reply and did not hug his mother back, but he didn't try and keep her at bay this time either. She held him close for a full ten seconds before he gently pulled away. Her brother Gunther had always been something of a stoic person, but Teresa could tell that even he was moved by his mother's heartfelt parting words.

"Goodbye, Mother," he said solemnly, and then Teresa led him and Savoyan out the kitchen, down some stairs, along a corridor, through a wine cellar, and to a small alcove with a door that opened onto the street behind the villa.

Carefully, she opened the door and scanned the misty street. It was empty.

"All clear," she said, keeping the door open only a crack. "Remember, the address is Viale Giulio Cesare 183. The apartment is six blocks north of the Vatican." She held up the key. "Now, before I hand this over to you, I need to tell you something. I haven't told Mother, but I have recently joined the Resistance."

"The Resistance? I don't believe it."

"Why not? I can fire a gun or set off a bomb just as well as you, Peter, or any other man."

"But you're a…a…"

"Girl," said Savoyan, finishing for him.

"Yeah, that's right, you're a girl."

"Oh, please. You have been gone for seven years—*John Bridger*—and if you haven't noticed, I am now a full-grown woman. I know what I'm doing, and I'm telling you that I have signed on to fight the Germans, the same as you."

"My God, you're serious. You really do want to kill Krauts." He smiled at her, appraising her in a different light. "Okay, you've won us over with your determination, Little Sister. But I've got to be honest with you, killing Hitler's finest is a man's work. Now give me that key."

"No, not until you admit that a woman can fight as well as any man. There are many of us among the partisans, and we want to kill Nazis just like you. And soon we will be."

"All right, I can tell by that look in your eyes that you're not going to give an inch on this. So you win. A woman can kill a Kraut just as good as any man."

"I agree one-hundred-percent," said Savoyan. "By the way, who did you enlist with?"

"I am a member of the *Gruppi di Azione Patriottica*—the Patriotic Action Group, Central Command. It is one of the military groups of the National Liberation Committee. We call it GAP for short."

Bridger smiled at her. "Quite a chip off the old block."

"I told you that I can fight as well as any man."

"I can see that. You are definitely the colonel's daughter."

"Yes, but which colonel?" quipped Savoyan. "The Italian pro-monarchist partisan or the ruthless Nazi."

"I suppose I have learned from them both. After all, each one of them has been a father to me at one time or another. But make no mistake, I hate both the

Nazis and Fascists with all my heart and soul, and I support the Communists."

Savoyan smiled. "Define irony: a descendant of Roman black nobility is actually a Communist partisan. You are full of surprises, Teresa, there's no doubt about it." He looked at her brother. "Hey, why don't we give her a chance to work with us? I don't have a problem with Communists, and neither does my boss 'Wild Bill' Donovan."

"No way. She's not going to be part of our operation."

"Wait, just hear me out. You and I haven't lived in Rome in years. Not only does Teresa know it far better than us, but her father the colonel is the head of the overall Resistance. She would be an ideal cutout and courier for us here in Rome."

"You want the young *Pasionara* to get killed, is that it?"

"No, I think she could be useful."

She dangled the key before him seductively. "Remember, I haven't given this to you yet, Brother."

"Come on, what Peter is suggesting could get you killed. Frankly, I don't want that on my conscience."

"Don't treat me differently because I am a woman." She waved the key. "Which is it going to be? Am I in or not? If the answer is yes, you get this."

He shook his head with skepticism before relenting. "Okay young *Pasionara*, you're in. But you had better be careful. Extremely careful."

Feeling a rush of excitement, she handed over the key and kissed him on the cheek. Acting the part of the gentleman, Savoyan then held out his hand. "We'd better make this official. I, Lieutenant Savoyan, duly appointed chief of the Office of Strategic Services, Rome Branch, do hereby swear you in as a full-fledged OSS operative acting on behalf of the United States of America. The date is October 16 of the Year of our Lord 1943. Congratulations, Private Di Domenico."

"Private?" protested Teresa. "Why not corporal?"

"Okay, corporal it is."

She raised an imaginary champagne glass. "Now let's have a toast."

"To what?" asked Savoyan.

"To driving the Nazis out of Rome and winning the war."

Bridger grinned at her. "I can drink to that. But you had better promise me one last time that you'll be careful out there. Now that I've seen you again, I don't want anything to happen to my little sister."

"I promise," she said. "But you had better be careful too."

And with that, she gave him a final hug, opened the door, and sent them off into the drizzly gloom, feeling a sense of purpose and renewal, as if she and her brother were now a part of history. They were not cursed at all, but rather soldiers with important roles to play in the forthcoming liberation of Rome.

CHAPTER 13

TIBURTINA RAILWAY STATION, ROME

OCTOBER 18, 1943

STANDING ON THE WOODEN PLATFORM above Tiburtina Railway Station, Hollmann stared down at the Jews being herded like cattle into the twenty-car freight train bound for the east. He felt sorry for them. Unlike his comrades in arms in the SS, he didn't believe there was an international Jewish conspiracy, or that international Jewry was the sworn enemy of the Reich. And he certainly didn't believe that Jews should be treated like rats and sent off to slave labor or extermination camps. But that was precisely what was happening before his very eyes at 1357 hours on a Monday afternoon in Rome's San Lorenzo District. He tried to tell himself that he had done everything in his power to stop this abomination from happening, but he knew that wasn't true. Like the Pope and Rome's ineffectual Jewish leaders, he wished he had done more to avert this tragedy, or at least done things differently.

And now it was too damned late.

Suddenly, a voice startled him from behind. "What are you doing here, *Standartenführer*? Don't tell me your friends at the Vatican have made a last-ditch effort to rescue the Jews?"

He turned to see Lieutenant Colonel Kappler, chief of the Rome Gestapo. "No, I am here strictly as an observer. But what are you doing here? Could it be, Herbert, you have come to witness firsthand the evil you have wrought?"

"You know perfectly well that I tried to stop this from happening. I tried to get these Jews sent to labor camps here in Italy."

"Oh, so you regard your gold ransom scheme to have been a charitable endeavor, I imagine?"

"It would have saved their lives. They raised the fifty kilograms of gold, but my superiors would have none of it. I tried to put a halt to this by interceding with the highest authorities. You think I wanted this? Look at this mess." He pointed down to the crying Jewish women and children being herded at gunpoint into the box cars, and the snarling and barking German Shepherds pulling on their leashes and frightening them to death. "Do you think that I am so heartless as to want something like that? If you do, then you don't know me at all."

"So you have come here to pray for their souls?"

"No, more out of curiosity and a little bit of guilt. I should have tried harder to stop this. This is not Germany or Austria. Rome's Jews should not have been touched. They are poor and hungry and do not deserve this kind of treatment."

"Oh, but in Germany and Austria they do, is that it?"

"Don't lecture me about morality, Colonel. What has happened here has taken place under the very eyes of His Holiness and before the entire Catholic world, and even the Pope himself was unable to stop it. Himmler and Eichmann have made a bold statement and made a mockery of the Vatican and the very idea of an Open City."

"That, at least, is one thing we can agree on." He pulled out a Lucky Strike and lit it with an engraved Zippo lighter. Hollmann smoked only American cigarettes, obtained on the Roman black market through pilfer or exchange from Allied POWs, and wouldn't touch a vile Eckstein, Sigarette Nazionali, or Galuoises. "I'll admit you have a certain broadmindedness, Herbert. But you are still a ruthless bastard. So don't try the saintly act with me."

He saw instantly that his words had struck a nerve. The scar at Kappler's jaw flared in the sunlight, and his gunmetal-gray eyes darkened.

"Why just last week you told me that you regard the Jews as our enemies," Hollmann continued. "You said that because they changed nationalities as the situation demanded, they were disloyal. You also said they are to blame for all wars. Surely you haven't forgotten saying those very words, Herbert?"

Kappler said nothing. Again, the snakelike scar etched into his face reddened.

"You are a Jew hater, Herbert, and you are as responsible for this as anyone." He waved his hand down at the boxcars. "You don't really differentiate between German and Italian Jews, or between Jews that have converted to Catholicism and those that have not. You have said that all Jews—whether disassociated, baptized, or mixed—are the enemy. Did you not tell me that just last week, Herbert?"

"You shouldn't talk to me like that, *Standartenführer*."

"Why is it whenever you are agitated, the scar on your cheek becomes inflamed? It reminds me of the way the Führer spews saliva from his mouth when he gets overexcited during his speeches."

"You talk like a traitor."

"No, I talk like the cynic I happen to be, at least on occasion." He looked down again at the Jews being loaded into the boxcars. "This sobering day happens to be one of those occasions. And besides, Herbert, my SS rank allows me to say what I please. I am a loyal soldier. I just don't approve of killing Jews. It makes us seem so low, and it goes without saying that history will judge us poorly. I mean, look down there. Tell me, where is the honor in that?"

Kappler followed his gaze. "This is Captain Dannecker's doing, not mine. Yes, I cooperated with the roundup, but I had no choice. Unless I, too, wanted to be stuffed into one of those boxcars down there. I am not the one who lied and told the Jews that they are going to a labor camp. I am not the one who said that everyone would be given a job, according to his or her skills, and those who could not work, the children, and the elderly would be supported by the rich paying for the poor. Dannecker did this so he could steal from the rich and poor alike whatever valuables they might still have on them. You and I know perfectly well, Hollmann, these people are on a one-way ticket to the furnaces in the east."

"So it is certain that it is Auschwitz then?"

The Gestapo chief nodded. Hollmann took a pull from his Lucky and slowly blew out a cloud of bluish smoke.

"It is a sin against humanity. These people are no more a military threat to the Reich than a flock of sheep, and yet, look at all this effort expended by the SS. It's no wonder we are losing this war. They should be rounding up Resistance members and escaped Allied POWs instead of wasting their time on those miserable wretches down there being packed into those damned cattle cars."

"It would appear that you and I have more in common than you would care to admit, Colonel."

"No, Herbert, you and I are nothing alike. As I've told you before, you have a certain broadmindedness about you. But as soon as you feel you are up against a traitor or enemy of the Reich—it doesn't matter whether they are a German, Jew, or foreigner—you are absolutely pitiless. You turn into the blind instrument of your beloved, implacable Gestapo. Don't forget, I know you."

"As I warned you before, talk like that could get you a room in my basement at Via Tasso."

"Then arrest me."

"As you have said, your rank protects you. And somehow, I don't believe General Wolff would appreciate you in my basement with all those rats. Everyone knows you are his protégé, as well as Himmler's erudite man in Rome and the Reich's military liaison with the Vatican and black nobility. So, it would appear that you are beyond the reach of anyone except the Führer himself. But you are still a dangerous man, Colonel Hollmann. One of these days, that mouth of yours is going to get you into trouble and you won't be able to talk yourself out of it."

"Iconoclasm runs in my family, I'm afraid. Except for my younger brother Walther. He is fighting at the front right now and happens to greatly admire our little Bohemian Corporal the Führer. Yes, you and my brother Walther would get along just fine, Herr Kappler."

"What is his unit?"

"He is a major in the Hermann Göring Division."

"The Hermann Göring? Those are crack troops. It must be a great honor for him to be an officer in such a magnificent division. Meanwhile, we are stuck here in Rome. I have requested a transfer to a combat assignment on several occasions, but unfortunately I have been rejected every time. Himmler insists that I am too valuable and must stay here in Rome."

"Consider yourself lucky. Here in the Eternal City, the enemy doesn't shoot back at you when you shoot at them."

"Not yet anyway. But the partisans will be fighting back soon enough. The Italians are lazy, but they are not as passive as those Jews being deported down there without a flicker of protest. Still, I would rather be fighting at the front than battling partisans, arresting spies, and sitting here watching old men, women, and children being handled like cattle. There is certainly no honor in the latter."

"Indeed, there is not, *Obersturmbannführer*. Indeed, there is not."

Suddenly, down below there was a commotion alongside the freight train. The doors had been bolted shut and the train was ready to leave. But somehow, a Jewish woman had managed to run past the guards and was pounding her fists on the boxcars and shouting out a man's name.

"My God, is she actually trying to get on the train?" gasped Hollmann.

"She must be trying to find her husband or family," said Kappler.

"I wish she would just save herself."

"She doesn't know she is going to die. She just wants to be with her family."

"Well, it is a tragedy all the same."

He and the Gestapo chief stood there breathless, watching. He saw what appeared to be her husband and others calling out to her from the slats in the box car, warning her to flee.

No, don't do it! Don't get on that train! If you do, there is no coming back!

But the woman, thinking of nothing except reuniting with her family, was not about to be dissuaded. After she had pleaded with two guards, they opened up the box car and let her board the train. Then the doors were again bolted shut and, at precisely 1405 hours, the whistle blew and the guards all down the line stepped back from the track. In a final emotional flurry, passengers pushed notes and letters to loved ones through the wooden slats and air holes with pleas to the finders to collect and deliver them. Then the twenty-eight car train began to chug down the arrow-straight track pointed northeast, towards the crematoriums of Auschwitz, and soon disappeared from sight.

He and Kappler glanced at one another. He felt sick inside.

"This should not have happened," he said. "If God actually gave a damn about Germany, he would not have allowed us to become monsters like this."

"The Father of Rome and Jewish leadership did no more than we did. They allowed their own Roman citizens to be rounded up and hauled off to Auschwitz. Foà and Almansi failed to destroy the community lists and didn't even warn their people to disperse and hide. And whatever protest Pius issued, it wasn't enough."

"Yes, but Pius and the Italian people are not the ones murdering the Jews. This travesty before us is what Nazi Germany does to God's children. And we have been doing it for years now. Do you still want to be part of this?"

"I have no choice. It is my sworn duty to support the Fatherland. If not, then I am a defeatist."

"There are worse things in the world, Herbert, than refusing an order."

"You are talking like a traitor again."

"Then so be it, because right now I certainly feel like one. By any definition, what has happened here in Rome these past three days is a sin against God."

They fell into silence. Hollmann took a final drag of his American cigarette, tossed it onto the sidewalk, stamped it out with the heel of his gleaming black SS boot, and exhaled the smoke. He knew he shouldn't have come here. The Roman roundup and deportation was deeply unsettling, and the whole thing made him feel raw and shameful inside. But for his own sanity, his own guilt, he had felt the need to come to Tiburtina Station and bear witness to the deportation. As a fervent Roman Catholic, he knew it was akin to self-flagellation, a way to purge the demons that had seized hold of him and his countrymen and turned them into evil.

"We are done here, Herbert. There is nothing more that can be done for those people. They are in the hands of God now."

"Yes," agreed Kappler. "But unfortunately, God doesn't seem to care much for the Jews. Otherwise, he wouldn't have allowed this to happen."

CHAPTER 14

VATICAN

OCTOBER 18, 1943

POPE PIUS XII, THE VICAR OF CHRIST, stared across his desk at Sir D'Arcy Osborne and realized, by the way the British Minister to the Holy See was staring at him, how terrible he looked. This morning, when he had dressed in his holy vestments, Pius had looked at himself in the mirror and, to his dismay, what he saw peering back at him appeared like a skeletal apparition. His complexion was sallow, his emaciated cheeks were sunken like craters, and his quicksilver eyes bore deep shadows from lack of sleep. Now, out of politeness, Osborne looked away, obviously not wanting to offend him in his own papal study. Feeling on edge, the Pope licked his lips, clenched and unclenched his hands, and cast a furtive glance at the gently ticking Rococo clock against the wall, as if time was running out.

And indeed it was.

The Jewish death train had left Tiburtina Station over an hour ago, he had learned from Secretary of State Maglione, and over a thousand souls, most of whom were women and children, were headed for either a crematorium or slave labor in the east. The Pope and Osborne both knew that. And they also knew that, whatever behind-the-scenes protests the Supreme Pontiff had made to prevent a holocaust for more than a thousand of Rome's citizens, his words had amounted to nothing.

Absolutely nothing.

It made Pius angry at the injustice of it all. The base cruelty of Adolf Hitler, the mass murderer whose tyrannicide he had fully authorized, ceased to amaze him. And the only way to end all the insanity, sooner rather than later with the Allies still thousands of miles from Berlin, was to forcibly remove the tyrant from power.

It was the only way.

"Your Holiness," said Osborne in a reverential tone. "I mean no disrespect. But don't you think that your policy of not taking a public stand against the Nazis has placed an unnecessary strain on you and the Vatican. It seems that it will end up emboldening the German occupiers."

Pius felt a flicker of disapproval cross his face, but he maintained his composure. Despite his haggard appearance, he looked saintly in his white robe, jewel-encrusted silver crucifix, and Piscatory Ring of the Fisherman. He tented his fingers into a steeple on his spacious desk, his eyes taking in everything and missing nothing as he studied the British minister's face.

"Embolden the Germans?" he posed rhetorically. "Embolden them to do what?"

"To perform even worse atrocities. What I am trying to say is how vile do the Nazis have to be until a public denouncement is made?"

"You know perfectly well, Minister, I cannot call out the Germans explicitly by name. Hitler would simply embargo, suppress, and discredit any papal protest."

"By what means?"

"The Germans would claim the protest was counterfeit. Or they would use it as vindication of the national broadcast Goebbels's issued years ago warning that the Holy Father and Church spread exaggerated atrocity tales."

"I believe you underestimate your moral authority, Your Eminence."

"And I believe you underestimate the vengeful nature of Hitler and his Nazis, Minister. But there are diplomatic constraints as well. If I speak out against the concentration camps, I would be violating the Concordat." He was referring to the 1933 treaty between the Holy See and Germany that regulated relations between the Catholic Church and the German government, both guarantying and limiting the Church's rights in the implementation of its ministry. "If I violate our agreement, the Nazis will not only take harsh action against Catholics in Germany and the occupied countries, but they will likely bring even more vicious reprisals against the remainder of the Jews hiding out in Rome. By our estimates, there are at least seven to ten thousand more still living in the city, and perhaps more. If I speak out, I will only make the situation worse for Catholics and Jews alike. Hitler is a madman, a madman who flies into an uncontrolled rage at the slightest provocation. I am sorry, Minister, but the only actions I can take to help the Jews of Rome and Europe are to offer them refuge in Vatican properties, monasteries, and convents, give them humanitarian aid by providing funds for food, clothing, and medicine, provide them with baptism certificates and Vatican papers identifying them as Catholics, and make appeals on their behalf through official diplomatic channels. And then, once I have done all those things, I can pray for them, which in the end is probably the most important of all."

The British envoy nodded. From Father O'Flaherty, Osborne was well aware of the Pope's extensive humanitarian efforts thus far during the war. From his intelligence sources inside the Vatican, Osborne was also well aware that Pius had worked hard with the three principal German diplomats in Rome—the German Ambassador to the Holy See, Baron von Weizsäcker, his closest aide Albrecht von Kessel, and the acting head of the German embassy, Consul Möllhausen—to terminate the Jewish roundup and deportation. Even now with the death train having left Tiburtina Station, the three diplomats, who in private Vatican chambers were strenuously opposed to Nazism, were still frantically working to control the damage to German-Curia relations that the ill-advised roundup and deportation posed. But Osborne still firmly believed that the Pope should have delivered a vigorous public protest. It wasn't the first time the British Minister had felt this way. They had been through this debate on several occasions since the beginning of the war, when they had first met in secret regarding the plot to remove the Führer from power and install an anti-Nazi government.

"If I protested the treatment of the Jews," continued the Pope, "I would have to denounce the atrocities of Stalin and the Soviet Union against the Catholics of Poland and elsewhere. As well as their brutality towards German prisoners of war. I would also have to speak out about the Katyn massacre," he added, referring to the 1940 massacre in which the Big Red Army, at the time an ally of Nazi Germany under the Ribbentrop-Molotov Pact, murdered over twenty-thousand Polish officers. Stalin and his political cronies in the Kremlin tried, unsuccessfully, to blame the mass murder on the Germans, while the Allies had remained conspicuously silent about the massacre during the past four years in order to preserve their fragile alliance with the Soviet Union.

"But the Germans have been deporting Jews to Auschwitz and other death camps for the past two years. Surely, that is enough to draw public condemnation."

"Minister, I know that this terrible situation has put everyone in the city on edge, both Jew and Gentile alike. But I am still under pressure from many quarters to condemn the abuses perpetrated by the Red Army against Catholic civilians all over Eastern Europe. How can I pick and choose when both sides have committed depredations?"

"We are all painfully aware of the Russian atrocities, Your Eminence. But surely they cannot be compared to the mass extermination of Jews taking place in Poland and Germany?"

"I agree with you that they are not the same. But I still cannot issue a public appeal on behalf of the Jews anywhere in the world that explicitly criticizes the Nazis. All I can do is work quietly behind the scenes for the simple reason that direct intervention will provoke Hitler and worsen the situation for both Jews and Catholics. I know this man—and he is a monster."

Osborne started to respond then thought better of it, and they fell into an uncomfortable silence. The Pope knew that the British dignitary understood and largely sympathized with his predicament; but it was equally obvious that the British minister—and the man he served, Sir Winston Churchill—still wanted him to issue a strong public condemnation. That had been the Allied modus operandi since the beginning of the war. Pius knew perfectly well that both Great Britain and the United States sought to exploit him for their war aims as a propaganda chess piece and make the Germans look bad before the eyes of the world. Of course, the great Western powers steadfastly claimed that they only wanted him to speak out against their common Nazi oppressor for the simple reason that it was the moral thing to do, consequences be damned; but what they really wanted was to capitalize on the Pope's worldwide influence to win the propaganda war. But the independent-minded Pius would never put Stauffenberg and the German Resistance movement, Europe's Catholics, or the Church itself at greater risk than they already were just to win the propaganda war for the Allies, not when both sides were committing atrocities.

Remember, he reminded himself, *if Hitler is dead then Nazism is dead. The Führer is the engine that drives the machine, and no Himmler or Göring could ever replace him. That is why it is imperative that Stauffenberg succeed. And that is precisely why you are taking these grave risks.*

"Your Holiness, under what conditions would it be impossible for you to remain here in the Eternal City and continue to remain silent about the abominations of the German occupiers? After all, the Germans have refused to recognize the Open City status and have rounded up more than a thousand Roman citizens, many within a few hundred feet of the Vatican? At some point, wouldn't it be better for you to just leave?"

"I will never leave Rome unless forcibly removed."

"And if the Germans round up a thousand more Roman citizens? Two thousand? Three?"

"As I just told you, I will never abandon my beloved city or its people unless I am removed by force."

"What about General Stahel and Kappler? Surely, you don't trust them?"

"I have no complaints against them with regards to the Vatican. They have been quite diligent about respecting our neutrality. And, as you are well aware, we have friends in the German embassy that are sympathetic to our unique circumstances here in Rome."

"Your Holiness," said Osborne in his most respectful yet quietly urgent voice, "your moral influence extends not only to the large Catholic population of Europe, but encompasses the entire world. I would urge you not to underestimate that moral authority, in case in the course of coming events an occasion might arise for taking a strong line."

"I think that perhaps, Sir D'Arcy, you overestimate my ability to control the events around me. Do you really believe that anyone can stop Adolf Hitler from doing as he pleases? My biggest concern now is the insufficient police forces in Rome."

"There were sufficient German forces two days ago to shut down the whole city and allow the Nazis to go from home to home rounding up Roman citizens."

"Yes, but these severe measures are bound to stir up unsavory elements of the population, driving some into the arms of the Communists."

"Is that really the most pressing item given the current situation?"

"These deportations are going to create problems. I have already spoken to Ambassador Weizsäcker requesting to have more police on the streets."

"You want more German police in what is supposed to be an Open City?"

"In the absence of adequate police protection, irresponsible elements might commit violence in the city. Communist bands are stationed in and around Rome at the present time. They are biding their time to move in and seize power. I am concerned about what will happen with the food situation in the city with these undesirables on the prowl. They could gain control of the city during the period between the inevitable German evacuation and the arrival of the Allies."

"You are worried about *il tempo di nessuno*—the time of no one," said Sir D'Arcy, reciting the phrase that had taken hold of the Vatican since the beginning of the German Occupation, the dreaded time between the German withdrawal and Allied takeover when "no one" would be in charge. At that time, the city would be left to "irresponsible or turbulent elements" and "godless Communists," as the Pope and his closest advisors nervously referred to them.

"Yes, I am worried. That is why two weeks ago Cardinal Maglione met with Ambassador Weizsäcker to express my misgivings. As the protectors of both the Vatican and Rome, the Germans have the responsibility to provide sufficient police forces to maintain public order and prevent insurrection. The German ambassador assured me that he would speak with General Wolff and Field Marshal Kesselring about this matter. The threat posed by the Communists and other irresponsible elements is very real."

"Well, I'm sure the Germans and their Fascist counterparts will prove to be more than willing to expand their anti-partisan police forces in Rome. Not out of a sense of duty, but in retribution for the Allied advance. Whenever the Allies push forward along the front, the police take it out on the people. So who are the law-abiders then?"

The Pope didn't answer. Instead, he launched immediately into another point of irritation. "I have also instructed every parish priest in Rome to speak to his congregation in my name urging their parishioners to be calm and self-possessed in whatever circumstances they might find themselves. People need to know that self-control, devotion to duty, and moderation are needed above all in times like these. We cannot have irresponsible elements dictating our fates or in charge in any way before the arrival of the Allies."

"Excuse me, Your Eminence, but I believe it will take the Allies a few months to make their triumphal march into Rome. The British Eighth and American Fifth Armies are barely past the rain-gorged Volturno River. Which means that they are more than a hundred miles from the Eternal City. Herr Kesselring will certainly have something to say about the rate of the Allied advance towards Rome in the coming weeks."

"Wasn't it your Mr. Churchill who called Italy the 'soft underbelly' of Europe and claimed that the Allies would have Rome by Christmas?"

"Well, yes, but Winston has a tendency towards hyperbole and is overly optimistic. Italy is a mountainous country with unpredictable winter weather and swollen rivers. And war is the most unpredictable of human endeavors."

"No, it is the most ignoble of human endeavors. It also leads to great instability. That is why these Communists and Allied war planes wreaking death and destruction trouble me so." He looked towards the ceiling, as if appealing to a higher authority. "Will there, Heavenly Father, be no end to these unholy measures?"

"With all due respect, Your Holiness, it is the Nazis and their Fascist puppets that we have to fear most—not a handful of Italian Communists or errant Allied bombers."

"That may be, but what those British bombers did in San Lorenzo in July was a crime against humanity and God himself. Fifteen hundred innocents were killed or wounded in that Allied bombing fiasco."

"It was indeed a tragedy. But it was an accident and, therefore, pales in comparison to what the Germans did earlier today at Tiburtina Station."

"Yes, that is true. But you know I can't say that publicly." He rose from his chair, signaling Osborne that the meeting was over. "Regardless of what you think, Sir D'Arcy, I have not underestimated my moral authority. I have long agreed with you, your prime minister, and President Roosevelt that it is a weapon I can wield against Hitler and his henchmen at critical moments. But please don't mistake my pragmatic public silence for inaction. You know better than anyone how strenuously I have supported removing the Führer by any means possible. I, sir, stand behind any German government except one with Hitler."

His steely gaze locked onto the British minister like one of the aerial bombs he so dreaded exploding in his sacred Rome. He then made the sign of the cross and spoke in a quiet voice.

"*Che Dio ri protegga,*" he said. May God protect you.

"Thank you, Your Eminence. But I think a more appropriate prayer is: May God protect us *all* from the Nazis."

CHAPTER 15

PIAZZA DI SPAGNA

OCTOBER 19, 1943

PULLING ASIDE THE BLACKOUT CURTAIN, Captain John Bridger peered down at the piazza and knew he was dealing with the real Roman Resistance. It was after the 6 p.m. curfew. Partisan sentries were posted in the shadows all around the piazza, keeping an alert eye out for German night patrols, snooping Gestapo agents, and Fascist police. The lookouts were posted near the Early Baroque *Fontana della Barcaccia*—Fountain of the Ugly Boat—at the base of the piazza. They were posted in front of legendary English poet John Keats's house and at set intervals along the 135-step staircase that led from Piazza di Spagna to the church of Trinità dei Monti. And they were posted all around the perimeter of the sacred church at the top of the Spanish Steps. Dressed in dark clothing, they carried carefully concealed submachine guns, hand grenades, and automatic pistols wrapped as common parcels in editions of *L'Osservatore Romano*. The Vatican newspaper was the only non-Fascist daily in Rome allowed by the occupiers and the most widely read paper in the city.

He let the curtain fall back in place, turned away from the window, and looked at Savoyan. This was their first official meeting with the partisan leadership and they were both nervous. He then took a moment to study the men he was about to address and bring into the fold of U.S. intelligence operations in Rome.

Four of the leaders in attendance were prominent anti-Fascist political figures representing the Military Council of the *Comitato di Liberazione Nazionale*—the National Liberation Committee, or CLN, an umbrella group representing the six liberal, anti-Fascist political parties dedicated to resistance against the German Occupation within the city. The other two leaders were from the conservative *Fronte Militare Clandestino della Resistenza*—the Clandestine Military Front of the Resistance that was backed by Churchill and the British. The head of the group—a tall, distinguished-looking man with regal bearing—was his stepfather and his sister Teresa's biological father, Colonel Giovanni Vassalli Di Domenico. The Military Front commanded by the respected, fifty-year-old aristocrat was the most well-armed and well-trained partisan organization in Rome representing King Victor Emmanuel's and Marshal Pietro Badoglio's monarchist government in exile in Brindisi. But that brought the group into direct conflict for the control of post-war Italy with the anti-monarchist CLN. The CLN fielded through its military council—dominated by the Action Party, the Socialists, and the Communists—a well-organized and powerful fighting outfit that sought freedom for all Italians, not just the black nobility closely aligned with the monarchy and Vatican.

Bridger knew it wouldn't be easy to get the two groups to cooperate. The alliance between the conservative Military Front and liberal CLN was a fragile one at best. United solely by their hatred of Nazism and Fascism, the two groups bickered constantly both internally and with one another. They reportedly spent as much time arguing as they did gathering intelligence and fighting against their common enemy. That enemy was not only the SS but Kesselring's occupying German Army, as well as the repressive Italian police forces that supported the Nazis and sought retribution against those that had opposed Mussolini.

Bridger cleared his throat to speak to the assembled men. "These are dangerous times and I thank you all for coming tonight," he began in fluid Italian, calmly sizing up his audience as he spoke. "My name is John Bridger. I am a captain in the First Special Service Force, a joint American-Canadian commando unit completing final training in the U.S. The rest of my cohorts are scheduled to arrive here in Italy in the coming weeks. I know you have all taken great risks to meet here after the curfew. I look forward to working with you to aid the war effort and to defeat the Germans who have taken over your country, as well as the Fascists that support them. I am here under the personal orders of General Clark, Commander of the Fifth Army, and Colonel Frederick, commander of the First Special Service Force. My job is to assist Lieutenant Savoyan here on my right in setting up an Allied intelligence network in Rome. The lieutenant is acting under the direct orders of General Donovan, head of the Office of Strategic Services. Lieutenant Savoyan is the acting chief of the OSS in Rome. When I leave the day after tomorrow, he will be responsible for coordinating and directing all intelligence activities on behalf of the OSS and Fifth Army in Rome. Our goal here tonight is to discuss how the Roman Resistance networks represented by all of you can aid the Fifth Army and OSS in intelligence gathering, disrupting enemy communications, and taking out key military targets."

Here he paused. The Resistance leaders stared back at him long and hard. All of the men were older than him and Savoyan, and they didn't look the least bit impressed. The sole exception was his stepfather, Colonel Di Domenico, whom he hadn't seen in seven years. The big Italian colonel looked vaguely amused to see his young American stepson lecturing Italians about obtaining intelligence in their own country. Looking out at his audience, Bridger once again realized that unifying all of these politically disparate brigands was going to be even more difficult than he had thought.

"Why should we obey you?" asked the Communist Party leader Giorgio Amendola of the CLN Military Council, echoing Bridger's own fears. "You look like you just got out of diapers."

Bridger tried not to let his surprise show on his face and offered up a challenging smile. "I am not asking you to obey *me*. I am merely a military liaison and an observer for the Fifth Army. General Clark wants eyes on the ground behind enemy lines here in Rome, and as you can see, I speak Italian as well as at least half of you." This drew a ripple of contentious laughter. "But if you genuinely want to help win the war, then you *do* need to obey Lieutenant Savoyan here on my right. Because he happens to be in charge of OSS Rome. Which means that, from this moment on, he *is* the official intelligence link between Rome and the Fifth Army."

All eyes turned to Savoyan, whose face visibly reddened.

Amendola sniffed, "He looks even younger than you. What does he know about intelligence here in Rome?"

Savoyan stepped forward. "I know enough to make sure that we don't have another Naples when the Germans abandon Rome," he said, in perfect Roman-Italian. "That is unless you want St. Peter's, the Colosseum, and Hadrian's Tomb destroyed, or the limbs of your women and children blown off from booby-traps planted all over the city. I was there when the Allies landed in Naples and saw the Nazis' handiwork firsthand. They destroyed not only the port and all utility facilities, but hundreds of historic buildings. Many bombs continued to explode well after the Allied armies had driven the Germans off and taken control of the city."

Riccardo Bauer of the Action Party wing of the CLN held up his hand. "All right, you have made your point. We all want to protect Rome from destruction. Even the colonel and I can agree on that much." He looked at Di Domenico. "Right, Giovanni?"

"That is correct, Riccardo." His thoughtful gaze reached out to everyone present. "We all want Rome spared and to drive the Germans from the city."

"That is what my government and our allies want as well," said Bridger, pleased that they had established something they could all agree on. "But I'm afraid our armies are still a hundred miles from Rome and the day of liberation is a long way off. After the New Year for certain."

"That long?" snorted the pugnacious Amendola. "Why I thought Churchill promised that Rome would be added to the British Empire by Christmas?"

"Yes, tally ho, old boy," quipped Socialist leader Sandro Pertini of the CLN. "Hop to it, you lazy Italians, and be quick about it. Smartly now!"

Everyone laughed at the spot-on impression of a lordly British officer. "That was good, I must admit," said Colonel Di Domenico affably, but with a note of warning. "But I wouldn't be so quick to condemn our British allies in the Eighth Army. The Tommies have already spilled more blood in this war than the Italian Army has in the past century."

"Well, they can bleed some more on their way to Rome," said Amendola. "All we care about is making Rome uninhabitable for the Nazis and saving her from destruction."

There were nods and head bobs all around from the liberal CLN Military Council Resistance leaders.

"You just let me and my people worry about safeguarding buildings, bridges, and utilities when the time comes," said Colonel Di Domenico.

"Who do you think you are talking to?" bristled Amendola. "You don't order us about."

The colonel held up an apologetic hand. "That is not what I meant. I only meant that I have a plan for safeguarding the city when the time comes."

The blue-eyed, forty-eight year old Milanese Riccardo Bauer of the liberal

Action Party smiled. He had been imprisoned twice during the rise of Mussolini's Fascism and it showed in the deep lines of his face. "That is good to know, Colonel," he said sardonically. "But just so you know, we, too, have plans to protect the city."

"I'm sure you do," said Bridger, trying to wrestle control of the meeting again. "But as I've just told you, it is premature to be making plans at this time for a German withdrawal. There will be a long fight from the Garigliano River to Monte Cassino, and then from there all the way to Rome."

"The Allies taking Rome might be a long way off,' snapped Amendola, "but when it happens, we sure as hell won't be fighting for those sacks of shit King Emmanuel or Badoglio hiding out in Brindisi."

A chorus of agreement rumbled through the group.

"My colleague Giorgio's tongue is sharp, but his point is a good one," said the ever-diplomatic Bauer. "A few days before your arrival, Captain Bridger, Badoglio demanded by radio that the CLN submit to his command."

"Of course, we rejected it," snapped Sandro Pertini. "We are not fighting for the King or his puppets."

Bridger held up his hands, calling a timeout. He realized that he and Savoyan had underestimated the extent of the rift between the CLN and the Military Front. "Now hold your horses, gentlemen," he commanded in a loud voice that brooked no opposition. "The job that Lieutenant Savoyan and I have here is purely military, and I will tolerate no further bickering from any of you—and that includes my stepfather Colonel Di Domenico. What General Clark wants is a united Resistance movement that has the same goal as the Fifth Army—and that's to kick the crap out of the Germans and drive Kesselring out of goddamned Italy. What you all do as far as politics is your own business. But if you're going to bicker like an old married couple, you're going to have to do it on your own time. Our enemy is the German Army, not one another. Our American troops are dying to the south by the tens of thousands. They're spilling their blood to liberate your country from Hitler, Mussolini, and all of the jack-booted thugs you seem to grow over here in Europe like fucking weeds. Most of our troops were drafted by Uncle Sam and never wanted to be here in the first place. They would much rather be back home with their gal sipping a cold one and taking in a Cagney movie instead of being shot at by Krauts and freezing their asses off over here. So all Lieutenant Savoyan and I are asking you to do is to put aside your differences for the time being and focus every ounce of your effort into defeating the Nazis and their Fascist lapdogs. Can we count on you? Are you with us?"

The room went totally silent. Bridger was worried that he might have overreached and become a little too preachy, but he saw from the faces that several of the Resistance leaders, battle-hardened men much older than him, were actually quite moved. They knew that they needed to put aside their petty differences if they were going to drive "Smiling Albert" Kesselring and his German goons from their homeland. Now was the time to put aside their quarrels and join together to destroy their common enemy by whatever means necessary.

His stepfather took a step forward. "I am with you." He looked at Amendola and the other CLN leaders. "I am with all of you. I will be there for you when you need me, and the Military Front will not let you down. We will work together as partners. Together, we will wreak havoc on the enemy, and drive Kesselring and his army first out of Rome and then out of all of Italy."

Bridger looked at the men and saw nodding heads all around. Through seasoned diplomacy, his stepfather had helped unite them. The man was a natural leader, and this was how Bridger remembered him when he had lived in Rome with him, his mother, and Teresa. At six-foot four-inches and two hundred pounds, the colonel had a hugely forceful physical presence that took the air out of a room and made people gaze in awe. Unfortunately, his commanding presence and leadership capabilities had also drawn the attention of the Gestapo and Fascist police and Di Domenico was much sought-after by the enemy. He had to remain in constant hiding, and even attending a meeting such as this posed grave risk.

"We are all with you, Captain Bridger," said Riccardo Bauer, and his words were echoed by the other CLN leaders.

For the first time, Bridger allowed himself a little smile. "Music to my ears, gentlemen. Now let's get down to the details. The first step is to set up a radio link with our friends in the Fifth Army."

CHAPTER 16

PALAZZO BELLOMO

OCTOBER 21, 1943

PEERING OUT A CLOSED WINDOW overlooking Piazza Navona, Teresa shook her head in disgust. Two poorly disguised Gestapo plainclothed agents were parked out front, and beyond loomed a marching German foot patrol. With a flick of her wrist, she closed the drapes. Turning away from the window, she drew a mental image of the *Pietà* at St. Peter's Basilica—Michelangelo's impassioned Carrara-marble statue of the Madonna clutching the dead Christ—and wondered if her beloved city would ever be rid of the hated Nazis. Like the monsters of Greek mythology, they were terrorizing Rome.

The Italian government, in exile in Brindisi, had declared Rome a demilitarized "Open City" and the Germans had reaffirmed it; yet every day, Nazi patrols just like those in the piazza shuffled past her window, and several nights a week the walls of buildings quaked as the Wehrmacht lorries, trucks, and tanks rumbled through the streets of the city towards the southern front. When would it all end? Teresa often wondered. When would Italy be free from the yoke of Nazi repression? When would the Allied liberators finally get here?

Abruptly, her thoughts were interrupted by her mother's sharp voice.

"Where were you last night?"

She tried not to let the surprise show on her face. "I don't know—where were you last night?" she fired back.

Her mother crossed her arms. "You were out late. The curfew is six p.m."

"Yes, well you know our saying here in Italy. *Fatta la legge, trovato l'inganno.*" No sooner have you passed a law than you have found a way around it.

"It is not right to make light of things in war. These are desperate times."

"That must be why we are down from five full-time servants to two."

"You don't talk to me like that, young lady. Where were you last night?"

Teresa felt delicious satisfaction anticipating what she was going to say. "If you must know, I was at a Communist partisan meeting," she said tartly.

"Don't joke with me. Where were you?"

She couldn't believe that her mother thought she was jesting. It made her angry. "I just told you where I was: a Communist meeting. It was held at Ponte Sant'Angelo in the *centro storico*. I am a member of the *Gruppi di Azione Patriottica*. The GAP is one of the military groups of the National Liberation Committee."

"I know perfectly well what the GAP is."

"Good, then you know that we are going to drive the Germans and Mussolini's Fascist pigs from Rome and reclaim our homeland."

Her mother stepped forward and slapped her face—hard. Teresa nearly fell to the floor.

She glared at her defiantly. "What, Mother, you don't like the new me? You didn't actually think I would be content to bring fresh sheets and clothes to Father O'Flaherty for the rest of the war when others are actually *fighting* in the Resistance?"

"But you are of nobility."

"You can take your nobility and shove it down the toilet."

"How dare you talk to me that way!"

"No, how dare you talk to me as if I am a child! I am twenty-one years old and am a partisan fighting for the GAP now. I don't take my orders from you or father. My commander Spartaco is the only one I need to obey."

"My God, who has planted these subversive thoughts in your head?"

"No one planted anything. All you need to know is that I am a partisan now—just like Father."

"Your father is not a *partisan*. He is a full army colonel!"

"He is a wanted former intelligence officer who has gone into hiding. Seriously, Mother, you say the word partisan as if it leaves a bad taste in your mouth. But that's what Father is—a partisan. In fact, he is the leader of the Military Front. The only difference between us is our rank and what we are fighting for."

"That is nonsense. You don't know what you're talking about."

"Father and I are both fighting to end Fascism. But while he fights for the King and Marshal Badoglio who fled Rome for the safety of Brindisi, I fight for all of Italy and the Risorgimento."

"The Risorgimento? You don't know anything about the Risorgimento."

"*La mia patria era la patria del Risorgimento*—my country is the country of the Risorgimento, the country of democracy and liberty. That is what I am fighting for, Mother. After twenty years of Fascist brutality, it is time for a rebirth. What the Resistance is fighting for is not to preserve the damned monarchy or simply get rid of foreign oppressors. It is a fight on behalf of Italy and all Italians. Liberals and Conservatives, Communists and Monarchists—indeed everyone except Fascists!"

"Good heavens, who has brainwashed you into espousing these dangerous ideas?"

"Why you and I, of course!" said a new voice.

Teresa turned to see her father the colonel standing in the open doorway with Father O'Flaherty and the silk-top-hatted family butler Vincenzo. Her father was dressed in shabby civilian clothes, gold-rimmed spectacles, and a peasant's hat and he had grown a thick moustache, but he was so tall and distinguished-looking that the disguise did virtually nothing to conceal his aristocratic identity.

"Father!" she cried with delight.

She dashed to him and they embraced as her mother looked on with a worried scowl and Father O'Flaherty grinned his carefree Irish smile.

When Teresa and her father pulled apart, the marchesa stepped forward imperiously. “How long have you been standing there?” she asked her husband.

“Long enough to know that I have been gone too long.”

“Did you hear that your daughter has become a Communist partisan?”

“Has she now? She is a real *Pasionara*, eh?”

Teresa crossed her arms. “I am not here to be made fun of. I am a *Gappista* and demand to be treated with respect.”

His expression turned serious. “You should know that the first rule of a soldier is that respect must be earned. It is not given automatically.”

“Oh please stop, Giovanni, you’re just leading her on. And what are you doing sneaking into your own house like this? You know the Germans are watching us at all times now. There are Gestapo agents right out front this very minute.”

“That’s why the monsignor and I came in through the wine cellar and old catacombs.”

O’Flaherty stepped forward politely. He wore round steel-rimmed spectacles, a cloak, a sash, and wide-rimmed black hat, which he tipped courteously. “I apologize for the intrusion, Marchesa,” he said in his thick Irish brogue. “But I’m afraid we have an emergency on our hands.”

“What kind of emergency?” asked Teresa, noticing that her father and the Vatican pimpernel were perspiring. They must have exerted themselves navigating their way through the maze of catacombs that interconnected with the servant’s quarters behind the palazzo as well as the wine cellar.

“We have come for my gold coin collection,” said her father. “To fund the Military Front and Father O’Flaherty so he can continue to hide his POWs. These are terrible times and we need money desperately for the Resistance.” He looked at his wife. “I would have called, Bianca, but the Gestapo has tapped the phones. And I did not want to risk sending a messenger with the police surveillance.”

“It is my fault, Marchesa,” said O’Flaherty. “I was most insistent. With all of the escaped Allied prisoners wandering into the city from the abandoned camps, and with the recent roundups of Jews, the *carabinieri*, and anti-Fascist Army officers, I’m afraid we have been inundated with refugees and our finances are dwindling.”

Teresa looked at the Irish priest, saw earnest sincerity in his kindly blue eyes, but also a hint of humor and mischief. Father Hugh O’Flaherty was quickly becoming as much of a threat to the German occupiers as her father’s Military Front or the CLN. He arranged for funds, disguises, false identity cards, food, and accommodations for escaped Allied POWs and war refugees on Vatican-protected extraterritorial properties, monasteries, and convents. The network was known as the Escape Line and its clandestine work was approved by the Pope as part of his overall plan of secret resistance. The Escape Line was quietly supported behind the scenes by Teresa and her parents; Prince Filippo Andrea Doria Pamphilj; Count Salazar; Sir D’Arcy Osborne; John May, Osborne’s resourceful butler; a new escaped British POW who had just snuck into Rome named Major Sam Derry; and other courageous individuals willing to risk their lives on behalf of the war effort in Rome.

"Of course, we will do everything in our power to help, Father," said Teresa's mother. "You can count on us. I am just concerned about my family's safety."

"I understand, Marchesa." He bowed his head. "I apologize for putting you all in danger, but I'm afraid it couldn't wait."

"We need to get to that coin collection," said the colonel. "But first, Teresa, you must tell me about your new role as *Gappista Pasionara*. If I don't at least try to talk some sense into you, and get Father O'Flaherty to do the same, I'm afraid your mother will never forgive me."

"She has been running around with Communists," said the marchesa derisively. "They have corrupted her."

Her father looked at her sternly now. Though he was more judicious than her mother, clearly he didn't approve either. "Is it true, Teresa? Have you joined the GAP?"

"Yes, Father. My group leader's name is Spartaco. He is brilliant."

"Is he now? Is he so brilliant that he can save you from the Gestapo? Does he have influence with Colonel Kappler at Via Tasso? Because if he does, maybe I should work for him instead of the Military Front. Will this Spartaco you seem to have so much faith in let me join up?"

"You are making fun of me. But I am not a little girl anymore."

"No, you are far more dangerous than that. You are a young woman who does not know what she is getting herself into. When the GAP attacks soldiers on the streets of Rome, the Germans take reprisals against whoever lives in the neighborhood where the attack occurred. Are you prepared to have five, ten, or twenty innocent Romans shot for a single German on a foot patrol you take down?"

Teresa realized that she hadn't even thought about German reprisals. Though she had come to terms with the possibility of her own death, it was unacceptable to her that others—friends, colleagues, or even citizens she did not know personally but were still fellow Romans, the very people she was fighting for—might suffer in retaliation for her attacks. On the other hand, how could one surrender to German blackmail? How could one renounce every act of war and just passively accept whatever military and political violence the Nazis imposed?

"You are combating the enemy in the Resistance, too, Father. And even Mother supports Father O'Flaherty and his Escape Line. So why shouldn't I fight just like you?"

"Because the Germans will kill you—that's why." He turned to O'Flaherty. "Father, please tell this young *Pasionara* what goes on at Via Tasso."

"I know what goes on there. I don't need the Father to tell me."

"With all due respect, I would prefer not to get in the middle of a family quarrel," said O'Flaherty with a deferential smile. "One of you might get a wee bit upset and decide to wallop me, and I'm afraid I haven't been in the ring in years."

"*Mama Mia*, you are no help at all Padre," said the colonel. "Daughter, if you are such a fearsome Resistance fighter, what are the three most important principles of partisan warfare?"

"Don't play these games with her. You'll only encourage her," protested her mother.

"The three essential principles of partisan warfare are mobility, surprise, and audacity."

Her father blinked with surprise, following up quickly with a grin of approval. "Most impressive. Obviously, you're a lot better at listening to Communists than your own parents. And what size operations are the best in partisan warfare?"

"One should never undertake complex operations involving large-scale planning and many different people. Small group actions involving three to six people are best."

"Give an example?"

"Very well. How about spreading four-pointed nails along a road frequented by enemy troop and supply traffic?"

"Mother Mary, why she's a chip off the old block!" exclaimed O'Flaherty.

"You two must stop this at once. You're not helping at all," again protested the marchesa, her dark eyes blazing.

But to Teresa's satisfaction, her father ignored her mother and looked intently at her. "What about attacks on Fascist leaders? How is this best accomplished?"

"Fascists should be handpicked from nearby towns or areas outside of one's own place of residence. This is to not only limit police searches and seizures, but to protect your fellow partisans. Once identified, they should be put under surveillance to learn their movements prior to attack."

"Very good. And what other actions can be taken against the enemy to aid the war effort?"

"Cutting telephone lines, creating landslides to block roads, hurling grenades into munitions convoys, ambushing motorcycles, bombing barracks, attacking supply lines and command posts, blowing petrol tanks, and sabotaging enemy vehicles. The Wehrmacht must be made to understand that it is not the master of Rome, and that behind every tree and bush lurks a hostile population that is willing to kill and die to win the fight for Italy's honor. The Fascists must be targeted just as aggressively. That includes spies, enemy agents, provocateurs, and actual collaborators. They cannot be allowed to move through the city with impunity. In short, we must impose the conditions that will make Rome a truly Open City, not only to defeat the enemy but on behalf of the Risorgimento."

"There she goes again with her talk of the Risorgimento," exclaimed the marchesa. "Please get her to stop! Why you're even worse than the Communists who have turned our daughter into a *Pasionara*!"

The colonel shook his head emphatically. "No, she is simply her mother and father's daughter. She is doubly stubborn."

"You are doing nothing but inciting her. My daughter is of royal lineage, and I did not raise her to be a fomenter of rebellion in the streets." She glared at O'Flaherty. "And you, Father, you should be ashamed of yourself."

"My humble apologies, Marchesa. But the fact remains that the lass has a will of her own. I don't think my words will have any effect on her, and in fact, could make matters worse. That is why I must leave it to you and your husband to decide what is best for young Teresa here."

Her mother shook her head in dismay.

The colonel looked sternly at Teresa. "You are twenty-one and can decide matters for yourself. But I will offer you one parting word of advice. If you are going to serve your country in this battle for Rome, you must tell no one that you are in the Resistance and be extremely careful, alert, and exercise good judgment at all times. Can you promise me that you will do that?"

"Yes, Father, I promise."

"Good. Now Father O'Flaherty and I must retrieve our coins and leave at once." He leaned down, kissed her on the cheek, and took her in an embrace. Then he did the same with his stunned wife before she could object. "I am sorry, Bianca, but I must be off. A Resistance fighter can never rest."

She stood there open-mouthed. "And what of our daughter?"

"I can handle myself," said Teresa. "If my father and brother can fight on behalf of Rome then so can I."

"She has a fire in her just like you, Bianca." Then he took Teresa by the hand in parting. "May God protect you," he said, crossing himself.

"Che Dio ri protegga, Papa," echoed Teresa. May God protect you as well, Father.

CHAPTER 17

PIAZZA LOVATELLI
OCTOBER 21, 1943

WHILE WAITING TO MAKE OSS-ROME'S FIRST RADIO TRANSMISSION, Captain John Bridger plucked the four-pointed nail from the table and looked it over. The device consisted of two iron rods with sharply pointed ends, each as wide as a heavy-duty nail but twice as long, bent in half at right angles, and soldered together as interlocking V's. When thrown onto a paved or dirt road, the nail always came to rest with three points directed towards the ground like a tripod and one point sticking straight up to puncture tires. Bridger was impressed.

"So this is the little contrivance that is causing the Germans so much trouble," he said to Peter Savoyan and Cervo, their new OSS recruit and Allied double agent. The Rome police lieutenant secretly ran the new Radio Vittoria that provided the only direct link between U.S. intelligence in Rome and the approaching Fifth Army.

Cervo nodded. "Smiling Albert and General Wolff are already up in arms over these babies," he said, taking the four-headed nail from Bridger and twirling it in the light. "Two dozen of them are enough to slow enemy traffic to the front to a crawl and immobilize an entire German convoy for hours. They are especially damaging for trucks driving fast downhill. Or where there are a lot of curves. The drivers cannot react in time. The tires on ten or more vehicles can be shredded before the convoy can come to a halt. Sometimes the trucks even crash and pile up on one another, forcing the Germans to get out, clear the gridlocked roads, and change out the tires before they can resume driving again. In the meantime, they are exposed to machine-gun fire and grenade attack from hiding partisans. Or even strafing from Allied fighters during daylight hours."

"No wonder the Germans are incensed," said Bridger, impressed. "I'm glad our side's the one that's got them."

"Partisans from Frascati and the other hill towns of the Castelli Romani snared some twenty trucks a few days ago," said Cervo with pride. "They spread the nails over the southbound lanes of the Via Casilina, Via Ardeatina, and Appian Way, causing quite a pileup. The Germans have outlawed the nails. They are threatening to take severe punitive measures against those who live along the roads where acts of sabotage are taking place."

"Bastards. They'll gin up any excuse to murder unarmed civilians." Bridger glanced at his watch. "Oh, shit, it's four. Time to transmit."

He went to the window and checked the street below, while Savoyan stepped to the window in the *gabinetto* and verified that the coast was clear. They were in

Cervo's friend Ivanoe Falcioni's third floor apartment, one story below the roof, which allowed for a clear radio signal for sending and receiving transmissions. Once the all-clear sign was given, Cervo grabbed his radio headset and prepared to send today's Radio Vittoria message on the special transmitter-receiver sitting on the work table. It was a hand-keyed Morse apparatus, about the size of a suitcase, tuned by quartz to a single preset frequency, and powered by batteries that gave it about twenty watts.

Over the next few minutes, with Bridger and Savoyan assisting, the Italian set up his distinctive "call sign," adjusted the transmission frequencies, checked signal strength, and completed several more steps to ensure direct communication between Radio Vittoria Rome and OSS Naples, and then sent OSS Rome's first encoded message along with his security check on 14,120 kilocycles. The message was limited to five hundred letters broken into five message parts of six typewritten lines. Each message took just under a minute to send. Bridger was impressed with Cervo; the man was indeed a very competent radio operator.

Once they obtained "message received" confirmation from OSS Naples, Cervo signed off and the three of them gave a little cheer. They had successfully sent their first radio message to the Fifth Army, and OSS Rome was officially up and running. The message provided the first estimate of the number of German military personnel in Rome, as well as a brief description of the key German command posts in the city, the state of the Roman partisan movement, and news of the new four-pointed device that was causing havoc on southbound German troop deployments. But even more importantly, the triumvirate seemed to have developed an effective system for intelligence acquisition and transmission behind enemy lines. CLN would provide the raw intelligence on the ground; Savoyan, as the new head of OSS Rome, would translate, edit, and format the output into concise telegraphese; and Cervo would encode and transmit the messages, in accordance with the designated radio plan, from a different location at 0900 and 1600 hours each day.

The intelligence that they were now able to provide would help tip the scales of war in the Allies favor on their road to Rome.

Suddenly, they heard a noise outside the apartment.

Bridger stepped quickly to the window. A gunmetal-silver Fiat 500 Topolino and a German troop transport had pulled up next to the curb outside the apartment next to a surveillance van with a revolving aerial on the roof. A young captain in a jet-black SS uniform stepped from the Topolino and began barking out orders. A dozen German soldiers with rifles began jumping out of the truck and running towards the entrance to their apartment looking out onto Piazza Lovatelli.

"Shit, another roundup!" exclaimed Savoyan, now peering down at the street through the crack in the curtain along with Bridger and Cervo.

"No, I don't think so," said Bridger. "Look at that surveillance van. This time they're here for us."

"Where did the damned thing come from? It wasn't there ten minutes ago."

"And this is only our first radio transmission," pointed out Cervo. "There's no way they could have triangulated our position so quickly."

"They could if they routinely sweep this part of town and have been driving up and down the street," pointed out Bridger. "Or maybe there's another transmitter in the area that they've been tracking." But it didn't matter: the damned van was down there, antennae twirling, and Germans were pouring into their building.

"I only know of the Military Front's Centro X Radio," said Savoyan. "Like us, they move around daily. But they couldn't be here at Piazza Lovatelli, too, could they?"

"I don't know, possibly. All I know is we have to get the hell out of here."

There was no time to follow the regular escape plan. Instead, they quickly stashed the radio in its small leather suitcase, grabbed their snub-nosed Berettas and spare magazines, and dashed for the door, leaving all of their other belongings behind. The most important thing was not to surrender the radio and spare quartz crystals to the enemy.

Opening the door, they darted down the hallway for the stairs that led to the roof. When they reached the landing, Bridger heard a door swing open and loud voices below. He and Cervo looked down over the railing and saw the SS captain in black leather and a handful of soldiers glowering up at them from several floors below.

"Halt!" shouted the officer.

Cervo's eyes bulged wide with fear. "*Merda*, its Priebke! Hurry, we have to get out of here!"

"Kappler's number two, the Torquemada of Via Tasso?" gasped Savoyan as they tore up the stairs to the roof. "Jesus Christ, that's just our luck!"

Feeling his heart rate click up a notch at the prospect of being taken alive by the Torquemada himself, Bridger burst through the roof door shoulder first—

And instantly tripped over a small knot of bearded Jewish men, and a boy not more than twelve years old, hiding under an improvised lean-to tent.

He yelled out a warning in Italian, "Get the hell out of here! The Gestapo are coming!"

He and his two comrades quickly stepped over them and darted to the edge of the roof. The gap between the two buildings was perhaps five or six feet. Bridger didn't hesitate and jumped immediately to the adjacent roof. His partners backtracked several paces for a running start and followed behind him. The three of them cushioned their fall by tucking their bodies, crash landing, and rolling onto white terra cotta tiles, dislodging a few and sending them clattering to the street thirty feet below. By the time they had scrambled to their feet, Priebke and his troops had reached the rooftop they had just vacated and began to spread out, searching for them. Spotting the fleeing Jews, the Germans opened fire on them, taking down an old man and the boy with shots delivered in the back.

Bridger returned fire at the Germans with his Beretta, catching one in the arm.

He turned to Savoyan and Cervo. "You two go on! I'll hold them off!"

"No way. We're not leaving without you!" cried Savoyan.

"The hell you're not. Go and that's a fucking order!" he shouted back as a bullet whistled past their ears. "Get Cervo and the radio out of here now!"

"We're not leaving you!"

"Halt or we will kill you where you stand!" shouted Priebke, glaring at them fiercely.

Bridger scowled at him and opened fire, missing. "I said move your ass, Lieutenant, and that's a goddamned order!"

"Fine, we'll meet up at the rally point!" said Savoyan with obvious reluctance. "Good luck!"

"Don't worry about me. I've got these bastards right where I want them. Now go!"

They shot off the lock to the cupola, threw open the door, and disappeared from sight as Bridger popped in a fresh 8-round magazine into his Beretta, jumped up, and opened up on the enemy again, receiving a blistering answering fire from Priebke and his men.

CHAPTER 18

PIAZZA LOVATELLI
OCTOBER 21, 1943

THE GERMAN BARRAGE forced him to take cover. Bullets pinged and ricocheted noisily all around him. Every few seconds, he rose up and delivered counterfire to hold the enemy at bay on the adjacent rooftop, aiming for the steel tortoise-shell helmets popping up like jack-in-the-boxes. But it was hard to hit the bastards when they were constantly moving from one position to another and only exposing themselves for a fraction of a second when they returned fire. But at least he was preventing them from jumping over onto his rooftop; and, after reloading a second time, he was even able to drive them back behind the perimeter wall.

Priebke and three of his men took cover behind a protruding dormer window. After reloading a spare magazine, the Gestapo captain maneuvered forward to a new position and let loose with a rapid burst of gunfire from his sleek Mauser *Hahn Selbstspanner* pistol.

Bridger returned fire before diving behind the wall again. He quickly found himself exposed to not just Priebke, but a pair of soldiers armed with rifles and another with a lethal Schmeisser MP 40 submachine gun—what the First Special Service Force called a "burp gun"—firing from the southwest corner of the adjacent building. Bullets whirred past his ears like hissing snakes, driving into a decorative scalloped wall attached to the cupola and ripping up chunks of plaster and terra cotta roof tiles.

Soon the firing slackened, giving him a brief opportunity to again reload and survey his surroundings. He definitely couldn't stay here. The wall and cupola offered no protection if the Germans moved onto one of the adjacent rooftops, where they would also be able to fire down upon him.

He had to get off this damned rooftop or he was a dead man.

The lull ended and the Germans again poured into him with a vengeance. A fusillade of bullets tore into the wall and cupola. Bridger returned fire and then turned and dashed to the edge of the roof. This time the gap between his building and the next one over was closer to eight feet and he would need a running start.

Another flurry of shots buzzed all around the rooftop.

Fighting against his natural survival instinct, he dashed back in the direction of the maelstrom of lead, stuffed his pistol in his pocket, and made a wild dash for the edge. As he flew through the air, he caught a glimpse of a pair of German soldiers on the street below pointing rifles up at him. Then he struck the roof of the adjacent building, slamming down hard on his hands and knees.

To his dismay, he lost his grip and began to slide down the sloping roof.

He clawed desperately at the terra cotta tiles, but he was unable to slow his rapid descent.

My God, am I really going to die by falling off a roof?

Thankfully, his feet caught in the gutter. But it started to give way and the Germans began firing at him, not only from the street below but from the rooftop he had just vacated, as Priebke and his detachment scrambled into firing position.

With dismay, Bridger realized he was a sitting duck.

It was then he felt a burning sensation in his arm.

Damnit, I'm hit!

He quickly realized he had only been grazed, but it still burned like hell. He struggled to climb back onto the rooftop.

But the gutter detached from the roof under his weight.

Desperate now, he swung his body up and onto the more gently sloped section near the dormer. From there, he was able to scramble up to the peak with enemy bullets peppering the tiles and sending sharp slivers of fired clay into his panted legs.

He ran along the peak like a high trapeze artist, balancing himself by holding out his arms and placing one foot after another along the narrow shingle path. With one false step, he'd tumble down the slope and plunge thirty feet onto the street below. Bullets zipped past his ears and all around his feet terra cotta tiles exploded and clattered over the edge. But still he ran on, unable to return fire.

All he wanted to do now was survive.

When he reached the end of the roof, he saw that the next roof was too far to attempt a jump. Cursing his luck, he chanced a look over his shoulder. To his surprise, Priebke had climbed up onto the cupola of the adjacent rooftop and was firing down at him from his elevated position. There was a gleam in his eyes like a killer wolf as he squeezed the trigger.

Damn! How did he get up there so fast?

Bridger ducked down and returned fire twice, but both shots missed as the SS captain took shelter behind the cupola.

Another fusillade rang out and chunks of roof tile erupted into the air.

Again, Bridger returned fire.

And then he felt a blow, like an expertly delivered jab punch, followed swiftly by a burning sensation along his right side. He fell back heavily and slumped against the broken chimney, feeling a rush of warm blood inside his shirt. Looking down, he saw a growing red blot along his ribcage.

It was not a grievous wound, but it still burned like hell and was bad enough that it would eventually slow him down and limit his ability to fight back. The Germans knew it, too, and were yelling excitedly, "*Ich habe ihn! Ich habe ihn!*"

He heard thudding noises and the sound of loose roof tiles crashing onto the street below. The bastards were jumping over onto his roof, moving in for the kill.

He tried to think, but his brain was muddled from the bleeding, rush of adrenaline, and strong possibility that he was about to die a violent death. The Germans were so close now that he could hear their snorting and grunting. Driven by pure animal instinct, he swung the gun up and leapt out from behind the chimney, his Beretta blazing in his hand. He heard a heavy groan as a beefy sergeant took a shot in the stomach.

I have to get off this damned rooftop.

Climbing to his feet, he squeezed the trigger two more times to cover his retreat. Then he slid down the west face of the roof to the dormer, grappled his way around to the window, and kicked it in.

The glass shattered on impact. A young woman with three children in rags cowered behind a dilapidated bed. Warning her to hide, Bridger dashed through the apartment and scrambled into the hallway. He needed to get onto the street on the north side of the piazza, on the opposite side from the German soldiers that had been shooting up at him.

He ran to the stairs. To his dismay, he heard the sound of charging feet and sharp voices, coming from below. He popped in a fresh magazine, turned, and ran down the hallway in the opposite direction towards a set of back stairs with a large window. He quickly realized that he should not have come this way either as he saw a pair of German soldiers lowering themselves down from the rooftop and climbing through the window. Schmeisser light submachine guns were strapped to their shoulders.

He froze, his life flashing before his eyes. But before they spotted him, he dashed down another corridor.

Frantically, he searched for an escape route. At the end of the corridor, he saw a set of doors that opened onto a small veranda overlooking the back side of the building.

He dashed for the doors.

But just as he was about to reach for the brass door handle, he spied a pair of Germans who had climbed down onto the veranda and were now creeping in from the west. He threw himself to the side of the wall so they wouldn't see him and scanned the corridor, grappling to find a way out.

Damnit, I'm trapped!

He reached out and quickly checked the doors. At least they were locked.

But the Germans weren't deterred. The officer in the cap ordered his enlisted comrade to use the butt of his rifle to break through the glass. Then the officer reached a hairy-knuckled hand through the broken window to open the door.

Rather than use his gun, Bridger opted for a weapon of quiet stealth. He withdrew his V-42 commando knife from its horse-hide sheath. The pride of the First Special Service Force, the weapon consisted of a sixteen-inch-long, double-edged, double-hallow-ground stiletto blade of high-carbon steel with a leather grip serrated with fine V-grooves and secured by a pointed steel "skull-crusher" pommel. It made the legendary knife invented and wielded by Jim Bowie at the Alamo look like a toothpick.

The officer in the cap unlocked the door and started to open it.

As he started to enter the building, Bridger pulled him into the corridor and slashed his throat. His right hand moved from left to right across the throat, severing the carotid artery and sending up a mist of blood that sprayed against the window. Bridger tossed the officer to the floor, where he made hideous gurgling sounds while clutching his throat. The German soldier yelled out in alarm and raised his rifle to fire, but Bridger struck him in the face with a heavy blow with the steel pommel end of his V-42. To his surprise, the soldier collapsed onto the floor and lay motionless.

Bridger took a moment to catch his breath. Looking beyond the unconscious soldier at the dead SS officer, he couldn't believe that he had actually killed a man. At the same time, he felt a sense of relief. His grueling, year-long indoctrination as a commando at the FSSF training center in Montana was paying dividends in his first concerted action of the war.

Hearing voices and stomping boots down the hallway, he quickly put away his knife, stuffed the officer's cap down his shirt as a makeshift dressing for his bleeding wound, and reloaded his Beretta.

He went to the large window on the other side of the door and looked down onto the street below. *How the hell am I going to get out of here?* Somehow, he had to get down to the street and disappear into a crowd of people.

There was a flash of movement and the glass window shattered. A pair of German soldiers with submachine guns swung into the room like chimpanzees, landing on the floor along with the broken glass.

His two adversaries quickly scrambled to their feet. One of them raised his Schmeisser to fire, but Bridger was ready with his Beretta. He put a shot in the German's shoulder, knocked the gun from his hands, and shoved him out the broken window. The man screamed in terror as he fell to the pavement. Surprisingly undeterred, the second German squeezed the trigger of his weapon.

But the Schmeisser jammed.

The German cursed and came at Bridger like a demon possessed. He was a fierce-looking specimen of Aryan perfection: tall, blond, blue-eyed, broad-shouldered, his teeth gritted savagely. Bridger raised his pistol to fire, but the German came at him swinging the weapon like a club before Bridger could get a shot off.

The first blow struck Bridger on the crown of his head, stunning him for an instant. The second knocked his Beretta from his hands. And the third caught him in the midriff near his gunshot ribs. He gave a howl of agony, but was able to grab the spare Schmeisser dropped by the other soldier and raise it to block the next blow. Again, his adversary swung the submachine gun at him, but this time the two metal weapons collided. Then, in great spasm of motion, they swung their Schmeissers at one another, connecting one instant, missing the next, until each of them had been struck a half dozen devastating blows to their faces and bodies.

Then, as the brawny German stepped close enough to get him in a heavy chokehold, Bridger shifted the position of his machine pistol to point over his shoulder and managed to squeeze off a round. His adversary cried out in pain, staggered back, and with a hard shove from Bridger, he, too, fell out the window. Bridger rushed to the broken window to take a look and was surprised to see that, by some miracle, both Germans were still alive. They lay groaning on the cobblestone street, badly wounded and immobile.

Now he heard voices down the hallway. The Germans had heard the gunshots and were coming for him.

Wounded himself, terrified, and exhausted but unwilling to surrender to the enemy, he scanned the street below for an avenue of escape.

Besides the two incapacitated Germans, there was no one on the street except a middle-aged Italian man and woman far down the block hurrying to get out of the area. The enemy had not been prepared for a rooftop escape and must have still been searching the building proper and the piazza side of the rooftop.

He climbed out onto the veranda. Along the side of the building, he spotted a drainpipe.

He didn't have time to test it. He suspended himself over the edge, gripped the two-inch pipe with both hands, and began to descend to the street below.

When he was ten feet off the ground, he jumped down and landed on the pavement. Hearing shouting voices coming from the building and around the corner, he headed in the opposite direction from the sounds.

Across the street, he saw a narrow passageway that led between two buildings. If he could get in there and make his way to the south, he should be able to make it to the church of *Sant'Ambrogio della Massima*, where Father Colucci would be able to hide him.

He dashed across the street and into the opening between the buildings, pausing a moment to look back over his shoulder for pursuers.

There was no one.

Feeling a wave of relief, he turned on a heel and dashed down the alleyway in the direction of the church. Behind him as he ran, he could hear the sound of voices and the shuffle of boots, but the sounds were a ways off and were growing fainter.

When he reached Via dei Funari, the city opened up before him and again there were people on the streets. He kept moving at a solid clip, but slow and casual enough not to draw attention to himself. He made sure to keep the German soldier's cap pressed up tightly against his wound to staunch the flow of blood. Luckily, his suit was dark blue so the blood stains were not overly conspicuous. To the south, he saw the reassuring cupola of the church.

Just a few hundred feet more.

He started to turn right at Via della Tribuna di Campitelli. But on the southeast street corner, in front of a trattoria, a pair of uniformed Fascist police gave him a wary eye. Pretending not to notice them, he turned left instead of right and headed in the direction of Trajan's Forum, not wanting to lead them to the church in case they followed. He walked at a brisk pace yet with as nonchalant an air as possible, praying they would lose interest.

At first they just studied him closely. But after a moment, they seemed to recognize that he had been wounded or that he was acting suspiciously and started after him.

Damnit.

He picked up his pace. After twenty paces, he glanced discreetly over his shoulder at his pursuers to gauge their threat. Unfortunately, they were walking faster and clearly on his tail.

He considered his options for escape. He couldn't risk a shootout with Priebke and his men nearby, so somehow he had to find a way to give these policemen the slip. Up ahead and on his left, he saw another narrow side street that headed west. He might be able to lose them by darting into a house, shop, or trattoria. Or should he just cross the street, double back, and head for the church, hoping he could lose them along the way and sneak inside unseen?

He opted for the side street.

Again, he subtly glanced over his shoulder. The policemen were still in pursuit, but they appeared reluctant to take him. They seemed to be assessing the threat he posed or trying to figure out how best to apprehend him without getting themselves killed. They had yet to blow their police whistles so it was clear that they were either playing it cautious or unsure of themselves. He lengthened his stride, wanting to put some distance between himself and them without raising the alarm and breaking into a full run.

Thirty feet. Just thirty more feet. If they corner me, I can pull my gun on them and hopefully scare them off.

He darted for the side street, turned the corner, and—

From seemingly out of nowhere, something big and heavy swung out and thudded against the side of his head. Feeling a sudden flash of searing pain at his temple, he fell hard to the pavement.

A minute later, he looked up and shook away his blurry vision. Slowly, an immaculately dressed SS officer in black leather with a red swastika armband and a Mauser pistol came into focus along with four German soldiers pointing submachine guns at him.

It was Priebke.

Kappler's right-hand man—the dreaded Torquemada of the Rome Gestapo himself—peered down at him with a grotesque curvature of the mouth that made it appear as though the man was smiling when in fact he wasn't. It was a crocodile's smile.

The officer clicked his gleaming, polished boots together like a courtly gentleman. "Allow me to introduce myself. I am Captain Priebke of the Gestapo. It will be my honor to introduce you to your new lodgings at Via Tasso—a place that, I regret to say, will be your last residence on earth."

CHAPTER 19

GESTAPO HEADQUARTERS OCTOBER 21, 1943

AS HOLLMANN ENTERED KAPPLER'S OFFICE, he noted that the lieutenant colonel's *sanctum sanctorum* at Number 145 Via Tasso was fussily immaculate. It was also still pleasantly scented with fresh roses cut from his garden and placed in a vase in his office by Helen Brouwer on Monday morning, a task which his dutiful and buxom mistress performed for him every week without fail. Hollmann found the Gestapo chief busy examining an Etruscan vase. The black-figure hydria was from early 5th century B.C. Tarquinia, and it displayed an intricate arrangement of painted cloaked figures from Greek mythology alternating with palmette motifs. Hollmann knew that Kappler had bought it from a wealthy Jewish collector who lived near Vatican City, and he had paid precisely what it was worth plus a reasonable commission. It struck the former art history student Hollmann as fitting that the only things he and the Gestapo chief had in common were their mutual appreciation of fine art and their love of Rome.

Kappler's face showed the usual consternation mixed with impatience as he looked up to see his new guest. He carefully placed the priceless Etruscan vase onto his desk and leaned back in his high-backed black leather chair, which bore an emblem of the *Parteiadler* of the Third Reich—an eagle violently clutching a swastika in its claws. On the wall behind his desk were photographs he had taken, including one of him with his beloved Wolfgang, his genetically engineered child selected from Himmler's *Lebensborn* program. On the index finger of his right hand was a steel ring decorated with a death's-head and swastika that bore the inscription, "To Herbert from Himmler." Kappler wore the glittering ring like a badge of honor.

"These unannounced visits are becoming annoying," snorted Kappler. "What brings you here this time, *Standartenführer*?"

Hollmann gave an exaggerated bow and plopped himself in the finely upholstered chair across the desk from Kappler. "Why, Herbert, here I stop by to fill you in on the latest diplomatic developments and you treat me like a crazy uncle. Does this mean we are not friends?"

"I do not have time for your sarcastic sense of humor. What is it that you want?"

"I told you. I have come to fill you in on the latest diplomatic developments. It seems our beloved Reich came much closer to dodging a bullet than you and I had anticipated."

"Speak clearly. What are you trying to say?"

"Apparently, the Father of Rome was so upset about the fate of his Jewish children that he actually prepared an explicit public condemnation of the roundup."

"But there was no official protest in the Vatican paper, or any pronouncement on the radio."

"I have it on the word of a very reliable source that Pius actually drafted a written protest to denounce the treatment of the Jews. But apparently, at the last minute, he burned the draft statement. He was afraid that, should the SS occupy Vatican City, it would provide justification to exact reprisals against Jews and Catholics. Not only in Rome but throughout Europe."

"It sounds like Allied propaganda to me to silence our foreign office."

"No, I don't think so. The public stand against the arrests—so greatly feared by our embassy here in Rome and in Berlin—never materialized. Our most delicate Vatican-German relations have been maintained, at least for the time being, because the Pope was talked out of it by people he trusted. Don't you see, Herbert, he wants to do more, but is being advised against it."

"By whom?"

"He was apparently dissuaded from going public by both leaders of the Jewish community here in Rome and by a group of German bishops. The Jewish leaders were said to be worried that speaking out would only make matters worse for the thousands of Jews hiding in church properties across Rome. The German bishops, for their part, were concerned that such a protest would create a 'serious crisis of conscience' among German Catholics."

"Both reasons make sense. According to the records we were able to obtain from the Jewish leaders, there are as many as ten thousand Jews still at large in the city and immediately outlying areas. We know perfectly well the Pope has authorized them to be hidden in Vatican extraterritorial properties protected under the Lateran Treaty as well as monasteries and convents. But I am not after Jews, as you well know, *Standartenführer*. I am after bigger fish: partisans, military deserters, and Vatican spies, both foreign and domestic."

"Yes, and that is another reason I am here, Herbert. How are your policing efforts coming along now that the Vatican has asked us to step up our efforts in the city?"

"It is still early in the occupation yet, but it is going well. We arrested a key Resistance member only a few minutes ago. Captain Priebke is interrogating him as we speak."

"In the basement?"

Kappler looked at him insolently. "Where else do we interrogate our prisoners?"

Hollmann felt a little chill nip his spine. He hated the dreaded basement of Via Tasso—and yet he was intrigued in a voyeuristic way about the horrors that went on down there. "Is the prisoner former army or Communist?"

"We don't know yet. But I am quite certain Captain Priebke will be obtaining that information shortly in our new, state-of-art interrogation room. We call it the Torture Chamber and now have three special isolation cells—Isolation Cells 1, 2, and 3—right next door so that we can give our guests the attention they deserve."

He underscored the words with a harsh smile that made Hollmann cringe.

"I would like to see this prisoner and your new interrogation and isolation center in the basement for myself. General Wolff asked me to conduct a formal inspection last week, but with the roundup I never got around to it."

Kappler stiffened in his chair. "The general requested an inspection? This is the first I've heard of it. Why wasn't I notified?"

"That would defeat the purpose, now wouldn't it, Herbert?"

"I've told you before not to call me that. You should address me as *obersturmbannführer*. That is my military rank."

"Very well, colonel it is. Now show me to the basement. General Wolff made it quite clear that I am to perform a thorough inspection. And I must confess, I am a bit curious."

"I'm afraid I cannot allow it. I will need to see specific orders from the general."

He rose from his seat and waved his hand dismissively. "If you don't show me to the basement, then I will just have to poke around down there by myself. General Wolff's verbal orders to me were quite specific. Do you want me to have to call him and have him pulled from an important meeting with Field Marshal Kesselring? Well, do you, Herbert?"

Kappler licked his lips, weighing his options. Several tense seconds passed. Then, coming to a decision, he opened a desk drawer, reached for a key, and withdrew it.

"Follow me," he said. "I will show you the basement."

"You do know that all of Rome has heard the grisly tales of what goes on down there. Already you have struck fear into the entire city."

"Yes, but I give you my word of honor, as an officer and gentleman, that I have personally never tortured anybody within the confines of this building."

"I guess then, in the eyes of God, that makes you a saint."

Kappler smiled thinly. "No, but it does not make me the devil either. What I do, I do for the Reich. But you, Herr Hollmann, you appear not to have a country to fight for. And for that, I pity you."

CHAPTER 20

GESTAPO HEADQUARTERS
OCTOBER 21, 1943

"WOULD YOU LIKE A CIGARETTE? I have Sigarette Nazionali, Dunhill, Galuoises, or Camel—which would you prefer?"

The voice was impeccably polite, chivalrous, and delivered *auf Deutsch*—but what Bridger felt most of all was the undercurrent of menace and manipulation. The Nazi fuck was trying to find out, first, if he spoke German, and, second, what type of cigarette he preferred, which might give away his nationality. Both of these tidbits of information might prove useful during interrogation. He had already decided that he would give Priebke nothing—not a single shred of information, except what he wanted him to know to deceive him or throw him off balance. It didn't matter if the bastard and his SS goons viciously tortured him or not, he wouldn't tell them a single thing. But then again, he knew that no man could withstand torture indefinitely, especially when wounded.

He looked dumbly at his inquisitor, pretending not to understand. In addition to Priebke, there was an SS lieutenant, sergeant, and two privates armed with Schmeissers in the interrogation room. *"Cosa?"* he asked. What?

Priebke repeated what he had said, this time in English.

Bridger shook his head—feigning incomprehension.

The Torquemada of Via Tasso then spoke in Italian, to which Bridger responded by accepting a *Sigarette Nazionali*. Then, in a fluid middle-class Roman dialect, he added, "But how do you expect me to smoke when I'm strapped into a chair with my hands tied behind my back?"

The Gestapo captain's mouth curled into the smile that wasn't a smile at all. "Oh, I think you will manage." He lit the cigarette and stuffed it in his mouth.

Bridger spit it out at him.

The burning tip of the cigarette struck Priebke near the eye and his hands flew to his face. "You swine!" he shrieked in German. "You burnt me, you bastard!"

Bridger just sat there tied to his chair with an expression of "Fuck you" on his face.

With Priebke's screaming voice echoing in the cool, dank interrogation cell, the SS sergeant stepped forward and smashed Bridger in the stomach with a heavy wooden club. The SS lieutenant quickly followed up by bashing him in the face with a smaller, but still lethal, truncheon. Bridger's head snapped back violently. Priebke howled in pain for a few more seconds before realizing that he was making a fool of himself and had received only a minor burn. He angrily stamped out the burning cigarette on the floor and stepped up to Bridger, who did his best to look unafraid though he was scared shitless. He knew he was about to endure the beating of his life. But he had to keep the Torquemada and his cohorts off balance by reversing the roles and being the unpredictable aggressor, especially since they would beat the crap out of him regardless of how much he told them. After all, this was Gestapo headquarters, not a convent.

"How dare you spit a cigarette in my face?"

Bridger continued to respond in Italian: "Untie me, you dim-witted German. I don't belong here."

The lieutenant and sergeant stepped forward to deliver more face and body blows, but Priebke held up a hand. "I can see that you want to play this the hard way. But you should know one thing: with me you're going to have to talk. You will probably be shot anyway, but you can avoid needless suffering by telling me what I need to know." He inspected the card he had removed from Bridger's wallet. "It says here that your name is Franco Fiorentini and that you are a member of the Honor and Combat Society. So you are a loyal Fascist, are you? That's why you were shooting at me and my men, Franco? That is your name, right, Franco?"

"Yes, and I don't know anything. Honor and Combat—that's my group. Long live Il Duce."

"You killed one of my men and wounded five others. I seriously doubt that you are a loyal *Fascisti.*" He tipped his head towards the sixteen-inch long First Special Service Force knife in the leather scabbard on the table. "I don't recall members of the Honor and Combat Society carrying weapons such as this." He pulled the knife from the scabbard and held it up in the artificial light. "Where did you get this?"

"I work for the SS. I am an informant for Colonel Hollmann, General Wolff's number two. He gave that knife to me. Now untie me. Like I told you before, I don't belong here. I am an SS operative."

Priebke's eyebrows went up; clearly he hadn't expected that he might be dealing with an informant. He looked nervously at his four subordinates. Then, after a moment, he seemed to recover his balance, shook his head, and laughed nervously, as if it was all a joke.

"So you are an informant working for Colonel Hollmann, are you? Nice try, Franco, but I think not."

"All right, don't believe me. But mark my words, the colonel's going to be angry when he sees what you've done to his top informant."

Now Bridger saw Priebke's expression deepen with worry and self-doubt. The SS captain realized that he was not dealing with an ordinary prisoner and the conventional approach might not work. It also seemed to dawn on him that his prisoner might be telling the truth.

"You are a very unusual man," said Priebke with a trace of admiration as he slipped a pair of shiny brass knuckles onto his right hand. "What is your name? Is it really Franco? Because, for some reason, I don't believe you. I'm sorry, but you just don't look like a Franco to me."

"I'm Franco all right."

"Where are you from? What part of Italy?"

"I'm sorry, but I'm not allowed to give out any information except my real name. Colonel Hollmann insisted that I maintain my cover at all times, even in front of other informants and members of the German Police and Army."

"So you and Colonel Hollmann are close then?"

"Very close. In fact, closer than you can imagine. And as I said, he is going to be very angry at you for torturing his top informant."

"Well, I suppose that is a risk I will have to take."

The lieutenant standing next to Priebke licked his lips nervously and leaned towards his superior officer to speak quietly in German. "Should we check with Villa Napoleon, Captain, just to be sure?"

"No, damn you. The man is desperate and obviously lying."

"But, sir, isn't it possible—"

"I said no, Lieutenant Groner!"

"You should listen to the lieutenant," said Bridger in perfect German. "You're all about to be knee deep in shit."

Speaking *auf Deutsch* had turned the tables, Bridger saw at once. The Torquemada's face showed surprise, followed swiftly by irritation; he was not used to his charges speaking to him in fluent German, or his interrogations disrupted by the men whose bones he was about to break.

"You speak German. That would make you a spy, a traitor, or both."

"No, I am an SS operative. In fact, I'll bet I've done a lot more than you to win the war for the Fatherland."

Bridger saw that it took all of Priebke's self-control not to lash back in anger. "I don't think you understand how this works, Herr Fiorentini," he said in a calm voice that carried an undercurrent of violence. "I do not like liars. In fact, I detest them and enjoy inflicting unspeakable pain upon them. Now I am going to ask you questions and you are going to answer them, or you will be tortured in the most horrific fashion imaginable for days, weeks, perhaps even months. You need to understand that at this moment you are in control of your own fate. You have the choice of pain or kind treatment, a firing squad or a reprieve."

"But you already said I am going to be shot. How can I get a reprieve if I am to be executed?"

"Most likely you will be shot, but I was just using a figure of speech."

"A figure of speech? You don't look smart enough to know what such a thing is. But you do have a nice car. I like your Topolino very much. You know I am a good friend of the Fiat family?"

"Are you now?" The smile that wasn't a smile reappeared. "I am a most reasonable man and I must admit I do find you amusing, but I fear that you are beginning to test my patience."

He stepped forward calmly and punched Bridger in the face with his brass knuckles. There was tremendous power in the blow, and Bridger heard his nose crack. He felt an excruciating pain, but forced himself not to make the slightest whisper of sound. The captain then struck him a second blow. Bridger saw blood cascade down his face onto his already bloody sharkskin suit and pants. Within seconds, he was soaked with a fresh layer of blood.

"You will answer my questions. Where did you learn to speak German?"

"As I've told you, I can't disclose such information except to the colonel. He is my control officer."

"Stop these damned lies. In the end you will talk. Everyone does, even men far more stubborn and brave than you. The only question is how long you can last before I break you and you tell me what I want to know. Now tell me about your radio and what partisan cell you are from."

He said nothing, just smiled at his adversary.

Priebke punched him again with the brass knuckles, ripping away a chunk of flesh from his cheek and drawing a torrent of blood from his battered nose. The Torquemada then motioned for his brutal comrades to join in. With sadistic smiles, the lieutenant, sergeant, and two privates stepped in and delivered a series of savage blows to his face and stomach. After a minute, Priebke ordered them to stand down and they drew away, red-faced and out of breath.

With blood streaming down his face and his rib wound reopened and bleeding, Bridger defiantly chuckled. "Is that the best you can do?" He knew his only chance was still to keep the captain and his men off balance since they would beat him mercilessly anyway.

As Bridger had hoped, Priebke licked his lips nervously and fidgeted with his bloody brass knuckles, his expression one of extreme discomfort and vexation. He looked like he was the one being tortured.

Bridger's suspicion had been confirmed: the great and terrible Torquemada was no Torquemada at all. When it came to the dark art of military interrogation, he was a babe in the woods. He was still learning, still finding his way along, still probing and testing the boundaries of inflicting punishment. He was no counterintelligence expert at all, merely an experimenting brute in a black uniform who had garnered some success breaking the weak and terrified since the Italian capitulation and start of the German Occupation. No doubt most of his previous victims had broken down and talked by now, which explained his frustration and annoyance. Many probably gushed forth with everything they knew before the first blow was even struck, so frightened were they of the brass-knuckled Torquemada and his violent Nazi sidekicks.

But if this Nazi fuck actually had the slightest idea what he was doing, Bridger knew, he would have blindfolded him and delivered blows to his shins, knees, elbows, and other hard parts without striking the face or risking harming vital organs. That way, Bridger could be interrogated indefinitely while under extreme agony without risking dislocating his jaw or damaging the brain, which could prevent obtaining any useful information and result in his accidental death. Also, with the blindfold, every blow would come as a terrible shock and the dreadful anticipation between blows would be agonizing.

"You are going to tell me the names and code names of the two men that escaped with you from the apartment in Piazza Lovatelli, as well as the names of all other persons in your Resistance network."

Bridger shook his head. "As I've already indicated, I am under strict orders to maintain my cover at all times and can only talk to the colonel. So you'd better go fetch him."

Priebke stepped forward and punched him in the balls with the brass knuckles.

With great effort, he stifled a yell of pain. His balls burned as if under a blowtorch. Maybe he was wrong about the "keep-them-off-balance" approach.

"You know these men. You know their names, code names, and addresses. I need you to give me their addresses."

Again he said nothing.

Priebke motioned to his brutish cohorts. This time the two privates pounded him in the stomach with their weapons. Bridger slumped in the chair and lost consciousness. They threw a pail of water on him and he came to again. He looked up groggily at his tormentors; one of his eyes was swollen shut and Priebke's face was distorted, surreal.

"What is the name of your Resistance cell? Is it the CLN or Di Domenico's Military Front?"

Bridger said nothing.

The Torquemada punched him in the nose again, drawing a cascade of blood.

"Which one is the radio operator? Is it you, or one of the two that got away?"

He remained silent.

Priebke motioned again. This time the Gestapo lieutenant delivered a hard blow to his shins with his truncheon. The blow made a sickening thud and Bridger couldn't help but let out a small groan of agony.

Now the captain spoke in a gentle, soothing voice. "I know that one hurt. Just remember, only you can make the pain stop."

Bridger smiled through a mask of fresh blood. "You are going to wish you had never laid a hand on me. The colonel is going to be very angry. You have made a serious mistake."

"Please, Captain, we must check with the colonel," the lieutenant appealed a second time, his face visibly pale at the prospect of inciting Hollmann's wrath.

"Damn your cowardice, Lieutenant Groner. I said no and that's an order. He is just playing with us. He is a desperate man and will try anything."

Now even the sergeant looked worried. "But what if he's telling the—?"

"He's not, damn you! Now shut up and let me continue my interrogation." He inched closer to Bridger, so close that Bridger could smell schnapps mingled with bratwurst on his breath. "Now what are the names of the two men with you?"

"There were no other men. It was just me."

"What is your radio code name?"

"I don't know what you're talking about."

"What is the name of your cell?"

"I am a loyal Fascist. You saw my Honor and Combat card. You have the wrong man."

"Where did you get that long knife and the Beretta pistol?"

"The colonel gave them to me."

"What are you doing in Rome? What is your mission here?"

"I am an informer for Colonel Hollmann. He knows me personally."

"Liar!" He drove his brass-knuckled fist into Bridger's thigh, giving him an excruciating Charlie Horse. "Who do you make radio contact with?"

"I don't know anything about a radio."

Again, Priebke punched him violently with his brass knuckles, this time in the chest. Bridger felt the wind knocked out of him and, for a full minute, he could not speak.

"Damn your insolence!" hissed the Torquemada, fuming. "You will answer my questions!"

"No, I will not because I am only allowed to talk to Colonel Hollmann. He is my contact here in Rome."

"Stop this foolishness. Who is your main contact in the Resistance?"

Bridger said nothing.

"Is he a cutout that you have never met? Do you only know him by a code name?"

"I don't know what you're talking about."

"Does the radio belong to Radio Vittoria or Centro X?"

"You've lost me. Can I please go to my cell? You have broken my nose."

Priebke gritted his teeth; it was all he could do to maintain his self-control. "I have had enough of your lies! You will answer my questions!"

He pretended to walk away, but then turned and delivered a savage blow to Bridger's jaw, cleaving away skin and opening up a new gash on his face that poured with fresh blood.

Suddenly, there was a presence in the room and a voice. "What is going on here, Captain? I believe the goal of our interrogations is not to kill the prisoner."

Through his one good eye, Bridger looked up to see Priebke's commanding officer, Lieutenant Colonel Kappler that he had been briefly introduced to when he had first arrived at Via Tasso. But what made his heart soar with relief was the man standing next to him.

It was his father.

Having taken the colonel's advice and used his name with the German police upon his arrest, Bridger had been banking on his father's eventual intervention, for the Gestapo would have to check on his claim that SS Colonel Wilhelm Hollman was, in fact, his control officer sooner or later. He had known since his capture that his father was his only hope of getting out of Via Tasso alive, and even that was a low probability.

But his father had told him to do it and it was all he had.

Hollmann stepped forward. "I am here at the order of General Wolff. Who is this man, Captain Priebke? And why is he covered from head to toe in blood?"

"We rounded him up an hour ago at Piazza Lovatelli. There were three of them, but we only caught this one. They had a radio and had just transmitted before we broke in. We caught them with our roving antennae."

But Bridger saw that his father was no longer listening. As he took a step closer, a look of recognition came over his face, followed swiftly by shock.

"This piece of shit actually said that he knew you, Herr Colonel. He has a Fascist membership card, but I know it's a fake. It says his name is Franco Fiorentini. I mean, he actually had the gall to say that he's working for you as an informant. He also said that you gave him his Beretta and that big knife there. Can you believe that he would—?"

But the words never had a chance to finish coming out of Priebke's mouth as

Bridger saw his father erupt with a violent fury that he had never seen before, at least not by any human being. With surprising quickness and strength, his father punched Priebke in the nose, striking him with the full weight of his solid chest and legs. Then he reached out, clasped his throat in a vice-like grip, drove forward, head-butted him in the face, knocked him off his feet to the concrete floor, and fell on top of him like a pouncing lion. Within seconds, he had him pinned to the floor, closed off his windpipe, and was choking the very life out of him.

"What on earth are you doing?" cried Kappler, and he rushed to the aid of his second-in-command. "Stop this at once! You're killing him!"

But to Bridger's surprise, even the Gestapo chief had no luck pulling him off. His father was like an enraged wild animal, and there appeared to be no way for Kappler to stop him. Weaned in a culture of rigid hierarchy and obedience, none of the others in the room made a move to help Priebke; they just stood there with mouths agape, watching his father the full SS colonel choke the life out of their less-feared and less-important captain, while Kappler tried, unsuccessfully, to restrain him. For the first time in his life, Bridger saw what a lethal killing machine his father truly was; and he knew in that illuminating instant why he himself had chosen to be a commando and why he was so damned good at it. True, his mother was as dangerous as a woman could possibly be, but the fierce determination and single-minded purpose that he was witnessing right now was a gift that he had inherited from his father. There was no doubt about it. Bridger was both terrified and intrigued by that fact as he watched his father choking the life out of the Torquemada of Via Tasso.

"Help me! Help me!" cried Kappler, realizing that, all alone, he was powerless to stop the colonel from killing his man.

By now, Priebke was purple-faced and appeared to be on the verge of death, and it was only then that the lieutenant and other three Germans intervened. They jumped in and tried to pull his father off Priebke, but his father was in such a state of fury that it took a full minute before they were able to yank him free of the captain.

He stood there restrained by all five men, fuming and puffing and red-faced, sweat pouring down his face as Priebke clutched at his ravaged throat, moaned and groaned, and greedily sucked in air. The Torquemada's face still had a purplish-blue hue like an oxygenless newborn infant, and blood gushed from his head-butted nose.

No one said a word.

Bridger watched with pride as his father jerked himself free of the clasp of his restrainers. His SS skull-and-crossbones insignia glinted defiantly from his lapel under the bright lights of the interrogation room. Kappler and his men continued to stare at him with a mixture of awe and fear, equally as stunned by the violent fury they had just witnessed as Bridger.

And in that visceral instant that he would remember for the rest of his life, Captain John Bridger realized that he had never stopped loving his father.

CHAPTER 21

GESTAPO HEADQUARTERS
OCTOBER 21, 1943

HOLLMANN glared at Kappler and his men, giving them his evil commanding officer's eye, while trying to figure out a way out of the mess he had just created for himself. At the sight of his own flesh and blood being sadistically tortured, he hadn't paused to think. Instead he had simply reacted, as if driven by some primitive instinct. In his moment of blind fury, all he had wanted to do was to rescue his son and strangle the life out of his offspring's tormentor. That was the only thing that had mattered to him.

But now he was in a terrible predicament.

He had overreacted in front of Kappler and his men, allowing his paternal emotions to get the better of him, and now he had to find a way to rectify the situation. Unfortunately, he couldn't undo what he had done. Somehow, he had to convince the Gestapo chief and others that his son was not a partisan or Allied spy at all, but rather a bona fide intelligence asset working for the SS, or better yet, him directly. Gunther had to be an undercover agent to be preserved at all costs. Luckily, his son had wisely taken his advice and claimed he was working as his personal operative, though unfortunately Priebke hadn't believed him. But at least the stage was set.

Still, it was not going to be easy. However, Hollmann knew he had one critical advantage: he was General Wolff's right-hand man as well as the eyes and ears of Himmler inside Rome and the Vatican. Kappler and his men were his official subordinates in a Nazi culture steeped in unquestioning obedience and unfaltering submission to authority, and they would be reluctant to risk drawing the ire of the top SS brass.

Wolff and Himmler were his ace cards.

He composed his face into a mask of professional indignation as he picked up the card lying on the table along with an open wallet, loose pocket change, a rosary, and the knife and scabbard. "Captain Priebke, get on your feet, damn you! This man is my agent! Why have you treated him this way?"

The Torquemada was still clutching his throat and struggling to breathe. He was not yet able to speak. For the time being, Kappler wasn't interfering. He stood there with his arms crossed, waiting to hear the explanations on both sides.

"Did you hear me, Captain? This man is my top counterintelligence asset in Rome, with direct access to the Vatican, and yet, for some unexplainable reason, you've dragged him in here in broad daylight under the eyes of the entire city and practically killed him! What do you have to say for yourself? I can assure you that

General Wolff will not be pleased when I make my report to him!"

Still purple-faced and gasping for breath, Priebke rose to his feet and stared in shock at him and Kappler. "This man…he's…he's really one of our agents here in Rome?" he blubbered, his voice still weak and raspy from being choked.

Hollmann looked over the fake name on the Honor and Combat Fascist membership card: Franco Fiorentini. "No, he's not one of ours, you fool—he belongs to *me*. He is my double agent and a source of vital information to the Reich. Do you realize what you have done? You may very well have blown his cover."

"B-But, sir, he and his accomplices killed one of our men and wounded five others. If this man is your informant, then he is lethal."

He looked at his son sharply. *You killed a Gestapo operative and wounded five others! Damn you, Gunther! I may not be able to get you out of this after all!*

He looked at Kappler, knowing he was the one that he had to convince in order to get his son released and make it out of the basement of Via Tasso alive. "I realize that this is a regrettable situation, *Obersturmbannführer*. But I'm afraid my orders to Agent Crusoe were not to break cover under any circumstances." The name had popped into his head based on *Robinson Crusoe*, his son's favorite adventure tale as a boy growing up in Innsbruck that he had read to him often. He shot his son a furtive glance to make sure he would remember the name. "He has close ties to the Vatican, and is the source of the information I relayed to you earlier regarding the Pope. If men were shooting at him, it was his job to shoot back."

Kappler squinted. "Crusoe? Is that his code name?"

"Yes."

"He didn't tell us that," said Priebke.

"Of course he didn't. He's under strict orders not to tell anyone his code name. My agents are not in the habit of giving out such things, even when undergoing interrogation. But he did tell you that he was working for me, correct?"

"Yes, but I thought he was lying."

Kappler was frowning and shaking his head. "Just who is this Agent Crusoe and why haven't I heard about him until now? I have my informants too, Colonel, and I have never heard this man's name mentioned until today."

"He is my agent and a cutout for the Vatican."

"What is his relationship to the Vatican?"

"I'm afraid that is classified."

"This man has killed one of my men and wounded five more. He is going to undergo further interrogation. And once he tells us what we want to know, he will be summarily shot for being an enemy of the Reich."

Hollmann saw that his grip on the situation was slipping away. He flashed Kappler a lethal glare then looked sternly at Priebke. "You two will stand down and obey my orders immediately and drop this matter. Or I will contact not only General Wolff, but Himmler himself, and they will have you on the next train to the Russian front. Do you really want to take the chance of irking the High Command again after your gold fiasco with General Kaltenbrunner? He refused to accept the gold payment you sent him and told you to arrest the Jews anyway." Kappler gave a look of surprise. "Oh yes, Herbert, I know all about it. So what is to become of you? The Red Army is breaking through on the Lower Dnieper and the Führer, as is his custom, has ordered our forces to hold to the last man. Who knows, perhaps you and captain Priebke could earn a posthumous Iron Cross when you are shipped to the east?"

A look of fear came over Priebke's face. "The Russian Front?"

Hollmann glanced at his son strapped to the chair and saw a ghost of a smile. *You bastard, don't you realize what this is going to cost me covering for you like this? Why the hell am I even doing this? Is it solely because you're my son?* He looked hard at Kappler, who still appeared unconvinced. "I hear the Dnieper River Valley is very pleasant this time of year—only ten below freezing at night. At least there will be plenty of Russian artillery shells to keep you warm."

"Stop your threats, Colonel. This supposed *agent* of yours killed one of my men and put five others in the hospital with serious wounds. We cannot just let him walk out of here. How will my men be replaced?"

"I would think you and Captain Priebke would be more worried about how *you* will be replaced here in Rome when you are shipped off to Mother Russia."

"What the colonel means to say is that we are upset about the losses," said Priebke, trying to ameliorate the situation.

Hollmann shot him a look. "Did I ask your opinion, Captain?"

"No, sir, but I—"

"Then shut up." He waved a dismissive hand. "You all are dismissed except Colonel Kappler."

Priebke's face reddened. "But, sir, I didn't mean to—"

"I said you are dismissed, Captain." He turned to the others. "That means all of you."

Priebke's face stiffened with mild protest, but he said nothing and started for the door along with the lieutenant, sergeant, and two guards.

But before they reached it, a knock sounded at the door and the desk sergeant's face poked in. "Colonel Hollmann, there are two people here to see you."

"Send them away! Can't you see I am busy?"

"But it is the marchesa and your daughter. They told me to tell you that it is urgent and they have valuable intelligence information for you."

He tried not to look surprised. Somehow his ex-wife and daughter must have found out that Gunther had been taken into custody and, pretending to be informants, they had come here to ask him to intervene on his behalf. But how did they find out that Gunther had been arrested by Priebke? And how did they know Hollmann was here at Via Tasso instead of his headquarters at Via Napoleon?

"Tell them I will meet them outside, Sergeant." Then to Kappler he said, "I am taking Agent Crusoe into my personal custody on behalf of General Wolff. If you let this matter drop, I see no reason for you or your men to be subjected to further inquiries or for an official report to be filed with the *polizeiführer*, or higher authorities." Here he paused, letting the looming threat of Wolff, Himmler, and Kaltenbrunner linger in the air, like a foul odor. "Well, Colonel, what is your answer?"

Kappler looked at him long and hard; the battle of wills between the two men was a chess game. "Very well, Wilhelm," he said in a chivalrous tone after a moment's reflection, addressing him deliberately by his first name in the same prickly manner Hollmann normally did to him. "We will consider this matter settled, for the time being. But you owe me now."

"Owe you? Owe you what?"

The Gestapo chief gave a knowing look. "Vital intelligence." He looked at his son. "From your valuable source here."

"On what exactly?"

Kappler allowed himself a smile, and the red dueling scar on his cheek gave a little throb. "Why the Roman Resistance, of course. You and your operative here, Wilhelm, are going to help me break it."

CHAPTER 22

VILLA NAPOLEON

OCTOBER 21, 1943

"I DON'T KNOW WHAT YOU THINK YOU'RE DOING, WILHELM," snapped Marchesa Bianca Manuela Di Domenico, "but you must release our son Gunther immediately."

Our son, Teresa thought to herself as she looked at her fiery-eyed, imperial mother then at her studiously calm, dignified father sitting behind his cluttered desk. What a contrast they were. She couldn't help but wonder how such a pair of opposites had ever been attracted to one another in the first place. Her father sat with his hands folded in his lap, looking on with a mixture of amusement and admiration at this emotionally charged woman who had the audacity to tromp into Gestapo headquarters and summon him like an errand boy. Teresa could only hope that he would be reasonable and that her tempestuous mother wouldn't do anything to anger him. So far he had been magnanimous; at this very moment, per her father's instructions, her brother Gunther was being patched up by a doctor in one of the sumptuously-appointed rooms of Villa Napoleon.

Smiling courteously, he pulled out an American Lucky Strike from the full pack lying on his desk next to a copy of *Popolo di Roma.* The newspaper displayed photographs of Kesselring and Kappler on the front page. Lighting his cigarette with his silver Zippo lighter, he took a puff and blew the smoke across his desk towards her mother. She frowned and waved the smoke away.

"You never fail to amaze me, Bianca," he said wistfully. "Here you are addressing the second-ranking member of the SS in all of Italy, a senior officer of a foreign power that occupies your city in time of war, and you treat me like a stable boy. Do you really think you are in a position to demand anything?"

"How dare you speak to me like that?"

"Very well, I apologize for my insolence," he said with playful sarcasm, and he took another puff, inhaling deeply. "By the way, how did you know that Gunther was taken prisoner and brought to Via Tasso?"

"That is none of your business."

"It most certainly is my business if you want to entertain the slightest possibility of getting what you want from me. That is why you are here, is it not, to secure your son's release from me here at Villa Napoleon?"

"If you think I am going to beg then you have—"

"That's enough, Mother. You are only making matters worse," interjected Teresa. She looked sincerely at her father, hoping to garner his equanimity. After all, despite the fact he had concealed both his previous marriage to a Viennese woman and his carousing ways during her youth growing up in Innsbruck, he had been an honorable police chief and devoted father during those years. "I was on my way to visit Gunther in Piazza Lovatelli when I saw him picked up by the Gestapo. I returned home at once to inform mother."

"So you saw him after our visit several days ago and knew where he was hiding out?"

"Don't you dare answer—"

"We're not going to be able to hide anything from him, Mother." She looked back at her father. "The answer is yes."

He nodded approvingly. "You should listen to *our* daughter, Bianca. She has a gift which God, no doubt due to his very busy schedule, regrettably didn't have the time to bestow upon you. It is the gift of diplomacy."

The marchesa's dark eyes flashed with fire. "Damn you, Wilhelm, she is not *your* daughter, and if you think I have come here to be insulted by—"

This time Teresa cut her off by raising her hand as well as her voice. "I said that's enough, Mother! You need to let us handle this!" Before her mother could object, she again made eye contact with her father. "What information do you need from me to secure my brother's release? You know that I would do anything."

He gave a look of bemusement. "Anything? Anything is a strong word, Teresa, and one that should be assiduously avoided in wartime."

He was suave, Teresa had to admit, but still frightening in his black SS uniform with a ring of cigarette smoke hovering above his head like a crown on a king. In the back of her mind, she wondered if he was toying with her and her mother, and was actually planning on having them put under arrest and held hostage at Via Tasso.

"I know you would like us to tell you where Colonel Di Domenico is hiding out, but the truth is Mother and I don't actually know. He has insisted upon keeping it a secret."

"I believe you. But I wasn't going to ask you that question. I was going to ask you if you had joined the Resistance. Otherwise, why would you be visiting your brother at Piazza Lovatelli?"

Teresa felt her breath catch in her throat; he had taken her off guard. "Me, joining a Resistance group? Do you know how ludicrous that sounds?"

"Don't treat me as if I am a fool, Teresa. Just remember this. If you have joined the partisans, you will have a very short life expectancy."

She gulped hard.

His expression was surprisingly tender. "You see, I want you to live through this war, marry a good husband, and have children and grandchildren even if I don't get the chance to see it all. I want these things for you because you are my daughter and I love you. In fact, I have always loved you since the day you were born."

Her mother was out of her chair and on her feet. "I told her you—you are not her damned father! Now stop terrorizing my daughter with all this talk about a short life expectancy!"

He waved his hand dismissively. "Sit down, Bianca. I am not terrorizing her. I am simply making you both aware of your current situation. Kappler's men will leave no stone unturned when it comes to breaking the Resistance. You need to know that as well as prepare for it. What you have seen these past few weeks is just the beginning. It is going to get worse, I promise you. I warned you two the other day and you need to heed my warning." His eyes narrowed on her haughty mother. "Do not make any further contact with the Allies or the partisans—especially your husband the colonel—or you will find yourself an unwilling guest at Via Tasso or Regina Coeli Prison. If you do not heed my advice, there is nothing I can do for you. For I have already used up my nine lives getting Gunther out of that rat-infested basement. So you will not be able to count on me as a guardian angel from this point forward—either of you. This is your final warning."

He rose from his chair and began pacing in front of his window with his cigarette. The October sun caught his reconstructed face, giving it a strange, otherworldly glow. In that moment, he didn't look like the father Teresa had grown up with at all, but rather some sort of alien wax-figure. She thought of the family curse, and couldn't help but feel that there was some truth to it. What had brought them all together again here in Rome had to be some sort of destiny. And yet, it couldn't be divine providence at the hand of a benevolent God; no, this unexpected reunion was too dark and dangerous and closely linked to their treacherous past to be anything but the fulfillment of the curse.

"Father, we both appreciate your looking out for us and for the warning." Out of the corner of her eye, she saw her mother cringe, but she ignored her. "Given your senior position in the SS, you have been more than fair. But we are here about Gunther. Are you going to release him?"

"I am still deciding what to do with him."

"Can you not see it in your heart to release him? If you do, I give you my word that Mother and I will make him leave the city and that you will never see him again, at least until the war is over. Please Father, can you help us? Or at least can you help *me*?"

He looked at her for a long moment in silence, as if peering into her soul. Then he turned away from her and stared out the window onto the SS-barricaded, heavily guarded street below. The room was so quiet that Teresa could swear she would be able to hear a pin drop.

It was at that moment a knock was heard at the door, startling her.

"Why speak of the devil," said her father. He looked at her intently. "I am going to give you and your mother what you want, Teresa, but I am warning you two that you had better keep playing this the right way. As I told you before, the subject's name is Franco Fiorentini. He is an Italian agent under my control here in Rome, and you two do not know him. In fact, you've never seen him before in your life. Is that clear?"

"Yes, yes," agreed the marchesa. "We won't say a word."

"You'd better not or we shall all get the firing squad." He straightened his uniform. "Come in."

His aide appeared at the door and clicked his heels. "Colonel, I am delivering Agent Crusoe as ordered."

"Very good, Lieutenant Vogel. That will be all."

As the young officer stepped away, Teresa saw her brother appear at the door and her heart leapt with relief and joy. His face was badly cut and bruised, but the blood had been wiped clean and the doctor had sewed up many of his facial lacerations with stitches. He had also been given a fresh set of clothes. Still, he looked awful. His nose was swollen and appeared to have been broken, and he still looked peaked from blood loss. But he was able to move about under his own power and appeared coherent.

She glanced at her mother, who looked beside herself with outrage. They both waited for the door to close before going to him.

"You look much better," said the marchesa, taking him by the arm, "but I still can't believe what these Nazi brutes have done to you."

"It would have been a lot worse if Father hadn't intervened. If it wasn't for him, I might very well be dead."

Father—so he still thinks of him as "Father" too, thought Teresa. She stepped forward and gave her brother a gentle hug, careful not to press against his wounds. Her father then waved everyone to the finely-appointed chairs in front of his desk. When they were all seated, her brother posed a question to her father.

"What I'd like to know is why you did what you did? You came within an inch of strangling that son of a bitch Priebke to death."

"You know perfectly well why I did it, and I would do the same for your sister." He turned his gaze towards her and gently inclined his head. "But that does not mean that you two, or your mother, have a free pass. In fact, Gunther, there are conditions that you must meet to secure your release today."

"I told you my name is not Gunther."

"Yes, of course, you are John Bridger now. A captain in the First Special Service Force—a highly-trained, joint American and Canadian commando unit consisting mostly of gangsters, roughnecks, backwoodsmen, and convicts."

"That's an exaggeration. But how did you know that?"

Her father drew on his Lucky, blew out a cloud of bluish smoke towards the ceiling, and looked at the American cigarette appreciatively. Then he gave a knowing smile and gently tapped the file sitting on his desk. "I have learned a thing or two since I last saw you."

"But my training, my unit…that's all classified information."

"Come now, did you really think that with twenty-five years of police experience under my belt I would not know how to obtain classified information? To be that incompetent I would have to be French."

Teresa couldn't help but smile. It pleased her to know that her father still had a sense of humor, even if he was fighting for her enemy the Germans.

"All right," said her brother with a stubborn look on his face. "What are these conditions of yours?"

"I need some information from you if I am to release you. I do not want it for military purposes, rather to satisfy my own curiosity. I promise that I will tell no one what you disclose to me. But I will need your word as an officer and a gentleman that you are telling the truth."

The marchesa rose from her seat. "This is preposterous. You can't expect him to give up secrets. And, besides, how can he trust that you will release him at all?"

Her brother answered for her father. "Because I saw what he did to Captain Priebke in the basement. You know, Father, having me as a son is bound to get you in trouble in this war."

"It already has. I am on extremely thin ice. Kappler expects to obtain useful counterintelligence information from me via you, or he will no doubt call Herr Himmler himself. For all I know, he might be calling him this very minute. At the very least, I will now have to watch my back with both Kappler and Priebke. But if I had to do it all over again, I wouldn't think twice about it."

"Good to know, but just don't expect me to do the same for you if you're in a similar fix. To me, you're not just the enemy, you're something far worse."

"And what is that?"

"A Nazi. And so is your brother Walther. Where is he by the way? Fighting the Russians?"

"No, he happens to be right here in Italy. He is at the southern front north of Naples."

"I always liked Uncle Walther. It's too bad he's fighting for a bad cause, like you."

"You can tell him that to his face next time you see him. He is a major in the Hermann Göring Division." He smiled devilishly. "Your G-2 Intelligence is already aware of this no doubt, so I am not giving away top-secret information."

"Bailing me out of jail and filling me in on Uncle Walther doesn't make you my friend. You're still a damned Nazi, and so is Uncle Walther."

"I can see the Americans have trained and brainwashed you quite well. But did you really need to kill one of Kappler's men and wound five more?"

"I had no choice. They were shooting at me."

"The will to survive is a powerful motive." He stamped out his cigarette in the Sigarette Nazionali ashtray on his desk and looked at his watch. "Unfortunately, our time is running out so here are my questions. First, did your American superiors assign you to be a spy here in Rome, or to be a bodyguard and escort for the actual spy?"

"Sorry, but that's two questions."

"That's all right, I have my answer. You blinked."

"I what?"

"You blinked when I said the part about the bodyguard. So that's how I know that your only purpose in coming to Rome was to insert your OSS agent comrade. He's obviously trying to establish an intelligence network to communicate with General Clark's Fifth Army. Which brings me to the reason I am letting you go."

"And what is that?"

"By now, you have no doubt completed your mission and were planning on leaving Rome soon anyway."

Teresa's mouth fell open at precisely the same instant as her brother's. How in the world did her father figure all that out? He was obviously more than just a competent police detective and liaison officer. He was as clever as Sherlock Holmes, and it suddenly dawned on her that, if he so chose, he could pose as much of a threat to the Roman Resistance as Kappler. As her father had made clear, the recent roundups of the Jews, anti-Fascists, and *carabinieri* by the Gestapo and

Fascist police represented just the beginning of what would soon escalate into a major battle between the partisans and German occupiers.

At the same time, despite the potential threat her father posed, she found herself intrigued by the man more than ever before. Watching him in action, she found herself feeling a mixture of sympathy, respect, and loathing. She could tell that he was torn by his duty as an SS officer and his need to protect his son. But was he helping Gunther out of love, or to redeem his honor before his family? Is that why he was lying to his fellow SS officers and subordinates, to save his own flesh and blood? Or did he have an ulterior motive?

If he did have another motive, did it have something to do with why her father and mother had tried to kill one another eleven years ago? It had always seemed odd that her mother had threatened to leave her father and take her two children with her to Rome and then, when her father had refused to allow it, she had tried to kill him. It seemed too drastic and didn't make sense. Sometimes, she wondered if the reasons Gunther had given her for her mother's violent behavior on that terrible day had nothing to do with why the marchesa had shot her father. Could there be another reason entirely? Something that her mother had kept hidden from her all these years? And what of the family curse? Was it real, or was it merely a figment of everyone's imagination?

"We are running out of time," said her father, looking at his watch again and breaking her from her thoughts. "All I am asking you to do, Son, is to leave Rome immediately. Your compatriots in the Allied Resistance will, no doubt, know how to get you to the Fifth Army in Naples. So that's all I want. I want you to leave Rome right away."

"That's it, I agree to leave Rome and you let me walk? What about Mother and Teresa?"

"They are free to go at any time."

There has to be a catch, thought Teresa. Her mother echoed her fears.

"You're holding back something," hissed the marchesa. "I just know it."

"I am not holding back anything. You should know, though, that henceforth in my official reports you will all be given code names and be described as my personal informants. And it will state, explicitly, that you three have provided valuable counterintelligence to me on a regular basis."

Her mother rolled her eyes melodramatically. "I knew there had to be something."

"After the stunt I just pulled at Via Tasso, I myself will be under suspicion from the Gestapo. Going forward, I will need something to explain my puzzling behavior. But I do not expect anything else from any of you. However, my terms do come with a separate warning to each of you—and you should know that these are the last warnings I shall give you."

"What are they?" asked her brother, leaning forward in his chair.

"If you ever get caught in Rome again, I will not be able to save you. That's why you must leave at once."

Teresa nodded. "And what about Mother and I?"

"If you two continue to aid or take part in the Resistance, even in a small way, you will eventually find yourself paying a visit to Colonel Kappler's grand hotel at Via Tasso. Your brother Gunther—who fancies himself an American Special Forces commando named John Bridger—was a guest there for less than a half hour and look at his face. As you can see, it is no longer a dashing Errol Flynn face. So take my advice and stay as far away from partisan activity as possible. Or you will look a lot worse than Captain Bridger here."

Her brother nodded. "Sounds like reasonable advice. And now, before we go our separate ways, allow me to impart a final warning to you, Father." Though the tone was affable, there was a look of danger in his ice-blue eyes. "When I return to Rome after we defeat your army, I'd better not find you here in the city."

"And why is that?"

"Because I may not be as generous as you."

"Meaning?"

"I just may be put in a position where I have to kill you."

His father looked at him, appraising him in a different light.

"You may be my father, and you may have just saved my ass, but you are still my sworn enemy. And there is still the family curse."

"Oh, that is nonsense and you know it," said her mother to him. "There is no family curse."

"Only a fool doesn't believe in curses, Mother. The Church has taught us that for centuries. And whether we like it or not, this family is cursed. I saw the fear in your eyes that day. You believed the curse was real then—and you believe it now."

"Stop this at once! We don't need to revisit that day!"

"Oh, but we do, Mother. When you pulled that trigger, you doomed us all. Remember what Father said. No one would be spared from the curse, not even Teresa's father Colonel Di Domenico, or the Bellomo family. You do remember, don't you? You know *I* do. I was outside on the deck listening to every word."

Her mother leapt to her feet. "This is outrageous! I refuse to sit here and listen to this! The beating you sustained has muddled your brain!"

"No, I'm perfectly lucid, Mother. And Teresa and Father know perfectly well what I'm talking about. Because of what you did, our family is cursed. That's why I left you and went to America. I didn't want a hex on me in this life or any other, so I got as far away from you all as I could."

"If we have all been put under a family hex, then why have you been rescued by your own father?" asked Teresa. "Why are you no longer at Via Tasso being savagely beaten, but here safe and sound with your old family?"

"She has a point," agreed her father.

"Our being reunited is intended to lure us into a false sense of security. Mark my words, nothing has changed. We are still cursed and our day of reckoning is coming. And it's coming sooner than you think."

"What's...what's going to happen to us?" asked Teresa, feeling a little fearful at the certainty in his voice.

"Tragedy, that's what."

"Tragedy?"

"Yes, the war here in Italy is going to destroy us," he said. "The war is going to destroy us all."

PART 2

THE WINTER LINE

CHAPTER 23

FIRST SPECIAL SERVICE FORCE HQ
ITALIAN ARTILLERY SCHOOL BARRACKS
SANTA MARIA (CAPUA-VETERE)
CENTRAL ITALY
NOVEMBER 28, 1943

"THE GOAL of Operation Raincoat," declared Lieutenant Colonel Robert Tyron Frederick, Commander of the First Special Service Force, "is to drive the Germans off their forward positions along their Winter Line, pushing them back beyond the Rapido and Upper Garigliano Rivers. We, gentlemen, are the spearhead of the operation. To break the German line, we have to take this rugged chain of heavily fortified mountains extending northeast from Camino-Difensa halfway across Italy. From there, we take the Liri Valley and make the big push for Rome. We take Rome and we've bagged our first Axis capitol. Then it's only a matter of time before we're marching through the streets of Berlin, yanking down every Nazi flag in sight. Is that something you debauched devils would enjoy doing?"

There were head nods all around and a bawdy chorus of cheers from the staff officers and regimental commanders filling the briefing room. When the cheering died down, Frederick—a 1928 West Point graduate known for his mediocre record as a cadet in the grand tradition of Ulysses S. Grant and George S. Patton—pointed to the oversized aerial photographic map on the wall showing Allied and Axis positions and movements.

"The key to cracking Kesselring's line is for us to take these two mountains here that have up until now stalled the Fifth Army's advance to Rome. They are Monte La Difensa, known as Hill 960 with an altitude of 3,120 feet, and Monte La Remetanea, which we call Hill 907 at 2,948 feet above sea level. These two salients are connected by a heavily mined ridge and capped by a pair of smaller knobs. Once both objectives are taken, the other mountains in the range will become vulnerable. The Germans will have no choice but to fall back. Taking these two heavily fortified positions won't be a picnic, but this is what you have spent the last year training for and we *will* succeed."

There was another round of rowdy cheers. Bridger looked around at the faces of the other officers. Like him, they were anxious about what lay ahead, especially since they were being given a job that had proven too daunting for several much-larger units. But after enduring a brutal training program where more than half the men had washed out, the surviving diehards cared less about their odds of survival than about finally getting the opportunity to kick some serious Kraut ass. And they were especially willing to do it for the man in front of them. A commander who had, for the past year now, molded them into a lethal combat unit and made them feel like they could do the impossible.

That was Lieutenant Colonel Robert Tyron Frederick's special gift.

"As you know, we have sent forward several reconnaissance parties to the 36th Division front. They have scouted out the middle and upper reaches of the main Hill 960 Difensa objective. Our patrols have worked all the way to the base of the peak and thoroughly reconnoitered the route we will take during our attack." He again pointed to the map. "Using ropes, we will make our ascent at this cleft on the north side of the peak. At daylight, we will be exposed to long-range machine-gun fire from the surrounding hills. The objective is to make it the top of 960 undetected at night, and then proceed across the mountaintop with the assault at dawn. Colonel MacWilliam will be commanding the lead battalion."

"Well, here's to a coffin or a brevet, chaps," said MacWilliam, a mild-mannered Canadian history professor in peacetime who would now be leading the main attack. "What about the enemy dispositions? Who are we up against?"

"G-2 has good intel on the bogeys." Frederick again used his pointer. "In this saddle here, between Maggiore and Difensa, including the outlying positions on Hill 960 itself, we'll be facing the Third Battalion, 104th Panzergrenadier Regiment. Some two hundred fifty men. In addition, about one-half of the Third Battalion, 129th Panzergrenadier Regiment, occupies our two objectives, while the other half is strung across the Hill 709 saddle into the British sector. In reserve for these positions are the 115th Reconnaissance Battalion and the Hermann Göring Division."

"Hermann Göring, you say?" snorted another Canadian officer. "Those bastards can bloody well fight."

"They sure as hell can," said Frederick. "That's why we have to get up and onto that mountain and take it quickly before the Hermann Göring reserves can be brought into play."

Bridger wondered if he might catch a glimpse of his Uncle Walther in the coming battle. What would he do if he saw him? Would he shoot him dead if he had him in his crosshairs?

"What about the artillery in the area, sir?" he asked, realizing that he had no desire to kill his Uncle Walther, whom he had enjoyed growing up.

"The Germans have over a hundred pieces," responded Frederick. "With this artillery, they can cover both of our mountain objectives as well as those of the British. The Germans also have the new *Nebelwerfers* in large numbers, so once we take the enemy positions we will have to take cover quickly." He was referring to the German's six-barreled mobile rocket launchers that Allied soldiers called, with a mixture of trepidation and respect, Screaming Meemies.

"Fuck, those things are lethal. We're going to have to dig deep into those rocky crevices before they pitch into us," Bridger overheard a fellow American regimental officer say to a Canadian officer.

Frederick continued: "As I have stated, Colonel MacWilliam and the Second

Regiment will be the lead element responsible for attacking and taking Hill 960. The First Regiment will be assigned to reserve. The Third Regiment will have double duty: its First battalion will serve as litter bearers and supply carriers for the assault regiment, and the Second Battalion will be used to augment the attack if necessary." He clapped his hands together. "So there you have it, gentlemen—the broad brushstrokes. As you can see, we are the spearhead of the operation that will, God willing, open the road to Rome. Now it is time to work out the details. But first are there any questions?"

The briefing room went quiet. Looking up at the map, Bridger realized that the job they had been given was a hundred times more dangerous than any of the training exercises they had endured back at Fort Harrison in Helena, Montana. He had even heard whispers among some of the officers in the 36th Division that casualties of fifty percent were expected, which made it a virtual suicide mission. But no one else in Uncle Sam's Army was going to do it; the other units had already failed, so it was up to the Force.

There were no questions. Frederick launched into the operational details and, twenty minutes into the briefing, as it dawned on the officers how ridiculously daunting the assignment truly was, they began asking questions. Lots of questions. Until finally, they were all exhausted and their brains could take no more. D-Day was then set for five days, on December 2, and all troops were to move out of the bivouac area under cover of darkness on the night of December 1. They would use ropes to make the ascent up the final, nearly vertical face of Hill 960, and mule trains would supply the attacking brigade up to the base of the mountain. All identification was to be removed except for pay books and dog tags. The attack would come at dawn on the morning of December 3, and it would be preceded by an all-night artillery barrage to soften up the German defenses before the big push to the mountaintop.

Bridger looked at the aerial photographic map with the little color coding showing their route to their two objectives. It all looked so easy up on a wall map. Like a child's tin soldiers spread out on a little mound of dirt. But in practice, he knew it was going to be far more difficult to take those rugged mountains in biting cold and with the German machine guns, mortars, and goddamned Screaming Meemies bearing down on them.

When they were all dismissed, he headed outside into the cool, muddy night. The rain had briefly subsided and he stared up through the broken clouds at the cryptic outline of the new moon.

The Roman Moon.

He took out a dirty bandanna, dipped it in his canteen, and wiped it across his face, feeling the coolness of the water reinvigorate him. Behind him, he could hear the quiet industry of the camp: men checking equipment, honing knives, cleaning firearms, spreading out bedrolls, packing supplies, talking in low tones in their tents. Further off, someone blew on a lonesome harmonica. He took a deep breath of the night air, listened to the peaceful murmur of the camp. He sighed. It seemed strange to find such tranquility in a country where so many men were dying violently and crying out for their mothers as they drew their final breath.

And yet, looking up at the silhouette of the moon, he felt special being a

Forceman. The 2,500-man brigade—made up of two-thirds Americans and one-third Canadians—had been formed in 1942 by Frederick as an elite guerrilla force specifically for winter mountain combat. Now that the Force was in Italy, its military function had broadened, and it was to be used to make swift surgical strikes against enemy outposts, to tie up large numbers of German combat troops with nighttime raids, and to perform impossible missions no other Allied outfit had the ability to carry out. The unit's original emphasis in training had been on mountaineering, skiing, and delivering hard kicks to the groin; and the Forceman's credo, borrowed from the British Handbook of Irregular Warfare, held that "every soldier must be a potential gangster." The name Special Service Force was conceived by Frederick to conceal its military mission and fool outsiders, both foreign and domestic, into believing it had to do with frivolous GI entertainment.

The call-out order to fill the brigade had specified that the enlisted men be "rough, tough and unafraid of anybody or anything." What Frederick got was some of Canada's finest soldiers and a hefty number of American lumberjacks, Canadian prospectors, and assorted ruffians, adventurers, misfits, cutthroats, and ne'er-do-wells of both nationalities emptied from stockades, or who volunteered in order to join an elite unit. When Bridger had showed up to commence his training in Montana, he had heard one volunteer admit that he hadn't been sure of his acceptance into the outfit because he didn't have a criminal record. Over the past year, Bridger had found that he liked training and fighting with a bunch of motley American and Canadian gangsters. Though there had been some early friction between the two groups of North Americans early on in the training, they had by the fall of '43, after a mission to Alaska, become a brotherhood. Now at La Difensa and La Remetanea, they would be blooded in combat for the first time against an equally tough and well-trained German adversary, including his Uncle Walther and the formidable Herman Göring Division.

He continued to stare up into the dark night sky and vague outline of the new moon, thinking about the Roman god Mars and the protective power of the Roman Moon; of seizing Hills 960 and 907 and driving the Germans back from their redoubtable Winter Line; and of taking Rome and being reunited with his mother and sister. And then he thought of the threat he had made to his father.

"I just may be put in a position where I have to kill you."

Would he really kill his own father? He thought back to when he was fourteen in Innsbruck, when his mother and father had nearly murdered one another before his eyes. He would never have thought his parents capable of such a desperate act. And yet, they had each shot one another twice in anger. Was he capable of being as cold-blooded and violent as his mother and father, whose blood flowed through his veins? He realized that he already knew the answer to that question: he had already killed one German and wounded five others in a matter of minutes. He had no problem killing the enemy if he had to, he realized. And over the next few days, he would have ample opportunity to do just that. He thought again of his Uncle Walther. Would he be able to kill him if they faced one another in battle and he knew that it was his uncle standing across from him?

"It sure is a fine night," he heard a voice behind him say.

Startled, he wondered how someone had been able to sneak up on him so quietly. But he relaxed when he saw it was just Colonel Frederick. The commanding officer was smiling pleasantly.

"A little jumpy are we, Captain? I apologize. I didn't mean to scare you."

He stiffened ramrod straight. "It's nothing, sir. I was just thinking."

"About the mission? You're going to play a big role, John."

He cleared his throat. "Actually, Colonel, I wasn't thinking about the mission. I was thinking about my father and my uncle."

"I know your father is an SS colonel and right-hand man to General Wolff. But who is your uncle?"

"He is a major in the Hermann Göring Division we'll be facing in the next few days. His name is Walther Hollmann."

"I've got to say, that's a lot of soldiers for one family, John." He smiled. "I read your report. I must tell you that I'm glad you made it out of that basement alive."

"My father got me out of there. I was lucky."

"Quite an unusual act of mercy for an SS colonel. But then again, you are his son."

"What I was thinking about, sir, was how just before I left Rome I threatened him."

"You threatened him after he saved your bacon?" Bridger nodded. "Why you have even bigger balls than I thought. Perhaps I should have you lead the assault on Difensa."

"I believe the proper name is Hill 960, sir. We don't want to give anything away to our enemies if captured and interrogated."

"I wouldn't worry about that, Captain. From what I saw of your OSS debriefing, it appeared to me that you gave as good as you got during your interrogation. Even before your dad showed up."

"Yes, but I was only in that room for maybe a half hour."

"You can thank your father for that next time you see him. So what did you say to dear old dad when you threatened him?"

"I told him that he had better not be in Rome when we defeated Kesselring's army and I returned to the city, or else I would…." He stopped short.

"Or else you would what?"

"Or else I might be forced to kill him."

"Sounds like something out of Hamlet or Macbeth."

"Are you a literary man, sir?"

"No, I was a piss-ass student, and that was on a good day. I always just wanted to play sports and chase girls, though my parents force-fed me German, Latin, the cello, and classical literature, including Mr. Shakespeare, whenever they got the chance. That's why I lied about my age and ran away to sea at the age of fourteen. Most of the time, I hated my own father. He used to whip me with a cello bow."

"Sorry to hear that, sir. Growing up, I worshiped my father. But I don't anymore. Now he's the enemy. And so is my Uncle Walther."

"Well, one of those enemies just sprung you from a Gestapo jail." Frederick gave a knowing smile. "Seriously, you wouldn't really kill your old man, would you?"

"Only if I was forced to. But I meant it when I said it."

"I'll remember not to cross you, Captain. I actually want to live through this war."

They chuckled and stared up at the faint outline of the new moon. It hung high above a hill amid a spangle of stars. A few splotchy clouds floated above the jagged outline of a bombed-out building, showing the destructive effects of the war in bold relief. Standing next to the soft-spoken yet intense lieutenant colonel, Bridger felt the man's quiet power. The thirty-six-year-old son of a San Francisco doctor was like a father to him and had led an adventurous life. He had joined the California National Guard at the tender age of thirteen, sailed to Australia as a deckhand on a tramp steamer at fourteen, and graduated from West Point at twenty-one. It was rumored that he had made his first parachute jump after only ten minutes of instruction wearing bedroom slippers, and that in combat the only things he carried with him were his rifle, Nescafe, cigarettes, and a hand-written letter in Latin from the bishop of Helena, commending him as "altogether worthy of trust."

Now that, thought Bridger, was an eccentric son of a bitch worth fighting for.

The colonel caught him looking at him and smiled. "What are you thinking about, Captain?" he asked quietly, before returning his gaze to the silhouette of the moon.

"I'm thinking about the Roman Moon."

"The Roman Moon, you say?"

"Yes, sir. The Italians believe that in wartime, when the moon is new or full, they are protected by the Roman gods of war. That they are, in effect, invincible. The Italians say it goes all the way back to the days of the Legions."

"You're talking about Mars and Juno?"

So you weren't such a mediocre student after all, were you? Bridger nodded. "The Roman partisans say the gods are watching over all of us—not just the Resistance but the Allies—in our battle against the Germans. They say that we are the righteous ones in this war, and that is why we will defeat the Nazis and continue to be protected by the Roman Moon. That's what the Italians say. Of course, it's just an ancient myth, but I like it just the same."

"I like it too, John. It makes me feel better about our chances in the coming days."

"To the Roman Moon then, sir."

Frederick grinned. "To the Roman Moon, Captain Bridger. And to Mars and Juno. May they watch over us all."

CHAPTER 24

MONTE LA DIFENSA (HILL 960)
CENTRAL ITALY
DECEMBER 3, 1943

FOUR DAYS LATER, AT 0445 HOURS, the lead brigade fanned out along the northeast rim of the German-held fortress dubbed Hill 960, moving into final assault position. Reaching the crest, Bridger peered up over the rim into the saucer-shaped depression that he had studied in the reconnaissance photographs, but all he could see was pitch black. It was still too early for even a glimmer of predawn light. A thick bank of heavy fog had settled in during the night, concealing the rocky eminence and the ridge extending to Hill 907. But he knew the enemy was close; he could smell the odor of cooked sausage and burnt coffee coming from the Germans' mess area.

Like a legion of snakes, the different sections of the advance brigade crawled up the final cliff face and, singly, broke over the rim. With the rain drumming steadily down his helmet and poncho, his face blackened and uniform dirt-stained to maintain a cloak of invisibility to the enemy, Bridger took a moment to thank his lucky stars. It was a miracle that he and the other six-hundred Forcemen in the assault brigade had made it up the mountain without freezing to death, tumbling onto the jagged rocks below the massive face, or being detected by the enemy sentries posted along Difensa's craggy crest.

Now they stood poised to attack the crack troops of the 104th Panzergrenadier Regiment and 115th Reconnaissance Battalion—some of Hitler's finest along the Winter Line—and the goddamned Krauts had no idea what was coming.

He couldn't believe that, so far, the colonel's risky plan was actually working and surprise was still on their side. It was the thing they needed most. That and luck.

Or were the Germans waiting to draw them into a trap?

He took a deep breath of the chill night air, waiting impatiently for the order to attack. He and the other members of the Second Regiment, First Brigade, clung to the rim of the football-field-sized depression in front of the enemy's perimeter entrenchments and the ledges below the crest. The sweat from their exhausting ascent had frozen to their bodies in the frigid air. The men had spent the night climbing hand over hand in the spitting rain with mountaineer ropes, as a friendly artillery barrage burst above them on the crest. To Bridger, it had looked as if they had been climbing towards Hell instead of Heaven. The whole mountain had exploded with shells, appearing as if on fire.

After midnight, they had come within earshot of the forward German entrenchments and began to scale the final cliff face. It was a bear, jutting upwards at a seventy-degree angle for at least a thousand vertical feet. But Bridger and the other six hundred members of the assault force managed to scramble to their designated attack position at the crest without losing a single soldier. They owed it to their brutal training in Montana during the preceding year. That was what enabled them to grope to the top of La Difensa in the darkness with seventy-pound packs strapped to their back, clinging to nothing but slippery, frozen rock notched with thin crevices. And it was their training that then allowed them to patiently wait for hours in the freezing rain before launching their attack.

Bridger cast an ear in the direction of the enemy. Since the Allied shelling had ended several hours ago, the only sound coming from the Germans was the regular tracer blast of a Schmeisser "burp gun" firing at fifteen minute intervals as a signal to the mortars on the nearby slopes, as well as the occasional roar of a distant mortar round or artillery shell. But that's all he had heard from the enemy since the Allied shelling had stopped, and no concentrated enemy fire had been directed at the approaching force as it scaled the final cliff face.

But again Bridger wondered: Was it deliberate? Did the Krauts know they were coming? Were they waiting in silence to draw them into a trap?

He felt a presence next to him and heard a whispering voice. "All companies are nearly in position, Captain. We're moving forward in silence to the final rally point. Knives and bayonets only. Pass the word to Colonel MacWilliam. We will commence the attack at 0600."

It was Frederick. The presence of the colonel gave Bridger a feeling of reassurance, like being reunited with an old friend.

"We're going to catch them with their pants down and give 'em hell, John. Godspeed."

"Yessir," he replied, suppressing a shiver in the cold air. He rose from his crevice and slipped forward on stiff legs in the darkness in search of the Canadian commander.

He found MacWilliam further up the edge of the saucer, chewing on a C ration down behind an outcrop of wet, slippery limestone. After he relayed the message, the Canadian gave a signal and the Second Regiment started forward again, inching closer to the hundreds of German troops concealed in the maze of underground emplacements and foxholes on the crest of the mountain fortress. The enemy still had not detected their presence or raised an alarm. The only sounds were the distant rumble of artillery from both sides and, along the rim of the mountain, the soft gurgle vented by unlucky German sentries as their throats were severed by the Forcemen gliding past the forward positions in the darkness.

And then, quite suddenly, it all went to shit.

There were loud rumbling and clanking noises up ahead to his left. Bridger stopped in his tracks to listen, desperate to know what the hell it was. And then he knew.

It was rocks tumbling downslope.

A lot of rocks.

"Damnit!" a Canadian voice up ahead whispered bitterly. "The Jerries have rigged a rockfall!"

"Everyone, hold up! The rocks are unstable all around that pillbox there!"

"I'm slipping!" muttered another soldier, this time an American.

Now Bridger heard a whole wall of rocks give way and muffled cries of alarm. In the darkness, he saw the silhouette of a tangle of bodies sliding down into a ravine to the sound of jostling stones.

It was a trap.

Suddenly, loud voices shouted out in German and then, like lightning, the blackness of the night sky was transformed into a surreal blaze of red and green flares and explosions of mortar and heavy machine-gun fire. Then the blinding flash of two magnesium flares lit up the entire mountain like Fourth of July fireworks, throwing the approaching battalion in an oppressive glare, like actors caught in unexpectedly bright stage lights. A curtain of Schmeisser machine-pistol fire erupted—the weapon fired at a cyclic rate of over a thousand rounds per minute—followed quickly by individual sniper blasts from the forward foxholes.

Seeing men from One Company diving for cover all around him, Bridger quickly ducked behind a knob of slippery marlstone and jerked out his Thompson light machine gun tucked beneath his rain poncho.

The battle for Monte La Difensa was on.

CHAPTER 25

MONTE LA DIFENSA (HILL 960) DECEMBER 3, 1943

GRITTING HIS TEETH, he returned fire with his Tommy at the gun flashes coming from the German forward position. A heavy grunt signaled a hit. Then, right beside him, he heard a quick intake of breath and knew that a fellow Forceman had taken one. In the blink of an eye, one fallen Kraut and one fallen comrade—it seemed an unfair swap.

He let loose with another burst, saw One Company charging forward into the maw to his left and attempting to flank the enemy, as McGinty's Two Company swept into action on the right. Behind him, Forcemen were pouring over the rim, moving fast and furious through the cold mist, though they seemed like wriggling worms moving in slow motion in the flickering gunbursts and overhead flares. The black-faced troops, soaking wet and covered in mud and grit, lugged light machine guns and mortars and began to emplace them into rocky defiles and shallow gullies to cover the advancing riflemen.

With flares bursting into the night and concussive explosions from the enemy mortars and machine guns blasting his ears, Bridger picked his way forward with One Company towards the main German position on the peak of Hill 960. In the flashes of light, he saw that advance platoons were furiously engaged with the enemy at the complex of caves and pillboxes built into the rocky heights. The Germans had emplaced several heavy machine guns to cover the northern approaches, and they blasted away at the oncoming wave of attackers with relentless fury, the bullets knocking down men and chipping away slivers of jagged rock that were as lethal as flak.

Taking cover behind an outcropping, Bridger realized that Frederick hadn't been exaggerating during his briefing: the German position was literally a goddamned fortress. He couldn't believe that the howitzers that had seemed to pulverize the mountain and turn it into a raging inferno had barely put a dent in the fortifications. Hell, they hadn't even cracked the hard limestone of La Difensa.

Popping in a fresh 20-round box magazine, he opened fire with his Tommy on a machine-gun nest just below the main pillbox. He couldn't tell if he had hit anything, but he did hear loud shouting and cursing in German between the bursts of return fire. He and a small group of Forcemen exchanged shots with the Germans for several minutes until Fisher, Bernstein, and another trooper whose name he did not know tossed grenades up at the position.

This time the Germans went silent.

A moment later, a series of enemy mortar rounds struck nearby with a deafening roar. Bridger felt a shard of rock blasted loose from an outcrop drive into his upper arm like a flint arrow point. He took cover to wait out the barrage, while a medic fashioned a bandage for him and gave him a shot of morphine. When the smoke finally cleared, Sergeant Fisher was blinded in his eye from the stone fragments and several other Forcemen were killed and seriously wounded. The dead included his friend Private Casey, who could have stayed behind as a cook but had insisted on serving in a combat platoon. A direct hit by a dud mortar bomb had cracked open his skull and spilled his brains. With the aid of the medic, Bridger helped Fisher and another man to their feet and guided them to the rear, stumbling through the pre-dawn darkness and confusion of battle as the mortar shelling picked up in intensity.

Here he found the colonel directing mortar fire in front of his forward command post and radio communications center on the shelf below the rope scramble.

"How's it look up front, John?" asked Frederick, yelling over the din of battle.

"One Company is heavily engaged along the ridge line, just below the peak, and Two Company is flanking right. But it's a fortress up there, sir. Last night's aerial display hasn't cracked through the rock at all. It's going to take some doing to take that hill."

"Well then, we'd better get up there and join Two Company."

"Shouldn't you stay here at your command post, sir? They're taking heavy mortar fire and those machine guns in those damned pill boxes are really letting us have it."

"You know me, John. I need to see things for myself."

"Yes, sir. But if you get hit, don't say I didn't warn you."

"I would never do that, John. You lead the way."

They dashed forward and linked up with Sergeant McGinty and Two Company just as the first streaks of dawn broke. Since Bridger had returned to the rear, McGinty had made unexpected progress with his section's right flanking move to knock out the crest defense of the enemy. And to the left, Bridger saw that One Company had consolidated to within a football field of the peak and was beginning to clean up a ridge supporting part of the heavy machine-gun complex. The men were still under fire from the enemy mortars, but had made considerable gains since the last time he had seen them. Now Two Company got back into the mix and swept in on the Germans' left flank, moving steadily uphill.

But the enemy responded in full measure.

A mortar exploded nearby, followed by the roar of machine guns and grenades and even rocks thrown from a nearby foxhole from a German soldier out of ammunition, which drew laughter from Bridger and two other Forcemen and a look of admiration from Frederick. The enemy hastily swung their pieces on the advancing company and improved their positions on the higher ground, bringing up a dozen machine-pistol men to snipe. Advancing rapidly with his Tommy firm against his hip, Bridger took down one German, then another, as he and the other attackers crept over the final limestone lip.

They were met by an explosion of Schmeissers.

Outgunned, they began losing men fast. Bridger saw two men fall, then a third and fourth, and a whole group of Forcemen were driven back as their faces were peppered with rock splinters from ricochets.

"Jesus Christ!" shrieked Frederick. "Where the hell did they come from?"

"I don't know," cried Bridger as they dove for cover. "But we need more suppressing fire."

"No, we need to outflank the bastards!"

He was right, Bridger saw at once. He and the colonel quickly issued orders to Sergeants Van Ausdale and Fenton, who had both led the company up from the assembly area as advance points. Frederick had Van Ausdale gather up eight men. He then ordered a nearby machine-gun squad to lay down fire, called for three mortar rounds from the company emplacement, and led the improvised section over the ledge in an assault on the entrenched German positions.

The daring Van Ausdale, a hard rock miner from Arizona with dark skin and high cheekbones attesting to his Apache ancestry, screamed like a banshee and charged. Bridger and the others, including old Frederick himself, quickly followed suit, dashing up the eminence right behind him using grenades and bayonets to dispatch the enemy and secure the captured positions. Soon, they had taken three enemy redoubts and the firing slackened sufficiently to enable McGinty to remove his wounded.

But they still hadn't taken the final peak.

Bridger scanned through his binoculars, wondering what it was going to take to clear the damned Germans off the bloody mountaintop.

He was forced to duck down as a pair of enemy machine guns began rattling to the front with such volume that Frederick ordered several men onto a firing line for support. When the closer of the two machine-gun nests changed out for more ammo, the colonel had the section advance on the first position. To Bridger's surprise, the gun crew surrendered intact. They then drove on to the second position, where Van Ausdale and Bridger silenced the crew with a pair of grenades.

When the smoke cleared, Bridger saw that only one of the Germans was still alive, and even he was in bad shape. Grenade fragments were embedded in his forehead and he sucked in his breath with a loud wheezing sound. While they waited a minute to decide their next move, Bridger grabbed a fresh Tommy magazine from his pouch and jammed it in place.

It was then he felt a throbbing sensation in his arm. Looking at his torn jacket, he saw where ricochets of flying rock slivers had cut through his uniform and made a series of gashes along his forearm. It was as if he had been cut repeatedly by a knife blade.

"You're going to have to have that looked at, John," observed Frederick.

"And *you're* going to have to have *that* looked at." He pointed at the colonel's scalp line beneath his helmet where a mortar splinter had cut a deep gash.

The colonel smiled. "We'll go in together, John."

"You've got a deal, sir."

Lieutenant Finn Roll, a Norwegian assistant intelligence officer, came up. He and Frederick talked and then set off together, leaving the others behind. Bridger and Van Ausdale waited a few more minutes for more sections to join up and to allow the men to reload their weapons before moving forward again. Methodically, they wormed their way up the hill.

Halfway up, Bridger found an unexpected change. The fog parted and the smoke cleared and he saw that Colonel MacWilliam and One Company had, by some miracle, already taken the German stronghold. The gunfire had slackened to a sporadic pop from a handful of remaining snipers, and the enemy was surrendering en masse.

Shouting with delight, he dashed to the top.

All along the crest he saw surrendering Germans in rain-soaked field gray stepping out of caves, pill boxes, trenches, and from behind rocky outcrops with their hands in the air. Beyond the mountain fortress, farther down the ridge, the enemy streamed down the hill like a herd of fleeing mountain goats, running madly away from the crest and tumbling down the slope, in a hurry to escape across the connecting ridge to the Force's second objective, Monte La Remetanea. Of course, it would take an hour or so to consolidate the Difensa stronghold, to clean out remaining snipers, reorganize the sections, platoons, and companies, and to dig in against the inevitable counterattack. But the first part of their mission was accomplished.

Against all odds they had taken Hill 960: the massive, impregnable Monte La Difensa that several other crack army units had failed to take and had been driven from in abject humiliation. Bridger couldn't fucking believe it.

"Holy shit, Colonel—we did it!" he roared triumphantly, throwing his arms around MacWilliam. "We goddamn did it!"

The colonel patted him on the back. "We sure as hell did, didn't we!" snorted the Canadian effusively. "But we still have to take that son of bitch down there."

He pointed down the long spiny ridge to Hill 907, La Remetanea, where Germans in *feldgrau* and mountain camo were now reforming in strength. The second eminence looked every bit as formidable as the fortress they had just lost at least fifty good men taking.

Bridger nodded. "You're right," he said. "It's not going to be easy."

"Unfortunately, there's no avoiding it. We have to take her."

Over the next few minutes, they watched as the enemy took cover all along neighboring La Remetanea. Meanwhile, squads of Forcemen cleaned out the last of the German snipers and other holdouts in the foxholes before rallying at the crest of the saucer-shaped depression with Bridger, MacWilliam, and the others. When the large party had assembled, the men raised their weapons and gave a loud cheer that echoed all across the mountaintop, reverberating all the way down to the defeated, scowling Germans.

But the cheering was abruptly cut off by the demonic whistle from one of the German *Nebelwerfer* six-barrel rocket guns that unleashed a reign of terror in the Italian skies. From the sound, it was coming out of the west.

"Screaming Meemie, get down!" cried Van Ausdale. "It sure didn't take those sons of bitches long!"

Bridger listened to the long, drawn-out moaning sound and felt the blood curdle in his veins. It sounded like the projectile was heading straight for them, but it ended up exploding further to the south, closer to the cliff face and rope scramble. But with daylight upon them and the break in the fog, they were now vulnerable to counterattack. Surprisingly accurate mortar and sniper fire began to menace them from the adjoining mountain complexes and Hill 907. Not wanting the men to become sitting ducks, Colonel MacWilliam ordered the section to press on to the second objective and continue the attack despite heavy casualties.

"Let's go!" he shouted once the column had formed up, and he and his staff began racing towards the edge of the plateau.

A mortar shell explosion rocked the summit basin, shaking the ground like an earth tremor and stopping MacWilliam and the five men in the advance with him in their tracks. When Bridger looked up, he saw nothing but pulverized rockdust mist where only a moment earlier six men had been standing.

Suddenly and without mercy, the full-scale German artillery counterattack was on. The entire saucer-shaped depression was pummeled with explosions from both artillery and mortars. Bridger and the others quickly took shelter in the maze of trenches, foxholes, and concrete pillboxes deserted by the Germans.

Five minutes later Frederick reappeared.

With shells exploding all around, Bridger told him about the taking of the summit and the death of MacWilliam and the others. He found the colonel more saddened by the loss of so many good men than the attainment of a critical military objective that for weeks had defied the Fifth Army.

Frederick then turned away to confer with Major Thomas about ammunition stores, and he ordered that the attack on neighboring La Remetanea be postponed until more ammunition, food, and water could be brought up from the rear.

Once he had issued his orders, he turned back to Bridger. Standing against a craggy backdrop of what the men were now calling Million Dollar Mountain, with shells and sniper fire raining down, the sky drizzling, and the air bitingly frigid, the colonel looked as famished and dirty and wet and miserable as any of his men.

"We've done well, John. We did in two hours what the brass said would take three days."

"Yes, sir. No one can ever take this one away from us. We earned this."

"But it's still just a goddamned hill. We lost too many good men for this to be some great victory."

"Yes, sir. Too damned many. But we did take the son of a bitch."

"Yes, John, that we most certainly did."

Minutes later, when the firing briefly abated, he and Frederick returned to the colonel's protected command post on the shelf below the rope scramble. A wounded private with a missing eye was working his way down the mountain praying out loud, "The Lord is my shepherd—he shepherds me hither, thither, and yon." From the shelf, they signaled Second Regiment by radio to hold up any further advance until the ammunition packers arrived. Then the colonel radioed the supply officers in the caves down the trail to get the packers started with ammunition, water, rations, blankets, and litters for the wounded.

"And one last thing, Colonel Adams," Frederick added at the end. "Don't forget to send the whiskey and prophylactics."

"What the hell do your men need whiskey and condoms for?" fired back Adams. "Don't tell me those Krauts have a goddamned brothel tucked away in the caves on top of that Godforsaken mountain?"

"No, we need the whiskey for warmth and fortitude, and the rubbers to keep the rain out of our rifle barrels. We're going to be in for another hell of a fight up here, so see to it. I don't care how you get it all, but I want six cases of whiskey on this mountaintop by day's end—and five hundred goddamned condoms."

"Yes, Colonel! It will take six hours to haul it all up to the top, but it will be there!"

Frederick hung up. Bridger peeked over the saucer-shaped rim at the battlefield, peering through his field glasses through the broken mist and steady rain. The Germans were now showering death upon them with an all-out barrage of heavy mortar and long-range sniper and artillery fire. The mountaintop shuddered violently from the exploding shells. Though Frederick had sent the men into the vacated pillboxes for shelter and the Force was dug in for counterattack, Bridger couldn't help but feel the situation had changed. Instead of being on the offensive, they were now on the defensive, which was not the Forceman way.

Instead of the hunters, they were now the hunted.

It was going to be a long, hard fight all right. They were definitely going to need the whiskey and prophylactics.

CHAPTER 26

MONTE LA REMETANEA (HILL 907) DECEMBER 6, 1943

SEVENTY-EIGHT HOURS LATER, on the fourth day of the battle for the pair of mountaintops, Bridger stared at the grime-covered, haggard, bleary-eyed face of Robert Tyron Frederick. He had a new nickname for him: "the Fighting Colonel." Though twice wounded, Frederick had continued to lead the men from the trenches and rocky caves since taking Monte La Difensa, and he had demonstrated an uncanny ability to be everywhere at once on the battlefield, directing both men and mortar fire. He was unlike any field commander Bridger had ever known or heard about, short of Stonewall Jackson, and that's why he had given him the nickname. It had already spread among the men and appeared to have stuck. Frederick was "the Fighting Colonel," and if the military powers-that-be were ever smart enough to promote him, he would be "the Fighting General."

Frederick leaned forward and handed him a sheath of paper. "Please take a look at this, John. Tell me what you think."

Bridger took the slip of paper from him. On it, he saw that Frederick had scribbled out a dispatch in heavy pencil for the command post far below the mountain for relay to General Walker, 36th Division. The message read:

> Situation at present: Dec. 6-1200 hours. We have troops down to our left boundary at the saddle and have consolidated for defense of the area south of La Difensa (Hill 960). Our attack to the west against Hill 907 has progressed beyond the crest of 907. We are receiving much machine-gun and mortar fire from several directions, principally from the draw running southwest from La Difensa, from west foothills of Maggiore and from north slopes of Camino. We are endeavoring to place artillery support fire on the troublesome areas but it is difficult due to very low visibility and the British restrictions on our artillery fire.
>
> I shall push the attack to the west on past Hill 907 as far as condition of men will permit. Men are getting in bad shape from fatigue, exposure, and cold.
>
> German snipers are giving us hell and it is extremely difficult to catch them. They are hidden all through the area and shoot bursts at any target.
>
> Please press relief of troops from this position as every additional day here will mean two more days necessary for recuperation before next mission. They are willing and eager, but are becoming exhausted.
>
> Communications are heart-breaking. Mortar fire (and travel on trail) knocked out lines faster than we can repair them. Every time we transmit by radio enemy drops mortar on location.
>
> German reinforcements approach up draw southwest of Camino, but I am unable to tell whether they are reinforcing or attempting to organize a counterattack.
>
> In my opinion, unless British take Camino before dark today it should be promptly

attacked by us from the north. The locations we hold are going to be uncomfortable as long as enemy holds north slopes of Camino.

PS. I am OK, just uncomfortable and tired.

Bridger looked up when finished reading.

Frederick raised a bloodied brow. "What do you think, John? Do you have anything to add?" His voice was surprisingly soft and gentle.

He shook his head. "No, sir, that sums it up." He handed the message back and looked at his wristwatch. "I'm going on patrol. As you say in your message, we need to drive these bastards off this mountain."

"Indeed we do," said Frederick, and he took the paper from him and started looking it over again. "Good hunting, John. I may see you out there."

"Yes, sir." He left the command post and met up with Staff Sergeant Van Ausdale, the part-Indian tracker and prospector from Arizona and best scout in the Force. They headed out on anti-sniper patrol to clear a spur below Hill 907.

Halfway down, they came upon a pair of German corpses behind a pair of boulders, lying stiff and gnarled. The stench of death made Bridger gag. Van Ausdale, who in his late thirties was older and more experienced than the other men, made a joke how poor Fritz and Dieter weren't really dead but had been transformed into wax figures that would one day be a carnival attraction. The men laughed, the smell didn't seem so bad any more, and the patrol moved on.

Five minutes later, they came under fire from an enemy sniper.

"Take cover!" yelled Bridger.

But it was too late as the Forceman on point took a bullet to the face, splattering blood, bone, and brain onto the rocks.

The startled squad, well-spaced and not bunched up, quickly dove by ones and twos behind a row of jagged boulders.

A bullet whizzed past Bridger's ear. As he ducked, a second round zoomed past and ricocheted off the rocks.

Then it went quiet for a moment.

Another shot whistled past his head. This time when he ducked, a huge German panzergrenadier who had to be six-foot-five inches tall materialized from out of nowhere and came at him screaming like a madman and swinging a machine pistol. Bridger rolled away to avoid the blow, suddenly afraid for his life. The Kraut had come upon him so quickly there was no time to raise his gun to shoot. But as the giant swung at him a second time, Bridger heard three thumping sounds and the man stiffened and then slumped forward onto the rocks with a triumvirate of bullet wounds in his back. The German went still.

Bridger looked up to see who had saved his ass. The Native American-Dutchman Van Ausdale stood crouched down low with a smoking rifle.

"I owe you one, Van. What the hell was that Kraut thinking? Why did he come at me like that?"

There was shooting on both sides now as the sniper and patrol exchanged shots. "He must have been out of ammo," said Van Ausdale, keeping his head down. "Either that or he was hungry. Look at the size of that son of a bitch. He probably eats about ten pounds of food per day."

"Ate, Van. Past tense."

Keeping in a crouch, Van Ausdale kicked him to be sure. "Yep, you're right. Dead as a doornail."

"He reminds me of the giant in *Jack and the Beanstalk* lying there like that."

"I always liked that one. The goose that laid the golden egg."

There was a gunflash to their right and they heard someone roar, "I got him! I got that sniping son of a bitch!"

Further down the slope, Bridger saw through the break in the fog a group of Germans dashing down the hill to safety. The air was filled with rat-tat-tat and pinging sounds as bullets plucked after the escaping enemy combatants, but no more Germans went down. Bridger, Van Ausdale, and the others followed after the German patrol, but eventually drew heavy fire and were forced to take cover.

After a few minutes, Bridger decided that they had had enough and they started back to base. He sent a platoon runner ahead to report the loss of Sergeant Wibben.

Halfway up the spur, they heard the crackle of a rifle.

He ordered the patrol to fan out and move forward through the heavy fog. A moment later when it cleared, they came upon the runner along the trial. Fortunately, he was only lightly wounded in the arm. But as they started off again, they received heavy fire from a German rifle pocket where the fog was thickest.

After several minutes of exchanging fire with no advantage gained by either side, the fog swirled in again, concealing them from the enemy. Knowing this might be their only chance to dislodge the Germans, Bridger called for the platoon to charge the enemy position.

They moved forward in a mad-dash frontal attack, yelling as much to scare the enemy as to relieve their pent-up emotions, their battle cries echoing through the curtain of mist like the terrifying Rebel Yell. After their fourth consecutive day of combat, getting almost no sleep, and losing so many of their fellow Forcemen to the enemy, they would ask for no quarter and give none in return.

With the concealment of the fog and their unconventional yelling, they were able to throw the Germans off guard, scare the crap out of them, and quickly overtake their position. Bridger heard an officer barking out orders and the men screaming in terror as the Kraut sniper company was cut to pieces by BARS and Johnny guns, M1s and Bridger's Tommy gun. So completely demoralized was the enemy that half of its force withdrew under the overpowering wave that poured in on them. Enemy "potato masher" stick grenades were picked up and thrown right back at the Germans with devastating consequences. The Forcemen had fixed bayonets and many used them, tearing through the snipers with all of their anger and frustration from being cooped up, frozen stiff, and under constant attack for the past four days of fighting.

It was all over in less than two minutes.

As was the new Force rule, no prisoners were taken.

When it was over, Bridger sat down on a boulder and watched the lucky few that had managed to escape retreating down the hill in confusion and disarray through the breaks in the fog. He was surprised to see that, between the German dead and survivors, the enemy had outnumbered him and his men nearly three to one. What the platoon had done had been almost suicidal, and suddenly he felt exhausted. The others were spent just like him. No one said a word or made a cheer as the routed Germans dashed down the scree slope into the valley below.

Once his unit had collected themselves, they left the dead Krauts where they lay, gathered up their wounded, and started up the trail back to Hill 709 again. On the way, Bridger was surprised to come across Colonel Frederick. He was leading a small group of his own, and appeared to be checking up on the various anti-sniper patrols clearing the mountain. He and his squad were in an area off the main path where another patrol of Forcemen had been recently ambushed and several men killed. The bodies were being placed side by side on the trail so that they could be transported back down the mountain to the rear.

Bridger quickly reported to Frederick. As they were talking, without warning a German sniper unloaded on them thirty yards away from between two boulders, shooting down a Forcemen and an unarmed medic with a Red Cross emblem on his helmet.

"Goddamnit, that's enough!" cried Frederick angrily. "Follow me!"

Bridger and two others went with the colonel to the left, and six more men to the right. Once they had outflanked the German, they split up into four different groups and opened up on the sniper from multiple positions. In less than five minutes, the lone sniper had tied a white flag to his gun and held the barrel-end up in the sky in surrender.

"Hold your fire! Hold your fire!" cried Bridger, who was the closest to the man. Though the Force credo was to take no prisoners, the German sniper was waving a white flag, and Bridger wasn't about to shoot an enemy soldier who was obviously surrendering.

But the firing didn't stop so he repeated the order.

"Hold your fire, goddamnit! He's surrendered!"

This time the firing stopped.

Behind him, Bridger heard Frederick say to a soldier, "Let me have your rifle, son."

Bridger spun around. "Wait, sir, what are you doing?"

But the colonel wasn't listening. With the agate eyes of an outlaw gunfighter, he took careful aim with the rifle, pointing it at the German's head.

Bridger tried to wave him off. "No, sir, no!" he cried. "The son of a bitch is waving a white flag!"

The shot struck the German in the forehead, killing him instantly. The crackle of the rifle echoed off the boulders and down into the valley below.

A silence fell through the ranks. Bridger stood there stunned. To see the man that he worshiped above all others, this paragon of all that was great and venerable about the Force, come unhinged like that made him feel sick inside. This, most certainly, was not Lieutenant Colonel Robert Tyron Frederick's finest hour. In anger, he had fired at an unarmed enemy surrendering with a white flag. It was a blatant violation of the Rules of Warfare.

Damn you! Damn you for not being better than the rest of us!

No one said a word until Frederick finally spoke. His jaw was set in a stubborn line, and Bridger saw in his haggard face all of the pain and suffering and bitter anger of the past four days of battle.

"No one is going to kill my men and get away with it—not if I can goddamn help it," he seethed quietly. "Especially not some son of a bitch who guns down an unarmed medic."

The Fighting Colonel tipped his head solemnly down at the medic with the readily-visible Red Cross symbol on his helmet and jacket. Then he handed the rifle back to the soldier, his lip quivering with emotion.

His gaze met Bridger's, and Bridger saw the shame in the colonel's bloodshot eyes. The mountaintop went totally still and quiet. For several seconds, there was nothing, no sound at all, only the distant roar of artillery. And then, like a snowball slowly gathering in size, the grimy hands barked blue from the frigid mountain air began clapping, the sound rising and rising and rising until it held a quiet thunder all its own. For two full minutes, a dozen unshaven, grimy, weary-faced men stood on the spiny ridge and clapped their half-frozen hands. Then they all stiffened and, as one, gave a crisp salute.

A moment earlier, Bridger had felt outrage and anger; now he couldn't help but be moved. He looked into the eyes of Sergeant Van Ausdale of Arizona and Private Eugene Forward from Montreal and he saw what they saw. In their eyes, what their commander had just done was not breaking the rules or a war crime at all, but simply enforcing the First Special Service Force code. If an enemy sniper was going to kill Forcemen and think that he could immediately surrender and expect mercy, well he had another thing coming to him. And that was even truer if the son of a bitch was going to shoot down a non-belligerent medic clearing away the dead and wounded.

He looked into Private Forward's eyes. "*I don't care what rule the colonel broke,*" the young Canadian seemed to say, "*that damn Kraut knew that he was murdering an unarmed medic. So fuck him and the train he rode in on!*"

Frederick kneeled down next to the dead medic and gently closed his eyes. "This has gone on too long. We need to get our boys off this mountain," was all he said.

In somber silence, they picked up the bodies of their dead comrades, lent an arm to the wounded, and hobbled back up the hill to the command post. All along the way, Bridger thought of Sherman's maxim that war is hell. But Sherman was wrong, he realized. War in the mountains of Italy in frigid winter, on the brutal road to Rome fighting against a ruthless enemy like the goddamned Nazis armed with weapons of mass killing, was a hundred times worse.

When they reached the mountaintop to deliver the dead and wounded, the clouds parted briefly. Bridger stared out with Frederick in silence at the drab-gray, rugged winter landscape. It dawned on him that all the fighting he had taken part in these past four days would probably be nothing but a blur; and the only thing he would remember would be the men he fought alongside and the ground itself. With the first opening rounds of mortar and machine-gun fire, this place where he and the Germans had done battle had been forever changed. Monte La Difensa would no longer stand alone as a part of the natural landscape or a place to visit. Once men had fought and died on a piece of ground, that ground was no longer the same. It stood with the bravery of the men that had fallen, with the blood spilled on both sides and the tragedy it brought to a thousand different families. It became more than just a place; it became a part of history.

Hills 960 and 907 were, now and forever, a part of history.

He looked at the Fighting Colonel staring off at the battlefield. He wondered if he was thinking the same thing. Looking at the tired, bloodied face, he was reminded of *Charles O'Malley: The Irish Dragoon*, his favorite book as a boy growing up in Austria along with *Robinson Crusoe*. Quixotically, he had thought war such an honorable thing back then, and it still was in its way. But the unspeakable horror of war, the death and destruction and cruelty he had witnessed in just these last four days alone, was something that he knew he would never be able to forget. With the honor and bravery came the barbarism—you could not have the one without the other—and from now on, each and every time Bridger took to battle, he knew that some part of his humanity would die right there along with the men that had fallen alongside him.

The colonel's soft voice broke through his thoughts. "I shouldn't have done what I did back there, John. May the Lord forgive me."

Bridger looked at him. "That wasn't you, Colonel. That was someone else."

"God, I hope so," he said. "God, I hope so."

ψψψ

It would be another three days before reinforcements arrived at Mount La Remetanea. When they came, Bridger, Frederick, and what remained of the First Special Service Force hobbled back down the mountain at only two-thirds the strength of what they had fielded when they had first started scaling the cliffs of La Difensa. But the German's formidable Winter Line was broken and the Allies were one step closer to their objective on the long, hard road to Rome.

PART 3

THE RESISTANCE

CHAPTER 27

VATICAN

DECEMBER 15, 1943

IT WAS THE SEVENTH SECRET MEETING between Pope Pius XII and the British Minister to the Holy See regarding the assassination of Adolf Hitler, and it was very much like a spy novel.

As per the previous meetings, Sir D'Arcy Osborne—codenamed "Mount"—was required to follow exacting cloak-and-dagger procedures to ensure his clandestine audience with the Chief. He had been instructed to disguise himself as a monsignor by wearing a long black cape, silver-buckled shoes, and scarlet sash, provided to him hours earlier. He was cautioned not to utter a word unless spoken to by the two hand-picked escorts that would deliver him to the Holy Father. And he was required to bring his diplomatic credentials and leave his writing materials in his apartment, as he would have to make it through two checkpoints and would not be allowed to make any official documentation of the meeting.

At twenty minutes past midnight, a light knock was heard on the door to his diplomatic quarters and he was quietly led by a black-cassocked intermediary to the Apostolic Palace. At the front entrance of the palace and again upon reaching the Papal Apartments, he was required to present his credentials to a Noble Guard. At the Apartments, the intermediary then handed him off to the *Maestro di Camera*, Monsignor Arborio Mella St. Elias, who slipped in noiselessly on the thick carpet from an adjacent room. The head of Pope's private household then escorted the British envoy to an antechamber outside the Papal Library. Here the maestro paused to look at his wristwatch and conduct a silent countdown to the appointed hour. At precisely half past midnight, Mella genuflected just inside the adjoining door to the library and motioned Osborne to do the same. Then, after crossing himself three times, he quietly opened the door and led the minister into the book-lined corner room, with three tall windows, overlooking St. Peter's square. The room was only dimly lit, and the fountains below were shrouded in darkness due to the blackout.

When he saw Sir D'Arcy enter the room, Pius looked up from his solid oak desk with the white Olivetti typewriter and cream-colored telephone. The minister took his seat in one of the cane-backed chairs in front of the desk. They exchanged polite conversation for a minute or two before Pius launched into a description of the newest German Army plot to liquidate Hitler. Little did Sir D'Arcy Osborne know that his entire conversation with the Chief this night was being recorded by a state-of-the-art audio-surveillance system that, for the next seventy years, would remain one of the Vatican's best-kept espionage secrets.

ψψψ

Two minutes before their historic meeting, at precisely 12:28 p.m., in a secret control room in a ninth-century dragon-toothed tower next to the Vatican Gardens, a Jesuit operative flicked a simple switch on a wall covered with frescoes. The switch activated a white lamp on a new type of eavesdropping device—called a Marconi-Stille recording machine—in the adjacent room. Once the machine lit up, the Jesuit technician waited a full minute to warm the cathodes before turning the control knob to the "record" position, as he had done on many prior occasions in the service of the Vatican's clandestine wartime eavesdropping operations.

Pope Pius XII, Holy Father to both the free and German-occupied world, and Sir D'Arcy Osborne, the British Minister to the Holy See, were now officially being recorded for the ages.

The Pope had had the advanced audio-surveillance system hard-wired in 1939 by Guglielmo Marconi, inventor of the radio and an important contractor to a rapidly-modernizing Vatican under Pius XII. The purpose of the spy system was to allow the Pope to secretly record wartime conversations of Axis and Allied representatives interacting with the Holy See, as well as members of the German Catholic Church involved in the plot to remove Hitler from power. By having his high-level diplomatic meetings recorded verbatim and by converting the source materials into master transcripts, the Chief ensured that his work on behalf of the Allies was properly documented and that he would be able to refute any distortion of his views.

The largest audio recorder ever built, the Marconi-Stille magnetic recorder-reproducer was almost as big as a Fiat. The machine consisted of two large mechanical drums, special ribboned "razor wire" tape for making the sound recordings, and an electric motor to wind the tape. The recordings were "stored" on the tape by magnetism so that they could be re-broadcast and transcribed at any time. The "razor wire" tape was sharp and dangerous; it was reported that if it somehow managed to break free, it could actually behead the technicians. For this reason, the Jesuit operatives who taped the recordings on behalf of the Pope worked the machine only by remote control from the safety of an adjacent room. Because a half-hour recording used 1.8 miles of spooled steel, the machine's operators had to keep numerous spools on hand to keep pace with the Vatican's secret wartime recordings.

Marconi and his special Vatican engineering staff provided the overall design per the Pope's eavesdropping, recording, and spy tradecraft requirements. The actual microphone was hidden in a hollowed-out copy of Thomas Aquinas's *Summa Theologica*. The hiding place had been expertly fashioned by Father Leiber and placed on the bookshelf just above the Pope's desk. The condenser device was plugged into a portable pre-amplifier that was disguised as a simple brown leather briefcase. The pre-amp was, in turn, connected to wires that ran to the recording and listening post. This stable link of coaxial cables passed unseen through a special water-proof tunnel, beneath a *pomerium* of stately oak trees in the Vatican Gardens, up the tower walls, and into the recording chamber, per Marconi's clever design.

And it was here—in an inconspicuous ninth-century dragon-toothed pinnacle looming above the Vatican Gardens—where the secret plots of the Holy Father and his extended Church of Spies were forever preserved.

ψψψ

With the preliminaries complete, Pius looked into the eyes of Sir D'Arcy, wondering how much of the ongoing conspiracy he should disclose. He decided to begin with only generalities, and see where that would lead before requesting the British envoy's official support, as he had done in the past two plots to have the Nazi leader removed from power.

"I have been approached again in secret by reliable intermediaries of the German military circle," he began. "There is a new plan afoot. I wanted to brief you on it and see where you and your government might stand in this matter, given the present state of the war. As you are well aware, despite my religious scruples as the Holy Father, I have concluded that Hitler's assassination is a lesser moral evil than the Führer remaining in power."

"I understand, Your Eminence. Are you, this time around, in a position to disclose the identity of the Resistance members?"

"Not at the present. But I can disclose that it is the same group of well-known and important German generals backing the plot, and that they are led by a new and energetic member."

"So the German Resistance has a new leader?"

"Yes. He is a very well respected and admired colonel in the Wehrmacht. But that is all I can tell you, at least for the time being."

"I can appreciate the need for discretion."

"The SS refers to this clandestine network as the 'Black Chapel.' They have already rounded up several high-ranking members of the group and locked them in prison. It is said that they are to be used as bargaining chips in the event of an Allied victory and Axis defeat."

"The Gestapo is merciless. And not just here in Rome."

"Precisely, Minister. They are ruthless. That is why I cannot divulge this officer's name or the names of any of the other conspirators. I could not bear to be the cause of any of these brave men's deaths if any of this should come out. But I can assure you that they are quite powerful, and the new plot is not to be taken lightly. And, as we get closer to an actual target date, I will be able to disclose the names of the actual parties, to ensure that the plot is taken one-hundred-percent seriously by your British government."

"Are you at liberty to brief me on any particulars of the plot and the plans for the post-Hitler government? What I mean to say is has anything changed since the last failed attempt that I should be aware of?"

He felt a little twitch at the word *failed.* The British envoy was talking, of course, about the bomb that had been placed on Hitler's plane last winter. Unfortunately, the explosive device had frozen at high altitude and failed to detonate.

"The only change is that the plotters now recognize that, given the recent Allied victories, the Western powers cannot guarantee the territorial integrity of a post-Hitler Germany. They have, therefore, abandoned pursuit of that objective given the current military situation in the east and here in Italy."

"I see."

"Other than that, there has been no change on the part of the anti-Hitler plotters that I am aware of. Their plan is still to start their coup in Catholic Munich, Cologne, and Vienna rather than in Protestant Berlin, in order to have the strength of numbers behind them. The Reich would have at first two governments, and most likely a civil war largely between those backing the Wehrmacht and those backing the SS. The anti-Hitler Wehrmacht faction would install a military dictatorship that would, once victory was assured, be replaced with a democratic state. Once the new regime could speak with authority, it would make peace. The plan's backers want to know if the British government can back off the Allies 'unconditional surrender' position initiated by Roosevelt to provide the basis for genuine peace talks. The anti-Hitler faction wants an honorable surrender."

Osborne responded only with a delaying nod, and Pius could tell that he needed a moment to process the stunning new information. They fell into a thoughtful silence as the British minister considered the plan. The Pope couldn't help but wonder if he was not risking too much, not only for himself but the Holy See, in continuing to pursue his agenda of removing the Führer from power. After all, what he was doing was without question one of the most dangerous undertakings in the history of the papacy. He had already participated in two plots to kill Hitler, and now he was actively taking part in a third. In the process, he was putting not only his own life, but other lives, in danger. A secret group of German Jesuits were acting under his orders as political organizers, couriers, and cutouts reporting to his closest advisors. Father Leiber and a good many other people from his inner clandestine circle would be in serious jeopardy if his involvement in the ongoing plot to overthrow Hitler was discovered.

"I have to be quite honest, Your Eminence. I remain skeptical that the Germans can deliver."

"It is a gamble to be sure. But they are even more determined to succeed this time. They have had enough of Hitler and his Nazi brutes for ten lifetimes."

"But the new approach is still open to all the old criticisms. It contains no guarantees of authenticity, or of success, or that a new German government will be more trustworthy or less aggressive. And the most vital question—whether the anti-Hitler plotters are willing to commence talks before the coup—appears not to have been given the consideration it deserves. There is also the delicate matter of conveying the plan to the Americans. We might even have to get the French involved, and you know how much London and Washington loathe having to deal with de Gaulle. And as you are also well aware, Roosevelt is even more adamant about unconditional surrender than the prime minister."

"I understand your misgivings, Minister, and realize London and Washington don't see eye to eye on this matter. In my view, unconditional surrender is an obstacle on the path for peace. But make no mistake, the German plotters are determined to succeed this time. The new leadership to which I refer has rejuvenated the Resistance movement, and this time I am confident they will succeed."

"But even if they pull off a successful regime change, Britain and most certainly the United States will never allow the German war machine to be left intact."

"No doubt. But if the coup succeeds, the Wehrmacht faction will voluntarily disarm once the Nazis have been neutralized and civil order is restored."

"I have other concerns as well. If the plotters really want regime change so badly, why don't they simply get on with it? Their situation can't possibly get any worse than it already is with Hitler in power."

"They want British assurances. That is why you and I are talking again about all this, Minister."

"I must admit it seems like déjà vu. As I told you up front during our first two go-arounds, this is going to be a tough sell for His Majesty's Government. And even if we do buy in to the plan, we have to get the Americans to do so, too. They will have to be fully briefed, and only then will we be able to move forward."

"Throughout this conflict, your country and the United States have constantly attempted to get me to publicly and forcefully condemn Nazi Germany. You know that in my heart, I want to do this. But as you know, these requests have been a thorn in my side since the beginning of the war. They have placed a burden on me in my attempts to try and bring about peace as a neutral party above the fray. And yet…and yet I have stood by you. I stood by Roosevelt on Lend-Lease and the Soviets, and I have worked behind the scenes with you, in secret, at grave risk to myself and the Holy See, to try and remove Hitler and his Nazis from power. I just want to bring about peace in this terrible conflict. I ask that you now take this matter to the higher authorities you deem necessary in your government. And please let them know that no one in the Secretariat of State—not even Maglione, Tardini, or Montini—has been told about this plan to remove the Führer. But you, Minister, you have been fully briefed."

"I appreciate the great risk you are taking, Your Holiness. If the Nazis ever found out what you were doing, it would completely destroy the Holy See's official position of neutrality. Even worse, it would confirm Himmler's and Goebbels's suspicions of the Vatican as a den of spies. The prime minister, too, is aware of the grave risk you are taking and applauds you for your efforts."

"I do not care about the risk to me, Minister. I fear what might befall others. But this must be done. Despite the Red Army's recent victories in the east, Nazi Germany still possesses a powerful army that will resist to the bitter end, especially with the uncompromising policy of unconditional surrender and the threat of punishment and retribution hanging over their leaders. Eliminating Hitler seems to me to be the only way to bring this terrible war to an end sooner rather than later. I know that this plot, like the two others before it, is probably doomed to fail. But if there is even one chance in a million of removing Hitler from power, and thereby serving the purpose of sparing lives, then it will have been worth it. My conscience simply cannot allow me to ignore such a possibility, however minuscule."

"I must say, Your Eminence, that your passion in this matter has made an impact on me. From what you have described, the German initiative is perhaps more genuine than I first believed."

"Thank you, Minister."

"By the forceful way you have lobbied for this coup, I can assure you that I will contact London and they will issue a formal response. If the principals in Germany have both the intention and the power to perform what they promise, His Majesty's Government will certainly consider any further inquiries they, with you acting on their behalf, might make."

"Very good, Minister. But I must reemphasize the need for absolute secrecy. As we have agreed upon previously, you must leave no trace of what we have discussed here on paper. Except what you choose to report of tonight's meeting to your superiors in London."

"I promise I will draft the letter myself and will make no copy."

"And Maglione, Tardini, and Montini must know nothing. The maestro will contact you to follow up in a fortnight."

Osborne rose from his seat, realizing that the meeting was concluded. "This means a great deal to you, I realize, Your Eminence. But remember, removing Hitler from power and obtaining peace is what we both want."

"If it can save lives from this abominable war that has robbed us of our humanity, then it needs to be done." The Chief then looked towards the ceiling. "In the name of the Holy Father, it needs to be done."

CHAPTER 28

CINEMA BARBERINI, ROME
DECEMBER 18, 1943

TERESA LOOKED THROUGH the light December drizzle at the cinema door for the hundredth time, feeling the imminent danger of what she was about to do. She crossed herself and prayed, appealing to the Holy Father, as she summoned all her courage and tried to exorcise her self-doubt. She had never killed anyone before and hoped that, when the moment of truth came, she would not lose her nerve.

She reminded herself again to be calm and methodical. She could not allow her emotions—or the fact that she was about to kill actual human beings with lovers, friends, and families—to affect either her judgment or execution. She was part of the Resistance now, and her comrades in the *Gruppi di Azione Patriottica* had to know that they could rely upon her to carry out an attack with no slip-ups to help drive the German occupiers from the city.

She looked down at her hands; to her dismay they were trembling. How would she be able to steer her bicycle and accurately fire her Sten when her hands were shaking?

She took a deep breath to steel herself, keeping her eyes fixed on the cinema door. *Damnit, why is it taking so long?* The film should have been over by now, and the Germans should have been walking out into the street and climbing back into their transports to return to their barracks.

She looked down the street at her comrade Giuseppe Valenti, nicknamed Beppo, hiding out in the shadows of the doorway across the street. The plan was for him to launch the initial attack from the north by riding in on his bicycle and tossing a *spezzone*—a homemade TNT-filled pipe bomb—at the Germans as they exited the Cinema Barberini and piled into their vans and trucks. Film showings were held twice weekly at the cinema exclusively for the occupying troops before they left for the front. The plan called for attacking the Germans when they were relaxed after having enjoyed themselves at the movie. Once Beppo's opening *spezzone* attack was launched, Teresa would peddle in on her bicycle from the opposite direction and open fire with her Sten, finishing off the wounded and killing as many more as possible while the Germans were momentarily crippled and thrown into disarray by the bomb. The key to the attack was complete surprise. Suppressing cover fire would be provided by Roberto and Vincenzo, who were across the street from the cinema and out of sight. It was their job to open fire on the Germans if they somehow figured out in advance what was happening and shot at Beppo and Teresa, and also to cover their retreat.

She looked at her watch and again muttered under her breath: *Where are the*

Germans? The film should have ended ten minutes ago. Was the cinema showing a second film tonight for some reason?

And then suddenly they were there.

At first, it was merely a handful of regular soldiers in gray uniforms, the raw troops that had recently been brought up and were about to be shipped off to the southern front. They laughed and joked as they stepped out into the cool December night, pausing outside the cinema to light up cigarettes and talk. But the number swiftly grew to a dozen soldiers…then two dozen, three dozen, and finally close to fifty men, the ranks filled by not only enlisted men but Wehrmacht officers and even SS officers wearing black uniforms with death's-head insignia like her father wore.

My God, she thought with sudden horror, was it possible that her father was here? What would she do if she saw him? Would she freeze up, or kill him where he stood with her Sten? Or would Beppo get him first with an exploding bomb?

She felt a surge of dread at the thought.

But there was no time for emotion.

Beppo had already mounted his bicycle and now started peddling towards one of the vans that a large number of German soldiers were starting to pile into. In the darkness, Teresa could tell that the driver and soldiers were preoccupied with their joking and laughter and hadn't noticed him approaching yet. The vehicle looked like it would hold fifteen men. With all of the Germans packed into the tight space, it would be a massacre.

Taking a deep breath to steady her nerves, she set off on her bike with the Sten resting on the handlebars.

It was then she saw her father step out of the cinema.

She felt her legs abruptly stop peddling, as if they had a will of their own. For an instant on the slippery street, she lost control of the bicycle and almost crashed into a wild cat that had suddenly appeared out of nowhere. But she was able to recover her balance and keep peddling. *What should I do?* But she already knew the answer. She could not botch her part of the mission and leave her comrade Beppo to do the job all alone. She had to finish the attack in accordance with the plan. If that meant killing her father, the enemy, then so be it.

With renewed determination, she picked up her pace, riding hard towards the Germans, her legs pumping furiously.

She saw Beppo pull up next to the van boarding the soldiers to take them back to their barracks. From the pocket of his raincoat, he exposed the upper part of the bulky, one-kilogram-TNT *spezzone* so he could light the fuse; he then lit the fuse while the bomb was still half-concealed in his pocket. The *spezzone* contained an eight-second fuse so Teresa needed to time it perfectly by hitting the Germans from the south no more than a few seconds after the initial blast when they were still in a state of disorganized panic. If she was too early, she might alert the Germans; if too late, they might have recovered from their initial shock and open fire on her.

She again accelerated. As she did, she stole a look at her father. His back was to her, but she could tell it was him by his uniform and the way he stood and smoked his cigarette. To her horror, he began walking towards the van.

My God, she thought, *is he about to be blown to bits before my very eyes?*

She suddenly felt a sickening feeling inside and wanted to warn him.

She peddled faster.

Next to the van, Beppo started to pull the half-concealed *spezzone* from the pocket of his raincoat. But when he tried to free it, the bomb got tangled in the lining of his jacket. Teresa could see his mind frantically working. For a desperate moment, she had an apocalyptic vision that he would give up and simply rush into the Germans—the bomb, his bike, and all.

Then he somehow managed to rip the sizzling bomb free, toss it beneath the gas tank on the underbelly of the van, and pedal briskly away.

She saw her father raise his hand and call out for Beppo to stop as he stepped towards the window of the van.

"No, Father, get out of there!" she screamed in German.

His head turned towards her and their eyes met.

But it wasn't her father at all! It was an officer that, in his black uniform, merely looked like him!

Now that she was closer, she could see now that the man was slightly younger than her father and didn't actually look that much like him, though their builds were very similar. With his SS cap pulled down low over his eyes, the dark SS uniform, and the poor illumination outside the cinema, his face had been obscured and she hadn't gotten as good a look at him as she had thought.

The bomb went off.

The blast shook the street and the van burst into flames, sending up a fireball that lit the Baroque façade of the cinema in brilliant hues. The windows of the cinema and buildings on either side blew out, spewing glass in all directions like flak.

Feeling the searing heat of the blast on her face, Teresa saw instantly that at least a dozen Germans, including the man she had mistaken for her father, had to have been killed or severely injured by the explosion. Those that hadn't been decimated by the initial blast were stumbling from the burning van on fire. In a fraction of a second, the peaceful street and sidewalk had turned to complete pandemonium as soldiers ran for their lives, knocked one another down, dove to the pavement, and screamed out in holy terror.

"*Mein Gott! Ich sterben! Helft mir!*" Teresa heard a burning officer shriek as he fell to the ground and struggled along with two soldiers to put out the flames. *My God! I'm dying! Help me!*

She couldn't believe her eyes and felt a wave of revulsion. If this was war, did she really want to be part of something like this?

Then she saw an officer with a Luger spot the retreating Beppo and take aim at him with the weapon.

She had to protect Beppo, who was peddling desperately to make his getaway down a side street.

The officer opened fire, his pistol crackling into the night above the screams of the burning and wounded.

Teresa charged in on her bicycle from the south, gripping the trigger of her Sten to fire.

Abruptly, the German officer turned towards her as he heard her coming from the opposite direction. Their eyes met. There was a split second of uncertainty as he recognized that she was a woman and tried to gauge whether she posed a threat or not. Then, erring on the side of caution, he turned towards her and opened up with his Luger.

She felt a momentary sense of panic as she realized the element of surprise was lost and she and Beppo might both be killed. Then, summoning a calm she didn't know she possessed, she took aim with her Sten with her right hand, while continuing to guide the bicycle with her left, as she had spent hours training to do. The British-made Sten Mark II 9-mm submachine gun was the weapon of choice for Resistance fighters in Occupied Europe. It had a compact barrel, light weight of seven pounds, and 32-round detachable box magazine that could be fed from the underside of the weapon. Easily concealed beneath a jacket and at night able to blend in with the frame of a bicycle, the only drawback of the weapon was that it tended to jam at the most inopportune moments.

Like right now.

She squeezed the trigger, but nothing happened. The Sten had failed to feed due to a jammed cartridge in the magazine and the damned gun didn't fire.

She cursed her miserable luck.

The German let loose again with his Luger. Forced to swerve the bicycle to avoid being hit, Teresa very nearly crashed.

She felt a burst of adrenaline seize hold of her body and suddenly felt out of breath. Fearing for her life, she tried to fire again, but the weapon was still jammed.

You've got to be kidding me!

The Luger spurted again.

The bullet tore through her baggy coat, just missing her midsection. It was only because she was a fast-moving target on a bicycle that she hadn't yet been hit.

Her only chance was to unjam the Sten while she rode and then return fire.

Removing her left hand from the handlebar and guiding the bicycle only with her legs, she quickly and expertly yanked out the magazine, tapped the base of the magazine against her knee, re-inserted the magazine, recocked the weapon, and took aim as she had been trained to do when the gun jammed.

Then she squeezed the trigger, and this time the Sten fired.

She took down the officer with a spray of bullets. There was a spurt of blood, his body stiffened, and the Luger dropped harmlessly to the sidewalk. She swung the Sten over and unloaded at a clump of German officers that had jerked out their pistols and were attempting to sight her and Beppo. She saw two more go down just as Roberto and Vincenzo stepped in to deliver suppressing cover fire from the south. With the Germans dodging and ducking the barrage, she took a hard left onto the cross street. Once she made the turn, she emptied her magazine in a final delaying-action burst over her shoulder, gripping the wheel with her left hand. As she rode away, she crouched down low like a Siena *Palio* rider, presenting as small a target as possible to the enemy as the bullets plucked after her in the darkness.

As she clattered down the street, she nearly ran over an old man who had stepped out under a street lamp and witnessed the attack.

Perhaps noticing her fair complexion, blonde hair, blue eyes, and British Sten gun in the light of the street lamp, the old man cried out encouragingly, "*Bravo, Inglesina! Bravo!*" while waving his arms in triumph.

Recovering her balance, she rode on. When she was three blocks away and had caught up with Beppo with still no one following them, she had two thoughts. The first was that what she had done was inhumane and sickening. The second—and far more overpowering—was self-acknowledgement that she was a true Resistance fighter now. Having nearly been killed and taking down several of the enemy in combat, she had most assuredly earned her stripes.

She even had a new partisan name.

From this point forward, she would be the *Inglesina*.

The English Girl.

CHAPTER 29

VILLA NAPOLEON

DECEMBER 19, 1943

"THE OLD MAN died, you say, before you could finish the interrogation? Is that what you're telling me? So you don't even know why she is called the *Inglesina*? Now that could have been useful information."

Hollmann let his words resonate and allowed his glare to linger on Pietro Koch, head of the Fascist *Reparto Speciale di Polizia*—Special Police Unit—better known as the *Banda Koch*, or the Koch Gang. The man was dressed in his customary foppish civilian suit and his hair was matted down with a thick coat of brilliantine. With orders from the highest police official in the new Mussolini puppet regime, the twenty-five-year-old adventurer was an ex-army officer of the Grenadiers of Sardinia and product of mixed Italian and German ancestry who spoke both languages fluently. He had only recently arrived in the city to lead a new anti-Resistance Fascist police force to rival the Gestapo in rounding up undesirables and subjecting them to brutal truth-through-torture techniques. In the short span of the past week, Hollmann had already discovered first-hand that the man was nothing but a loose cannon and violent thug who should have been behind bars.

"The old man said she had fair skin, light hair, and blue eyes and that is why he called her the *Inglesina*," said Koch in a defensive tone.

"Yes, but why the English Girl?" fired back Hollmann, concealing his irritation behind a scholarly expression. "There are many fair-skinned, light-haired, blue-eyed Romans with mixed blood. No, it must have been something else. Did she speak to him in a British accent? Was it her British Sten gun? Did the old man once live in England and know what British are like? Did he get a look at the man on the bicycle who threw the bomb? These are the types of questions that would have been good to have answers to *before* our elderly detained witness expired. Normally when a man is coughing up blood from his lungs, it is a good time to stop an interrogation. *Capiche*?"

Koch's eyes narrowed with indignation. The self-titled "Doctor" who had not one iota of medical training thought himself an important man, a conquering hero returning to Rome, and didn't appreciate being talked to this way. But Hollmann didn't give a damn if he had offended the bastard. Though the self-proclaimed doctor was in essence an ally, Hollmann didn't trust him, nor did he approve of his regrettable combination of stupidity, overzealousness, and brutality, the latter of which appeared to exceed even that of the Torquemada of Via Tasso seated next to him. But Hollmann knew Koch and Priebke would both serve a useful purpose in the coming days as informants, as the *Banda Koch* and the Gestapo began their joint large-scale crackdown on the recent partisan attacks. And General Wolff wanted eyes and ears on the ground close to the action. Everyone in the city, including the Pope, knew there was going to be some form of retaliation for the recent attacks.

There had been three of them in only the past two days. On December 17, an important German officer had been shot at point-blank range on the streets of Rome in broad daylight and his briefcase stolen from him. He died on the way to the hospital, and the contents of his briefcase were taken by the partisans, including detailed maps and blueprints of power and communications grids used in German antiaircraft emplacements in and around Rome. Then yesterday on the 18th there had been two attacks. The first was a *spezzone* bombing at a favorite trattoria of the Germans and Fascists near a German command post and barracks in the Prati district, in which eight German soldiers were killed. The second was the attack at the Cinema Barberini by the *Inglesina* and her male accomplices that resulted in the death of eight German soldiers and the serious wounding of fifteen others. In Hollmann's view, the three bold strikes by the partisans in the most heavily fortified parts of the *centro storico* represented a coordinated attempt to drive the German Army from Rome.

In response, Kappler and Koch intended to retaliate in kind with a massive counterattack against the Roman Resistance to deal it a crippling blow.

He looked at Priebke. "Captain, did you and Dr. Koch canvas the neighborhood around the cinema a second time to find out if anyone else saw anything? The attack claimed nearly twenty-five casualties. Someone must have seen something, and a second pass-through can often lead to new eyewitnesses."

"I canvassed the neighborhood and thoroughly questioned the people," Koch answered for him. "No one but the old man saw anything."

Hollmann looked at him sharply. "You're quite certain?"

"Yes, I am certain."

"Then you are a fool. Because of your stupidity, the key eyewitness in the cinema attack is dead. How's this for an idea? Why doesn't Captain Priebke here host you as his personal guest for a few nights at Via Tasso? I'm sure he'd be more than happy to set you up with your own soundproofed room and show you some of his special techniques. The Captain, as you know, has developed something of a reputation in our fair city for his expertise, which it seems you are only too eager to emulate. The difference is, Captain Priebke knows how to inflict the maximum amount of pain possible, while still managing to keep his victims alive for weeks or even months, rather than have them die right away like your poor old man. That is because, unlike you, he is a true master of the dark arts. Though you should know that I, from first-hand experience, find his particular skill set unsettling."

At this, the good "Doctor" visibly paled and his eyes fell to the floor.

Hollmann smiled bloodlessly. "I can see that it has finally dawned on you, Dr. Koch, that *we*—not you—are the ones in charge of the Eternal City."

"I apologize for my rudeness, Herr Hollmann," the now-cowed head of the Fascist political police squad mumbled meekly. "I wasn't thinking."

"Indeed you weren't, but like me, you have mixed Italian and German blood so one cannot expect miracles. In any case, I accept your apology." He reached across his desk for a coiled Jurassic ammonite, originally discovered by Pliny the Elder near Pompeii, and idly looked it over while leaning back in his high-backed leather chair. "Now, Dr. Koch, since you will be working together with us and will require our cooperation to combat these new partisan threats, I would like to know if you have any specific ideas or approaches moving forward. It is clear that a message needs to be sent to the partisans. Messages can be very persuasive—if properly administered. Too harsh a response and you turn the people of Rome violently against you. Too little and you look weak and incompetent and the enemy comes after you more aggressively. I can tell you, officially, that General Wolff wants a measured but decisive response, and he wants to make sure that I am personally kept in the loop on all planned activities in this regard. I am, as always, his eyes and ears here in Rome."

Koch nodded and gave a knowing smile. "I did have one idea."

"Yes, Pietro, what is it? I can see a light bulb has gone off in that brain of yours."

"I was thinking of hitting the Vatican's extraterritorial properties."

He raised an eyebrow. "Come again, *Herr Doktor*?"

"I have reviewed the plan with my men. It calls for a mass roundup at the off-site Vatican properties that are under the protection of the Curia."

"You're referring to the residences with protected extraterritorial status."

"Yes, Colonel. We both know that many influential anti-Fascists, military officers, labor leaders, and Jews who escaped the October roundup are being harbored on these properties."

Hollmann couldn't believe that Koch had come up with such a bold idea all by himself.

"Go on, Pietro. For once you seem to have captivated my attention."

"We would start off by hitting the Seminario Romano. It is next to the Basilica of San Giovanni in Laterano and is the main hiding place of many anti-Fascist elites. We have reason to believe that Ivanoe Bonomi is there."

"Ivanoe Bonomi, the head of the CLN?"

"Yes, and not only him, but the heads of four of the other six parties in the Resistance coalition. There are also many prominent Jews hiding out there."

"I am well aware of the prominent enemies of the Führer and Il Duce hiding at the Seminario Romano and other Vatican extraterritorial properties. What intrigues me is that you think you can just knock down the door, barge in, and start hauling away Roman citizens from these properties without any adverse diplomatic repercussions. Are you unaware of the fragile relationship between the Vatican and the German consulate here in Rome? The criminal elements you have described are hiding out in these properties precisely because they are safe there."

"No, they just *think* they are safe."

Hollmann stared at him for a long moment. Then he rose from his chair, went to the window, and stared down from his well-appointed corner office at a newspaper blowing down the empty street. "I'm afraid you are wrong, Dr. Koch. They *are* safe there. The Führer and General Wolff have both made it clear that the

Vatican and its extraterritorial properties are not to be tampered with—at least for the time being. But what is fair game and not safe for Rome's anti-Fascist Badogliani are the off-site Vatican-controlled properties that are recognized by treaty, but do not have extraterritorial status. If you strike anywhere it should be there. They most certainly won't be expecting it."

"All right, assuming me and my men lead the raid, what will the German involvement be?"

Hollmann looked at Priebke.

"Colonel Kappler has informed me that you will lead the raid, Dr. Koch," answered the captain. "You and your Special Police Unit will be in charge from start to finish. The SS must be seen as having no involvement whatsoever in either the planning or execution of the raid. We have to at least pretend to respect the sovereignty of the Holy See. But I will be on hand as a plainclothed observer along with a few of my men."

"Very well, that sounds like a plan," said Koch, grinning like the overzealous psychopath every instinct told Hollmann the man was. He couldn't help but wonder what General Wolff had gotten him into? Could this brutal miscreant before him be counted on to keep the SS's involvement a secret and not botch the job? With the Koch Gang turned loose on the anti-Fascists, there was bound to be excessive violence and destruction of property. In that case, the raid could utterly backfire. He could very well be blamed by Himmler and Wolff for overstepping his authority by failing to respect Vatican neutrality and sovereignty.

"To avoid upsetting current diplomatic relations, what properties would you prefer that we hit, Colonel?" asked Priebke, as if reading his mind.

"I was thinking of the Seminario Lombardo, the Pontifical Institute of Oriental Studies, and the Russicum Institute. Those are the religious institutions next to the Basilica of Santa Maria Maggiore. Our intelligence indicates that many high profile ex-soldiers, Bolsheviks, Jews, and other enemies of the Reich are hiding out there. Consider this the opening salvo in our war to purge the Resistance from our fair city."

"I can't wait," said Koch, his dark beady eyes gleaming with the icy fire of a true zealot. "When do we hit them?"

The question was left hanging as a hard knock sounded on the door.

"Yes, what is it?" snapped Hollmann, irritated at the interruption.

His aide, Lieutenant Vogel, poked his head in. "Colonel, I apologize for the intrusion, but it seems there has been another bombing attack."

Hollmann shook his head in indignation. "Where this time?"

"It happened fifteen minutes ago at the Hotel Flora. Seven men have been killed and more than fifteen have been wounded, including two staff at the hotel."

"The Hotel Flora? But that can't be. The security there is the best in Rome." In fact, because the Flora was the headquarters not only of the German High Command but also the German War Tribunal, it was ringed with multiple checkpoints, mounted police, and heavy machine-gun nests that should have rendered the hotel an impregnable fortress. "How many partisans were there this time, and just how the hell did they penetrate our checkpoints?"

"There were four of them and they rode in on bicycles."

"Bicycles again? Was the *inglesina* among them?"

"No, the guard doesn't think so. But one of the four was a woman."

"My God, we're being picked off by fucking women?" snorted Koch. "This is an outrage!"

"Don't worry, we will make them pay for this," said Priebke.

Hollmann wanted more details. "How many bombs this time?"

"They set off three pipe bombs, but only two blew up. The ground floor of the hotel was devastated."

"My God, this is outright war." He looked up at his aide. "Thank you, Lieutenant. Please have my chauffeur bring up my car. I want to take a look at the crime scene."

"*Jawohl, Herr Colonel,*" and he was gone.

Hollmann looked at Priebke and Koch. "Very well, gentlemen, we all know the plan. We will strike at the Seminario Lombardo, the Pontifical Institute, and the Russicum Institute. A firm reprisal where they least expect it and think they are safe is the only thing that might actually deter these partisans."

"Do you think the Vatican will make a public protest?" asked Priebke.

"Did the Pope protest the October roundup?"

"Well, no, at least not publicly. But there was concern that he might."

"Yes, but in the end he said absolutely nothing on Vatican Radio or in *L'Osservatore Romano*. Based on his past behavior, I would wager that he will again not make a formal public denunciation."

"Or perhaps this time," countered Priebke, "Pius will surprise us all and actually lift a finger to protect his children, the good *and* bad citizens of Rome. In any case, if he again does nothing, then we will know that when the time comes we can push him even further."

"Why you make it sound as if he's Hitler's Pope," said Koch.

Hollmann shook his head. "No, he is most certainly not that. But this policy of silence when he is vested with the authority of God to protect the weak and helpless is mind-boggling. But perhaps this time, *he* will speak out publicly and we will all be sent off to a labor camp for overstepping *our* authority."

Priebke and Koch fell into silence as they mulled over the disturbing possibility. Hollmann wondered how the Pope and people of Rome would react to the raid. Would they be active or passive this time? Which way would His Holy Eminence go? Would he protest and make things difficult for the occupiers, or continue his pattern of careful silence when his own Roman citizens were being rounded up and incarcerated? Would the planned raid on the Vatican-administered properties be a lightning rod that would result in more violence and chaos?

Koch broke the silence. "When will we hit them, Colonel?"

"On Tuesday," said Hollmann. "We will hit them on Tuesday. And remember, when it's all over the SS were never there."

"Don't worry, Colonel," said the self-proclaimed "Doctor" and ruthless leader of the Koch Gang. "Nothing bad is going to happen. It's going to be a walk in the park."

CHAPTER 30

SEMINARIO LOMBARDO DECEMBER 21, 1943

IT WAS 10 P.M., well after curfew, and Teresa and Peter Savoyan were drenched from the rain. After rapping on the brass door knockers in the prearranged signal for the fourth time and not receiving a response, she glanced again worriedly at the head of OSS-Rome. Then she nervously scanned the street outside the Seminario Lombardo, searching for the prying eyes of the SS or Italian Police. It was taking too long for someone to answer the door. Even under the concealment of a dark rainy night, she didn't like being out after curfew. She felt vulnerable and exposed. Though the streets were deserted and she couldn't spot anyone suspicious, she had the feeling they were being watched.

Or was it her imagination?

She had cropped her hair short and dyed it black. But even so, since her and Beppo's attack two nights ago at Cinema Barberini, she had been seeing Gestapo agents and Fascist *Polizia* lurking in every doorway. She was still coming to grips with the paranoia and secrecy—not to mention the violence—of being an undercover Resistance fighter. Then again, the whole city was on edge after the four recent attacks that had claimed the lives of more than thirty German soldiers and wounding of dozens more, including a handful of innocent Roman bystanders that happened to be at the wrong place at the wrong time. Only this morning, the Nazi occupiers had issued another punitive ordinance bringing the curfew down to 7 p.m. and prohibiting the use of bicycles after 5 p.m.

She looked up at the warning placard posted next to the door printed in Italian and German. It read: "This building serves religious objectives, and is a dependency of the Vatican City. All searches and requisitions are prohibited." The notice was signed by General Rainer Stahel, the German Military Commandant of Rome, and had been posted on ecclesiastical buildings throughout the city, including the Pontifical Institute of Oriental Studies and Russicum Institute next door. Tucked away safely inside the seminary, beyond the placard, were some two-hundred powerful enemies of the Nazis and Fascists, including her father and other ex-military figures. Peter Savoyan was about to join them. She was moving him to what they hoped was a safer location than the one he had just been forced to vacate, due to a nosy apartment neighbor looking to make some extra lira as a Gestapo informant. Unfortunately, with the whole city on edge from the recent partisan attacks, Teresa knew that placards alone would hardly keep the police from banging down doors and dragging people in for questioning at Via Tasso or Regina Coeli—the infamous Queen of Heaven Prison.

The door cracked opened and the face of a young priest appeared. "Quickly, come inside," he instructed them once he recognized Teresa.

She cast a furtive glance around once more to make sure the coast was clear and they ducked inside. The priest threw the lock and led them through the rear of the chapel, where mass was being held and several nuns in steel-blue habits with ample skirts and wide-winged coifs were praying before a large crucifix of Christ and an open coffin. From there, they headed down a passageway past several simply furnished ecclesiastical rooms and finally to a "secret room" in the cellar. There they found Teresa's father Colonel Di Domenico and Father O'Flaherty sitting on an intricately carved wooden bench talking. The young priest closed the door and left them.

"Is it safe to meet in a basement?" she asked. "Only one way in and out."

Smiling knowingly, her father stood up, stepped to an oversized triptych in the style of Fra Angelico, and felt along the panel on the right, releasing some sort of lever. The panel slowly retracted to open into a hidden doorway that led to a narrow passageway and a winding metal staircase. To Teresa's surprise, the stairway appeared to ascend several floors of the seminary.

"That is our escape route should the need arise," said her father jovially. "But of course, it won't be necessary for such theatrics since our esteemed Father O'Flaherty here has what is known as 'the luck of the Irish.' Nothing bad ever happens when he is around."

"That's good to know," said Savoyan. He stepped forward and offered his hand to the bulbous-nosed monsignor, who wore his usual steel-rimmed spectacles, cloak, sash, and wide-rimmed black hat. "I'm Lieutenant Savoyan of the OSS. Thank you for making the arrangements for me to stay here for a few days until I can locate safe lodgings."

"The pleasure's all mine, Lieutenant. I know the Germans and Koch's new Special Police Unit aren't making life easy for anyone. One half of Rome may be successfully harboring the other half in these perilous times, but it is still a living hell and daily struggle for survival for us all."

"Please sit," said the colonel.

They all took seats at the wooden table in the center of the room. It was covered with a tablecloth, pair of candles, a pitcher of iron-tainted water, and four glasses. Her father looked at Savoyan.

"What news do you have of the Allied advance on the Winter Line?"

"You didn't know? The Fifth Army is marching on Monte Cassino."

"That is good news. But they still won't be here by Christmas as Mr. Churchill guaranteed."

"No, they won't be here by Christmas. The prime minister should never have suggested otherwise. It is a hard slog through those mountains in winter."

"Blustery fellow, that Churchill," said Father O'Flaherty with a devilish grin. The Irishman was known to take digs at the British whenever possible, having lived through the "Irish Trouble" in the 20s and 30s. "But what I'd like to know is the word on the streets after these recent partisan attacks? The Pope and all of us at the Vatican would hate for there to be reprisals against innocents."

Teresa looked at him with a trace of defiance. "If you want to know the mood of the city, then I shall tell you. The partisans have made it quite clear that they will not accept Nazi blackmail as an option."

"That type of thinking tends to get innocent people hurt, my dear."

"That may be. But to not attack the Germans and Fascists for fear of reprisal is to renounce the struggle from the outset—and that *we* will not do."

As soon as the words left her mouth, she realized she had given herself away and they would know she had taken part in the recent partisan attacks. Her father and O'Flaherty were looking at her intently. She had known the other night at Cinema Barberini that she had crossed a line and there was no going back. She felt different now, liberated and fiercely determined, and she knew it showed on her face, indeed in her whole manner. She had long been disenchanted with her coddled aristocratic life, and joining the Resistance and fighting for the Risorgimento was her way of rebelling against authority and gaining her freedom.

She was a true partisan now. Not only that, she had been blooded. And her father and Monsignor O'Flaherty knew it.

"You were there, weren't you?" said the colonel accusingly.

She said nothing.

"You don't have to say a word. I can see it in your eyes."

She looked away, maintaining her silence. Now Father O'Flaherty was looking at her worriedly.

"What have you done, Teresa?" asked her father.

It was several seconds before she spoke. Then, in a soft voice filled with restrained but evident pride, she recounted the attack at the cinema from beginning to end. When she was finished, the room was silent for a full minute. It was the monsignor who broke the silence.

"Heavenly child, if what you say is true then that means you are the *Inglesina* that everyone is talking about."

Her father's mouth fell open. "You? You're the *Inglesina*? Do you realize what you have done? The Germans will not stop until they destroy you. There is already a one-hundred-thousand lira reward out on your head."

"Dear Lord, that's nearly seven thousand dollars," said Savoyan. "At that price, I may have to turn you in myself."

"This is no joking matter," interjected her father, his owlish brows turned downward and his mouth creased into a frown. "Teresa, do you know how serious this is? These attacks have already stirred up a hornet's nest. From a credible source in the Swiss Legation, Father O'Flaherty has learned that the SS police forces in Rome are about to be increased from four hundred men to two thousand. Two thousand! Because of these attacks, the Gestapo and this new Koch Gang are going to punish many innocent people. They will be busting down doors, rounding up anyone without a German accent, and sending them to labor camps. Or torturing them at Via Tasso or Coeli Prison. If you think the roundups of the Jews and *carabinieri* were bad, wait until you see this. This is going to be all-out war and the city will be torn apart. Is that what you want, to see Rome destroyed?"

That was the wrong question to be asking, Teresa thought. The real question was why hadn't every Italian united to drive the Germans out of their country. For the next few minutes, she and her father argued bitterly, with Father O'Flaherty and Peter Savoyan occasionally putting in their two cents and eventually forcing a truce. Teresa found her father infuriating. Of course, she wanted to help save her beloved city from destruction. But the reality was the Germans had taken over Rome, were in no way respecting its Open City status, and had to be stopped. She was not about to be told what to do. As a GAP operative, she was an integral part of a fighting army—an army that was every bit as important to defeating the Nazis as those on the front lines. In her eyes, she was on equal footing with Peter Savoyan working for the OSS, her brother fighting for the Fifth Army, and her father carrying out the struggle on behalf of the Military Front. She had one duty and that was to keep on fighting—not for the ineffectual Badoglio or the Pope, but for Mother Italy and the Risorgimento.

Now that was something worth fighting for!

Suddenly, the young priest reappeared, this time at the doorway to the secret passageway.

"Come, you must leave," he said with quiet urgency. "The police are here."

"The police?" asked Father O'Flaherty. "But this is a Vatican property. The seminary and all the buildings around it are protected."

Her father shot Teresa a sharp look. "After recent events, it appears not." He turned back to the priest. "How many of them are there?"

"The building is totally surrounded. I would say there are at least fifty men. A dozen have just barged their way onto the premises, including the leader who identified himself as Pietro Koch. He claims to be the head of the Special Police Force and said he is looking for enemies of the state: army deserters, criminals, Communists, and Jews. I saw them come in from the second floor balcony. They fooled us by having a fake priest knock on the door."

"So it is the *Fascista*, not the Gestapo? Are you sure that the Gestapo aren't with them?"

"I didn't see any SS uniforms. But they could be wearing regular clothes."

"Shit, it *is* the *Banda Koch*," cried Teresa. "I know now why I had a bad feeling when we first got here."

"Don't curse like that," grumbled her father. "It is not ladylike."

"I'll curse whenever I want to. I am a soldier just like you. And if there's one thing I know about soldiers, it is that they curse. A lot."

"Well, I don't like it. But what's even worse is that you have led the police here. You and the lieutenant were not vigilant and must have been followed."

"With all due respect, Colonel," countered Savoyan, "we didn't lead anyone anywhere. We were not followed—I made damn sure of that."

"And so did I," said Teresa.

Suddenly, a thumping and crashing sound and terrified screams could be heard coming from the floor above.

"Quick, my friends," said the young priest gravely. "They are tearing the place apart and rounding people up. We must hurry."

CHAPTER 31

SEMINARIO LOMBARDO

DECEMBER 21, 1943

WHEN THEY REACHED the third floor, they had to sneak back through the passageway into the main building since the secret escape route didn't go to the fourth floor. As they stepped into a corridor, a terrified nun came running up to them.

"The police have removed the rector from his study. They are swarming the seminary, Colonel. You must leave at once or they will capture you."

"We will take the fourth floor bridge to the Institute. Can you delay the police?"

Suddenly, a voice down the hallway sounded in fluent Italian. "Halt! What are you doing?"

They came to a stop. Teresa's eyes shot down the corridor. It was the head of the Koch Gang himself—his dark corvine face, thickly brilliantined hair, and dandy gray suit lending no doubt that it was the infamous Doctor Koch in the flesh. The man had only been in town for ten days and already he and his Special Police Unit had struck fear in the hearts of Romans to rival Kappler and his Gestapo. According to CLN reports, Pietro Koch and his band of ruthless outlaw officers had already hunted down more than fifty Jews, Communists, and known anti-Fascists and were subjecting them to brutal torture and interrogation. Moving in his wake were several uniformed policemen and four men in civilian clothing, making up a small but well-armed attack force. Teresa recognized Kappler's number two, Erich Priebke, among them wearing plain-clothed *Fascisti* attire. She knew exactly who they were because she and Beppo had seen them just last week at the Hotel Excelsior having a drink with her German father Colonel Hollman, Kappler, and the new commandant of Rome and replacement for General Stahel, General Mälzer.

"Stop where you are! Do not move!" commanded Koch a second time, and this time he pulled out his gun.

Seeing her father reach for his Beretta that he kept concealed under his waist belt, Teresa started to make a move for her own gun.

"No, Colonel," whispered Father O'Flaherty, gripping him by the gun hand. "There can be no shooting in the seminary. We cannot give the authorities a reason to raid without impunity. The Pope will issue a strong protest to this treaty violation."

Koch, Priebke, and their men stepped warily towards her and the others, pistols trained on their chests.

"If we stay here, the police will lock us up and torture us, or send us to labor camps," said her father. "We need to make a run for it."

O'Flaherty gave a fatalistic smile. "On three then."

"You all go to the bridge. I will lead them back down to the cellar," said the young priest.

"I will go with you," said Teresa. "We need to split up and force Koch and his gang to do the same."

"Stay where you are!" Pietro Koch warned again, his gun trained on her father, whom he seemed to recognize now that he was closer.

"Shit, he knows who you are," she whispered.

"I thought I told you not to curse. It is not ladylike."

"And I told you I am a soldier just like you and will curse whenever I want."

"We've got to go—our time is up," said Savoyan. "One, two…"

On three Savoyan, her father, and O'Flaherty dashed for the stairs that led to the fourth floor bridge across to the Institute, while Teresa and the young priest broke left down a branching hallway. As the priest slid open the panel that led back to the secret passageway, he and Teresa both looked back at their pursuers. Priebke and three other men, who, like him appeared to be Gestapo agents wearing civilian Italian attire, had chosen to pursue her, while Koch and the others had gone after her father's group, which the good doctor no doubt considered the bigger game. Priebke yelled, "Halt!" in surprisingly fluent Italian, and when they didn't, he opened fire with his Mauser pistol.

The bullet screamed past her ear and thunked into the wall, exploding stucco chunks and dust. Teresa blew out a sigh of relief that the bullet had missed, but then she realized that she and the priest were cornered unless they could slip inside the secret passageway and close the door behind them.

What should I do? Take my chances with surrender, or make a run for it?

The priest held up his hands in surrender. "Please don't shoot." Then to her he whispered: "Go on into the passageway, my child. God has chosen this for me. You must save yourself. I will seal off the panel behind you and buy you perhaps a minute or two. Go now!"

Another bullet rang out, whistling past and driving into the stucco wall.

"Stay where you are!"

The priest started walking towards Priebke and his men, momentarily blocking her from their view. She ducked into the secret passageway, closed the door behind her, took a hard right, and hurried down the winding stairs, taking them four at a time in frantic leaps and bounds. Behind her, she heard shouting voices as the priest was being berated for aiding her escape.

On the second floor, she turned off and dashed through a separate narrow passageway. Reaching the end, she came to a paneled secret door that led to the chapel the young priest had led her and Savoyan through upon their arrival. She opened the door.

The chapel was now filled with more than twenty people—including a priest, four nuns, and close to two dozen seminarians or men posing as seminarians—participating in a prayer service. Thankfully, there were no enemy policemen.

But behind her now, she heard the heavy thumping of the boots of Priebke and his men. The young priest had bought her only a brief respite, just as he had said, and they were coming up fast behind her.

She had to make a quick decision whether to hide or try to outrun them.

In the third row of the chapel, one of the nuns called out to her, "Quick, over here! We will hide you!"

She dashed over to them, passing on her way the priest in his vestments making a sermon and the formerly empty open casket that now held the body of a dead man. The nuns rose to their feet, pulled up their ample skirts, and quickly instructed her to crawl down onto the floor and hide beneath them.

Feeling her heart thundering in her chest, she dropped to the floor of the pew as instructed, making sure that she was completely covered by the lengthy black habits of the four sisters. When she was fully concealed, the priest returned to his sermon.

But his voice abruptly stopped as Priebke and his men stomped into the chapel.

"What is going on here?" demanded the priest. "This is a house of God and I must protest!"

Teresa heard Priebke's winded voice. "Where did she go, Father?"

"I don't know what you're talking about?"

"Don't lie to me. Where the hell did she go?"

Teresa heard a loud whack followed by a cry of pain from the priest and a collective gasp of surprise from the worshipers in the chapel.

"I'm only going to ask you one more time. Where did she go?"

"She ran out the door," said one of the nuns, pointing. "Now what is this about?"

"You are harboring fugitives. You must clear this chapel at once!"

"We will do no such thing," protested the priest defiantly.

Teresa heard a clicking sound and then the report of a pistol.

"The next one goes into your chest, Father. Now everyone out of the chapel and into the hallway!"

"We will not leave," said one of the nuns. "We have come here to pray for the dead."

There was a lengthy silence: it was a standoff.

"All right, you holy sisters can stay, but I want all the men out now! Don't make me shoot this damned priest!"

"May the Almighty have mercy on your soul," said the priest. "Very well, clear the chapel. Sister Gabriella, you and the other nuns can stay but everyone else out now."

It took a minute to clear the room. When Priebke and his men were gone, the nuns whispered to her that the coast was clear.

She rose to her feet. "Thank you," she said, and she made her way quickly back to the secret passageway. Maybe she could hide herself in there until the police went away or make her way to the bridge on the fourth floor that led to the Pontifical Institute.

"Good luck to you, my child," said one of the nuns. "These are terrible times. May the Almighty watch over you."

"Thank you, Sister. Go in peace."

As Teresa headed for the door to the passageway, the supposedly dead man in the coffin suddenly jumped up and hopped out of the contrivance, very much alive.

She nearly jumped out of her skin. "You scared me half to death. You were playing dead that whole time?"

The middle-aged man winked. "They caught me off guard and I had to think quickly."

"Halt, what are you doing there!" a voice shouted.

Teresa turned towards the doorway. It was Priebke again, pointing a gun at them.

"Don't shoot, I surrender!" cried the man.

"So we have brought you back to life, eh? Put up your hands!"

When the man did as commanded, Teresa stepped quickly through the open door and into the secret passageway. Priebke opened fire, but the shot missed her and struck the door as she closed it behind her. Fearing for her life, she dashed up the winding staircase and ran back up the stairs the way she had come before. This time when she reached the third floor, though, she turned right into a corridor instead of left into the main hallway, heading in the opposite direction from where she had first been spotted by Koch and Priebke. Her path was illuminated by a single light bulb hanging from a wire in front of a decorative stained-glass window at the end of the corridor. Slowly, the voices and commotion outside in the main third-floor hallway receded behind her.

She threaded her way down the dark, cramped passageway, past rows of shelves containing what appeared to be ecclesiastical icons and relics until she reached the stained-glass window. Here the passageway dead-ended and there was nothing but the window and a wooden chair leaning against the wall.

Why is there a chair here?

She scoured the walls and ceiling. In the faint light, the outline of a trap door was just visible. Presumably it led to some sort of crawlspace or attic. Maybe she could get to the fourth floor from here and then make her way to the bridge. She pulled out the chair, stepped up onto it, and tried to push open the trap door, but it wouldn't budge.

She tried again.

Still nothing.

She heard a creaking sound and what sounded like a light footfall down the passageway. She turned her head in the direction of the sound.

But in the deep shadows, she saw nothing except the single glowing bulb at the end of the corridor. It was swinging lightly. She wondered: *Did I accidentally touch it?*

Feeling a sudden shudder of fear, she drove her shoulder into the trap door hard. This time she felt the door give way.

But the delivery of the blow made the chair teeter beneath her feet and she started to lose her balance. Feeling a wave of panic from the sound down the hallway and now the wobbly chair, she pushed aside the wood sheet of the trap door and started to pull herself up into what she could tell was a surprisingly large crawlspace. A sudden burst of relief poured through her: it was a perfect hiding place.

All she had to do was hurry and climb up there and set the door back—

Suddenly, she felt her legs grabbed from below in a tight grip. She tried to kick her way free, but felt herself yanked down and then allowed to freefall to the floor.

Her back hit the floor hard, and the air left her lungs in a terrible whoosh. For a second, she was unable to breathe or see who had jerked her down. Then suddenly, she felt herself pulled to her feet and shoved up against the wall.

Now, up close, she could see the man's face.

It was Pietro Koch!

Dazed, terrified, and with the wind knocked out of her, she couldn't believe how quickly her luck had turned.

"Ah, it is the pretty girl who tried to escape. Well, you will not be escaping now, I can assure you."

He laughed wickedly, exposing gleaming white teeth. It was then that she realized something was terribly wrong, something much worse than being caught and interrogated by the police. There was a look in his eyes like a wild dog.

Kicking the chair towards the stained-glass window, he slapped her face hard—harder than any blow she had ever been dealt before—and grabbed her in a bear hug. As she struggled to pull away, he spun her around so that she was facing away from him and clasped a hairy-knuckled hand over her mouth. Then, using his powerful arms, he shoved her towards the chair beneath the stained-glass window with the image of Christ and the Virgin Mary.

She tried to fight him off, but he was too strong, his grip like a vice.

Keeping his hand cupped over her mouth to keep her from crying out, he pulled her back hard at the waist and doubled her over the chair. A bony hand slid up her skirt and jerked down her undergarments, practically tearing them off her body.

"You have been a bad girl," he leered. "You are a traitor masquerading as a servant of the Lord and I am going to have to punish you."

He licked her ear.

She screamed. She wanted desperately to kill him. But first she had to get away?

He shoved his way inside her.

"Oh, sweet St. Peter," he moaned. "So wet and so young. You were ready and waiting for Pietro, weren't you, my child?"

Using all of her force, she jerked back and shoved him away.

But he overpowered her again, jammed his way inside, and doubled her over the chair, panting like a dog.

She tried to break free, but he pinned her against the chair, pushing down hard and nearly crushing her with his weight.

In and out. In and out.

God, help me! God, please!

The backrest of the chair broke from the downward pressure.

Suddenly, he let out a low bovine groan and she saw his face in the distorted reflection of the window, grotesquely contorted in a rictus of pain and pleasure.

Desperate, she grabbed a piece of the broken backrest with her free hand, jabbed him in the eye by thrusting a sharp end back over her shoulder, and jerked free from his clasp.

Badly wounded, he screamed in agony and fell back away from her as he sprayed himself and the floor with fluid.

She picked up the broken chair and smashed him over the head.

He fell to the floor, throwing his hands up to protect himself.

She clubbed him twice more with one of the chair legs. Upon the second blow, he fell to the floor, hit his head hard, and didn't make a sound. She kicked him in the stomach three times for good measure.

When she was finished, she collapsed against the wall to catch her breath.

She looked at Koch, laying on the floor unconscious with his pants at his ankles and cum all over his front side and the floor.

She wanted to kill him.

God, did she want to kill him!

But she didn't. Instead, she used the window sill to climb up into the crawlspace, navigated her way to the fourth floor, and took the bridge to freedom. Unlike eighteen others who were captured and hauled off to be brutally tortured under interrogation, she had narrowly survived the very first *Banda Koch* raid.

CHAPTER 32

HOTEL EXCELSIOR, ROME
DECEMBER 22, 1943

TAKING A BITE of his exquisitely prepared veal scallopini with lemon and capers, Hollmann leaned across the dining table and quietly asked Priebke, "Did anyone recognize you?"

From his guilty expression, Hollmann knew they were fucked.

"Who was it?"

The young Nazi captain looked around the room, scanning for eavesdroppers before replying in a low voice. "You're not going to believe this, but I think it was your daughter."

"Teresa? Are you sure?"

"She's dyed her hair and dresses differently than I've seen before, but it was her. Do you want to know who she was with?"

This was getting worse by the minute. "Who?"

"Colonel Di Domenico, Father O'Flaherty, and the OSS man I nearly captured in Piazza di Spagna."

It took great effort for Hollmann to hold back his shock and anger. His daughter was mixed up with the wrong people and playing a very dangerous game. At this rate, it was doubtful that he would be able to protect her much longer. "They were at the seminary too?"

"Unfortunately, they got away just like her."

"Too bad. Arresting the head of Badoglio's Military Front, the Vatican leader of the Escape Line, and an OSS agent on the same night would have been quite a haul."

"I don't think they recognized me, but your daughter definitely did."

"Were Lieutenant Bachmann and the others aware of my daughter's presence at the seminary?" he then asked, referring to the other three disguised Gestapo officers that had accompanied Priebke and the Koch Gang on the raid.

"No, I didn't say anything to them and they don't know what she looks like."

"Did you tell your boss Kappler that you saw her there?"

"No, Colonel. I have not told anyone but you."

"Good, that's the way we're going to keep it. My daughter is not a topic of discussion for the SD or the local Italian police. She doesn't exist. Do you understand me?"

"Yes, sir."

Hollmann set down his fork, delicately wiped his mouth, and leaned across the table. "I'm afraid I'm going to have to be even more blunt, Captain. If you breathe a word of Teresa's presence at Seminario Lombardo to anyone, especially *Obersturmbannführer* Kappler, I will personally kill you. That is, after I cut off your balls and throw hydrochloric acid into your eyes. Do you understand me?"

Priebke gulped hard. "Yes, Colonel."

"And your wife, Alicia, and your two young boys, George and Ingo, will never be seen or heard from again. Now, have I made myself clear?"

Priebke had visibly paled. "Please do not hurt my wife and sons. Six months ago when I started working for you, Herr Colonel, I swore an oath of allegiance to you, and I promise you again right here and now that I am your obedient servant in all things. My first loyalty is to you—even above that of our Führer."

"I am certainly not naïve enough to believe that, Erich. But because your lust for promotion knows no bounds and you would sell your own mother to become head of the SS, I do believe you will be true to your word. Just remember, my daughter is a valuable source of intelligence information to me and me alone, and is strictly off limits to anyone else. She is not to be considered the enemy, but rather my personal informant."

"I understand, Colonel, and as I say my loyalty is to you. But if you would please allow me to speak freely?"

"As you wish."

"Others in positions of authority here in Rome may not see things as you and I do."

"You are referring to your boss Kappler and our new military commandant of Rome, that fat drunk Mälzer?"

"Yes, Colonel."

"I am fully aware of the risks that I am taking and assume full responsibility." He resumed eating his veal scallopini, plucking up an oversized caper and delicately forking it into his mouth. "Now, how do you know that my daughter recognized you?"

"By the way she looked at me. But I didn't know it was her at first. In fact, not until this morning when I was shaving did I realize who she was. Her hair was dyed dark-brown and cut short, and her clothing and whole manner were so different than what I had seen previously. I didn't realize it was your Teresa. She fooled me."

"What do you mean her manner was different?"

"She doesn't look like the daughter of an aristocrat any more. She looks like an ordinary Roman. Of course, I have only seen her twice before today. The first time when you showed me your ex-wife's home when we first started surveillance. And then there was the other time."

"What do you mean *the other time*? Don't tell me you were following her?"

"No, of course not. I saw her at the opera when I was with my wife. It was before the October roundup."

He blew out a sigh of relief. But could he trust Priebke? That was the most important thing: could he trust the son of a bitch now and for the foreseeable future? Or would the young captain—who appeared to be doggedly loyal but was first and foremost a violent torturer, a flagrant womanizer, and a rabid social climber—betray him? After all, the dapper counterespionage officer was cheating on his ravishing young wife Alicia with not only the famous silver-screen actress Laura Nucci, but another young, nubile *Fascista* woman from the fashionable black set whose name he did not know. So how could Priebke possibly be trusted when he was dishonest not only to his wife and mistress, but his boss Kappler?

The answer was he couldn't be trusted at all, and Hollmann would have to constantly watch his back.

They both took a sip of Merlot and returned to their sumptuous meals. Even during war time, the Excelsior's fine restaurant frequented by German diplomats, SS, and Wehrmacht officers served some of the best food in the city, at prices that were unaffordable to all except the wealthiest Romans and the Nazi occupiers.

"So far you've told me who escaped. But how many prisoners did Koch actually take during the raid?"

"Eighteen total."

He frowned. "Only eighteen? Our estimates place the number hiding out at the seminary and neighboring Vatican buildings at two hundred."

"They only got eighteen. The prize catch was Giovanni Roveda."

He nodded approvingly. The trade-union leader was a high-ranking official of the Communist Party and outspoken anti-Fascist.

"The other prisoners were military officers, working age men with falsified documents, and Jews. Most of them were young men evading the forced-labor and military draft. They were pretending to be seminarians and were exposed as frauds by one of Koch's agents."

"Who?"

"A renegade Tuscan monk named Alfredo Troia. He posed as a priest, calling himself Don Ildefonso. He made them all recite the Ave Maria to decide who the imposters were. He smoked out at least eight of them that way. You should have seen their faces."

"Yes, I can imagine," said Hollmann, but inside he felt sympathetic to them. While some of those rounded up were no doubt genuine enemies of the Reich, some were just young men trying to live through a war that was gobbling up millions on both sides. It was a tragedy, really.

All of a sudden, there was a noticeable change in the air. For some inexplicable reason, Priebke began licking his lips and looking very nervous, as if he had something important to say but was afraid to say it. Having worked with the captain since the Mussolini rescue this past summer, Hollmann had come to know him well enough to be able to read his mind.

"Is there something you want to tell me, Erich?" he asked gently, using his given name to put him at ease.

"Yes sir, but I am afraid to tell you. It's about Koch."

"You already told me that he and his men ransacked all three properties—the Seminario, Pontifical Institute, and Russicum Institute. They stole everything they could get their grubby little hands on."

"*Ja,* Colonel, it was a free-for-all. But what I also wanted to tell you was that they tormented many of the people beyond what I would consider…" He left the words dangling.

"Reasonable?"

"Yes. Reasonable is the right word."

"What did they do?"

"They stole all the art, jewelry, and religious objects they could get their hands on."

"You already told me about that. What else happened?"

He hesitated. "I think Koch himself raped one of the women."

Hollmann felt a wave of revulsion. "My God. Don't tell me it was one of the nuns?"

"No, that's just it…I…I think it was…I think it may have been…"

Hollmann jumped up from his chair. "No, not Teresa!"

Inadvertently, it came out as a shout, and suddenly everyone in the restaurant was staring at him. He quickly smoothed his SS uniform, looked apologetically around the dining room, and sat back down, composing himself into a mask of calm. But inside he wanted to strangle Koch! Striking an alliance with the man had been a deal with the devil from the beginning, but this exceeded his worst nightmare!

Priebke licked his thin lips. "When my men and I found Koch, he was laying on the floor unconscious. He had a battered eye, his trousers were around his ankles, and there was semen all down his front. When I asked him who had done this to him, he said it was the young woman with Colonel Di Domenico and he vowed to fuck her in front of his men and then kill her—slow and painful."

Hollmann's jaw clenched tight. It took every ounce of his self-restraint not to curse God out loud. But at least Teresa had fought the bastard off and he had not been able to consummate the act. Somehow that brought him relief.

"I am sorry, Colonel. Koch is a ruthless bastard—he knows no boundaries. But at least he doesn't know that Teresa's your daughter and he was never able to finish what he started. She beat the daylights out of him, that's for sure. Wait until you see his face."

Beneath the table, he balled up his fists in his hand. God did he want to kill the monstrous fuck! He knew that the punishment Kappler allowed Priebke and his other officers to mete out at Via Tasso crossed the bounds of human decency, but it was war time, the prisoners they interrogated were the designated enemies of the Reich, and it was their sworn duty to obtain information on the Resistance from the prisoners in order to save German lives. It was their responsibility, their duty to help win the war, and there was no doubt that the Russians, British, and Americans used harsh methods to obtain information, too. But what the self-described Doctor Koch and his Gang had done was truly heinous and made the Gestapo seem like child's play. Somehow he had to make Koch pay. But how?

"*Scheisse*, there he is right now!" gasped Priebke, his expression showing visible alarm.

Hollmann looked to his right and saw the dark-skinned police chief walking swiftly towards his table, a heavy bandage over his right eye. He felt his body tense up with rage.

I am going to kill you, you son of a whore! I am going to kill you dead!

He started to rise from his seat, his hands balled into tight fists.

Priebke reached out and grabbed his arm. "Please sir, we will get even with him for this. But the time is not now. Please don't react, or it will raise questions in Koch's mind, and we already have enough enemies to contend with here in Rome. Please, Colonel, you must listen to me."

It took great effort, but after taking a deep breath he was able to sit back down and pretend to be calm. Priebke had a good point. It would not be to his advantage to make a public scene. Besides, he had to get more information on what had happened between Koch and his daughter before he decided on what course of action to take. But how could he possibly control his temper when all he wanted to do was take Koch by the throat and strangle him to death?

The mixed Italian-German walked up in his foppish suit, his dark hair slicked back with brilliantine. "*Buon appetito*, gentlemen," he said jauntily despite the prominent bandage covering his eye. "I can see you are celebrating our first great coup together."

"Shut up and sit down!" Hollmann commanded him, glaring fiercely, his voice just low enough not to be heard by the mostly German diners at the surrounding tables.

The police chief's dusky, corvine face registered shock; he obviously had expected to be treated as a conquering hero by his new allies, not as a dog to be kicked around. But he was not about to challenge the second leading SS officer in all of Occupied Italy. He did as instructed, timorously taking his seat.

Hollmann launched into his assault without preamble. "It has come to my attention, Dr. Koch, that you have violated every shred of human decency in this attack of yours upon the Seminario Lombardo and other Vatican properties."

"But it was under your orders that I—"

"Keep quiet! If you interrupt me again, I will have you arrested!"

Koch snapped silent and retreated into his seat, looking more like a frightened skunk than a triumphant police chief. Hollmann let the tense silence smother him a moment, watching him squirm in his seat like a terrified schoolboy before a headmaster.

"You have flagrantly abused your authority, Doctor, by allowing yourself and your men to behave like scoundrels. It is one thing to bust in and round up Resistance members and draft evaders—it is quite another to plunder religious artifacts, abuse priests and nuns, and rape innocent women."

Koch looked sharply at Priebke, as if betrayed.

"Don't blame the captain for your disgraceful conduct. As we both know, he was there as an observer on behalf of Colonel Kappler and myself and is under strict orders to report every detail of the raid to me personally on behalf of General Wolff."

Koch stared down into the table. "Yes, Herr Colonel."

"That's better. Now tell me about this young woman you raped and do not deny what you did. First off, what possessed you to conduct yourself and risk the wrath of the Vatican in such a reprehensible fashion?" Koch started to protest, but Hollmann held up a hand, silencing him instantly. "Answer me honestly and without holding back the details, or I will have you incarcerated at Via Tasso under Captain Priebke's care. And we both know how efficient the captain is with a pair of brass knuckles. You may proceed when ready, Doctor."

Suddenly, tears came to Koch's eyes and he looked around the room desperately, as if looking for a way to escape.

"Don't even think about it. I will hunt you down like a dog and I can promise you that you will be kept alive for months and undergo the most severe torture imaginable. Now answer my damned questions accurately and without prevarication, or your life as you know it is over."

He began quietly sobbing. "What have I done to anger you so? Who is this woman?"

"I will ask the questions, you cowardly swine. Now get a grip on yourself—we don't want to make a scene in front of our lunch guests. I can see a pair of officers from Field Marshall Kesselring's staff right over there."

It took Koch a full minute to regain his composure. He then told the story of his attack on the young woman and how she had ultimately fought him off before he could finish what he had started. He was ashamed of what he'd done, he said, which Hollmann knew was a lie. The only thing the ignominious *Doktor* Koch was ashamed about was that he had to suffer the embarrassment of being beaten up by a woman, creaming all over himself, and being found by the Gestapo knocked unconscious with his pants around his ankles and soaked from his own cum.

"Now I know you're wondering who this young woman is that you have violated," said Hollmann when Koch was finished with his confession. "What is so important about her, you are no doubt asking yourself? Well, the answer is she is an extremely important informant of mine."

Though still terrified, Koch couldn't help an expression of skepticism. "She's an informant? That's what this is about?"

"Yes, and she also happens to be my daughter—or she was once anyway. She has infiltrated Colonel Di Domenico's Military Front and when the time comes, she is going to help me capture him and his key associates. The colonel, you see, is her biological father. She has lived the last decade in Rome after being raised by me and her mother in Austria. Her mother, my ex-wife, is the Marchesa Di Domenico."

Koch shook his head in disbelief and crossed himself. "My deepest regret, Herr Hollmann. I had no idea she was your daughter."

Hollmann smiled bloodlessly. "If you *had* known, Pietro, you would be dead. The only reason you're alive right now is because my daughter is the one who triumphed over you, not the other way around. And because you are going to prove extremely useful to me from here on out. You see, I own you, Pietro. You will do my bidding whenever and wherever I please. *Capiche?*"

"Yes, Herr Colonel. My deepest apologies."

"The marchesa and my daughter Teresa are not to be touched by you or any other police force here in Rome. We have them under surveillance and they are our responsibility, not yours. If you so much as look at them the wrong way or mention what we have spoken of here today, you will be arrested and your police unit will be disbanded. I am holding you personally responsible for the health and safety of both the marchesa and my daughter Teresa. If anything happens to them—anything at all—you are the first person that will be arrested. Do I make myself clear?"

"Yes, Herr Colonel. Again my humblest apologies."

"In the future, when I call upon you, Doctor—and rest assured I will be calling upon you—you will do exactly as I say."

"Consider me your obedient servant, Colonel."

"Oh, you're going to be a lot more than that, Pietro. Now get the hell out of here before I change my mind and decide to shoot you myself."

"Yes, Herr Colonel." He rose from his seat quickly and started to walk away.

"Oh, and Pietro, please remember that we have a very big file on you and your extended family. I'm talking about your parents, brothers, sisters, aunts, uncles, nephews, cousins, both on your father's German side and your mother's Italian side. We know their names, where they live, everything, Pietro. Do you understand?"

His lips were trembling. "*Ja,* Herr Colonel. I understand everything you just said."

"Good, then you may go back to your rat hole."

CHAPTER 33

PALAZZO BELLOMO, PIAZZA NAVONA
DECEMBER 22, 1943

FROM HER BALCONY overlooking the piazza, Teresa gazed out at the leaden winter sky and felt the oppressive burden of the Occupation. She felt like lashing out at the enemy again, and regretted not having killed Pietro Koch last night when she had had the chance. She had allowed her humanity, her compassion, to get the better of her and vowed to never let it happen again.

She couldn't afford to let it happen again.

After all, Koch was still out there, and the next time he might kill her.

Her thoughts were interrupted as a sleek Mercedes-Benz pulled up in front of Palazzo Bellomo. The massive luxury car looked utterly foreign on the streets of a city that was becoming an increasingly desperate place to live with roundups, bread rations, curfews, and endless restrictions on everyday life, the most recent a police posting only this morning outlawing bicycles altogether due to the recent bombing attacks. An Italian chauffeur stepped out and opened the door for a strikingly fit and handsome middle-aged man, wearing an immaculate jet-black uniform, Teresa immediately recognized as her father.

As he strode purposefully towards the Palazzo's front door, she felt herself shudder at the sight of him. But a voice deep down inside told her not to worry. If her father had come here to arrest her, he wouldn't have showed up with only his driver. She studied him as he walked: he was a commanding, impressive-looking man, and his loose-fitting SS colonel's uniform with the death's-head insignia only added to his aura of command. All the same, her knees felt weak and her mouth went dry at the sight of him in his Nazi uniform.

Feeling her heart flutter in her chest and a sudden lightheadedness, she stepped back inside her room, closed the balcony door behind her, and went downstairs. With her mother out getting her hair done, the family butler Vincenzo and house servant Carla were the only ones at home with her right now, which was probably for the best. If her mother was here, she would probably say something to insult her father and they might be in real trouble.

Wearing his tailcoat and white gloves, Vincenzo went to answer the door when the bell rang. Whenever the German or Fascist police visited Palazzo Bellomo, his explicit instructions from the marchesa called for him to politely say that no one was home. But Teresa would talk to her father. Despite being a partisan, she was under her father's unofficial protection and might actually stand to learn something from him to aid the Resistance.

She stepped quickly to the door as the butler opened it. "I'll see the colonel,

Vincenzo. Thank you," she said.

He shot her a worried glance. "Are you sure, my lady?"

"Yes, the colonel and I will be meeting in the main sitting room. Please bring us some refreshments."

He moved off and she opened the door. "Welcome, Colonel," she greeted him. "Please come inside. Would you care for some wine?"

He appeared a little startled at her affability, but recovered quickly. "Yes, that would be fine," he said graciously.

He stepped inside, bowed cordially without, thankfully, clicking his heels—overzealous boot-clicking was another thing that irritated Teresa about the damned Nazis—and then they made their way to the sitting room, where she showed him to a seat beneath the Tintoretto, while she sat in a Queen Anne chair. The gilded leaf ornamentation running along the ceiling glimmered like Ghiberti's bronze doors to the Florence Baptistery that Michelangelo had affectionately called "the Gates of Paradise."

"So, Colonel, what did you want to see me about?"

"Your hair looks darker? Did you dye it recently?"

"My hair is sandy blonde and always has been. You know that."

"Yes, but did you color it recently? It looks a little darker than usual."

My God, he knows, she thought with horror. *He knows I'm the Inglesina!*

"No, Father"*—wait did I just call him father?—*"I did not color my hair. I know you are with the SS and details are part of your job, but you are grasping at straws."

"I'm sure you're right. It is just my imagination."

"Why are you here, Colonel?"

"What, you're already dispensing with *Father*?"

"That was a mistake."

"It was no mistake. It was a Freudian slip. I will always be your father, Teresa. As will Colonel Di Domenico, whom I'm sure our mutual nemesis Kappler will be welcoming as a guest in the basement of Via Tasso very soon. Seeing as he is the most wanted man in all of Rome."

"You'll never catch him."

"I'm sure that's true. But Kappler will. He's a bloodhound and won't stop hunting for the old fox until he has found him."

He smiled charmingly and she wasn't sure what she wanted to do more: marvel at his bravado or shoot him down for working for the monster Himmler. Then they both fell silent as Vincenzo entered with a tray containing an open bottle of Pinot Nero, cultivated from the Collio Goriziano region, and two glasses. He poured them each a glass and left. She took a sip of the wine, and then watched with surprise as her father downed his whole glass, gave a sigh of satisfaction, and set the empty wine glass on the table.

"That was quite refreshing," he said.

He leaned forward in his seat, took her by the hands, and looked at her with a serious expression on his face. "I don't want to beat around the bush, Teresa. I know what happened to you last night at the Seminario Lombardo. I want you to know how sorry I am and also how proud I am that you gave the son of a bitch what he deserved."

At first, she pretended not to understand, but then she saw from his sympathetic expression that he knew precisely what that ruthless bastard Koch had done and had come here to console her. It made her angry that he knew, angry that he had a window into such a humiliating incident in her life, an incident that she hadn't told anyone, not even her mother, about. Feeling violated with having to relive the horrible experience, she pushed his hands away and jumped up from her chair.

"How dare you come here and act as though you are my father?" she snapped. "Are you so delusional as to think that I want your sympathy?"

He looked genuinely hurt. "I just told you. I am your father, Teresa, whether you like it or not. I am the one that raised you. I am the one that read books to you and taught you how to ski, play tennis, and to climb mountains. Your mother certainly wasn't there for any of those things. I loved you the day I first set eyes on you, and I love you still to this day."

"Shut up! I hate you! You are not, and never will be, my father!"

"I wouldn't be here if I wasn't your father, Teresa. But I haven't come here just to say I am sorry for what happened to you. There is another reason as well."

She said nothing, waiting for him to tell her. But she *was* intrigued.

"I have come to ask your permission for retribution."

"Retribution?"

"Koch is a monster and should pay for what he has done. If you want me to execute him, I would be more than willing to do so to punish him for his transgression. Do not ridicule me by calling me a violent, loathsome Nazi—any father would do the same for a daughter that he loves. I will kill Pietro Koch. Just give me the word. But I will not do it without your permission."

"If I would have wanted him killed, I would have done it myself. I had the chance."

"I know you did. Captain Priebke is the one who found Koch knocked out on the floor unconscious and he gave a very precise description of his condition. You gave the self-proclaimed 'Doctor Koch' quite a beating. But you stopped short of killing him, and the reason you did is because you are a good person. You do not kill helpless human beings. That is what makes you and me both quite different from Pietro Koch, Teresa."

"Actually, I question whether you are any different from Koch at all. Your tongue may be more refined, but what makes you any less a monster than Koch?"

"God Almighty is the only one who can answer that question. And he will have his judgment day, I can assure you."

"That's the first true thing you've said."

"A man must pay for his sins."

"Are you talking about the supposed family curse?"

"Perhaps I am. All I know is that one day I will have to pay for my sins for the Reich, as will my brother, your once-beloved Uncle Walther. As you know, he is fighting for the Hermann Göring Division a hundred miles to the south. But Koch is an altogether different animal. He should pay for his sins now, I think. That is why I want to know if you want me to kill this man."

"I've already given you my answer."

"Is your answer final?"

"Yes, I do not want you to kill him. I just want to forget about the whole thing."

"I am sorry that it happened. Now there is something else that I need to talk to you about. I know that with you at Seminario Lombardo last night was your father, Colonel Di Domenico, Monsignor O'Flaherty, and the OSS man that was seen with your brother. The Gestapo identified them."

"I don't know what you're talking about."

"Don't insult my intelligence by pretending to be innocent. I know where you were last night and who you were with, and I can promise you that this information is enough to put both you and me before a firing squad. However, I am after much bigger game. I am also aware that you know that Kappler arranged for four of his officers to accompany the Koch raid as observers. You recognized Captain Priebke and perhaps some of the other men. I will not ask you how you obtained this information, but I will tell you that you are playing a dangerous game and it is only a matter of time before you are caught. Now as both your father and an SS colonel, I am urging you to stop."

"I have done nothing wrong. I was simply visiting the seminary, and the Koch Gang and your German Gestapo men barged in and violated a Vatican property. There is a sign posted on the front signed by General Stahel himself that protects the seminary. And yet Koch and the Gestapo were there last night in open violation of the general's orders. Pius will no doubt be upset when he learns that the Gestapo has violated his orders. So I ask you, who are the lawless criminals here?"

"An excellent rhetorical question in a time of peace, but we are at war. Did you or anyone else tell the Vatican of the Gestapo's presence at the seminary?"

"I haven't spoken to anyone. But I will tell you that there may have been others beside myself that recognized Captain Priebke. The man has quite a reputation in Rome for his wandering eye with wealthy, unattached Fascist women. I have even heard a rumor that he is the film star Laura Nucci's lover."

"You are well informed. The man is a regular Casanova."

"I wonder what his wife would think about that." She took a sip of wine. "I am still not sure why you have come here. You have no proof I have done anything wrong. Being at the seminary does not make me a criminal. If anyone should be arrested, it is that vulgar monster Koch who tried to violate me. Otherwise, why else would you want to kill him?"

"You are a persuasive arguer, Teresa. And whether you think I deserve it or not, I will take a large measure of the credit for that. Your mother was always an emotional volcano, a Vesuvius always erupting. But your powers of calm deductive reasoning…now those you got from me."

"Oh, yes, the SS colonel. What a happy upbringing with you and mother shooting one another in anger. I still don't understand why she did it. What was it that drove her so far over the edge? I know it wasn't just because you had a previous marriage and threatened to take me and Gunther away with you. So what was it that drove her to such violence?"

"I'm afraid only your mother knows the answer to that question. All I know is I did the best I could and it still wasn't good enough. I am about as flawed as a husband and father can be."

"Yes, but why did she shoot you? What pushed her so far over the edge that you were forced to abandon all hope of ever seeing your children again and undergo plastic surgery to wipe away your past? What would drive a woman to shoot down her own husband in cold blood like that?"

"I told you, I don't know."

Taking a sip of wine, she reached out and touched his smooth, plastic-like face, so much like a wax figure.

"You are a formidable young lady. But the mistake you are making in all this is thinking that you and I are on equal terms. We are not. There is a war going on and we occupy this city. We are the law—we make all the rules and decide who shall live and who shall die. The only reason you and your mother both have not been locked up, or put before a firing squad, is because of me. You are safe only as long as I say you are safe and as long as I am safe."

"So now you're threatening me? First you wanted to avenge me, now you want to lock me up in Via Tasso. Which is it to be, *Father*?" She said the word coldly, making it sound cruel and shameful.

He reached out and gently touched her hand. "You know I would never harm you. But the situation is precarious. You are openly challenging the police authorities here in Rome—both German and Italian. The truth is, Teresa, you are a GAP partisan."

She gave a challenging look. "You have no proof of that."

"I don't need proof to know that you are the *Inglesina*. I know what thirty years of police instincts tell me."

She felt a sudden shortness of breath. *How could he possibly know?*

"I know it was you at the Cinema Barberini, Teresa. I knew today at lunch when Captain Priebke described what you looked like. It puzzled me at first. But then once I took into account your dyed hair, your change in clothing, your different manner, I realized the transformation you had made since the last time I saw you. You are a partisan, and you and three other GAP comrades-in-arms led the attack at the cinema that resulted in the killing and wounding of over twenty men."

"You don't know that. In fact, you don't know anything about me. You haven't been my father for more than ten years. And now that there's a war on, you return to my life and want to look out for me?"

"Those men you killed had wives and lovers back home, and several of them were fathers of young children."

She wagged a finger at him. "Don't toy with my emotions and try to fill me with guilt. Those damned Nazis deserved to die."

He rose from his chair and looked at her sadly, his face a morass of concern and fatherly love.

"In war no one deserves to die," he said softly. "I love you, Teresa. That's why I want you to stop before you are killed—or, God Forbid, you end up like me."

CHAPTER 34

VATICAN

DECEMBER 22, 1943

THE CHIEF SHOOK HIS HEAD IN DISMAY. Cardinal Maglione, the Vatican secretary of state, had just briefed him on last night's raid at Seminario Lombardo and the other Vatican properties. The news was bad—very bad. Unable to believe what he had just heard, he sighed with resignation and placed his white-skullcapped head in his hands. He wondered how the Almighty Father could allow such Machiavellian ruthlessness to take place in his beloved city when its citizenry was already suffering beyond imagination.

"No place is safe anymore, Your Holiness. The German and Fascist police forces have no respect for the ecclesiastical institutions of Rome—it is as simple as that," declared Maglione to wrap up his briefing.

Distraught at this latest flagrant abuse of power by the occupiers, Pius rubbed his temples to drive away the demon of a headache that was beginning to take root inside his head. How could the situation have deteriorated so quickly? In only three months, the Germans had taken over as the undisputed masters of Rome, seizing all power and authority through martial law and in the process making a laughingstock of the Curia. But the worst thing—as evidenced by the October roundup, last night's raid, and all the other atrocities being committed on a smaller scale on a daily basis—was that he was powerless to stop them.

It ate away at him, like a festering wound that refuses to heal. The Holy Father of Rome—the *defensor civitatis* that the citizenry was counting on in this desperate time of war—had no more authority over the German occupiers than a peasant from the Trastevere. He felt not merely angry, but ashamed. Was he truly so impotent that he could not even help his own people?

Every day the Germans were becoming more powerful. Even before the raid, the Vatican had received information from a trustworthy source that the SS police force in Rome was about to be increased from four hundred to two thousand men. Moreover, according to the informant, a diabolical plan had been spawned to use the augmented police force to make a city-wide, house-to-house search to root out all able-bodied males for labor service at the Italian front or in Nazi Germany. Most disturbing was the revelation that convents, monasteries, and even treaty-protected Church properties would not be exempt from this latest planned Nazi roundup, which would be the fifth or sixth in only the past two months.

It was a tragic situation, made even more tragic by last night's devastating raid. But even more shocking was the renewed possibility, revealed by another secret source, of an even more ambitious raid on Vatican City itself. Were Hitler and his Nazis again seriously considering kidnapping him and shipping him off to Lichtenstein in a cattle car?

"This war," he lamented in his high-pitched voice, "is making old men out of all of us. Do kindness and generosity have no mercy in this land?"

"Hitler knows nothing of mercy, Your Holiness," replied Maglione. "If there is one thing we have learned these last few years, it is that he cannot be trusted. And like the Bohemian Corporal, this new head of the Rome Secret Police is just as untrustworthy and dangerous."

Pius nodded. Though he and his secretary of state did not always see eye to eye, Maglione was still his most trusted advisor and he always gave his counsel the consideration it deserved. But what Pius didn't know was that his second was believed by the OSS to be the Curia's top high-level pro-American, and with the Allies inching closer to Rome every day, his influence on the Pope was highly desired by FDR, Churchill, and their diplomatic representatives in the Vatican.

"What Koch has done is a clear treaty violation," pointed out Pius. "Those buildings serve religious objectives and are dependencies of the Vatican recognized by General Stahel himself."

Maglione folded his hands in his lap. "It's highly unlikely Koch acted alone."

"I agree. But do we have any evidence the Germans were the ones actually pulling the strings?"

"There is some indication that Kappler's men may have been present. But other witnesses are not so sure. Father O'Flaherty believes at least two Gestapo operatives were at the seminary, but he is not one hundred percent certain."

"Regardless, you will have to talk to Weizsäcker and make my displeasure known," he said, referring to the German Ambassador to the Holy See. "See him today if possible. We need to know if Kappler was behind this, or if this Koch acted on his own volition."

"Yes, Your Excellency. Should the new *stadtkommandant*, the replacement for General Stahel, be contacted as well?"

"What's his name again?"

"Mälzer."

"No, just talk to Weizsäcker." With his bony fingers, he pushed aside a small pile of papers on his neat and tidy desk. "Tell me about this Mälzer. Can we expect trouble from him?"

"I would not be optimistic. According to one of our reliable Swiss informants, he is said to be a man of poor character."

"How so?"

"He is reported to be both a gourmand and carousing bacchanal. He is fifty-five years old, fat as a cow, and would be quite laughable if he wasn't so dangerous. He apparently enjoys shooting people before firing squads by day and imbibing vast quantities of schnapps by night. He has already issued his first edict in response to the recent partisan bombing attacks: he has banned bicycles."

"Banned bicycles?"

"He has declared that the contraptions are no longer allowed on the streets of Rome." He pulled out one of the posters that had been put up all over the city. "It says right here that 'from this moment on, without exception, the use of any bicycle anywhere in the territory of the Open City of Rome is prohibited. Transgressors will be shot without regard to who they are and without prior notice. The bicycle will be requisitioned with no right of compensation.'"

So now the Nazis have taken away bicycles, he thought derisively, as Maglione leaned across his desk and handed him the poster. He read it over before handing it back to the cardinal with a heavy sigh. These were dark days indeed for the Eternal City. The winter of the Occupation had arrived and, with all of the new restrictions and shortages of water, coal, and food, the beleaguered citizens on the streets were calling it the "Christmas in captivity." He couldn't help but feel embarrassment that the city of his birth, the cradle of Roman civilization, had sunk so low that people were persecuted and starving and begging on the streets by the thousands. Rome was anything but an Open City: the occupiers were holding the entire town hostage and using it as a staging ground and supply line to the Cassino front, where Kesselring had thrown up his new Winter Line.

Still, he couldn't help but blame the Resistance for stirring up the occupiers.

"It is clear that these raids by the police would not be happening if it wasn't for the irresponsible elements in the city," he said to Maglione.

"You are referring to the partisans?"

"They are the ones driving the authorities to these audacious attacks." He saw from the cardinal's face that he was skeptical. "What, you do not agree?"

"You must remember, Your Eminence, that the partisans believe they are fighting to free themselves from the yoke of Nazi oppression. Whether that is actually true or not, I leave that to His Holiness to decide."

"Without order there is nothing but violence and chaos. I wonder if these Communists and Socialists understand that."

"There are many partisans besides the Socialists and Communists—and what unifies them is their desire to drive the German occupiers from the city and to wipe out the Fascists. But I do agree with you that their actions have placed a burden on us here at the Vatican."

"Yes, but we must still help those in need. That is our most important task in these perilous times."

"On your orders, our convents, monasteries, seminaries, and other institutions have thrown open their doors to those seeking refuge. But it's only fair to point out that these places of refuge are becoming a problem for us with regard to maintaining our coveted impartiality. They are becoming overcrowded, which makes it more difficult to hide people from the Gestapo and Koch Band. The situation is fast turning into a crisis."

Though the Pope had personally ordered Rome's religious institutions to provide refuge to all those in need, he and his inner circle had known back in October that at some point the Vatican and its religious refuges would be stretched to capacity, at which time the risks might outweigh the benefits. Now the dreaded moment had arrived. However, the rescue efforts were critical to the survival of thousands of people, and he was not about to allow them to be halted. The Church's refuges continued to ease the tremendous pressure on Rome's citizens and escaped Allied POWs mounting each and every day.

"There is the question, Your Holiness, of whether we should warn those hiding out in the extraterritorial properties that they are not secure and suggest that they move. I am talking about the Allied POWs, Italian labor- and draft-evaders, and others hiding out in our ecclesiastical buildings."

"Are you suggesting that we urge them to change lodgings?"

"That may be the only path open to us if we want to maintain our sovereignty. We are walking a dangerous line, Your Eminence, sheltering so many. We are at overflow capacity already and our independence as a neutral entity is at stake."

"Has it truly come to that?"

"If it hasn't yet, it may soon enough."

"Then see to it that people are warned, but we cannot support a policy of expulsion. These people are in a desperate situation and have nowhere else to go."

"Yes, Your Excellency."

From Maglione's pensive expression he could see that his secretary of state still had something on his mind.

"What is it, Luigi?" he asked softly. "What is it that troubles you?"

"With all due respect, Your Eminence, I do not know if the Germans will ever respect our authority if we do not speak out more firmly against them. This is the first attack on a Vatican property—and I can promise it will not be the last. That is what troubles me most about our present situation. I see them pushing us harder and harder, tightening the noose around our necks and becoming more audacious every day in testing our resolve."

He felt a watery feeling in his stomach for he knew Maglione was right. The Germans would push him as far as they could. That was why he had become so deeply involved in the three plots to kill Hitler; without the great tyrant gone, the Nazis would continue to wreak death and destruction across all of Europe. Eliminating Hitler was the only sure way of striking back and weakening them. He thought of a quote from Peter 5:8-9: "Be sober, be vigilant; because your adversary the devil walks about like a roaring lion, seeking whom he may devour. Resist him, steadfast in the faith, knowing that the same sufferings are experienced by your brotherhood in the world."

"I know what you are saying," he said to Maglione after reflection. "At some point, you have to stand up to a bully or he will not stop his bullying."

"We are at a crossroads, Your Holiness. We need to stand up for the sanctity of the Holy See, for all of Rome, and for all of humanity. We must call out the oppressors while at the same time pretending to be neutral and impartial. Some in the Curia say that the Germans don't respect anything but military might. But I think your moral authority carries more weight than a hundred armored divisions."

He appreciated the praise, but the thought of taking Hitler publicly to task in a high-stakes manner made him feel older than his sixty-six years. More importantly, such an approach deviated from the time-honored tradition of the Holy See, and had backfired repeatedly against Napoleon in the last century and Hitler in the present war. Since the *blitzkrieg*, taking a vocal stand against Nazism had proven to actually put more lives in jeopardy in Poland, the Netherlands, and elsewhere, though standing up against Hitler in a united front had succeeded, to some extent, by the bishops of France in preventing further atrocities against Jews.

"We have had this discussion before and we have always agreed that we need to work quietly behind the scenes to achieve our aims and ensure our survival."

"I understand that, Your Eminence, truly I do. But if we do not lift our voice in protest for this raid on our very own properties protected by treaty, are we not just encouraging the perpetrators of repression to even more brazen violations?"

"There is no other path open to us but restraint and measured silence. As you've said yourself, we are dealing with a madman as unpredictable as a tempest. We cannot risk violating our coveted image of neutrality by raising his ire—not when the British and Americans drop bombs within a stone's throw of St. Peter's and the Russians take part in crimes that are just as reprehensible as the Nazis. If we are too outspoken, we risk losing everything."

What he left unsaid to his secretary of state—who was not in on the Vatican plot to remove Hitler from power—was that any public accusation against the Führer and his demented Thousand-Year Reich would put Stauffenberg, his plotters, and the entire Catholic population of Greater Germany in jeopardy. And that Pius would not do. He remembered back to 1942 when the Dutch bishops had spoken out against Dutch Jews and workers being kidnapped from their homes and deported. In response, the SS had promptly rounded up 40,000 Catholics of Jewish descent and shipped them east to death and slave labor camps, sending a clear message to Pius and the Vatican not to meddle in German affairs.

"But maybe we *should* risk everything," countered Maglione. "After all, one day history will judge us not only based on our actions—but our *inaction*. After all, the security of the German occupiers is not tied to us. If the partisans attack the Germans, that is their business, not ours. The more tolerance we show for the Germans and anti-partisan police through our silence, the tighter the yoke is drawn between us and our oppressors."

"Our problems are not just due to the occupiers. Every day the war draws closer and closer to our fair city. Every day we have to endure losses, suffered mostly by the poor, from Allied air attacks. Every day most Romans have only half of the food they need to survive. And now on top of all this, we have these partisan attacks that drive the Germans crazy with retribution."

"But surely something can be done? The Germans are the enemy, not the partisans or Allies that will soon be at our doorstep to liberate Rome."

He frowned. The simple truth was he didn't want the Allies to be the liberators of Rome. As the *defensor civitatis* and a son of the Eternal City, he wanted that honor for himself. Over the past four years, he had repeatedly tried to forge a peace agreement between the Allied and Axis powers, but had failed. In the last year alone, he had been in essence rebuffed by the Allies—whom he had been secretly supporting throughout the war—through their "unconditional surrender" policy. He had also hoped early on that the city of his birth would not be bombed during the war, since it would mean so much to his prestige afterwards if it could be said that the city had been spared out of respect for the Holy Father. But he had achieved neither of his wishes, and now the Germans had rebuffed him, too, by brazenly taking over his city and using it as a staging area for their troops.

But there was still *one way* that he could affect the outcome of the war. And that was to be the primary Allied diplomatic agent in the plot to remove Adolf

Hitler from power and the mediator in setting up a viable post-Nazi government.

"All I can do, Luigi, is urge the people of my diocese to remain calm, exercise moderation, and abstain from any inadvisable acts that might provoke even worse misfortunes."

"But is that enough in these perilous times?"

"I don't know the answer to that. But don't forget that we are already quietly supporting the Resistance even as we claim impartiality. Our attitude towards the partisans may be lukewarm at best because of our fear of Communism and German reprisals on the civilian population, but as you well know, that hasn't stopped us from being in regular contact with the Resistance. Nogara and Ronca both have been working closely with the partisan leaders on a number of fronts."

He was referring to Bernardino Nogara, the Vatican's financial director, and Roberto Ronca, rector of the Roman Seminary, who acted as the Vatican's representatives to the Roman Resistance *Comitato di Liberazione Nazionale*. Most of the CLN, including leading Communists, were secretly quartered in the Holy See's Lateran Palace complex. The extraterritorial enclave was run by Ronca, who was sympathetic to the growing partisan movement. Nogara liaised with the CLN on behalf of the thousands of escaped Allied POWs, former Italian Army officers, anti-Fascist politicians, Jews, and other civilian refugees being secretly hidden by the Pope and his Church of Spies. The network of refuges included Rome's many monasteries and convents, Vatican extraterritorial properties like the Basilicas of the Lateran, San Paolo, and Santa Maria Maggiore, and the Vatican itself.

"Yes, Your Eminence. I know all about the fine work these two have done for the refugees behind the scenes. But I still don't think we can continue to stand by in the face of pure evil either. If we do, are we not complicit ourselves?"

"What would you suggest we do, Cardinal Maglione?"

"We need to break ranks with the Germans and call them out for their inhumanity in a subtle yet convincing fashion. Is that not what you would do if you knew there would be no reprisals against the Church or Rome for speaking out? Is that not what God Himself would want you to do? Surely the Almighty does not want us to close our eyes to Nazi and Fascist brutality here in Rome?"

He thought again of Stauffenberg and his plot of tyrannicide. A part of him desperately wanted to tell the secretary of state the truth about the deep, historically unprecedented conspiracy he had been involved in these past four years. But more than anything else, removing Hitler from power demanded public silence and utter secrecy. After all, in this momentous time in history, he led not a Church of Saints, but a Church of Spies.

"Sometimes we have to maintain silence in the face of wickedness for the greater good, Luigi," he said with a knowing expression on his sharp, ascetic face. "And you have to trust me, right now is one of those times."

"But is it, Your Holiness? Is this not instead the time to stand up for what is morally right regardless of the consequences?"

"No, it is not," he replied sternly. "There is too much at stake."

And then he thought: *If you only knew, Luigi. If you only knew.*

PART 4

THE DEVIL'S BRIGADE

CHAPTER 35

ANZIO BEACHHEAD, WESTERN ITALY

FEBRUARY 1, 1944

JOHN BRIDGER, promoted on January 30 to major, looked out from the officer's deck of the LCI—Landing Craft Infantry—at a school of dolphins racing through the Tyrrhenian Sea.

Five sleek torpedo-shaped miracles of nature with bottle-nosed beaks and gray dorsal fins glinting in the sunlight. They moved alongside the vessel with disarming ease, leaping out of the water every so often, carefree smiles clinging to their snouts as if there was nothing they'd rather be doing than racing against a 300-ton U.S. naval vessel.

What Bridger liked most about them was their sense of merry freedom: they made the war seem far away.

A familiar voice behind him pulled him from his reverie.

"Just look at them. Now aren't they the lucky ones."

He turned to see his commanding officer, Brigadier General Frederick, also recently promoted for distinguishing himself against the Wehrmacht in the rugged Apennines of Central Italy. Only two years earlier, he had been a mere major; now at thirty-six, he was the youngest general in the U.S. Army. With an unassuming manner, he slipped his hands over the railing, peered down at the dolphins, and grinned.

"Why is that, sir?" asked Bridger. "Because they get to swim around all day?"

"No, John, because they don't even know what the hell war is."

"Yes, sir. I see what you mean."

They both chuckled and watched the playful creatures for a minute longer before turning their attention to the approaching Anzio-Nettuno coastline, which was about to serve as the new base of operations for the First Special Service Force. The bay was packed with massive Allied supply vessels, Liberty ships, smaller landing craft including LSTs, and destroyers. Beyond the docks and beaches spread the growing Fifth Army encampment along the reclaimed Pontine Marshes. One of the flattest pieces of ground in all of Italy, the area was referred to by GI's as the "billiard table." The days of "refitting and recuperation" for the Force following Operation Raincoat were officially over, Bridger thought with some regret, knowing that as soon as he hit the beach a new cycle of fighting and killing would begin anew. It was all part of the new "Operation Shingle"—the amphibious end-run from Naples to the Anzio-Nettuno beachhead thirty-five miles southwest of Rome. This latest operation—originally conceived by Churchill, who had over-optimistically guaranteed the Allies would take the Eternal City by Christmas and who had naively referred to the Italian theater of operations as Hitler's "soft underbelly"—was intended to outflank the German forces of the Winter Line and enable a concentrated attack on Rome. Instead, in the past ten days, the Fifth Army had barely budged off the beachhead, clinging precariously to a strip of savagely contested real estate that extended a mere three miles inland and was under constant German artillery, mortar, and aerial bombardment.

Frederick said, "I wanted to inform you personally of our orders, John, before I addressed the other officers."

"Yes, sir," replied Bridger, keeping a wary eye on the explosions of the German 88 shells in the distance. The detonations were growing louder as the LCI closed in on the coast. "Where have we been assigned?"

"You see that big canal off to the right there." The general pointed at the long, prominent ditch that drained into the ocean, bounded by a few scattered farmhouses. "It's named after that Fascist son of a bitch Mussolini. We've been assigned to take up a position along the canal and hold the right-hand sector of the beachhead."

"How big is our sector?"

"About eight miles long."

"That's a lot of ground to patrol for twelve hundred men, sir."

"One quarter of the beachhead to be exact. Which makes our sector twice the length of any other division in VI Corps."

Bridger raised a brow. "If you don't mind my asking, sir, how are we going to patrol an area that size with only twelve hundred men? We're a brigade—not a division."

"I don't think the brass understands that yet. They think we're goddamned invincible or something."

"It's FUBAR, sir. And now the army, in its infinite wisdom, has decided to deploy a mountain combat unit to the flattest land in all of Italy, to guard a canal. Seems like a piss-poor allocation of government resources, if you don't mind my saying so, sir."

"You're a major now, John. You're not supposed to bitch so much."

"Just speaking freely, sir."

"Congratulations again on your promotion. At least you've got the good sense to bitch up the chain of command. To tell you the truth, when our orders came through I thought the same thing as you. After all, we were trained to fight as skiers, parachutists, and mountain climbers not footsloggers. I thought to myself what the hell is General Clark thinking? But then I looked at the bright side."

"Yeah what's that, sir?"

"By making us part of the Anzio end run instead of keeping us at Cassino, we get to enjoy a beach instead of those ice cold mountains."

Bridger looked towards the Mussolini Canal. A pair of mortar shells blasted out huge chunks of earth on the west side of the canal, where they would soon be pitching their tents and setting up their mess area. "I don't know, sir. I've got to say that piece of ground over there looks awfully exposed to German mortar fire. This isn't going to be any picnic on the beach."

"We'll just have to dig in deep, I guess," said Frederick with a devilish grin. "And get in and out of that water quickly when we do take a dip in the ocean."

They watched a few more mortar shells explode along the canal before turning their attention to the myriad supply and attack ships anchored off the Anzio headlands. South of Nettuno, Bridger saw the charred hulks of a freighter and lesser ships that had been beached and set aflame after recent air attacks. The hard landings and piers of Anzio were jammed with unloading ships, while in the port proper anchored freighters were discharging via DUKWs. In the sky further to the east, a dogfight began between a German fighter and an American fighter.

The Forcemen on the LCI deck began waving and cheering at the dogfight.

Frederick said, "We're not just going to sit idle on that canal, John. We're going to constantly probe the enemy for weaknesses and push him back." He pointed to the vast open tableland south of the canal where there was nothing but scattered farmhouses with few trees. "There's three miles of heavily mined lowland in the hands of the left wing of the Hermann Göring Division. We're going to push those bastards out of our front yard and give them nightmares so they can't sleep at night."

"That's what I like to hear, sir. But how do we expect to put the fear of God into a crack unit like the Hermann Göring when we have to guard eight miles of front with twelve hundred men. Math was never my strong suit, but I believe that works out to around one Forceman per twelve yards of frontage. That's pretty damned thin to cover the whole right flank of VI Corps."

"We'll have to be creative, Major."

"How do you plan to do that, sir?"

"I don't know yet. I'm still working on it. But I have come up with this."

He pulled out a paper sticker the size of a playing card and handed it to him. The sticker contained the symbol of the First Special Service Force—two crossed lightning bolts with a dagger pointing upwards through the middle—and a phrase in German that, translated into English, said: "THE WORST IS YET TO COME."

"It's going to be our calling card, John."

"Calling card?"

"For the Krauts. Whenever we kill a German soldier behind their lines, we're going to place one of these stickers on his helmet or forehead. I've had a thousand of these cards printed up. And I've got another thousand, in the form of red stickers, emblazoned with our Force spearhead symbol. We're going to post them on buildings and fenceposts behind enemy lines. Yessir, we're going to give those Hermann Göring boys a little taste of American terror. We're going to scare the holy fuck out of those Kraut bastards and make them wish they had never joined Hitler's army."

Bridger watched as the American pilot took evasive maneuvers against the Nazi fighter bearing down on him. The German Messerschmitt Bf 109-F in pursuit looked particularly menacing with its battle camo and black iron cross brandished across the fuselage. "Psychological warfare," he said. "I like it, sir."

"In the spirit of Sun Tzu and von Clausewitz. Once the Krauts get a little taste of our hospitality, I wager that the word will spread quickly within their ranks. We're going to steal in on them at night like ghosts, kill and capture as many of the enemy as possible, and sneak back behind our lines without making a peep or leaving a trace except our calling cards. They're going to fear us *and* remember us, John. But they're never going to know just who in the hell we are. They're going to think we were spawned from the goddamned devil himself."

Bridger saw the gleam in his eye. The Fighting General was dead serious.

"Some in our own army may come to view us as lunatics in uniform, John. But I don't give a damn what they think. We are not going to sit idly by on the defensive. I will be ordering reconnaissance patrols and harassment raids by day and night, and I will be instituting offensive tactics to demoralize the enemy and energize the men at every turn. These Forcemen calling cards are just the beginning."

"It will be fun to play the bogeyman instead of the Nazis for a change."

A cheer went up from the Forcemen as the Messerschmitt took a hit of machine-gun fire, burst into flames, and nosedived into the azure blue Tyrrhenian Sea. Bridger and the general took off their hats and waved them in the air triumphantly along with dozens of others.

"They're going to bloody well remember us, John. We're going to put the fear of God in them. They're going to see us in their nightmares until we take Rome, by thunder."

"I can't wait, sir. When do we start?"

"Tonight—I want you to lead the first raid tonight."

CHAPTER 36

HERMANN GÖRING DIVISION HEADQUARTERS

LITTORIA, WESTERN ITALY

FEBRUARY 10, 1944

SITTING in front of his younger brother Walther's desk, *Standartenführer* Wilhelm Hollmann wondered if an imposter had somehow taken over his brother's body. His brother's eyes were bloodshot and ringed with dark circles, his hand trembled as he smoked his Eckstein front-line-issued cigarette, and his body appeared unnaturally gaunt. Hollmann could swear his brother had lost twenty pounds since the last time he had seen him. That had been back in early December in Rome when Walther was on leave.

He couldn't help but wonder: *Is the war truly going this badly?*

After all, his brother was a veteran commanding officer in one of the Reich's best-trained and most-feared military units—the vaunted Hermann Göring Division. So how was it possible that he looked more like a shell-shocked private than a major in the best Wehrmacht division in Italy, a unit that rivaled the crack Waffen-SS? What had happened to him? It couldn't be the current military situation here at Anzio. After all, it was the Allies that were pinned down under heavy, non-stop artillery fire on a narrow beachhead and were about to be driven back into the sea.

"You look terrible, Walther. What is wrong with you?" he said without preamble as he pulled out a Lucky and lit it with his engraved Zippo lighter.

His brother took a long pull from his Eckstein, his fingers trembling. Artillery roared in the distance; from the sound it appeared to be their own 88s. "There was another raid last night by *die schwarzen teufel*—the black devils," he said in a monotone. "They killed seven of my men…slit their throats from ear to ear. We never hear the damned devils when they come."

"What do you mean the black devils?"

"The enemy with the blackened faces that come only at night. They appear out of nowhere in their strange uniforms."

"Strange uniforms?"

"In addition to camouflage blackface, they wear fur-lined parkas and baggy cargo trousers and they carry all manner of weapons. They have a knife with a blade that is more than a foot long, and they slit the throats of my men with it. In the past week, I have lost nearly sixty men. Sixty men killed or captured by those black devils! And we have killed only three of theirs without capturing a single one alive—and that was the first and second night we encountered them. Now they are smarter. We never see or hear them coming until it is too late."

Hollmann felt a chill up his spine; the way his brother described the cold-blooded bastards made them seem like some sort of supernatural demons or ghosts of the darkness. "Well, who the hell are they?"

"That's just it—we don't know."

"Are they British or American?"

"American and Canadian, we think. But they are not like other Allied soldiers we have captured. They are clearly an elite unit, but where the hell they came from or what they are called we still don't know. They moved into the Allies' right flank along the Mussolini Canal last week, and they have been on the warpath ever since."

Hollmann was listening intently. He had the sneaky feeling the crack enemy outfit his brother was referring to was his son's commando unit, the joint American-Canadian First Special Service Force. He had been tracking the movements of the unit since its presence in Italy had become known by German intelligence, both the SS and Abwehr. They had fought in several battles in the mountains south of Cassino in December and must have recently been thrown into the right flank at Anzio. It meant that the Allies were growing desperate on the narrow beachhead. The time was ripe for a fierce German counterattack to deliver a crippling blow and drive the Allies back into the sea.

"How do you know that they are American and Canadian?" he asked, intrigued by the sudden turn of events and, most especially, the possibilities.

"They leave stickers behind our lines bearing an Indian spearhead symbol with the words "USA" and "Canada" on them. They slap them on buildings, fenceposts, vehicles, and equipment. Unless they're trying to trick us, these stickers are the symbol for their elite unit. They also leave behind death stickers to strike fear in us."

"Death stickers? What do you mean?"

From his desk drawer, he grabbed a sticker containing a symbol with two crossed lightning bolts, a dagger pointing upward through the bolts, and a phrase in German: *DAS DICKE ENDE KOMMT NOCH!*

Hollmann took the sticker from him, looked it over, and repeated the catchphrase to himself in English.

THE WORST IS YET TO COME.

"They stick them to the helmets or foreheads of my dead men when they slit their throats. I am telling you these are not men—they are demons of the night."

"Come now, it is all just psychological warfare. We do the same thing."

With trembling fingers, his brother raised his cigarette to his lips, inhaled a huge puff, and clenched his teeth as the smoke slowly drained from his nose. "Yes, but the difference is when Goebbels makes one of his little propaganda pitches, people don't end up with their throats slit. You haven't seen what these bastards do with your own eyes. I'm telling you, we've covered these black devils with flares, tank fire, and heavy machine-gun fire and it has had no observable effect. Every morning this week, I have seven to ten men dead with their throats slit or missing from their guard posts. The American artillery then opens up on us all day long with uncanny accuracy from the intel these devils are able to obtain on our positions at night. Their big guns work us over all day long and then at night the bastards sneak back across No Man's Land and kill us one by one in silence. I tell you they are fucking ghosts—we never hear them coming."

"You must stop this. They are not Supermen."

"Oh, but they are. They have already driven us from a dozen farmhouses that we once used as forward observation posts. They fire bazookas at us to divert our attention while demolition crews sneak up in the dark and set explosive charges. Up in smoke the houses go with my men trapped inside. These *schwarzen teufel* seem to get their kicks out of driving us upstairs and then blowing the farmhouses out from beneath us."

"You sound like a defeatist, Walther—and you know what Kesselring thinks of defeatists."

"Don't give me that nonsense. These bastards are Supermen, I tell you. I thought we were a crack unit until I witnessed these demons firsthand. They have driven our outposts back nearly a mile in only a week."

Hollmann studied his brother's haggard face as he took a deep pull from his cigarette. This brigade of black-faced brigands had definitely rattled him. Hollmann had always thought the Americans were poor fighters compared to those of the Reich or the experienced Tommies, but it appeared that they had improved considerably since their early debacles at Kasserine Pass and Meknassy Heights in North Africa. But this new Devil's Brigade was obviously something far different. They must be some sort of shock troops, like Skorzeny's elite Waffen-SS unit that carried out the successful rescue mission that liberated the deposed Mussolini from captivity in Northern Italy. But still, wasn't his brother exaggerating the threat they posed? How could they have gotten into his head so quickly?

"You've got to buck up, *Brüderlein*—Little Brother," he admonished him gently. "You make these black devils sound like Supermen when everyone knows it is the Hermann Göring Division that is composed of true *Übermensch.* My God, don't you realize that from the Alban Hills all the way here to Littoria, we have the Allies in our gun sights and trapped on the coast. With one dedicated counterattack, we can cut them to pieces and drive them back into the sea."

"It is not as easy as you think, not with the black devils all around."

Another shell exploded in the distance. His brother's desk vibrated, and a ripple propagated through his coffee as if on the surface of a pond.

"But on the whole, the Americans and British must be in poor shape. Their morale must be terribly low right now clinging to the beachhead like survivors aboard a life raft. Why the Führer himself has called Anzio an 'abscess' that must be excised from Italy's body to preserve the Third Reich and keep Rome in German hands."

"You don't know these murderous bastards. They are not human, I tell you."

Seeing that his brother had come completely unglued, Hollmann held up his hands and apologized. "All right, Brother, I understand. They are a formidable opponent. I am sorry for stirring you up like this. Perhaps it would be best to change the subject to the reason for my visit. There is more going on in this sector than these marauding black demons."

His brother impatiently stamped out his Eckstein stub in the ashtray on his desk. "What do you want then? As you can see, I am busy."

Hollmann frowned. "I am your older brother and a colonel in the SS. You need to treat me with the respect I deserve, Major."

His brother's bleary red eyes fell with shame. "Yes, I am sorry. These devils have unnerved me. I can't sleep at night."

"I am sorry, Brother. But know that I am here to help you as well as to ask for your help. Remember, *blot ist dicker ales wiser*." Blood is thicker than water.

"I apologize, Brother."

"I accept your apology. Now my intelligence information indicates that the Allies are using the Mussolini Canal and its network of shallow ravines as a rally and evacuation point for escaped POWs. General Wolff has instructed me to verify this for him."

"Yes, one of our patrols caught a group attempting to sneak through to the Allied lines the other night. The canal is a prominent geographic marker—that's why they use it."

"The Escape Line is run by an Irish priest named Father O'Flaherty. He works at the Vatican and he's developed into something of a nemesis for Colonel Kappler, the head of the Rome Gestapo. General Wolff wants this Escape Line here in the south to be terminated."

"What do you want me to do?"

"I want to question your POW captives."

"But they are long gone. We handed them over to the SS two days ago."

"Damn, I need to know more about the Escape Line."

"What do you need to know exactly?"

"I need to know who besides O'Flaherty is involved. I need to know how the Allied POWs make contact with the Resistance when they arrive in Rome. Is it handled only by O'Flaherty or are there others? Do they use cutouts with codenames that cannot be linked to other agents?"

He paused a moment as several closely-spaced artillery explosions thundered in the distance. They sounded like they were from the Allies this time.

"I also want to know how they get through our lines. Are there bribes and payoffs? Do they use codenames and alternate routes if necessary? What are the Resistance cell names? Can you help me, Brother?"

"Yes, we can talk to my interrogators and you can have access to our reports. Do you need them right now?"

He looked at his watch; it was after 2200 hours. "No, it is late. We can start tomorrow. Right now, I would like to hear more about these black devils. How do you plan on stopping them?"

"I don't have the foggiest idea. We've tried everything and they still have pushed us far back from our original line. These bastards are not human, I'm telling you."

His brother's panicky voice had returned and he held up his hands again to calm him down. "I believe you, *Brüderlein*. I believe you," he said in a mollifying tone. He pulled out his pack of cigarettes. "Here, have a Lucky Strike. American cigarettes are the best."

Stamping out his smoke in the ashtray, he handed his brother a Lucky, grabbed another one for himself, and lit them with his Zippo. They sat back in their seats puffing on their American tobacco for a minute without talking. Hollmann was pleased to see his brother calm down. He was a fine officer and it pained him to see him so rattled. This Devil's Brigade had certainly gotten inside his head. Kesselring's forces should have been able to push the enemy back into the sea, since every square foot of the Allied position was within range of German artillery; and the veteran Hermann Göring Division should have been more than a match for this Devil's Brigade. But somehow, this stealthy enemy was able to sneak undetected behind German lines by night and gain sufficient intelligence on the division's dispositions to supply its own artillery with valuable target information, which they then used to bomb the hell out of them during the day.

How ironic it was that his son Gunther was probably one of these American black devils that had turned his brother into a blubbering fool.

He had an idea. "Let's take a walk outside, Walther. Some air will do us good."

After initial reluctance, his brother consented and they stepped outside into the peaceful light of the full moon. The shelling had stopped and the cold air smelled briny like the sea. Smoking their cigarettes, they walked to the edge of the woods. Hollmann noticed that his brother was looking around nervously, as if the enemy might pop out and attack at any moment.

He felt sorry for the poor bastard.

"Brother, I have some important information for you with regard to this *Schwarzen Teufel Brigade.* Their real name is the First Special Service Force. It is an elite commando unit recruited among American lumberjacks, Canadian prospectors, and assorted ruffians of both nationalities. They were trained in Montana and are highly skilled in mountaineering, skiing, hand-to-hand combat, and nighttime infiltration. Their motto is 'every soldier must be a potential gangster.' You are right. They are as close to supermen as we are going to see in this war. But as Superman has his krypton, so too do these Forcemen have their Achilles heel. You just have to find out what that is, and I promise I will help you do just that."

"My God, you knew who these bastards were all this time and you didn't tell me?"

"I wasn't one hundred percent certain at first, but now I realize that it must be them. How many elite American and Canadian units are there? Now they are leaving calling cards. They want you to know who they are so that you will fear them. Their reign of terror has begun."

"It most certainly has. But there's something I didn't tell you either."

"What?"

"The black devils have taken over the village of Borgo Sabotino that only a week ago was a quarter of a mile behind our lines. They have turned it into a big brothel."

Hollmann suppressed a laugh. "A whole village?"

"Yes, and they have renamed it 'Gusville.'"

"Gusville? That is a strange name even for the Allies. What does it mean?"

"We don't know. But yesterday one of our patrols saw a sign hanging at Borgo Sabotino that said 'Gusville.' Obviously, they renamed the town after some American or Canadian bigwig named Gus. In any case, the black devils have taken over Borgo Sabotino and turned it into a brothel. There are all kinds of women there and the men get drunk at the bar they have created. It is like the Wild West. They have even put up their own street signs."

"Street signs?"

"The main street is called Tank Street, and another street is named Prostitute Avenue. Our tanks hurled shells at them yesterday and blew up one of their buildings. But they called in artillery support and took out two of our Mark IV's within minutes. This Devil's Brigade—they seem to have luck on their side."

"Luck comes only to those who earn it. We should give this First Special Service Force, if they are in fact the black devils, a little of their own medicine. Do you have patrols going out tonight?"

"Of course, but I am afraid of losing more men. I have lost a whole company in a week."

"I want to go on a patrol and catch one of these devils for myself. Then I can interrogate him about his outfit and the Escape Line here at Anzio."

"Sounds dangerous, Brother. I would advise against it. You have no idea what you are up against. It is hell out there in No Man's Land."

"I need a prisoner and this may be the only way to prove to you that these bastards aren't supermen. Now where are your patrols heading tonight?"

"One is in Sussuno, the other east of Borgo Sabotino."

"Don't you mean Gusville?"

"This is not fun and games, Brother. These black devils will stop your heart without you hearing a peep. They are like Indians the way they sneak up on us. It reminds me of the Karl May books we used to read when we were boys."

"You give them too much credit. Tonight we have the moon on our side."

He pointed up to the pregnant, fluted-yellow ball in the night sky with a halo of milky white light around it. It was a mesmerizing thing of beauty.

"The moon is on our side, you say?"

"Yes, when it is new, or full like you see now, the Italians call it the Roman Moon. It is said to protect warriors during an upcoming battle. Tonight it will protect us like the Roman Legions of old."

"The moon will protect us? Now who is the superstitious one?"

"It is not superstition, *Brüderlein*. I tell you these dusky black devils are in for a good whipping and we will do it by the light of the Roman Moon."

"But how do you know that the moon protects us, and not the Allies?"

"I don't know. It's just a feeling I have. At least for tonight."

"I'll believe in this special moon of yours if and when we defeat the enemy. Until then, it is nothing but an old Roman myth."

"I don't think so, Brother. Mark my words, tonight the Roman Moon will be with the Reich."

CHAPTER 37

MUSSOLINI CANAL AND SESSUNO FEBRUARY 10, 1944

UNDER COVER OF THUNDEROUS ARTILLERY FIRE, Bridger crept forward through the night, his baggy cargo pants and hooded wolf-fur-trim parka rippling in the winter breeze that had picked up in the past half hour. The assault force consisted of a hundred blackfaces from Fifth Company, Second Regiment, commanded by Captain Adna Underhill. At 2000 hours, they crossed the Mussolini Canal at Bridge Five and marched eastward along both sides of the main road towards their target: the small town of Sessuno, where a bulked-up company of Hermann Göring Panzergrenadiers was reportedly garrisoned.

The Germans had the advantage of armor, while Forcemen had surprise on their side. Or at least that's the way Bridger figured it. They were also armed to the teeth. On their right sides, they carried Colt .45-caliber M1911A1 semiautomatic service pistols in their holsters; on their left, 20-inch long V-42 fighting knives in tied-down scabbards; and in their hands, M1 rifles with fixed bayonets at the end of the barrels, Thompson submachine guns, or more cumbersome Johnson light machine guns—affectionately called "Johnny guns." Despite all their lethal weaponry, they moved swiftly and silently. There was not even a chuff from their boots on the cold, hard ground or from the elkskin moccasins favored by the smattering of Native Americans, from both sides of the border, in the assault unit.

One of those Indians creeping forward alongside Bridger at the head of the column was a brooding, barrel-chested scout by the name of Sergeant Tommy Prince, an Ojibwa Native of the Saulteaux tribe who had spent most of his twenty-eight years on the Brokenhead Reservation at Scanterbury, Manitoba. He was a hulking figure with a broad face, crow-black hair as thick as prairie grass, and mahogany skin that needed no camouflage—but most importantly, he was a natural-born Kraut killer. Like Sergeant Van Ausdale and the other Forcemen with Indian blood, Prince had acquired significant skill at hunting, tracking, and wilderness survival as a youth and he brought this skill set to the army. With a special talent in scouting, stalking the enemy, and close-quarter combat, he was determined to fight the Germans as an Ojibwa warrior, never failing to wear his silent moccasins or scalplock into battle.

Bridger had taken part in a patrol just last night where he had witnessed firsthand the havoc wrought by the descendent of the Saulteaux patriarch Chief Peguis. Sergeant Prince had slit the throats of three sleeping German sentries with his V-42, while letting one escape unharmed by only counting coup on him and stealing his Mauser submachine gun. But even more importantly, when the Indian scout had killed one of the Germans, Bridger had heard the surprised Kraut gasp, as his throat was being sliced open, the words that would soon become legendary throughout Italy.

The dying German had gurgled, "*Schwartzer Teufel.*"

Black Devil.

That's what had started all the craziness. Then later that morning, a captured German private had, unprompted, referred to the night raiders as the "Black Devil's Brigade" during interrogation by intelligence officer Finn Roll; and later that same day, a German lieutenant's diary that had been recovered was translated by Bridger referencing the "Black Devils" that stole in unseen and unheard at night, employing cold steel as their primary weapon of intimidation. Suddenly, a nickname was born for the Forcemen—a name that, for the first time, didn't piss them off and they actually liked. The new nickname caught on like wildfire, spreading across the Anzio beachhead faster than mail call. Now everyone in the embattled Fifth Army was calling them by their new moniker.

They were the "Devil's Brigade."

A sound came from the brush up ahead. Prince put up a hand in the moonlight, halting the company. Bridger ducked into the shadows of a bush next to the road as everyone took cover, thinking back to what he had heard two hours earlier over the radio from sexy-voiced Axis Sally: "Boys, there's no use going out on patrol tonight because we're waiting for you." *Actually,* he thought, *it's the other way around: we're coming for you, you Kraut bastards. Again.*

THE WORST IS YET TO COME.

The all-clear signal was given and they started off again, a single column on each side of the road. The artillery barrage on Sessuno continued, the shells whistling overhead and roaring as they exploded in the outlying farmhouses and town center. The night air was cool and smelled of petrol fumes and cordite. As they shuffled along, Bridger prayed he wouldn't step on a goddamn Bouncing Betty. The German antipersonnel mine had three prongs and, when triggered, bounced up several feet and exploded ball bearings, cut glass, and metal shavings. The Betties were far worse than the German *Schu* mines and would blow your balls off, or rearrange your stomach or face into a picture of hell.

A half hour later, they came to a halt three hundred yards west of town. Sessuno was a crossroads and major German thoroughfare for both supply trucks and heavy armor, and they were fortunate to have avoided detection by the enemy's forward positions and alarm company patrols. When the scheduled artillery cover stopped, Underhill radioed for another fifteen minutes of shelling so the assault force could creep in closer to the enemy outposts along the edge of town. The goal was to attack the Germans, seize the village, and occupy it for the night, thereby leading the enemy to believe that a major Allied breakout from Anzio was in the works.

As the artillery barrage resumed, the patrol crept forward until it reached the edge of the Allied shelling zone. The strategy courted death from friendly fire, but ensured that they would maintain the element of surprise by attacking from an unexpected quarter. Bridger, taking part on the raid as Frederick's HQ staff officer and observer, then listened as Underhill huddled up the officers and quickly issued the attack orders.

"Lieutenant Ivey and Second Platoon will lead the attack up the Bridge Five-Sessuno Road, while First and Third provide cover fire on the flanks. Take out their goddamned machine-gun nests with the Johnnies. The three mortar crews will also cover the advance. First and Third Platoons will then hit them on the left and right at the same time. We go one minute after the shelling stops. Major Bridger, do you have anything to add?"

"Just one thing. We need to take Sessuno before they counterattack with their reserves. When they come, it'll be from Littoria to the southeast. It's only three miles away and they have heavy armor—a dozen or so Mark IV's—that will be coming in hot."

"Anyone else have anything?" asked Underhill.

No one did.

"All right. Keep up a hot sustaining fire with those Johnnies. Stay low, keep moving, pinpoint Jerry's fire, and take him down. In a half hour, this goddamned town is going to be ours for the night. Hopefully, they'll have something to drink stiffer than *vino*."

There were grunts of ascent and head bobs all around. Bridger looked at Sergeant Prince and said, "You ready to kill some Krauts, Kemosabe."

The brawny Ojibwa grinned. "Fuck yeah. Tonight I might even take a scalp or two."

That brought a roar of approval from the Forcemen.

Then they went quiet, all blood and guts. They waited and waited and then waited some more until, finally, the artillery pounding stopped, the forward signal was given, and three platoons of black-faced marauders, armed to the teeth in their baggy outfits, charged into the village.

ψψψ

Bridger went with Ivey's Second Platoon up the main road.

They immediately met stiff resistance from the German guns and mortars targeting the lane. The machine gunners flipped back their camouflage nets and let fly a thunderous clatter of blue and white tracers. Suddenly, flares illuminated the whole sector and mortar bursts blossomed across the contested road. While First and Third Platoons angled towards the two machine-gun nests, the German's fire was accurately centered on Second Platoon and instantly inflicted a heavy toll.

Letting loose with his Tommy at the enemy gunners crouched behind sandbags, Bridger saw Sergeant Butler to his left ripped apart like a buzz saw across his chest. Then to his right, he saw Lieutenant Ivey go down with a bad stomach wound.

The attack quickly faltered.

With the help of Sergeant McGinnis, he dragged Ivey into a ditch, covering his body as a German mortar round came in and blasted his eardrums.

And then a great and wondrous thing happened.

Friendly guns roared and barked all along the road from all three platoons at once in a massive barrage of counterfire augmented by the mortar crews. The next thing he knew, the two flanking platoons were swooping in on the gun pits and silencing two of the machine guns with a handful of timely thrown grenades.

Bridger quickly led the counterattack.

Screaming like a banshee, he stormed into the town with thirty men from Third Platoon. On his left was the Ojibwa scout, Sergeant Prince, also letting loose with a war cry and a lethal spray from his Thompson on full automatic. The assault had force and momentum and sheer will behind it, and the Germans in their coal-scuttle helmets turned in panic, spilled into the crossroads, and tried to flee.

Those who tried to escape south in the direction of the nearest German-controlled town, Borgo Piave, were mowed down with automatic weapons fire from Third Platoon waiting in ambush at the intersection.

Bridger followed up with a smaller squad and made a frontal assault on a pair of farmhouses, killing a dozen more of the enemy and taking three prisoners. By the time he emerged, most of the enemy resistance had ceased and the scattered pockets of Germans were routed from houses and barns with bazookas and grenades.

By then it was midnight. It had taken less than a half hour to seize the town.

They began a house-by-house mucking operation. A defensive belt was laid down south, east, and north of Sessuno, while the wounded Captain Underhill set up his headquarters and reserve in a building at the crossroads. While the Forcemen liberated the Italians of their food and liquor and the Germans of their Schmeissers, Mausers, and *Gott min Uns* belt buckles, Bridger counted the enemy dead and wounded. The final tally was forty-eight dead and seven prisoners of war, four of whom were lightly wounded and one badly.

A death sticker—*THE WORST IS YET TO COME*—was placed on the forehead of every dead German, and Indian-spearhead stickers with the words "USA" drawn horizontally and "Canada" vertically were stamped to buildings and guard posts all over town.

The mission had been a complete success. In fact, it was a rout. But Bridger knew the German counterattack was coming.

And the Krauts would be coming in hot.

CHAPTER 38

SESSUNO
FEBRUARY 11, 1944

HE AND PRINCE hijacked a Volkswagen *Kübelwagen*—the German bucket-shaped equivalent of the U.S. "Jeep"—and drove it to a farmhouse on the outskirts of town where there was a good view to the southeast towards Littoria. This was the direction that the enemy counterattack, if it came, would likely originate from, and Bridger wanted to observe the German response to the FSSF raid with his own eyes on behalf of HQ to gauge the unit's combat readiness and response time. Parking the vehicle, they lit up Camels, walked past a riding horse and two plough horses in the stalls, climbed up into the second floor loft of the barn, slid open the big south door, and were instantly bathed in bright moonlight.

With no sign yet of the German reserves, Bridger stared up at the pockmarked, silvery-yellow orb, feeling its transcendent power.

"That there, Kemosabe, is what's known as a Roman Moon," he observed.

The Native Canadian nodded. "I heard the Italians talking about it in Borgo Sabotino. They said it would protect us in battle as it did their Roman ancestors. I thought they were pulling my leg—seeing as I am a superstitious Indian and all."

"What do you think now?"

"I think those dagos weren't fooling. We just destroyed an entire company of Hitler's finest. I mean, we tore through those bastards like shit through a goose. They never knew what hit 'em."

Bridger nodded. "I figure it the same as you. If Ares is on the side of anyone, it's got to be us dogfaced bastards from the US of A and Mother Canada, plus our Limey friends. After all, we're the ones who are liberating this country on behalf of the descendants of the ancient Romans."

The Ojibwa stared up at the moon with a gleam in his eyes, his chin jutting out like a cliff of resistant sandstone. "All my life, I have wanted to be a warrior and do something to help my people recover their good name. Here in Italy with the Force, I have that chance every goddamn day."

"That's why you've got to stay alive. So you can keep getting that chance."

"Yes, sir, Major. I'll do my best."

He took a puff from his Camel. "I'm just glad you're on our side. I've never seen anybody as lethal with a knife or Tommy as you. You truly are a natural-born Kraut killer, Kemosabe."

"That's what they call me, and I take it as a compliment. Sometimes I wonder, though, if the killing comes too easy."

"Lately, I've been wondering the same thing myself."

"So what do you do?"

"I remind myself that these Nazis are ruthless bastards that deserve what's coming to them. I tell myself that they're the ones who started this damned war and they have to reap what—"

He stopped right there as the Indian raised his hand abruptly, signaling for silence. Had he heard something?

They stopped and listened.

This time Bridger heard it: a light footfall coming from the ground below.

He slowly withdrew his Colt from his holster rig as Prince unsheathed his V-42 knife from his scabbard. Keeping their Tommies strapped to their backs, they crept to the edge and looked down into the dark barn below, which was illuminated by only a sliver of moonlight slanting in through the half-open door.

Bridger probed the shadows, but couldn't see anything except the vague outline of a field plough, a pair of harnesses, and a pile of farming equipment. A horse in one of the stalls below gave a snort.

He watched and waited a full minute before moving to his right and taking cover behind a clump of hay. Prince stole his way to the ladder and started easing his way down, rung by precious rung, to the ground floor. Silent as a mouse.

The light chuff of feet across straw rose up through the rafters, and the horse snorted again. Then the sound of the footsteps stopped.

Bridger continued to scan the shadows, keeping his pistol aimed downward, but he didn't see or hear anything except the two plough horses and the single riding horse snorting and pawing in their stalls. They seemed agitated.

He felt a tickling sensation on the back of his neck, as if someone was watching them. But who the hell was it? Did he dare call out in German? Or was it one of the boys from the Devil's Brigade trying to scare the shit out of them? But why would anyone pull a stunt like that after the battle they had just fought?

He watched Prince. The Indian stepped down onto the straw floor of the barn, tiptoed to the left on silent moccasins, and disappeared into the shadows.

Heart hammering in his chest, Bridger crept down the other ladder, coming in from the other direction. When he reached the matted straw floor, he froze.

He heard a snorting sound to his right. Turning, he saw in the bleached moonlight the huge eye of one of the big plough horses. It raised its ear, turned its head, looked right at him, and stepped forward until its massive head and jaw projected out of its stall. He went up to the horse and ran a hand through its mane, trying to keep the animal calm. Meanwhile, Prince checked towards the back of the barn, his V-42 drawn like a miniature saber.

Bridger heard low whispers behind him in the opposite direction from the Ojibwa.

He froze and scanned the barn.

The sounds stopped. But he had pinpointed where they had originated from. The whispers had come from the first stall near the barn door, where the smaller riding horse was penned.

But it was dark and he couldn't see a damned thing. Unsure if the new interlopers were friend or foe, he tiptoed forward, keeping his Peacemaker aimed at the stall but holding his fire. But if they were Forcemen, why would they be hiding out and whispering? They had to be Krauts or Italians.

"Halt! Who goes there!" he called out first in Italian then *auf Deutsch*.

Now he heard the jingle of a harness or bridle. But it was still so dark he couldn't make anything out.

Then he heard the riding horse in the stall snorting and pawing.

"Throw down your weapons!" he warned again in both languages, and this time he squeezed the trigger, aiming high.

He heard voices and saw the massive head of the horse and above the equine the outline of what appeared to be not one, but two, riders mounted on its back.

He fired the Colt a second time.

Now the horse reared up in panic, tossed its head wildly, and threw the two riders. They fell back hard against the rear wall of the stall and collapsed in a heap.

Bridger fired again. This time he heard a heavy grunt and knew he had hit a target. Terrified, the horse broke through the flimsy stall and loped off in panic, charging through the open barn door and bolting out into the moonlit night.

Covering the stall with his gun, Bridger shouted out in German, "Don't move or I'll shoot again!"

"Don't shoot! We surrender!" cried a voice in aristocratic English, and Bridger thought to himself, "Holy shit, did I just shoot some Limey officer?"

Bridger fought against the panic as his fingers clenched his pistol and he stepped forward to see who he had shot. "Come out of there with your hands up!" he commanded in English.

"All right, we're coming out! Don't shoot!"

The two figures stepped forward, one of them helping the other. Prince came up beside him, his V-42 knife exchanged for his Tommy gun, which was aimed directly at the midriff of the uninjured one to the left. Slowly, they emerged from the battered stall and their faces became visible in the moonlight.

Bridger's jaw dropped.

"*Mein Gott*, is that you, Gunther?" cried the one on the right in the Wehrmacht major's uniform. He was clutching his shoulder and supported by the other man, who was bedecked in a jet-black SS uniform.

Prince looked at Bridger with shock. "What the hell? This Kraut officer knows you? And why did he just call you Gunther?"

He was still unable to believe his eyes and couldn't bring himself to speak. But pleasant childhood recollections of a fishing trip in the Austrian Alps outside Salzburg with the two men before him brought him quickly to his senses. As before in Rome, he couldn't help but feel that it was destiny that had brought them all together in this war-torn locality in Central Italy.

He responded to the sergeant. "He called me that name because he's my uncle and that is what I used to be called growing up in Austria."

The Ojibwa looked confused. "This son of bitch is your uncle? Are you shitting me?"

"Nope, and it gets worse, Sergeant. The SS colonel standing next to him is my goddamn father."

CHAPTER 39

SESSUNO
FEBRUARY 11, 1944

HOLLMANN felt like an idiot. He had demanded that his brother Walther take him on a raid this evening so that he could capture and interrogate one of the black devils—but instead he had to suffer the ignominy of being taken prisoner by one of them. But it wasn't just any black devil. The charcoal-faced, baggy-uniformed commando who had just captured him and his brother happened to be his own estranged son. A more embarrassing fate he could not imagine for a father in time of war.

He looked down the barrel of his son's pistol, thinking about the curse. Or was his and Walther's capture at the hands of his son attributable to random chance? No, it couldn't be; this had to be destiny. But it seemed to be more than that. In the back of his mind, he couldn't help but feel it was some sort of payback for not only what had happened back in Innsbruck, but for fighting for Nazi Germany, as if God Almighty Himself was taking him to task for his accumulated lifetime of sins.

You have been captured by your own son, you swine. It doesn't matter that you saved his life in Rome. This is the fate you so richly deserve—this is your curse for all you have done in this world!

"I need to get Walther to a medic," he said to his son. "He is badly wounded."

"You really thought you were going to get away on a horse? This isn't the Wild West, you know."

"It worked when Old Shatterhand did it, did it not?"

"You do realize that you're talking about the novels of a German writer from fifty years ago who made his career writing Westerns, yet never once set foot in the American West. No wonder Germany is losing the war."

"You can dispense with the American bravado, John Wayne. Your uncle is hurt and needs a doctor." He glanced at the burly Native American sergeant standing next to him. "Or would you and Cochise here prefer a medicine man?"

The big Indian pointed his Tommy at him. "Don't be calling me no Apache, or I'll shoot you where you stand. I'm an Ojibwa of the Saulteaux tribe."

Bridger shrugged. "Sergeant Prince here is a regular Kraut killer and descended from a long line of chiefs in Canada, so I wouldn't make him mad if I were you. He's killed two or three of your Hermann Göring boys practically every night this week. And he enjoyed every minute of it."

"I sure as hell did," agreed the Ojibwa. "Killing Krauts is even easier than killing deer."

"I'll be sure to remember that," said Hollmann, eyeing the Indian warily. "Now we need to see to Walther. He is badly hurt."

"No, it's not as bad as I thought. I'll be fine," said his brother. "The bullet went clean through. I just need a dressing."

"We'll get you what you need," said Bridger. "But first hand over those weapons, slowly now. Sergeant, disarm them and see to a field dressing for the major. I am going to interrogate them."

"Right here?"

"Yes, Sergeant. Do you have a problem with that?"

"No, sir. But aren't the Krauts coming?"

"That's why I'm going to interrogate them. With your permission, Sergeant."

Now that's the American army for you, thought Hollmann with amusement. *A mere sergeant questioning the orders of a major. No wonder the Allies are still clinging to the beachhead!*

After he handed over their weapons, he and the sergeant attended to Walther's gunshot wound. Hollmann doused the wound with schnapps from his flask and, with the sergeant's help, he applied a makeshift field dressing out of a pair of rags found in the barn. His brother was right: the bullet had missed the bone and the wound, though it had bled profusely, wasn't as bad as either of them had thought. When they were done applying the field dressing, he and Walther were made to sit down with their legs crossed on the floor of the barn with guns trained on them.

After a moment, his son stepped forward and hovered over him aggressively. "So, Colonel Hollmann, what are you doing in this neck of the woods? Last time I checked a map, Rome was thirty-five miles to the north. I sincerely doubt you got lost."

"I was visiting your Uncle Walther. I brought him two cases of Chianti and thought we'd sit around and drink, but instead we ended up here."

"You didn't answer my question. What the hell are you doing in Sessuno?"

"Pardon the American expression, but piss off."

Bridger—or was the son of a bitch still Gunther?—kicked him with his heavy boot and pointed his pistol at him. "Start talking, pops. Last time you and I had a chat was after I was beaten senseless at Gestapo headquarters. What are you doing so far away from home? And don't lie to me, or I'll have Sergeant Prince scalp you. I am not joking either. He literally lives for that kind of shit."

Hollmann looked again at the Indian and could tell that his son was dead serious. "Very well, I happen to be checking into an Allied Escape Line that for the past month has used the Mussolini Canal to sneak POWs back behind Allied lines. I also wanted to see the First Special Service Force in action for myself and perhaps take a prisoner or two for interrogation."

His son smiled sarcastically. "Is that right? How's that going for you?"

"Badly, as you can see," said his brother Walther, grimacing in pain. "Do you have any damned morphine? My arm is throbbing."

"Sorry, Uncle Walther, we're fresh out of morphine—and sympathy too. You'll have to try the British Eighth Army. They should be in Cassino about now."

Hollmann shook his head. "It will be months before they take Cassino, and by then you will be wiped clean off this beachhead."

"I seriously doubt that." He turned to the Indian. "Sergeant Prince, would you be kind enough to climb back up to the loft and keep an eye out for the enemy. Their armor should be coming up any minute now."

"Yes, sir. But shouldn't I keep an eye on these two?"

"My father and uncle aren't going anywhere. If they make one false move, I will shoot them down like the dirty Nazi scoundrels they are without batting an eye."

"Yes, sir. Sounds like you have a close-knit family." Grinning, he left them and climbed up into the barn loft.

Hollmann tried to read his son's mind. He was most certainly not going to allow himself and Walther to be captured by the Allies and shipped off to North Africa, and then to the United States or England, to work like a slave in a POW camp. There had to be some way to fool Gunther and get out of this situation. His son had already made one poor decision by remaining here to interrogate him and Walther; instead, he should have been driving them back to his unit that had taken over the town. Out here, more than a mile from the town center, he and the Indian were vulnerable. The planned counterattack would come any minute now and cut them off—and not necessarily just from Littoria. Somehow, Hollmann realized, he had to distract them so they lost track of time and could be trapped.

"Tell me about this Gusville," he said to his son as if genuinely interested. "All our troops are talking about it. Is it true that you and your men have taken over the town and turned it into a giant brothel?"

"Hey, what do you know?" exclaimed Prince from the loft, taking the bait. "The Krauts already know about Gusville."

"You're damn right we do," Hollmann called up to the Indian enthusiastically. He looked again at his son. "Tell me about it. Are the women there as pretty as they say? And who is this Gus anyway? Is he a general or a Hollywood actor? Or maybe he is a U.S. senator?"

"Yes, tell us, Gunther," said Walther, adroitly realizing that his brother was trying to buy time and now playing along with the charade. "Who is Gusville named after?"

"Not any goddamned general, actor, or senator, I can tell you that. It's named after Gus Heilman."

"Who the hell is Gus Heilman?"

"A measly lieutenant in the First Regiment who played football at the University of Virginia and started up a tavern in Charlottesville. Gus Heilman's only claim to fame is he likes to drink, fuck, and fight—and usually in that order."

They all laughed. Looking at his son's lighthearted expression, Hollmann knew that he and Walther had him. His son may have been a fierce and well-trained commando named John Bridger now, but he was still a young man. And young men were gullible.

Hollmann pretended to be surprised. "They changed the name of Borgo Sabotino because of a lieutenant?"

"Well, yeah. Gus is very popular and it was his idea to make the town our own. He and the others in Second Company decided it would make a good home base, so after driving out Hitler's finest, they elected to stay there. They had seen enough of Anzio to decide it made no sense not to have a place to relax with booze and women. So they created their own Deadwood and appointed Gus the mayor."

"A man after my own heart. I sure as hell hope he got promoted."

"No, not yet. But the guy is absolutely nuts. I mean, how crazy do you have to be to start up a new town a quarter of a mile behind enemy lines?"

"I would like to meet this Gus Heilman," said Walther, maintaining the charade. "He sounds like an interesting fellow."

"And crazy as a loon. One of his first acts was to appoint other officers to different positions, including head of sanitation, chief of police, and social coordinator. There are already three good bars open in town."

"Tell us about Tank Street and Prostitute Avenue," said Hollmann, stringing his son along. "Our advance patrols have seen the new street signs. How did Gus and his crew come up with those names?"

"More importantly, are there really young sporting ladies all over town as it is rumored?" asked Walther like a salacious schoolboy.

"You don't know the half of it," Sergeant Prince said from above. "One of our guys snuck in a half dozen lovely ladies on a boat from Naples."

Hollmann looked at his son and feigned a look of surprise. "What? They actually smuggled in women on a boat?"

"I couldn't believe it either. But now there are women from the surrounding countryside, too. They just love us Americans. That's why we have to have nightly raids behind German lines. We have to obtain enough food and booze not only for us, but to keep our lovely ladies in a reasonable state of comfort. There's a war going on, but they won't have it any other way."

"Yeah," agreed Prince, "otherwise they might—"

He stopped right there, leaving the words unfinished.

"Oh shit," he said. "The Krauts are coming! Fuck!"

"What?" cried Bridger. "You're messing with us, right?"

"No, sir. The road is swarming with Krauts! We've got to get out of here!"

Hollmann watched as his son's expression turned from alarm to anger. "Goddamnit, I told you to keep an eye on the road!"

"I swear I only looked away for a minute!"

"What's the enemy strength?"

"I count eight vehicles, including two tanks, coming in from the east, and eight to ten coming up from the south. A pair of half-tracks are out front of the southern column. They're hauling ass, too."

"Get your butt down here!"

"Yes, Major!"

Hollmann suppressed a gloating smile. The German reserves were pouring in as expected. If the Allies didn't pull out immediately, they would be crushed by the counterattack. There was not a moment to waste. With any luck, they would be cut to pieces as they retreated down the Sessuno Road back to the Mussolini Canal. But if that happened, there was a strong likelihood that Bridger and his

Indian cohort would be captured or killed. He didn't want that to happen, and realized that he had to do something to prevent it.

"You've got to get the hell out of here now," he implored his son. "You and the sergeant can make it if you leave me and Walther behind."

Bridger wheeled and glared flints at him and his brother. "You sons of bitches! You knew they were coming, didn't you! You tricked us!"

"We knew nothing of the sort!" said Walther, thinking quickly on his feet. "There are no tanks coming up from the south because they have been moved to the coast. The only armor you see is coming from the east."

"Well, there are half-tracks. Now get on your feet!"

"You need to leave us here, or you will die," protested Hollmann. "Walther is injured. He is just going to slow you down. You must leave now!"

"The Krauts are coming like bats out of hell, Major!" warned Sergeant Prince. "What should we do?"

"The first thing is to get you butt down here!" Then to the two brothers. "You two, get on your fucking feet before I shoot you both! *Komm, komm, los, los!*"

Hollmann held up his hands. "Easy, Son, we are getting to our feet. But remember, your Uncle Walther is injured. He is just going to slow you down."

"Don't call me *son,* you bastard!"

"All right, all right, just be reasonable!"

"Fuck you! Get up!"

He jabbed them with his Thompson. Hollmann tried to protect his brother, but the nose of the submachine gun drove into Walther's wounded shoulder. Giving a cry of excruciating pain, he collapsed back to the ground.

"I said get up! *Schnell, schnell!* Let's go, we're taking the Volkswagen!"

The big Indian pulled Walther to his feet, hoisted him over his shoulder like a potato sack, and began carrying him towards the vehicle. Hollmann's mind worked frantically for a way to escape as his son prodded him towards the *Kübelwagen* at gunpoint. If he and Walther got inside that vehicle, anything could happen. They could be taken prisoner by the Americans and shipped off to a POW camp, or be blown to bits by the German counterattack. Either way, it was a terrible roll of the dice and their future was uncertain at best.

He had to find a way to seize control of the situation. He glanced back over his shoulder at his son, and was poked again in the back.

"Keep moving! Keep moving!"

He couldn't believe this was once the sweet little boy that he had swam and sailed boats with in clear alpine lakes and skied with at Innsbruck and Grindelwald. All he saw now was a dirty, grim-faced American GI who looked and behaved more like a gangster than a soldier.

Damn you, Gunther! Is it fate that has brought me here? What have I done in this world to deserve this?

He felt another hard jab from behind.

He turned around to protest.

But his son was having none of it. "You two have ten seconds to get in that goddamned wagon. Or I blow your fucking brains out!"

CHAPTER 40

SESSUNO

FEBRUARY 11, 1944

WITH SERGEANT PRINCE BEHIND THE WHEEL, they raced back towards the town, passing olive trees and scrub oak that appeared blurry in the headlights. The heavy gears of the open-topped *Kübelwagen* grinded and the tires squealed across the Sessuno Road as the Ojibwa punched into third. Bridger had crammed his father and brother into the front seat next to the sergeant, and he now covered them with his Tommy from the back. The partially armored, camouflaged Volkswagen was a chariot among dog carts on the dirt road. But Bridger wasn't sure if it would be fast enough to elude the machine-gun fire of the armored half-track that suddenly appeared on their left flank. The Germans opened up with a mounted M-42 from fifty yards, the bullets clattering against the rear of their vehicle like a handful of gravel thrown by a giant.

"Stay down!" he yelled over the roar of the engine. Then to Prince: "Go faster, goddamnit! And that's an order!"

The Ojibwa pressed the gas pedal to the floor, yelling at them all to hold on tight as they started into a curve on the road.

Just before the turn, another enemy barrage swept in like heated needles, cleaving out sharp slivers of bumper metal from the back of the *Kübelwagen.* As they swung into the curve, Bridger answered with fire of his own. The driver of the *Sonderkraftfahrzeug* half-track, one of the German Army's fleetest light-armored fighting vehicles, was forced to turn the wheel hard to his right to avoid the burst from the Thompson.

"Take that, you bastards!" shrieked Bridger with delight.

His father frowned. "Cheer all you want, but you and your squad will never get away. You have no damned armor."

"Shut the hell up. When I want your opinion, I'll ask for it."

And then he wondered: *What if I just let him and Uncle Walther go? What if I decided to just live and let live? Would I get in trouble with the brass? Could Prince keep quiet if we made it a secret?* But with the enemy practically upon them, it was already too late to set them free, he realized. Plus he and Prince would be bagging an SS colonel and a Wehrmacht major, quite an impressive haul for one night's work behind enemy lines.

Another crackle of German machine-gun fire. Bridger heard the snarling whine of bullets and a flurry of ricochets off the *Kübelwagen.* Prince again jammed his foot down upon the accelerator and tore off down the dirt road.

But the half-track was fast. Though lagging behind, it was still speedy enough to keep within effective machine-gun range.

"Faster, Sergeant, faster!" commanded Bridger over the roar of the barking machine gun.

The vehicle surged forward like a racehorse, but the road was filled with potholes and loose gravel and it took all of Prince's dexterity to navigate through it all. As they roared over the rough ground, they churned up a cloud of dust, which Bridger hoped would serve as a smokescreen and allow them to elude the damned machine guns.

The front tire hit a bump. They bounded in the air and came down hard just before a curve, and the sergeant was forced to slow down to control the vehicle.

Bridger opened fire on the enemy. The Germans started to return fire but the M-42 jammed. The gunner in his moldering field gray gave a curse and threw up his hands in anger. But just then, a new pair of fleet German *Kübelwagens* broke from the trees and appeared on their right flank.

One of them swung in and rammed them from behind.

The impact jerked their heads forward and snapped them back violently. Bridger heard his uncle groan in agony as his wounded shoulder was driven into the steering wheel.

"Hurry, we've got to get to our lines!" yelled Bridger over the sound of the straining engines.

"I tell you you're not going to make it," said his father. "You're just going to get us all killed."

"I thought I told you to shut the hell up."

"I am your father and the senior officer in this car—and I will decide when it is time to shut up. You should be worried about not getting us all killed."

"Okay, quit your bickering, you two," said the Ojibwa, gripping the steering wheel hard. "We're going to get out of this pickle by—"

His voice was cut off as a single bullet zipped past his head, drove into the windshield, made a small hole, and exited without shattering the glass. The Germans were now shooting at them with rifles from their *Kübelwagens*. In response, everyone in the car ducked down, keeping their heads just below the tops of their seats. Another flurry of shots: this time one of the bullets smashed into the side view mirror, tearing it from the racing vehicle.

The Germans were hot on their tail and showing no signs of letting up.

"Goddamnit, I can't shake them!" cried the Ojibwa.

"You've got to do something, Kemosabe! They're coming in again!"

"I'm going nearly sixty miles an hour on a dirt road potholed like the surface of the moon! What more can I do?"

"As your superior officer, I am ordering you to shake the bastards! Imagine they're Custer and his bloodthirsty cavalry coming after you!"

"Okay, that'll do it!" He slapped his foot down on the accelerator and gave a high-pitched war cry.

Suddenly, one of the German *Kübelwagens* exploded like chain lightning and burst into flames as it was struck by a mortar round. Bridger caught a glimpse of the soldiers inside struggling to escape the burning vehicle as they were engulfed by a flaming inferno. Up ahead, he saw that Third Platoon had deployed to meet the anticipated German counterattack.

He tapped his father with the nose of his Thompson. "Still sure we're not going to get away?"

"The odds are against it. They're coming up fast."

He pointed behind them to the remaining German *Kübelwagen*—rushing in like a shitstorm from hell—that had shot forward to take the place of the one that had been destroyed.

Suddenly, they were raked with a hailstorm of plunging machine-gun fire and depressed-trajectory, small-arms fire not from only the *Kübelwagen*, but a speedy half-track the Germans called a *Schützenpanzerwagen* that had joined the fray. Meanwhile, the Third's mortar crews, realizing Bridger and company were struggling to outrun their pursuers, unloaded on the Germans trailing behind them. Now both sides were being strafed by small-arms and mortar fire.

And then an unexpected thing happened.

The half-track roared right up next to them, the driver realizing that he would be better protected from the Allied mortar fire by swinging in close to the fleeing enemy.

Bridger looked over at the determined face of the driver. The granite-jawed German with the bristly mustache gritted his teeth and swung the *Kübelwagen* towards them like a quick-darting shark.

Prince swerved right to avoid the impact, but to no avail as the heavy scraping sound of metal on metal echoed into the night. Hitting the accelerator, the Ojibwa was able to pull away. With engines straining, the vehicles sent up jet streams of dust that coalesced into one large ribbon that appeared iridescent in the bright moonlight.

But then the front left tire hit a huge rut from an exploded land mine. The *Kübelwagen* bounded in the air, coming down hard and swerving to the left as the Ojibwa struggled to keep the vehicle under control. A moment later, they were jolted again by the German vehicle, which pitched them in their seats.

Prince jerked right again to avoid being hit. Bridger looked over at the German driver again: his face was taut, his concentration nursed to the highest level. Bridger fired his Tommy at him and the face and its Hitler mustache dissolved in a spray of blood. The German vehicle spun out of control and crashed into a poplar tree.

The Ojibwa gave a rowdy cheer. Bridger was about to do the same when a German Mark IV tank materialized from the trees fifty yards ahead, along their right flank.

"Tank, two o'clock!" he shouted as he saw the turret swinging towards them.

"*Scheisse!* Get down!" screamed his father.

"Good Lord, are we to be killed by one of our own?" shrieked his uncle.

The tank fired.

The first shell missed the Volkswagen, but blasted out a monstrous hole in the dirt road and sent up a cloud of dust and dirt. His view obstructed, Prince swerved crazily and plunged part-way down a sloped berm next to a rainwater-filled drainage ditch on the far side of the road.

The second blast, though it missed too, laid waste to a sycamore tree as the

Ojibwa struggled to keep the vehicle from sliding into the ditch.

The third shell crashed near the vehicle just as all four wheels regained traction on the dirt road. The *Kübelwagen*, though stoutly built, was kicked out at nearly a ninety degree angle by the explosion, as if struck head-on by a freight train. It nosed into the side of an olive tree, veered to the right, and flipped twice before coming to a halt upside down with the driver's side dipping towards the road.

Bridger and the others were trapped inside the vehicle. All around them, machine guns and mortars from both sides continued to rattle with violence. He felt blood trickling down his face as well as a throbbing pain in his head and shoulders. But he was all in one piece and fully mobile.

"Sergeant Prince, you all right?"

"My wrist hurts like a motherfucker, but that's it, sir. It got caught in the damned steering wheel."

"Father?"

"I hit my head, but I'm all right."

"Uncle?"

"I'm in a bad way."

"How bad?"

"I've been shot a second time and I think my legs are broken."

"What?" cried his father in disbelief.

"Just leave me here to die. There is nothing more for me on this Godforsaken earth. I am sorry, Brother, for letting you down. I curse this damned war. Just let me die."

"Never!" Bridger heard his father roar, and he felt a pride in his father's stubbornness. "What kind of man would I be if I let my own brother die? I'm getting you to a medic!"

"No, I am finished. This war has killed me. And it will kill all of you, too, if you don't get out while you can."

"Shut up, Brother! You talk like a defeatist!"

"Yeah, shut up, Uncle!"

"Shhh," whispered Sergeant Prince. "The enemy is close. I can hear them creeping up."

The vehicle went quiet and no one moved a muscle. Listening intently, Bridger heard footsteps, barely audible with all the machine-gun and mortar-fire. Then he saw who it was: a young, beefy German soldier in a coal-scuttle-covered head and *feldgrau* uniform, Schmeisser machine pistol in hand. His youthful eyes blazed with intensity. He was a private and his body was crouched down low, his head twisted at a sharp angle away from his massive body. He inspected the open space between the driver's side door and the ground, running a hand along the bottom of the upturned *Kübelwagen.*

Another *panzergrenadier* joined him and Bridger heard the guttural language of his Innsbruck youth.

"Someone may still be alive. If they are, we should try and get them out of there. The captain said to bring back prisoners."

"No, I think we should just shoot them."

Bridger heard the clicking of the Schmeisser as it was made ready to fire. Holding his breath, thinking he was about to die, he took his father's hand and held it reassuringly. Their eyes met. *If I am to die, I want to be with you at the end,* his expression said plaintively. He wanted him to know how much he had loved him during their times together as father and son, should this prove to be their last moment on earth together.

An officer called out to the German soldiers and they turned. He ordered them to see if anyone was alive and take prisoners.

Like the others, Bridger continued to hold his breath. He could smell actual blood now, most likely his uncle's, a sweet and sickening stench that somehow mingled with the smell of gasoline from the ruptured fuel tank. His heart palpitated wildly, threatening to explode, but he was helpless, crammed upside down trapped in a car seat. He could hear the clatter of machine guns and mortars in the distance, and a vague rumbling sound like an approaching truck.

One of the German soldiers leaned down and started poking inside the *Kübelwagen*. The nose of a Schmeisser poked beneath the vehicle, like the head of a cobra, and a helmeted head appeared and stared at them.

Bridger closed his eyes and squeezed his father's hand. As he did, he heard his uncle moan in pain and then suddenly the rumbling sound was right on top of them, loud as a passing train. The German soldier retracted his head abruptly. Bridger saw his body and the other soldier's suddenly lifted off the ground, like football players upended in the air. There was a violent collision followed by a flash of rubber and metal as a half-track caromed past, dragging the two surprised Germans across the road. Bridger realized that Third Platoon must have gotten their hands on a half-track of their own and driven through the trees to rescue them. The collision was followed by a tremendous explosion and a wave of searing heat as a mortar round landed nearby and blew up another German vehicle rushing onto the scene.

Suddenly, the entire town and outlying areas were lit up by flares and mortar fire. The flames from the German vehicle rose twenty feet in the air in the foreground, the swelling black fuel cloud bending south in the light breeze. Bridger and the Ojibwa climbed out of the battered *Kübelwagen* and stared at the fire and the strobe-light-like flashes of the battle beyond, mesmerized. It reminded Bridger of the Fourth of July fireworks he had watched in Livingston, Montana, when he had been on weekend leave a year and a half ago.

A moment later, still watching the unfolding battle scene, he heard the crackle of underbrush behind him. He turned to see his father dragging his uncle to the safety of a nearby olive grove along the muddy ditch.

And he couldn't help but smile.

CHAPTER 41

VATICAN
MARCH 1, 1944

"THEY CALL THEM THE BLACK DEVILS, YOUR EMINENCE," said Father Robert Leiber, Pius's private secretary and closest advisor. They were sitting in the unheated, drab workroom of the papal *appartamento privato* going over the latest war news. The Jesuit priest codenamed Gregor wore his black soutane, the Bishop of Rome a simple, gray-white work tunic rather than his formal holy vestments. "Apparently, they have made quite a lasting impression on Kesselring's troops at Anzio. The Germans are terrified of them, or so our sources tell me."

"Who are these men?"

"An elite American and Canadian force. Everyone is calling them the Devil's Brigade."

"It appears Satan fights now for the North Americans. If these men are so valiant, I wish they would make their way to Rome more quickly. Nazi terror has increased these past few weeks and the Allies cannot get here soon enough."

"They are coming as fast as they can, Your Eminence. We must remember that the Allies are over here spilling their blood so that we can all be free."

"Of course, you are right, Robert."

They settled into silence. The simple truth was he was growing tired, so terribly tired, of this protracted war that had engulfed Europe, and much of the world beyond. He was tired of the endless killing, of the hungry mothers and children begging on the streets, of his godly children—Jew and Gentile alike—having to hide out like vermin from the Gestapo and Fascist police to avoid being sent off for labor service or to the death camps. He was tired of the constant appeals by both sides—the Axis and Allies—for him to speak out on their behalf and publicly castigate the enemy.

He was so very tired of it all.

And yet, he wished he could do more for the people of Rome; more to ease the suffering of the weak and powerless crowding every corner of war-torn Europe; more to help his beloved Catholic children in Poland, Germany, France, Italy, the Balkans, and elsewhere, as well as the Hebrews who deserved a far better world than the one that Hitler and his nefarious Nazis were forcing upon them.

He thought of the sacred words from Psalm 51: *Miserere mei Deus secundum magnam misericordiam tuam.* Have mercy on me, O God, in your great mercy.

It was nearly the end of winter, and the situation in Rome, indeed in all of Italy, was growing worse by the day. The Allies were stalled at Anzio and Monte Cassino. The German occupiers added daily to the misery of the city with their endless arrests, torture, and reprisals. And the relentless air bombings of what was supposed to be an Open City kept everyone on edge. With nearly a million displaced war refugees from the surrounding countryside now making Rome their home, the beloved place of his birth had turned into a city of parentless children, spies, double agents, informers, torturers, fugitives, and hungry people.

Sometimes, he wondered if he could take it anymore. And so he prayed.

Alone in his private chapel, he prayed for the war to end and for peace. He prayed for all those—on both sides of the conflict—that were suffering. He prayed that the demons that had taken over the soul of Hitler would be exorcised by a munificent God Almighty, and barring that, that Stauffenberg would be successful and the tyrant would be no more. And in the dead of night, he prayed that he might one day locate and excavate the very bones of Saint Peter buried beneath the basilica. Yes, St. Peter would guide him and show him the way through this moral crisis that had taken over his life, the entire world, and his very being.

But unfortunately, praying was never enough.

The war was a disaster, and the last month had been particularly painful for him. On February 10, the Allies bombed his papal estate of Castel Gandolfo, resulting in five hundred casualties among the thousands of innocent Jews and Christians hiding out there. On February 15, the historic monastery of Monte Cassino was reduced to rubble from heavy American-led air raids. Not a single German soldier was killed; the only casualties were two hundred thirty Italian civilians seeking refuge in the monastery. On February 16 and 17, heavy Allied air raids on the German positions in and around Rome reverberated all over the city, shaking the ground like an earth tremor and driving the populace to take cover in fear. And on February 16 through 19, the German Fourteenth Army had led an all-out attack on the Anzio Beachhead, nearly driving the Allies back into the sea. The attack had so demoralized the Allies that General Lucas had been sacked only a week ago and replaced at Anzio by General Truscott.

Feeling depressed, he looked at Father Leiber. He knew that the private secretary who enjoyed privileged access to him found him aloof and taciturn these days. He also knew that Leiber regarded him as an overly sensitive perfectionist when it came to papal diplomacy. Pius couldn't argue with that assessment. He *was* a solitary man and mystic, a leader yes, but also ascetic, occasionally rigid, and fanatically driven in his work, so much so that he rarely slept and ate very little. Since the war had started, he had lost more than thirty pounds and, though over six feet tall, he now tipped the scales at only one hundred twenty. He ate alone, always, with only his pet bird perched atop his skeletal shoulder; and he rarely spoke to his inner circle of papal advisors in a leisurely and relaxed manner, so consumed was he with the war and combating Hitler.

But if you only knew how much I feel inside, Robert, you would see what I truly am. When I witness the human suffering of this war, I suffer more than you can ever imagine. I feel, Robert, I truly feel.

Have mercy on me, O God, in your great mercy.

Leiber broke the silence. "I also have news of Stauffenberg, Your Holiness. He is coordinating his operations with Count Preysing." Konrad von Preysing was the bishop of Berlin and a rabid anti-Hitlerite. "He and Stauffenberg met at

Hermsdorf, reportedly for more than an hour."

"And?"

"Bishop Preysing sanctioned the plot. He said that he could not absolve Stauffenberg in advance from what he was going to do, but he gave his personal blessing as a priest."

"If Stauffenberg succeeds, we will need all of the German bishops behind us."

"Bishop Preysing has agreed to serve as a papal delegate following the coup, while as before Müller would seek an armistice through you." Josef Müller, the longtime anti-Hitler plotter and German Catholic lawyer, was to serve as the Vatican's special emissary to the post-Hitler government, with the title and status of ambassador-designate. His role would be to work with the Pope and Holy See to mediate with the Allies, but unfortunately that was looking to be more and more difficult due to his incarceration in an SS prison since last April. Müller was set to be tried by the SS in court in two days, and Pius knew he could very well end up swinging from the gallows.

"The unconditional surrender demand of the Allies will make things difficult," said Pius. "But the British are still open. Skeptical but open. We will need to ensure that our communications with the bishop are secure."

"Yes, Your Holiness. I will write Bishop Preysing personally to make sure." He cleared his throat. "There is also the matter of Müller."

"You are talking about the coming trial?" queried Pius.

"Yes, Your Holiness. It is being billed as a showdown of the Wehrmacht and Abwehr versus the SS."

"How strong is the prosecution's case?"

"Our contacts believe that it is a fifty-fifty proposition. It could go either way. The prosecution will argue that Müller abused his authority as a military spy to conspire, through his Church friends, with the enemy. The charges against him are high treason and they are requesting death by hanging."

"Oh my. The stakes are huge, as we expected."

"As you are aware, Müller has an exceptional military record. The chief of Hitler's own bodyguard detail is testifying on his behalf regarding his character. It is, therefore, expected that Judge Biron will require solid proof of high treason before he would allow the hanging of a man with such an exemplary record."

"Yes, but no doubt the SS will warn the court that Berlin's highest leadership circles will be monitoring the proceedings, and especially the final decision. The whole spectacle could turn into a kangaroo court."

"Our sources say that Judge Biron is expected to retain his independence and not agree to rubber-stamp decisions made outside the court."

"What will be Müller's defense?"

"He is expected to say the accusations are rehashed hearsay from discredited figures with personal grudges against him. His primary defense will be that an inquiry investigated and rejected their charges years ago; otherwise, how could Müller have continued to occupy one of the most sensitive and important intelligence posts in the Reich? He will maintain that he acted on the orders of his superiors, in the interest of his country, as his bosses testified previously."

"But will the prosecution be able to produce evidence to the contrary?"

"Our sources say no."

"Then why aren't the odds better than fifty-fifty?"

"Because we are dealing with the SS. There is the fear that even if Müller wins the case, the SS will just arrest him on new charges."

"So what is to prevent that from happening?"

"To keep Müller out of Gestapo custody, the Wehrmacht is planning on re-arresting Müller and returning him to the Lehrterstrasse prison. It is apparently the only way to keep him safe."

"The SS are beyond ruthless. The word Machiavellian comes to—"

He stopped right there as he heard the sound of heavy airplanes.

In the name of St. Peter, not again!

He rose from his chair and stepped out onto his balcony, with Father Leiber two steps behind him. Up in the pewter sky, he spotted six German Focke-Wulf fighter-bombers with black Nazi crosses on white backgrounds. In the next instant, he saw six bombs, one from each aircraft, hurtling towards earth like falling geese.

He couldn't believe his eyes. Were the Germans actually bombing the Vatican?

A series of tremendous explosions shook the ground in the Saint Damaso Courtyard of the Apostolic Palace. Within seconds, the Court of Saint Damaso itself turned to a raging inferno and the courtyard was littered with debris. The flames rose fifty feet into the air, the swelling black cloud mushrooming upwards like something out of Dante. He saw Swiss Guards running to escape the flames, as the fire spread outward and began devouring the perimeter vegetation in the courtyard.

"Courage and Loyalty," he said aloud, reciting the motto of the oldest standing army in the world that had guarded the Vatican for centuries. "Has the world gone completely mad?"

He watched in horror as the smoke cloud blew south into St. Peter's Square like a malevolent calling card delivered by Herr Hitler himself. The cloud hovered in the air above the Bernini colonnades and bold line of white paint demarcating the limits of Vatican City and physical boundaries of Pius's Nazi-enforced prison. On the other side of the curved white line stood German soldiers in black boots and steel helmets, armed with submachine guns. They were jabbering and pointing up at the roaring fire and plume of smoke as if it were an exciting display; and he hated them for their banality, hated them for their casual acceptance that a violent world such as this was not pure madness, but rather a circus-like event to be applauded with oohs and ahhs, hand clapping, and shouts of glee.

"When will it end, Robert? When will it all end?"

"When Claus von Stauffenberg succeeds or the Allies take Berlin. That's when it will be over, Your Holiness."

He stared into the infernal flames, shaking his head sadly. "Yes, you're absolutely right. That's when this hell on earth will end—and not a moment before. And now we must get down there and help those poor people. Let's go, Robert. And if we cannot lend a helping hand then we shall pray for them. It's the least we can do."

PART 5

FOSSE ARDEATINE

CHAPTER 42

VATICAN

MARCH 19, 1944

AS TERESA WAITED with her mother in the papal antechamber to speak with Pius, she stared out the window with sorrow at her ravaged city. The winter of the Occupation was proving interminable and grim—and she had grown to hate the Nazis with all of her being. In fact, she would like to see them all dead.

In recent weeks, the city's population had begun to actually starve. The daily bread ration was down to two slices per person, from loaves made with ground chickpeas, maize flour, elm pith, and mulberry leaves. With so many mouths to feed, the city's prodigious wild cat population shrank to virtual extinction as people were forced to eat felines to survive. The vast majority of food and clothing was only sold on the black market, and prices had quadrupled since the New Year. The German retreat to the Gustav Line hindered efforts to feed the hungry population, for the bulk of the city's granary lay south of Cassino. The destruction of supply trucks by Allied warplanes further complicated the task, as Vatican convoys hauling supplies from Northern Italy were often mistaken for German transports and machine-gunned by Allied aircraft.

With most public services virtually defunct, Rome was like a besieged city. Electricity supplies were erratic: alternating neighborhoods went without power two nights per week. All winter long people had felled trees and hacked away at park benches for firewood. The city smelled of sweat and urine, and lice had become ubiquitous. Tuberculosis and infant mortality were on the rise. Getting washed regularly was a luxury for all but the privileged living in the neighborhoods seized by the Germans. Drinking water was often unavailable, and even the houses of the rich grew infested with germs and insects. On downtown sidewalks water-sellers peddled potable water, women hocked their furs, scholars their books, children their tattered shoes, and others everything from gramophone records to empty bottles.

But sickness and starvation were nothing compared to the terror wreaked by the Gestapo and Fascist police forces upon Rome's citizens. The Gestapo, Koch Gang, and a newcomer Fascist Chief of Police named Pietro Caruso, a murderous bungler and lout who had arrived to the Eternal City a month earlier, enacted a ceaseless campaign of raiding, torture, and extermination. Since the beginning of the year, the police presence in Rome had been greatly augmented by the addition of five hundred German soldiers and more than a hundred policemen to the savage Koch and Caruso units. Mass roundups of males, young and old alike, occurred on a daily basis as civilians of every stripe were plucked from trams, pulled from the *centro storico*, and rounded up in the Via Nazionale for labor battalions or a prison cell. The interrogators at Via Tasso, Pensione Jacarino, and Via San Vitale where Kappler, Koch, and the new *Questore* Caruso ruled their fiefdoms extracted confessions through pure savagery. The continuing torture techniques of choice were brass knuckles, bright lights, pins through the penis, blowtorches, and pulling out mustache hairs by means of screws and a steel bar.

Half of Rome was said to be hiding the other half, and Teresa knew it was close to the truth. According to CLN estimates, more than five thousand souls were being hidden in Roman convents, monasteries, and the Vatican, including large numbers of Jews. Telephones were tapped throughout the city. Five hundred Fascist eavesdroppers in the central exchange reportedly listened in on local phone calls, inducing the wealthy to speak in code in the acquisition of black market food.

In Rome, no place was safe. In fact, it was so dangerous that her father Colonel Di Domenico had been captured two weeks earlier and was being held at Via Tasso. Word had reached her and her mother from sympathetic Italian personnel working at the Gestapo headquarters that he was undergoing brutal torture on a daily basis. Dragged repeatedly between Isolation Cell One—a cold, unlit, windowless room—and the Torture Chamber, he had reportedly been beaten and whipped with chains, punched with brass knuckles so hard his jaw was broken, and blowtorched on the soles of his feet. And yet he had not talked. The rumors of his inhumane treatment and fortitude at the hands of his captors had spread throughout the city all the way to the Vatican. Which was the reason for her visit with her mother: to politely beg the Pope to intervene on her father's behalf.

But what broke Roman hearts more than anything else, Teresa knew, was the Allied-German stalemate at Anzio and resultant sense of hopelessness. The euphoria over the Allied landings in late January and hopes for a swift liberation had long faded, giving way to despair and resentment that was only exacerbated by all of the hunger, sickness, and oppression on the streets. The slogan about the Allies being just around the corner had been replaced by cynical graffiti on city walls proclaiming, "Americans, hold on! We'll be there soon to liberate you!" The six brutal months of the Nazi Occupation had sharpened Roman snarkiness to a razor's edge.

Monsignor Nasalli Rocca appeared in the anteroom. "His Eminence will see you now."

He quietly led Teresa and her mother into the papal study. Behind his oversized desk Pius solemnly sat, dressed in his habitual holy white vestments with his skull cap snug across his small head and a shining cross of diamonds and sapphires glittering on his chest. As they bowed in genuflection before him, Teresa noticed that he looked even more gaunt and haggard since the last time she had seen him during the October roundup. Five months had passed since that terrible day, and his control over his holy city had been seriously contested at every turn by the Germans and their Fascist pit bulls. The war was taking the same terrible toll on him, she realized with despair, as it was the people of Rome: everyone—even the *defensor civitatis*—appeared powerless in the face of the Nazi oppressors.

Nodding for them to sit in the chairs facing him, he invited them to speak.

"Holy Father," her mother began, "I dare to come before Your Holiness to plead for a kindness that, if granted, would not only mean the salvation of one person and the joy of his family, but could have important implications for keeping public order in Rome."

"You are referring to your husband Colonel Di Domenico."

"Yes, Your Eminence. Before his capture two weeks ago, Rome was not bombed regularly and indiscriminately as it is now because he was in radio contact with the Allies on a regular basis. He directed the Americans to specific targets so that the bombings would not damage the city. He was in control of the military resistance of all the partisan groups. He was commander in chief of all the political parties, who were under orders from their own leaders to obey his commands in the name of sparing Rome undue violence and hardship and to spare innocent lives. If he could be freed from prison, the colonel that you have known for many years, would not only be in a position to save lives and maintain civil control, he could guarantee a smooth transition of power when the Germans withdraw from Rome and it is handed over to the Allies."

"He's being held at Via Tasso by Colonel Kappler, is he not?"

He looked intently at Teresa as the question was posed. She couldn't help but wonder if the Holy Father knew that she was a partisan and he was subtly showing his disapproval. But how could he know that she was the *Inglesina*? She wondered how the Pope would feel if he knew that not only was she a partisan, but she had taken a Communist lover. She and her *Gappista* comrade Beppo had become romantically involved over a month ago and she had been sleeping with him regularly.

"Yes, Your Eminence," replied her mother. "The colonel is being held at Via Tasso by Kappler. And unfortunately, we all know what that means. The tortures he is reported to be undergoing are inhumane."

He nodded sympathetically. Teresa could tell that he was well aware of the terrible atrocities taking place at Via Tasso.

"I have visited there several times, Your Eminence, as has Teresa. But Kappler appears to be irked by our presence. He refuses to even let us see him."

"We have been told of his condition by those sympathetic to his plight," quietly added Teresa. "He has been beaten so badly that he can only eat soft foods. And he has a constant fever."

The marchesa removed a letter from a folder and held it up in her hand. "I have put together a memorandum summarizing both his condition and why he should be released at this time. It is in everyone's interest, even the Germans. If he cannot be released outright, then at least perhaps the torture can stop and he be given favored treatment. He is working for order and for the greater good of Rome."

Pius did not take the memorandum. Instead, he nodded, steepled his hands on his desk, and contemplated for a few seconds, apparently going over in his mind what the memorandum likely contained. Teresa thought her mother had made a convincing argument for her father's release by invoking the maintenance of public order, the control of Allied bombings, and a smooth transition of power. True, she had been exaggerating her father's ability to influence events, but it was also true that if there was one man in Rome who could unite and maintain the respect of the disparate partisan bands, it was the colonel. As head of the Clandestine Military Front of the Resistance, he was a sterling leader and the powerful anti-Communist force so valued by the Pope, but he had also shown his ability to forget petty disagreements and work with the GAP. In fact, some in his own party found him too accommodating with the partisan opposition.

At last he spoke. Teresa held her breath.

"I promise you," he said, the sincerity and pain in his eyes readily apparent, "we will do everything possible for Colonel Di Domenico, truly, all that is possible. I don't know what results we will obtain, but we will neglect nothing that is within our power. Leave your memorandum with me." He motioned for the letter, which her mother quickly slid across his desk to him. "I will read it attentively and, as I have said, we will do everything possible to ease your husband's suffering."

"Thank you, Your Holiness—thank you," said the marchesa.

The Pope looked at her intently. "But I do have to ask you one question."

The breath seemed to catch in her throat. "Yes, Your Eminence."

"Would it not also be wise to make an appeal to your…ex-husband?"

"My ex-husband?"

"Yes, Colonel Hollmann. After all, as a high-ranking SS colonel, second only to General Wolff, he would be in a unique position to persuade Kappler to release your husband."

Her mother bowed with shame; her Annulment after the Innsbruck shooting had always been a convenient sham for her, and it wasn't the first time the Pope and the mighty Roman Catholic Church had reminded her of her transgression.

"No, I have not contacted Colonel Hollmann," she said.

"It seems to me that it would be worth a try. He is, of course, the SS liaison officer of choice in matters involving people such as yourself, Marchesa."

Teresa knew exactly what he meant: he was talking about the black nobility. She could tell her mother was struggling to keep from cringing; the last person she wanted to go begging to bail her husband out of prison was her ex-husband and Teresa's father the SS colonel. Looking at her mother, Teresa couldn't help but wonder, yet again, what had possessed her to shoot her father on that late summer day in Innsbruck.

Why did you do it, Mother? What is the real reason, and why have you kept it a secret all these years?

"My advice would be to contact Colonel Hollmann, Marchesa. He may very well be your best hope," said Pius. "But of course, I will do all in my power to help your husband in any way I can."

At this, he bowed his head, and Teresa saw a deeply lodged pain cross his ravaged countenance. This war would be the death of him, she swore, just as it would probably be the death of her poor father being tortured in the basement of Via Tasso.

"Go in peace," he said in parting.

Monsignor Rocca showed them out. Though her mother seemed relieved, Teresa was left to wonder if the Pope was pessimistic about his chances of securing her father's release, and that was why he wanted her mother to lobby Colonel Hollmann. After all, Pius had failed to save the Jews during the roundup, to stop the enemy raids on Vatican extraterritorial properties, to halt the Allied bombings of the railyards and the killing of innocent civilians, and to stop the Germans from plucking men off the street at random and sending them off to labor camps to die a slow, agonizing death. So why should she or her mother believe that he would have any success now?

It pained her to see her father in such dire straits and to see her beloved city like a prison under harsh German rule. God, did she hate these brutal Nazis, and that included her SS colonel father. She knew that he had been investigating Father O'Flaherty's and Major Sam Derry's Vatican Escape Line and that he had played a hand behind the scenes during the past three months in the raids on Vatican properties. Though he had shielded her and her mother from the Gestapo, Koch Band, and the new *Questore* Caruso, he was still a high-ranking Nazi, clever police detective, and a thorn in the side of everyday Romans.

She wanted desperately to lash back at the Nazis, to make them suffer as the people of Rome were suffering, to give them a strong dose of their own medicine. They had to pay with their lives for what they had done to her beloved city. To make that happen, she and her partisan comrades had to continue to answer terror with terror, vengeance with vengeance, blood with more blood. Who knows, she might even be forced to strike back not only at the Gestapo and Fascist police, but her own father, Colonel Hollmann.

In her gut, she could feel an epic struggle with the man coming in the near future. The underground war between the Resistance and Occupation police forces was growing more violent by the day, and she couldn't help but feel that everything was building to a final showdown between her and the father she had worshiped growing up in Innsbruck. True, it was just a feeling she had, but since joining the GAP and becoming a freedom-fighter, she had learned to trust her instincts. They had saved her life on more than one occasion since she had drawn her first blood at Cinema Barberini.

But first she had to convince the colonel to free her birth father, Colonel Di Domenico, from Via Tasso. Her mother would never be able to put aside her pride and make the request so it was up to Teresa to take care of the deed herself.

And she would do it today.

CHAPTER 43

VIA RASELLA
MARCH 23, 1944

THE MEN'S RAINCOAT Teresa carried made her feel conspicuously out of place. After all, it was *una giornata da B-17*—a B-17 day—the morbid name the Romans used to describe clear-blue-sky days that provided perfect Flying Fortress bombing weather for the U.S. Army Air Corps. The time was 2:44 p.m. The late March sun shone resplendently and the temperature was the highest of the year to date, warm enough that street children wore no shoes. And yet on this sunny day, Teresa carried a bulky raincoat—not to mention a concealed Beretta pistol in her pocket—as she pretended to study the headline of the newspaper pinned to the display rack outside the entrance of *Il Messaggero*. The newspaper was full of news about the major eruption of Mount Vesuvius near Naples.

Nearby, two plainclothed Fascist policemen stood out like sore thumbs. They had materialized like ghosts minutes earlier, making her feel nervous as a cat. But she didn't dare leave—not before completing her mission and going through with the attack. Via Rasella would be GAP Central's most audacious strike yet, and she wanted to take part in it and ensure its success.

But where were the targets of the attack? Why were the SS troops late when they had never been late before?

The whole mission had been built upon the Nazis' cross-town marching routine: every afternoon, without fail, the same column of over one hundred fifty troops from the Eleventh Company, Third Battalion, of the SS *Polizeiregiment Bozen* would goose-step through the center of Rome on their way back to their barracks after their target-range practice near the Ponte Milvio. As they marched, singing "*Hupf, Mein Mädel*"—"Skip, My Lassie"—a sappy ditty Romans found insufferably annoying, they would pass up the length of a narrow and enclosed city street, Via Rasella. The CLN had for some time now considered the constricted choke-point the perfect place for a deadly ambush.

The attack was supposed to happen at 2 p.m.

And yet, the clock would soon strike three and there was still no sign of the Germans, not even the distant strains of their favorite marching song. Why hadn't Pasquale given her the signal? Where could the normally punctual SS troops be?

She looked over at her fellow *Gappista* comrade, one of half a dozen partisans taking part in today's operation. Pasquale was standing by a nearby newsstand, pretending to be scanning the cover of *Popolo di Roma* just like her. Their eyes briefly met. He appeared to sense her agitation, because as they made eye contact he gave her a reassuring wink.

It was Pasquale's job to give Teresa and her lover Beppo, who was posing as a street cleaner, the signal to let them know that the SS troops were on their way. She would then walk swiftly to Via del Tritone, a main thoroughfare that ran parallel to Via Rasella, and then on to Via delle Quattro Fontane until she reached her designated support position at the junction with Via Rasella. With the Germans approaching the narrow Via Rasella choke-point and Teresa in position, Beppo would deliver the bomb that would kill as many of the enemy as possible. He had it carefully concealed beneath a thin stratum of rubbish in an old dust cart that they had stolen the day before. It was a homemade bomb of twenty-six pounds of TNT, topped by a twenty-five-second fuse and packed into a steel case stolen from the gas company, plus another thirteen pounds in loose bags and several iron pipes packed with explosives. Once it was detonated, a separate team of Gappists would finish off the attack with mortars and Stens, while Teresa would wait for Beppo with the raincoat—to cover up his street cleaner's uniform as they made their escape.

She looked at her watch again. Damnit, why was it taking the Germans so long? Would the whole mission have to be scrapped?

To her horror, one of the plainclothed policemen appeared at her side. Teresa quickly gripped the pistol in her pocket, bracing herself for a confrontation.

"Excuse me, *signorina.* Are you waiting for someone?"

She felt her whole body freeze up for a terrible moment before recovering her composure. "Yes, I am waiting for my fiancé," she replied. "He is at the Palazzo Barberini."

"Oh, I see," the other one said, looking disappointed.

The other one started to say something, but she delicately cut him off, pointed down to the newspaper, and began talking to them about the eruption of Vesuvius and potential disaster this might pose for Naples. This seemed to distract them and she began to feel calmer, though her heart was racing wildly.

"Why are you carrying a raincoat on such a hot day?"

"Oh, that." She waved her hand dismissively. "It is my fiancé's. I brought it with me to give back to him. I just had a stain removed."

In the reflection in the glass, she saw Pasquale start walking towards her from up the street. Her heart fluttered in her chest. *Is this it? Is it time?*

"What time is it?" she abruptly asked the policemen.

One of them looked at his watch. "It is 2:47, *signorina.* Is there some place you have to be?"

"Yes, I must go. Goodbye."

"Good day, *signorina.*"

Were they suspicious? She couldn't tell as she hurried away and passed Pasquale, who whispered something to her that she couldn't quite make out. She didn't dare look back, believing Pasquale's message was the signal for her to move. She quickly turned into the Via del Tritone and then down Quattro Fontane to take up her position for her lover Beppo's attack. Her heart pounded in every part of her body: the climactic moment was at hand.

Reaching Via Rasella, she stopped in the shadows of the great Baroque *Palazzo Barberini*, built in part from the stones of the Colosseum, and where both

Bernini and Borromini had made artistic history. Below, she saw Beppo sweeping the road halfway down the street, the dust cart in the middle of the road. She instantly cursed him under her breath. His blue street cleaner's uniform, worn-out patent leather shoes, and black-visored blue cap looked authentic, but he was sweeping in such a conspicuous, awkward manner that she was sure that somebody would blow the whistle. Even worse, by now she had been expecting to see the SS column marching into the bottom of the street, but there was still no sign of any troops.

She couldn't understand why they weren't there. Had something gone wrong?

A noise behind her suddenly startled her. In the garden of the Barberini Palace, she spotted some children playing soccer. Imagining the horrors of the little boys and girls being caught in the bomb blast, she crossed the street and, pretending that she lived in the palazzo, shouted at them sternly.

"You can't play ball in this garden!" She wagged an admonishing finger. "Go home and do your homework!"

They looked at her for a moment with surprise. Then, recognizing the note of danger in her voice, they dropped their game and scurried off, one group dashing right down Via Rasella.

"No, not that way!" she cried, but they ran on without looking back.

She shook her head, looked towards the heavens, crossed herself, and thought anxiously, *Una giornata da B-17.* The minutes ticked by, but there was still no sign of the Germans. What could have gone wrong? She paced back and forth at the entrance gates of the Palazzo Barberini.

Her breath caught as the same two plainclothes policemen approached her again. Damn, why wouldn't they leave her alone?

"What are you still doing here, *signorina*?" one of them asked her.

"Unfortunately, my fiancé is at the Officer's Club in the Palazzo," she lied, hoping they would not see Beppo and his rubbish cart a hundred yards below.

"He's been in there a long time. Or maybe he's not even in there and you are making this all up?"

"I would never make something up like that. I don't lie."

They laughed harshly. "The *signorina* doesn't lie!"

"I can't go in there," she explained, "because it is a men's-only club. So I have to wait."

"Well, why don't we wait with you," the one on the right said, tipping his policeman's cap and smiling through dingy yellow teeth.

She felt a flicker of desperation. How could she get rid of them?

Suddenly, she spotted a friend of her mother's walking on the other side of the Via Quattro Fontane, an elegant elderly woman with a glistening hairdo. Worried for the safety of her mother's friend just as she was the children, she quickly excused herself from the two policemen, raced across the street, and, after a brief conversation, instructed the woman to get as far away from Via Rasella as possible. Heeding her warning, the woman took fright and left.

It was then Teresa saw Guglielmo, another member of her GAP team, walking up the street towards Beppo, who was still pretending to be a street cleaner. As they passed, she spotted the head of the SS column as it turned into the bottom of Via Rasella.

Finally, the moment they had all been waiting for had arrived! But could they pull it off?

The clap of more than one hundred fifty boots on cobblestone carried up the narrow Via Rasella. The *Polizeiregiment Bozen* troops, marching three abreast, wheeled left onto the street from the Via del Traforo and burst into the annoying "Skip, My Lassie" that anti-Fascist Romans had come to detest. They were singing at the top of their lungs, their chests pushed forward like crowing roosters. Though the column was sprinkled with some older men graying at the temples, Teresa told herself not to feel any sympathy for them. After all, they were Nazis, not human beings. The unit had been formed in October 1943 of recruits from her birthplace of South Tyrol, the German-speaking part of the Italian Alps that, under the terms of a 1939 agreement between Hitler and Mussolini, had been incorporated into the Greater German Reich as the *Alpenvorland.* The 3rd Battalion had arrived in Rome early in February, attached as SS police to Kappler's Gestapo headquarters, but in practice was under Commandant Mälzer as part of Mackensen's Fourteenth Army. She studied them closely as they marched towards her in lockstep, singing in unison. She couldn't help but feel a little guilty for what was about to happen to them, but again reminded herself that they were evil SS troops that deserved everything they had coming to them.

They paid no notice to the moon-faced Italian street sweeper smoking a pipe and cleaning the gutter up ahead, now only fifty yards from the intersection with the Via delle Quattro Fontane. Holding her breath, Teresa watched her lover calmly lift the dust cart lid and touch his pipe to the fuse, carefully timed to detonate in the middle of the column. He then removed his black-visored cap, laid it atop the cart as a signal, and hurried up the street towards Teresa. Her heart in her mouth, she watched the SS troops gradually fill the entire street, tramping rhythmically towards Beppo's soon-to-be lethal cart when he disappeared from sight.

She was standing alongside a handbag shop on the southwest corner of the Via Rasella and the Quattro Fontane, preparing to take shelter from the blast and still straining to see him, when he suddenly appeared at her side. She nearly jumped out of her skin.

"Come on, we have to get out of here!" he cried, his face pale with fear.

She handed him the raincoat. As he started to hastily put it on over his overalls, she looked back towards the marching column again. To her horror, she saw the two policemen again. They apparently were still keeping an eye on her since she had been acting suspiciously. They started up the street to intercept her and Beppo.

She pulled out her Beretta to defend herself, but a city bus passed between them. The front of the column was now near the top of Via Rasella.

It was then the bomb detonated.

The explosion mowed down the column as if they were toy soldiers knocked down by a great gust of wind. Shards of broken window glass showered the street from the five-story buildings next to the column, along with smashed dishes, furniture, and dislodged stucco. The violent blast of air pushed her and Beppo forward and forced the bus driver to swerve out of control, drive up onto the sidewalk, and crash into a wall.

Spotting her and Beppo at the top of Via Rasella, the troops at the head of the column that had not been mowed down in the blast opened fire on them. Bullets pinged and ricocheted all around them and they were showered with bits of airborne stone, stucco, and tile from the blast. A finer cloud of dust and smoke from the explosion began to blanket the entire quarter like volcanic ash.

As they dashed away from the Germans, she looked back through the gaps in the smoke. Pasquale, Guglielmo, and the other partisans stepped out from concealment down the street and opened fire on the rear of the German column, lashing the company with Stens and mortar bombs converted into grenades. The second-phase barrage led the surviving Germans to assume that they were being attacked from the buildings, and they turned their rifles up at the windows of the five-story apartments facing the Via Rasella. Some of those with minor wounds staggered to their feet and fired wildly at the building facades. Other Germans tried to escape but were blocked by the partisans. Mortars exploded and guns rattled all around, echoing off the walls, mingling with the roar of the fire.

They had turned the terror back onto the occupiers more devastatingly than Teresa could possibly have imagined. She had no idea how many had been killed in the initial blast, but it had to have been thirty or forty. And there were many more wounded, screaming in terror and moaning in agony. The gruesome reality of the devastation made her feel nauseated; for a moment she thought she might vomit. But she was able to steel herself and they dashed to the west towards the river.

When they reached the Tiber's embankment, they saw frightened people jumping onto the circular trams. It seemed as if already the entire city feared what the Nazis would do in reprisal.

They followed the river south before turning east and walking briskly to the Church of St. Peter in Chains, where they paused to catch their breath. Beppo yanked off his street cleaner's uniform and tossed it into a dark corner.

"The Nazis are going to retaliate savagely for this," she said, gasping for air. "They will avenge this with a fury that, before today, I don't think either of us could have imagined."

He took her by surprise by pulling her close and kissing her. There were tears in his eyes—tears of co-mingled pride, sadness, and desperation—and she could tell that in this cathartic moment they were part of history.

"I know," he said. "We are going to have to leave the city. They are not going to stop until they have hunted us down and killed every last one of us."

"Then we will die," she said fatalistically. "But at least we will die together."

"And at least we will have died for something. *La mia patria era la patria del Risorgimento*," he said with a patriotic gleam in his eyes.

She leaned into him and they kissed again. "Our country is the country of the Risorgimento, the country of democracy and liberty. Long live Italy."

"And long live the Risorgimento. I love you, Teresa."

"And I love you, my sweet Beppo. I truly love you."

CHAPTER 44

VIA RASELLA

MARCH 23, 1944

HOLLMANN WAS SUFFERING THROUGH a late lunch at the Hotel Excelsior with Kappler and Lieutenant General Kurt Mälzer—the military commandant of Rome and a corpulent drunkard whom he detested—when word arrived of the carnage at Via Rasella. Hollmann immediately summoned his chauffeur, and he and Mälzer drove ahead to the bombing site in separate cars, while Kappler returned to Via Tasso to assemble Priebke and his other Gestapo officers to investigate the scene of the attack. Arriving minutes later to the site, Hollmann had Mario halt the Mercedes at the corner of Via delle Quattro Fontane and Via Rasella, and he jumped out of the vehicle.

He felt an instant wave of outrage as he caught his first glimpse of the destruction from the enormous explosion that had rocked the city. It was apparent that the Eleventh Company of the Bozen SS Third Battalion, which he had already been informed were the victims of the bombing, had ceased to exist as a fighting unit. The area was devastated. A huge hole was blown out of a stone wall, and an equally large crater perforated the ground. There were bodies and puddles of blood everywhere. Water from a broken water line surged from the demolished wall, flowing downgrade with the diluted blood of the dead and maimed.

The air was filled with cries from the wounded and curses for retribution. Soldiers and policemen ran up and down the street, brandishing submachine guns, yelling, cursing, barking out commands. Others were bursting into shops and houses, searching and ransacking them, dragging out men to the desperate cries of women and children, while others scanned the rooftops and windows for signs of the enemy. Small packs of SS soldiers were shooting frantically at upper windows, the crackle of their rifles carrying all the way to the Trevi Fountain and Palazzo Barberini.

He made a rough count of the bodies lined up in a row on the street: thirty or so dead with another fifty, dying or seriously wounded, among the blown-apart corpses and scattered body parts. In addition, two civilians had been killed by the blast: an old man and an adolescent boy. The body of the boy lay on the street on top of uprooted cobblestones near the huge hole caused by the explosion.

As he took in the devastation, shaking his head in dismay, Consul Eitel Möllhausen, head of the German embassy in Rome, came stomping up to him. The youngest chief of a German diplomatic mission at age thirty, he loathed Nazism and was reported to have a penchant for aiding Jews.

"That crazy Mälzer wants to blow up all the houses!" he exclaimed. "Damn him, he needs to be stopped!" He pointed down the street at the self-proclaimed 'King of Rome.'

Hollmann looked where the diplomat was pointing. Mälzer was pacing up and down the street bellowing, "Revenge! Revenge! We will raze the entire block!" His face was crimson, his prodigious uniform drenched with sweat, and he was flagrantly drunk. During their lunch together at the Excelsior, Hollmann had watched him toss back two bottles of Chianti, but he looked even more intoxicated now. At the sight of the carnage, he must have tucked into his personal flask of cognac, for he appeared stark raving drunk.

"Do you understand, Colonel?" pleaded Consul Möllhausen. "We can't blow up the building and shoot all of these people." He pointed to the men, women, and children being lined up and handled roughly by the soldiers in front of the gates of Palazzo Barberini. "Most of them probably had nothing to do with this, and that drunken lout wants to shoot them all!"

"Settle down, Eitel. I'll try and get him out of here."

"The man has lost his mind! He will blow up the whole area and kill all of these innocent people!"

"All right, but just settle down. I will take care of the situation, and I suggest you leave too."

"No, I'm staying. I don't trust Mälzer."

"Then at least let me do the talking and don't provoke him further."

They stepped quickly over to Mälzer. As he drew close, he could see that the commandant had been crying and was in a literal state of hysteria. He had to calm the son of a bitch down.

But Mälzer was beyond reason and cried without preamble, "You see, Hollmann?" He pointed frantically to the row of dead. "You see what they have done to my boys! Now I'm going to blow all these houses sky high!"

"We are not blowing up anything. Colonel Kappler will be here shortly and conduct a thorough investigation to determine who is responsible for this. You must return to your headquarters at once."

"Leave? I shall not leave." He glowered at the German consul. "Look here, Möllhausen—here are the beautiful results of your liberal politics!" he cried, again pointing to the corpses and body parts on the bloody street. "But all that is going to change now! I am going to blow up the entire block of houses! I have already given the order! I'm going to blow the whole thing up, I swear it! And I want to see who's going to stop me!"

Looking down the street, Hollmann saw that he wasn't bluffing. Wehrmacht engineers had in fact arrived and cases of explosives were being unloaded.

"We are not blowing up anything," he said to the blubbering commandant. "There could be women and children still in the buildings. To kill innocent people—that is *Schweinerei*—and Consul Möllhausen and I will not allow it."

"None of that is important to me! These houses are going up in smoke, even if tomorrow the diplomats get me fired!"

Hollmann stared at him incredulously. Tears were streaming down the commandant's face and he was clearly not a sane man. Hollmann quickly called out to the engineers and instructed them to put an immediate halt to their demolition work.

"What? What are you doing?" shrieked Mälzer.

"*My job*. And yours is to get a grip on yourself before I put you in leg irons and have you locked up at Via Tasso. You are fucking drunk as well as an embarrassment. You must leave at once."

"But my soldiers, my poor soldiers! I cannot leave! Not until I have killed them all!" He pointed to the gates of the palazzo. The men had been separated from the women and children, and they were all arranged in a line and being forced to stand with their hands above their heads, which Hollmann could see was pure torture for the elderly Romans. "They did this, or stood by while others performed their wicked deeds! They must be killed!"

"You must calm down. *Polizeiführer* Wolff is going to want cooler heads to prevail in this tragedy, as well as complete crime scene details on how it all happened. You will listen to me and stand down immediately."

"But my men! My poor men!"

"Do I have to drag you out of here kicking and screaming, *Herr Kommandant*, or will you leave quietly like a good German officer on your own volition. The choice is yours. You have five seconds to decide."

"Don't you threaten me! I'm going to blow up the whole neighborhood with whoever is in the houses! And you, Möllhausen, I'm going to throw you in jail!"

He called to one of his officers, ordering him to get Field Marshal Kesselring on a radiophone to ask for full powers to blow up the entire neighborhood.

"You can't do this, Mälzer!" countered the young anti-Nazi consul. "It isn't right! The actual perpetrators have long since vanished, and all you'll be doing is killing innocent women and children!"

The commandant turned away, ignoring him and relaying instructions to his staff.

Hollmann turned to Möllhausen. "This isn't getting us anywhere, Eitel. Let me handle this. Come, let me show you to your car and allow me to deal with the commandant alone."

For an instant, it looked as though the young man was going to resist, but then he agreed. Wanting him out of here as quickly as possible so he could stop Mälzer before he did anything crazy, Hollmann shuttled him quickly to his car. At that moment, Kappler arrived with Priebke and the rest of his men. He and Möllhausen walked up to them.

"That crazy Mälzer wants to blow up all the houses here!" said Möllhausen. "He needs to be stopped at all cost!"

Kappler said nothing in reply. His presence and that of his Gestapo officers in their SS uniforms had exercised a chilling effect on everyone, and even Mälzer and his officers had stopped talking to stare at the newcomers.

"He's not exaggerating, Herbert," said Hollmann. "Mälzer has completely come unglued and lost all control. I am going to put an end to these histrionics. I could use your help."

"Are you sure you're not exaggerating, Colonel?"

"No, I am not. Let's go."

Leaving Möllhausen, he and Kappler went up to Mälzer, who was still flushed and covered with sweat.

"You see, Kappler?" cried the commandant, pointing to the row of dead. "You see what they have done to my boys? Now I'm going to blow all these houses sky high!"

"As I have told you, General," said Hollmann as Kappler signaled Priebke and the rest of his men to take charge of the crime scene. "You will do nothing of the sort. Colonel Kappler will proceed with his investigation, and he and I both urge you to return to your headquarters. Don't we, Colonel?"

"You heard him, Commandant," said Kappler, for once in agreement and on his side. "There is nothing more for you to do here. You must not contaminate this crime scene and allow us to conduct our investigation without disruption."

"No, I am not leaving! These people must be lined up and shot!"

"I'm afraid I must insist, Commandant," said Kappler, and he took him aggressively by the elbow and led him to his plush Mercedes. Hollmann followed. As they helped him into his car, the bloated general, still overcome with convulsive weeping and looking like a mortally stricken beast, took one last look at the civilians lined up against the Barberini gates. He made a chopping motion in the direction of every man, woman, and child, as if beheading them.

"They are all to be shot! There can no other recourse!"

Then he roared away in his chauffeured car.

Shaking his head in disgust, Hollmann returned to the scene of the explosion along with Kappler. The Germans and Italian police were still emptying the houses on the street, not only of residents but of other contents. They were going from building to building, kicking in doors, dragging out residents and whatever could be dragged with them. Soldiers were still firing mindlessly at the high windows. Together, he and Kappler instructed them to stop and eventually restored order so that the Gestapo could commence its investigation.

It took Kappler and his men over an hour. Hollmann, the former police chief, watched them sort through the physical wreckage and explosive residue and conduct interviews with several of the surviving members of the Eleventh Company. The only incriminating evidence they found was a small red flag and an unexploded mortar shell. From its Italian origin and primitive detonator, Hollmann instantly ruled out the possibility of an Allied commando attack, which the new *Questore* Caruso and some of his police officers were suggesting. The surviving SS troops could add nothing; they had not seen anything suspicious and at first thought the bomb had come from the sky, then from one of the rooftops. Inspecting the rooftops along with Kappler, Hollmann found no evidence of the use of explosives or any other weapons. Based on this fact and the size of the bomb crater, he concluded that the bomb attack had come from the street. Kappler disagreed. He believed the bomb and subsequent mortar attacks had been launched from the fourth or fifth floor windows, which Hollmann thought was ridiculous.

When the Gestapo had completed its investigation, a sanitation crew arrived to scrub the bloody cobblestones with water and salt. Hollmann turned his attention to the two hundred civilians whom the mentally unhinged Mälzer had ordered executed. They were still standing at the front gates of Palazzo Barberini. Kappler reappeared at his side.

"What are you going to do with them?" he inquired of the Gestapo chief mildly between puffs of his Lucky Strike.

"Well, we're certainly not going to shoot them."

"Thank God for that."

"Cooler heads have prevailed."

He stared off at the Roman captives: virtually all of them old men, women, and children. German soldiers were still cursing at them and poking and prodding them with rifles to keep their hands up. He felt sorry for the civilians, knowing that most, if not all, of them had had nothing to do with the attack. He wondered if Teresa had had anything to do with it. If she did, she would be hunted down and shot. Today's attack had been far too audacious and bloody for there not to be vicious reprisals. And the reprisals, he knew, would be carried out by the man standing next to him, Lieutenant Colonel Herbert Kappler, who had proven over the past six months that he was more than capable of serving as the blind instrument of Nazi brutality and suppression when the occasion called for it.

"So what should we do with the prisoners?" Hollman asked him.

"I think they should be handed over to the Italian police. They can march them to the Viminale barracks and take them into custody for questioning."

"Yes, that is a good idea."

"This vile act was big in scale, well-organized, and undoubtedly carried out by the Resistance, not the Allies."

So you too, Herbert, believe this to be the work of the partisans. Astute fellow. "They obviously picked today—the twenty-fifth anniversary of Mussolini's founding of the Fascist movement—to make their bold statement."

"Many people must have been involved. We just have to catch one or two. Someone will crack. They always do."

"Yes, well you do your job, and I will do mine. I will be going now. I am off to Mälzer's headquarters at Corso d'Italia to make sure that fat bastard doesn't do anything more stupid."

"Hopefully, he has calmed down."

He took a deep pull from his Lucky. "One can only hope. But you are wrong about one thing."

"What is that?"

"Cooler heads have not yet prevailed. We are just getting started and you know perfectly well that our bosses will not show the least bit of restraint. There will be a serious *rappresaglia* for this bombing attack in the heart of Rome. I would not be surprised if the Führer himself weighs in on this one, and the punishment meted out will be swift and brutal."

"If you're right, then it would seem that there are only two questions: how much blood will flow, and will the bloodletting involve only the guilty parties, or perhaps innocents?"

"It's going to be a river of blood. You know that, Herbert. And you and I had better find a way to get the hell out of the way. Or I can promise you that our names will live in infamy—for a thousand years."

CHAPTER 45

GUSVILLE, ANZIO RIGHT FLANK

MARCH 24, 1944

BRIDGER slammed back his third shot of 180-proof alcohol from a bottle plainly labeled FOR THE USE OF U. S. ARMY MEDICAL DETACHMENTS ONLY, set down his Ernie Pyle column that he had just finished, and looked at Lieutenant Gus Heilman, the founder and duly elected mayor of Gusville as well as owner of *Gus's Bar and Grill.*

"You know what it says here. It says that Rommel wants to wage a 'war without hate.' *'Krieg ohne Hass'*, he calls it in German. I don't know about you, Gus, but I think it's a little late for that."

"I'm not much for politics, Major. But I do know that I'd like to shoot old Erwin Rommel and that paper-hanging son of a bitch Hitler both." He snatched the bottle of grain alcohol from him and took a gulp, washing it down with a generous slug of pineapple juice from an open tin can. "Now if that's what the Desert Fox means by 'war without hate' then I'm all fucking for it."

They were sitting in the parlor of what up until two months ago had been a modest country farmhouse, but had since been converted into Gusville's premier bacchanalian establishment. The *Bar and Grill* was located just off the main street of Borgo Sabotino, which the mayor of Gusville, in his first of many official acts, had renamed Tank Avenue. Sitting on his lap and holding his hand was a pretty young Italian woman, who happened to be wearing nothing but lacy undergarments and spoke only a smattering of English. Two other attractive women lounged on a nearby mattress with Sergeant Walkmeister; they too were scantily clad and happily attentive to his needs. In the main barroom, four stubble-faced Forcemen with Camels and Luckies dangling from their mouths sat around a card table playing a high-stakes game of Texas hold 'em.

Last night Bridger, who had been temporarily reassigned from General Frederick's staff to be the new commander of the First Regiment due to an officer shortage, had led a raid on the Germans, and he and the men were now relaxing and celebrating. They had killed and captured more than thirty of the enemy. In response, the Germans had pulled back their lines another two hundred yards early this morning to lick their wounds. In interrogating the German prisoners early this morning, Bridger had found out that they belonged to a new enemy outfit: the 735th Grenadier Regiment of the 715th Infantry Division. They were the replacements for the Force's nemesis, the vaunted Hermann Göring Division, along with a pro-Axis battalion of Italy's elite San Marco Marines.

Bridger took the bottle back from the irreverent mayor of Gusville and made himself a drink, pouring two fingers of alcohol in with a few splashes of pineapple juice. "Well the Germans can wait for my hatred until tomorrow because today I'm getting lit up like a firecracker."

"Me too, Major. I have even passed off my mayoral responsibilities."

"You don't have any mayoral responsibilities."

"Oh, yes I do. There are appointments to be made, taxes to be levied on units passing through our fine town, and wine, spirits, cattle, and chicken inventories to inspect. It's a damned tough job, but someone has to do it." He leaned in close to the young woman sitting on his lap to give her a kiss. "Right, baby?"

They kissed. When they pulled away, she giggled and said, "*Tutto bene, Gustavo. Tutto bene.*" And they kissed again.

Bridger smiled. "You're a cad, Gus."

"Add that to my list of accomplishments. My first report back in Helena said I was 'big, tough, mean, resentful, and lazy' and that I was a 'social misfit.' I take great pride in having overcome so many obstacles to become mayor of such an important town."

Bridger chuckled. He had a fine buzz going and Heilman was entertaining as hell. An enemy Panzer shell whistled overhead and exploded west of town, an overshoot. It was a warm, sunny day on the Anzio front and not a single German daylight patrol had been sighted. But the Krauts were still flinging in the occasional shell to keep them on their toes. The new German grenadier detachment, he knew, had to be angry at how badly they had been mauled last night. But more importantly, they had to be scared shitless of their new black-faced enemy directly opposite their left flank. When another tank shell blasted nearby, Bridger decided that he would lead another raid tonight to put the fear of God in the Germans. He would show them what he thought about Erwin Fucking Rommel and his 'war without hate.'

A voice slashed through his thoughts. "Attention!"

He didn't jump up or salute. Instead, he and Heilman both looked up through alcohol-soaked eyes at General Frederick and his aide, who had barked out the order.

"At ease, men," said the general with a carefree smile.

"Can I offer you a libation, General?" said Heilman with a welcoming grin.

"Why certainly, Mayor. Can I have the key to the town too?"

"Yes, sir, coming right up." Heilman pretended to toss him a key, gave an irreverent laugh, poured two fingers of grain alcohol into a dirty mug along with a finger of pineapple juice, and handed it to the general, who took it and sipped it slowly before giving an appreciative sigh.

"Now there's a cocktail that will put hair on your chest. Let it be said that the cup truly floweth over at *Gus's Bar and Grill* on Tank Avenue."

"Thank you, sir. Though the truth be told, I'm a bit out of practice. You see, when I was running my little bar and grill in Charlottesville, I used to mix all the drinks myself. But since then all I ever serve are screwdrivers, high balls, and red wine. So I'm really out of practice, sir."

"It tastes pretty damned good to me."

"Why thank you, General."

Bridger rose to his feet, feeling the blood and liquor rushing to his brain. "Do we have any orders, sir?" he asked, curious as to why Frederick was visiting the front lines, though he did so often enough and still took part in occasional nighttime raids deep into German territory. That was why they called him 'The Fighting General.'

"No, I just wanted to check up and see how you boys are doing."

"As you can see, sir," said Heilman through a toothy grin, "we have our hands full. We kill so many Krauts every night that we find it necessary to indulge in extreme forms of relaxation to get back into battle shape the following evening." He nodded towards the attractive Italian women lounging around the room. "Sherman said war was hell, but I'm afraid he only told the half of it, sir."

"Yes, I can see that…Captain."

"Captain? Why I'm no captain, sir, just a little old first lieutenant who nearly washed out of Officers Candidate School back at Fort Benning."

"Not anymore you're not. You have been promoted, Gus."

"Promoted? You've got to be shitting me, sir?"

"'Fraid not, Gus. Now you have the distinction of holding three titles: army captain, mayor, and saloon proprietor. I hope that's not too much to juggle."

"This is FUBAR, sir," said Bridger. "After all, we *are* talking about the same lazy bum who only joined the Force because he thought he was going to wash out of OCS, be shipped overseas as a lowly infantryman, and have his football star-bartender glory days come to a premature end."

"I am very much aware of Captain Heilman's colorful past, Major. In fact, when I first read his file, I thought I was reading a dime novel or a rap sheet. To say that our esteemed mayor of Gusville was a rebel and troublemaker…well, that would be putting it mildly."

"Thank you, sir," said Heilman. "It appears you know me better than my own ma."

The general grinned. "That's right I do—and never goddamn forget it."

"And to what may I ask, General, did my good drinking buddy here do to earn his promotion?"

"Captain Heilman has proved himself to be very resourceful. It seems that last night before your successful raid, Major, our newly promoted captain here led a group of Forcemen on another nighttime raid."

"Another raid, sir?"

"You weren't aware that our esteemed mayor of Gusville here invaded General Truscott's command post?"

He glanced at Heilman, who was looking guilty. "No, I wasn't aware of that, sir."

"He and his gang made off with more than a dozen casks of wine after disarming the military police guarding the place. Quite a haul, don't you think?"

Now he smiled at Heilman. *You wily bastard.* "You're right, he is very resourceful, sir. I will say that for him. Perhaps I was premature in my assessment."

The mayor of Gusville looked confused. "You're promoting me for last night, sir? Normally, wouldn't that be a court-martial offense?"

"I'm promoting you for your initiative, Captain. I admit it is a bit unconventional to promote an officer for stealing from his own army. But the fact is the raid was a success and General Truscott told me in person how impressed he was with the operation. Though he was mildly disappointed to have been liberated of so much fine Chianti."

Not sure what else to do, Heilman saluted. "Thank you, sir! I think?"

"You and your pals here in Gusville have become masters at not just raiding and killing Krauts, but at scrounging, begging, borrowing, and stealing from both sides. And now you've taken to gardening, too. I saw the plots outside filled with cabbage and potatoes. It has also been brought to my attention that while every other dogface on this Godforsaken beachhead is merely eking out an existence hiding out in foxholes and nibbling on crappy GI rations, Gusville's occupants dine regularly on fresh eggs, meat, and vegetables in addition to your consumption of various wine and spirits. Now word of your exploits has spread throughout the beachhead. Rather than cause resentment among our less opportunistic comrades in Third Division, your clever little enterprise here has become a morale booster. All in all, I have to say to you, Captain, that what you've done is very commendable. Very commendable indeed."

"Spoken like Stonewall Jackson himself, sir," said Heilman. "But are you sure this is not some kind of cruel joke and I'm actually going to be court-martialed?"

"I wouldn't joke about something like this, Captain. Congratulations on your promotion. Your bars should be in by next week. But you might want to hold off on putting them on for a while."

"Why's that, sir?"

"Because the Kraut snipers will likely start taking more of an interest in you than you'd like."

"Yes, sir. Thank you, sir."

"*Bravo, Gustavo!*" exclaimed the pretty Italian girl in his arms, and she gave him a big, wet kiss.

Frederick then looked at Bridger and said, "Actually, John, I did come by for another reason as well. I have news from Rome. Why don't we take a walk?" He ordered his aide to stay put and told him he'd come back for him.

Bridger felt himself sober up instantly. "Yes, sir."

They stepped outside the farmhouse onto Tank Avenue. The air smelled of cordite, cow manure, and the tangy scent of the sea as they started walking down the dirt lane pockmarked with German tank shells. A small patrol armed with Thompsons was just returning from No Man's Land with four prisoners and considerable booty: one Kraut was pushing a baby carriage full of potatoes; another bore a mattress on his back; a third carried a large crate of live chickens; and a fourth was herding a scraggly cow into town. *Ah, the spoils of war,* thought Bridger as he and Frederick looked at one another and grinned.

They came to a stop and the general's smile disappeared. "I wanted to tell you about Rome, John. Your friend Peter Savoyan with OSS reported in today. I thought you should know what's happening."

"What is it, sir?"

"The partisans bombed a marching column of SS troops yesterday at Via Rasella. More than thirty Krauts were killed and another seventy-five wounded. The Germans are expected to make fierce reprisals and the word is that Hitler is livid. No action has been taken yet, but Savoyan thinks the German response will be extreme."

"How are we getting this intelligence?"

"I can't tell you that, John. But I wanted to tell you that your family is in jeopardy. I'm sorry. I didn't want to spoil all the fun you and the boys were having after last night's raid. That's why I told Heilman about his promotion first. But the main reason I came to Gusville was to see you."

Bridger suddenly felt stone-cold sober. "What's happened to my family, sir?"

"Your stepfather was taken captive by the Gestapo two weeks ago. He's been imprisoned at Via Tasso."

"Jesus."

"That's not all, John. Your mother has been arrested, too, and was taken to the Gestapo's prison wing in Regina Coeli. I'm truly sorry, John."

Bridger felt the air leave him all at once. He had been dreading this day of reckoning for more than a decade now, the day when the family curse turned into something real and concrete. But there was no doubt about it now: the decisive day had come. He wondered if his father had anything to do with the arrests, or if it was Kappler or that brutal bastard Priebke behind it all.

"John, I'm sorry, but there's more."

Bridger braced himself. Though already drunk, he needed a stiff drink badly.

"Your sister is being sought by the Gestapo as well."

"Teresa? What has she done?"

"She is fighting for the Resistance. They call her the '*Inglesina.*'"

"She's the English Girl? My little sister? You've got to be kidding me."

"I'm afraid I'm not. But that's not all. She is believed to have taken part in the attack at Via Rasella. That's why the Gestapo arrested your mother and is tearing down half of Rome looking for Teresa and anyone else involved. Rome has become a war zone just like Anzio."

Bridger shook his head in disbelief. He knew his sister had brass balls, but a full-fledged partisan taking part in a bombing attack in broad daylight? She must have gone through some rigorous training after he had left Rome for her to be taking part in such a major Resistance operation. *Good for her,* he thought. *Good for her for taking the war to the Krauts on the streets of Rome.* He could only hope, though, that she wouldn't be caught like his mother and stepfather. There was no doubt Colonel Di Domenico was being cruelly tortured under interrogation, probably by that bastard Priebke that seemed to be Kappler's right-hand man. But what about his mother? Would the Fascist guards or the Nazis torture her as well? His own mother?

Now that the damned curse had reared its ugly head, everything was coming to a head now for his family. They had all been brought together in Italy during this bloody mess of a war, and now the day of reckoning he had predicted and been dreading had arrived. It was the will of God—or more likely, his opposite number Lucifer.

Frederick touched him on the shoulder. “I’m sorry about all this, John. I’m sorry I’ve come in here and ruined the festive spirit. I just wanted you to know. Savoyan has had to go into hiding just like your sister. He doesn’t know when he will be able to make his next radio communication.”

Bridger felt a spasm of anger: at his mother and father for being despicable human beings and instigating the goddamned curse in the first place; at the brutal Nazis and their maniac leader; at the whole shitty mess of a war that was taking his buddies from him and killing millions; at God Almighty for not coming to the aid of the weak and oppressed and for not punishing the wicked. After all, the sides in this war were clear cut and there was no debate about which side was right and which was wrong. It was black and white.

“I’m leading another patrol tonight,” he blurted, feeling the need for vengeance.

“John, you’ve led a dozen in the past three weeks. You need a break. In fact, I also came here to tell you that I’m taking you off the line and returning you to my staff.”

“No, I’m going out tonight.”

“Tonight?”

“Yep, and I’m not coming back until I’ve killed a dozen goddamn Krauts and slapped a sticker on every one of their foreheads!”

“John, no—you need a break.”

“No, sir. The worst is yet to come—and it’s fucking coming tonight!”

CHAPTER 46

GERMAN WING OF REGINA COELI PRISON

MARCH 24, 1944

PEERING THROUGH THE STEEL BARS, Hollmann saw his ex-wife shivering on the wooden bed rack of Holding Cell 23 in the Third Wing of Regina Coeli Prison. Her eyes were ringed with circles, her face lined with exhaustion, her once voluptuous body thin and frail. Though even the nobility of Rome had been suffering for some time now during the Occupation, he was still surprised at the extent of her physical deterioration since the last time he had seen her two months ago. But what struck him most of all was how out of place she looked in her surroundings. For probably the first time in her life, the imperious marchesa, this woman of noble blood and bearing, was truly a fish out of water and utterly defeated human being.

The wing was quiet as a mausoleum. The cell itself was cavernous and institutional, covered floor to ceiling in cold concrete. It was also windowless, and his wife had been given only a single blanket. The pungent stench of urine and excrement fouled the air of the cell block, adding a miasma of sickness and disease to the sense of gloom and isolation. She might as well have been a common murderer awaiting the gallows, and he was reminded of the fallen Napoleon banished to Elba. Yet, visiting her in person, he got no satisfaction from the sight of his once great and fiery marchesa reduced to a withered state.

When the pock-faced guard unlocked the prison door, she looked up at him and Hollmann saw the fire rekindle in her eyes, which somehow made him feel better.

"Get out of here! I am not talking to you!" she snapped, and he thought to himself that perhaps he was wrong and the walls of the prison would crumble around her before Regina Coeli got the better of his marchesa.

He held up a hand. "Settle down, Bianca. I come in peace." He turned to the guard. "Leave us and keep the door unlocked."

The guard looked worried. "Are you sure?"

"Yes, and when my visit in this foul place is concluded, you will bring the marchesa two more blankets and get someone to clean up this cell. I will have an officer from my staff return to conduct an inspection later this afternoon so you had better make sure to be thorough. Otherwise, I will have you locked up at Via Tasso. Have I made myself clear?"

"Y-Yes, Colonel," stammered the guard.

"Good, now leave us."

He turned back to his ex-wife. She still wore her usual haughty expression;

again the sense of normalcy made him feel better, though her stubbornness would make his task harder today. They watched one another for a long moment, like two panthers circling one another and sizing each other up, before he broke the silence.

"I came to tell you that last night Colonel Kappler was up all night compiling a list."

"A list? You came here to tell me about a list?"

"It is no ordinary list. It is a list of *Todeskandidaten.*"

"*Todeskandidaten*?"

"Candidates for death. He drew up a list of three hundred nineteen names from a master list of criminals currently in Via Tasso and other prisons throughout the city. His list has three separate headings: *Spionage*, *Kommunismus*, and *Jude*—Spies, Communists, and Jews. These are the men to be shot for the killing of the thirty-two German soldiers yesterday by the partisans in Via Rasella. The order is to be carried out by tonight."

"Why are you telling me this?"

"I have my reasons and they will become evident in the next few minutes."

"But no doubt the men on Kappler's list aren't the ones responsible for the bombing. The Gestapo couldn't possibly have rounded up the actual perpetrators so quickly, and there weren't more than three hundred partisans behind the bombing. So you're telling me that he is going to murder innocent people?"

"Yes. It is a travesty, and I tried to stop it but have failed. This reprisal is far out of proportion to what is necessary to maintain order. It also happens to be a direct violation of the 1907 Hague Convention on Land Warfare. But unfortunately, the Führer himself is involved, so all sense of reason has been thrown out the window. He initially demanded that thirty to fifty men be killed in reprisal for every one of the SS troops that died. Luckily, he was dissuaded from that excessive number, most likely by General Kesselring, and the ratio now stands at ten persons shot for every SS soldier killed."

"I still don't understand why you're telling me this? Is it your goal to make me detest you even more than I already do?"

"I am doing this because Kappler's list stands at three hundred nineteen souls. He is one person short, and the question is who the last person shall be?"

"*Dio mio*—you're not thinking about…is my husband on his list?"

"No, he is not. I have managed to keep him off the list for the time being. But I am feeling pressure from many sides."

"How so?"

"That is my business."

"Why are you telling me this? You want something from me, don't you?"

"Did you love him since the beginning, Bianca?"

"What?"

"Just answer my question. If you tell me the truth, I will do my best to ensure that the colonel is not added to the list. Do you understand what I am offering you here?"

She said nothing, her face a mask of proud defiance. But he did see a little gulp.

"Tell me now what I want to know and his life will be spared, even though it will cost me more than you can imagine. Was your love for him so pure that I never meant anything to you? Was it always Di Domenico that you loved desperately? Or was there ever a place in your heart for me?"

The cell fell silent. This time her lips trembled, but still she said nothing.

"The man is Teresa's biological father, Bianca. Tell me the truth and I promise I will do everything in my power to ensure that his life is spared. I cannot fault you for shooting me if your love for Di Domenico meant everything in the world to you and nothing else mattered but being rid of me and having him and the children together with you in Rome. That I can understand."

She looked down into the floor, her lips quivering. But she still could not bring herself to answer him.

"Tell me, Bianca. Is that how it was? Did you never love me and it was always him? Was your love for him so strong that you had to kill me so that you could be with him? Is that how much he meant to you?"

No answer.

"Tell me that's why you became so desperate that an Annulment wasn't enough and you had to kill me. Tell me that was the reason you did what you did that terrible day."

The cell remained silent, the only sound a faint creak from a pipe down the empty, cavernous hallway.

"Talk to me, Bianca. Tell me what happened. I need to know *why*. I have never been able to make sense out of it."

Still nothing.

"You never loved me! Say it, goddamnit! You never loved me!"

"I cannot say that!" she cried, jumping up from her hard wooden bed. "I was in love with you from the beginning and that is the truth!"

For a moment, he was too overcome with emotion to speak. Why did he want to know so badly? Why, after all these years, did he care? In the torment over the struggle for Rome—the torture and random violence, the bureaucracy, the relentless Allied and partisan bombings, the ever-present paranoia wrought by Hitler and Himmler even from afar—was he losing his mind?

His voice was soft, as it had once been between them in gentler times. "You were in love with me? But I thought you had always wanted to be with him?"

"No, it was you I loved!"

"Me? But what happened? You never talked about it before the shooting. I never even knew you were unhappy. I mean, we had arguments like all young couples, but I never for the life of me thought you wanted to kill me. And the way you went about it. It was as if I had pulled the gun on you. What made you commit such a desperate act?"

Her lips quivered again. "I didn't...I didn't want..." She left the words hanging.

"Didn't want what?"

"I didn't want...I didn't want to—"

"What is it? Out with it, woman!"

"I didn't want the Nazis to know that my children had Jewish blood!"

"What?"

"Your grandmother was a Jew! You tried to cover it up by falsifying the official government records in Berlin, Vienna, and Innsbruck, but my father's German lawyer discovered what you had done! You are a Jew!"

He just stood there in shock, unable to speak

"Don't you understand? With Hitler in power and the racial laws and Jewish boycotts in effect and getting worse every day, I didn't want to take the risk that the children would be persecuted! It was for them that I tried to shoot you dead when you said you would take them with you! I did it for them!"

My God, he thought. So that's what had driven her to commit such a desperate act. It had never had anything to do with his marital infidelities, her love for Di Domenico and the children, or because she and her powerful father were embarrassed that he had been married previously to another woman. Instead, she had tried to kill him because his grandmother was a Jew and his falsification of his family records, membership in the Nazi Party, and high rank as an Austrian police chief and wealthy landowner might not have been enough to protect him, her, or their children from persecution. He came from a reputable German and Italian family with ties to ancient nobility, and in 1932 at the time of the shooting, he had held millions of Schillings in the bank and extensive land holdings—and yet, because his grandmother had been a Jew, his entire life and that of his children had been in jeopardy. It was his Jewish heritage that had led his wife to try and kill him, so her children would not suffer discrimination and brutality on account of Hitler's monstrous racial laws. True, the laws didn't go into full effect until the fall of 1935 when Germany's Nuremberg decrees were formally enacted, but the marchesa had seen the writing on the wall in 1932 in Innsbruck and was not willing to risk her children's' lives or her own.

A part of him still couldn't believe it. But he knew it was the truth. Suddenly, all of her actions over the past eleven and a half years made complete sense. From the shooting, to the restraining order to keep him away from their children, to paying him off to silence him, to her moving to Rome with Gunther and Teresa to ensure that they were far away from Austria and Nazi Germany and in the safe haven of Rome with her father and their protective black nobility. After all these years, it had come down to the fact that he had posed an unacceptable risk to her and her children because of his heritage, because of his descent, and nothing more. In a way, knowing what was happening today to the Jews of Europe through Hitler's *Endlösung*, he could not blame his ex-wife for what she had done. He might very well have done the same thing if he truly believed that it would protect Gunther and Teresa.

"You don't know how much I loved you," he said. "I would have done anything for you if you had just asked me."

"Is that why you cheated on me with those young tarts in Innsbruck? Because you loved me?"

"You know none of that meant anything. I took advantage of the authority I wielded. It was you I always loved. In fact, I have never loved anyone else—even to this day."

Tears appeared in her eyes. "I feel lower right now than I ever thought possible. But it was my father who pushed me to do it with all his talk of what would happen to the Jews. He said that the children would never be safe as long as I was married to you. He said you would be the death of us all because of the Jewish blood that coursed through your veins. And in the end, he was right. Just look at what is happening all over Europe. The Jews and anyone who associates with them are not just losing their right to vote and their jobs, they are being exterminated. And it is not happening far away in Poland anymore; it is happening right here in Rome."

"But no one ever found out about my grandmother. I was never questioned by anyone about it."

"That's because you had policemen and political friends in high places and falsified the records, and because you joined the Nazi party early on and your family were practicing Catholics. All of those things protected you. But once my father's lawyer discovered the truth about your family's history, my father told me that I still couldn't take that chance."

"I should have known it would be something like this. I was blind. The police chief of Innsbruck, and here I was blind."

"Well, now you know the truth."

"Yes, I know the painful truth."

"The question now is what are you going to do about it?"

"Are you suggesting that I won't be true to my word to try and have your husband released from Kappler's custody?"

"I don't know. You tell me?"

"Di Domenico's life will be spared if I can help it. That I promise you."

"Kappler is a loathsome murderer to do this. What kind of man draws up a list of three hundred twenty innocent men to be shot down in cold blood for a military attack that took the lives of only thirty-two?"

"They are not innocent. They are jailed criminals and threats to the Reich. But you are right, most of them don't deserve to be executed, especially without a fair trial."

"Kappler is a murderer."

"Yes, and so are the partisans that killed the soldiers in Via Rasella yesterday. The battalion was made up of Austrians from the Tyrol. Many of them are middle-aged men with wives and children waiting for them back home. Their only crime was being called into service to fight a war that can no longer be won."

"The Pope will never stand for this. He will protest this and then where will you be? The tide of sentiment will be against you, and all you will have accomplished for your Führer is to enrage the people of Rome, the Allies, your own German diplomats, and neutral countries like Switzerland, Spain, and Sweden. How can you even fight for Germany when you have Jewish blood and you know what Hitler and your boss Himmler are doing to the Jews?"

"I am doing what everyone else is doing, including you. I am surviving. And as for your precious Pope, why hasn't he raised a single word of protest? It's as if he doesn't exist in this holy city—and it has been that way since last October."

"How dare you speak of His Holiness in that fashion?"

"How dare I? When it comes to protecting his own people, how dare *him*. Don't you see his agenda? All he cares about is maintaining order, keeping the

Communists at bay, and making certain his beloved Catholic children are not shipped off to labor or death camps. As long as partisan bombings and shootings on the streets of Rome don't erupt into a full-scale war that weakens the Germans while empowering the Communists, he doesn't care what happens. This time the Pope's own children, as he is fond of calling the Romans of his diocese, are to be shot. This is an unspeakable affront to the Holy Father, here in his very own backyard, the Eternal Holy City of Rome. And yet he remains silent. When it comes to saving his own people, the only thing this Pope has in his papal arsenal is his treasured *policy of silence*. That is why he is perhaps Germany's greatest ally here in Italy. When something bad happens to his own people, he does nothing but pray in silence."

"That is blasphemy! As you well know, he has been protecting thousands upon thousands of war refugees, Jews, and Allied POWs all over Rome and at his estate in Castel Gandolfo! And, despite your brutal tactics, you and your Nazis have been powerless to stop him! For every person you catch ten more are safely hidden away or aided in their escape from Italy!"

"Yes, his humanitarian works have been far-reaching. But he still has no more influence over events here in Rome or the ultimate fate of the city than you or I. We own him!"

"You never have and never will own the Defender of Rome, Wilhelm! And you are a monster and I regret ever having been married to you!"

He headed for the steel barred door. "I would not be so hasty in your judgment, Marchesa," he fired back, smiling thinly. "Your former marriage to this lowly Jew is the only thing keeping you alive."

CHAPTER 47

HEADQUARTERS OF THE COMMANDANT OF ROME

CORSO D'ITALIA

MARCH 24, 1944

AT FIVE MINUTES PAST NOON, Hollmann sat in front of *Stadtkommandant* Kurt Mälzer's desk with Kappler and SS Major Dobbrick, the commander of the 3rd Battalion who had miraculously managed to escape injury during the Via Rasella attack. The desk was cluttered with unattended paperwork; a plate of half-eaten dark bread, sausage, and smelly Limburger cheese; a pair of empty beer bottles and three empty glasses; and a half-drunk bottle of W & A Gilbey single malt Scotch whiskey with its cork and wax seal removed—all a testament to the self-proclaimed "King of Rome's" indolent management style. Hollmann had to suppress the urge to shake his head in disgust: the man was indeed not only a ticking time bomb, but a professional embarrassment to the Reich.

"So, Kappler," began Mälzer, his fleshy cheeks already ruddy from drink, "have you completed your death list?"

"Yes, I have the list of the *Todeskandidaten* right here, excluding of course *Questore* Caruso's fifty names. The Chief of Police has promised delivery by 1300 hours of the names of the criminals being held at his headquarters."

Kappler handed the list to the commandant. As Mälzer began to read it over, the Gestapo chief sat back in his seat, stifling an exhausted yawn. Hollmann knew he had stayed up all night putting the list of "candidates for death" for Kesselring's reprisal order and hadn't gotten a wink of sleep. Hollmann and Consul Möllhausen of the German Embassy had paid him a dead-of-night visit while he was leaning over the file cards, immersed in making his momentous choices of who would live and who would die.

"Listen, Kappler," Hollmann remembered Möllhausen saying, "if I were in your place my conscience would tremble. I do not know how I would act. But I certainly would feel myself at a decisive turn in my life. What you are doing goes way beyond war and Fatherland, and remember that one day you will be called to account before the tribunal of God."

The Gestapo chief had replied: "Möllhausen, I can only promise you I will do what I am able to do. And this is what it is: For every name that I write, I will pray three times that I have picked the right man for punishment."

Mälzer looked up from the three sheets of paper he had been flipping through. "I don't see Colonel Di Domenico's name on this list. He is a known enemy of the Reich and richly deserves punishment."

Hollmann looked at Kappler, who crossed his arms and gave him a skeptical look that said, "You're on your own, Wilhelm."

"He is not on the list because he is still under active interrogation," replied Hollmann. "I believe he is very close to providing us with useful information on the inner workings of the Military Front."

Mälzer frowned. "General Mackensen wants him on the list. You will need to find other informants and add Di Domenico."

Mackensen had ordered it? Damn, he hadn't seen that coming. "I'm afraid I can't do that. The colonel is too useful to me."

"Did you not hear me? General Mackensen has issued a specific order and it must be obeyed. But more importantly, you saw yesterday what was done to my men. They were blown to bits and the Italians have to pay for this."

"With all due respect, *Stadtkommandant,* I need this important informant kept alive until we have completed our questioning."

"We?"

"Colonel Kappler and I."

Mälzer looked at the Gestapo chief. "Are you in agreement, Colonel?"

"No, I am not. I believe Colonel Di Domenico is worthy of death and that General Mackensen's order should be carried out."

Hollmann shot him a glare. *You bastard! We had a fucking deal!*

"Very well, that settles it," said Mälzer. "I don't need to remind you how important carrying out this reprisal order is to our Führer. And let's not forget that he wanted fifty Italians shot for every soldier killed. Now we all know that Field Marshal Kesselring and Mackensen both believe the Führer's numbers to be excessive, but now is not the time for softness. These impetuous Romans have to be taught a lesson in order to scare them into submission and achieve the necessary deterrent effect. It hardly matters that none of the *Todeskandidaten* on your list were the actual perpetrators of the crime. Why a mere three hundred and twenty souls for yesterday's outrage is really an exercise in humanity. Indeed, killing only ten Italians for every German is an act of Christian kindness."

Hollmann tried to keep his tone controlled. "Di Domenico can serve a greater purpose to the Reich if he remains under my custody for interrogation."

"General Mackensen has ordered it and I will not argue any further, Colonel." He turned towards Major Dobbrick, the commander of the Bozen SS 3rd Battalion. "The list is complete, or soon will be, and we all know the importance of the mission at hand. The order comes from the highest authority, the Führer himself. It is now up to you, Major, and the survivors of the Eleventh Company to avenge your fallen compatriots. I hereby order you to execute all three hundred and twenty men on Colonel Kappler's list, including Colonel Di Domenico."

He underscored his patriotic flourish with a whiskey-soaked smile.

It was then that Dobbrick caught them all by surprise.

"I'm sorry, sir, but I cannot obey that order."

Taken aback, Hollmann watched as shock followed swiftly by anger overtook the commandant's fleshy face. "And why not, Major?" snarled Mälzer.

"My men are not trained for firing squad details. Plus they are rather inept."

"Inept?"

"Yes, they are old, as you know, and clumsy. I think they would botch the whole thing. They are also very religious, and full of superstition. They are Austrians from remote provinces in the Alps. As you know, such things are common in alpine men. Above all, there are now too few of them to carry out such a large assignment in so short a time. Wouldn't it be better for an all-German detachment to fulfill the necessary quota?"

Mälzer's face had reddened. "Is this some sort of joke, Major?"

"No, sir, it is not."

Hollmann frowned; though he was in the process of actively refusing an order himself, he did not want his subordinate Dobbrick to weasel out of his duty to carry out the Führer-directed reprisal. "Your unit was the one bombed by these partisans, Major. And yet you refuse a direct order to carry out the reprisal?"

"I am sorry, sir. I won't do it, and neither will my men."

"Very well. I am letting you know that as your superior officer in the SS, I will be filing an official complaint with General Wolff if you persist in this dereliction of duty. Does that change your mind?"

"No, Colonel. My men and I are not equipped for this type of thing."

He looked at Mälzer, and then at Kappler, but they were at a loss, both taken by surprise by Dobbrick's insubordination.

"I will call General Mackensen's headquarters and see what he has available," said the *Stadtkommandant.* He picked up the telephone, called Fourteenth Army headquarters, and spoke with Mackensen's Chief of Staff, Colonel Wolfgang Hauser, informing him that he needed a detachment of troops at once to carry out the reprisal. But Hauser refused, too, although unlike Dobbrick he offered no excuses.

"He won't do it," said Mälzer when he hung up the phone, clearly vexed. "He says it was the police who were attacked and, therefore, the police must carry out the reprisal. He referred specifically to the teleprint from OKW to Kesselring's headquarters, which states that the execution is to be by the SD."

"So who will fulfill the order?" asked Kappler.

Looking at him, Hollmann already knew the answer. *It's going to be you, you idiot! Don't you see?*

"I'm afraid it is up to you, Kappler," said Mälzer. "These men were acting under Gestapo orders. You must be the one to even the score for this atrocity."

Kappler looked at Dobbrick, whose eyes had turned down meekly into the floor. If the Gestapo chief obeyed, he would no longer be an officer making the best of a bad situation under an urgent timetable and putting together the list of *Todeskandidaten.* He would be something much worse. He and his men would be the actual executioners and would be accountable for war crimes, which the Allies were constantly reminding Germans and Italians alike now that they were stalemated at Anzio. On the other hand, if he refused, he would be relieved of duty, locked away in a prison cell or put before a firing squad just like the prisoners on his list, and his life as he knew it would be over. Wolff, Himmler, and the Führer himself would see to that. For all intents and purposes, if Lieutenant

Colonel Herbert Kappler—married man and father of a perfect "experimental" son of the *Lebensborn* Nazi baby farm—disobeyed the order, he would cease to exist.

"Well, Kappler, what do you say? Will you do it?" asked Hollmann.

The Gestapo chief hesitated, needing more time to think. Hollmann could see him cursing himself for being outmaneuvered. The thought of who would actually execute the men whose names he had placed on his list had never crossed his mind. Kappler had told Hollmann on more than one occasion that he had never actually killed anyone in his life, though he had proved his willingness to die fighting for the Fatherland. Five times since the war began he had volunteered for front line service, but all of his requests had been denied. His expertise as a police chief was required in Rome, maintained his SS superiors repeatedly. He had even gone above them directly to the Wehrmacht, only to receive a record-marring reprimand. Now that the initial worry over the bombing had faded, he was being told to execute not armed soldiers but the men and boys who bore the names on his list. Hollmann knew from talking to the Gestapo chief that he had come to know and respect many of them during their incarceration at Via Tasso and Regina Coeli. Men like Colonel Di Domenico and old General Simoni of the Military Front; the fifty-three-year-old Communist priest Don Pappagallo; Colonel Frignani and several other ex-*carabinieri*; Professors Pilo Albertelli and Gioacchino Gesmundo; and the crippled diplomat Filippo De Grenet.

Kappler cleared his throat to speak. "If you so order me, *Stadtkommandant*," he said in a firm but deferential voice, "I will place my men at your disposal."

Mälzer considered this a moment before shaking his fat head. "No, that won't do, I'm afraid. As the head of the Gestapo in Rome, it is your duty, Colonel, to set an example for your men. I know you are a man of conscience and even putting together the list was not easy for you, but you cannot expect your men to do what you have been ordered to do. These orders come from the Führer himself and absolve you of all blame. Besides, these men on your list are partisans, Jews, and other enemies of the Reich. They are expendable."

Hollmann scowled at him. "No one is expendable, Mälzer. No one—not in this war or any other. But you are correct to say that Colonel Kappler has no right to ask his men to do what he himself is loath do."

Mälzer looked intently at Kappler. "Then you will do it."

"Yes, with deep regret and great reluctance, I will do it."

"Good, I want Colonel Di Domenico on that list too. You will see to it."

"Yes, *Stadtkommandant*, I *will* see to it." He gave Hollmann a look of rebuke. The price that Kappler was extracting was that Di Domenico was on the list. As he stood up, he looked at Dobbrick, who was cowering in his chair, refusing to meet his gaze. "I also fully expect Colonel Hollmann here to file an official report to *Polizeiführer* Wolff about your insubordination, Major. You will be filing your report, won't you, Colonel?"

"I most certainly will," said Hollmann.

"Very well, I bid you good day. With only eight hours to fulfill the Führer's directive, I have a multitude of logistical and security problems to take care of."

"Good luck then, Kappler. Heil Hitler!" said Mälzer with a salute, looking like a sadistic Santa Claus without a beard.

CHAPTER 48

GESTAPO HEADQUARTERS

MARCH 24, 1943

HOLLMANN AND KAPPLER drove in separate cars to Via Tasso, where the Gestapo chief assembled the twelve officers in his command to brief them on the regrettable enterprise they would have to perform in their service to the Reich.

He got right to the point. Because the commander of the Bozen battalion had declined to carry out the execution of Hitler's order, today he and his men were to be the executioners of the three hundred twenty selected prisoners. Furthermore, all officers would have to take part along with the NCOs and enlisted men as a symbolic necessity indispensable to the maintenance of discipline. To Hollmann's surprise, all of Kappler's officers agreed with him and not a single one voiced an objection. Making it easier for them was the fact they had witnessed firsthand the carnage and suffering at Via Rasella yesterday. They had seen the body parts and blood caked to the street, and they had heard the anguished cries of the wounded men. Otherwise, they might not have been so amenable to executing such a large number of prisoners in reprisal for the bombing.

"I know this is horrible for all of us to have to do," Kappler went on to say, "but it is important that the men have the backing of the officers. That is why all officers will be required to fire one shot at the beginning and one at the end."

Priebke and the other officers nodded. Hollmann saw that they had accepted their duty—and their fate.

"Very well, there is much preparation work to be done. At present, I have two overriding concerns: speed and security. The reprisal must be completed by 2030 hours so we will have to round up the prisoners, load them onto trucks, and complete the executions in the next seven and a half hours. Security is best served by secrecy. Now it is my understanding from Colonel Hollmann here that the Vatican is aware of the ten-for-one reprisal order, but the partisans and citizens of Rome know nothing of what has been planned. Once we start loading the prisoners onto the trucks, the prisoners that have not been selected and are left behind at Via Tasso, Regina Coeli, and elsewhere, as well as the administrators and guards at these facilities, will have an idea of what is happening. There is nothing we can do about that. But we must keep the executions secret from the partisans and Roman citizenry until the very end. No one can predict the reaction of the Romans if they discover what is taking place in their midst. The partisans could organize an armed assault and the whole city could explode with violence. An attack such as the one at Via Rasella would rout our meager forces, which are inferior in both number and firepower to the pre-attack strength of the Eleventh Company."

"How many men do we have, sir?" asked Priebke, standing in the front row of officers.

"Seventy-four total. In addition to you dozen officers and myself, there are sixty NCOs and a single soldier at our disposal."

"If there are over three hundred men to be shot," asked Captain Köhler, "and there are seventy-four of us, how will we go about executions to finish in the allotted time?"

Hollmann thought: *What the hell am I doing here? This is madness.*

"I have already thought this out, gentlemen," replied Kappler, putting on a clinical front for his officers despite his qualms. "I have calculated the time necessary for executing each of the three hundred twenty, as well as the required arms and ammunition. Five hours will be required to complete the shooting at a rate of one prisoner killed per minute. We will divide up the men into platoons of five men each. Once each officer has shot their prisoner at the beginning, each NCO will shoot one prisoner by pistol, rotating through until near the end when the officers will again take care of their second target to maintain order and discipline. The bullets will be fired to enter the victim's brain from the cerebellum so that no bullets are wasted and death can be accomplished instantaneously. Captain Priebke, I am assigning you to be the keeper of the list. It will be your responsibility to make sure that everyone named is properly executed, and that once they have been executed their name is checked off the list. Captain Schütz, you will be in charge of directing the executions. Are there any questions?"

"Where will we perform the executions, Colonel?" asked Priebke.

Hollmann suddenly realized that Kappler had neglected perhaps the most important item. Executions were normally carried out at Fort Bravetta, by firing squad in the outdoor prison yard. But that would jeopardize secrecy with all of the noise and the bodies to be cleared away and buried, especially given the large number of *Todeskandidaten* to be executed. Disposing of so many corpses created a special problem. Digging a mass grave would take too long. So where could Kappler avoid having to dig a mass grave, while at the same time maintaining secrecy, even if only for a few days but preferably longer, to blunt the expected harsh partisan response and public outcry?

To Hollmann's surprise, Kappler was already one step ahead of him.

"We need a natural death chamber. Like a cavern or grotto. It needs to be big and it needs to be nearby because we are running out of time. We will also need to be able to set demolition charges around it to keep people from snooping around, at least for the short term. Does anyone know of such a place?"

Captain Köhler stepped forward. "I do, sir. There is a network of tunnels only a couple of miles away in the Via Ardeatina. It is among the Christian catacombs."

"Oh, yes, I know what you're talking about." Kappler looked at Priebke. "Those catacombs have long been abandoned, haven't they?"

"Yes, but they have been used recently by the Resistance. They were hiding their vehicles there until one of our informants reported it to us."

Kappler looked back at Köhler. "All right, Captain, I want you to proceed immediately to those catacombs in the Via Ardeatina. Take some engineers with you to make sure we can seal those caves off when we're finished. Go now!"

"Yes, Colonel—Heil Hitler!" and he was off.

After delegating out to Captains Schütz and Priebke the remaining details, Kappler ended the meeting and looked at his watch. Hollmann checked his, too, noting that the time was 1301. He and the Gestapo chief went downstairs to the mess hall. They didn't eat, but instead Kappler solemnly briefed his NCOs as he had done with his officers. After a few minutes, Schütz interrupted the meeting with news that another SS soldier from the Eleventh Company had died a few minutes earlier. That brought the total number of dead to be avenged up to thirty-three. Realizing that if he was to obey Field Marshal Kesselring's order he would have to find another ten men to execute, for a total of three hundred thirty, Kappler quickly finished the briefing and returned to his office.

Hollmann gave him a few minutes before going upstairs. Finding the lieutenant colonel shuffling through the paperwork at his desk, he closed the door behind him.

"You don't have to go through with this, Herbert. You are murdering innocent people who had nothing to do with yesterday's attack."

"You know it is too late, Hollmann. You tried to talk me out of it last night, but Kesselring and Mackensen have made it clear that there must be at least ten killed for every one of ours that was murdered."

"I can only say that, like Möllhausen, if I were in your shoes my conscience would tremble. If you go through with this, it will be a criminal act and not a simple reprisal of war. The Hague Convention makes it clear that we cannot kill indiscriminately in this manner. You know this, Herbert. And yet you still are willing to go through with it?"

"What else can I do? I have been ordered by my superiors as well as Hitler himself. I must do my duty for the Fatherland."

"But this isn't duty. This is mass murder. Most of the men listed as worthy of death have not been condemned to death by a judge or jury. They are innocents."

Kappler looked at him stoically.

"What we are doing here is totally and irrevocably wrong—and yet somehow you feel the utter wrongness of it is trumped by your sense of soldierly duty. Like you, I saw firsthand the bloody carnage at Via Rasella. I know what the partisans have done, and it both revolted and angered me. I know you are a loyal soldier and feel duty-bound to follow orders. But this is wrong, Herbert. And one day we are all going to live in infamy for it. People will not forget this atrocity. It will tarnish you, me, and every German not only here in Rome, but everywhere in the world for generations."

"I will pray to God then. There is nothing more I can do."

"There will never be absolution for this. Never."

"I know," said Kappler. "Absolution after Via Ardeatina will be impossible. But a loyal soldier must not shirk from his duty. In the end, he must obey his Führer."

CHAPTER 49

VIA ARDEATINA
MARCH 24, 1944

TERESA heard the rumble of the noisy truck engines before she actually saw any of the vehicles. Her first thought was that someone had talked under torture and the Nazis were coming to arrest her and Beppo, who lay napping in the straw bed beside her. Since the attack at Via Rasella, she and her lover had been hiding out in a farmhouse two miles south of Rome near the *Fosse Ardeatine*, hoping to keep a low profile until the ardor over the bombing had passed. She instantly shook Beppo, who looked up at her in sleepy-eyed startlement.

"Get dressed! I think the Germans are coming!"

Instead of obeying, he darted, still half naked, to the farmhouse window to have a look for himself. Teresa followed him and they both looked out the cracked window. A long caravan of heavy trucks raced along the dusty, pitted track leading to the quarry and catacombs a half mile to the south. But, to her surprise, she saw at once that they weren't German military transports, and, more importantly, that they weren't coming for her and Beppo. They were civilian conveyances that looked an awful lot like meat trucks. And they were in a hurry. They roared past like a whirlwind, their engines rattling and rubber tires kicking up a plume of ginger-colored dust, as if not a precious second of time could be wasted in getting to their destination.

She looked at Beppo. They both shook their heads, at a loss to explain what was happening.

"This is very strange," he said after watching the last vehicle disappear down the road. "But more importantly, it doesn't feel right."

"No, it doesn't," she agreed. Over the past four months she had learned to trust his instincts—but she trusted hers even more.

They quickly dressed and collected their Berettas. Teresa also snatched up her father's old pair of Italian Army desert field glasses from the 1936 Ethiopian campaign he had given her as a present. After grabbing their bicycles, for which they would have been shot by the occupiers on the streets of Rome but were allowed to use outside the city limits, they started riding off down the road in the wake of the settling cloud of dust, across the melancholy yet beautiful Roman Campagna. On their left, they passed the Catacombs of St. Calixtus before arriving to a hillock above the caves near the Catacombs of St. Oomitilla. There they saw a peasant in tattered, mud-splattered work clothes. He was crouched down in a stand of cypress and umbrella pines, peering down into the clearing where the trucks had pulled up outside the entrance to the caves. The man looked frightened when he saw them riding up from behind him on their bicycles.

"Don't worry, old man, we are not here to hurt you," said Beppo as they came to a skidding halt. He raised his hands to show he meant no harm. "We just want to see what is going on? What name do you go by?"

"I am Nicola D'Annibale. I mind pigs and don't want any trouble."

Teresa noticed that he still looked petrified. "Everything is all right," she said to assuage his fears. "We just want to see what these trucks are doing way out here."

"The Germans are bringing prisoners to the caves," he said, pointing down below. "Look."

Dismounting from their bicycles, they crept forward into the stand of trees with the pig farmer, whom she could tell wasn't so old after all, but just worn out from a lifetime of hard labor and probably the war. Together, the three of them looked down into the clearing where the meat-wagon-like trucks had pulled up. Teresa peered through her father's military field glasses.

Her jaw dropped.

An SS officer with a scar on his face was addressing a group of uniformed soldiers, some in black, others in *feldgrau*, while male prisoners with their hands tied behind their backs were being unloaded from the trucks. There was no doubt in her mind who the officer was and what he was doing here. It was the dreaded Kappler, and he was here to carry out the reprisal at the *Fosse Ardeatine* for Via Rasella. Standing next to him was Captain Erich Priebke and a pair of officers named Schütz and Köhler that were rumored to be as brutal as the infamous Torquemada, who reportedly performed Kappler's bidding in the basement of Via Tasso by day and romanced film star Laura Nucci by night. The Germans were obviously planning on using the labyrinth of tunnels cut into the reddish-brown earth—some a hundred yards long and fifteen feet high—to hide the bodies and cover up their despicable deeds. It was painfully apparent what future the gaping jaws of the tunnels would hold for the poor men in the trucks. Why else would more than fifty Gestapo men drive hundreds of tied-up prisoners to remote caverns outside the city if not to mass-execute them?

Her heart sank. Turning towards Beppo, she saw it in his eyes too. He didn't need the field glasses to know what was happening.

What in the name of the Holy Father have we done? Is this all that Via Rasella has amounted to, the murder of innocents?

"The officer in charge down there is Herbert Kappler, the chief of the Gestapo in Rome," she said to Nicola D'Annibale. "This is retaliation for the attack at Via Rasella. Those are innocent men in those trucks who had nothing to do with the bombing, and Kappler is murdering them."

"Yes, I know of this Kappler. We should get out of here. If they see us, they will kill us."

"You can go, old man," said Beppo. "But we are staying here to watch. What Kappler is doing is a war crime."

The rear door of one of the trucks rolled open and a group of doomed men, momentarily blinded by the low-hanging sun, were ordered to descend and stand waiting before the entrance of the cave. They had been tied together in pairs and were being sorted out in groups of five by another SS officer. She quickly scanned for familiar faces amongst the prisoners, praying that her father Colonel Di Domenico wasn't among those condemned to death. She didn't see him anywhere, but she did recognize her father's old war partner General Simoni of the Military Front and Father Don Pappagallo.

My God, she thought, *was the Gestapo now murdering priests?*

She looked again at Kappler. He was still addressing his men. Through the field glasses she could see him clearly; he was gesturing vigorously and pacing as he spoke, probably trying to reassure and instill courage in them for the gruesome task they were about to perform. Around the perimeter of the clearing, SS guards with submachine guns had been posted to keep civilians away.

Watching through the field glasses, it seemed to her as if a terrible nightmare was unfolding slowly before her eyes. Was there nothing they could do to stop this atrocity from happening?

Kappler stopped speaking.

Teresa held her breath.

He made a motion, as if giving an order. A platoon of five SS officers chose five prisoners, bound to one another, and herded them with the noses of their pistols and submachine guns into the tunnel. They were led by a sergeant holding a torch to illuminate the way into the dark tunnel.

"We've got to do something," she whispered defiantly.

"There is nothing that we can do," said Beppo sadly, and he took the field glasses from her.

She looked at the pig farmer D'Annibale. He crossed himself.

From inside the cave, she heard an explosion of gunfire. The shots were muffled by the walls of the cave but still discernible through the open entrance with the wind blowing their way and orifices in the rain-pitted rock that allowed sound to escape. Then nothing, no screams, no cries, nothing.

Only a morbid silence.

One of the prisoners awaiting his turn at death in front of the entrance shouted, "Italia!" in a booming voice. The sound carried all across the *Fosse Ardeatine* and others joined in until the SS guards bullied them into shutting up. Teresa saw Father Pappagallo among those near the entrance. He was standing in a group that included General Simoni and what looked like other military officers and perhaps partisans. He appeared to be giving blessings to the other men as they waited their turn to enter the caves. He was tied to a tall, fair-haired young man who didn't look Italian at all.

She felt tears welling in her eyes. She knew these men personally. They were good men and noble Romans and certainly didn't deserve an ending such as this. She looked again at D'Annibale, who was staring grimly at his pocket watch, as if he wanted to stamp this terrible moment forever in his memory.

"What time is it?" she asked quietly.

"Three-thirty-three." He shook his head sadly.

"St. Peter met Jesus here when he fled from persecution," said Beppo. "And now we are confronted by Nazi atrocities at this historic place. Keep a sharp lookout on those guards patrolling the perimeter. If they spot us, they will take us into those caves and shoot us down like dogs, too."

He was right, what they were doing was dangerous and could easily get them all killed. She crouched down deeper in the tall grass behind the cypress tree, feeling her breath quickening. Beppo handed back the field glasses and she looked down at the cave entrance. The five officers who had gone inside the cave reemerged and the next group was about to be brought forward into the gaping jaws of death.

Suddenly, there was confusion.

Padre Pappagallo, in an exhibition of what seemed to Teresa like superhuman strength, burst free from his ropes and began to pray, imparting a paternal benediction to all. When he did so, he lifted his hands and the fair-skinned man tied to him was suddenly freed. The German guards rushed in to restore order, but in the confusion the man ran for his life. He scaled the slope to a field above the caves, but quickly ran into the SS patrol guarding the perimeter. Then, for some inexplicable reason, he was escorted back by several Germans and thrown inside a truck.

"I wonder why they're letting him go?" said Beppo.

"I guess he's not supposed to be here. The Germans must have realized they had an innocent man."

"They are all innocent men."

"Yes, and no doubt they wish they could be as lucky as the one in the truck."

A minute later, another salvo of gunfire, again dampened by the cave walls, crackled into the late afternoon.

Another five men dead.

In that instant, a black Mercedes brandishing a pair of flapping swastikas pulled up and parked in front of the cave entrance next to the prisoner trucks. Teresa recognized the car instantly, and watched as her father, SS Colonel Hollmann, got out from the back seat with the aid of his Italian chauffeur. He spoke to Priebke, who seemed to be checking names off some sort of list at the entrance, and was pointed to one of the trucks, just as the five SS executioners reemerged from the cave. Her father said a few more words Priebke and then she watched with horror as he went to a nearby truck that the SS captain pointed him to. My God, was he selecting a victim?

"It's my father," she said to Beppo.

"Colonel Hollmann?" He took the field glasses from her and peered down at the scene. "So he, too, is part of this."

"And to think I once loved him," said Teresa sadly.

She felt the eyes of D'Annibale heavily upon her. But the peasant farmer said nothing. She took back the field glasses and peered through them, sickened yet at the same time curious, in a macabre way, to see whom her father would select.

The door slowly swung open and she saw a face.

She couldn't believe her eyes.

The man Hollmann helped from the truck was none other than her birth father, Colonel Di Domenico. His face was terribly swollen from the beatings he had sustained, and he had an enormous welt under his right eye. Despite his wounds, he had a heroic bearing about him as he shambled towards the entrance to the tunnel of death, his brutalized legs barely able to walk. Just before reaching the entrance, Hollmann had him stop and Priebke and the other SS officers saluted him.

And then he disappeared into the cave with Hollmann.

Teresa was unable to hold back the torrent of tears that poured from her eyes. To see these two men—both of whom had been fathers to her and that she had loved and worshiped growing up—finally square off in this tragic manner made her question if there was a God at all. How could her life—and, more importantly, theirs—have come down to this horrible moment? There just couldn't be a God if this were so.

There was a moment of great silence, like the calm before the storm, and then a single gunshot ripped through the cave and echoed out the open entrance. The terrible sound was attenuated by the cave walls but still distinct, carrying a squalid note of finality.

When Hollmann reappeared a moment later, he looked visibly shaken. She wanted to kill him. There and then, she vowed that one day she would—just as her mother had tried to do eleven and a half years earlier.

Teresa would fulfill the curse.

The murder of innocents at *Fosse Ardeatine* had to be avenged.

CHAPTER 50

VATICAN

MARCH 25, 1944

STANDING OUTSIDE THE OFFICE of Pope Pius XII at 9:43 a.m., Count Giuseppe Dalla Torre—the director and chief editor of *L'Osservatore Romano*—stared down at the Nazi communiqué from the Stefani wire dispatch received by the Vatican at 10:55 p.m. last night. He had already read it over ten times this morning and he still couldn't believe his eyes.

The Germans had always been vile and duplicitous propagandists, but this was a new low even for the deplorable disciples of Hitler and Goebbels. Clearly, the battle for Rome, at least on the part of Nazi Germany, had escalated to a point where the lines between humanity and barbarism had been erased. He read the German communiqué one more time and compared it to the front-page editorial that he had written for today's edition of the Vatican newspaper. His stinging editorial spared no words in protesting the bloody vendetta of the Ardeatine Caves. Quite simply, what had transpired at the caves was a massacre of innocents and a brutal act of infamy that, in his mind, would resonate in Italy for all eternity. In stark contrast, the German propaganda piece read:

> On the afternoon of March 23, 1944, criminal elements executed a bomb attack against a column of German Police in transit through Via Rasella. As a result of this ambush, 32 men of the German Police were killed and several wounded.
>
> The vile ambush was carried out by *comunisti-badogliani*. An investigation is still under way to clarify the extent to which this criminal act is attributable to Anglo-American incitement.
>
> The German Command has decided to terminate the activities of these villainous bandits. No one will be allowed to sabotage with impunity the newly affirmed Italo-German cooperation. The German Command has therefore ordered that for every murdered German ten *comunisti-badogliani* criminals be shot. This order has already been executed.

When he had written his editorial, he was confident he knew precisely how the Supreme Pontiff would react to the indisputable Nazi atrocity, which was why he had written his front-page editorial in stronger language than usual. Though time-honored Vatican neutrality and diplomacy had to be respected as always, especially in this great and uncertain time of war, he had no doubt that His Holiness would want a stronger-than-usual admonishment within the context of the newspaper's customarily ambiguous and careful language. He had worked very closely with the Holy Father, in a day-to-day relationship over many years, and was confident that he knew how the editorial should be written. Especially given the despicable nature of atrocity that all of Rome would be aware of by noon when today's edition came out. He knew the nuances of papal policy and he knew how to use cleverly coded language to express the Supreme Pontiff's attitudes via the printed word in the Vatican's daily newspaper, regarded by many as the most objective and accurate in the Eternal City.

He was planning on running the text of the German communiqué on the front page with his editorial, in italics to signal high authority from Pope Pius XII himself. How could the Holy Father not censure Kappler and his band of murderers in as unambiguous language as possible to make clear his far-reaching powers of authority? But somehow the Pope, after reviewing the galley, was displeased and had summoned Dalla Torre to his office, which he seldom did.

"His Holiness will see you now," pronounced Monsignor Nasalli Rocca stiffly. He had been the first one to brief both Pius and Dalla Torre on the atrocity at *Fosse Ardeatine* based on his talks with the prison guards at Regina Coeli last night. He had been there to take confessions from the male and female political prisoners in the Fourth Wing, and had learned from the Italian guards about the mass executions at the caves. Silesian monks had also crept into the caves—the Germans had attempted to seal them off with explosives last night—and observed hundreds of bloody corpses, which they had promptly reported to their superiors who had, in turn, swiftly informed the Vatican.

"Thank you, Monsignor," he said, and he was shown into the papal study, where he found the Pope sitting behind his desk ensconced in paperwork. Pius gestured for him to take a seat in the cane-backed chair in front of his desk.

By the Pope's expression, Dalla Torre could tell he was in even more serious trouble than he had thought.

ΨΨΨ

Pius waited for Dalla Torre to settle into his seat and took a moment to gather his thoughts. He tried to soften his expression to make the count feel more at ease. He could tell that the man was inordinately anxious, and he didn't want to come across too harshly. *Be firm, but not excessively stern,* he told himself.

He attempted a smile and cleared his throat before speaking. "Count Dalla Torre, thank you for coming over so quickly. I know that you are busy and that recent events have had an unsettling effect on us all here in Rome, so I will get right to the point. The editorial that you wrote for today's edition of *L'Osservatore Romano*, I believe, casts the Vatican in an inappropriate light. I regret to say that I have rewritten your original text almost entirely."

A look of severe disappointment appeared on Dalla Torre's face. "Holy Father, I humbly apologize if I have offended you and have failed to adequately represent your views. These are terrible times and I am sorry if I have overstepped my authority in some way."

"Well, what you wrote, while passionate and no doubt quite accurate, is just not diplomatically possible at this time. Here is my version."

He handed Dalla Torre the original galley with all of his changes. He knew that the newspaper's director and chief editor had never had his work so thoroughly edited, and it would be painful for him to see that virtually none of his original verbiage had been retained. He watched quietly as Dalla Torre read over the revised handwritten text immediately below the German communiqué from the Stefani dispatch. With the Pope's extensive changes, the Vatican text now read:

> In the face of such deeds every honest heart is left profoundly grieved in the name of humanity and Christian sentiment. Thirty-two victims on the one hand; and on the other, three hundred and twenty persons sacrificed for the guilty parties who escaped arrest. Yesterday we addressed a sorrowful appeal for serenity and calm; today we repeat the same request, with more ardent affection, with more fervid insistence.
>
> Above and beyond the strife, moved only by Christian charity, we call upon the irresponsible elements to respect human life, which they have no right whatsoever to sacrifice, to respect the innocence of those who as a consequence are fatally victimized; from the responsible elements we ask for an awareness of their responsibility, toward themselves, toward the lives they wish to safeguard, toward history and civilization.

When he was finished reading, Dalla Torre looked up. His face was red with outrage. He held up the revised sheet, waving it angrily.

"Your Holiness, with all due respect, this article says nothing. Even worse, it blames the wrong party for the violence. The Nazis murdered the three hundred twenty souls, not the partisans."

"But the partisans caused it. If not for the attack at Via Rasella, the massacre at *Fosse Ardeatine* would not have occurred."

"But the way you are interpreting good and evil is misleading, Your Eminence. Early this morning when I wrote my draft, I was convinced that you would want to protest the infamy of the Nazi atrocity right here in your own diocese. But the way that this is written now makes it clear that the 'guilty parties' are not the monstrous Germans of the Ardeatine Caves, but the partisans of the Via Rasella. This turns everything that happened upside down."

"If we publish what you originally wrote, Kappler and his Gestapo henchmen will be busting down our doors and shipping you, me, and everyone else off to Germany or Lichtenstein. Are you questioning my judgment?"

"I meant no insincerity, Your Holiness. But we have an obligation to the truth. The Roman Resistance is not the one to blame for what happened at the caves. The victims of the reprisal were not 'sacrificed for the guilty parties who escaped arrest' as it says here—they were murdered in cold blood by the evil Nazis. The Nazis are the ones who issued their vague communiqué without any explanation of the manner in which the three hundred twenty victims were selected, killed, prayed over, or buried. Were the men chosen from prison, or chosen at random from the roundups just before the Via Rasella attack? And what of the poor families of the people that the Germans murdered? Has anyone told them anything? Will they ever be told what has happened to their loved ones? I also realize that those who took part in the Via Rasella affair will be criticized for not giving themselves up to the Germans. But they were never asked to do so. The executions were announced by the Nazi High Command as a *fait accompli.*"

The Pope felt a wave of sadness. Of course, everything Dalla Torre was saying was true, which was what made it even harder for him. More than anything else, he wanted to speak out against the vile Nazis and tell the whole world how evil they were. But neutrality in time of war was not something that could be taken for granted and modified to suit individual circumstances. It was black and white, and had to be honored absolutely. Of course, he cared deeply about those that had been killed as well as their families. But deep down, he couldn't help but feel that the partisans had created a volatile situation by making such a bold statement on the twenty-fifth anniversary of the birth of Fascism, and that the only way to prevent further German excesses was for the partisans to restrain themselves.

Worked up now, Dalla Torre continued his protest: "The 'irresponsible elements' to which you refer—which you and I know is code to refer to the partisans—are not the cause of the slaughter of the three hundred twenty innocents. The Germans are the cause. And they should pay a price in the eyes of Rome, indeed in front of the whole civilized world, through a harsh editorial in our paper for what they have done."

Despite his best efforts, the Pope's thin, stern face compressed into a censorious scowl. "You know that is out of the question, Giuseppe. The Germans will come down upon us like an anvil. Do you really want to provoke them when the Allies are still bogged down at Anzio, thirty-five miles from Rome? I am sorry, my old friend, I cannot sit here any longer and argue with you. We must get today's edition out. I only called you here to inform you of my decision. I wish I didn't have to do it, but your article, as originally written, simply won't stand."

Dalla Torre bowed his head in genuflection. "I am sorry, Your Holiness, truly I am if I seem insubordinate. But I only wish to make clear that, like the Germans, we will one day be judged not only by history—but in the eyes of God—for our conduct in this war. If we move forward with this editorial as written, we are assailing the 'irresponsible' armed resistance and sending a subtle reminder to the 'responsible' Nazi occupiers not to stray. But we should be doing precisely the opposite: severely admonishing the Germans, while sending a warning to the partisans that their actions risk severe reprisals against innocents."

"My greatest fear right now is that the partisans will aggravate the situation by responding in kind to the occupiers and provoking the Germans into murdering more innocent people."

"Can you blame them after what the Nazis did?"

"That is not point, Count Dalla Torre. My goal is to stop further bloodshed. Can't you see that we are in a bind here?"

"But that is the problem, Your Eminence. Time-tested papal silence in the name of a greater good does not make sense in the case of this heinous atrocity. I know that you believe the Open City negotiations with the German Occupation forces and your quest for striking a separate peace between Germany and the West might be jeopardized by taking a strong stand, but that is precisely what is necessary. What the Germans have done is pure evil. It demands a firm reprimand before the entire world."

"But as always, we are limited in our response by diplomacy. What can possibly be done to exert influence over the German occupiers after the bloody challenge in Via Rasella? Right now, they are like their mad Führer: a wild, uncontrollable animal. The partisan bombing has done nothing but compromise my policies as well as my prestige among the German authorities. And you just said yourself what the Germans will do now: they will link this 'terrorist' action by the Resistance to the fate of the Open City. Despite the fact that we have nearly reached a settlement with *Feldmaresciallo* Kesselring, they will now use this against us and threaten to reexamine all aspects of the agreement. I don't know what the partisans thought they would accomplish by their unprovoked attack at Via Rasella. But all it has done is hurt everyone, including us here at the Vatican."

"I believe they undertook the attack in Via Rasella to provoke the occupiers into an excessively repressive act and to increase the people's hatred of the Germans. If that was their goal, they succeeded beyond their wildest dreams."

"My main concern is that a full-scale war will explode in the streets of Rome as a consequence of the partisan actions. That is what I fear most and, by necessity, all of my interventions must be aimed at avoiding such chaos."

"But the Germans are lying propagandists and murderers. There is no such thing as *comunisti-badogliani.* That is the term the Germans have created to turn the right of the Resistance against the left. The Communists and the Monarchists are a fragile coalition at best. Inevitably, after yesterday's Ardeatine infamy, the right will deny any such association to the left, and there's a possibility the whole Roman Resistance could be splintered in two."

"My priority is to save Rome from ruin and chaos. The attack at Via Rasella is going to be a serious blow to those efforts. Throughout all these months of the Occupation, I have been pressing the Germans to exercise moderation. At the same time, I have attempted to calm the impatience of the Romans, particularly the partisans. Now Via Rasella has changed everything. The Open City negotiations are the cornerstone of the smooth transition of power from the Germans to the Allies. I just hope this attack at Via Rasella hasn't ruined everything and the Germans won't threaten to withdraw from our nearly finalized agreement. They have already changed the curfew to 5 p.m. and the bread ration has been reduced from one hundred fifty to one hundred grams per day because of Via Rasella."

"Another unwarranted turn of the screw. That is the way these Nazis do everything—by coercive threats. I tell you we must, for once, stand up to them!"

With that, Pius rose to his feet at his desk, his normally pale face reddening to something approaching the color of the sapphires glittering on his chest. "I know how you feel, Giuseppe, and I can tell you that I feel much the same sentiment. But diplomatic concerns and the welfare of all of the Roman people, not just the partisans, must come first."

Again, Dalla Torre bowed his head in contrition. "My sincerest apologies, Your Holiness, but I feel very strongly about this. As do many Romans who worship not only their great city, but you, the one and only Father of Rome and Vicar of Christ."

And with that, he left Pope Pius XII alone in his papal chamber.

Alone with his conscience.

PART 6

THE ROAD TO ROME

CHAPTER 51

VATICAN

MAY 10, 1944

"DON'T WORRY. YOU LOOK FINE, GENERAL," said Hollmann to his boss reassuringly, though he was thinking that *Obergruppenführer* Karl Wolff looked like a gangly teenager who had outgrown his clothes.

He and Wolff were walking down a hallway of the Apostolic Palace on their way to the *sala delle udienze* of His Holiness. Having navigated a warren of halls and courts, they turned first left then right before boarding a creaking elevator bound for the Pope's papal library. Their escort was a priest in a black cassock with a magenta-colored sash and piping. The man's well-tailored livery couldn't help but make the general look even more ridiculous in Hollmann's eyes, but he didn't dare say this to his boss. Arriving to Rome for his scheduled meeting with the Pope with only a suitcase filled with conspicuous SS uniforms, Wolff had been forced to borrow a suit, shirt, and tie from his much shorter assistant. Through Hollmann's connection to Princess Virginia Agnelli of the family-owned Fiat automobile company, Wolff had gained an audience with Pius and hoped to win the favor of the influential Bishop of Rome for the uncertain days ahead should the Reich be forced to capitulate. Given the importance of the meeting, the second highest-ranking SS leader in Europe and head of all SS troops and German police in Italy was feeling self-conscious about his attire. But Hollmann didn't dare tell the tall, usually-dapper general that he looked like a badly-dressed Fascist policeman in his ill-fitting civilian suit.

Once they reached the papal antechamber, they were greeted by Father Pankratius Pfeiffer, a German national and the Pope's personal liaison to the Occupation authorities. The red-velvet waiting area was decorated with medallions of recent supreme pontiffs. Hollmann watched as the Bavarian priest gave Wolff a lesson in proper protocol in his audience with the Pope. As the Abbot-General of the Order of Salvatorians, Padre Pancrazio, as he was known in Vatican circles, had worked quietly but successfully with the Pope to save Jews and non-Jews alike from imprisonment and death during the war. He had befriended occupying troops housed adjacent to the Salvatorian motherhouse on Rome's Via della Conciliazione, and had been given carte blanche to work in the Pope's name as a liaison between the Vatican and the German military command.

"Are you ready?" the priest asked Wolff in German when finished.

"Yes," replied the *polizeiführer*.

"Before you see the Holy Father, there is one thing that I would like to ask you. Actually, it is a request from the Holy Father."

"What is it, Father?"

"The son of an old friend of the Pope's late brother is currently a prisoner at Via Tasso. He was arrested because of his radical left-wing tendencies and is facing the death penalty."

Given Padre Pancrazio's history during the Occupation, Hollmann could see where this was headed. "What is his name, Father?" he asked.

"The prisoner is Giuliano Vassalli. He was captured a month ago by Kappler's men, and is most assuredly not being treated well at Via Tasso. It is for that reason that the Holy Father places a high value on his release."

Withdrawing a pen and small black notebook, Hollmann proceeded to jot down notes. He knew that Vassalli was a high-ranking partisan, but didn't know much else about his background. There were whispers that Vassalli was working with the known OSS-Rome Chief Peter Savoyan, whom Hollmann hadn't seen since October and had gone into secret hiding to avoid capture, and Socialist intelligence operatives of the Savoyan-Malfatti spy network here in Rome. Others claimed Vassalli was the highest-ranking Socialist member of the Military Council, and that he had played a hand in the Via Rasella attack and other operations against German military and Fascist targets. Considering Vassalli's suspected background, Hollmann knew that his boss would be going out on a limb if he secured the release of such a dangerous partisan.

Wolff gave a nod. "I can assure you Father Pfeiffer that I will do everything in my power to honor the papal request for Vassalli's release. But from what I know of this man, I must warn you right here and now, the Holy Father may very well come to regret his request."

"That may be the case," said Pfeiffer, "but this is what His Holiness desires."

"In that case, I assure you we will do all we can, Father," said Hollmann, knowing that with his connections to the black aristocracy here in Rome he was not overstepping his authority with Wolff. "That is our promise to you."

"Thank you, Colonel. Now let me show you, General, to the Holy Father."

ψψψ

When Pius first laid eyes on his Nazi visitor, he felt his whole body wanting to coil up in self-defense. He knew that Wolff had played an important role in sabotaging Hitler's plot to kidnap him last fall and again in December, and thus must have some good in him. But he was still wary. For a decade now, the SS had been singled out by the Vatican as a particularly reprehensible and dangerous arm of Hitler's Third Reich. Its officials were for the most part unwelcome in the Holy See, though some discreet engagement out of the public eye was necessary to pursue humanitarian aims, generally through Father Pfeiffer. Which was why Wolff had been told beforehand that the meeting would have to be conducted in total secrecy and that he would have to wear civilian clothes.

It was true, Pius thought as he studied his new guest, that the Supreme SS *Polizeiführer* had implemented an "easy hand" approach to quelling partisan unrest here in Italy. But he was still a top-ranking official in the Nazi hierarchy. Wolff was the man most responsible for the safety of Vatican City and the Pope himself, as well as maintaining order in Rome, but he also served Himmler, formerly as his chief of staff and now as the commander in chief of the entire police and persecution apparatus in all of Occupied Italy. Not only that, mere weeks had passed since the Ardeatine Caves Massacre, and from his secret sources the Pope knew that Wolff, although he had not been directly involved in the tragic affair, had kept track of developments from afar. Those facts alone made him a man not to be trusted. And yet, Pius had to concede that the Nazi general could prove useful towards attaining the much-sought after peace that had thus far been so elusive. In fact, that was the sole reason he had agreed to the meeting arranged by Hollmann through the Fiat family in the first place.

Father Pfeiffer introduced them. Wolff stepped forward, bowed with cordial grace, and kissed the proffered Piscatory Ring. The German priest then took his leave and the Pope and SS commander were alone. As Wolff took his seat in the chair in front of his desk, Pius continued to appraise the man. The general was tall and handsome, with tightly combed blond hair that receded from a high forehead, piercing blue eyes with a hint of irony, thin lips, a strong chin, and a long blade of a nose that lent him the regal bearing of the elite of his day. All in all, he presented himself as an exquisite specimen of Aryan perfection, and Pius could see why Hitler and Himmler regarded the man so highly. He exuded a personal charm that gave the SS a human face and even a touch of glamour. And yet, the Pope couldn't help but notice that his clothes did not fit him at all. Not wanting to be disrespectful, he said nothing and forced his eyes to reveal nothing as well. But he was surprised. Did this man who faithfully served the Führer and had given longstanding service to SS headman Himmler not have his own civilian clothes for an important meeting such as this?

Clearing his throat to speak, Pius cast a final glance at the book spines on the library wall. He spotted the hollowed-out copy of Thomas Aquinas's *Summa Theologica* that concealed the room's secret microphone. His trusted Jesuit operatives were recording the entire conversation between him and Wolff, and he didn't want them to miss a single word. He then took an invisible deep breath and looked back at his high-ranking visitor.

"It is good that we can meet and discuss matters that are of potential mutual benefit to us both," he began in German. "But my primary goal as Supreme Pontiff is to alleviate the suffering of the people during these terrible times, and to find a way that peace may be achieved. With that in mind, I want you to know that I am personally unhappy with the treatment prisoners are receiving at Via Tasso under Lieutenant Colonel Kappler. Are you aware of the situation at Gestapo headquarters, General?"

Wolff licked his lips anxiously and replied in his native tongue. "To be perfectly frank, Your Eminence, I have not visited there in some time. And when I did, Colonel Kappler personally gave me his word of honor that he had never tortured anybody."

"I'm afraid that Kappler has not been forthcoming with you, his superior officer. There are atrocities taking place at Via Tasso on a daily basis. I know because Father Pfeiffer and others have visited there on numerous occasions and seen firsthand the work of the colonel's men. The officer known as Captain Priebke is known to be especially cruel with a pair of brass knuckles, I am told. He appears to take a perverse pleasure in meting out punishment to the prisoners. I want such behavior to stop."

"I promise to look into it, Your Eminence."

"Good, because I would also like to ask a favor. A favor that Father Pfeiffer, in his efforts to ease my burdens, has most likely already requested from you."

"You are referring to Giuliano Vassalli?"

"Yes. Unfortunately, he is facing the death penalty."

"That is my understanding. Father Pfeiffer said you want him released."

"Yes, I do. I can say that a demonstration of cooperation on your part would be viewed here in the Holy City as most helpful for diplomatic relations."

The SS general nodded. "As I informed Father Pfeiffer, I promise to look into the matter personally as soon as I finish here with His Holiness. I will do all I can, and that is my promise to you as an officer and a gentleman."

Despite his instinctive distrust of the man, he honestly believed Wolff would do all that was possible. But the real question was whether he could actually deliver and have Vassalli released. That was the real test of whether he had authority and influence here in Italy and might be of value in the effort to end the war. He decided to throw the Nazi a bone.

"I appreciate your goodwill in this regard, General. I must say that, finding you so amenable to cooperation, I cannot help but think how many crimes, how many injustices, how many offenses against the human spirit would have been avoided if you and I had sat down earlier."

"I couldn't agree more, Your Holiness. Which brings me to the main reason that I am here. I, like you, want this war to end and to seek peace."

"That is also good to hear. What are your feelings about the current situation in Germany with regard to continuing the war?"

"In my opinion, the political and military might of Germany and the Western powers will eventually be wasted away in this senseless war. A defeated Germany will plunge into chaos, while the real conflict with Soviet Russia and the Communists goes on, leaving us all in a state of total exhaustion."

"That is my feeling as well."

"Germany cannot win this war and will be dealt with as harshly as Versailles unless cooler heads prevail on the Allied side."

"In my view, unconditional surrender is a mistake. The policy is an obstacle on the path to peace, and it leaves no room for potential intermediaries. I would also add that the whole notion of punishment and retribution in the policy offers nothing but a lengthy prison sentence or a hangman's noose for senior SS officials like yourself. Which is, no doubt, one of the primary reasons why you, General Wolff, are now in my papal chambers. Am I right?"

"That is a logical assessment of the situation. But an even simpler answer is I firmly believe that you are the best person to engage the Western powers in a search for an early end to this war. That is the main reason I am here."

"What do you propose?"

"I promise to do whatever I can to help bring the war to an end. But the terms would have to be honorable, since I refuse to appear as a traitor. I am firmly committed to carrying out the mission entrusted to me to the very end and would like to open a line of communication with His Holiness to achieve an honorable end to this conflict."

"I must say I am both relieved and pleased to hear such an honest and open-minded appraisal of the situation. I believe this corresponds to the reality in Germany and generally speaking in the West."

"To achieve the aims I just expressed—an early end to the war with the West—I would be ready to risk my own life. But, because of the danger I face if my efforts were to be misunderstood, I would also be jeopardizing the lives of my family. So this is not an easy decision for me."

"Does Colonel Hollmann see the situation the same as you?"

"The colonel is the one who has made me see the light, so to speak. Germany cannot win this war, and further death and suffering on both sides is not justifiable in the name of humanity and God."

"You know that it will not be easy to test the waters regarding the possibilities of a compromise peace."

"Yes, Colonel Hollmann and I are all very much aware of that fact."

"The main difficulty lies in the fact that a part of the Allies bear an attitude that is not only anti-Nazi, but to some extent anti-German. It is a prejudice that will have to be overcome. But you do realize that it is your country's persecution of Jews, outspoken Catholics, and others that has made it so."

"Yes, I am all too aware of my countries failings. But I want to reiterate my agreement with you that the best way to end the war is an Allied-German alliance, without Hitler, to halt the Soviet advance in Europe. I also want to give you my word, as I gave you last December, that as long as I am head of the SS here in Italy, I can assure your complete safety here at the Vatican."

He knew what the general meant. As long as Wolff held his position in Italy, the Vatican's inhabitants were safe from abduction. From his Vatican spy network, Pius knew that Hitler had specifically asked Wolff in the fall of 1943 and again in December to prepare a full-scale plan to evacuate him and the Vatican art treasures to Lichtenstein. After several weeks of investigation, Wolff had concluded that an attempt to invade the Vatican and its properties, or to seize the Pope in response to a papal protest, would prompt a backlash throughout Italy that would seriously hinder the Nazi war effort. Wolff thus persuaded Hitler to drop his plan to kidnap him. The Pope knew that Hitler had only backed down because he regarded the Vatican and Catholic Church as the strongest social and political force in Italy, and he was convinced that its potential for thwarting the SS and making Germany look bad in the eyes of the world was immense.

"I appreciate your assurances, General. But know this. Whatever happens, I shall never leave Rome voluntarily. My place is here, and I shall fight until the very end for the Christian commandments and for peace. But if you are as serious about peace as I am, I will do everything possible to support your efforts in this regard. They correspond to my own ideas on the matter."

He then rose from his seat, signaling that their meeting was over.

"Thank you, Your Eminence."

"I will keep you advised through Father Pfeiffer as to when it would be possible to meet again and explore this matter further."

And with that, he reached for the phone at his desk to resummon the padre. As he made the call, he glanced back at his SS guest, thinking to himself what words best described this newest cog in the wheels of his Church of Spies. What came to him was this: *SS General Karl Wolff: political opportunist, like a rat jumping off a sinking ship and looking for a scrap of wood for a lifeboat.*

ψψψ

Waiting in the anteroom outside the papal library, Hollmann greeted Padre Pancrazio cordially as he reappeared. "They are finished, Colonel," the bristly-haired Bavarian informed him. "Come, please join the general for a farewell with the Holy Father."

"Yes, of course," said Hollmann. "After you, Father."

Pfeiffer opened the door and Hollmann stepped inside. He saw Pius behind his desk and Wolff standing across from him preparing to take his leave. The room overlooking St. Peter's Square was handsome, but simpler than Hollmann had expected. Packed bookcases lined the walls along with twelve paintings of lions, elephants, and other African animals. A crystal chandelier hung from the ceiling, and a plush Italian rug spread under foot. Three dark portraits by Dutch Old Masters peered down at him from niches.

He went forward to the desk and bowed formally. "Your Eminence."

"Colonel Hollmann. Thank you for arranging this meeting. It has been most productive. I bid you gentlemen good day, and hope that we can all work for peace in a productive manner."

"Thank you, Your Eminence," said Hollmann, surprised at how gaunt and haggard the Pope looked. It was said that he didn't eat any more than the Jews, Army escapees, and Resistance leaders he was hiding out in the Vatican and its extraterritorial properties. If that was the case it certainly showed.

"Colonel Hollmann and myself are ready to do everything in our power to bring the war to a rapid conclusion," said Wolff.

"Yes, and in bidding my own farewell, I would like to remind you that I, too, have embarked on a difficult road, fraught with peril to my own life."

"Yes, Your Eminence," said Hollmann. "The general and I both appreciate the difficulties you have faced and the sacrifices you have made in an effort to bring about peace in this war."

"Go in peace then, my sons. At some point, it is the only thing that will bring us salvation."

It was then Hollmann received the shock of his life.

Without warning, Wolff backed away two steps from the Pope, and instead of bowing politely or performing some such nicety, he abruptly stiffened, clicked his heels together, and raised his right arm in the official Nazi salute.

"Heil Hitler!"

The room went awkwardly silent. The Pope stood behind his desk in open-mouthed shock, his lean face a picture in moral outrage mingled with stupefaction. But then he gave a forbearing smile, as if to say that he understood that the general had made a simple faux pas.

Despite the Holy Father's attempts to mollify the situation, Hollmann couldn't believe his eyes and looked on in cringing amazement, his skin crawling. Even though he knew his boss had simply obeyed an ingrained reflex that was mightier than his will, he still considered it a severe lapse of judgment and a horribly gauche incident that reflected poorly on not only the general but himself. But before he or Wolff could utter a word of apology, Father Pfeiffer took the general by the elbow and swiftly escorted him towards the door.

Hollmann looked at the Pope, tipped his head deferentially to apologize for Wolff's lapse, bid him goodbye, and then closed the door behind them.

"Oh dear, I don't know what I was thinking," lamented Wolff as Pfeiffer led them through the anteroom.

"I wouldn't worry yourself over it," said the priest. "The Holy Father will understand and take it in the right way."

"I hope so. I don't know what came over me. I instinctively raised my hand in the Party salute. I guess I have become unused to civilian dress and it happened spontaneously. But I tell you, Father, it was meant as a sign of deference."

"As I said, the Pope will understand."

Hollmann saw things differently. On the Pope's face, he didn't see an ally in the struggle to bring a swift and honorable end to the war for Nazi Germany. He saw a man disgusted with Hitler and the Third Reich, who, if he could, would have them both removed from the face of the earth in the time it took a priest to genuflect.

"We're going to do what the Pope says," said Wolff worriedly, as they stepped into the elevator to head down to the ground floor. "We're going right now to Via Tasso, Wilhelm, and we're going to get Kappler to release Vassalli."

He could see his boss was agitated. "But, General, weren't you the one who said the Holy Father would likely come to regret his request?"

"The situation has changed. The Holy Father made the request in person."

"He did?" said Pfeiffer, clearly surprised.

"Yes, the Holy Father wants Vassalli released as soon as possible. And that, gentlemen, is exactly what we're going to do."

Hollmann couldn't help but smile. "I can see, General, that you did indeed have a most productive meeting. Now if we can just end this fruitless war altogether, wouldn't that be something?"

"Well, if you have any particular ideas, please tell me. Because right now, Wilhelm, I am all ears."

"As a matter of fact, I do have a little something in mind, General."

"You do?"

"Yes, and his name is Allen Dulles."

"Allen Dulles, you mean the—"

"Yes, the OSS chief in Switzerland. Trust me, General. When the time comes to strike a deal with the Allies, he is *our* man."

"Very good, Colonel. But let's lay the groundwork for our peace overture by getting Vassalli out of Kappler's little dungeon first. Shall we?"

CHAPTER 52

CISTERNA CANAL, ANZIO

MAY 23, 1944

CROUCHED DOWN IN A FOXHOLE, Bridger peered over the top into No Man's Land. He was anxiously awaiting the opening salvo signaling the first stage of Operation Buffalo—the long-awaited breakout from the Anzio beachhead. Stretched out alongside him, in a line extending more than a mile along the Cisterna and Mussolini Canals, were more than two thousand black-faced Forcemen; and further west, along a ten-mile long segment, another one hundred fifty thousand troops from VI Corps. Like their fathers a generation before them in the trenches of France and Belgium, they kept their heads down low from the German snipers and quietly talked while smoking their Camels and Lucky Strikes.

Bridger felt a watery feeling in the pit of his stomach. He always got a little jittery before going into battle, but he was far more anxious than usual this morning. He knew that today was going to be an epic fight that would determine whether the Allies would take Rome or slink back into the sea. After four months of stalemate at Anzio, he and everyone else wanted more than anything else to get the hell off this damned beachhead, even if it meant getting shot at by the Krauts.

Feeling antsy, he loosened his jacket collar around his neck. Then he fidgeted with the trigger guard of his Tommy and rechecked his ammo clip for the tenth time. A cool rain drizzled down upon his shoulders, and he heard a faint susurrus of wind sweeping up the coastal plain. Staring out at the blood red poppies poking up from the grass of No Man's Land, which he would soon have to cross under a furious German barrage, he was reminded of the WWI trench warfare poem "In Flanders Fields" that a Canadian lieutenant had given him in a poetry book. He felt a sense of foreboding, as if he had been thrown back in time. After all he had been through, was this his day to finally buy it?

We are the Dead. Short days ago
We lived, felt dawn, saw sunset glow,
Loved and were loved, and now we lie
In Flanders fields

Suddenly, the early morning calm was shattered by a thunderous roar and bright illuminating flashes against the sky as fifteen hundred Allied naval guns, howitzers, mortars, tanks, and tank destroyers opened fire. Bridger felt the ground beneath his boots quiver and tremble. He saw the actual shock waves shimmering across the dawn sky like heat rising off a desert floor. A mile in front of the canal, a wall of fire appeared as the opening salvo crashed into the German front lines. He saw a bright fiery spume erupt in the enemy-occupied town of Cisterna, the primary target of the cannonade since it was the key jumping-off position for the Buffalo offensive.

"Holy shit, I'll bet they can hear this all the way to Rome!" roared the burly Gus Heilman, crouching next to him.

"I sure as hell hope so!" said Bridger. "Eternal City here we come!"

"I don't think that town's big enough for both me and the Pope!" shouted the irreverent ex-mayor of Gusville.

"You can tell him that face to face when you see him!"

"I don't care if I get shot today! Just get me off this damned beachhead!"

They laughed the crazy Forceman's laugh—equal parts war-weary, cheeky, and fatalistic—but the sound was drowned out by the massive artillery barrage. In the foxhole with them was Sergeant Tommy Prince, the Canadian Ojibwa battalion scout. Raring to go, he and Bridger were scheduled to advance with Frederick's battalion headquarters. Further down the line, but within spitting distance, was Frederick himself and his staff, the Arizona miner Howard Van Ausdale, and the sardonic Norwegian Finn Roll, who skied and shot a rifle like an Olympic champion, which unfortunately would not come in handy today.

Tracer fire from the 50-caliber machine guns erupted, adding to the roar of the battle. To Bridger, it looked like a meteor shower as hundreds of reddish-white tails of light streaked across the sky from machine guns of every caliber pouring a hail of steel into the enemy positions. The muzzle blasts made his whole body vibrate like a tuning fork. Soon, towering clouds of smoke and dust blanketed the battlefield, brilliantly lighted from within by bursting shells.

By the time the yellowish dawn gave way to daylight, the guns ceased firing and he heard aircraft engines. Looking skyward, he saw more than fifty fighters and light bombers sweeping across the front. Through the dust and smoke, they attacked the already battered town of Cisterna, delivering a terrific pounding of any buildings not already reduced to rubble, as well as roads and enemy defenses.

It was a ferocious five-minute assault.

When the aerial bombardment was complete, there followed a momentary silence, broken abruptly by a second intense artillery and mortar barrage in support of the attacking tanks and infantry. At this second cannonade, Bridger and the other Forcemen all along the line cheered and waved their hats and helmets. There was nothing quite like a show of artillery and fighter-bombers to lift an infantryman's spirits before he was about to go over the top.

Still, Bridger wondered: Has my time come? After six months of battles and night patrols has my luck finally run out?

The artillery firing stopped. The field of battle fell preternaturally still and silent as the smoke drifted off, as if from a peaceful campfire.

Then the *Go* order was shouted all down the line.

With cotton mouth and a lurching stomach, Bridger climbed out of his foxhole and started forward into No Man's Land with the rest of the massive infantry army breaking out from the beachhead in the assault wave. All around him Forcemen spilled over the top, running and shouting. Further down the line where Third Regiment was attacking from across the Mussolini Canal, Sherman tanks and tank destroyers materialized like phantoms from farmhouses, straw piles, ditches, and underbrush, providing a screen for the advancing infantrymen and spurring them on.

But Bridger and First Regiment didn't have any armor.

With officers and NCOs barking out encouragement, the regiment managed to advance unmolested for two hundred yards before the Germans opened fire. Suddenly the *pop-pop-pop* of sniper and infantryman rifle fire was punctuated by the keening of machine guns and the deep roar of artillery. Despite the barrage that had clearly broadcast Allied intentions, Bridger saw a pair of sleepy Germans dressed only in dirty gray Long Johns jumping out of their foxhole to give battle.

To his right, Prince let loose with his Thompson, mowing down the Germans like dominoes.

"Give 'em hell, Kemosabe!" And then he added to the men behind him, "Keep moving!" knowing that to stop was to die.

They quickly came upon a machine-gun nest, tucked behind a sand bag and barbed wire in a copse of poplars. The Germans opened up at close range with a pair of MG-42s, taking down a handful of men to Bridger's left. Enraged, he led a small group to outflank the position, coming in from the trees on the right. But they had been spotted. The enemy let loose with a concentrated fusillade, the white-hot shrapnel cutting down branches and limbs with a retching crash and ripping up clods of dirt.

He and Heilman tossed in hand grenades.

Two explosions, one right after the other, and the machine-gun nest fell silent. They ran to the edge of the dugout. To Bridger's surprise, one of the Germans was still alive. He took aim and squeezed the trigger of his Thompson, but the weapon jammed. The German threw a potato masher grenade at him, hitting him on the cheekbone as he and Heilman ducked for cover. But instead of going off, the grenade bounced off his face, hit the ground, and rolled back into the trench directly towards the German. The last thing Bridger saw was the Kraut struggling to crawl away from the grenade like a fast-moving crocodile. A spout of earth flew upwards and then the Kraut was no more, his guts blasted from his body and spattered against the trench wall like spaghetti.

"Jesus Christ, that was fucking close!" gasped Heilman, climbing to his feet to take a look at the dead German.

Bridger looked down at the grimy, youthful face attached to the destroyed body. "He was just a kid. Look at him."

"Yeah, a little fucking Nazi. He's not going to get any tears from me—the little shit got what he deserved."

"Hell of a way to die for a kid, though. We'd better keep moving."

They continued on to the next advanced position, side-stepping skeletons in moldering field gray from previous forays into No Man's Land. But the German artillery had by now fixed on the onrushing wave across the broad front.

The shells were coming in hot.

In a sudden barrage, a shell exploded ten yards from Bridger. The concussion of the blast knocked him, Heilman, and Prince to the earth. When they arose and shook themselves off, they realized that they had been spared from getting hit by shrapnel from Art Arsennek, a rail-thin scrapper from Ontario that everyone had liked. Closer to the explosion, the unlucky Canadian had taken the brunt of the blast.

Bridger shook his head in despair: another good man gone. But there was nothing to do but keep pushing on.

With a squad of a dozen men, he dashed ahead, taking heavy fire from artillery and mortars until they approached what looked to be an abandoned German trench. They had already covered a half mile of No Man's Land and were sweating buckets. Suddenly Prince, up ahead on point, held up his hand and called a halt.

"Nobody make a move! We're standing in a mine field!"

Bridger looked around. He couldn't spot any mines, but he didn't have eagle eyes like the Ojibwa. The Bouncing Betties were the sons of bitches that everyone dreaded the most because they would blast your nuts right off. But they were hard to spot even though the ground was firm.

Someone behind him stepped towards him; with the artillery and mortar shelling all around, he must not have heard the scout instructing them to halt.

"Stop right there!" Bridger called out to the black-faced kid, one of the Ranger replacements whose name he didn't know. He waved his arms for him to stop, but he was too late. The kid took a step forward, and the next thing Bridger knew he was thrown in the air and instantly dismembered.

Shaking his head in anger, Bridger yelled up to Prince. "Sergeant, get us the fuck out of here now!"

"Yessir, Major, I'm on it!" and he calmly picked a path out of the mines for every member of the squad. As he stepped gingerly to safety, Bridger looked back at the mine field and couldn't believe no one else hadn't set off a detonation. He hated mines: they were random and cruel and, if they had your number, you were seriously fucked.

They pressed on, racing forward to get ahead of the bullets and shells raining down on them as much as to destroy the enemy and take Cisterna. They soon found the Germans retreating en masse, reeling from the massive coordinated attack all across the line.

An hour later, they had reached the first strategic prize of the advance: Highway 7, the lifeline of the German defenders. They had now effectively cut off Cisterna.

"Piece of cake," roared Heilman with bravado.

"Piece of cake, my ass," countered Bridger. "I'll bet we just lost twenty guys."

"I know it's a damned shame, but it's not my fault. I didn't start the war—the Germans did. All I know is I'm going to get my hands on a good stiff drink before this day is over. I'm mighty parched."

"You'd better hold your horses, Gus. We're not out of the shit yet," Prince reminded him.

"Maybe, but at least we're not still on that beachhead. That was the worst."

"That's a fact," said Bridger. "Come on, quit your jawing and let's keep moving."

He led the squad forward until they reached the railway line just south of Cisterna. There they again met stiff German resistance, this time from two packs of Tiger tanks along the Ninfa Road to their front, as other companies began trickling up from behind.

Oh shit, we're in for it now, he thought, still not seeing any sign of the Force tanks or tank destroyers that would at least give him and his men a fighting chance. He counted a total of nine among the enemy armor. *Too many.*

He looked at Heilman, whose eyes had grown as big as saucers. The mere cough of a German Mark VI Tiger engine was enough to send a shudder down any American or British soldier's spine. The behemoths were beasts from the Book of Revelation. With an 88-mm cannon and 100-mm thick frontal armor, the 60-ton Mark VI Tiger was superior to every other tank in the war possessed by either the Allies or Germans. Even the mass-produced American Sherman, with its 75-mm gun, or the vaunted Russian T-34, were no match for Hitler's weapon of choice for *blitzkrieg*—the massive, lethal Tiger tank.

"Take cover!" shouted Bridger as the lead tank in the pack of nine opened fire.

Bridger felt a swoosh as the projectile zoomed past his ears. Then the earth shook, an eruption of loamy sand spewed up from the ground, and men screamed in terror as they were pulverized by the blast. When Bridger next looked up, he saw an apparition that was as ghostly as it was grisly. A Forceman's helmeted head had been blown completely off with nothing remaining but his upper torso and guts splayed across a tangle of rolled-up concertina wire.

He shook his head in dismay: the poor bastard had taken a direct hit. It reminded him of the Headless Horseman from *The Legend of Sleepy Hollow*.

Now other Tigers moved into position and unloaded with their dreaded 88-mm guns, pinning the men down all along the railroad tracks and Mussolini Canal. Despite the protection afforded by the cinder brow of the rail embankment, several more from his squad were killed by the lethal blasts as the companies hunkered down along the railway line. Bridger wanted to hold the ground they had thus far gained, but with Tigers on the prowl, it was going to be tough.

To his surprise and relief, a pack of Shermans and Lieutenant Colonel Austin's motorized tank destroyers swept in from the left to give battle. The Forcemen cheered. But the cheering stopped abruptly as the Tigers proved to be impervious to the Sherman's 75-mm shells and the smaller anti-tank rounds delivered by the tank destroyers.

"Goddamnit!" shouted Heilman. "Why can't we catch a break?"

The indestructible German tanks kept advancing and firing, knocking down men left and right like bowling pins. Within minutes, they had laid waste to a quarter of First and Third Companies, as well as the bulk of the Force's tanks and tank destroyers.

"All hell has broken through up here!" Bridger heard a staff officer radioing to General Truscott's HQ on the beachhead. "The Germans have unleashed everything!"

At that moment, he saw a Tiger sight a Sherman behind a nearby farmhouse and let loose with a round. Not only did it penetrate the house, but it pierced through the tank and travelled another hundred yards until it exploded into a copse of trees.

"Jesus Fucking Christ!" hollered Heilman. "Did you see that, Major?"

"I sure as hell did! And that's why we're getting the fuck out of here! Give the order to fall back to the highway, Captain!"

"Yessir!"

There was no choice. They were clearly outgunned by the Tigers. The battle had degenerated into a bloody mess and it was time to beat a hasty retreat.

Once the order was passed along, the Devil's Brigade survivors lugged their wounded over their shoulders and retreated pell-mell back a quarter mile to hard-won Highway 7. En route, they came under a lashing fire from the Tigers as well as a handful of Panzer Mark V's that had appeared on the scene. Then, with the Germans smelling blood and moving in for the kill, they dug in.

It was then that the tide turned.

Air and artillery fire rained down on the German tanks and infantry as a fresh column of Allied tanks and tank destroyers drove into the enemy flank. The burst of friendly fire halted the German armored counterattack in its tracks, as all four of the Panzers and two of the Tigers went up in flames. Knowing they were whipped, the Germans did not press further and withdrew from the field, leaving their infantry to dig in between the highway and railway. With the new line established south of the highway, Bridger and the Force began laying antitank mines and digging foxholes.

Looking at the carnage and pockmarked battlescape around him, Bridger let out a mixed sigh of relief and dismay. They had broken out of the cursed beachhead and were finally on the road to Rome. But they had lost far too many good men doing it.

And tomorrow, the goddamn bloodletting would begin all over again.

CHAPTER 53

COLLE FERRO, CENTRAL ITALY
JUNE 2, 1944

"I AM HERE FOR MY BROTHER, Major Walther Hollmann. Per General Wolff's orders, he is being discharged to convalesce under my physician's personal care in Rome."

He handed the weary-looking *Oberarzt*—Senior Surgeon—his brother's hospital discharge papers signed by the head of the SS in occupied Italy himself. The muffled screams and groans of wounded men undergoing amputation in the front-line field hospital mingled with the dull roar of nearby mortars and artillery. With trembling fingers, the surgeon took out his wire-rim glasses from a pocket and looked over the release order. Beneath his bloody apron, he wore a uniform with three gold sleeve stripes and the *Äskulapzeichen* symbol worn by German military physicians, the Rod of Asclepius entwined by a snake stick. When the surgeon was finished, he handed the order to the sergeant manning the check-in and discharge desk, who spent an inordinate time examining the document before handing it back to Hollmann.

"Follow me," said the surgeon. "We will get your brother now."

He led him through the enlisted men's' hospital ward. They passed row upon row of maimed and wounded *panzergrenadiers*, medical patients, and those with extreme battle fatigue until he came to the officers' quarters, which contained a much smaller group of men. Hollmann spotted Walther right away, laying on his cot and staring off into space. A huge bandage was tightly wrapped around his neck and right side of his face, rendering only his mouth and left side visible. But thankfully, he was alive and could leave this dreadful place. When Hollmann had learned of his brother's severe injuries, on top of the ones he had received at Sessuno three months earlier, he had used his influence as a high-ranking SS officer to secure his release under his personal physician's care.

"Hello Walther," he said with a smile. "I am here to take you to Rome."

He saw his younger brother's eyes light up, which made him feel good inside and reinforced the idea that he was doing the right thing. Despite his nasty jaw and neck wound, Walther immediately sat up from his hospital bed and looked alert. He was already dressed in his full uniform with his mud-splattered boots on and appeared surprisingly ready to go.

"Let's go, I want to get out of here," he said without preamble. "The Allies will be here soon."

In that instant, Hollmann saw all the pain and suffering of the war in his brother's eyes. He quickly helped him gather up his things. After thanking the surgeon, they started through the hospital ward towards the front door. Outside and around the corner, he had left his chauffeur Mario waiting with his massive, sparkling Mercedes-Benz, ready to convey them back to Rome.

"Don't worry, everything's going to be all right, Walther," he said to assuage his brother as they stepped outside into the sunlight and turned the corner around the building where the Mercedes was parked. "Soon we will be in Rome drinking Chianti at the Excelsior—"

"They're trying to steal your car!" interrupted his brother. "Look!"

Hollmann saw that a Waffen-SS major and a captain had Mario shoved up against his Mercedes at gunpoint, while an SS sergeant with a machine pistol strapped to his shoulder was unloading objects from a second vehicle and stuffing them into the trunk of the Mercedes. Hollmann couldn't tell what the objects were, but by the careful way the SS man was handling them they appeared to be fragile. They were wrapped in rolled-up blankets and the sergeant was pulling them from a battered *Kübelwagen* with a flat tire parked nearby and placing them into the trunk of the Mercedes. Whatever these bastards had wrapped in the blankets had to be valuable for them to try and steal his car in broad daylight.

"Halt, release that man at once and step away from my car!" he yelled at them.

They looked at him insolently, as if he were a pesky fly that they needed to swat away. He saw right away that these were desperate men, and unfortunately there was no reason for them to respect his authority. After all, he was not wearing his customary black SS uniform, but rather a civilian suit in order to not stand out if he was captured by the partisans. Now that the Allies were converging on Rome, the partisans had become more brazen in their attacks along Highways 6 and 7. To further disguise himself, he had removed his twin SS car flags from his Mercedes, as well as secured to the roof a white sheet with a Red Cross symbol to dissuade Allied fighter-bombers from blasting him from the road during their daily raids on the main arteries leading to and from the Eternal City. That was probably why these SS men were trying to steal his car: they wanted safe passage into Rome for whatever they were stuffing into his trunk.

But what the hell was it?

The SS major stepped forward to cut him off. "In the name of the Reich, I am commandeering this vehicle," he shouted without preamble, like a man snapping for a mutt to get out of the way.

"You will do nothing of the kind. I am Colonel Wilhelm Hollmann and this is my staff car. I have orders from General Wolff himself to take this officer back to Rome immediately."

"If you are a colonel, then where is your uniform?" sneered the major.

"I chose not wear it today. But I assure you my papers are in order."

The major and the captain looked nervously at one another. Hollmann pulled out his papers and Wolff's orders from his jacket and held them out to the major. Ignoring them, the major signaled his two men. They turned their weapons on him and his brother. The major, too, withdrew his Luger.

"I'm afraid we're going to need your car, Colonel. My humblest apologies, but we have orders too." He motioned to the captain. "Get those keys from the driver and start the engine."

"I have them right here." He held them up.

"You are nothing but thieves," hissed Walther. "What have you stolen? Is it paintings you have under those blankets?"

So that's what they are, thought Hollmann. They had stolen Italian paintings, wrapped the canvasses up in blankets, and were now trying to hijack his car with the Red Cross sign on the rooftop so they could make it to Rome unmolested. Looking at their battered *Kübelwagen* with the flat tire, he realized they must have been strafed by Allied aircraft along the way to Colle Ferro. The Allies were closing in fast now that they had fought their way off their cursed beachhead.

The major frowned. "You three are coming with us." Then to his men: "Sergeant, finish your loading—and be quick about it. Captain, disarm these men and show them to our newly acquired transportation."

A moment later, Hollmann found himself weaponless and crammed into the front seat with his wounded brother next to him and Mario behind the wheel. All three of their captors had guns pointed at the back of their heads.

They started off down the road. But a few miles out of town, they came across an Italian peasant and his two sons herding goats along the road and blocking it off completely.

"What the hell?" shrieked the SS major. "Honk your horn at them!"

Mario punched the horn, but the animals didn't budge.

Overhead, Hollmann heard the distinctive drone of a squadron of American P-51 Mustang fighter-bombers. During the past nine months, he had learned to dread the sound of their approach. The major looked nervously out his window and up at the sky.

"Sergeant, fire your weapon and get those damned animals off the road!"

"*Jawohl, Major*!"

He stepped from the car and let loose with a burst from his Schmeisser above the heads of the animals, but only a few of them moved off the road. The old goat herder yelled and cursed at him to stop and waved his big walking stick angrily.

The buzzing sound overhead grew louder.

The sergeant looked up at the sky worriedly and stepped back to the window. "They won't budge, Major."

"Well then shoot them down, goddamn you!"

"Shoot them?"

"Yes, shoot the animals, damnit! We have to clear this road before we're blown to bits!"

"But why do I have to shoot them?"

The swarm of Mustangs was visible now, the strains of their engines filling the air with sound.

"Give me your weapon, you idiot—I'll do it myself!" To his partner in the back seat. "Cover them, Captain!"

He jumped out of the vehicle and grabbed the Schmeisser.

"We should try to make a run for it," whispered Hollmann to his brother in Italian. "This might be our best chance. They are just going to kill us anyway once we get near Rome."

"We wouldn't get ten steps," replied Walther, tipping his head towards the blond, pock-faced captain in the back seat covering them with his pistol.

"Stop talking, you two!" snapped the captain in German.

The major opened fire with a lethal spray into the herd of animals. In a matter of seconds, a half-dozen bleating goats had been shot down and a path cleared as the surviving animals scattered from the road. Then, as the major and sergeant were about to step back into the car, the old goat herder cried out. At the same time, the buzzing swarm of Allied aircraft swooped down to attack.

"No, not my Fabrizio!" exclaimed the old man over the roar of the aircraft engines. He knelt down in the middle of the road where one of his sons lay.

"You shot one of his sons, you murderer!" hissed Walther accusingly.

"I didn't mean to!" cried the major and he looked fearfully towards the sky at the oncoming Mustangs before jumping back in the Mercedes along with the sergeant. "It must have been a ricochet!"

"You're a thief and a murderer! You bastard!"

"Shut up, or I'll shoot you down like a dog!" To Mario. "You—get this car moving! Now!"

They started forward. The buzz was becoming deafening.

"*Mach schnell!*" screamed the major.

But the peasant father and his remaining son blocked the road defiantly. Mario slowed down and came to a halt.

"You've got to be joking!" bellowed the major. "Drive through them, you fool, or we'll all be killed!"

"No, don't do it, Mario," protested Hollmann. "They're just going to shoot us anyway, all for a bunch of artwork." He glared at the major. "What do you have rolled up in those blankets, a half dozen Tintoretto's?"

The Mustangs roared overhead like thunder, sending a shudder through the whole car. But then they banked left, passed them by, and disappeared over the tree line without dropping a single bomb or firing a round from their machine guns. After a moment, the drone of their engines faded away altogether. The Red Cross sign on top had indeed worked after all, Hollmann realized. But then the major said the words that sent a chill down his spine.

"All right, I've had enough of this! Everyone out of the car—now!"

"Oh shit, we've had it," whispered Walther in Italian.

"I'm sorry, *Brüderlein.* I'm afraid all I've done is get us both killed."

"Get out of the damned car! Captain, I want you and the sergeant to line them all up."

"All of them, sir?"

"Yes, damn you! What's wrong with you two? I have given you an order and we cannot have any eyewitnesses!"

"Yes, Major."

It took a minute to line everyone up. Hollmann stood next to Walther with Mario on their left and the unfortunate goat herder and his remaining son on their right. The old man crossed himself and prayed out loud as tears poured from his eyes and those of the young boy. They had stumbled into something that they had not expected. Opposite them stood the two Waffen-SS officers with their Lugers and the sergeant with his rapid-fire Schmeisser machine pistol. Behind them was a bank of tall, straight-trunked pine trees and a gently sloped hill lit up by the noonday sun.

"Ready!" declared the major in a booming voice.

"I'm sorry, Walther," said Hollmann. "I have ruined everything for us both."

"No, it is the war that has ruined us. I heard what happened at *Fosse Ardeatine*."

"Aim!" shouted the major.

"I tried to stop it, *Brüderlein.* The reprisal should never have happened. Not like that. I saw it with my own eyes."

"It's Hitler, Brother. He makes us do things we would never do on our own."

"Goodbye, Little Brother. And remember, I love you."

"I love you too."

"Fire!"

Hollmann had closed his eyes a split second before the salvo of gunfire he knew was coming, bracing himself for the bullet that would put him out of his misery.

But the firing didn't just come from the SS men.

Instead, most of it came from the nearby trees. When he opened his eyes, he saw the three SS men sprawled on the ground, blood oozing from circular wounds, wounds that nobody came back from; and when he looked to his right and left to see what fate had befallen his own condemned contingent, he saw that Mario had received only a grazing wound in the arm, his brother Walther had fallen to one knee with blood dripping from between his closed fingers pressed against his stomach, and the old man and the boy lay still in the grass.

What? How was he the only one without a scratch?

Then he saw a small band of partisans filtering out of the stand of trees to the south towards Colle Ferro. They carried Sten guns and were dressed like peasants as they emerged from the woods, all men except one. She was further away than the others, but even from a distance he could see that she was a handsome woman despite her gaunt frame, close-cropped dark hair, and mud on her face and clothing. She looked a bit like his daughter Teresa, but her hair was black as night, she was much too thin and rugged-looking, and she appeared too old and experienced, like a veteran soldier accustomed to taking out German patrols.

"Come Mario, we have to go. Help me get Walther to the car," he said, seeing that the partisans were waving for them to get in the car and drive away before more Germans came along.

He and his chauffeur dragged his brother to the Mercedes and plunked him into the passenger seat. Then Hollmann took off his jacket, slid in next to him, and pressed the jacket against his brother's wound, applying pressure, as Mario jumped behind the wheel, fired the engine, and drove off.

A moment later, when Hollmann looked in the rear view mirror, he saw the young woman peering at him through a pair of field glasses.

It was then he knew.

The partisan girl *was* his daughter Teresa, the *Inglesina*.

CHAPTER 54

VATICAN

JUNE 3, 1944

"THE PLOT TO REMOVE HITLER IS IN ITS FINAL STAGES. I am now in a position, Sir D'Arcy, to brief you on the details in order to secure British support."

Wanting his stunning announcement to strike home with maximum effect, Pius the Chief stared intently at his clandestine Allied go-between for several seconds before looking away. His eyes were drawn to the bookcase containing the hollowed-out copy of Thomas Aquinas's *Summa Theologica*, inside which resided a hidden microphone that was, once again, secretly recording a meeting with an important diplomatic representative. Then he looked back at Osborne. The usually calm and deliberate British Minister to the Holy See was on the edge of his seat. He peered back at the Pope with the suppressed exhilaration of an Eton schoolboy about to go home on holiday.

"So, am I to assume that you can now reveal to me the identity of this new leader that you referred to in our two previous meetings?"

"Yes, Minister, I can now make that information available to you, should you want me to disclose it."

"I most certainly would appreciate your disclosing it, Your Holiness."

"His name is Lieutenant Colonel Claus Schenk Graf von Stauffenberg. He is a highly decorated Roman Catholic officer of some distinction who was badly wounded in North Africa last spring. Like me and his brethren working alongside him, he believes that Nazi Germany is being led to ruination and that Hitler's removal from power is critical for the survival of the German State."

Osborne smoothed a wrinkle on his disguise for tonight's secret half-past-midnight meeting, a priest's vestments. "Can you tell me, what is the plan of this Stauffenberg and the German Resistance for removing the Führer?"

"Stauffenberg has taken over the planning and execution of the assassination himself. He and the other plotters are looking for a way to get close to Hitler. It is apparently not very easy."

"It is a well-known fact, even outside intelligence circles, that the Führer rarely appears in public these days and is only infrequently in Berlin."

"That is what my informants tell me as well. He spends most of his time at his headquarters at the Wolf's Lair near Rastenburg in East Prussia, and at Obersalzberg, his Bavarian mountain retreat near Berchtesgaden. He is always heavily guarded. That is why Stauffenberg must get close to him. Himmler and the SD have become increasingly suspicious of plots against Hitler. They no longer trust officers of the General Staff."

"As we both agree, getting close to the Führer is easier said than done."

"Stauffenberg is believed to be in line for promotion to the position of chief of staff to General Friedrich Fromm at the Reserve Army headquarters in Berlin. The position will enable the colonel to attend Hitler's military conferences, either at the Wolfsschanze in East Prussia or at Berchtesgaden."

"I see. So even though Hitler is closely guarded, Stauffenberg would have an opportunity to eliminate the Führer using a bomb or a pistol at close-range. Is the colonel willing to give up his own life for the cause?"

"I do not know. I would suspect not."

"So it will have to be a bomb then and he will have to leave it behind."

"I do not know these kinds of details, Minister. Nor do I want to know them. My role is purely to serve as a diplomatic liaison to ensure that the plot and the brave men behind it risking everything are taken seriously by your government. My overarching goal, as you well know, is peace. The widespread murder of both Jews and Gentiles across Europe cannot end without Hitler being removed from power. That is the *starting point* for any peace process and the termination of long-term suffering of the innocent people of this continent."

"I can see that you feel strongly about this matter."

"As I have told you on several occasions, Minister, I will support any government in Germany—as long as it is without Adolf Hitler."

"Yes, you are quite right. Those have been your exact words on several occasions. But if I am to pursue this with my government, I am going to need further details regarding the plot. How do Stauffenberg and the other plotters plan to get close enough to carry out the elimination of the Führer, and what steps will they take if the coup is successful?"

"The plan is called Operation Valkyrie. It has been in the works for six months now, but has recently been refined by General Friedrich Olbricht, General Tresckow, and Stauffenberg as the primary plan for staging a coup against Hitler. It is based on the operational plan of the Replacement Army."

"The *Ersatzheer*."

"Yes, Minister. The operational plan is to be implemented in the event that disruption caused by the Allied bombing of German cities causes a breakdown of law and order. Or in the event of an uprising by the millions of forced laborers from occupied countries being used in German factories."

"How will the plot work?"

"The plan is to mobilize the Reserve Army for the coup. Once Hitler is eliminated, a message will be broadcast to all military personnel. The message will announce that the Führer is dead and that a treasonous group of Party leaders is attempting to seize power for themselves by attacking German troops on the Russian front. To counter the coup, directives will be issued to all Wehrmacht commands for the seizure of government ministries in Berlin, Himmler's command post in East Prussia, German radio stations and telephone offices, and the concentration camps. Operation Valkyrie can only be executed under direct order from the commander of the Reserve Army, General Fromm, so he must either agree to join the team and carry out the plot, or be neutralized, if it is to have any chance of success. It is my understanding that Fromm, like many senior Nazi officers at this stage, is carefully biding his time to see how the war plays out. His foremost priority is his own survival. He neither supports the resistance nor provides information to the Gestapo. Accordingly, Stauffenberg and his colleagues believe he can be won over, and with the Reserve Army mobilized, they can seize control over communications and the government from the SS."

Sir D'Arcy let out a deep sigh. "I must say this is a more thoroughly detailed operation than I had anticipated."

"Yes, and that is what I would like you to convey to our mutual friend the prime minister. The Germans are serious, and they want to know whether they can count on British support or not. They need to have a Western power behind them."

"I understand, Your Holiness. And I can assure you that I will convey the importance of the operation to His Majesty's Government."

"There is one more thing."

"Yes, Your Eminence."

"The conspirators tell me that their time is running out. As I relayed to you in our last meeting, the SS have been tracking them. They have code-named the group the 'Black Chapel,' and they have several of the members under surveillance. With the clock ticking down, time is of the essence. They want reassurances that Great Britain will support the coup and follow through with the peace process if it is successful. That is why you and I have been holding midnight meetings in my papal apartments and I have been acting as a secret foreign agent for the past five years. This war has dragged on for far too long and it is time for peace. But there can be no peace without the elimination of Hitler first."

"Yes, I quite agree."

"There is one more thing that I would like you to put to the prime minister."

"Yes, Your Eminence?"

"I know that, whether Hitler is eliminated or not, the Allies are ultimately going to win the battle for Rome as well as the war. But I would caution the Allies about being too hard on Germany and Italy when this war is finally over. We all know what happened at the end of the Great War with the Treaty of Versailles. The world is at war precisely because of the draconian terms of surrender from that war. I acknowledge the justice of punishing war criminals, but at the same time I express the hope that the people of Italy will not be too harshly punished when this is all over. As a matter of fact, it would please the Holy See immeasurably if Italy was made a 'full ally' in the remaining war effort once the Germans have withdrawn and Rome is in Allied hands."

"I will convey your message to my government. But I must tell you up front that London will never agree to make Italy a full ally. Your country made a huge mistake in following Il Duce, and it will have to pay a price for that folly. Nonetheless, I will make your concerns known."

"Thank you, Sir D'Arcy." He folded his hands in his lap. "You know it is a curious irony that, on the one hand, the Allies believe I haven't been firm enough in standing up to Hitler and his Nazis or done enough to save the Jews; while on the other hand, the Germans claim that I am the mouthpiece and secret agent of the Western powers and the Jewish people. But I ask you, my old friend, how can I be both Hitler's Pope and Hitler's assassin? How can I simultaneously be reviled as a

Nazi supporter and an Allied benefactor? If I was truly what both sides say I am, I would have to be a double agent, wouldn't I? Do you honestly feel that I am a double agent working on behalf of Nazi Germany, Minister?"

Osborne chuckled. "Of course not, Your Eminence. You *are* an Allied secret agent but are most definitely *not* Hitler's Pope. In fact, you have built up quite a pro-Allied network of spies here at the Vatican. And you and I both know that the Holy See is the oldest intelligence apparatus in the world, with many centuries of experience in subterfuge and spy tradecraft."

"Oh, you've been reading too many spy novels, Sir D'Arcy."

"Guilty as charged. I must confess a fondness for Phillips Oppenheim."

"I enjoyed *Last Train Out* very much."

"His Holiness has read a spy novel? I must confess my surprise."

"I have read several, in fact. And I can see why you like Charles Mildenhall, the upper-class British adventurer-hero in the novel. He works for the Foreign Office in a role that is equal parts diplomat and troubleshooting spy. Sounds like someone I know."

"Sometimes life and fiction are inseparable, Your Eminence."

They smiled at one another, something Pius did only rarely and usually in the presence of children. He truly loved children.

"Before I take my leave, Your Eminence, I must also relay the latest request I have received from our Foreign Office."

"Yes."

"My government is still very troubled by the merciless persecution of the Jews throughout Europe."

"As are we here at the Holy See, Minister."

"My government feels that stronger censure from the Holy Father would go a long way towards reassuring the world where you stand morally and give added strength to the Allied cause on the home front to keep spirits up. In our view, a policy of silence must necessarily involve a renunciation of moral leadership and a consequent atrophy of the influence and authority of the Vatican. Without the maintenance and assertion of such moral authority, it is unlikely that there can a papal contribution to the re-establishment of world peace at the close of the conflict. I don't mean to sound unduly harsh, Your Eminence. But I want you to understand London's position. As we both know, Nazi war crimes have reached a level of cruelty and barbarism never seen before in the history of humanity. We feel that a public condemnation is desired not only by the world's Catholics, but also by its Protestant population."

Pius couldn't help but feel defensive. Since the fall of Poland, he had endured this very same lecture countless times not only from Osborne, but from Myron Taylor, Roosevelt's handpicked peace ambassador and personal envoy to the Curia, Harold Tittmann, the U.S. Chargé d'Affaires to the Holy See, and several other Allied diplomats from other countries who were more than happy to tell him how to run the Roman Catholic Church. He had even been subjected to the same hectoring from his own secretary of state, Maglione, and the editor of the Vatican newspaper, Dalla Torre. The names changed, but the debate did not.

"As I have made clear in the past, Sir D'Arcy, I have already condemned

Nazi war crimes. I did it during my Christmas radio address a year and a half ago. I made it clear what was happening to the Jews and other non-Aryans in the territories occupied by the Germans. My Christmas message was brief, but it was clearly understood. We do not need to assure the world that our love and our paternal solicitude lean towards all non-Aryans. The world already knows this. Furthermore, me and my Vatican brethren have decided that, when the circumstances advise or permit, to raise our voice on behalf of the disenfranchised again. But this matter has to be handled diplomatically."

"I understand that, but if you don't condemn Hitler and Germany by name, how can the world know for certain what you are referring to?"

"As I have made clear to you on several prior occasions, if I single out Hitler and Germany, then I must also single out Stalin and the Soviet Union. They are also committing unspeakable acts of oppression, persecution, and murder at this time. Certainly not on the scale of the Nazis, but they are horrendous nonetheless. You know whose side I am on. After all, we *are* in my papal library at two o'clock in the morning talking about a plot to *assassinate* Adolf Hitler. But I still have to maintain at least the appearance of impartiality before the rest of the world. To do that, I would have to condemn Stalin's crimes as well as those of Hitler. You and I both know just what those crimes are. I am talking about the massacre by the Soviet NKVD of Polish Army officers at Katyn, and the other atrocities in the Baltic States against Roman Catholics. Hundreds of thousands have been murdered by the Soviet killing machine. Not in the same numbers as the Germans are liquidating the Jews, but they are still criminal actions that would need to be publicly disclosed in order to preserve even the appearance of impartiality."

"Yes, I can see that we have reached a stalemate yet again on this matter. I understand your position, Your Eminence, but I'm afraid it will be met with disapproval from London."

"Why is that? I have made my position abundantly clear."

"It has to do with the Holy See's claims to be infallible in matters of faith and morality."

"Come now, Minister. We here at the Vatican have never claimed to be infallible."

"Yes, but you do present yourself as the world's supreme moral authority, the proverbial 'oracle of God,' do you not?"

"Yes, that is true."

"Then it is only right and just for people to expect that you speak out clearly against the greatest evil of our day and all history: the Holocaust of the Jews and other people suffering mercilessly at the expense of Hitler's Third Reich. Indeed, my government might even go so far as to expect that the Holy Office officially excommunicate Hitler, Goebbels, and Himmler. As well as the other German, Hungarian, Croatian, Lithuanian, and Slovakian mass murderers who have collaborated with them in their genocidal atrocities."

"I agree with you in spirit, but not in terms of practical diplomacy, Sir D'Arcy. If I am to condemn atrocities, then I have to condemn *all* atrocities. It is as simple as that. Are Mr. Churchill and the British Government prepared for me rail against the injustices of Stalin and his Big Red Army on Vatican Radio and

L'Osservatore Romano? Well, Minister, are they?"

"No, of course not. We cannot allow any specific condemnation of the Soviets. The Allied partnership must remain intact, and we can have nothing that threatens that."

"So your hands are tied, just like mine. As I have told you before, our explicit condemnations in the past have often either had no effect or made the situation worse. You recall what happened with the Dutch bishops?"

"Yes, when they broke ranks in 1942 with the leaders of the Dutch Reformed churches and publicly denounced the deportation of their country's Jews, the Germans responded by extending the deportations to non-Aryan Catholics."

"Precisely. Forty thousand people were sent east and never seen or heard from again. And you remember what happened last year when Secretary Maglione sent a list of protests to Ribbentrop against maltreatment of Poles by Germans?"

"The German Foreign Office refused to receive the note, arguing that this and Nuncio Orsenigo's complaints were out of order since they touched on German internal affairs."

"Nazi Germany is controlled by madmen. There is no reasoning with these people. I truly believe that I am doing as much as possible within the limits imposed upon me by the German leadership. If I speak out too strongly or frequently or even *unequally* in favor of the Allies, the Nazis will retaliate by intensifying their persecution of not only the Jews, but Catholics and the Church overall in both Germany and the territories under their occupation."

"I confess these are troubled times."

"I can further tell you that there is a great fear of a new, sustained Nazi *Kulturkampf* in the minds of bishops throughout Germany. The Nazis have killed so many. What's a few hundred thousand more? An individual life means nothing to them. It has no value. And that is why our first task must be to cut off the head of the snake. I tell you, we must eliminate Hitler. But no one can ever know that I have been a party to three plots to remove this terrible man from power."

"You're saying the Vatican will keep it a secret, even after the war is over?"

"Yes, my involvement in this tyrannicide must remain a secret forever, Minister. That is why, as always, you are not to produce official notes of any kind of this midnight meeting except what you yourself type up when you leave this room and forward to London."

"But don't you want the world to know, someday, what you have done?"

"No, the world must never know that I wanted peace so badly, that I loathed the cruelty and barbarism of mankind so desperately, that I was willing to go against the diplomatic precedents set by my church, as well as the will of God, in support of the elimination of another human being. What I am doing is, ultimately, a sin. And I'm afraid my own shameful pride will not allow me to be a sinner who publicly announces his sins to the world."

"But Hitler is a tyrant. He deserves to die."

"No one deserves to die. But we all *do* deserve to be rescued and loved by the Holy Savior."

"Even Hitler?"

"Yes, Minister, even Adolf Hitler."

CHAPTER 55

VALMONTONE, CENTRAL ITALY

JUNE 3, 1944

AFTER DRIVING OFF the last of the Herman Göring rear guard and taking Valmontone, instead of scrounging up some grub or catching a few winks of sleep, Bridger decided it was high time to clean and oil his Tommy. Five minutes into it, he heard a light tread of boots and a familiar voice say, "I've brought someone to see you, John."

He looked up to see Frederick with two unexpected new arrivals. At first, he didn't recognize the young woman, but as she stepped up to him he realized it was his sister Teresa. With her was a young Italian man with a heavy beard, wire-rim glasses, and the clothing of a partisan. His heart instantly leapt with joy at the sight of his younger sibling, whom he hadn't seen in six months and had heard no word from since March.

"Well, if it isn't my baby sister!" he roared, and he set down his weapon and bristle brush, jumped up from his makeshift seat of Valmontone rubble, and took her in his arms.

"Thank God you're alive, Gunther!" she said as they embraced.

"John Bridger, you mean," he said playfully. "Remember, I'm a gangster American, not a drawing-room European as you can tell from my sorry-ass uniform."

She giggled. "I'm sorry, I forgot."

He hugged her tighter. After more than a week of virtually continuous fighting since the breakout at Anzio, the feel of her vibrantly alive young body brought tears of joy to his eyes.

"I'm just glad you're alive. There's been no word for months," he said.

"As you can see, I'm still all in one piece. But others haven't been as lucky."

He wondered if she was talking about anyone in particular, but he was so ecstatic to see her that he didn't give it a second thought. They held each other for several seconds longer before gently pulling apart. He took a moment to take her in. She was remarkably different from when he had seen her last in Rome six months earlier. Her hair was dyed black, her face gaunt and crinkled from the sun, her body taut and wiry, and her clothing was not that of the titled Roman black set, but a country peasant. She looked very much the part of a hungry and battle-weary yet fiery-eyed Resistance fighter willing to die for the Risorgimento. But more than the physical transformation was the change in her manner and bearing. There was now a maturity and seasoned toughness that she had lacked six months ago. The sporadic reports he had heard about her from Savoyan were right: she was a

Roman Resistance fighter, not a rich Roman society girl anymore. No wonder the Nazis wanted her so badly: she really was the *Inglesina*.

Looking at her, he felt a burst of pride. In this terrible bloody war, she was a true fighter for a worthy cause.

She introduced him to her companion. His name was Giuseppe Valenti, but he said to call him Beppo. He looked to Bridger more like a young university revolutionary than a Resistance fighter. He wore a brown leather jacket and an Italian beret, and he was armed with a worn-out Sten.

"We're going to Rome, John," said Frederick when the introductions were complete. "Commanders Di Domenico and Valenti here have offered to lead us into the city and help us secure the bridges over the Tiber. What do you think of that?"

"I say it's damned good timing, sir. But how are we going to do it without armor?"

"Ah, but we do have armor, John. Task Force Howze will be lending us a hand.'

"Task Force Howze?"

"They're an armored group made up from the Eighty-first Reconnaissance Battalion and Thirteenth Armored Infantry under command of Colonel Howze. They'll be joining us for the final push into Rome to secure the bridges. We'll have a front running the width of II Corps to lead the assault with the support of the Howze group. We're going to be the first ones into the city, John. And with the help of your sister and the Resistance, no one's going to beat us to the punch. With that in mind, I'm giving you ten minutes for you two to catch up before our scheduled briefing in my new HQ."

"Your new HQ, sir?"

"The little church on the hill. It's practically the only building left standing in the whole town, but you should smell the jasmine and bougainvillea. Sure beats the hell out of cordite. Teresa will show you the way. By the way, why in the hell were you cleaning your gun? I thought I ordered you to catch some shut eye?"

"The weapon needed cleaning, sir. I can't very well kill Germans without a clean weapon."

"No, Major, I suppose you can't. I'll see you in ten minutes." He motioned to Teresa's companion Beppo. "In the meantime, Commander Valenti here will give me a rundown of the bridges on a map."

"It would give me great honor, General. But I still have one question."

"And what is that, my friend?"

"Why did it take you so long to reach Rome?"

"I don't know, Commander, but don't jinx us. We haven't made it there yet."

The young Italian revolutionary laughed and he and Frederick started up the hill. Bridger gave Teresa his seat on a pile of fragmented rubble, and took the broken block next to her. It sure as hell wasn't the Ritz. But at least it was in the shade and, with the Krauts in full retreat, the roar of the German 88s and *Nebelwerfers* had died down, rendering the demolished little village at least somewhat peaceful. Bridger knew, though, that it was only a momentary lull on the road to Rome. Kesselring's *panzergrenadiers* would make them fight for every goddamned inch of ground.

"I must say, Little Sister, you have grown up a lot since the last time I saw you. How long have you been in the field fighting for the Resistance?"

"Since December of last year. I took part in the attack on the Germans at the Cinema Barberini. That was my first operation."

"Well, tales of your exploits have become legendary. Peter Savoyan and Radio Vittoria have kept the OSS and us dogfaces at the front well informed. You're with the GAP, your *nom de guerre* is the *Inglesina*, and Kappler and his Gestapo and the Koch Band want you bad. You know you're lucky as hell to be alive, don't you?"

"I'm no luckier than you. The reports say that the Allies have suffered more than a hundred thousand casualties since landing in Sicily—and yet you are not one of them."

"You're right, and I owe it to blind dumb luck. I've lost a lot of buddies, more than I can count. This war is terrible. Ain't no doubt about it." He looked at her knowingly. "But at least you have found true love."

"True love? Me?"

"Don't act so innocent. How long have you and Beppo the revolutionary been lovers?"

"That's none of your business."

"January. I say you've been lovers since January."

She raised a brow and looked at him with cool challenge.

He smiled. "What?"

"You know what. You're being an overprotective older brother. What are you going to do, interrogate him or challenge him to an arm-wrestling contest to see if he's good enough for me?"

"Actually, I was thinking of a duel at thirty paces. My Tommy versus his Sten."

"Very funny. But I'm afraid wartime is not much of a time for laughter." She reached out and touched his hand. "I was going to tell you this when I first saw you, but you looked so happy and I was so excited to see you that I didn't want to spoil everything."

He could tell from her solemn expression that it was something bad. He felt guilty for joking around with her about Beppo. "What…what is it?"

"There's just no easy way to say it. Mother was killed last night."

It should have been like a mule kick to the gut, but after witnessing so much death and destruction over the past six months, it just made him feel numb. He shook his head in despair. He wanted to cry, but somehow he couldn't. Instead, he blew out a war-weary sigh.

"How did it happen? Was it the Germans?"

"No, it was a Fascist guard at Regina Coeli Prison. He beat her up so badly that he ruptured her appendix. She died two hours later."

Though he had grown estranged from his mother during the past seven years, he still felt bitterly angry. He vowed to kill the son of a bitch responsible for this when they took Rome. "Does this guard have a name?"

"Lorenzo Carmeli. Apparently, he began abusing her a month ago when he was moved to her wing. He used to work for us as a gardener and he recognized her."

"Carmeli, Carmeli…I don't remember him. But apparently you do?"

"Vaguely. He started working for us the summer after you went to America. He stole money from us and so Mother fired him. He had a wife and family to support and he never forgave her for getting rid of him. So he beat her so badly that he ended up killing her."

"What the hell has this war done to us all?" He blew out another heavy sigh. "I heard about what happened at the Ardeatine caves."

"I was there. I saw it with my own eyes."

"You saw them kill all those people? The BBC said there were more than three hundred murdered."

"I didn't actually see the killings. But I saw them lead the prisoners into the caves in groups of five and I heard the gunshots. And the next day, before they had completely sealed off all of the entrances with explosives, Beppo and I crept back to the scene of the crime with two Silesian monks. We saw the bodies. They had been shot in the back of the head and many of them had been beaten to death and decapitated. The Nazis butchered them. Some of the Italians and other non-Germans who work at Regina Coeli and Via Tasso said that, by the end, the SS were drunk out of their minds. Because they couldn't shoot straight, they had to bash in the skulls of the prisoners with their rifle butts and shoot them multiple times."

"Please don't tell me that our…our father, Colonel Hollmann, had anything to do with this atrocity?"

"He's not my father."

"At one time he was. All the same, don't tell me he was there at the caves?"

"Yes, he was at *Fosse Ardeatine*. But that isn't the worst part about it."

He held his breath.

"Colonel Hollmann killed my real father."

"My God. Did you see him do it? But I thought you didn't actually—"

"I didn't see him pull the trigger, but that doesn't mean I don't know what happened. I saw him take the colonel from the truck and lead him into the cave. A minute later, I heard the shot and the colonel did not come back out. Only Hollmann did."

"I'm sorry, Teresa. I'm sorry about all of this," he said, and he reached out and took her by the hand.

Her lip quivered. "It was our family's destiny that this should happen. The curse is real."

He said nothing. He didn't want it to be real, though he knew there was no escaping it now. Fate of the most malevolent kind had seized hold of their family, and one by one, they were being killed off.

"You know that it's true. What happened eleven and a half years ago in Innsbruck has cursed us all."

Again, he took a deep, war-weary breath. "I know," he said quietly. "I always knew it was real."

"Evil found an opening and pushed its way into our lives. That is why our mother—and my father, your stepfather—are dead."

"I always wanted to believe that we create the world around us. That we're not just characters in someone else's script. But when I see this..." He left the words unfinished.

"But we do control our own destiny, Brother. Don't you see? The evil that started that day in Innsbruck has come full circle here in Rome in 1944. Now is our chance to do something about it."

"What are you talking about?"

"Beppo and I are going to lead you and your men into Rome. General Frederick has said that the First Special Service Force will be leading the charge along with Task Force Howze. You know what that means don't you?"

"Yeah, it means we'll be the first to liberate Rome."

"No, Brother, it means that we have a chance to stamp out evil and put an end to the curse."

"What are you saying?"

"We're going to finish what Mother started eleven and a half years ago."

"We're going to shoot our father?"

"Yes."

He still couldn't believe what he was hearing, even if he had thought it before himself. "We're going to kill him dead? Colonel Hollmann of the SS? Our own father?"

"Yes. Brother. Only then can we put an end to the curse that began that terrible day in Innsbruck."

CHAPTER 56

VIA TASSO

JUNE 3, 1944

CALMLY SMOKING a Dunhill, Hollmann watched as Captain Priebke and two of his Gestapo thugs dragged Lorenzo Carmeli into the interrogation room and chained him to a set of iron-ring bolts drilled into the concrete wall. The room, illuminated by a single light bulb dangling from a string, was covered with dried iron-red blood on the floor and walls despite repeated scrubbings. Carmeli's arms and legs were spread apart to nearly maximum extension as he was restrained into place against the wall. The gag in his mouth was removed, but the blindfold was kept on so that, during his torture, every blow would come as a shock and every moment between blows would be filled with dreadful anticipation. This way, while the pain eased, Carmeli could only imagine the terrible horrors to which he would be subjected with the next blow.

The Regina Coeli Prison guard had committed the unpardonable sin of killing his ex-wife—and the dumb brute was about to pay dearly for his crime. But Hollmann didn't want to rush it. He let Carmeli stand there, chained to the wall, for several minutes, letting the anticipation build while he calmly finished smoking his British cigarette. Already he could see the effect the blindfold was having on his prisoner: Carmeli's legs were shaking and his head, which was free to move left and right, jerked around like a nervous bird whenever Hollmann, Priebke, or one of the other two SD men made a movement or whispered something to one another.

"So, Lorenzo," he began in Italian, using his silky smooth interrogator's voice, "were you unaware that the Marchesa Di Domenico was formerly my wife when you beat her so badly that you ruptured her appendix?"

The reply came quickly in a note of desperation. "I had no idea, Colonel. I swear before St. Peter."

"That's not what I heard. The other guards said that they warned you of the marchesa's importance here in Rome and also of her former marriage to me. They said that you boasted that you didn't care and were going to get even with 'the royal bitch' just the same."

"I tell you they are lying."

"No, it is you who are lying, Lorenzo."

He gave a little nod towards Priebke, who stepped forward with his brass knuckles and delivered a vicious blow to Carmeli's left knee. Hollmann thought he heard something crack, and Carmeli screamed in agony. After nine months of occupation, it was readily apparent that Priebke and the Gestapo had perfected their torture regimen to a fine art. Striking hard bony parts and joints like kneecaps, shins, ankles, elbows, shoulders, and ribs rather than the head or soft vital organs was now standard procedure. This ensured that a prisoner experienced unbearable agony without endangering his life or hurting him so badly that he was incapable of providing sought-after information.

"Now, Lorenzo," Hollmann continued after letting the pain subside for a moment. "Please tell me that you are going to stop lying to me."

The guard blubbered for mercy. "Yes, yes, I...I will tell you everything you want to know."

"Good, I am glad we have reached an understanding. Now, as to the reason that you murdered my ex-wife—"

"But I didn't murder her. It was an accident, I swear."

Again, he gave a little nod towards Priebke, who, with a fiendishly calm smile, delivered a savage blow to both shins, drawing howls of agony from Carmeli. This time Hollmann definitely heard the distinctive sound of shattering bone.

He waited a full minute before speaking, letting Carmeli moan and beg for mercy. Breaking a bone was an especially useful technique during interrogation: once a bone was broken, pressure or additional blows could be inflicted upon the damaged area to ensure excruciating pain for an extended period of time without resulting in death.

"Do you understand now, Lorenzo, that it is best not to interrupt me when I am talking?"

"Yes I understand, but please don't hit me again," he cried. "I beg of you."

"Then will you stop lying and answer my questions without interrupting?"

"Yes, yes, I'll do whatever you want. Just...just don't strike me again."

"Very well, I'm going to give you another chance. It is my understanding that you had it out for my ex-wife and that is why you murdered her. Apparently several years ago, when you were in her employ, you stole from her and were caught. She dismissed you and you were angry over being fired and sought revenge. Your reassignment to the Third Wing at Regina Coeli gave you the opportunity to gain your revenge. Is this all true?"

There was no answer.

Carmeli's lips were quivering, his hands trembling, but he still didn't want to admit what he'd done. He obviously feared receiving even harsher treatment if he confessed. Hollmann couldn't help but feel a modicum of pity for the poor bastard, but then he reminded himself what Carmeli had done to his once-beloved Bianca. True, the damned woman had shot him twice in cold blood and ruined his life. But for some inexplicable reason, a part of him had still never stopped loving the fiery, dark-eyed Italian from the black nobility; and he couldn't blame her when he knew that she had only tried to kill him to spare herself and the children from being associated with a Jew and incurring the wrath of the Nazis. He understood why she had done what she had done. Terrified of the pitiless abuse she and her children would likely have to endure due to his grandmother's Jewish heritage, she had temporarily lost her mind and tried to kill him. He had only learned the truth yesterday; and yet, knowing that she had had good reason for her actions somehow brought a sense of closure to the whole traumatic incident. And now, just when he had come to terms with it all and accepted it, she was dead.

"Wait, what's that, Lorenzo? I can't hear you. You must speak up."

A low moaning sound came from his trembling mouth, and Hollmann could see that he was crying beneath his blindfold. He signaled Priebke again, who gave a sinister smile and stepped forward to deliver another blow.

"No, no, please," cried Carmeli, hearing the approaching footsteps.

This time Priebke delivered a devastating blow to Carmeli's right arm, and Hollmann definitely heard the snap of bone.

Carmeli screamed like a wounded animal and fainted.

Hollmann waited a moment to make sure he was unconscious before commanding, "Wake him up."

One of the other SD guards picked up a bucket of water from the corner of the room and tossed the water in Carmeli's face. After a few seconds, he came to again and began moaning and pleading for mercy.

"This will all end when you tell me what I need to know," said Hollmann in a friendly voice, as if he was lecturing a small child. "You control whether it is to be pain or the relief of pain. If you are honest with me, I can even get you a doctor to give you a shot of morphine."

"Please…give it to me now and…and I will tell you everything I know."

"No, I'm afraid I can't do that, Lorenzo. You need to tell me what I want to know first."

"I'll tell you everything. Please, please, just stop hitting me."

"My ex-wife, Lorenzo…the reason you killed her was because she had fired you, correct?"

"Yes, I was angry at the marchesa."

"But it was you who stole from her. Why should you be angry with her when you were the thief? It was you, Lorenzo, who violated the marchesa, not the other way around. Wasn't it?"

"Yes, yes, it was me who was at fault. I stole money and jewelry. I was desperate. I owed money from gambling and I didn't know how else to raise it."

"You could have asked for it, Lorenzo. I doubt the marchesa would have given it to you because she is a proud, stubborn woman, but you could have at least tried."

"I...I don't know why you care so much about her, Colonel. I thought you hated her."

"Hate her? Why would I hate my ex-wife?"

"Because she shot you and stole everything from you. That is the story I heard. That is why I thought I would be doing you a favor."

"A favor? You thought you would be doing me a favor?"

"Yes, I thought she was an enemy of the Reich and that it was you who had her arrested and locked up at Regina Coeli."

"Kappler is the one who had her arrested, you fool, not me. And despite my previous rocky history with the marchesa, I would never want any harm to come to the mother of my children."

"Please, I am sorry…truly sorry for what I have done. I know I deserve to go to hell."

"Oh, you're going to hell all—"

He stopped right there as a knock sounded at the heavy iron door and a lieutenant appeared. "Colonel, I am sorry to interrupt the interrogation, but I wanted to let you know that your brother's surgeon called from Santo Spirito Hospital. He said your brother has taken a turn for the worse and has requested to see you."

"Walther is dying?"

The lieutenant nodded. "It appears he wants to see you one last time and settle his affairs. The surgeon, Dr. Weiss, instructed me to summon you straightaway. Again, I am sorry for the intrusion."

Hollmann felt a sudden stab of sadness and sympathy. He desperately wanted to see Walther before he passed from this earth. He turned to Priebke.

"I will leave you to finish up here, Captain."

"Yes, sir, of course. I offer my sympathies to you and your brother. He is a genuine hero of the Reich."

"Carmeli must not be killed. You can use the blowtorch, but you are to keep him alive until my return."

"And then what?"

"And then, when he has endured unspeakable suffering, I will let you kill him."

"Yes, Colonel," said Priebke, smiling. "It will be my pleasure."

CHAPTER 57

SANTO SPIRITO HOSPITAL

JUNE 3, 1944

AFTER PASSING UNDER the life-sized portrait of Hitler in the Via Tasso lobby, Hollmann dashed to his Mercedes. Mario was sitting in the car reading a copy of *L'Osservatore Romano* and sipping a real cappuccino from the money the colonel had given him as extra compensation for being wounded south of Rome. With his arm in a sling, the chauffeur quickly tossed aside his paper, fired the engine, and, once Hollmann informed him where they were headed, peeled off in the direction of Santo Spirito Hospital.

Along the way Hollmann thought of Carmeli. A part of him felt guilty for being so cruel to the poor bastard; but the other, more practical and darker, side of him told himself that the prison guard deserved whatever he had coming to him for murdering his wife. The man had let vengeance get the better of him—and, in the process, he had killed a poor helpless woman, a woman whom Hollmann had once deeply loved that was the mother of his children, a woman whose passing continued to produce strong, conflicting emotions inside him. Once again, he realized that, despite the violence and ugly aftermath of what had transpired between them eleven and a half years earlier, he had never stopped loving his beloved marchesa.

The streets of Rome were packed with sick and starving citizens, hordes of rail-thin refugees, and congested traffic. Escaping the city before the Allies took it by force were not only members of the SS and Wehrmacht, but the Fascist police, *Nazifascisti* elite, and soon-to-be-imprisoned collaborators. The Allied radio at Anzio had broadcast the names and addresses of spies and collaborators; Hollmann knew that many of them were fleeing northwards to avoid a firing squad. The question on everyone's mind—for both Rome's citizenry and its remaining Occupation leadership like Hollmann—was, of course, whether or not Kesselring would defend the city. Most of the signs suggested that he intended to do so. As of yet, the field marshal had not ordered a withdrawal and it appeared that Rome would soon be contested as fiercely as Stalingrad. But still, no one knew the answer yet—except Smiling Albert himself. And he wasn't telling.

As he weaved his way through the steady stream of dispossessed and traffic, Hollmann shook his head in despair. Rome had turned into a hideous facsimile of the city he loved. He almost didn't recognize it any more. Once the Allies had broken out of Anzio, Kappler's Gestapo, the Koch Gang, and Caruso's Fascist police had become possessed by a state of frenzy, searching and ransacking practically every inch of Rome and capturing dozens of key Resistance figures and male laborers for service in Germany and the Italian front. Now there were house-to-house searches and round-ups every day with men and boys regularly plucked off trams or trapped in bars and cafes. Partisans were being arrested and executed at Forte Bravetta by the score daily.

Looking out his car window, Hollmann saw the hate in the eyes of the people as he threaded his Mercedes with the twin Nazi flags through the maze of shambling masses, oxcarts, and stolen or requisitioned motorized vehicles. But there was also a look of utter sadness and defeat. With thousands of war refugees pouring into Rome daily and severe food and fresh water shortages, the existing population was in a state of crisis. In fact, they had been that way for more than a month now. Outside his car window, most everyone appeared as walking skeletons. But it wasn't just the Germans and Fascist police that were to blame, Hollmann knew. He had learned that in recent days, the Allies had once again turned down a Vatican proposal to feed the starving refugees and citizens of Rome, this time by sea using Spanish and Irish ships. With Clark's Fifth Army already on the outskirts of Rome, Roosevelt and Churchill were taking a hardline stance. They would not allow potential food stores intended for the suffering population to fall into German hands.

When they reached the hospital, Mario parked out front. Hollmann hopped out and dashed quickly up the stairs. He was blasted with bright ceiling lights as he stepped into the hallway of the second floor. He darted anxiously up one hallway, then another, until he found the officers' hospital room. He saw Walther on the second to last cot on the right. By some trick in the lighting, the figure lying underneath the hospital sheet appeared too small and fragile to be his younger brother. His neck, jaw, chest, and midriff areas were heavily bandaged. His eyes were open, but not at all lucid as he stared off into space. His chest rose and fell in a shallow rhythm that made it clear that he was on his last legs. A clear pouch containing IV fluids was suspended from a metal stand beside the bed, and a clear tube trailed beneath the bedcovers to his left arm. Pinned to the headboard of his bed were two medals: a Knight's Cross of the Iron Cross with Oak Leaves and Swords, and a Gold Wound Badge–First Class for having been wounded five times in battle. At the next bed beyond Walther's, Hollmann saw a priest giving last rites to a comatose officer covered in bandages.

He sighed with relief. He was not too late and would be able to see his beloved brother one last time.

He went to his bed and sat on the edge beside him. "Hello, Walther," he said softly. "I came as soon as I heard."

"Thanks, Brother," his younger sibling croaked in reply. "I am glad you are here."

Hollmann saw his eyes light up and it made his heart feel glad.

"Walther, you're going to make it. We Hollmann's are a tough lot. We don't die easily."

"I know we don't. But I don't want to live anymore even though they just promoted me to lieutenant colonel. Kesselring himself came by today and gave me that gold medal." He nodded up at the gilded wound badge pinned to the headboard. "I must say it doesn't make much sense promoting an officer for getting shot by his own army."

"It was an ugly scene, but thankfully we both survived and the paintings are in safe hands at the Vatican. You are going to pull through this tough time, mark my words. You are a colonel now just like me. Congratulations, *Brüderlein*—now you definitely can't die."

"Why not?"

"Because it is quite an achievement to have two colonels in one family. We must enjoy this, at least for a little while."

"Well, I don't care anymore about this war. I just want to die."

"You shouldn't talk like that."

"But it's the truth. I want to die."

Hollmann licked his lips; this was harder than he had thought. He looked at his brother and remembered back to all the wonderful times they had schussed down the slopes of Innsbruck together and fished for alpine trout and chased after young girls. He began to feel himself choking up.

He took his brother by the hand. "I don't want you to die, *Brüderlein.*"

Tears poured from his eyes and there was nothing he could do to stop them. He felt like a child again and tried to wipe them away, but it was no use. More came out, forming a pair of water falls tumbling down each of his cheeks.

"I don't want to be a part of this war anymore," said Walther. "The things I have seen…on both sides…I…" He left the words hanging.

Hollmann sniffled. "Me too, Little Brother. But even worse, I cannot help but feel that we are on the wrong side of history."

"We most certainly are." His brother's look sharpened to a razor's edge. "But you…you are far worse than even me."

He was taken aback. "What are you talking about?"

"*Fosse Ardeatine*. I heard you were there."

"Who told you that?"

"Your daughter Teresa told me."

"What? Teresa was here?"

"She came late last night, hours after you brought me here. She snuck into the city to see me. She said she saw me get shot by the SS on the road outside Valmontone and she knew you would bring me here to Santo Spirito where I would best be cared for."

"But why did she come to see you?"

"She said that with Rome about to fall and me getting wounded, she wanted to see me one last time in case I didn't make it."

"What else did she tell you?"

"She said she saw you at the caves that night. She said you shot her father Colonel Di Domenico. How could you have done such a thing?"

"I didn't do it. I was at *Fosse Ardeatine* that night, but I didn't kill anybody."

"I don't believe you." He sighed deeply. "Look at what this war has turned us into. You and I are both murderers."

"What are you talking about? What did you do?"

"I had a dozen soldiers who had surrendered shot in a field. They were goumiers, the French Algerians. I made them get down on their knees and had them executed by my men. They shot them in the back of the head outside Monte Cassino."

"My God, Walther. You ordered twelve surrendered soldiers to be executed and stood by while they were shot?"

He nodded guiltily. "There are other officers who have done far worse than us. I have seen them...you wouldn't believe the things I have seen them do to our enemies, especially the goumiers. That is what I find so disconcerting. We are not even close to the worst. That is why I would rather die than continue on with this fight. How much more vile can we Germans be in this terrible war?"

Hollmann gave a heavy sigh. There was a small mirror on the wall above his brother's bed and he caught his own reflection. He looked awful. His eyes were ringed with black from lack of sleep and red from crying, and the pallor of his skin was alabaster, like the walking dead.

In the fluted overhead lighting, his brother saw the damage too. "My God, what has happened to us, Brother? We used to both have so much hope and promise."

"I'll tell you what happened to me. My wife shot me, and I shot her back and my life was ruined and I lost my children and then this war happened. It is like a bad dream."

"I can't help but feel we are cursed. And now I just want to die."

"Cursed? What makes you say that we are cursed?"

"It is a feeling I have. A feeling deep in my bones."

My God, he thought miserably, *the family curse has seized hold of my poor brother Walther too.* He reached out and gently touched his face. "I don't want you to die, Walther."

"A part of me doesn't want to die either. But I have to do this for both of us."

"What are you talking about?"

"I am going to kill myself. That way I will atone for both of our sins."

"Walther, you are talking crazy. You are not yourself."

"Yes, I am." From beneath his blanket, his younger brother produced a Luger. He pointed the gun inward at his temple. "I am not crazy at all. In fact, I have never seen things more clearly in my entire life."

Hollmann raised his hands to stop him. "Don't do it, Walther. You don't want to shoot yourself."

"No, that's where you are wrong. I *do* want to die, as I have told you."

"Not like this, you don't. What about your children, Anna, Dieter, and little Hans? Don't you want to see them when you go home after the war?"

"What are you talking about? When we lose this war, there will be nothing left of Germany, or Austria for that matter. And why would I want to return to my children? I am an embarrassment and don't want to face them."

"But there must be something to live for?"

"There is nothing. I will take my life for the both of us."

He wanted to reach out and try and wrestle the gun from him, but he wasn't close enough and the attempt would probably backfire. "Listen to me, Walther," he said, trying to keep his voice calm and soothing. "Whatever wrongs you think you have committed, you are still a good man. It is this war that has turned us into barbarians. It happened to our father and our uncles in the Great War, and it has happened again a generation later. It is the war that is monstrous—not you or I."

"No, what I did to those goumiers and what you did at Ardeatine was pure evil. And don't tell me you weren't there or that you didn't pull the trigger. Teresa saw you and heard the shooting when you went inside. She said there were more than three hundred bodies piled up in that cave."

"What, she went into the caves?"

"Some Silesian monks led her and her lover to the bodies the next day."

"Her lover?"

"Yes, your daughter has a partisan lover. His name is Giuseppe Valenti, but she calls him Beppo. She said they are very much in love."

He thought: *Maybe I can distract him by keeping him talking.* "You met this Beppo?"

"No, Teresa came alone. But she told me all about him."

"My daughter is with the GAP, you know. She took part in Via Rasella."

"That at least was a military strike. What I did to those French Algerians outside Monte Cassino was far worse. You and I both deserve to be struck down by the hand of God Almighty himself for what we've done." He dug the nose of the Luger into his temple, as if he had reconciled himself to his violent fate.

Feeling a surge of mortal fear and dread, Hollmann raised his voice in protest: "You can't do this, *Brüderlein*! There is no reason to kill yourself!"

Several of the other patients and a nurse had overheard, turned their heads, and were now staring at them fearfully. The hospital room went deathly silent.

"You're right, Brother. There is no reason to kill myself until I've done one thing first."

Slowly, he withdrew the nose of the pistol from his temple and pointed it at Hollmann.

"What are you doing, Walther?"

"Why should I be the only one to die when we both deserve it? I should just end things now for us both."

Hollmann had no doubt that he would follow through with his threat. His face carried the fanatical gleam of conviction of a true zealot. The war had unhinged him, made him snap. Or was it the curse?

Damn, he thought. *How am I going to get out of this?*

His brother started to squeeze the trigger.

Suddenly, the nurse screamed. Walther looked up.

Fearing for his life, Hollmann lunged for the pistol.

But his brother, despite his wounds, was quick and opened fire.

Hollmann dodged to his left and turned his cheek. But he was unable to escape the bullet. He felt a burning sensation along his face that brought back a sickening déjà vu of when he had been shot by his wife. But he knew right away that the damage was nothing like that terrible day. Because he had turned his face at the last second, the bullet had only grazed him. But the gunshot wound still burned like hell. Shaking off the pain, he lunged at his brother to wrestle the Luger away from him before he could get off a second shot, but there was no need.

His brother was pointing the pistol beneath his own chin.

"We are cursed, Brother. May God have mercy on our souls," he said, and he squeezed the trigger.

Hollmann saw his brother's head suddenly jerk back as if knocked by a boxer's punch and then a misty spray of blood, bone, brain, and tissue blew out from the back of his head and splattered onto the wall above his hospital pillow. The nurse screamed again as his body slumped onto the bed like a slab of beef. A small army of guards, doctors, nurses, and orderlies flew into the room to see what the commotion was about.

Hollmann felt his burning face. It all seemed familiar. He would never forget the scalding sensation from being shot in Innsbruck. It was like having acid poured on his face. But the difference this time was that it was only a minor facial wound and he would not require reconstructive surgery.

Damn you, Walther! How could you try to kill your own brother and then take your own life?

And then he realized he knew the answer. It was his destiny in this world not to be shot down by his wife or brother, but by one of his own children, by Gunther or Teresa. That was his designated punishment under the family curse, and he would never survive a third attack on his life.

The next time it would be Gunther or Teresa—or perhaps both—that would finish what the marchesa had started.

Only then would the family curse be no more.

CHAPTER 58

VATICAN CITY

JUNE 4, 1944

AT FIVE MINUTES PAST ONE A.M., Cardinal Maglione, the pro-American Vatican secretary of state, smiled as he stared down at the German occupiers fleeing the city under a brilliant full moon. He stood on the apartment balcony with Pope Pius XII, bedecked in brilliant fleece-white robes. They had been unable to sleep because of all the commotion in the city with the Allies on the doorstep of Rome. The streets were filled with marching footsoldiers, grim-faced collaborators, and a hodgepodge of conveyances. Official military trucks, tanks, and motorcycles vied for space in the massive retreating column with requisitioned cars, bicycles, horse- and ox-carts, and even street cleaners. The lengthy procession snaked its way through the Piazza Venezia, up the Corso, across the Ponte Milvio spanning the Tiber, and along the Via Cassia and the Flaminia, the consular roads that had carried the Legions of ancient times to triumph. In the foreground, just beyond St. Peter's Square where it yields to the Via della Conciliazione, Maglione saw German Tiger tanks grinding along the thoroughfare, in yet another violation by Smiling Albert of the Open City. But for the first time since the German Occupation began in September of 1943, there was a difference: all the traffic was going the opposite direction.

"They are leaving at last," said Maglione, as the night sky lit up with a pulsing glow and the clatter of booming artillery sounded in the distance. "Now perhaps the smiles will return to the faces of the children."

Pius's pallid, gaunt face remained expressionless. "Not so fast," he said, frowning at the sight of the flashes in the sky from the artillery shelling. "Only a portion of Kesselring's army is in retreat. No doubt he is leaving a considerable force behind to harass the Americans. But there is cause for rejoice: thanks to the Heavenly Father, the city has been spared from destruction and the Germans have agreed not to turn Rome into Stalingrad."

"Yes, but the Open City ploy is nothing more than a means for Kesselring to have an escape route for his reeling army, and to deny the Americans the use of the city as a base of operations," said Maglione. "The general and Ambassador Weizsäcker have been bluffing for the past two days. The Germans never had any intention of holding Rome to the last man and allowing it to be destroyed. The field marshal just wanted to keep that as an option to allow his troops to escape to Florence in the dark of night, as he is doing right now."

The Pope nodded but said nothing. He knew Maglione was right; the Germans had been duplicitous since the day Italy had surrendered.

"Kesselring is not just an able general, but a clever one. An hour ago when the Germans first started pulling out, everyone here at the Vatican, me included, still thought there would be a battle for Rome. Weizsäcker informed me just a few minutes before midnight that the German withdrawal was not imminent. And now look at those streets down there. They are packed with German soldiers and Fascists desperate to leave the city. Just look at them. Yesterday, they were strutting about like peacocks and wreaking unspeakable cruelty on all of Rome. Today, they have been burning documents, gathering their loot, and quietly skulking out of town. Or so I am told by our informants."

Again, the distant menace of heavy guns flashed across the moonlit sky. Pius stared down at the column of massive Tiger tanks rumbling down the road beyond St. Peter's Square. He shook his head in disgust. He thought: *So much death and destruction; so many lives wasted. And for what?*

Maglione said, "*Elefante* is the code word signifying the Allies entry into Rome. It was radioed from the BBC in London yesterday. The German rear guard is putting up stiff resistance south of the city, but the Americans are getting close."

Pius listened to the booming guns. "The German resistance cannot last with so many soldiers leaving. I should think the Americans will be here by tomorrow, or the day after at the latest. I just wish they would hurry."

"You fear that Rome will be in the hands of…irresponsible elements?"

"Yes, I do. Right now the largely Communist partisans are the most powerful military force in Rome—certainly more powerful than those hapless Germans down there on the streets stealing away in retreat. What is to keep the *Communista* from taking *de facto* possession of the city? The Germans appear to be leaving, but they are not gone yet."

"All the same, their reign of terror has ended and they are abandoning the city."

"Yes, that is true. It is a triumphant day for good over evil. It has taken an eternity but the day of liberation is at hand."

They fell into thoughtful silence. The Pope reflected on the Allies' policy of unconditional surrender towards Nazi Germany. Though he hated to admit it, he knew now that it had been the right decision. The fruits of the stubborn policy were plainly evident on the streets below: Hitler's defeated army slithering out of Rome. Only an hour into the exodus, Pius had already received detailed reports from his spies on the ground. The retreating Wehrmacht soldiers were wild-eyed, unshaven, unkempt, battered, and strangely quiet. There was no singing or attempt at military formation. They showed signs of the last two weeks of constant battle: the thousand yard stare, faces blackened with soot, uniforms stained with blood, the shambling gait with many hobbling along on crutches and dragging small ambulances packed with wounded. Whereas last September the Germans had brazenly goose-stepped their way into Rome armed to the teeth and singing songs, this time they looked like skulking dogs. How many of them, he wondered, still believed in the promise of Hitler's Thousand-Year Reich?

Maglione was looking at him.

"Do you regret, Your Eminence, not having been able to broker a peace between the Allies and Germany, or to have Rome declared a true Open City?"

His gaunt face assumed a wistful expression. "How could I not? Look at how much pain and suffering our Roman children have had to endure because of the Germans. And the Allies have not been blameless. Look what happened at San Lorenzo and Monte Cassino and all the other places where the Allies accidentally bombed our churches and artistic treasures. No side can claim the absolute moral high ground when it comes to war. War is an ugly thing. Unfortunately, it is the ugliness that resides in all men."

"Yes, war is a terrible thing. But there is no comparison between the Allies and the Germans and there never has been. The partisans have always said the Allies are our liberators—the Germans our destroyers. I think they are right, and we should never have treated them the same in the name of papal diplomacy."

"Yes, the Allies are our liberators. They spilled their blood to set us free here in Rome. But we had no choice but to remain neutral, or we would have put even more innocent victims of war in jeopardy. And in the end, Luigi, we did our part to defeat Nazi Germany here in Rome. We may have done it behind the scenes, but we were there all along, fighting beside the Allied Army."

He pointed towards the Tiber at the retreating Germans limping through the city like rats deserting a sinking ship, across ochre and amber roofs, to the Quirinale palace and the Campidoglio, and to the white Victor Emmanuel monument, symbol of the unification of Italy and the overthrow of papal temporal power.

"That is the result of our handiwork, as well as that of the Allies and God Almighty himself. Together, we have *all* driven out the barbarians."

"Yes, Your Eminence. This is our Altar of Resistance."

Again, they fell into thoughtful silence. Even though he had fought hard for Rome and its people, Pius knew he could have done more. He was supposed to be the *defensor civitatis*, but he knew in his heart he had not fully lived up to his title as the defender of Rome. In the name of papal silence, he had not protected all of Rome's citizens; some had been sacrificed so that the vast majority could live another day. But he could find comfort knowing that most of the Jews living in Rome had survived the German Occupation because of his direct efforts. He had intervened to halt the German deportations during the *razzia*. He had himself raised, or assisted in the raising, of substantial sums of money to aid in the relief of Jews wishing to escape Occupied Italy. He had given clear verbal instructions for the Vatican's properties to be opened to Jews, escaped POWs, and other war refugees, and for the convents and monasteries of Rome to provide hiding places as well as false identification papers. He did not know the exact numbers, but Tardini and others had told him that more than four out of every five Hebrews had escaped the original roundup and were still hiding out in Rome or outside the city.

But still. Four out of five wasn't enough. He wished he and the Church could have saved more. *Defensor civitatis*—and yet he had not been able to save many helpless women and children in their time of greatest need, not just in Rome, but in Poland, France, and the other occupied countries. Since the first day German tanks had rolled into the city, Hitler and his Nazis had made a mockery of him and forced him to abandon many of the moral principles he held dear.

He looked at Maglione. "I must confess to you, my old friend, that I cannot help but regret the silence. I know it has proven to be the best and only way when it comes to protecting people and saving lives, but it still pains my heart that throughout this war some people have had to be sacrificed for the greater good of the many."

"Do you wish you had spoken out more strongly?"

"Sometimes I think I should have stated at the beginning of the war that I would denounce all atrocities—whether from the Allies or Axis powers. This would have been no violation of the Lateran Treaty and our coveted neutrality. Such a public declaration would have given me the opportunity to speak out more strongly against the Germans for the simple reason that Nazi atrocities have always been a thousand times worse than those of the Allies."

"You would have been able to make the case that there is no moral equivalency between the Allies and the Axis."

"I believe so. It would have allowed me to be morally honest and declare what the Nazis and Russians have done is not the same as what the British and Americans have done."

"It sounds simple, but in practice it would not have been so easy. The Allies have begged you not to speak out about Stalin and the Soviet atrocities, so your hands are still tied."

He gave a heavy sigh. "It would appear that I cannot win. I am Hitler's Pope on the one hand—and the destroyer of Hitler and Nazism on the other. What a strange world we live in, Luigi, that a man can be two polar opposites at once in the eyes of his fellow man."

"But in the end, you know you have always been on the side of the righteous. You have always been on the side of humanity and the Allies."

Pius nodded, his liquid brown eyes taking on a puissant gleam as somewhere to the south a series of artillery shells exploded, sending flashes across the moonlit sky. He stared up in transcendent awe mingled with sadness at the full Roman Moon as the shells thundered in the distance. He hated this war, loathed it with all of his being. But somehow the sight of the full moon with the flashes of artillery beneath it was awe-inspiring. It was as if the Holy Spirit was telling him something.

"Yes, it is true that I have always fought for the Allied cause," he said, thinking about the irony. "But no one knows that, Luigi. And I don't know if they ever will."

CHAPTER 59

ROUTE 6 - VIA CASILINA
OUTSKIRTS OF ROME
JUNE 4, 1944

BRIDGER FELT THE WIND cuffing his face as he sped along the Via Casilina, the historic road that had once connected Rome to ancient Casilinum near modern-day Naples. With him in the open-topped half-track were General Frederick, his sister Teresa and her fellow partisan Beppo, the lead scout Sergeant Prince, two radio operators, and the general's aide and driver. In front of them, Forcemen clung to the decks of Howze's massive Shermans at the head of the advance column. Making up its snake-like tail were more tanks, trucks, and footsloggers from the Third Regiment.

Although he had hardly slept in the past week, Bridger felt a soaring feeling inside as they neared the Holy City of his youth and the Allies' single-minded obsession for the past nine months. From Commanding General Mark Clark on down, the whole Fifth Army had become infected with Rome fever as it pushed further and further up the Liri Valley and set its gaze on the shimmering dome of St. Peter's Basilica. Now the moment they had all been anticipating since stepping onto Italian soil was about to become reality.

They were going to take Rome, the first Axis prize of the war.

As the column rolled up to a big blue and white ROMA sign marking the city limits, Frederick called a halt. The tanks and trucks pulled up along the side of the road. Looking at his watch, he said to his aide, "Captain McCall, send the following message to headquarters. 'We entered Rome at 0620 hours.'" As the aide radioed the message, Frederick turned back towards Bridger and the others standing in the rear of the half-track.

"Looks like we're the first ones into Rome. What do you say to that?"

Bridger grinned. "I say it's been a long time coming. But it sure feels good."

"I think we can all agree on that," said Teresa. "But I don't think they do." She pointed ahead to a rear guard of perhaps three hundred German troops, a clutch of enemy tanks, and a heavy concentration of guns in a deep roadblock along the city's edge.

"Now those boys do look like they mean business," observed Frederick.

He immediately deployed the Howze Force tanks and his troops into battle positions as the Germans opened fire.

Within a matter of seconds, the lead tank was hit and a second was set afire by German anti-tank guns from behind a stone wall. The Force took cover in ditches and behind houses as the Shermans wheeled away and took evasive action into the fields. With Teresa, Beppo, and the Ojibwa scout Prince, Bridger moved forward with a reconnaissance patrol to ascertain the enemy's positions. But the wall of anti-tank, automatic weapons, artillery, and now sniper fire from the Germans concealed in the buildings and behind stone walls made it impossible to probe closer than fifty yards, and they were forced to turn back.

Peering through his binoculars, Bridger wasn't surprised to see that the rearguard element they were up against was their usual nemesis, the Hermann Göring Division, along with the 4th Parachute Division they had encountered in the past week. To his dismay, the scene quickly turned to a long, drawn-out infantry battle. The German resistance proved stout. The fighting raged on without visible progress as Frederick withheld ordering his artillery to blast loose the roadblock for fear of inflicting unnecessary casualties upon the civilians caught in the crossfire. It was unlikely that they would be securing the bridges over the Tiber today, thought Bridger with regret. Kesselring had left behind his two best divisions in Italy to protect the rear of the retreating Fourteenth Army.

An hour later, a convoy of two armored cars and six jeeps came driving up. From the vehicles tumbled out Generals Clark and Keyes to a flurry of salutes, along with four other officers and a phalanx of photographers and newsmen. To Bridger, the tall, photogenic Clark was the opposite of Frederick in every respect. His face was clean-shaven, his cap was set at an angle perfect for a photograph, his uniform was immaculate, and everything about him seemed fastidious. He was certainly no fighting general like the leader of the Devil's Brigade.

And right now he looked irritated.

"General Frederick," he inquired with Keyes, Commander of II Corps, standing next to him. "What's holding up the First Special Service Force?"

"There are strong rearguard posts to our front with tanks and artillery. And we've also got mines and snipers. I'm holding off our artillery until I know I won't be killing innocent civilians." He pointed to the map spread out on his jeep as the journalists and photographers crowded around them, flashbulbs began popping, and the newsreel crews began filming. "They're all over the area: old men, women, and children. I've called in aerial observation to clearly identify the German strongpoints so we can spare the civilians. But we're still sorting it all out."

"Well, I wouldn't hesitate to use the artillery if you need to," said Clark. "We can't be held up here too long."

"Yes, sir, I've already committed my reserve regiment to putting pressure on the roadblock," he said, again pointing to the map. "My other two regiments in the suburbs to the east are making an end run west into Rome with some tanks to get to the bridges over the Tiber."

"Sounds like a plan, but let's take a look and see what we're up against."

"Yes, sir, but keep your head down. These boys are shooters."

"Follow me, General, I know a safe route," said Bridger.

He led the high-ranking group up a low hill for a better view that afforded some protection from the enemy firing, which had slackened in the last few minutes. But along the way, a group of photographers and cameramen asked the trio of generals to pose for a picture beside the reflector-studded, blue-and-white road sign that read ROMA. Bridger glanced at Teresa and they both smiled: they knew that history was being made and they were part of it.

"What do you think, Bob? How about something to remember this occasion by?" asked Clark.

Bridger could see that Frederick would rather just get on with the job at hand, which was to attack the enemy and break the roadblock, but he humbly relented. After all, it was a historic occasion.

"Sure, General, why not?" he said.

The three generals stepped forward and posed under the huge sign with the big, bold letters to popping flashbulbs and rolling film cameras. It was a magnificent scene, and again Bridger and Teresa looked at one another and smiled.

When the photographers were finished, Bridger saw Clark turn to Frederick.

"You know what, Bob," he said, putting a bony-fingered hand on his shoulder. "I sure would like to have that sign in my command post. It would make a great souvenir. Will you get it for me?"

Seeing that his commanding officer was hesitant, Bridger quickly volunteered. "Oh, I'll get it for you, General."

He and the half-track driver started for the vehicle to get a hammer so that they could take down the sign. It was three feet tall by six feet wide and would take two people.

But Bridger hadn't taken two steps when a sniper's bullet blew through the metal face with a sharp bang. He stepped protectively in front of the trio of generals, making sure they took cover in the ditch before diving to the ground himself along with the gaggle of photographers and newsmen. The clatter of gunfire sounded again. Bridger heard a flurry of sharp pings against the sign and bullets whistling overhead as they all clung to the ditch. The shooting went on for several minutes until Bridger, with Teresa's help, led the three generals on all fours down the hill to a safer position two hundred yards away behind a shelled farmhouse.

As they rose to their feet and dusted themselves off, Frederick said, with obvious satisfaction, "That, General Clark, is what is holding up the First Special Service Force."

"That may be," said Keyes, "but we certainly don't want one little old popgun stopping us."

"I think it's a little more than that, General," said Teresa, looking proud and tough in her partisan's uniform. She wore the distinguishing armband of the Roman *Partigiani* that bore the green, white, and red of the Italian flag with the full name of the CLN spelled out around it. She didn't look the least bit intimidated in the presence of three American generals. "But I will help you get to your bridges tonight. You can count on it."

"Now there's a gal with spunk," said Clark, sizing her up and liking what he saw despite his bristling impatience to take Rome as quickly as possible on behalf of his beloved Fifth Army. "If I were you, Bob, I'd listen to her."

"I have been for the past two days, sir. She's my newest scout and Major Bridger's sister. She knows Rome like the back of her hand."

"Well good. Then she should have no problem leading you to those bridges tonight. We've got to get into Rome—and we've got to get in there tonight. In the meantime, I'm going back to Anzio."

"Yes, General," said Frederick, and he saluted.

Bridger watched as Clark climbed back into his jeep with his staff and bevy of journalists and photographers for the thirty mile drive back to the safety of Anzio. There would be no triumphant entry into the Eternal City this afternoon for the Commanding General of the Fifth Army that some disparagingly referred to as "Markus Clarkus."

As the general and his convoy headed south on Route 6, Frederick turned to Keyes. "Why the hell is he chomping at the bit so hard?"

"Well," said the general, "our boys are going to be invading France soon and we've got to take Rome before then. General Clark wants to get his name in the papers before the news is swamped out by the invasion of France. That's why we need a frontal assault down this damned road and we need it right away."

Bridger looked at Frederick. Good soldier that he was, he said nothing about how he felt about Clark's mania for self-publicity or being ordered by his superior officer Keyes to make a frontal assault. But his face said it all.

"We'll get to those bridges, General," said Bridger. "Teresa and I know another way into the city."

Frederick smiled. "Thank you, John. Maybe you and your sister should be running this army." He gave Teresa a little wink.

She returned the wink in kind. "No, General, I think it is you who should be running it."

"You think so, huh?"

"Yes, sir, I do. If you had been running this campaign from the beginning, the Allies would have taken Rome six months ago instead of today."

He raised a brow. "We're still not there yet."

"Yes, but you will be by tonight because we will show you the way."

CHAPTER 60

PONTE REGINA MARGHERITA, ROME

JUNE 4, 1944

BY DUSK, the German rear guard in the outer precincts melted away, and Bridger set out for the Tiber with Frederick and seven others in a half-track and radio jeep. With Teresa and Beppo acting as guides, they were part of a larger Force assault group whose objective was to secure as many of the bridges spanning the historic river as possible, if still intact, and to determine if they were wired with explosive charges. For those booby-trapped, the explosives were to be quickly defused to secure the bridges for heavy motorized crossings.

Within the city, little organized resistance remained except for snipers, scattered tanks and flak wagons, and a few recalcitrant strongpoints along the river. Although Rome was falling swiftly, Bridger saw at once that it was also turning into a bedlam of confusion. One minute, ecstatic Italians clogged the streets by rushing from their houses to offer gifts and deliver kisses to the American liberators; the next minute, they dashed back inside as Germans and Roman Fascists still sympathetic to the Nazi cause sniped away at the approaching Allies from concealed positions in the maze of alleys and streets.

They followed the Via Casilina until reaching Piazza di Porto Maggiore. Here they were slowed by a tipped-over oxcart and nest of snipers for several minutes. Then a window sash flew open, an excited voice shrieked, "*Americano! Americano!*" and Romans by the hundreds swept into the street despite the sniper fire. They quickly mobbed the half-track and radio car, as well as the stalled traffic behind them. Bridger looked at Teresa and Beppo and they laughed. It was like comedy opera. The road quickly became so congested with shouting and cheering Romans offering wine, plates of spaghetti, and kisses that they turned west and headed towards the Colosseum. When they passed the ancient gladiatorial arena, one of the Forcemen next to Bridger said, completely straight-faced, "My God, they bombed that too!" Everyone in the half-track laughed uproariously. From the Colosseum, they struck north towards Piazza del Popolo. Bridger noted the *S.F.Q.R.—Senatus Eopulusque Romanus*—proudly stamped on monuments and manhole covers all along the route. He remembered back fondly to the many childhood holidays he had enjoyed in the city and the four years he had lived in Rome as a teenager, and it felt as though he was returning home.

With Teresa and Beppo leading the way, they pushed on, ducking the occasional snipers, nudging their way through the hysterical crowds, and driving like bats out of hell whenever the road opened up. When they were forced to slow down or come to a halt, delirious Romans flung themselves at their vehicles. The *signoras* smothered them with kisses, offered bowls of hot shaving water, and handed them *vino* in glasses, in pitchers, in bottles, and even in kegs. Emboldened by the sight of the liberators, the Italian men swooped in with ancient rifles and red sashes, clapped their liberators on the back in tones of bibulous revelry, and stalked off with bravado in search of Germans and Fascists.

Just west of the Piazza del Popolo, they came to a stop at their destination. To his relief, Bridger saw, in the radiant Roman moonlight, that the triple arches of the Ponte Regina Margherita were indeed intact.

"All right, everybody out. Secure the bridge and check for mines," commanded Frederick to the team, before pulling Bridger and Teresa aside next to the half-track.

"What is it, sir?" asked Bridger, surprised.

"I know we have a mission to secure these bridges," said the general in a serious voice, addressing them both. "But you two also have another mission and that is to take your father into custody. That is if he's still around."

"Hold on, sir, now you want us to go get him? But before you said—"

"I know what I said, Major. But what if he hasn't left the city? If he's still here, it should be you two that arrest him for *Fosse Ardeatina*. He needs to be punished. You can take my jeep."

"And what if we don't want to arrest him?" asked Teresa.

"You can't just shoot him."

"Why not? After what he did, he deserves to die."

"No, he needs to be put on trial before the entire world for what he did at those caves. To kill him is to be just as bad as he is. Maybe he's fled north already, but maybe he hasn't. In any case, you two should be the ones to arrest him if he's still here."

"All right, sir," said Bridger, seeing the logic despite his and Teresa's desire to take justice into their own hands, "we'll go once we've secured the—"

His voice was cut off by a sharp staccato of machine-gun fire.

"Take cover!" shouted Frederick, and he dashed for the protection of a bridge support.

Across the dark river, Bridger saw another spurt of tracer fire from a German squad. The driver went down as a spray of bullets rattled against the side of the radio jeep and half-track. Bridger quickly dragged him behind the jeep then returned fire along with Teresa, Beppo, and several Forcemen, who had taken positions along the bridge and behind the vehicles.

The night sky above the triple arches of Ponte Regina Margherita lit up with tracer fire. The shooting roared and echoed across the Tiber. And then suddenly, Bridger saw a confused battalion from the 88th Division blunder into the scrap and start to open fire on their unit instead of the Germans.

"Jesus Christ, stop shooting!" he yelled, waving his arms so they could see him. "We're on the same fucking side!"

But they still failed to recognize that he and the others were friendlies. Now their unit was caught in a cross fire.

To his right, he saw Frederick empty the clip of his .45 at the Germans then go down as a bullet tore into his right thigh. Another pierced his right arm and then a third bullet entered just above his left knee. Sinking to the ground, he crawled along on one knee, leaving a trail of blood a foot wide behind him as he made his way for the protective cover of the bridge.

Bridger dashed out to help him, the bullets dancing at his feet, ricocheting off the pavement.

"I'm okay, I'm okay!" cried Frederick.

But Bridger didn't see how he could even move. He was bleeding badly from his shirt and pants. With the help of Teresa and Captain McCall, who quickly dashed forward, he pulled him to safety behind a half-track. Then he crept forward to a better position behind the jeep with his sister, and they opened fire on the Germans on the far side of the bridge. At the same time, the 88th, finally recognizing that they weren't the real enemy, unleashed a fierce suppressing fire at the Germans.

Bridger emptied his Tommy at the same time Teresa fired her Sten. He saw three Germans go down in the burst. Then to his left, he saw Lieutenant Mitchell's Third Regiment platoon coming up in reserve. The enemy swiftly withdrew, leaving behind several dead and badly wounded.

"Let's go—let's take the bridge!" he yelled to Mitchell.

With their total force now twenty strong, he, Teresa, and Beppo charged across the bridge. A dozen Germans threw up their hands in surrender and the bridge was quickly secured by Sergeant Chaffeur and another Forceman. Walking over the captured position, Bridger counted five German dead and six wounded.

"Wait, what about them?" said Teresa, pointing to the northwest.

Bridger looked up to see a group of over one hundred Italians in Fascist Blackshirt uniforms assembling up the street. They had gathered around an apparent leader who was berating the group in angry Italian. It looked as if the Italians were screwing up their courage for a counterattack.

"I believe you two should have the honor of showing your fellow Romans who the new sheriff is in town."

"It would be my pleasure," replied Teresa.

She and Beppo stepped forward, calmly pointed their machine guns at the wavering Fascists, and ripped loose with a round over their heads. The enemy broke and scattered to a man.

With the bridge secure and the enemy driven off, Bridger, Teresa, and Beppo returned to General Frederick. They found him praying over the fallen half-track driver, who bore a gaping gunshot wound in his shoulder. Bridger didn't know his name, but the young Canadian had attached himself to the Force without orders and had proven his worth more than once during the day's fighting. Frederick seemed to have taken a special liking to him.

"I'm sorry, General," said Bridger. He looked at the general's arm and leg wounds; he was a mess. "We've got to get you to a hospital. You're in bad shape."

"We shouldn't have rushed it, John," he said quietly, and Bridger saw that there were tears in his eyes. "We rushed into Rome and now boys like this have been killed unnecessarily. What a waste."

"I am sorry, General," said Teresa. "But all of Rome is grateful for what you have done. My people have been living like animals and dying in this city for months, and now you and your men have given us life again. All of Italy will never forget what you Americans and the rest of the Allies have done to liberate our city. You are heroes in the eyes of Rome."

"Thanks, I have to admit that makes me feel better. But we still shouldn't have rushed it all for the glory of a lofty few." He sighed heavily. "Oh well, you two don't want to hear me bitching any longer. Now what in the hell are you two still doing here? I thought I told you to go after that father of yours?"

"Sir, we need to get you to a hospital first."

"And the quicker the better," said a new voice. Bridger looked up to see a medic. "Those wounds needs to be cauterized and bound."

"I don't have time," said Frederick, and he rose to his feet unsteadily and started to hobble towards the bridge. "John, Teresa, what are you still doing here? Get in my damned jeep and go take Colonel Hollmann into custody, if he's still here that is. Now that's a goddamned order!"

"He's right," said Teresa solemnly. "We need to at least try." She turned to Beppo. "I'm sorry, but my brother and I have to do this alone."

"I understand," he said.

Frederick stopped hobbling and came to a halt. "If you do find him, you can't kill him. That, too, is a goddamned order. You must take him into custody."

"Sorry, but I can't promise anything," said Teresa, looking stubbornly at the Fighting General with the backdrop of the Roman Moon shining radiantly above the arches spanning the Ponte Regina Margherita.

"Neither can I, sir," said Bridger. Then to Teresa: "Come on, Sister, let's go."

CHAPTER 61

VILLA NAPOLEON

JUNE 4, 1944

STANDING ON THE BALCONY outside his office, Hollmann stared up at the luminous orb perched above the Holy City like a bright Christmas ornament. He recalled the legends of how, during the new and full moon, ancient Roman warriors had been protected by the gods. The ancients may have been protected, he thought reflectively, but his retreating German army certainly wasn't. He adjusted the bandage on his face from his gunshot wound. It still deeply saddened him that his younger brother had tried to kill him and then taken his own life in front of his eyes. Poor Walther. He had loved the man, and now this terrible war had ruined him and made him commit suicide.

It made Hollmann wonder if he even wanted to live anymore himself.

He looked down upon the streets below. All day long, he had observed from his balcony the long columns of soldiers, oxcarts, commandeered automobiles, motorcycles, and horse-pulled artillery pieces creaking up the narrow streets and highways of Rome. Hollmann knew there was no way the gods could possibly smile upon the rabble he saw shambling and hobbling in shamed silence through the historic city. The beleaguered Roman citizenry had actually been kind to the retreating soldiers, although they were immensely relieved to see them leaving. They gave them watered-down lemonade, wine, and cigarettes—but they had done so out of pity, not respect.

He pulled out his last Dunhill, lit it with his silver engraved SS lighter, took a long pull, and blew out a bluish-tinged cloud. A clatter of machine-gun fire could still be heard towards the Tiber to the west. The night sky was lit up by distant flashes of mortar and artillery fire, as well as dive-bombers chasing after the receding army. At Via Tasso, his nemesis Kappler still had dozens of prisoners locked away in cells. Minutes ago, Hollmann had informed him that tomorrow, once the liberators secured the city, the prisoners would have to be let go per General Wolff's orders. Giuliano Vassalli, the Resistance-fighter son of the Pope's friend, had already been released through the intervention of Wolff, who had made good on his promise to Pius and commanded Kappler to release the young Communist to the care of Father Pfeiffer.

Hollmann knew that he should have left Rome hours ago. But something—something deep inside him—made him stay.

"Father," he heard a familiar voice behind him say. It was the voice he had wanted—indeed had expected—to hear, and the person behind the voice was the reason he had stayed behind.

"I knew you would come," he said, turning around. "Oh"—he gave a little start—"I see you've brought your brother."

They were pointing submachine guns at him.

"Do you want to talk first?" he inquired mildly, blowing cigarette smoke through his nose. "Or would you prefer to just get it over with?"

They said nothing. He saw the hate in their eyes, but he could tell that they also still feared him and were a touch uncertain. Deep down, it hurt to see their loathing.

He stepped inside the room and gestured towards the chair at his desk. "May I sit down?"

His son nodded. "Just keep your hands where we can see them."

"Of course," he said gingerly. He took his seat and folded his hands on the desk as instructed. His Walther PPK lay within reach to the right on his desk; his daughter eyed it warily, but did not make any effort to take it away.

"We are here to arrest you," said his son, and they took a step forward and stood erect with their weapons leveled on his chest.

"No, you're not. You're here to kill me."

The noses of his son's Thompson and his daughter's Sten moved a little left until they were aimed directly at his chest. His daughter said, "After what you've done to my countrymen, you deserve to be shot down like a dog."

"Perhaps. But you should know before you shoot me that your mother was killed two days ago."

"We know. We found out yesterday. It was you who killed her, you bastard."

"I did nothing of the kind. In fact, I avenged her death."

"You signed her death warrant when you put her in Regina Coeli."

"I didn't put her in there. Kappler did. Because of you and your father Colonel Di Domenico, he claimed she was an enemy of the state and had her arrested. I protested, of course, but to no avail."

His daughter glowered at him. "Mother was no enemy of the state. You and Kappler don't know the first thing about the Resistance. Why you couldn't even catch me, your own daughter, you Nazi pig."

He said nothing, kept his gaze on the submachine guns pointed at him.

His son was looking at him. "How did you avenge Mother's death?"

"I killed the bastard who did it. I stuffed my pistol in his mouth and pulled the trigger—and I felt damned good when I did it, too. I may have my flaws, but loving your mother wasn't one of them. Eleven and a half years ago that woman tried to kill me, and yet I still loved her all these years. Now why is that?"

"You'll get no sympathy from me, you bastard," said Teresa. "You murdered my father. I saw you in March at the *Fosse Ardeatine*. You took the colonel from the truck, walked him into the cave at gunpoint, and murdered him in cold blood. He had nothing to do with Via Rasella—but I did."

"I know you did. And this may come as a shock to you, but I didn't kill your father, Teresa."

"Oh yes, you did. I saw you escort him into the cave and then I heard the shot."

"There was a gunshot, but it wasn't me who fired it."

"Then who was it?"

"It was your father. I gave him the honorable way out."

"The honorable way out? You mean he pulled the trigger himself?"

"He was the only one. I tried to have his life spared, but Mälzer and Kappler would not allow it. So I struck a deal with Kappler. He was coerced by higher authorities to see to the execution, and because of that, he said he was duty-bound to include the colonel on his list. I said that the only way he could be on the list was if he had the military honor of taking his own life. Quite frankly, after everything he had endured at Via Tasso, even Kappler was quite moved by him. He was a true officer and warrior. He deserved an honorable end, and unfortunately, that is all that I could get for him. I couldn't manage to have him set free, which is what he deserved. But I was at least allowed to let him die honorably. Your mother would have wanted it that way."

"You're lying. You're just trying to win over my sympathy so that you can save your own skin."

"No. What I am telling you is the truth, whether you like it or not."

"Even if it is the truth, you're still a Nazi pig who deserves to die."

She pointed the Sten at his face. His right hand reached for the top drawer, slowly.

"I wouldn't do that if I were you," said his son.

He reached in the drawer anyway and snatched up a white manila envelope.

Without the slightest hesitation, his daughter pulled the trigger. The bullets from the Sten whizzed within an inch of his right ear and shattered the glass window behind him, sending a racket into the Roman night.

But he didn't even flinch. After seeing his brother kill himself before his very eyes yesterday, there was no fear left in him.

Instead, he calmly raised his hands above the desk where they could see them. He still clutched the envelope.

"What is that piece of paper that you would risk your life for?" asked his son.

"It is my final will and testament. I had a lawyer draft it up today. I have left everything to you two children. All of my property and money. When you add it all up, it's quite a tidy little sum. Over two million of your American dollars, Major Bridger."

"We are not your children," snapped Teresa.

"Perhaps not now. But you once were."

"You are not and never were my damned father."

His son held up a hand. "That's enough, Teresa. We need to take him in."

"Not a chance," she said stubbornly, her hands tightening on the Sten. "You'll have to shoot me first."

"We're not going to shoot him down like an animal. That's exactly what the Nazis would do."

"I don't give a damn. He may not have murdered my father, but he still played a role in the killing of more than three hundred people at *Fosse Ardeatine*. And the rounding up, torture, and deportation of hundreds more since last October's roundup. Those people were innocent and he killed them. He needs to pay for his crimes."

"I believe you are confusing me with Colonel Kappler. You wouldn't be the first person to do that, my dear."

"You may not be a Kappler, but you still need to pay for your crimes."

"And he will pay," said Bridger. "But not like this. We're better than this, Sister. We're better than"—he looked at his father—"them."

Hollmann clapped his hands together, simulating applause. "Bravo, my son. That was quite a performance. You Americans are certainly the embodiment of perfection and we Nazis the personification of evil. That must be why your Negroes are lynched from trees in Alabama and your slant-eyed Japanese-Americans have been imprisoned behind barbed wire in the American West. Because you are such perfect people."

"Shut the fuck up, or I'll shoot you myself."

"Go ahead and get on with it then. What are you two waiting for?"

He watched as his daughter frowned coolly. "He's twisting everything around. We need to just get it over with and shoot him."

"We're better than this Teresa. I've been killing Germans for the past six months and I'm tired of it. We need to take him in."

"There is another way," said Hollmann, saddened to see that his children he had always loved, and loved still, had turned into the almost unrecognizable creatures he now saw before him. Unfortunately, that was what war did. It made rational people make irrational decisions, forced good people to become bad, and turned people and families against one another. Even already broken families like his. On some level, he knew, there were no winners, only losers, when it came to war. Somehow everyone lost, including his own children.

"What is the other way?" asked Bridger.

"A soldier's death with a pistol." He looked at Teresa. "Like I gave your father."

Her eyes blazed like her mother's. "Not a chance. I don't trust you."

"Don't you understand, Teresa? I stayed behind so you could catch me. I want to atone for my sins on behalf of the Reich. But I also want you two to know about your inheritance and for my end to be a soldier's end."

"You don't deserve a soldier's end. You're nothing but a common murderer."

"As I told you, I murdered no one." He looked at his son, appealing to him with his eyes. "If you ever loved me, the least you can do is honor my last will and testament by taking the money and allowing me to die a soldier's death. Then this old Jew will be no more."

"Jew? What are you talking about, Jew?" demanded Bridger.

"That's what I thought. Your mother never told you."

"Told us what?" asked Teresa.

"The reason she wanted to leave me and take you children away from me. And later, when I refused, the reason she tried to kill me. You mean you truly don't know?"

His son and daughter looked at one another. "No, neither of us knows what you are talking about," said Teresa.

"My grandmother, who died before you were born, was Jewish. Your mother didn't want you children to suffer persecution for being Jewish because of your grandmother. That is why she became so desperate and tried to kill me. It was for you."

"You're lying! This is a trick to deceive us!" cried his daughter.

"No, it is the truth. Your mother told me at Regina Coeli Prison."

"Why should we believe you?" asked Bridger. "You have no proof."

"My lawyer in Vienna has the proof. As the chief of the Innsbruck police and a Nazi Party member, I was able to get hold of the family records of both Walther and I and have them replaced before the racial laws came into effect. Walther and I joined the Nazi Party before Hitler rose to power. Your uncle and I weren't 'Septemberlings.' That's the Nazis' derogatory term for those who didn't join the party until after Hitler took office following the successful elections in September 1930. So Walther and I were above suspicion to begin with. But we wanted to be assured of being safe, so I took advantage of my Nazi Party and police chief status and purged the records for the both of us. And yet, that still wasn't good enough for your mother or her domineering father. They didn't want to take the chance that my dirty little secret would be discovered. So she tried to kill me."

"My God," gasped his son. "So that's why she shot you? Because you had Jewish blood?"

"She knew I would have been classified as a *Miscalling*, a hybrid. A person not classified as a Jew, but who has some Jewish blood. I was a *Miscalling* of the second degree because I had only one Jewish grandparent. But that still would have officially barred me from continuing on as chief of police, and I would have been excluded from most professions, all political organizations, and any position as a military officer in the event of war. Nazi officials considered plans to sterilize *Miscalling*, although it was never done. As it has turned out, all *Miscalling* in Germany, Austria, and elsewhere have been incarcerated in slave labor camps or deported to death camps. The racial laws became effective in 1935, so your mother accurately foresaw the risk. She could see the future, and to be honest, I can't blame her for what she did. If I had been in her shoes, I would very likely have done the same thing to protect you children."

They both just looked at him. Now he could see that they felt pity for him. Seeing pity on their faces made him want to die even more.

"The simple truth is I have nothing left to live for. I am not really Jewish, and Germany is going to be turned into a country of peasants. Your mother is dead and my brother Walther committed suicide yesterday before my eyes. And you two want to either lock me away in prison or see me hang. What's the point in going on?"

His daughter licked her lips, staring at him hard. "Uncle Walther is dead. But I just saw him two nights ago at the hospital. He was alive."

"Well, he is dead now. He took a shot at me, and then he shot himself. Why do you think my face is covered with this bandage? Why don't you allow me to say goodbye to you and then let me die a soldier's death. All hope is gone for me."

"You really want to die?" asked Bridger. He looked at his sister. "Maybe he does deserve that much, Teresa."

"After *Fosse Ardeatine*, I don't think so."

"Rome is under American occupation now. If he wants a soldier's death then I think he should have it."

The room went deathly silent. He stared intently at his daughter as she trained the muzzle once again on his chest. Keeping his eyes on the Sten, he slowly raised his hands above his shoulders.

"All I am asking for is to die the same way as your father, Teresa. I do not ask for forgiveness, but I do want you both to know that I love you. I have loved you since the first day I held you in my arms. And I will never forget either of you—even if I am condemned to hell in the afterlife. Which I no doubt will be on account of the curse."

His daughter said nothing, didn't move a muscle. And then a slight nod of the head. "All right, go ahead. But don't try anything funny."

"Use your pistol," said his son.

"Yes, of course," he said softly. He reached across the desk and carefully removed his nine-millimeter from his death's-head holster.

Then he placed the nose of the pistol directly under his chin, as his brother Walther had done, so that the bullet would enter just above his Adam's apple and blast upward directly into his brain.

"Goodbye, my children. I am sorry for everything that has happened. I will always love you," he said.

Looking them in the eye, he imagined them when they were both young and idolized him. Those had been the best years of his life, he reflected fondly. He felt tears coming to his eyes.

Suddenly, his son held up his hands. "No, wait!" he cried. "We can't let him do this!"

"No, he needs to pay for his sins!" protested Teresa.

"We just need him to surrender. He could work for the Allies in intelligence. He's a senior officer in the SS for crying out loud. And more importantly, he has Jewish blood. So do you and me, Teresa."

He turned his Thompson on her.

Her mouth fell open. "You would shoot me? Your own sister? I knew we were cursed, Brother, but this? Why you're just as much of a devil as he is."

"It has to end, Teresa. It all has to end right here and now."

He lowered his weapon and looked at his father. "Put the gun down. Please, Father, just put it down."

Hollmann felt tears rolling down his cheeks. He wanted to reach out and hug them both. His beautiful children that he had always loved and had never stopped loving.

"We're a family, goddamnit," said his son. "And families have to stick together. You're going to surrender to us, Father, and you're going to do it right now. There is no fucking family curse. It's Hitler and the war, goddamnit. That's what has changed us all and turned us away from what is right. Goddamn Hitler! We can choose to be whatever we want to be. There's nothing holding us back but our own fears and prejudices. There is no curse, and there never was one!"

Hollmann looked at his daughter, who was still pointing the Sten at him. Her lips trembled and he saw a hint of tears in her eyes.

"We have to do this, Teresa! We are—all of us—better than this! There is no family curse and we are better than Hitler and the goddamned Nazis! All of our suffering is because of him! But this can't go on! The persecution and killing and dying has to stop! And it has to stop right now! For our family, it ends right here and now, goddamnit!"

The room came to a standstill. Hollmann carefully laid his pistol on his desk and stared at his daughter, surrendering himself before her, giving himself up to her mercy. Looking at her with her mouth taut and the Sten pointing straight at him, he saw his life pass before his eyes.

The anxious seconds ticked down.

"You're right," she said finally. "A family has to stick together. Especially in times like these. Will you surrender to us, Father? Can you promise to try and become good and help the Allies win this war?"

"Yes," he said. "I am yours, my children."

"Good," she said, lowering her weapon. "There just may be hope for all three of us after all."

CHAPTER 62

ST. PETER'S SQUARE

JUNE 5, 1944

ON MONDAY JUNE 5, THE OFFICIAL DAY OF LIBERATION, church bells rang all across the Holy City and the Roman people rejoiced and sang and shouted, "The Americans are here! The Americans are here!" The triumphant Fifth Army rolled into town like the Legions of old—creating a joyous wall of sound that cleansed the air of the roar of dive-bombers, machine guns, mortars, and artillery. Jubilant Romans filled the streets all the way from Porta San Giovanni to the Spanish Steps, from San Lorenzo to St. Peter's Basilica, providing a crescendo of human voices on every street corner and alleyway. More than a quarter million people were expected to gather at the Vatican later in the day to celebrate the momentous occasion. During the afternoon, placards in Italian were posted and handed out door-to-door that cried, "Come to St. Peter's at six o'clock to thank the Pope." Adults and children alike had motored all around the city in loudspeaker trucks broadcasting the heartwarming message.

After visiting Frederick at the field hospital and bivouacking late last night in the Roman suburb of Tor Sapiens, Bridger secured a pass and spent the day with Teresa and her lover Beppo. They navigated through the haunts of their youth, helping her locate missing friends, and assisting with the transition of power to the Allies. With the streets and piazzas jammed with monstrous crowds, they proceeded at a snail's pace in his requisitioned officer's jeep. Wherever they went they were cheered, applauded, and showered with roses. Bridger was genuinely moved as old men grabbed and kissed his hands, women sobbed tears of joy, and little girls and boys waved impromptu American flags and ran along the jeep cheering and yelling, *"Viva gli Americani!"*

Everywhere he went the newly liberated Italians cheerfully posed the question to him and his fellow dogfaces: *"We are so happy to see you at last. Why did it take you so long?"* But he didn't have an answer for them, at least not yet, so his stock reply was, "Well, we're glad to be here now!" He made sure to underscore his response with a big, old Yankee grin.

He was surprised to learn from his sister that Rome's civilian population had expected the Allies to roll right into Rome within days after the Anzio landings back in January, more than four months ago; and that, when the Allies had become bogged down on the beachhead, the whole city had become severely depressed.

But the one thing he did know was that today—the day of liberation that he had looked forward to for months—was a great day for the world.

It was a great day for the beleaguered Romans who had endured so much hardship and brutality at the hands of the *Nazifascisti*; for the Pope who had done so much to protect the beloved city of his birth and help so many Romans despite being caught in the middle of an inhumane war; for the U.S. Fifth Army, British Eighth Army, and all of the other Allied forces that had slogged from Salerno to Rome, fighting off freezing snow and rain and rugged mountains and Anzio Annie and Stuka dive-bombers and Screaming Meemies and SS death squads as well as Kesselring's crack Wehrmacht troops; for the partisans like Teresa who had fought bravely to redeem Italy's honor and drive out the German occupiers; and for the tens of thousands of Allied soldiers who had been wounded and crippled and had never made it to the Eternal City to witness firsthand this historic moment.

As a representative of democracy, decency, and success, Bridger felt like he and Teresa had accomplished something great. The heartfelt adulation of the Italian people stirred something deep inside him, and he knew his sister felt it too. From the depths of despair and starvation, the Romans were now delirious with hope for the future. Because of him and his kid sister the Resistance fighter, and other men and women like them.

But he also felt a sense of loss. His mother and stepfather were dead, and so was his uncle Walther whom he had at one time cared about deeply. He had lost hundreds of fellow Forcemen, many of whom he knew well, in the bloody battles from La Difensa to Rome. Many of them he had seen killed in action before his very eyes. When he thought about all the death and suffering, when he reflected upon all those he had loved and cherished on both sides, the joy he felt inside at the liberation was offset by a profound feeling of loss.

At 5:15 that afternoon, Bridger and Teresa were escorted by Father O'Flaherty to the rooftop of the British legation so they could view the Pope's six o'clock speech. Wearing civilian clothing to preserve the guise of Vatican neutrality, they mingled, drank champagne, and ate hors d'oeuvres with the monsignor, Sir D'Arcy Osborne, Major Sam Derry, and several prominent Italian political refugees who had been given shelter in the Vatican through the Escape Line for Allied POWs, Jews, and other Nazi enemies during the past six months.

Still battle-fatigued and with his stomach still shrunken from emergency rations, Bridger felt a bit out of place and overwhelmed by the whole experience. The atmosphere of old-world English courtliness and all the attention lavished upon him by Sir D'Arcy and his guests made him feel uncomfortable, as if he had to be on his best behavior. But after two glasses of champagne and some canned sardines and crackers, he felt himself loosen up and his stomach felt better. He and Teresa joked and laughed and he politely answered questions about the Devil's Brigade. Everyone wanted to know about the legendary outfit, the first Allied unit to reach Rome, and all the battles it had fought from Monte La Difensa to the Eternal City. He was, once again, glad that he had his sister by his side even if he had lost so many others to crippling wounds and death. And he was also glad that he and Teresa had done the right thing for their father. Colonel Hollmann had officially surrendered himself to Bridger at precisely 2147 hours last night and was being held at the makeshift German officer's POW camp at Tor Sapienza.

ψψψ

At six p.m., a ceremonial draping was thrown over the parapet of the central balcony and the great bell of St. Peter's ceased to toll. Pope Pius XII, the defender of Rome, stepped forward to the roar of the crowd of three hundred thousand strong.

Wearing his snow-white skullcap and robes, he felt the sacrosanct power of the moment and the momentous energy of his beloved Roman children. He waited to soak it all in before speaking, calmly basking in the adulation and then raising his hand to silence the crowd. This moment did not belong to him, he knew, but to everyone that had sacrificed in the long, terrible battle for the liberation of Rome. Looking down at the packed square and beyond the skyline of the Holy City, he had never witnessed a more epic or majestic scene in his entire life.

Torrents of sunlight slanted across the great dome of the Basilica and lent a golden hue to the sea of humanity below. With all of the Italian and American flags—as well as the banners of the Monarchists, Communists, Socialists, Christian Democrats, and other parties that on this special day had come together as one—it looked to him like a garden in full bloom. Stubbly-faced soldiers in dusty, olive-drab battle-dress were sprinkled throughout the massive crowd, looking on in boundless wonderment. The multifarious crowd seemed to shimmer in the late afternoon's transcendent glow.

When the square had quieted, the Vicar of Christ spoke, his high-pitched but resolute voice rising up from the amplified microphone.

"On this historic day for Rome and the world, yesterday's fear has been replaced by today's new hope."

Though the crowd had been quieted only seconds before, the people were so exultant that they let loose with a roar of approval.

"Instead of unimaginable destruction Rome has been granted salvation."

The crowd cheered again.

"The Eternal City has been saved by divine mercy inspired by the intent of both belligerent parties to seek peace not affliction."

St. Peter's Square thundered with cries of support.

"I would like to thank God, the Trinity, and Mary, Mother of God, for saving all of us Romans. I bow before the Apostles Peter and Paul for protecting the city in which they, too, have impregnated its soil with the sweat and blood of their martyrdom."

Again, the crowd cheered and this time he had to hold up his hands to quiet the people.

"I call on all Romans to put aside their thirst for vengeance and strive for brotherly love. I urge you all to forget any thoughts of retaliation and reach out to those who have been your enemies."

Again, his heartfelt words delivered over the microphone brought a crash of applause.

Now, he raised his hands in a heavenly appeal.

"*Sursum corda!*" he cried. "Lift your hearts!"

The crowd kneeled before him and cheered.

"May the Holy Father bless you, one and all!" he said in conclusion, and he turned and disappeared from the balcony in a wake of white silks.

As a great roar rose up from three hundred thousand throats, the Supreme Pontiff—Roman-born Eugenio Pacelli—was so moved he wanted to cry. He loved Rome. He loved its people, Jew and Gentile alike, and he admired them for their sacrifice under the horrific German Occupation. He also wished, in his heart of hearts, that he had done more for them in their hour of greatest need. But most importantly, he wished he had succeeded in eliminating Hitler for them and for all of humanity long before this historic day of June 5, 1944. Then the people of the world wouldn't have had to endure so much suffering.

But at least the new plot was still in play. Stauffenberg was set to strike any day now.

He looked at his fellow secret agent, Father Leiber, codenamed Gregor, at his elbow. They were alone. "What did you think?"

"It was a great speech, Your Eminence. Very much to the point."

"You know what I was thinking the whole time?"

"What, Your Eminence?"

"I was thinking to myself in German, *Wir gedenken des Führers, uns zu entledigen.*"

The Jesuit priest nodded and repeated the words in English in a conspiratorial voice. "'We are thinking of the Führer, that we may be rid of him.' Somehow, after Colonel Stauffenberg's most recent communication, I thought you would say that, Your Eminence."

"Come, Father, let's talk in my study," said the Chief. "Rome has been liberated, but there is still much work to be done. Much work to be done indeed."

ψψψ

As the Pope disappeared from the balcony and the crowd roared its approval, Bridger looked at Teresa. Seeing the tears streaming down her face, he felt the stirring power of Pius's words. After months of grueling fighting and agonizing anticipation, he and his sister both felt awe in the presence of such splendor, pageantry, and sense of spectacle and theater.

He could have felt bitterness that the Pope had thanked his "side" only, while commending the evil Nazis as much as the Allies. He could have felt outraged that Pius had given all the credit to God, the Trinity, Mother Mary, and the Apostles Peter and Paul for saving Rome instead of the Allies and the Roman Resistance that had actually liberated the city. He could have felt angry that the defender of Rome had not acknowledged what was plainly evident: that it was the Allied boots and tanks on the ground and planes in the air that had driven the hundreds of thousands of German soldiers out of Rome and ultimately spared the sacred city. And he could have been outraged that the Pope had made no mention of the hard-fighting partisans that had, in a supporting but still crucial role, tied up German divisions at critical times, harassed their relief columns, and provided crucial intelligence to thwart the Nazi war machine and thus save Rome.

Bridger could have been deservedly angry about all of these things. But instead, the veteran warrior didn't care.

Pope Pius XII could give all the credit for saving Rome to God and the others if he wanted to. After all, after being flouted, manipulated, deceived, and strong-armed by the Nazis on countless occasions during the past nine months, the Pope was to be applauded for simply surviving and saving countless lives during the conflict. It was all right with Bridger if the cheering masses in the square below credited Pius with leading the effort to liberate the city when, in actuality, it had been the hard-fighting black devils and dogfaces, supported by the partisans, that had won the day for all Romans. After all, the people of Rome needed their own hero to believe in. What mattered most was that the Pope had, without question, made a difference in the Allied war effort. As Teresa had made clear to him, the Pope had stood by his people in their time of crisis and not abandoned them like the Italian king and his royal circle; and he had personally opened the doors of the Church to any and all war refugees.

That was worth something. In fact, it was worth a lot.

He looked at Teresa. "What do you think, Little Sister?"

She wiped the tears from her eyes. "It was deeply moving. But I think that, by omission, he took a lot of credit for what you and your army did."

"And what *you* and *your army* did as well."

"Yes, but that is to be expected. We're the 'irresponsible elements' as the Supreme Pontiff is so fond of calling us. But I don't care. What matters most is Rome is free, free at long last."

"You're right, that is what matters most."

He reached out and hugged her. With smiles on their faces, they stared down at the ebullient crowd, still cheering above the glittering dome of the basilica.

"I am happy for you." He then nodded towards the crowd. "And I am happy for them. They deserve this moment."

"It has been a long time coming."

"Yes, it certainly has. But I am most happy for you and me. We made the right decision to spare father's life and take him into custody. And one day, when this terrible war is over, I hope you and I can see him and be a family again."

"Believe it or not, I hope so too."

"What a remarkable day. I believe a celebration is in order."

They looked up to see Father O'Flaherty, wearing his friendly Irish smile, Sir D'Arcy, the British officer Sam Derry, and a pair of gaunt, noble-looking Romans that no doubt had been hiding out in the Vatican like countless others during the German Occupation.

"Yes, my good monsignor, a celebration is certainly in order," said Sir D'Arcy, looking spry and dapper in his dark tailored suit. "There is ample champagne up here on the roof if you want to stay, but I feel it only fair to warn you that my personal valet Mr. May has reserved the extremely good stuff in my quarters downstairs. What do you say?"

Bridger smiled. "I like it up here, Minister. I'm going to have to go back to the killing fields up north tomorrow, so if you don't mind, I'd like to stay up on this here rooftop for a while longer and not have to think about the war."

That quieted everyone. "Yes, of course," said Sir D'Arcy soberly.

"Sorry, I didn't mean to spoil the festive atmosphere. I just think it's beautiful up here."

"Indeed it is," said Major Sam Derry. "How about a toast to the liberation of

Rome then?"

"Hear, hear!" echoed Sir D'Arcy and Father O'Flaherty.

Bridger smiled. Everyone except the monsignor, who didn't drink, raised their champagne glasses. Then they all gave a little cheer.

When the voices died down, the elderly Italian gentleman standing next to Sir D'Arcy said, "By the way, Major Bridger, I've been meaning to ask you one thing."

He smiled politely. "Yes, what is it?"

"Well, we are all, of course, overjoyed to see you. But why did it take you so long?"

Staring at the shimmering golden dome of St. Peters, Bridger thought back to the long, hard road to Rome: to all the rain and mud; to the grim cobalt skies and forbidding ridges and ghostlike clouds that unveiled and then quickly concealed the enemy; to the nighttime raids and long chess match with the Hermann Göring Division at Anzio; and finally to the breakout and taking of the first Axis capital. Then he looked at Teresa. When she smiled at him, he knew the answer.

And it could be only one thing.

"Because so many of us died to set you free," he replied, thinking of General Robert Tyrone Frederick, the Devil's Brigade, and everyone that he had lost along the way to the Eternal City of Rome. "That's why we took so long, sir. Because so many of us died to set you free."

And with that, he and Teresa smiled at one another again, and he thought of his father. Despite this terrible war and their dreadful past in Austria, he hoped—truly hoped—that one day the three of them could put it all behind them.

And be a family once again.

AFTERWORD

In the eyes of historians, novelists, and the public at large, the battle for Rome and Italian Campaign of 1943-1945 has long been eclipsed in importance by the Nazi Occupation of Poland and France and the Normandy D-Day invasion. Yet, the Italian Campaign was the only theater of operations that included a major world leader, Pope Pius XII, caught up not only in the middle of the fighting but in the midst of a Nazi occupation; and it involved the most diverse assemblage of nationalities and differing races among the Allied and Axis armies during WWII. The Italian Campaign—or the *Guerra di Liberazione* (War of Liberation) as Italians prefer to call it—included not only Americans (including Native-Americans, African-Americans, Hispanic-Americans, and Japanese-Americans), British, and Germans in the fighting, but also Italians (on both sides), Austrians, Yugoslavians, French, Moroccans, Canadians, New Zealanders (whites and Maori), Poles, Norwegians, Nepalese, Indians (all faiths), South Africans (white, Asian, black, Zulus), and in the air forces, Australians, Rhodesians, and others. The war in Italy was a truly multinational and multiracial affair in a truly global war.

It was also supremely bloody, with some of the most furious fighting of the war and over a million total casualties, including more than 300,000 Allied and 500,000 German casualties and over 150,000 Italian civilians killed, including partisan fighters like the fictitious Teresa Di Domenico in the novel. When the remnants of the First Special Service Force were examined by unit physicians in early June 1944 after taking Rome, the doctors reported that the men in the vaunted Devil's Brigade were "listless, perilously close to exhaustion, and infested with lice." There is a reason that the American troops in Italy were called "dogfaces" and that historian Eric Morris's seminal book on the Italian War of Liberation is titled *Circles of Hell, The War in Italy, 1943-1945*. Ernie Pyle, the legendary U.S. war correspondent who lost his life during WWII, captured the fighting thusly: "Few of us can ever conjure up any truly fond memories of the Italian campaign. The enemy had been hard, and so had the elements." The late great Audie Murphy, Hollywood actor and one of the most decorated American combat soldiers of the war, fought at Sicily, Anzio, and the battle for Rome. It should come as no surprise that his autobiography is entitled *To Hell and Back* and he suffered from post-traumatic stress disorder, slept with a loaded handgun under his pillow, and looked for solace in addictive sleeping pills. After the long, grinding battle that finally resulted in the liberation of the Eternal City, Murphy deflatedly recalled, "We prowl through Rome like ghosts, finding no satisfaction in anything we see or do. I feel like a man reprieved from death; and there is no joy in me."

The road to Rome was indeed a hard one. But, as history has shown, there was a damned good reason for the fighting. The Allied conquest of the Mediterranean wasn't merely a notch on the tomahawk for taking the war's first Axis capital and a city of great strategic importance for its roads, rail lines, and airfields. The liberation of Rome was of immense psychological value as well and broke the offensive power of Hitler's Reich once and for all, forcing Nazi Germany to fight thereafter on the defensive without any hope of victory. But for the "black devils" and "dogfaces" on the killing fields, there was an even more important reason to wage war on Italian soil: to fight for democracy and stomp out totalitarianism. As a Japanese-American soldier with the 100th Battalion wrote from Italy: "I really belong to the great American Army here and feel that I am part and parcel of the forces that are fighting for the kind of America we always dreamed of back home." When the Allies took Rome, the normally war-weary Ernie Pyle reflected sublimely upon the moments of "overpowering beauty, of the surge of a marching world, of the relentlessness of our fate." Ultimately, the Allied liberators and Italian partisans fighting alongside them were fighting for something loftier than just freedom from the yoke of Nazi repression. They were fighting for freedom and decency and democracy itself—and they damn well knew it.

Humanity should never forget the sacrifices of the heroes who helped liberate Rome and fought in the Italian Campaign, and we should especially resist the temptation to consider Italy a backwater to the glitz and glam of Overlord and Normandy. This book pays tribute to the Allied soldiers of all nationalities and the Italian partisans who fought the good fight in Italy; and to Pope Pius XII and the members of the Catholic Church that risked everything to save countless Jewish and non-Jewish lives. Despite some of the perceived imperfections, in the eyes of history, of Pius, the Vatican, the Roman partisans, and the Allied historical figures depicted in this novel, they are all heroes in my view for taking a stand against Hitler and Nazism.

Below I tell the story of what became of some of the important historical figures (on both sides) presented in this novel following the liberation of Rome and end of the war.

Pope Pius XII (Eugenio Pacelli, the Chief) and the Vatican

The Pius Wars began in earnest in 1963 when playwright Rolf Hochhuth released his controversial drama *The Deputy,* portraying Pope Pius XII as a cold-blooded hypocrite who remained silent about the Holocaust. Since that time, the Bishop of Rome has remained a controversial figure with outspoken supporters and detractors. As has been made apparent since the beginning of this book, this author takes neither side. I treat him critically and at the same time with some degree of admiration, emphasizing both his perceived failings by those who worked closest with him (Leiber, Maglione, Osborne, and Dalla Torre) and his deep involvement in the plots to remove Hitler from power and his heroic efforts, behind the scenes, to rescue the persecuted during the war.

Pope Pius XII's valiant efforts to eliminate Hitler and save lives must always be weighed against the one great indictment against him. As stated by Robert A. Ventresca, author of *Soldier of Christ*, the most comprehensive and balanced biography of the Pope, "Perhaps no failure—personal or pastoral—was greater than Pius XII's inability or unwillingness to lend his singular authoritative voice to arouse the individual and collective conscience in a humanitarian defense of European Jews before and during the war.... This is not to say that he was anti-Semitic or hard-hearted in the face of the catastrophe that befell Jews and others during World War Two. We know that he was neither of these things. It was simply that he failed to appreciate how a word from the foremost spiritual leader of the Christian world could serve as a powerful symbol and practical impetus for action during the war, and for atonement and reconciliation after."

The historical record is clear enough on Pius to conclude that he was a heroic yet flawed religious leader who guided the Catholic Church during an extremely perilous time. From that perspective, he was perhaps no better or worse than Franklin Delano Roosevelt or Winston Churchill. For all of his greatness, Roosevelt will forever be tarnished for unfairly interning Japanese-Americans, not speaking out early enough against German oppression of Europe's Jews, and his failure to perceive, or not take seriously enough, the full extent of the post-war threat of Stalin and Soviet Communism. Similarly, the legendary Churchill is remembered not just for uniting his great country during time of war, but for his loose tongue regarding top-secret intelligence matters, his meddlesome and opinionated personality, and for putting Britain's stodgy imperialism and pride ahead of the Allied war effort, as shown by his obsession with the Mediterranean theater and Balkans and his overzealous promotion of British Generals Montgomery and Alexander. Meanwhile, Pius has his supposed "silence" regarding Nazism and the Holocaust while being fixated on halting the spread of Soviet Communism; and his potential indifference towards, or at least inexcusable lack of knowledge of, what U.S. intelligence referred to as the Vatican "Rat Line" that allowed post-war Nazi and Ustaši war criminals to escape justice and flee to South America. When you consider the facts about each of these three larger-than-life figures, the reality is inescapable: they were—all three of them—flawed yet great men. In the time of the greatest war and moral crisis the world has ever known, they all united their people and stood up against Adolf Hitler and the Nazi war machine in their own unique way. Maybe Pius could have done more, but anyone with an ounce of fairness in them surely agrees that he should be recognized at least as much for what he actually *did* during the war as for what he *didn't do* or what he *should have done*.

For all of his flaws, Eugenio Pacelli was most certainly not "Hitler's Pope." When it comes to Pius XII, there are five critical numbers—40, 55, 3, 4,000, and 85—that every historian and writer needs to acknowledge first and foremost in their assessment of the man. The first number, 40, is the number of speeches Eugenio Pacelli gave in Germany as papal nuncio between 1917 and 1929 that unambiguously denounced Hitler and the emerging National Socialist ideology. The second number, 55, is the number of official protests Pacelli lodged with Hitler and the Nazi regime while serving as Vatican secretary of state, a time in which the German press lampooned him as his predecessor Pius XI's "Jew-loving" cardinal and "Jew lover in the Vatican." The third number, 3, represents the number of plots in which Pope Pius XII was directly involved to remove Hitler from power through political assassination. The number 4,000 represents the estimated number of Jews that respected Holocaust historians Sir Martin Gilbert, Renzo De Felice, and Meir Michaelis maintain found refuge in the Vatican and its religious institutions during the German Occupation of Rome. And lastly, the number 85 represents the percentage of Italy's Jewish population that survived the Holocaust as a direct result of the efforts of Pius and the Roman Catholic Church, the highest survival percentage of any country in Europe except Denmark. In my view, every historical text written by every author on Pope Pius XII needs to start their narrative with these numbers (and perhaps other numbers as well). In fairness to history and Pope Pius XII, the objective numbers must be acknowledged up front prior to passing judgement.

Having said that, I fully agree with the fair and widely-respected Ventresca that, "Pius XII *could* have spoken out more clearly, more explicitly, to denounce the Nazi persecution of Jews and others, including Catholics. He could have directed Catholic agencies and the Catholic faithful to make anti-Nazi resistance a religious crusade or the rescue of Jews and other victims a religious duty. So, yes, Pius XII could have done things differently. But we can never say with certainty that a different approach would have produced a different outcome. The approach he chose—to avoid public confrontation and thus avoid a greater evil, as he put it—is all we have to go by. How do we assess this approach? That is the question."

I also agree with intelligence expert Mark Riebling's judicious but critical assessment of the historic figure. In his seminal book, *Church of Spies: The Pope's Secret War Against Hitler*, Riebling makes clear the "long, epic history in which Pius was deeply involved in trying to remove Hitler from power." But in trying to tell the story of the Chief's valiant struggle against Hitler, he maintains that "there is no evidence he was doing it for the Jews. What was really driving Pius was the plight of Germany's Catholics." Riebling further maintains that "the Vatican's view wasn't that much different from the views of governments and other institutions. You had the *New York Times* put a story about gas chambers in its back pages." While sympathetic to Pius and his efforts to remove Hitler from power, he then goes on to state, "The Pope was someone who saw the church in a certain way" and believed "that it couldn't afford to lose any more prestige. He believed that if he spoke about morals during the war and everyone ignored it, it was all over for the church. He should have said what the truth was and dealt with the consequences."

How will history ultimately judge Pius XII? In 1965, Pope Paul VI opened his cause for canonization, and in 1990, John Paul II declared Pius a Servant of God. Pope Benedict XVI then furthered Pius's cause for sainthood by declaring him Venerable in 2009. Pius XII's elevation to Venerable status elicited howls of protest from international Jewish groups, including the World Jewish Congress, because of the Pope's controversial "silence" regarding the Holocaust, specifically his failure to publicly speak out during the October 16, 1943, *Judenaktion* and the March 24, 1944, Ardeatine Caves Massacre (75 of the 335 victims murdered by Kappler's Gestapo were Jewish). In contrast, no less than Albert Einstein praised Pius and the Vatican for its efforts in combating Hitler's Third Reich: "[Only] the church stood squarely across the path of Hitler's campaign of suppressing the truth. I have never had any special interest in the church before, but now I feel a great admiration and affection because the church alone has had the courage and persistence to stand for intellectual truth and moral freedom."

Some claim that the Vatican is in a rush to make Pius XII a saint before the 1939-1945 wartime archives from his papacy are opened to historians. But most historians (including the late Sir Martin Gilbert) agree that until the Vatican's wartime archives are opened, all talk of Pius XII's canonization needs to be postponed. According to Riebling, the Vatican's reluctance to release all of its papers and transcripts of the secret recordings made during the wartime Pius's pontificate is evidence that the Holy See "clearly has stuff they're holding back." He concludes by saying, "I think it's important for secular scholars to check the Vatican's work."

This author wholeheartedly agrees.

Open the vaults so the world may truly see this heroic yet flawed man—Roman-born Eugenio Pacelli, Pope Pius XII, the Chief of the Vatican's wartime Church of Spies.

General Robert Tyrone Frederick and the First Special Service Force

Following the liberation of Rome, the First Special Service went on to fight in Southern France before being disbanded in December 1944. The modern American and Canadian Special Forces trace their heritage to the Devil's Brigade depicted in this book—the colorful gang of black-faced ruffians, rabble-rousers, and roustabouts from both sides of the border that struck fear into the hearts of the German Army during WWII. In 2013, the United States Congress passed a bill to award the First Special Service Force the Congressional Gold Medal. The Force officially received the medal on February 3, 2015.

In late June 1944, Robert T. Frederick was promoted to major general. At the same time, he announced that he was leaving the beloved unit he had created, trained, fought alongside, and bled with in the Italian campaign to organize and train an airborne force for the Dragoon landings that would take place in Southern France in August 1944. He went on to command the U.S. 45th Infantry Division from December 1944 through February 1945; the unit saw heavy combat in French Alsace. The youngest general to command a division-size unit in WWII, he was awarded two Distinguished Service Crosses and several other decorations. He is the only U.S. serviceman to receive eight Purple Hearts in the war, which earned him the moniker as "the most shot-at-and-hit general in American history." No less than Churchill himself called him "the greatest fighting general of all time" and proclaimed that "if we had had a dozen more like him we would have smashed Hitler in 1942."

According to John Nadler, author of *A Perfect Hell: The True Story of the Black Devils, the Forefathers of the Special Forces*, Frederick ended the war a bona fide star destined for an important role in the post-war army, but his success in the European theater in 1944-1945 proved to be almost an impediment in peacetime and he did not take well to army politics. After serving in several U.S. and overseas posts, he tendered his resignation from the army in 1952 at the age of forty-five. In the words of his daughter, he had come to the end of his endurance and his "mental, physical, and spiritual expenditures in war were catching up with him." He drifted into retirement, purchasing land in California and becoming "a gentleman farmer." When the legendary exploits of the First Special Service Force were immortalized in the 1968 film *The Devil's Brigade*, Frederick was portrayed by actor William Holden.

He died from heart failure in 1970 at the age of sixty-three, having never fully recovered from his numerous battle wounds or from being poisoned by gas fumes in his quarters at Anzio, an accident that caused enlargement of his heart. The architect of the Devil's Brigade was interred at the cemetery of San Francisco's Presidio, the military base where young Frederick a half-century before had first dreamed of soldierly glory. As Nadler says, "Today Robert Tyrone Frederick's career remains both an ideal and a cautionary tale: a style of leadership that was unique, inspired, brilliant, and tragically costly."

According to eminent WWII historian Carlo D'Este, "it was the outstanding leadership of men like Frederick that prevented the Germans from annihilating the Anzio beachhead. He was one of the most respected and fearless American commanders, and his accomplishments in organizing and commanding the Anglo-Canadian First Special Service Force were unparalleled. Like Darby with the Rangers, Frederick was the heart and soul of his unit and the right man for the very difficult task of creating and training the most successful unconventional unit ever fielded by the United States Army in World War II."

Captain Gus Heilman, First Special Service Force

During his pre-war career as the freewheeling owner of the Cavalier Bar & Grill, Graham M. "Gus" Heilman tried to pull every political string that he and his doggedly loyal clientele could dream up to stay out the Army. Yet ironically, the former University of Virginia football star, college-town tavern owner, and iconoclastic FSSF officer went on to become a genuine war hero in WWII. Following the Italian Campaign and breakup of the Force, Heilman continued to serve under Frederick in the 45th Infantry Division. He also continued to miraculously survive some of the bloodiest battles of the conflict and was twice wounded in France.

By war's end, he had risen to the rank of lieutenant colonel and had earned the Purple Heart with Oak Leaf Cluster, the WWII Victory Medal, the Silver Star, and the Bronze Star. Following the war, he returned to Charlottesville, married, started a family, and enjoyed a successful career as a banker instead of a tavern owner. A picture of Heilman taken near the end of the war shows a young, strapping Tom-Berenger lookalike (Heilman was in his late twenties at the time) bedecked in his officer's uniform with an irreverent "What me Worry?" grin that brings a smile to my lips and makes me proud to be an American every time I look at it. The legendary, hard-fighting, and hard-drinking founder and mayor of Gusville died in Charlottesville, Virginia, on November 29, 1996, two years after his wife Elsie passed away and just shy of his 80th birthday. He is buried at Arlington National Cemetery, Virginia, Section 65, Site 980.

Sergeant Tommy Prince, First Special Service Force

Following the war, Sergeant Prince—who fought throughout WWII as an Ojibway warrior and was a descendant of Salteaux Chief Peguis—was summoned to London. There he was invited to Buckingham Palace and decorated with the Military Medal and Silver Star by King George VI himself. According to Nadler in *A Perfect Hell*, he then "returned to the Brokenhead Reservation, one of only three Canadians to possess both the Silver Star and Military Medal. His other citations included the Italy Star, the 1939-1945 Star, the France & Germany Star, the Defense Medal, and the Canadian Volunteer Service Medal with Clasp, making him one of the most decorated native soldiers to emerge from the Second World War." Upon his return to Canada, he picked up right where he had left off before the war, returning to the life of a logger. But the Ojibway warrior who had wreaked hell upon the Nazis with the V-42 combat knife invented by his commander Robert T. Frederick was never able to adjust to civilian life. He died a broken and destitute ex-soldier in a veterans' hospital in 1977.

General Mark Clark and the Allied Army of Italy

After capturing Rome, General Mark Clark succeeded British General Alexander as the commander of the Allied armies in Italy. But he was badly in need of rest and was gripped with an intestinal infection. Whatever elation he derived from the liberation of the Eternal City quickly dissipated as the Germans retreated north of Florence to the Gothic Line, where the Allies were held in check by the crafty Kesselring in yet another bloody stalemate until the spring of 1945. He received his fourth star in March 1945 at age forty-eight, becoming the youngest of the thirteen U.S. officers to wear that rank during WWII. But the Italian campaign would haunt him for the rest of the war and beyond. In October 1953, Clark retired from the U.S. Army after a career that spanned thirty-six years. From 1954 to 1965, he served as president of the Citadel, the military college of South Carolina. He died in 1984, shortly before what would have been his eighty-eighth birthday. According to Rick Atkinson, author of *The Day of Battle*, "He would remain among the war's most controversial commanders, a man whose very name more than a half century later could cause brows to knit and lips to purse."

Giorgio Amendola and the Italian Resistance

Following the liberation of Rome, the National Liberation Committee (*Comitato di Liberazione Nazionale*, CLN) continued on as the political umbrella organization and main representative of the Italian Resistance movement fighting in Occupied Italy. The multi-party partisan entity led the government of Italy from the liberation until the first post-war general election in 1946. The partisans continued to coordinate strategy, cooperate with the Allies, administer liberated areas, and appoint new anti-Fascist officials to positions of authority to rebuild what the Germans had destroyed in their northward retreat across Italian soil. The CLN organized the uprisings in northern and central Italian cities, including Milan in April 1945, which fell to the partisans before Allied troops arrived.

Giorgio Amendola would continue to serve as the Communist leader of the Military Council of the National Liberation Committee and commander of CLN GAP's throughout Occupied Italy until the end of the war. Afterwards, he served as deputy for the Italian Communist Party from 1948 until his death in 1980. He became known (especially in the 1970s) as one of the leaders of the party's right wing, which espoused gradual removal of the ideas of Soviet Communism and Leninism and supported alliances with the more moderate parties, especially the Italian Socialist Party, a concept later called Eurocommunism. An author later in life, he died in Rome at age 72, after a long illness. His wife Germaine Lecocq, whom he met during his French exile in Paris and who helped him to write his last work, died a few hours after. Amendola will always be remembered as one of the great Italian partisan leaders of Italy's *Guerra di Liberazione*.

Sir D'Arcy Osborne

The chivalrous British Envoy Extraordinary and Minister Plenipotentiary to the Holy See served at the Vatican until 1947. Throughout the war, he was the British government's key diplomat involved in the three Vatican-supported plots to assassinate Adolf Hitler, as well as the most direct Allied liaison to Pope Pius XII. Using the code name "Mount," he also continued to be an important contributor to the Escape Line. The notorious Escape Line continued to be led by Monsignor Hugh O'Flaherty, French diplomat François de Vial, and British Major Sam Derry through the liberation of Rome and the eventual capitulation of the German forces in Italy. The Escape Line was instrumental in helping conceal an estimated 6,000 vulnerable people in Rome during the war from the Nazis (4,000 at the time of the Allied liberation in June 1944), including large numbers of escaped Allied POWs and Jews.

During and after the war, Osborne spoke both admiringly and critically about Pius's wartime conduct. The Pope had confided to him that he feared history would judge him harshly for his failure to speak out more vehemently against Nazi atrocities. In late 1942, Osborne wrote his now famously stinging line in his diary, "The more I think of it, the more I am revolted by Hitler's massacre of the Jewish race on the one hand, and, on the other, the Vatican's almost exclusive preoccupation with the...possibilities of the bombardment of Rome." Osborne understood the reasoning behind the Pope's reluctance to speak out publicly against Nazi atrocities, but he did not entirely approve. He attributed Pius's "silence" to the Pope's policy of "meticulous neutrality between the warring countries." In a secret report to Churchill in July 1945, Sir D'Arcy was particularly scathing in his criticism, describing Pius XII as "timorous, irresolute and averse to irrevocable action." According to Ventresca in *Soldier of Christ*, Osborne was conflicted in his assessment of the Holy Father. "It is impossible not to admire the saint or to like and respect the man," wrote Sir D'Arcy, but it is "less easy to esteem the diplomat, the politician, the Pontiff."

According to Ventresca, long after the war, amid the gathering controversy over Pius XII's wartime role as described in Hochhuth's 1963 play *The Deputy*, Osborne offered a much different and highly flattering portrait of the embattled Vicar of Christ. "So far from being a cool (which, I suppose implies cold-blooded and inhumane) diplomatist," the British envoy wrote in a 1963 letter to *The Times of London*, "Pius XII was the most warmly humane, kind, generous, sympathetic (and incidentally saintly) character that it has been my privilege to meet in the course of a long life." Osborne went on to highlight the Pope's capacity to empathize with the "human suffering" caused by the war and his universal compassion and charity for all peoples, "quite irrespective of nationality or faith." The British minister concluded that the enormous challenges facing the wartime Pope were exacerbated by the effective limits of his papal power. After all, Osborne asked, "what could he effectively do?" In recent years, as it has become clear that the Pope was deeply involved in three plots to assassinate Hitler and was directly responsible for saving countless Jews and other war refugees from persecution, this appears to be the judgment of history.

Monsignor Hugh O'Flaherty

As a senior official of the Roman Curia and major figure in the Catholic resistance to Nazism throughout the war, O'Flaherty was responsible for saving thousands of Allied soldiers and Jews through the Escape Line approved by Pius XII. When outside the Vatican, O'Flaherty wore various disguises, and his ability to evade the traps set by Kappler and his Gestapo earned the monsignor the nickname "The Scarlet Pimpernel of the Vatican." When Kappler ordered the white line to be painted in St. Peter's Square to signify the limits of the Holy See, he made it clear to O'Flaherty that the priest would be liquidated if he crossed it. In fact, the two adversaries took part in a dangerous game of cat-and-mouse throughout the 1943-1944 German Occupation that *Altar of Resistance* only barely touches upon; the story of this exciting battle of wits will have to await another novel.

The secret battle between O'Flaherty and Kappler was portrayed in the 1983 television movie *The Scarlet and the Black*, starring Gregory Peck as O'Flaherty, Sir John Gielgud as Pope Pius XII, and Christopher Plummer as the evil Kappler. The film follows the exploits of O'Flaherty, and Kappler's cleverly diabolical attempts to catch the Irish priest, from the beginning of the German occupation of Rome to its liberation by the Allies. It is clear that Peck (the Scarlet) is having a blast outwitting Plummer (the Black) in his role as an Irish priest and Vatican spy.

After the war, O'Flaherty received a number of awards, including the U.S. Medal of Freedom and the Commander of the Order of the British Empire. He was also honored by Canada and Australia. A scratch golfer in his younger years (hence the codename "Golf"), O'Flaherty died on October 30, 1963 at the age of 65 and is buried in Cahersiveen, Ireland. There is a monument in Killarney town and a grove of trees dedicated to the memory of the Scarlet Pimpernel of the Vatican in the Killarney National Park. A commemorative plaque was unveiled in May 2016 at the Vatican honoring O'Flaherty as a "tireless defender of the weak and oppressed" and for his instrumental efforts in helping to rescue and protect an estimated 6,000 vulnerable people in Rome during the war.

Lieutenant Colonel Herbert Kappler and the Gestapo

Following the German surrender in May 1945, Kappler sought refuge in the Vatican, but was arrested by British authorities and eventually turned over to the Italian government in 1947. After spending ten months in Regina Coeli Prison, he went on trial by an Italian military tribunal in May 1948 for war crimes for the Ardeatine Caves Massacre and his extortion scheme of extracting fifty kilograms of gold from Rome's Jews. According to historian Robert Katz in *The Battle for Rome*, this latter charge was "the closest anyone would get to obtaining justice for the monstrous roundup, deportation, and extermination of the Jews caught in the October 16 razzia." Five of Kappler's men, three officers including SS-Captain Erich Priebke and three NCOs, were to stand trial with him. But Kappler's longtime number-two man in Rome had managed to escape and it was not until 1996 that the Torquemada of Via Tasso would face criminal justice.

Obersturmbannführer Kappler was found guilty on all charges. The Ardeatine Caves Massacre was deemed a war crime for the barbaric manner in which the Italian prisoners were executed. In the trial, it became clear that they had been led into the caves in groups of five and shot in the neck, and when the bodies had begun to pile up, that many had been forced to kneel down over the bloody, mutilated corpses of their comrades before they were, in turn, executed. Furthermore, Kappler had provided his SS exterminators with cognac to steel their nerves and the Germans, becoming drunker and drunker, had become grotesquely sloppy, blowing away heads from bodies with multiple gunshots (thirty-nine of the corpses were later found decapitated from gunshot wounds). Consequently, Kappler was sentenced to life imprisonment in the Gaeta military prison with almost no possibility of parole, the severest penalty under the postwar Italian constitution, and received an additional fifteen years for the gold extortion charge. Kappler and his first wife divorced while he was serving his sentence.

In 1959, Kappler converted to Catholicism, largely due to the influence of his old Vatican nemesis, Father O'Flaherty, who baptized him. The monsignor regularly visited the former SS chief in prison, month after month. The Irishman was Kappler's sole visitor and the two would spend time discussing literature and religion. After converting to Catholicism, Kappler married Anneliese Wenger Walther, a nurse who had carried on a lengthy correspondence with her Nazi lover before wedding him at a prison ceremony in 1972.

By 1975, at the age of sixty-eight, Kappler was diagnosed with terminal cancer and was soon transferred to a military hospital in Rome. Appeals by his wife and the West German government to release him were denied by Italian authorities. Because of Kappler's declining health and his wife's nursing skills, Anneliese Kappler was allowed to regularly visit him during his time in the hospital. On August 15, 1977, Kappler was smuggled out in a large suitcase by his wife and apparently unwitting *carabinieri* and transported to West Germany. The cancer had reduced the fearsome ex-Gestapo chief to a weight of less than 105 pounds at the time. The Italians demanded that Kappler be returned, but the West German authorities refused to extradite him and, due to his ill-health, did not prosecute him for any further war crimes. Six months after his remarkable escape, Kappler died at home in his native Stuttgart on February 9, 1978, at the age of 70.

Captain Erich Priebke and the Vatican Rat Line

In post–war trials, Kappler's second-in-command in Rome was set to be tried for his role in the Ardeatine Caves Massacre, but he managed to escape from a British prison camp in northeastern Italy in 1946. After his escape, the former SS-*Hauptsturmführer* lived with an Italian family, received a second baptism by a local priest, and eventually made his way from South Tyrol to Vatican City in Rome, where he found protection under Bishop Alois Hudal. The Austrian was one of the chief architects of the Vatican's underground "Rat Line," which, apparently unknown to Pope Pius XII, allowed prominent Axis officers and political leaders, among them accused war criminals, to escape Allied trials and denazification by blending in with the mass of legitimate war refugees seeking a new life overseas. Hudal made false travel documents for German officials who had been involved in war crimes, and he supplied Priebke, his wife, and young sons with falsified visas to travel to Argentina.

According to Katz in *The Battle for Rome*, Priebke's post-war Rat Line experience was typical. Traveling with his wife and two small boys, Priebke was given a Red Cross passport, courtesy of the Vatican, and safe passage out of Genoa. The Priebkes crossed the Atlantic on an ocean liner named San Giorgio, arriving in Buenos Aires and beginning a new life. Former U.S. Justice Department Nazi-hunter John Loftus estimates that in the post-war years approximately 60,000 war criminals disappeared down the Vatican Rat Line in this manner to Argentina—"the single largest smuggling route for Nazi war criminals." Despite his war crimes, Priebke lived in Argentina as a free man for nearly fifty years and it was not until 1997 that the Gestapo officer would face justice.

In April 1994, Priebke was approached as he was getting into his car in Argentina by American TV newsman Sam Donaldson, who innocently inquired if he could talk to him for a moment. The trim, grandfatherly-looking gentleman known by friends and family as don Erico made the costly mistake of answering yes. On the street, Donaldson and his team proceeded to interview and film the Gestapo torturer who had cheated on his wife and wooed Italian film star Laura Nucci in 1944. After initial hesitation, the former Nazi admitted who he was and spoke openly about his role in the Ardeatine Caves Massacre. He justified his actions by saying that he only followed orders from Kappler and that, in his view, the victims—from 14-year-old boys to 75-year-old men—were terrorists. He admitted that he had been the one responsible for making sure that all the prisoners were brought to the caves and executed, and to check them off the list once they were dispatched. Don Erico was thus unmasked by Donaldson as ex-SS Captain Erich Priebke, and the fugitive from justice since 1947 was placed under house arrest, extradited to Italy, and subjected to a war crimes trial which lasted more than four years.

According to Katz, during Priebke's house arrest and subsequent lengthy trial, it became evident that Kappler's number two had managed to live for nearly a half-century in blissful freedom under his real name as the well-respected proprietor of Bariloche's Vienna Delicatessen. Prospering in Argentina, Priebke had traveled widely on a German passport, including vacation jaunts with his wife to New York, Paris, and twice to Italy. His various interviews and testimony were important in establishing the inner workings of the post-war Rat Line in spiriting the Mengeles, Eichmanns, and lesser but still vile offenders like Priebke out of Europe. The former SS captain made it clear that the Vatican's refugee-aid operation was run by Nazi-sympathizing prelates like Hudal dedicated not only to assisting war refugees but actual Nazi war criminals. "I want to thank the Catholic Church for their help," he told the Buenos Aires *Daily Clarin* in May 1994.

On July 22, 1997, the Military Tribunal of Rome found Priebke guilty of war crimes and crimes against humanity under international law for the Ardeatine Caves Massacre. He was sentenced to life without parole without being subject to any statute of limitation. However, the sentence was reduced, in consideration of his age and other extenuating circumstances. Priebke was to serve fifteen years under house arrest. He died in Rome in 2013 at the age of 100, from natural causes. The Vatican issued an "unprecedented ban" on holding the funeral in any Catholic church in Rome. Priebke's body was buried in a secret location at a military base near Rome after his remains were refused to be accepted by both the Argentinian and German governments.

Pietro Koch

Following the fall of the Eternal City to the Allies, the self-proclaimed doctor and former head of the Rome Special Police Unit (Koch Gang) continued his reign of torture, terror, and murder in Florence and later Milan. During the course of the war, Koch was behind hundreds of murders of Italian patriots. Fearful of his violent extremism, Mussolini had his close ally Renzo Montagna arrest Koch for his excesses in October 1944. He soon fell into Allied hands and, on the first anniversary of the liberation of Rome, June 4, 1945, he was tried in a makeshift courtroom at the University of Rome by an Italian High Court of Justice formed to punish Fascist crimes. He claimed he was sorry for his sins and asked for forgiveness, abandoning his previously strident atheism in a newfound declaration of his firm belief in God.

The court did not care. He was convicted of six charges that same day for high crimes against the Resistance, including torture, deportations, and "handing over numerous patriots to the German SS to be massacred in the Fosse Ardeatine." The swiftly delivered sentence was death by firing squad.

On the afternoon of the execution, Koch knelt in the grass at Fort Bravetta and received the last rites. He then rose and calmly took his place before the firing squad, refusing the proffered blindfold. Minutes later, seventeen rifle bullets tore through him, removing the entire cap of his skull and hurling it over the wall behind him. He was not yet twenty-seven years old.

AUTHOR'S NOTE

Altar of Resistance was conceived and written by the author as a work of historical fiction. Although the novel takes place during World War Two and incorporates actual historical figures, events, and locales, the novel is ultimately a work of the imagination and entertainment and should be read as nothing more. The names, characters, places, government entities, armed forces, religious and political groups, corporations, and incidents, as portrayed in the novel, are products of the author's imagination, or are used fictitiously, and are not to be construed as real.

With that disclaimer up front, it is still useful to allow readers a little peek behind the curtain to separate scenes based on actual historical events from highly fictionalized scenes, and real-life figures from invented, or highly fictionalized, characters. As stated in the "For the Reader" introduction at the beginning of this book, more than fifty actual historical figures populate the pages of *Altar of Resistance*, and many of these characters figure prominently in the events depicted in the novel. For these actual living and breathing historical figures, I have tried to recreate them and their worlds with meticulous fidelity. Where possible, I have taken their actual wartime quotes, or large portions of their actual words from transcripts, documents, and other quoted materials. At the same time, however, the book's characters are part of my overall imaginative landscape and are, therefore, ultimately the fictitious creations of the author, reflecting my personal research interests and biases.

Several fictional characters are based upon actual historical figures or composites of historical figures. Readers familiar with the 1943-1944 battle for Rome will recognize that Colonel Wilhelm Hollmann is based primarily upon *Standartenführer* and *Doktor* Eugen Dollmann (August 8, 1900 – May 17, 1985), the famous Waffen-SS colonel and diplomatic liaison officer for Rome's black nobility in 1943-1944. My fictitious Hollmann is also, secondarily, based upon Consul Eitel Friedrich Möllhausen, the thirty-year-old acting head of the German Embassy in Rome and nonmember of the Nazi Party with a penchant for aiding Jews, who also appears as himself in the novel. History and fiction have provided us with more than enough rabid, despicable Nazis, so I wanted to create a character that was a German patriot but opposed to the worst excesses of the SS and Holocaust, as history has shown both Dollmann and Möllhausen to be. The fact that the real-life Colonel Eugen Dollmann was an actual senior SS officer opposed to both the 1943 *Judenaktion* and severe Nazi reprisals following the Ardeatine Caves Massacre makes him all the more interesting as the basis for a fictional character.

Like my fictional SS colonel, the real-life Dollmann was an erudite Bavarian *bon vivant* from an aristocratic background, right-hand man to General Karl Wolff, and the official liaison officer between the highest echelons of the SS and the Fascist hierarchy, Roman aristocracy, and Vatican. Most importantly, the real-life Dollmann was the exact opposite of Kappler and the two reportedly clashed often and despised one another, the Gestapo chief considering the refined Dollmann a drawing-room soldier who flitted about Rome's high society doing as he pleased. According to historian Robert Katz, author of *The Battle for Rome* and *The Talented Doktor Dollmann*, the Forrest Gump-like Dollmann was—in his various roles as a German spy, conspirator, secret envoy to the Vatican and the Allies, and interpreter to Hitler and Mussolini—an eyewitness to an incredible number of drama-filled moments of crisis, battle, and betrayal during WWII. He "had the uncanny talent of being everywhere in Nazidom whenever history was being made—a clandestine intelligence agency unto himself," observed Katz.

Working with his boss Wolff, Dollmann played an important role in the surrender of the German forces in the Italian theater on May 2, 1945, six days before the final German capitulation. The legendary OSS spymaster Allen Dulles who handled the surrender from his post in Switzerland called him "the ubiquitous Dollmann" and "an intellectual, highly sophisticated, somewhat snobbish and cynical." Dulles regarded Wolff's protégé as a silver-tongued gentleman who "knew how to be everybody's man, but only in high places." An Italian countess who met Dollmann in German-occupied Rome said of him: "He was tall, slender and elegant, not at all a German type. With perfect grace, he kissed my hand and invited me to sit beside him...I hated him!" According to Katz, for his role in the surrender of Kesselring's Army, Dollmann was given assurances of special consideration by the Allies and was later cleared of any war crimes. In 2000, many years after his death, the CIA released documents that confirmed the long-held suspicion that at war's end Dollmann had gone on to serve as a source for Allied Intelligence.

In addition to the fictional Colonel Hollmann, several other characters are based partly on actual historical figures. Teresa Di Domenico is based partly upon the heroic partisan *Gappista* Carla Capponi (known as Elena), who took part in the Via Rasella attack and other field operations against the German occupiers in 1943-1944. Teresa's mother in the book, Marchesa Bianca Di Domenico, is based upon the Marchesa Fulvia Ripa di Meana with regard to her relationship to the Pope. The real-world Marchesa di Meana was a long-term friend of Pius XII; she enlisted him in her one-woman battle to have her cousin, the Resistance leader Colonel Giuseppe Cordero Lanza di Montezemolo, spared from Kappler's tortures at Via Tasso. Teresa's biological father and the marchesa's husband, Colonel Giovanni Di Domenico, is based loosely upon Colonel Montezemolo, a patriot and royalist who did seek accord with the liberal National Liberation Committee in an effort to drive out the German occupiers and liberate Rome. Teresa's fellow freedom-fighter and lover in the novel, Beppo (Giuseppe Valenti), is based loosely upon Elena Capponi's real-life lover Rosario "Sasà" Bentivegna (code-named Paolo), a partisan-medical student. The two brave, real-world Italian partisans ended up marrying one another and raising a daughter together. Finally, Lieutenant Peter Savoyan is based loosely upon Peter Tompkins, the actual American Fifth Army intelligence officer and head of Office of Strategic Services (OSS) Rome.

Handpicked by "Wild Bill" Donovan, Tompkins didn't arrive to Rome until January 21, 1944 (I have Savoyan inserted into Rome with Bridger just before the October roundup on October 16, 1943).

With regard to the historical events of the novel, I have tried to place the actual historical figures in a given scene and have used, to the extent possible, their actual words based on transcripts, documents, and other quoted materials. The rare exceptions are (1) when I place a fictional character based on a real-life figure (i.e., Hollmann for Dollmann) in a scene where the real-life historical person instead of my fictional character was present; and (2) when I place a fictional character in a scene where he or she is there simply to act as a point-of-view character. Below I have summarized the major historical events from the 1943-1944 Italian Campaign which have been faithfully recreated in the scenes in the novel, or are discussed by the characters in the book either through dialogue or interior monologue. The major historical events are presented in chronological order:

October 1943

Oct. 14 (?). Vatican City. Chapter 1. A historically documented secret meeting was conducted in mid-October between Pope Pius XII (codename: the Chief) and Father Leiber (codename: Gregor) regarding the removal of Hitler from power and Pius acting as post-war mediator between Nazi Germany and the West. As was his custom and like the true secret agent he was, the Pope really did burn the paper file that Leiber gave him to read describing the Hitler operation. However, the precise date and time of the meeting has, to the author's knowledge, not been recorded. I have given the date as October 14, two days before the Jewish Roundup in Rome.

Oct. 16. The Roundup, Jewish Ghetto, Rome. Chapter 6. In a house-to-house sweep of the ghetto and other neighborhoods, more than one thousand Jews are seized during the morning and early afternoon. The task is made easier for the Nazis because the community lists and addresses were, regrettably, not destroyed by Ugo Foà, President of the Rome Jewish community, and were obtained by the SS.

Oct. 16. Vatican. Chapter 7. Meeting between Pope Pius II and Princess Enza Pignatelli Aragona Cortes, who was the first to inform the Pope of the ongoing Jewish roundup. At the end of the meeting, the Pope calls Secretary of State of the Holy See Maglione, instructing him to immediately summon Baron Ernst von Weizsäcker, the German Ambassador to the Holy See, for a meeting with the intent of lodging an earnest protest. I have the fictitious Teresa Di Domenico at the meeting as the point-of-view character and friend of the princess.

Oct. 16. Vatican. Chapter 11. Meeting between Cardinal Maglione and German Ambassador Weizsäcker. In this chapter, I have Maglione later recounting his late morning meeting with Weizsäcker to Pius in his papal study, rather than the actual meeting, to maintain the Pope as the central Vatican point-of-view character. According to Raleigh Trevelyan, a young British lieutenant during the Italian campaign and author of the excellent *Rome '44: The Battle for the Eternal*

City, the cardinal's "prompt protest to Weizsäcker, on the Pope's order [was] instrumental in alerting Berlin and Hitler to the possibility of a disastrous break with the Vatican, and the round-up of Jews was halted." As Trevelyan states, "8,000 Jews had originally been marked for elimination," indicating that Pope Pius XII was directly responsible for saving nearly 7,000 Jewish lives on the much-disputed day when he supposedly remained "silent" and "did nothing."

Oct. 18. Tiburtina Railway Station. Chapter 13. The tragic deportation of the 1,007 Jews, crammed into boxcars and shipped northeast by rail to Auschwitz, is told through the fictional eyes of Hollmann and Kappler (who was not likely to have been there in real life given that he was opposed to the roundup and deportation for practical "police security" reasons). The poor woman who pounded on the boxcars until she located her family and was reunited with them in this scene was Costanza Calò Sermoneta. Tragically, she, her husband, and five children were gassed by the SS at Auschwitz two days later on October 20.

Oct. 18. Vatican. Chapter 14. Meeting between Pope Pius XII and Sir D'Arcy Osborne, British Minister to the Holy See, regarding the brutal German Occupation and Jewish roundup. Afterwards, Osborne (codename: Mount) reported to his diplomatic superiors in London that "it was of the opinion of a number of people that [the Pope] underestimated his own moral authority and the reluctant respect in which he was held by the Nazis because of the Catholic population of Germany; I added I was inclined to share the opinion and I urged him to bear it in mind in case in the course of coming events an occasion might arise for taking a strong line."

November-December 1943

Nov. 28. Italian Artillery School Barracks, Santa Maria (Capua-Vetere), Central Italy. Chapter 23. First Special Service Force (FSSF) Operation Raincoat briefing by Colonel Robert Tyron Frederick. The military objective of the operation was to drive the Germans off their forward positions along their Winter Line, pushing them back beyond the Rapido and Upper Garigliano Rivers.

Dec. 3. Monte La Difensa, Central Italy. Chapter 24. FSSF commanded by Frederick conducts nighttime, one-thousand-foot-plus rock climb in cold rain and takes Hill 960 after savage fighting.

Dec. 6. Monte La Remetanea, Central Italy. Chapter 25. FSSF takes adjacent Hill 907 following four days of relentless artillery bombardment, mortar fire, and sniper attack. At the end of the six total days of fighting, a full one-third of the Force (532 men) is listed as dead or wounded, including Frederick, who was wounded twice during the battle.

Dec. 18. Cinema Barberini, Rome. Chapter 28. Italian Partisan GAP Central bombing attack on German soldiers outside the movie theater, killing eight and wounding fifteen.

Dec. 19. Hotel Flora, Rome. Chapter 29. GAP Central bombing attack devastates the ground floor of the hotel and kills a number of Germans, although the occupiers keep the death toll secret.

Dec. 21. Seminario Lombardo, Rome. Chapters 30-31. In reprisal for the recent partisan attacks, a mixed formation of Fascist and Gestapo agents make the first collective raid on the Roman Resistance. The Seminario Lombardo and two other Vatican properties known to be harboring influential anti-Fascists and military officers are targeted. Koch and his *Banda Koch* are present along with SS-Captain Priebke and three other Gestapo agents wearing plainclothes to avoid being identified by the Vatican. The Koch-Teresa rape scene and O'Flaherty's presence are fictitious. The very-much-alive man who feigned death by hiding out in the coffin was real. Unfortunately, he was captured by the brutal Koch Gang.

February 1944

Feb. 1. Anzio Beachhead, Central Italy. Chapter 36. First Special Service Force arrives to Anzio following successful amphibious Operation Shingle. The elite unit is placed on the Allied right flank to guard the Mussolini Canal against the vaunted German Hermann Göring Division.

Feb. 10. Sessuno, Central Italy. Chapters 37-40. The Fifth Company, Second Regiment of the FSSF, commanded by Captain Adna Underhill, seizes the village of Sessuno during a nighttime raid. The Germans are mowed down with automatic-weapons fire, "falling like leaves in a windstorm." The Sessuno raid and other nighttime FSSF attacks along the right-wing at Anzio in February scar the psyche of the veteran Hermann Göring Division and lead the Germans to nickname the FSSF raiders as *die schwarzen teufel*—the black devils. Allied soldiers and U.S. war correspondents at Anzio are quick to pick up on the new moniker, and the FSSF swiftly becomes the greatly feared and admired "Devil's Brigade" later made famous on the silver screen by William Holden and Cliff Robertson.

Feb. 10. Castel Gandolfo, Central Italy. Chapter 41. An Allied air raid of the papal estate results in five hundred casualties among the thousands of innocent Jews and non-Jews hiding out there under the Pope's protection.

Feb. 15. Monte Cassino, Central Italy. Chapter 41. A massive Allied air raid destroys the sixth-century monastery founded by St. Benedict on top of Monte Cassino.

Feb. 16-17. Rome. Chapter 41. Heavy Allied air raids on German military targets in supposedly "Open City" of Rome. The city is, in fact, being used as a transportation hub and staging area by Field Marshal Kesselring for his army.

Feb. 16-19. Anzio. Chapter 41. The Germans launch a new offensive (Operation Fischfang), supported by Tiger tanks and inflicting heavy casualties. On February 22, with the Allies battered by Smiling Albert and clinging precariously to the Anzio beachhead, U.S. General Lucas, commander of Allied forces at Anzio, is replaced by General Truscott.

March 1944

March 1. Vatican. Chapter 41. Mysteriously, six bombs from identified German aircraft drop on the Saint Damaso Courtyard of the Apostolic Palace, turning the courtyard into a raging inferno and littering it with bomb debris.

March 3. Josef Müller trial at the Supreme Court in Berlin. Chapter 41 involves a fictitious meeting between the Pope and Father Leiber that takes place on March 1, 1944, during the German airborne bombing of the Vatican (a known historical fact). However, the subject of the meeting was not fictitious. I have the Pope and Leiber discussing the forthcoming trial of Josef Müller that took place on March 3, presenting the full details of what actually happened during the trial as pre-trial supposition. Müller (codename: Herr X) was the courageous leader of the German Catholic Resistance to Hitler. He was imprisoned by the Nazis in April 1943 and Pope Pius XII kept tabs on his welfare during his imprisonment through Leiber and the Roman cutouts.

March 19. Vatican. Chapter 41. Meeting between Pope Pius XII and Marchesa Fulvia Ripa di Meana. The long-term friend of the Pope was trying to enlist him to take action on behalf of her cousin, the Resistance leader Colonel Montezemolo, who was being held captive and subjected to brutal torture at Via Tasso. In the book, I have my fictional marchesa, Bianca Di Domenico, and her daughter Teresa meeting with the Holy Father instead of Marchesa di Meana.

March 23, 1943. Via Rasella, Rome. Chapters 43-44. Timed to the twenty-fifth anniversary of the founding of Fascism, Roman GAP Central partisans explode a bomb into a heavily armed marching column of 156 SS military police, killing 32 (one additional SS policeman will later die from his wounds, bringing the total death toll to 33).

March 24, 1943. Headquarters of the Commandant of Rome, Corso D'Italia. Chapter 47. Meeting between Kappler, General Kurt Mälzer, the Commandant of Rome, and Major Hellmuth Dobbrick, the police battalion commander of SS *Polizeiregiment Bozen* attacked at Via Rasella. The three German officers determine who specifically will carry out the 10-to-1 reprisal order and execute the 320 prisoners (called "candidates for death") for the Via Rasella bombing. The real-life Dollmann was not present. I have placed the fictitious Colonel Hollmann there since he is the major German point-of-view character.

March 24, 1943. Gestapo Headquarters, Via Tasso 145. Chapter 48. Kappler and his officers develop the plan to liquidate the 320 prisoners, deciding to carry out the death sentences via gunshot to the back of the head at the Ardeatine Caves, where they can conceal the crime from the Roman citizenry. When a thirty-third member of the SS *Polizeiregiment Bozen* dies from wounds sustained during the Via Rasella attack, Kappler is forced to add another ten innocents to his list of "candidates for death." The real-life Dollmann was not present during these machinations and the point of view is from the fictitious Colonel Hollmann.

March 24, 1944. Ardeatine Caves Massacre. Chapter 49. Kappler and his Gestapo death squad carry out the execution of a total of 335 prisoners at Rome's Ardeatine Caves. In groups of five, the victims are led into the caves with their hands tied behind their backs and shot in the neck. As the bodies pile up, prisoners are forced to kneel over the bloody, mutilated corpses of their already-dead comrades before being executed. During the killings, it is found that an error has been made and that five additional people who were not on the prisoner list have been transported to the caves. They are held off to the side until the 330 original prisoners have been executed, at which time Kappler decides to have them shot too. As the mass execution event turns into a grisly affair, Kappler provides his men with cognac to steel their nerves. But the Germans become so sloppy drunk that they literally blow away the prisoners' heads from their bodies (as noted previously, thirty-nine of the exhumed corpses were later found to be decapitated from gunshot wounds). Priebke is responsible for the list and crosses off prisoners' names as they are shot and killed. History has found him guilty of murder because of the additional five people executed who were not on the list of the 330 condemned to death by the 10-to-1 rule. Priebke's trial strongly focused on these extra killings performed to cover up the crime and leave behind no living eyewitnesses. The sole Italian eyewitness to the Ardeatine Caves Massacre, and even then only from a distance from the cave entrance, was the farmer Nicola D'Annibale depicted in the novel. The scene is from the perspective of the fictitious Teresa, who watches in horror alongside D'Annibale along with her lover and fellow partisan Beppo.

March 25. Vatican. Chapter 50. Meeting between Pope Pius XII and Count Giuseppe Dalla Torre, director and chief editor of the *L'Osservatore Romano.* The two men are in sharp disagreement with regard to how forcefully to protest the Ardeatine Caves Massacre in the Vatican newspaper, with Dalla Torre wanting to issue a strong condemnation of the Nazis and the Pope declaring that the partisans are the "guilty parties" whose "deeds in Via Rasella" have caused the sacrifice of 320 innocent victims (actually 335).

May 1944

May 10. Vatican. Chapter 51. *Polizeiführer* Karl Wolff, the head of the SS in Italy, meets alone and in secret with Pius in the papal study while Colonel Eugen Dollmann, who had arranged the meeting, waits in the antechamber. In the book, I substitute Hollmann for Dollman. For an hour, the Pope and Wolff talk about the German atrocities at Via Tasso and how peace might be achieved between Nazi Germany and the West, with Wolff offering his services to the Pope should he be willing to act as intermediary. At the Vatican's request, Wolff agrees to release Giuliano Vassalli, a leftist Roman partisan leader and son of an old friend of the Pope's late brother, who is being held at Via Tasso. On June 2, prior to the liberation of Rome, Kappler reluctantly releases Vassalli, per Wolff's order, with a stern warning: "You can thank the Holy Father that you're not being sent to the wall, which is what you deserve, Vassalli, right? Don't ever let me see you again."

May 23. Cisterna Canal, Anzio. Chapter 52. The much-anticipated Allied breakout from Anzio during Operation Buffalo. The FSSF battles its way across No Man's Land to control Highway 7, a major thoroughfare to the Eternal City, taking many casualties.

June 1944

June 4. Route 6 – Via Casillina, outskirts of Rome. Chapter 59. Generals Frederick, Mark Clark, and Keyes gather on a hill for a Fifth Army photo-op. Markus Clarkus requests that the "Fighting General" Frederick retrieve a reflector-studded, blue-and-white road sign that reads "ROMA" as a war souvenir when the group comes under heavy sniper fire. With bullets clattering off the road sign, the group of high-ranking generals is forced to take cover in a ditch. Not one to be thwarted, Frederick manages to recover the sign once the sniper fire slackens and dutifully gives the present to Clark.

June 4. Ponte Regina Margherita, Rome. Chapter 60. Tasked with penetrating the city limits and securing all six of Rome's main bridges, the FSSF is the first Allied unit to reach the Eternal City, winning Rome for the Fifth Army. After driving into the city, the Forcemen encounter stiff resistance from a German rearguard patrol at the Ponte Margherita, where Frederick is badly wounded in the shoulder and leg.

June 5. St. Peter's Square. Chapter 62. The liberation of Rome and legendary speech by Pope Pius XII to 300,000 faithful from his papal balcony. He is hailed by the hearty throng in the square as the *defensor civitatis*, and later privately scorned by the U.S. and British governments for failing to condemn Nazi Germany or adequately pay homage to the Allies who have given their lives to liberate Rome. But it is a glorious day as the Allies have won the Eternal City, driving out the brutal Nazi occupiers and once and for all answering the Italians' all-important question, "Why did it take you so long?" Of course, as Audie Murphy knew only too well, the answer could only be: "Because so many of us died to set you free."

SOURCES AND ACKNOWLEDGEMENTS

To develop the story line, characters, and scenes for *Altar of Resistance*, I consulted over a hundred archival materials, non-fiction books, magazine and newspaper articles, blogs, Web sites, and numerous individuals and visited most every real-world location in person. These principal locations included numerous physical settings in Rome and Central Italy. All in all, there are too many resources and locations to name here. However, I would be remiss if I didn't give credit to the key historical references upon which *Altar of Resistance* is based, as well as the critical individuals who dramatically improved the quality of the manuscript from its initial to its final stage. Any technical mistakes in the historical facts underpinning the novel, typographical errors, or examples of overreach due to artistic license, however, are the fault of me and me alone.

I relied heavily upon seventeen references dealing specifically with the Battle for Rome and German Occupation of that city, the First Special Service Force, and the papacy of Pope Pius XII during the Second World War. The four most invaluable references for the overall Italian Campaign and battle for Rome were Raleigh Trevelyan's *Rome '44: The Battle for the Eternal City* (1981), Robert Katz's *The Battle for Rome: The Germans, the Allies, the Partisans, and the Pope, September 1943–June 1944* (2003), Rick Atkinson's *The Day of Battle: The War in Sicily and Italy, 1943–1944* (2007), and Carlo D'Este's *Fatal Decision: Anzio and the Battle for Rome* (2008). For the FSSF, I found the following four books of great research value: *The Devil's Brigade* by Robert Adelman and George Walton (1968), *The First Special Service Force: A War History of the North Americans, 1942-1944* by Robert Burhans (1996), *A Perfect Hell: The True Story of the Black Devils, the Forefathers of the Special Forces* by John Nadler (2006), and *The Black Devil Brigade: The True Story of the First Special Service Force* by Joseph Springer (2001). These four outstanding works brought Robert Tyrone Frederick and his gang of black-faced ruffians to life. With regard to Pope Pius XII, I knew I would be treading in dangerous waters between raving cheerleaders and ranting critics, so I relied most heavily on those texts by respected researchers that seemed to provide a balanced and well-rounded perspective, or that at least presented convincing arguments with ample supporting documentation. Even then, the authors tended to fall into either pro-Pius or anti-Pius camps so I had to tread carefully. In my mind, the most well-researched and convincing books on the controversial Pope, and the references that I primarily relied upon for my conceptual model of this most controversial leader, were the following: *Soldier of Christ: The Life of Pope Pius XII* (2013) by Robert Ventresca; *Church of Spies: The Pope's Secret War Against Hitler* (2015) by Mark Riebling; *The Papacy in the Age of Totalitarianism, 1914-1958* (2014) by John Pollard; *The Righteous: The Unsung Heroes of the Holocaust* (2002) and *Hitler's Pope?* (2006) by Sir Martin

Gilbert; *A Cross Too Heavy: Pope Pius XII and the Jews of Europe* (2011) by Paul O'Shea; *Britain and the Vatican during the Second World War* (1988) by Owen Chadwick; *The Myth of Hitler's Pope: How Pope Pius XII Rescued Jews from the Nazis* (2005) by David Dalin; and *The Pope's Jews: The Vatican's Secret Plan to Save Jews from the Nazis* (2012) by Gordon Thomas.

Readers knowledgeable on the subject of Pope Pius XII will no doubt recognize that these nine works, taken as a whole, paint a detailed and sometimes contradictory picture of a most complex human being, one who at times merits our admiration and at other times our disappointment and criticism. I earnestly hope that this second book in my WWII Trilogy provides a full and complex portrait of the man; after all, Pius was a complicated and conflicted world leader in perhaps the most abhorrently violent and complex time in human history.

In writing the novel, there were many excellent historical books and articles in addition to those listed above from which I drew facts and inspiration. The interested reader is referred to the following additional sources. The list is especially useful for those who would like to know more about the Italian Campaign and German Occupation of Rome in 1943-1944, the legendary "Devil's Brigade," and Pope Pius XII.

General WWII Politico-Military and Italian Campaign: *Anzio: Italy and the Battle for Rome—1944* by Lloyd Clark (2006); *Circles of Hell, The War in Italy, 1943-1945 (1993)* by Eric Morris; *Breakout and Pursuit: U.S. Army in World War II: The European Theater of Operations* (2012) and *United States Army in WWII – The Mediterranean - Salerno to Cassino* (2013) by Martin Blumenson; *United States Army in WWII – The Mediterranean - Sicily and the Surrender of Italy* by Albert N. Garland and Howard McGaw Smyth (2013); *The Second World War* (2005) by John Keegan; *Italy's Sorrow: A Year of War, 1944-1945* by James Holland (2008); *Rome Fell Today* by Robert Adelman and George Walton (1970); *Calculated Risk* by Mark Clark (1950); *Dogface Soldier: The Life of General Lucian K. Truscott, Jr.* (2010) by Wilson A. Heefner; *Franklin D. Roosevelt: The War Years, 1939-1945* (2016) by Roger Daniels; *Ernie's War: The Best of Ernie Pyle's World War II Dispatches* (1986) by David Nichols; *To Hell and Back* (2002) by Audie Murphy; *Wild Bill Donovan: The Spymaster Who Created the OSS and Modern American Espionage* (2011) and *Disciples: The World War II Missions of the CIA Directors Who Fought for Wild Bill Donovan* (2015) by Douglas Waller.

First Special Service Force: *First Special Service Force 1942 – 44* (2006) by Brett Werner; *The Last Fighting General: The Biography of Robert Tyrone Frederick* by Anne Hicks (2006); *Once Upon a Wartime: A Canadian Who Survived the Devil's Brigade* (1996) by Peter Cottingham; *The Supercommandos First Special Service Force, 1942-1944* (2000) by Robert Ross; *Matters Canadian and the Problem with Being Special: Robert T. Frederick on the First Special Service Force* (2003) and *We Move Only Forward: Canada, the United States, and the First Special Service Force, 1942–1944* (2006) by James Wood.

German Occupation of Rome and Roman-Vatican Resistance: *Hide and Seek: The Irish Priest in the Vatican Who Defied the Nazi Command* (2011) by Stephen Walker; *A Spy in Rome* (1962) by Peter Tompkins; *The Rome Escape*

Line: The Story of the British Organization in Rome for Assisting Escaped Prisoners-of-war 1943-44 (1960) by Sam Derry; *Saving Italy: the Race to Rescue a Nation's Treasures from the Nazis* by Robert Edsel (2013); *The Talented Doktor Dollmann* (1967) and *Death in Rome* (1968) by Robert Katz; *The Interpreter: Memoirs of Doktor Eugen Dollmann* by Eugen Dollmann (1967); *The Italians and the Holocaust: Persecution, Rescue, and Survival* (1996) by Susan Zuccotti and Furio Colombo; *The Italian Resistance: Fascists, Guerrillas and the Allies* (2009) by Tom Behan; *Top Nazi: SS General Karl Wolff, The Man Between Hitler and Himmler* (2005) by Jochen Von Lang; *Women and the Italian Resistance: 1943-1945* (1997) by Jane Slaughter; *Forgotten Battles: Italy's War of Liberation, 1943-1945* (2001) by Charles O'Reilly; *The Scarlet and the Black: The True Story of Monsignor Hugh O'Flaherty, Hero of the Vatican Underground* (2009) by J.P. Gallagher; *The Vatican Pimpernel: The World War II Exploits of the Monsignor Who Saved Over 6,500 Lives* (2008) by Brian Fleming; *The Memoirs of Ernst von Weizsäcker* (1951); *Rome's Resistance* (2016) by Kevin Doyle; *Nothing Sacred: Nazi Espionage Against the Vatican, 1939-1945* (2003) by David Alvarez and Robert A. Graham; *Heroic Wartime Irish Priest Honored at the Vatican* (2016) by Edward Pentin.

Pope Pius XII: *The Archive Holds the Answers* (2008) by Sir Martin Gilbert; *Inside the Vatican of Pius XII: The Memoir of an American Diplomat During World War II* (2004) by Harold Tittmann, Jr.; *Rethinking 'Hitler's Pope': A Q&A With Mark Riebling* (2015) by Sam Harris; *The Pope's Dilemma: Pius XII Faces Atrocities and Genocide in the Second World War* (2015) by Jacques Kornberg; *Under His Very Windows: The Vatican and the Holocaust in Italy* (2002) by Susan Zuccotti; *Pope Pius XII and World War II - The Documented Truth* by Gary L. Krupp (2010); *The Moral Costs of Inaction* (2015) by Gerald Steinacher; *A Cross Too Heavy: Some Thoughts on Pope Pius XII and the Jews in 2012* (2012), *Media Spin and "The Pope's Jews"* (2013), and *John Pollard, Pope Pius XII, and Paul O'Shea:* Pollard Review of *A Cross Too Heavy: Pope Pius XII and the Jews of Europe* (2013) by Paul O'Shea; *The Unsilent Pope* (2004) by William Doino, Jr. and Joseph Bottum; *Catholics Confronting Hitler: the Catholic Church and the Nazis* (2016) by Peter Bartley; *Hitler's Pope: The Secret History of Pius XII* (1999) by John Cornwell; *Hitler, the War, and the Pope* (2010) by Ronald Rychlak (2010); *The Catholic Church and the Holocaust, 1930-1965* (2000) by Michael Phayer; *Pius XII and the Second World War according to the Archives of the Vatican* (2003) by Pierre Blet; *Pius XII, the Holocaust and the Revisionists: Essays* (2006) by Patrick J. Gallo; *The Vatican in the Age of the Dictators, 1922-1945* (1974) by Anthony Rhodes; *Was Supposedly Pro-Nazi Pope Pius XII a Secret Anti-Hitler Plotter?* (2015) by Desmond O'Grady; *Review of Mark Riebling, Church of Spies: The Vatican's Secret War against Hitler* (2015) by Mark Edward Ruff; *Pius XII on Trial* (2014) by Katherine Campbell; *Pius XII Wanted Hitler Gone, But He Didn't Plot to Have Him Killed* (2016) by Francis Phillips; *Book Review Church of Spies: The Pope's Secret War Against Hitler* (2015) by Joanne McCarthy; *Church of Spies by Mark Riebling: A Pope's Enigmatic Silence* (2016) by Barney Zwartz; *WWII Pope's secret scheme to assassinate Hitler: Historian claims Pius XII was the centre of elaborate plot to have the Führer killed (2015)* by Kieran Corcoran; Review of *The Papacy in the Age of Totalitarianism, 1914-1958* (2015) by Lauren Faulkner Rossi; *Stalled Sainthood: Strategic Silence of Pius XII Still Begs Study: Mark Riebling's "Church of Spies" Brings Us Closer to Understanding* (2015) by Russell Saltzman; *Pius XII and the Jews: A defense* (2001) and *A Righteous Gentile: Pope Pius XII and the Jews* (2003) by David G. Dalin; *Did Pope Pius XII Help the Jews?* (2007) by Margherita Marchione.

I would also personally like to thank the following for their support and assistance. First and foremost, I would like to thank my wife Christine, an exceptional and highly professional book editor, who painstakingly reviewed and copy-edited the novel. Any mistakes that remain are my fault, of course.

Second, I would like to thank my former literary agent, Cherry Weiner of the Cherry Weiner Literary Agency, for thoroughly reviewing, vetting, and copy-editing the manuscript, and for making countless improvements to the finished novel.

Third, I would like to thank Stephen King's former editor, Patrick LoBrutto, for thoroughly copy-editing the various drafts of the novel and providing detailed reviews.

I would also like to thank Austin and Anne Marquis, Governor Roy Romer, Ambassador Marc Grossman, Betsy and Steve Hall, Rik Hall, Christian Fuenfhausen, Fred Taylor, Mo Shafroth, Tim and Carey Romer, Peter and Lorrie Frautschi, Deirdre Grant Mercurio, Joe Tallman, John Welch, Link Nicoll, Toni Conte Augusta Francis, Brigid Donnelly Hughes, Peter Brooke, Caroline Fenton Dewey, John and Ellen Aisenbrey, Margot Patterson, Cathy and Jon Jenkins, Danny Bilello and Elena Diaz-Bilello, Charlie and Kay Fial, Vincent Bilello, Elizabeth Gardner, Robin McGehee, Bill Eberhart, and the other book reviewers and professional contributors large and small who have given generously of their time over the years, as well as to those who have given me loyal support as I have ventured on this incredible odyssey of suspense novel writing.

Lastly, I want to thank anyone and everyone who bought this book and my loyal fans and supporters who helped promote this work. You know who you are and I salute you.

ABOUT THE AUTHOR AND FORTHCOMING TITLES

Samuel Marquis is a bestselling, award-winning suspense author. He works by day as a VP–Principal Hydrogeologist with an environmental firm in Boulder, Colorado, and by night as a spinner of historical and modern suspense yarns. He holds a Master of Science degree in Geology, is a Registered Professional Geologist in eleven states, and is a recognized expert in groundwater contaminant hydrogeology, having served as an expert witness in several class action litigation cases. He also has a deep and abiding interest in military history and intelligence, specifically related to the Golden Age of Piracy, Plains Indian Wars, World War II, and the current War on Terror.

His thrillers have been #1 *Denver Post* bestsellers and received national book award recognition. His first novel, *The Devil's Brigade* (formerly *The Slush Pile Brigade*), was an award-winning finalist in the mystery category of the Beverly Hills Book Awards. His follow-up *Blind Thrust* was the winner of the Foreword Reviews' Book of the Year (HM) and Next Generation Indie Book Awards and an award-winning finalist of the USA Best Book and Beverly Hills Book Awards (thriller and suspense). His third novel, *The Coalition*, was the winner of the Beverly Hills Book Awards for a political thriller and an award-winning finalist for the USA Best Book Awards. *Bodyguard of Deception*, Book 1 of his WWII Trilogy, was an award-winning finalist of the USA Best Book Awards in historical fiction. His fifth book, *Cluster of Lies*, won the Beverly Hills Book Awards in the regional fiction: west category and was an award-winning finalist of the USA Best Book Awards.

Ambassador Marc Grossman, former U.S. Under Secretary of State, proclaimed, "In his novels *Blind Thrust* and *Cluster of Lies*, Samuel Marquis vividly combines the excitement of the best modern techno-thrillers." Former Colorado Governor Roy Romer said, "*Blind Thrust* kept me up until 1 a.m. two nights in a row. I could not put it down." Kirkus Reviews proclaimed *The Coalition* an "entertaining thriller" and declared that "Marquis has written a tight plot with genuine suspense." James Patterson said *The Coalition* had "a lot of good action and suspense" and compared the novel to *The Day After Tomorrow*, the classic thriller by Allan Folsom. Other book reviewers have compared his WWII thrillers *Bodyguard of Deception* and *Altar of Resistance* to the epic historical novels of Tom Clancy, John le Carré, Ken Follett, Herman Wouk, Daniel Silva, and Alan Furst.

Below is the list of suspense novels that Samuel Marquis has published or will be publishing in the near future, along with the release dates of both previously published and forthcoming titles.

The World War Two Trilogy
Bodyguard of Deception – March 2016 – Award-Winning Finalist USA Best Book Awards
Altar of Resistance – January 2017
Spies of the Midnight Sun – January 2018

The Nick Lassiter – Skyler International Espionage Series
The Devil's Brigade (formerly The Slush Pile Brigade) – September 2015, Reissue April 2017 – The #1 Denver Post Bestseller and Award-Winning Finalist Beverly Hills Book Awards
The Coalition – January 2016, Reissue April 2017 – Winner Beverly Hills Book Awards and Award-Winning Finalist USA Best Book Awards
The Fourth Pularchek – June 2017

The Joe Higheagle Environmental Sleuth Series
Blind Thrust – October 2015 – The #1 Denver Post Bestseller; Winner Foreword Reviews' Book of the Year (HM) and Next Generation Indie Book Awards; Award-Winning Finalist USA Best Book Awards, Beverly Hills Book Awards, and Next Generation Indie Book Awards
Cluster of Lies – September 2016 – Winner Beverly Hills Book Awards and Award-Winning Finalist USA Best Book Awards

Thank You for Your Support!

To Order Samuel Marquis Books and Contact Samuel:

Visit Samuel Marquis's website, join his mailing list, learn about his forthcoming suspense novels and book events, and order his books at www.samuelmarquisbooks.com. Please send all fan mail (including criticism) to samuelmarquisbooks@gmail.com.

Made in the USA
Lexington, KY
08 July 2017